I0590143

THE HERETICAL DARK

William Zimmerman

This book is a work of fiction. Names, characters, places, and incidents are the product of the author's imagination or are used fictitiously. Any resemblance to actual events, locales, or persons, living or dead, is coincidental.

Copyright © 2025 William Zimmerman

Cover art and design by Marta Obucina

All rights reserved.

The scanning, uploading, and distribution of this book without permission is a theft of the author's intellectual property. If you would like permission to use material from the book (other than for review purposes), please contact will.zimmerman.j@gmail.com. Thank you for your support of the author's rights.

ISBN: 979-8-9990730-0-6

For Claire
Your support is everything to me

1

"You know the worst thing about war?"

Aethan didn't answer. They were supposed to be quiet, but Bulwark wasn't deterred.

"It ain't the usual. It ain't the violence. It ain't losing friends. It's this. Squatting in the jungle. Sweating so bad you feel like you're swimming, but so thirsty you'd drink your mate's piss."

"You ever been shot?" Aethan asked.

"Nah, I'm too quick," Bulwark said.

Aethan swiveled on his haunches to look at the big man squatting to his right. Were it not for the pipe in the man's mouth casting an orange glow on his face, Aethan wouldn't have seen him. His clothing, like Aethan's, was dark green to blend into the vegetation all around them. His matchlock rested against his shoulder, the butt pressed into the mossy turf. Aethan was a tall man, but Bulwark was a head taller and twice as wide. The orange glow made him look like a grinning demon from a Dominion storybook. Aethan could just make out the man's fingers, undulating in the dark, clacking his slaver bones softly together.

It was day, but they were in the Greenwall, and the canopy was so thick that night was perpetual. If he looked up, he would have seen the little pinpricks of light that managed to sneak through the leaves, looking like stars, twinkling on and off as the leaves rustled in a wind that Aethan couldn't feel. When the wind blew above, there was no breeze below. When storms raged, the rain was redirected by the branches and flowed down the tree trunks in rivulets, picking up poisons and parasites on its descent. To drink it was suicide. The Greenwall had no seasons: no winter, no spring, no fall, only a wet summer that constantly smelled of decay.

"Then how would you know which is worse?" Aethan asked.

Bulwark's demon face grinned. He blew out smoke and the glow swelled.

"My boots ain't been dry since we got here. If I got shot, I could go home."

"To be buried maybe."

"Death don't scare me," he said and then motioned with his chin to the jungle around them. "I'm already in hell."

"Hush now," spoke a tiny voice to Aethan's right. "Captain said we was to keep quiet."

"You gonna make me, Weed?" Bulwark grumbled.

The girl squatted a few feet to Aethan's left. Aethan could barely make her out.

"Captain will," the girl said.

Weed was young, too young to be fighting, but the revolution made no distinction between age or gender. All had the right to serve the call for freedom. All had the right to die for the Freelands.

Aethan lifted his chin and watched the twinkling of the canopy above him. It was best not to think of such things. It was better to think of the sweat that poured out of him, that never evaporated, that only gathered to drip down his back and pool in the seat of his pants like he'd pissed himself. That thought was easy enough to focus on.

Was this why he'd left? To die of dysentery? Is this why the old woman, Ashatee, had forbidden him from going?

No, Aethan thought, she had been explicit in her reasons.

"Little tattle tale," Bulwark said.

"Captain will hear you himself if you keep at it," Weed answered, getting louder as she got frustrated.

"And what will he do? Send me to some paradise prison up north?"

"The captain could—"

2

A ripple came down the line of Freelanders. Bulwark touched two fingers to Aethan's shoulder, and Aethan passed the signal down, touching two fingers to Weed's. She cut herself off mid-sentence. Two fingers. The Dominion was coming.

"Thank the damn fates," Bulwark grumbled, shoving his slaver bones into one pocket. "Let's ruin some northern dogs."

Aethan lifted his own matchlock rifle, carefully maneuvering to keep the long barrel from getting caught in the vines overhead, and swiveled back to the big man. Bulwark held the embers in his pipe to the match on his gun, and then Aethan touched his match to Bulwark's until it flared to a glow.

"Ready, little tattle tale?" Bulwark asked, tapping his pipe against a tree and stowing it in a bag at his hip.

Weed nodded but said nothing.

"Just shoot, reload, and shoot. Leave the charging to us," Bulwark said.

He and Aethan had long knives at their belts. The Dominion depended on their guns, and guns were useless once you got past their barrels.

Another hand signal flashed down the line, three fingers this time, and Aethan pushed forward through the plants, watching the match on his gun to make sure it didn't get wet and go out. The jungle rustled around him as the other Freelanders did the same, and then a pale light began to show through the undergrowth.

Before them was the Amaranthine road, an ancient slab of granite that cut through the jungle and whose width prevented all but the most persistent trees from reaching across it. He still could not see the sky, but enough light came through that it felt like a late evening. The road was part of a network that ran all over the continent, stretching from the Greenwall in the south to the city of Sheras at the northern edge of the Ryker Dominion, from the sea in the east to the deserts in the west. The Greenwall was said to be full of the roads, but most had been long overgrown by creeping vines and brush, and not even the Dominion would creep deeper into the Greenwall than it had to.

The northern front was a quagmire that had congealed into a bloody stalemate, so the Dominion went around. Their ships dominated the seas and they shipped soldiers around the Freelands and into the Greenwall itself. Then they hacked away the jungle until the Amaranthine road revealed itself and marched straight into the Freeland's belly. Aethan's people viewed the Greenwall with too much darkness and horror to imagine that the Dominion could come through it, but they did. The bluebacks pushed all the way to South Harbor, and almost broke the revolution then and there before Old Chainbreaker conscripted the chaff of the Freelands and stymied the advance.

Now the Dominion was overextended and fighting in a second front far from its borders, a front that it could only reinforce from this road. That was why Aethan crouched in a place where more Freelanders died to snake bites and fever than they did from blades and bullets: to cut off the Dominion. To starve the bastards out.

"Down," Bulwark whispered.

Aethan settled on his stomach, grimacing as the wet ground soaked into his shirt. Bulwark lay on his right and he could just see Weed's frizzy hair poking up from the leaves on his left. They lay on the edge of a small ridge that ran alongside the road. It was a good place for an ambush.

He could hear the marching now, a vague rumble in the distance, barely distinguishable from the rustling of the leaves, and Aethan felt something stir in him. When they had left New Freedom, when their hodgepodge troop was ordered down into the Greenwall, Old Chainbreaker himself had spoken to them. Aethan had been in a crowd ten thousand strong, sweating at attention, and Chainbreaker's voice had carried across the field.

"Their Pale God drives them to seek dominion over all and to break the backs of those that would not be yoked. We will not be yoked, but though their god will wrath and wail and spit its fury, neither will our backs break. We Freelanders have no religion, for we will have no Master. But if a god does dwell within our hearts, let that god be neither mercy nor love nor justice. Let it be vengeance."

That was why Aethan had left Ashatee's hut by the lake, so that he could be the vengeance of his forefathers. The old woman had kindled in him a power that would put all the guns in the line to shame, a power that could be turned against the Dominion and burn them out of the Freelands like the cancer they were.

They will never accept you. Ashatee had said. *They will use you, and then they will kill you when the using is done. In the end, normal people are always afraid, and they would rather have you burn.*

Aethan shook the memory away. He knew she was right. He had heard of witches being burned in the countryside, but the revolution *would* accept him when it saw how useful he could be, how dedicated he was to protecting the Freelands. He just needed the right opportunity. Until now it had all been raids in the dark and violent and quick skirmishes amongst the leaves. His power would have had no great benefit in those chaotic and claustrophobic places, but now the rumbling was growing louder than a few dozen supply wagons, and Aethan knew this would be no small raid. He looked down at his hand gripping the barrel of his gun and saw that it was trembling.

"That's too many," Weed whispered.

"Shut up," Bulwark hissed.

"It was only supposed to be supplies," Weed breathed.

Aethan saw her lift her head to look at him. He met her eye and mouthed "down." She disappeared beneath the green.

Aethan reached a hand into his pocket to rub at his own slaver bones. The last real battle he'd been in was on the south bank of the Freeflow, before he'd met Ashatee, and he'd almost died there when a Dominion shot had gone through his thigh.

The din of the boots rose, and then the first soldiers came into sight. They came in ranks of eight with a drummer at every fourth row who rapped at his drum with each step. They walked all in unison, swaying with the beat, and the hands that weren't holding their matchlocks swung in time with their step. Aethan's breath caught in his throat as rank after rank materialized out of the gloom.

This was no supply caravan.

Someone had screwed up, badly. Aethan's troop of the too young and the too old numbered maybe a hundred, and already twice that number of Dominioneers had walked by. Aethan readied himself for the retreat, to slink back into the dark before–

The captain's bugle blared and Aethan's troop opened fire around him. The enemy were only some ten yards away and the heavy Freelander shot ripped into their sides and on through to the soldiers behind. The air filled with smoke and screams. Aethan squeezed his own trigger and the gun slammed back against his shoulder. The drummer was no longer beating, and the footfalls devolved into madness.

Another bugle sounded and Bulwark bellowed. He leaped down the embankment, leaving his gun behind and pulling his long knives from his belt. Aethan scrambled after him, fumbling at his own blades.

They tore into the Dominion soldiers, slicing open bellies and throats and groins. A Dominioneer before them leveled his gun, but the match hadn't been lit, and when he pulled the trigger, it only mashed against the firing plate. Bulwark stabbed him in the chest.

The enemy's order had entirely devolved. Officers drew swords and moved their mouths, but Aethan could hear no words. All was madness and panic, and the Dominioneers fled into the jungle, or stood frozen, or clutched at their own wounds.

It was a rout, yet when Aethan cut down a man, there was always another behind. More shots sounded behind him and the smoke in the air whirled. Dominioneers were flung to the floor, but others were turning to fight. Across the road, an officer had gotten a group of soldiers into a double line. The first rank jostled with the Freelanders, fending them off with bayonets, while the line behind primed their guns and lit their matches.

If the Dominioneers regained their order, then Aethan's troop would be slaughtered. If ever there was a time for drastic measures, it was this time. This was his chance.

Aethan dropped to a crouch and looked at the ground, but instead of blood and road, he saw Ashatee's lake in the forest. He saw the ripple of a pebble dropped into still water, and he focused on the tiny waves until the sounds of battle were out of his awareness, and he found the corridor within.

Aethan didn't know if the corridor was a real place or just a trick of the mind, but he navigated it all the same, turning at one intersection and then another until the door appeared before him.

It was a massive thing, appearing to him like the cold marble mausoleum he'd crawled into as a child. He'd fallen and broken his leg. He'd lain there for three days before his father had found him, half frozen and more than halfway to dead. The door within him was that same tomb's door, and the sight of it filled him with dread.

Such was the nature of the door within, Ashatee had told him. It did not want to be opened, and it used whatever tricks it could to prevent it. The mausoleum filled Aethan with an old terror, but Aethan was stronger than fear. He was a Freelander, protecting his people from the Dominion who wanted the Korkin empire back, who wanted the Freelanders to be slaves again. He was a child of the revolution, and he would not let fear rule him. He gripped the door's handle and heaved against its bulk.

It opened, and behind was nothing.

Truly nothing. A blackness entirely void of light. There were no dimensions to it, no sign at all that it was anything more than a two-dimensional nothing, and yet it was deep. It seemed to him unimaginably vast and completely beyond his comprehension.

Aethan subvocalized the words Ashatee had taught him, and their symbols appeared before him in a spidery, silver script. They hung suspended against the darkness, morphing as his meaning was amended with rules and conditions. The words were old, older than humanity if Ashatee were to be believed, and even she did not understand them. Not entirely. What she did know, and what she taught Aethan, was that there was no room for double meaning in this tongue. The darkness demanded clarity.

Aethan finished his recitation, setting the parameters and the conditions, and then called the darkness forward. The void burst forth, pressing past the mausoleum door in a river of black, through the hanging symbols, and into the corridors of Aethan's self.

He emerged from within and the sounds and sights of the battle assaulted him. Screams, smoke, violence. He had practiced this, and his attention had only been away for a few moments. The line of Dominioneers had lit their matches and were leveling their guns. On the outside, Aethan pointed at them, and on the inside, he changed a symbol. The air in front of him burst into flame and he flung it forward in a plume of fire. The Dominioneers burned. He swept his arm towards another clump of Dominioneers and the fire claimed them too, along with a Freelander who'd been grappling too close. Aethan had no time to worry about one casualty though. He felt the darkness roiling through him and he was vengeance, a demon from the Dominion's own hell come to drag them screaming from life. A soldier charged him, and Aethan flicked his wrist and the soldier burned too.

Ashatee would have chided him for using his hand as an anchor. She would have stood still while the death played out around her. A child she would have called him, a child playing with matches in a house made of paper.

Aethan spun and flared and pointed and killed and when he caught sight of Bulwark staring at him, dumbstruck, Aethan felt his own smile widen.

"Come, friend," Aethan called, laughing as he did. "We have killing yet to do!"

Then the volley came.

It ripped through them. The bullets whistled past and impacted trees, cracking the wood like thunder. They impacted the Amaranthine road and ricocheted through the growth. They impacted men, Freeland and Dominion both, and flung them back. Bulwark cried out and spun to the ground. A spray of blood followed him and spattered across the road. Aethan turned and saw a line of Dominioneers standing from their knees and falling into well-ordered gaps between columns of ready soldiers. The new front line knelt and pointed their matchlocks forward. Aethan reached out his right hand towards the line.

Another plume of heat spat forward, and half the column was engulfed in flame, but as he swept his hand to end them all, the other half fired. A bullet tore through the chest of a Dominion regular. A bullet ruined a Freelander's shin. A bullet ripped through Aethan's outstretched hand.

Aethan spun with the impact, his shoulder wrenching around behind him, and fell to the ground. He couldn't feel his hand. He couldn't feel his arm, and then he felt everything all at once. He rolled over and pulled his hand in front of his face. The pointer and middle fingers were gone, and the ring finger hung uselessly by a bit of flesh. Blood gushed out in little spurts. Aethan screamed.

Another volley turned the air into daggers. Men died. Bulwark lay several yards away crawling on the ground.

Aethan had to do something. He was going to die. Shadows on

the smoke swirled as the bullets tore through them, dancing like devils in the firelight.

He pushed to his knees and the next volley tore half his ear off. A man lurched through the twilight towards him, an infantry sword raised high. Aethan pointed at him and fire erupted forth. They were everywhere. He swung his arm to the left and the flame spread out in a great arch. There wasn't enough, there wasn't enough, he was going to die!

Aethan went back within and heaved at the great mausoleum door. Wider. Wider! The river of darkness became a flood. More bullets flew. Aethan tore the symbols out of the air. There was no time for precision. He heaved the door even wider and its frame warped out of shape.

Heat exploded outward from him. The air combusted, and the bodies nearest him blew into dust. The shock wave hit the trees on either side of the road and rent them from their roots. A circle of hell expanded outwards from Aethan in an instant.

Too much.

The world around him was only fire. He shut his eyes, withdrew within, and heaved the door closed. The darkness reacted, its flow suddenly reversing, streaming back through the door and back into the void, racing out of the world, out of him, and just before the door fully closed, the last tendril of darkness tucked itself away behind it. Then there was silence.

Aethan opened his eyes.

The world around him was desolated. There was nothing near him. Just a glassy substance where the road had been. A bit beyond bodies lay charred and broken. The jungle on either side of him for a hundred yards had been blown apart to broken timbers and the jungle beyond that was an inferno.

He pushed to his feet and cried out in pain when he pressed up with his ruined right hand.

He went to the nearest body, a large blackened thing in a heap, missing half its limbs. He nudged it over with his foot. It was Bulwark. Or at least, it could be. The person's face was gone, along with much of the bone beneath. Aethan turned and vomited on the granite.

He collapsed to his knees and screamed. His hand seared with pain, but he had to stop the bleeding or he would die. Die like Bulwark and Weed and every other person around him. All of his regiment. All of the Dominion soldiers.

He pulled his belt from his trousers and clumsily cinched it around his forearm. He looked around. The Amaranthine road was hot, he could feel its heat coming up through his shoes, but not enough for what he needed. His eyes fell on glowing metal near a body. It was a knife.

The leather grip had burned away, and the wooden pommel with it. But the blade itself remained, albeit somewhat deformed now, glowing a dull orange. Aethan staggered towards it, clenched his teeth around the end of his belt, and pressed the remains of his hand against the sword.

He passed out from the pain.

"Get up," a familiar voice said to him.

He opened his eyes and stared at the thatch and pitch roof of Ashatee's hovel. Mist rolled around him. The old woman had left the door open. She liked to do that in the mornings sometimes to wake him from sleep. Life, she said, was the accumulation of heat. It was what separated us from stones.

"But what about fire?" Aethan had asked, thinking himself very clever. "By that logic fire is alive."

"And who is to say it is not?" she had asked. "It grows. It eats. It dies."

"I say so. And so would many others."

"Ah," she had said. "But what do you and many others have in common?"

"What?" Aethan asked.

"You are all idiots."

Aethan rolled over to look across the one room hut and out the open door. The old woman sat upon the threshold, her back to him, looking out over the lake and shivering. With a word, she could summon a flame and burn away the fog around her. Her mastery went beyond the fire. She could command the darkness to pull reeds from the lake and weave them into a blanket. She could see a deer and command it to die and for the skin to pull itself into a coat. She could do all these things, but instead she chose to shiver.

She was brilliant in her knowledge of the Darkness, but here was one area that Aethan knew himself to be more intelligent. With power like hers, power he did not believe existed before she'd saved him, she could rule the continent. She could rip the Ryker Dominion from the world and protect the revolution once and for all.

Instead, she chose to shiver.

"And to what end would I dominate?" she said, facing away from him as she spoke.

Reading minds was not a trick he knew she possessed, and he quickly filtered through his thoughts the past few days, wondering what offense she might have gleaned.

"What would you do with the Pales if you could?" she asked. Her voice seemed so far away.

Aethan threw off the blankets and felt the air prickle his skin. He pushed himself to sitting and winced. His right hand burned for some reason. He flexed it and pushed it from his mind.

"Revenge our people," Aethan said.

"Our people?" she asked.

He wondered why she did not look at him. "The Freelands. The sons of slaves."

"I am no son of slaves."

"You know what I mean," he said.

The air warmed, and Aethan wondered if the old woman had finally called the Darkness to heat the room.

"Do I?" she asked.

"The daughters of slaves too. You were that. You cannot deny. You were a slave yourself! How can you sit and do nothing when you know the cruelty of the Pales? With the Darkness, you could fix the world, or, at least make great changes."

"Like the Amaranthine?" she asked.

He closed his eyes and took in a deep breath. She was always like this: intransigent and unwilling to give on a single point. Even unwilling to *make* a point, only questions questions questions.

His feet were wet.

Aethan opened his eyes and saw that he stood in the shallows of the lake. The mist was gone, burned away by the afternoon sun which beat down with sweltering heat. Ahead of him stood the hovel and in the shadow of the doorway, Ashatee sat, her face cast into darkness. Another one of her tricks that he had not yet seen.

"If you leave, you will die," she called out.

"I will not die!" Aethan yelled back. It was important that she understand. "I will use what you've taught me to fight for what is right!"

"And what is right, young wolf?"

"Freedom."

"And what is freedom?" she asked.

"I will not play this game, Ashatee. I will not be baited!"

"And yet you are. And yet you leave."

"I do not leave," Aethan said, tugging his pack's straps over his shoulder. "Not yet." The air was sweltering and muggy. Strange for the Shafala.

Finally, Ashatee A'alan stood. She walked towards him, but the sun was behind her and cast a harsh shadow over her face.

"Why do you leave?" she asked. She was close now, steps away, and he still could not see her face.

"To do my part."

"Of what, young wolf?" She reached up and grasped him by his shoulders. She was a small woman, only coming up to Aethan's chest, but she stood at eye level now and a sweet scent wafted from her. He still could not make out her shadowed face. The shadow was too harsh and the sun over her shoulder too much in his eye. The smell made his stomach growl. Meat thick with fat, roasting on the fire.

"Of the fight, Ashatee," he said.

"Of death, Aethan," she responded.

Aethan shook his head, but the woman turned him in a pivot, her grip like iron on his frame, and the sun came to light up her face.

It was burned to ruin. The skin melted away and blackened bone shown through her cheeks. One eye stared at him, bleeding from its socket, while the other oozed, deflated and sagging down her face. He recoiled and struggled against her grip, pressing against her body with all his might. The clothing tore away and her skin sloughed off with it, like muck from a pond stone.

"For it is death that you will find, and you will kill all the world. But then," the charred skull said, "what is death after all?"

2

Only two people Carlotte knew had ever disobeyed her mother
directly: her father, when her mother had ordered him not to die,
and her sister, Elspeth, when her mother ordered her not to leave.
Now that Elspeth was back, her mother didn't even try. Carlotte's
entire regimented life was put on hold by Elspeth's decree. She
didn't even go to her classes.

The gardens around their tower were expansive, and Elspeth
chased Carlotte through them in the way that she used to before
she'd left, before Carlotte had grown older and such antics had
become inappropriate. They ran and played until they collapsed,
exhausted in the sun, and then when they became too hot, they
curled up underneath a thick willow. The branches came down
around them like it was only the two of them in all the world. They
ate treats that her sister had taken from the kitchen, and Carlotte
watched the sun glittering through the gaps in the leaves, her head
resting on her sister's thigh while Elspeth lay against the trunk of
the tree.

"Mother is mad at you," Carlotte said. Elspeth did not answer.
"Is it because you left?"

"In part," Elspeth murmured. She traced her fingers along the
edge of Carlotte's ear.

"Why did you go?" Carlotte asked.

There was silence then, except for the sounds of the birds in the branches above them, and when Carlotte looked up at her sister she saw that her gaze was far away.

"Elspeth?"

Her sister looked down, the distant gaze banished.

"To study. To learn."

"About the Amaranthine?"

"In part."

"Why?" Carlotte asked. "History is so boring."

Elspeth laughed and it blended with the chattering of the birds in the trees.

"Classes and tutors are the first part of learning, but going out and discovering... that is the spark that makes life worth it. All this," and Elspeth waived at the canopy of branches, "this and the city beyond and the Dominion... It's all so fragile. The world works around us, and we bend like this tree, and when the wind grows harsh we break." Elspeth snapped her fingers. "And like the willow, we don't know what it is that bends us. We only feel its force."

Elspeth's face grew dark and Carlotte worried that she had asked the wrong question and ruined the afternoon.

"It's all so fragile," Elspeth repeated, just above a whisper, and her look was distant again as though she could see through the tent of branches and out into the world.

A woman peeked her head into the dome of leaves and then ducked away. She was a servant checking up on them for their mother. Most of their servants were women then. Her mother said the young men who used to serve them dinner had been needed for the war in the south.

"I know what they say about me," Elspeth whispered and Carlotte looked back up at her sister. Elspeth's eyes were trained on the spot where the woman had been. "I heard it. Even in the mountains it came to me, and I see it here, but they are all fools."

Carlotte said nothing. She was well aware of what they said about her sister. She'd heard them too, though not directly. When the other Ryker lords and their children came to DeSheras functions and her mother was out of ear shot, they wondered at Elspeth and what she had been doing in the mountains.

"Fools who bury their heads in the sand."

Carlotte squirmed, and Elspeth put a firm look on her face. She pinched some dirt between her fingers and then rubbed them together until a single grain remained.

"If the garden is all knowledge, then this grain is all we know. There is so much of the world that passes by us unseen, and it is up to you..." She flicked the grain away and poked Carlotte on the nose, "to learn everything you can so that you can discover more of it. God put us on the earth to learn."

Carlotte pinched up her face.

"But I hate class."

Elspeth looked down at her for a long moment.

"I think we'll skip class again tomorrow. I want to show you some things."

The next day Elspeth woke Carlotte at dawn and pushed her into a carriage. Carlotte ate pastries and sausages as they rolled through the city, and Elspeth sipped coffee that had been smuggled across the front lines. When they arrived at the edge of the city, horses and a small retinue of soldiers and servants waited for them. They mounted up and rode, and while they did so Elspeth talked to Carlotte of the world. She quizzed Carlotte on the laws of physics, on mathematics, and on the flora and fauna around them, and though Carlotte feared the day would become dull, she wanted very much to impress her older sister and did her best to answer. Elspeth corrected her when she was wrong and enlightened her when her understanding was weak and made Carlotte feel intelligent. Soon she was having fun, and Elspeth began to show her things Carlotte's tutors hadn't. They sat before a lake and splashed it with their hands, watching the ripples and describing their motion as they interacted with each other. They calculated the height of a tree using a stick and the sun's shadow, and Elspeth climbed it to drop rocks, making Carlotte time them and calculate their acceleration. Then they sat down to a prepared picnic, and Elspeth talked to Carlotte about things neither understood.

They watched a flock of birds and wondered at the way they all turned simultaneously. They wondered at what caused the wind and why rain fell. They talked about life and what separated it from death and what separated the higher forms of life from the lower.

They talked, and the hours of the afternoon drifted away while servants erected a pavilion by the lake so they could lounge and watch the water.

"Would you like to see something I found in the mountains?" Elspeth asked as the shadows of the pavilion grew long.

Carlotte nodded and Elspeth shooed the servants and soldiers away. She dropped the rolled fabric on the sides of the pavilion so that all Carlotte could see was the water in front of them, and again Carlotte felt as though it were only them in the whole world.

Elspeth pulled up the rug and cleared away a section of dirt that had no grass. She dug a finger into the earth and drew. It was simple, a dot with two arcs around it, radiating outward in opposite directions, like an eye with the lids off set.

"What is it?" Carlotte asked.

"Light."

Carlotte didn't understand, but unease crept into her. Elspeth had gone north to Amaranthine ruins deep in the mountains, and that had not made sense to Carlotte. She knew her sister and she knew that the past was not what interested her. It was not the past they had discussed during the long nights spent stargazing atop their tower. It was the future, and the glory that they could make in it. For Elspeth to have gone to the ruins, she must have been looking for something.

"The Amaranthine symbol for light?" Carlotte asked.

"No," Elspeth murmured. "It's not their language. It is something older I think." She looked up at Carlotte. "Can you keep a secret?"

Carlotte nodded and felt her stomach drop. She could hear the whispers of the other Ryker lords and ladies, whispers about her sister's obsessions. Elspeth reached into her pocket and pulled out a small metal ball with an eyelet attached to its surface. She held it out and Carlotte opened her hands. Elspeth dropped it, and Carlotte cringed like it would burn her, but it did not. It was just a ball.

"Look at it," Elspeth urged, and Carlotte brought it to her eye. Its surface was not perfectly smooth. There were lines that ran from the eyelet to the opposite pole. Carlotte looked up at her sister.

"I found that in the mountains where the ice never melts," her sister said. Then, she bent at the waist, put her face near Carlotte's hands, and whispered something Carlotte could not hear.

The sphere in Carlotte's hands moved, and she gave a little squeak. Its surface retracted on itself, separating into tiny sheets at each of the lines and withdrawing beneath each other to reveal a brilliant light beneath.

Carlotte gasped and brought one hand up to shield her eyes. The plates continued to withdraw until it was a tiny stack of metal in the shape of a crescent moon, with a pebble of white light suspended at the center. Carlotte looked up at her sister. This was wrong.

"Magic doesn't exist," Carlotte breathed.

"Magic is just a word," Elspeth said. "Look closer."

Carlotte did not want to, but neither did she want to disappoint her sister, so she forced herself to look into the light. She felt it blinding her to the world around them, but as she stared, she saw at its core the symbol Elspeth had drawn in the dirt.

"Magic..." Elspeth paused, choosing her words before she said them. "This force... is real. This exists. Your tutors have lied to you."

"God says it does not," Carlotte said.

Elspeth shook her head.

"The priests say it does not and priests are men. God created it, and God wants us to understand."

"But..." Carlotte began. She could not look away from the light and the symbol in its center. "But magic destroyed the Amaranthine."

"Ignorance destroyed them. A gun may kill its master, but should we refuse to understand how black powder works? Of course not."

Elspeth reached out her hand and closed Carlotte's fingers around the pebble. She felt it squirm like a cockroach, closing back into its silver sphere. Elspeth leaned in close and held one hand to Carlotte's face. Carlotte saw the red lines in her sister's eyes and the dark pouches beneath them. She smelled the faintly rotten scent of Elspeth's breath.

"Your tutors would tell you we largely understand the world, but do not be fooled, Carlotte. There are parts of this world that we can't begin to comprehend. Not yet. We Rykers seized power with knowledge, but we ignore a force more powerful than all the black powder in the world.

"The inquisitors-" Carlotte began, but Elspeth finished for her.

"Are fools. Before the fall, Amaranthine power was beyond imagining. They created golems of mud and steel that walked. They conquered the continent with land ships that rolled across the earth on great wheels." Elspeth drew even closer and Carlotte pulled away without thinking, but Elspeth grabbed the back of Carlotte's head and held her close. "They built a device that could heal sickness and dismemberment, that could bring the dead back to life. Kel Shoatone."

Carlotte shook her head.

"It means the 'Re-creator' and it was in a place called Lok Secrak. There were references to it in the ruins. Records of Amaranthines sent there for healing."

"That's impossible," Carlotte breathed.

"With God," Elspeth murmured, shifting back on her heels, "Anything is possible, and with God, all things are understandable."

They were silent for a moment, and then Elspeth raised the dropped sides of the pavilion and called for wine. Carlotte stuffed the metal pebble into a pocket on the breast of her dress. It lay there against her chest, unnaturally heavy while the servant poured wine for Elspeth and a smaller glass for Carlotte.

Conversation was sparse for a while, but then picked up and Elspeth had Carlotte again wondering at the mysteries of the world. When evening came they mounted their horses and trundled back to the carriage. Carlotte did not want the day to end and she knew that when it did, things would not be the same. Elspeth had ridden ahead of her caravan to come home early, and the caravan was to arrive the next day, bringing with it all that Elspeth had found in the mountains. Things would not be so carefree then. Elspeth would have work to do and Carlotte would have classes to attend.

When the carriage pulled to a stop, the driver knocked twice to announce they had arrived, but Carlotte grabbed Elspeth's hand before she could open the door.

"What did you say to make the light?"

Elspeth smiled mischievously and leaned in close.

"Lix."

"How does it work,?" Carlotte asked, and joy filled Elspeth's eyes.

"We have to figure it out. You and me. You need to learn everything you can so that you can help me."

They parted ways on the seventh landing. Carlotte went to her room, sad that her normal life was to resume the next day, but her sister's returning had brought a light into her dark, monotonous world, and it made the future seem bright and full. So, Carlotte sat hunched in her bed with the blankets in a tent above her, whispered the word to open the pebble of light, and imagined the future that she and her sister would discover.

The caravan did come the next day and the stairs of the Tower DeSheras were filled with laborers hefting large boxes up to Elspeth's laboratory on the tenth landing. When the last laborer left, Elspeth withdrew inside and closed the door. She stayed inside all through the day and though Carlotte hoped that she would rescue her from her mathematics lesson, she understood her sister's obsessions. Before Elspeth had left, she'd been known to spend days locked up in her laboratory, eating meals left at the door.

The next day she was absent from the dinner table again and then the next, her mother's face growing more dour with each empty chair. After dinner, on the third night, Carlotte climbed the stairs to the top of the tower and put her ear to the laboratory door. She heard nothing, so she climbed back down before anyone saw her snooping.

The fear she'd felt when Elspeth had first shown her the pebble vanished, and now Carlotte found herself disappointed each morning when it was not Elspeth who woke her, but some servant. She longed for Elspeth to take her up into her laboratory and invite her to discover the secrets of the Amaranthine, but Carlotte knew Elspeth would let her in when the time was right. So Carlotte studied harder, and devoted herself to learning everything her tutors could teach her. Her mother approved, and when a butler had come at dinner on the fifteenth day to tell her mother that Elspeth hadn't eaten her lunch or dinner, her mother brushed it aside and said that no amount of mania from Elspeth would distract her from Carlotte's merit.

Elspeth didn't eat her next breakfast either, or her lunch or dinner, and on the night of the seventeenth day, Cainia DeSheras climbed to the top of the tower and rapped on Elspeth's door. There was no answer, so Carlotte's mother told her to wait at the landing and asked the maid to unlock the door.

Her mother screamed, and Carlotte ran from the landing, tearing around the maid's attempts to block her, and froze at her mother's side. The room was littered with Elspeth's books and Amaranthine artifacts, all burned to ash. The walls were black with fire. Everything was destroyed, and at the center of the desolation was Elspeth's corpse, lying on her back, dried foam all down her chin and a broken vial at her side.

PART ONE

SHERAS - TEN YEARS LATER

3

"Where you headed, peasant?"

Aethan lifted his head. He hadn't seen the man resting in the shade of the ramshackle building, but now Aethan could see the deep blue of his coat and trousers. A blueback.

"Boneman?" The blueback asked and then nodded when Aethan pulled his horse, Toktok, to a stop beside the building.

Aethan shifted in his seat. This was the first person he'd talked to since... since he'd left the Freelands three weeks before.

"Freelander," Aethan said. The speech felt like gravel in his throat after so long in silence. Toktok wasn't much for conversation.

The blueback carried a matchlock rifle and used it like a staff, its tip coming even with the tricorn hat on his head.

"Right..." the man narrowed his eyes. "What's a Boneman doing north of Domsar?"

Aethan stared at him, unsure of how he was supposed to respond. "Trading," he said eventually.

"Trading what?"

"Do you want to see?"

"What's that, boy?"

Aethan looked down at the soldier who couldn't have been more than a few years older than Aethan himself and felt that old familiar hatred flare up in him. He pushed it down though. Nothing good ever came from it.

"Do you want to see?" Aethan said, louder this time. The man scrunched up his face even more, eyes squinted into little slits.

"Yeah, I think you'd best show me."

Aethan shifted the reins to his right hand and reached back to undo the knot holding the oilcloth over his cart.

"A Boneman gimp! Now there's something. You fight in the war? Maybe it was me that blew your hand off!"

The man cackled at the thought, and after a moment, Aethan went back to unhitching the knot. His right hand clutched the reins between his thumb and pinky, the only fingers on that hand the bullet had left. He ignored the jibe. The man's opinions were worth nothing.

Aethan threw the oilcloth back and revealed neat rows of shiny matchlock rifles nestled in straw; quality arms from the forges of Wesley & Son's in the Freelands. The blueback whistled.

"Guns?"

Aethan nodded.

"The peasants here can't buy guns, Boneman."

"They aren't for the peasants."

The man raised an eyebrow.

"They are for the Armory in Sheras," Aethan said.

The gunsmiths in Sheras were said to be buying up all the iron they could, which could only mean the Dominion was arming, and when arms were being bought, Freelander arms, especially Wesley and Sons' firearms, could be sold at a premium. No gunsmith in the Dominion could make a matchlock that stood up to a Wesley and Sons.

"A Boneman gimp selling guns to the Mareshal?"

"Is there a law against it?" Aethan asked, knowing full well there wasn't. The soldier burst into laughter, sounding a bit like a barking dog.

"Hell, you Bonemen really do grub for gold don't you?" the man said between guffaws.

Aethan felt the temperature rise in his cheeks but said nothing.

"Well, Boneman. You can't just sell guns to the Mareshal either. You need a permit to transport goods on Dominion roads."

Aethan tossed the oilcloth back over the weapons and fished a parchment out of his coat pocket. The blueback made a show of looking it over. Aethan didn't think he could read.

"Well, off you go then," the man said and handed the paper back.

"Is there... an inn here?" Aethan asked after a moment. He did not typically stay at inns. They were expensive, and every coin spent was a coin less in his pack. The Dominion wind was cold though, and the thought of a bed and a warm meal was hard to ignore.

"An inn? I've no idea," the soldier said.

"But... aren't you stationed--"

Then he heard the scream. A woman's scream, and the distant jeering of a crowd.

"Nah. Ain't stationed in this shit hole," the blueback said, as though the scream was nothing but a bird call. "Just passing through with the inquisitor."

Aethan's core seized and for a moment his breath was stuck in his chest. He considered turning his horse then and there and taking his chances riding through the fields that surrounded the little town. No. That would only lead to attention, and a broken axle besides.

The screams grew louder and the blueback noticed Aethan's discomfort.

"What's the matter? I heard you bonemen draw and quarter your witches."

Aethan nodded. The Freelanders did all sorts of things to accused witches and Aethan had seen several of them. A people did not need God to hate.

"You soft for them or something?"

Aethan shook his head. "I've just no taste for it."

"Well, you chose a bad time to come here then. Woman had it coming though. Claimed she worked ungodly powers to heal folk."

A likely story. No one would claim they worked ungodly powers. Not even in the Freelands, where the Dominion religion was only a story. The woman was more likely some herbalist. Some widow with no one to stand up for her.

Aethan gave a curt nod and smacked at the reins, lurching his cart forward.

"Get a good look for me!" the blueback shouted after him. "I'm always stationed too far to see anything good!"

The street was empty. There were no old people looking through windows or men leaning against doorways. There were no children running through the streets or wives hanging clothes to dry underneath the eaves. He heard the people though. Their jeers were loud and only grew louder as Aethan rolled through the town with its buildings looking like shacks rammed up against the old Amaranthine road that gave the place purpose.

The screams of the woman reached a high pitch, and then he could smell her. Burning hair and cooked meat. No matter how far he roamed, it seemed he would never escape the smell of burning bodies.

Aethan considered riding down one of the muddy alleyways that split off from the main road. He could skirt whatever this thing was, avoid the whole damned affair, pass through this town like a ghost, with no one save that lone blueback to testify to his presence. No. He should look. As a reminder. As a warning to himself. Aethan reached into his pocket to touch the slaver bones there. It was always important to remember how bad things could get.

The screaming had stopped by the time he reached the square, really just a large patch of dirt next to the road that had nothing built on it. It was full of people, more people than Aethan would have thought could come from a place this small. Some twenty men in starched blue coats ringed the crowd, and in the middle of the whole mess was the pyre. Aethan smelled burning hair and meat, and another smell that seemed out of place: lavender and sage. He felt a small scratching at the back of his throat. The pyre was a mound of branches and brambles with a long log sticking up the middle. Through the flames, Aethan could see the shape of a body. His stomach turned. He was glad he had not eaten.

Beside the stake was the inquisitor. Their order was impossible to miss, with their black coats trimmed in white, and their knee-high riding boots. They wore the same tricorn hats that were popular all over the dominion, but they wore a white feather in theirs, contrasting against the black.

This one stood close to the flames, close enough that the heat must have been painful like he suffered with the woman. His nose was long and hooked down, like a hawk's beak. The man turned then, and his eyes caught Aethan's for just a moment, marking the newcomer to his theater. He cleared his voice.

"This... woman," he said, barking the word like a slur, "is just a woman!"

The crowd quieted and the inquisitor drew his eyes across every one of them. Their heads bowed as he did so, only to rise again when his gaze had passed.

"How do I know this?" he asked.

The crowd did not answer.

"I know this because there is only God and his grace! There are no ulterior powers. There are no supernatural evils. There are. No. Witches." He said, hitting each word like he beat them on an anvil. "There are only these," he jammed his finger at the bonfire. "Only those that would pretend otherwise. That would play on you and stir up blasphemous thoughts. This woman was a fraud and a temptress. A temptress away from God. A temptress for your soul."

Aethan wondered if she had been a witch. If perhaps she had some small door within her that she drew from. But no. It was unlikely. It did not work like the story books. There was no smattering of power that leaked out untrained. No unassuming boy found power flowing out with his teenage rage. One had to have the door within, and one had to be taught to open it, and to give it direction. If this woman had been trained, then she would not have let herself die here. This was just a woman who they'd decided to make an example of. Though... Ashatee had spoken of those who chose to die instead of defending themselves. That was something Aethan had never understood. For all his pain and regret, he had no interest in letting others kill him.

"Who was she?" Aethan asked, reaching down to tap a man's shoulder who stood just before him.

The man glanced back. "An old healer woman. A witch."

"Of course," Aethan withdrew.

No, this woman was no witch. Using the darkness to heal would take incredible precision. Aethan had never seen it done. As powerful as Ashatee was, she'd used herbs and bandages to heal Aethan when she'd found him. If this woman could heal she would have been powerful indeed, and this lot--

Aethan's thought trailed off as he noticed several members of the crowd glance back at him with sneers on their faces. The inquisitor was staring him down.

"No witch or evil will get you while your faith in God is strong. All you need fear is the path away from God. The southern path of the old Korkin empire. It is they and their Godlessness, leaking across the border and corrupting people like this woman. They who call for war and death and suffering."

Aethan clicked his tongue and tapped gently at Toktok's hide with the reins. The smell of burnt flesh came on him again, and his stomach churned. He needed to leave now. He should not have talked to the man. He should not have come through the town at all. He should have taken his chances traveling through the fields that surrounded it. Broken axles be damned. It was not worth the risk.

There was no inn for him here. There was no inn in the world for him. There was only the goal. Fifty pounds of gold and he would buy up some land in the east, at the edge of the Freelands, by a lake that no road, Amaranthine or otherwise, led to. He wouldn't have to see people anymore. He wouldn't have to bear witness to the way people treated each other. He wouldn't have to watch the cruelty, and the neglect, and the hatred. The world could go on turning without him. Fifty pounds of gold and he could furnish the house, and stockpile it, and build a landing in the water where he could fish and sit and be alone until he died in ignominy. Where his body could lay undiscovered for generations.

Aethan passed the other edge of the town and saw another blueback watching this bit of road. He leaned in the shade and did not stop Aethan from leaving. Aethan waited until the man was several hundred yards away, and then leaned forward and felt for the satchel of coins underneath his seat.

It was exactly where he always kept it. The feel of it calmed his nerves. Forty pounds, Aethan reckoned. It had been forty-seven before he'd bought up his cargo to make this last venture northward, and when he sold the cargo, he reckoned it would be fifty strong. He'd thought long and hard before he'd spent it. What really was forty-seven to fifty? But no, he'd settled on fifty and he would get his fifty. He squeezed at the tough canvas, feeling the coins rubbing against one another. The coins were from all over. Freeland Stones embossed with the Revolution's scythe and ax, Dominion Rakes with the Mareshal's scowling face, Bergshalen Queens with the Mad queen's profile, and some coins even from across the desert, from the peoples who had sold Aethan's people to the Korkin so long ago. The faces didn't matter. Currency was fickle, but gold was always worth something, and fifty pounds of it was worth quite a lot.

Fifty pounds of gold, and he'd never smell humans burning again.

That night, when Aethan ate salt pork and hardtack by a little fire just off the road, he withdrew into himself and walked the corridors of his soul until he was at the door.

It was still the mausoleum, but ever since the Greenwall it didn't stand in the graveyard. Now it rose out of the jungle, encrusted with creeping vines and shaded by the Greenwall's canopy. The door was lit from below where the desolated land burned, and bodies littered the ground. It was not realistic. Aethan remembered that day very clearly and the bodies had been burned almost beyond recognition, but here, Bulwark's face was clearly visible through the blistered and bubbled skin. Weed lay beside him, one eye wide with terror while the other oozed out of her socket. He could smell them burning, and his body began to shake. He didn't open the door. He hadn't opened it in more than a decade, not since the massacre.

He turned and left, withdrawing back into the world and his little fire, the scent of flesh still lingering in his nose.

"Fifty pounds," he whispered. "Fifty pounds."

4

"What do you pray for?"

Carlotte opened her eyes but did not turn her head. She considered her answer for a moment, and then placed the little dowel into the flame of the first candle and lit a second beside it.

"Knowledge," she said.

"Knowledge?" Harold repeated. "Well, I'd be happy to tutor you."

She frowned, but before she could speak, he went on.

"Though I think more would be learned if you tutored me."

Carlotte gave a short but genuine laugh.

"You play on the edge, Monsieur Orlient."

"Please, Carlotte," he said, moving forward to stand directly beside her. "It's very rude to forget my name."

"I didn't forget it."

"Why else would you call your fiancé by his family?"

She laughed again and he moved even closer. They were both looking forward at the statue of the Saint in front of them, so it wasn't terribly improper. There was some privacy in the back of the Cathedral, but not so much that it would cause very many whispers.

"Parsaille is a strange choice," he said.

"Oh? And why is that?" Carlotte asked.

The artist had carved the statue's face with delicate curves and painted her cheeks with a lovely rose, and they'd angled the saint's gaze upward, rising gently towards the heavens.

"She was a woman of science," Carlotte said and from the corner of her eye she saw Harold nod.

"But she knew nothing of love or family. Ended her line, you know. She threw away a powerful legacy in Domsar."

"She also designed the aqueducts there. The ones in Sheras are based on hers. Her work in sanitation has saved thousands of lives. She changed the Dominion for the better... family lines end all the time, but she is remembered here," Carlotte said and it was Harold's turn to laugh.

"Nothing is eternal, I suppose."

"Well said."

"And the other candle?" Harold asked, "What was it for?"

She scowled. It had been a silly thing, a selfish choice to light it, but it felt so good to give into the dream, if only for a minute. For a moment she considered telling the truth, but only in the way that she considered standing up in the middle of mass and screaming, or taking off her dress and running naked through the streets. Foolish little girl thoughts.

Carlotte turned and he turned with her and they were suddenly very close together. It was no longer appropriate, but it was effective and it was necessary.

"What does Carlotte DeSheras need other than knowledge?" he asked and she took in a fragile breath and looked up at him through fluttering eyelashes. She could smell oranges, his cologne, and another deeper, mustier scent that must have been his own. It was vaguely rotten.

"Love," she lied, and looked into his eyes. She smiled and felt the blood rush to her cheeks in what she hoped was a rose as pleasant as the paint on the saint's face.

He smiled too and then gave a little cough. They both stepped back as though they'd only just become aware of how close they'd been.

"Would you come to my home for tea?" he asked. He bit the corner of his lip.

"I wish I could," Carlotte said, "But I've got work to do. Science waits for no woman."

"Surely you could spare a half hour to make my day brighter?"

Carlotte shook her head with a girlish laugh.

"We'll be married soon enough and then you won't be able to get rid of me."

"I would never want to," he said.

"I'm sorry. I know how long teas at the Orlient's actually take and I've got the exhibition tonight. I really must prepare."

"If I know Carlotte DeSheras, I know she'd have been prepared days ago, surely--"

"No, Harold, I'm sorry," she said with a bit more finality than she intended, "But I really must be home."

There was a moment of silence and then Harold nodded.

"Of course," he said. "Until tonight then."

He gave a stiff, shallow bow, and then turned and walked away. Carlotte took in a deep breath and let it out slowly, watching her fiancé stride away. She'd been too harsh. She should have turned him down more gently, and the fact that she didn't know how she could have done so did not look good on her. She turned back to the saint.

"Anything you could teach me about dealing with men?" she asked.

There was no response. Parsaille wouldn't have been the saint to ask such a question to anyway. She'd forsaken men for God.

The second candle had been silly. She shouldn't pray for things she couldn't have. That's what children did. Women knew that the choice one didn't have always looked better, but only because you couldn't see the downsides. Carlotte was not Saint Parsaille, and Saint Parsaille hadn't been Carlotte DeSheras. Saint Parsaille had never really needed her womb.

Carlotte stuck a finger in her mouth, rubbed the wet against her thumb, and then pinched out the second candle.

"God!" she hissed and snatched her arm back, resisting the urge to stick her fingers back in her mouth. She'd never gotten the hang of that trick. She always held the wick for a moment too long. Carlotte looked up at the saint's face, muttered a prayer of forgiveness for her language, and turned to leave the cathedral.

The statue of Saint Parsaille was at the back wall, behind the enormous stage ringed in gold filigree. The stage was lit by the great windows high above, and as she walked around the edge, passing by alcoves with other saints, she felt as though she were walking in darkness. She could see easily, the light diffused well enough, and the prayer candles that flickered beneath the statues cast light, but it all paled in comparison to the brilliance of the stage with the midmorning sunlight glittering from the gold canopy and the archbishop's pulpit. It was almost difficult to look at after spending so much time with Parsaille. She should have left long ago. She shouldn't have stayed long enough to give Harold the chance.

The pews were empty except for a few minor Rykers who sat in their unimportant seats in the center of the massive chamber. Carlotte had no doubt most of them had moved up from where they'd actually sat during the service. It was common enough among the unimportant who wanted to be noticed.

The ones who sat with their hands drawn together and their heads bowed were almost certainly putting on a show, but the few who looked up at the ceiling, their mouths twitching in silent repetition while their fingers counted through the beads in their hands, may have been honest. It was a position Carlotte herself assumed when her faith wasn't as hard as she needed it to be.

On the ceiling was a mural spanning the length of the cathedral and Carlotte knew it almost by heart. There was God, painted as a bearded giant, pointing down at the fabled Amaranthine Capitol perched on top of the mountain. Fire rained down upon it, and at God's command, angels flew through the city's streets and pulled the screaming Amaranthine citizens up to their judgment. At the center of it all, at the very tip of the mountain, was the council that ruled the old empire, wielding their sorcery in defiance. A great serpent of flame emerged from their hands, but instead of biting at the giant in the sky, it turned back, its mouth open wide, ready to consume those who dared challenge God.

Carlotte's great grandfather had painted it. A few hundred hired artists did most of the brushwork, but when the people of Sheras looked up at the painting, at God, they did so through Carlotte's family's name. Her family *was* the city, and since her sister's death, Carlotte was the last DeSheras. That was why she could not do as she pleased.

She lingered by a decorative pillar that bore no weight and looked up at the painting, up into God's accusing eyes. She whispered a prayer for her sister's soul, and then hurried out of the Cathedral.

Four armed men in the DeSheras livery flanked her as she stepped through the door. They kept perfect distance from each other and from her as she descended the enormous steps of the cathedral. The outer shell of the cathedral and its foundation were actually older than the city itself. The cathedral, like the stairs that led up to it, and the wide main street of the city that carried on a hundred yards into the sea, were left over from that same Amaranthine Empire that God had cast down. It was all made of the same white granite that did not seem to age, and all of it had been made to match the Amaranthine's outsized egos. The steps were each over a foot tall, and even with the half steps the church had installed between the originals, it always made Carlotte feel like she was about to bowl over and roll down to the street below. It took a people who thought themselves greater than God to build so impractically.

"Lady."

Carlotte spun around, hand to her heart, and found her lady's maid, Saara, standing just behind her, one massive Amaranthine step above, dressed in the same livery as her guards. Carlotte narrowed her eyes and stepped up to be on even footing. Carlotte was very aware that her maid was three inches shorter than her, and thirty or forty pounds heavier. Saara stood with a slight hunch to her shoulders, like a bull slowly considering a charge.

"I really must get you a bell."

Saara nodded and the tight bun that the woman always wore bobbed with the movement. The small black ribbon that held it together seemed to pull the skin of her face back with it.

"I've called a carriage--" Saara began but Carlotte cut her off.

"Good, I need to be back at the tower. I need to be away from here."

Carlotte's mind was still on her sister, Elspeth, and she needed to clear her head.

"Your mother would like a word," Saara said and motioned off to the side.

Carlotte followed the gesture to see her mother standing higher up on the steps, speaking with her own assistant, Enriq, and surrounded by guards.

"What about?" Carlotte asked, and Saara shrugged. Carlotte considered ordering Saara to call up the carriage anyway. If she ordered it Saara would do it, and Carlotte's mother would never make a scene. The thought was nice, but it also left her feeling a little sick. She was being petulant. She could feel the rumbles of a tantrum crawling up her throat. Children were supposed to obey their parents. It was in the holy books and God would not have put the rule there if he didn't want it so.

Carlotte whispered a short prayer for patience and climbed back up the stairs.

Her mother nodded as she approached, and Saara, Enriq, and the guards stepped back. They turned their heads away.

"Mother," Carlotte said, and gave a small curtsy.

"Why did you say no to Harold?" her mother asked.

Of course her mother knew what she had said. Her mother always had someone watching.

"The exhibition is tonight and I need to prepare."

Her mother frowned.

"You are already prepared."

"I can never be prepa--"

Her mother held up her hand and Carlotte stopped talking.

"You're being childish. Send word that you changed your mind. You need to get used to obeying your husband."

"He's not my husband yet, Mother," Carlotte said.

"All the more reason for you to get used to it."

"But mother-"

Her mother placed a hand on Carlotte's shoulder and pulled her face close to Carlotte's.

"The Lord God said that women should obey their husbands."

"I know what the books say--"

"But," Carlotte's mother interrupted, gripping her shoulder even tighter. "You are the Heir DeSheras." Her mother hissed out their family name, holding on to the s at the end. "He is taking your name, and he must take your direction, but you must obey him." Her mother smiled and pulled back, turning her grip on Carlotte's shoulder into a pat.

"It is difficult. So you should get the practice."

With that, her mother descended the stairs. Enriq and the guards fell into formation around her. A carriage pulled up with the green and purple DeSheras colors and Enriq pulled down the step ladder just in time for her mother to mount it.

The tantrum was still in the back of Carlotte's throat. She could feel it.

"Madam," Saara said from just over her shoulder. Carlotte turned and found the woman standing again one step above her. "To the tower then?"

Carlotte shook her head and turned back to the street, suddenly much too tired to insist on being on even ground.

"Apparently I'm going to tea."

Carlotte drank a glass of black tea imported from across the desert and then had a small glass of coffee from the Freelands before taking a few bites of a chocolate cake baked by one of the finest bakeries in Sheras. After that, she, accompanied by Harold and some twenty other guests, moved to a different drawing room on the west side of the Orlient's manor where the light was better and had some crispy flake pastries made of stacked wafer dough and honey. While Carlotte drank a green tea that tasted like mint and ginger and that bit the back of her throat, they all talked about the state of the Dominion. The Lady Orlient then led the ladies on a circuit through a gallery while the men began to smoke. Carlotte had been in the same gallery just the week before, but all the paintings were new and most had been imported from Domsar. Carlotte recognized the artists' names. Everyone did.

An hour later they joined the men for cocktails and wine in the library where they all sat on tufted leather chairs and listened to a vocalist who sang sad songs about the war, though Carlotte wasn't sure which one.

"Do you like singing?" Harold whispered into her ear. He was sitting just behind her and she could feel his fingers gripping the back of her chair.

"I prefer strings," Carlotte said.

"Ah. Next week we will have the violinist, Visoletta. She's playing this month at the Grand Theater. She doesn't do private performances you know, but mother saw to it."

Carlotte nodded but didn't respond. She kept her eyes focused forward.

"You'll love it," he said.

"I hope I can make it," she said.

"Of course," he whispered, and leaned back into his chair.

When the singer was done, they had a selection of cheeses aged in caves, and salted meats with a jam glaze, prearranged in bite-sized portions on top of crispy bread. They went out onto the veranda and Carlotte had a white tea that tasted like acai berries from the Freelands with a bit of clear wheat liquor that poured like syrup. There were jugglers and a trio of acrobats who stacked themselves on top of each other and formed suggestive poses. Harold's arm snaked around hers, and she clasped it as was appropriate. The Lord Orlient caught their eye and tapped his nose in warning, but then winked.

They went back inside to a third room which had windows on the ceiling and a large fire at one end, and servants served them snifters of port and an herbal tea that smelled of cinnamon and tasted like allspice and dram.

Carlotte looked up at the clock that stood against the wall behind the Lord Orlient. She'd arrived at eleven and it was nearly four. If she was there much longer she'd have to go upstairs and change for dinner. She knew the Lady Orlient had several closets on demand for such eventualities. Carlotte had used them before.

She sighed and took a sip of her tea that had grown cold. She didn't actually need to prepare for her exhibition. Harold and her mother had been right that she was prepared, and Carlotte tried to remind herself that this was good for her. This wasn't wasted time. Social ties were just as important as scientific progress. When she was the Lady DeSheras, most of her time would go to this sort of thing.

She glanced at the clock again and sipped. She grimaced. It was a travesty that no one had invented a tea cup that kept the tea warm. Perhaps if she built a compartment on the bottom where a hot coal could be placed...

The Lord Orlient barked a laugh that jolted her out of her musings.

"Military is the secret, the only secret, to a nation's success. Without their military the Freelanders wouldn't be so free and the Korkin Empire would still be around. Because of their military, the Freelanders have a right to exist. It is the foundation for any nation to exist. Without it you don't get to choose your name because someone else chooses it for you."

"Well of course," said the Lord Aeshire, a older Ryker in a long white coat with blue frills down the front. Carlotte couldn't remember where his money came from. Something to do with farming. "I don't think anyone could argue, but what you really speak of is power and the military is just one wing of that power."

"Just one wing?" the Lord Orlient boomed. He was a barrel chested man, with long mustaches as was the current style for Ryker men. His hair line had receded to a severe widow's peak, and he kept it cut close to the scalp. He was standing with his foot up on the bench that ran along the edge of the fireplace. He adjusted himself to look directly at Aeshire.

"Politics, Science, Economy--" the Lord Aeshire began, but the Lord Orlient barked over him.

"Lets see how much all that matters when a troop of the Marshal's own marches into your town. All those things support the military. They are the means and the military is the end! How does politics, science, or economy stand up to the long barrels of the Mareshal's muskets!"

"Especially if you made the muskets?" Lady Aeshire said, seated just behind her husband. She took a sip from her cup and looked over it at the Lord Orlient. There was a moment of silence, and then Harold's father guffawed and slapped at his knee.

"Especially then, Lady! Especially then!"

The room tittered.

"The Military certainly suits you," the Lady Aeshire said. "If only my husband could convince the Mareshal to kill with stalks of Barley."

The room erupted into laughter, with the Lord Orlient laughing the loudest. Carlotte remembered then. The Aeshire's controlled the ale trade in Sheras and much of the Northern Dominion. She should have remembered that right away. Her mother would have. Carlotte lifted her cup to her lips, remembered it was cold, and set it back down. Perhaps they could just keep a hot poker nearby and when the tea cooled they could jab it in the cup to reheat--

"Carlotte?"

Her head snapped up, a delicate smile pinned as tight to her face as the Mareshal's flag was to the wall. The room was looking at her.

Shit.

"Your research? Carlotte? Lightning isn't it," Harold said beside her.

Carlotte took a breath to compose her thoughts. "It is, Monsieur Orlient, in a way. It started there and has taken some pleasant turns."

"Wonderful, simply wonderful," The Lord Orlient rumbled, "though it sounds inconvenient. Much like studying the stars, lightning is so dependent on the weather!" He boomed a laugh and several others took it up.

"Actually, my work is mostly in my labs."

"You study lightning indoors?" the Lady Carrell said from the other side of the semi-circle. She was a relatively minor Ryker, but Carlotte had been at her last exhibition on alchemical corrosion and found the woman brilliant. Their family... owned tenements in the outer city, or maybe inns. Carlotte turned in her chair to face the woman directly.

"Yes, technically--"

"She studies lightning in fishes!" Harold interjected. "She's shown them to me and they're very interesting!"

Carlotte opened her mouth to retort, but took a sip from her cold tea instead. She was an adult and adults didn't say rash things. No matter how much they wanted to.

"Lightning in fish?" the Lady Carrell said.

"Shaker fish!" Harold exclaimed, and then placed a hand on Carlotte's arm. She assumed the gesture was meant to be reassuring.

"Mostly knife-fish from down past the Freelands," Carlotte said.

"You must explain," the Lord Aeshire said.

"I believe..." Carlotte began, choosing her words, "that lightning is the same force that you can feel when you touch a shaker fish. Only smaller. Much smaller."

There was a pause as they all considered this. The Lord Orlient sat down in his chair and leaned forward, resting his considerable weight on a whale bone cane in front of him.

"The same force? And how did you come to this conclusion?" he asked.

"I--"

"She can make it! Small. Tiny lightning. I've seen it in her lab," Harold exclaimed.

"Tiny lightning? Really?" the Lady Carrell said. "How?"

"You'll have to see tonight," Carlotte said, "assuming this tea ever ends."

The room laughed, and Carlotte smiled. She was doing well. Her mother would've been proud.

"Tiny lightning!" the Lord Orlient mused. "Lightning! I wonder, is there a military application?"

"Why?" the Lord Aeshire cut in. "Will you buy up all the clouds then?"

"Ha! ha! Too expensive to get the mine carts up into the sky! I'll let someone else mine the clouds. The price of iron has doubled for three years straight. My administrators have plenty to do!"

"Only because you keep pushing all this military nonsense. The farmers have to use wooden plows because all the iron goes to the Mareshal," the Lord Aeshire fired back in good jest. The debate over militarization continued and Carlotte's attention drifted slowly to her lab in the tower, to the work she could be doing. Every second counted. She looked over at the Lady Aeshire, sitting pretty as a princess by her husband's elbow. Married almost half a century but back straight as a cedar beam. The Lady was still brilliant and still did good work, but her treatise on acids and bases, her crown jewel which Carlotte had read several times in her own research, had been written before she'd married. These years of engagement were Carlotte's last prime research years before she would be broadsided by wifely duties and childbirth. Thank God she wouldn't have to rear the things. Small mercies for wet-nurses. If only they could bear the children too.

Carlotte shivered and sipped at her cold tea.

"Carlotte," Harold whispered. She could feel his breath hot on her neck. The conversation was still rolling on in front of them, all revolving around Harold's father, whose voice, like a bull's stampede, demanded everyone's attention.

"Would you like to see my laboratory?"

Carlotte's stomach dropped a little, and the refusal came swiftly to her lips, but she stopped it before it went out. Seeing someone's workshop was almost synonymous for inappropriate behavior in Ryker circles, and while she'd kissed him on a balcony of her tower, and in the alcoves around the church, it had always been the briefest pressing of lips. They'd never been alone, not truly, in a workshop all by themselves with nothing but honor between them. And yet, she was his fiancée, and there were things she was expected to do now and in the future, and it was expected that she would do them well and with pride.

She lifted the cup to her lips and drained the last of it, feeling the grainy dregs on her tongue. She rose from her seat, and with all the grace and practiced splendor of the Mareshal's own daughters gliding off to the washroom, she left. Harold would follow a minute or two after when enough time had passed to keep up transparent pretenses.

There was a cart just outside the drawing room, and atop it was an array of crystal decanters filled with various liquids. She sniffed a few of them, settled on a brown one with strong vapors, and lifted it to her lips. She paused then, considering the wisdom of her choices, and then took a swallow. It was as hard as it smelled and it was all she could do not to spew it across the wall, but once the shudders withdrew she took another full swallow. She needed the courage.

Harold came out of the room and stopped when he saw her putting the crystal down. She gave her best mischievous smile and he returned it with a wink. He grabbed the crystal from the cart and took it with him down the hall. Carlotte followed.

The Orlient estate was one of the largest in the city, larger even than the De Sheras tower, though only in square footage. It was no accident. Nothing was an accident with the Lord and Lady Orlient. Harold turned, turned, turned, and went down a flight of stairs. Carlotte tried to keep a map in her head as they went, and wondered if Harold was intentionally going a roundabout way just to show off how large the manor really was.

He drank from the decanter as he walked, and when he handed it back to Carlotte, she took another drink that went down easier than the first two had. He led her down a hallway that seemed familiar, and then ducked through a door, and the Orlient laboratory opened up before her. She stopped at the threshold, taking it all in, while Harold walked to the center of the room with his arms spread wide.

"Welcome to the forefront of war."

The room was large, at least two hundred feet long and fifty across. Armaments of every make and design lined the long walls, and tables ran down the room's center, covered in tools and half-completed firearms. An unlit, hooded forge sat against the far end of the room. Carlotte caught the smell of black powder on the cold draft that flowed from it.

"Are you cold?" Harold asked, stepping back towards her. "When the forge is on it gets quite hot."

She shook her head and raised the bottle to her lips, taking a fourth swallow. It tasted sweet.

"I have all the warmth I need."

"Yes," he said. "I see." He glanced down at his toes.

"A forge so close to black powder. Isn't that dangerous?"

Harold's face brightened and took her hand and pulled her into the room.

"It's a new design you see. There, the hood catches sparks, and when the forge is aflame, the billows draw the air in from outside and push it through the top, so the flow of air keeps the sparks contained."

"Nothing gets out?" she asked.

"Well, occasionally, but we do our work with the powder at that end and we only do that when the forge is cold."

"Ah." It seemed a needless risk to keep the forge inside, but this was admittedly not her specialty. She turned to look at the barrels of powder that lined the short wall beside the door and stopped.

"What is that?"

Harold followed her gaze to a large painting that covered much of the wall behind the barrels. It was painted all in reds and oranges, and it showed an explosion of fire. Men with dark faces dressed in Freelander uniforms flew through the air along with splinters of wood and metal from barrels in the painting's center. The trees were bent back, or ripped from their roots entirely with the blast. The men's faces were full of surprise and pain.

"It's... Pendlehurst, I think. My father had it commissioned some time ago."

Carlotte stepped closer to it. There was an inscription on the massive burgundy frame.

"The Inferno at Greenwall." Carlotte looked up at the explosion and then back at Harold, who seemed amused by her amusement. "Pendelhurst's imagining?"

"He interviewed some soldiers who came upon the scene. There's another somewhere of the aftermath. My mother had it in one of the galleries for a time. My father liked this one though. Thought it showed the grandeur of what we do. My father ignited ten barrels of black powder for Pendelhurst to see, you know. Explosions are terrifying, let me tell you. Louder than thunder."

Carlotte gazed at the canvas.

"It was black powder that did it? I read the inferno cleared a half mile of jungle. Can black powder do that?"

She felt his gaze on the side of her face.

"With enough of it, I imagine. The Freelanders must of had a big stockpile there."

"A stockpile in the middle of the Greenwall?" She cocked an eyebrow at him and he shrugged.

"Somethings can't be understood."

"With God, all things are understandable."

"You have a better explanation?"

Carlotte remembered when the news of the inferno had reached Sheras. She had a bulletin from it in her library still. She'd been just a girl... right after her sister had...

Carlotte turned away from the painting. The alcohol was making her dramatic.

"No. Of course not," she said. "So what's all this then?"

His face lit up.

"Come look." He pulled her towards a table in the middle of the room and swept the tools aside. He picked up a small firearm, no longer than her forearm and held it out to her.

"Pretty," she said. The barrel had been stained black and the handle was made of carved ivory.

"That's my work," Harold said, blushing with pride. "But tell me, what do you see?"

Carlotte almost said "a gun" before she realized that he was testing her. She hated it when men did this, but she gave the gun a good look anyway. It never helped to chastise them, and Harold had a patronizing look in his eye that she wouldn't let him earn.

It really was beautiful. On closer inspection the handle had been carved into a scene of war. Tiny men rushed towards the barrel with bayonets. For a few moments, "gun" was all that she saw, but then-

"There is no match," she said. Carlotte thought the study of powder and gunsmithery a bit basic, but she did understand how firearms worked. A pipe with a small hole at one end and a bigger hole at the other had a metal ball stuffed into it on top of some black powder. Then fire was introduced at the small hole, usually by a slow burning match attached to a trigger, and the powder exploded, pushing the metal ball out. Powerful but inaccurate, and useless if the match went out. Slow to load, expensive to make, and these little hand-cannons were worse than the longer version. Harold nodded and smiled but didn't say anything. He wanted her to go on. Carlotte suppressed a sigh and took the weapon from his hands.

It was heavy. She looked closer at the mechanism on the trigger where the match should have been. There was a metal plate and a little vice, reared back like a snake with a rock in its teeth.

"Flint," she said. When the trigger was pulled the flint would strike the steel, make a spark and light the powder. No match needed.

She lowered the gun and looked at Harold who was smiling wide enough his head might have cracked in half.

"That's actually genius," she said. "Does it work?"

"It does," he said. "Would you like to see? I keep it loaded."

Before she could answer, he stepped behind her and put his arms around her shoulders. He held her hands from either side and pressed his face next to hers. The bristles of stubble scratched at her cheek.

"Arms straight, keep your elbows strong."

"Harold, I--"

He pulled her arms out in front of her, pointing the gun down the length of the room at several large targets to the right of the forge.

"Breathe and pull the trigger."

"Harold--"

"Pull!" he hissed and mashed her finger against the trigger. The snake reared back and then struck the metal plate. Sparks flew and the gun cracked so loud Carlotte let out a little scream. The bullet missed the target and clanged against the forge, chipping a chunk out of the stone masonry and sending bits of rock and dust flying.

Harold laughed, and Carlotte squirmed out from under his arms, releasing the gun into his hands. She stalked over to the table where she'd left the decanter of liquor and gathered herself. There was silence for a moment.

"I'm sorry," he said. "That was too much. I see that now."

"It wasn't too much, it was... I could have done it myself. I didn't need you to press the trigger for me," she said.

He placed the gun down on the table.

"Well, what do you think of all this?" he asked after a moment. She wanted to hit him in the face, but of course she couldn't. He'd been inconsiderate but what could she expect? He was a man, a Ryker man with the world open in front of him. She could detest it all she wanted, but it wouldn't change her future for the better.

Carlotte looked around the room again, at the painting and the firearms on the walls. It really was brilliant, mounting flint on the trigger mechanism. Such a little, simple thing that no one had thought of before. At least, no one so far as she knew. She placed herself in this workshop and wondered if that same brilliance would have stricken her.

"It's very impressive, Harold. It will make killing so much more efficient."

"Thank you," he said, and took a step closer to her. She shifted back and bumped the table behind her. "It really means a lot. You are the most magnificent woman in this city and if you think it's remarkable, then it really must be."

There was a vulnerability in his eye. For a moment the bravado was gone and she saw an earnest love-struck man in front of her. He was everything a woman should want. He was brilliant, educated, powerful and had the kind of face that girls gossiped about. The stubble outlined his jaw and the afternoon light that came in through the skylights gave his skin a healthy glow. His lips were large and she wondered how they would feel in a real kiss.

She grew queasy imagining it, and she willed the feeling away. This man was God's plan for her and she had no right to disagree with God. She needed to give it a chance. It was her duty to do so.

He took another step forward and she did the same. She forced a look of longing onto her face and when their hands touched she rose up onto her toes and kissed him. It was more than a peck, but it was not forceful. It was soft and a bit wet. His arm snaked around her back and he pulled her up against him and she felt the stubble again, scratching at her chin. His tongue pressed against her lips and after a moment's hesitation, she let it in and their tongues touched. The nausea rose in her again, but she pushed it from her mind. This was normal. All of this was normal and expected and proper. Maybe not proper in the open, but it was the proper sort of thing that young ladies and men were supposed to do when they were alone. Her own tongue was frozen in her mouth but his made up for it, slithering over hers like a squid entrapping a fish. She held that position for a few more moments and then squirmed her hand between their bodies and pushed him gently away. He did not give at first, but after a moment he relented and their mouths pulled apart.

She settled back onto her heels and looked up at him through her eyelashes. It hadn't been so bad. Not really. She'd done her part and now only needed to go back to the social pleasantries.

"That was nice," she said and then bit the edge of her lip. "I'm hap--"

He bent down and pressed his face back into hers. Perhaps the lip bite had been a bit much. She let it go on for a few moments more, and then pulled away again. She opened her mouth to speak, but before she could get in a word he grabbed her around the waist with both hands and hefted her onto the table with more strength than she thought he possessed. She let out a yelp of surprise and he smashed his lips against hers, squishing them against her teeth, and shoved his body between her legs on the table. A hand grasped her breast and clawed at the fabric that covered it. Carlotte tried to cry out, but he pressed her down onto the table, mouth jacked to hers so hard she couldn't breath. His other hand was between her legs, fingers probing randomly at her vagina through her shift.

It all happened so quickly, and she thought how silly that excuse had seemed to her before. She had thought it was what girls said who didn't want to take responsibility for their actions, and here she was, pressed on her back on a work table in the Orlient manor. Her, the Heir DeSheras, feeling unmarried fingers clawing at her.

She pushed her hand between her legs, but his body was pressed against her and she couldn't find a way in. She tasted blood in her mouth. She couldn't breathe. Her other hand was pinned underneath her and his face was so close to hers that his eyes were one blurry mass. His hand found its way past her shift. She felt him scrabbling at her pubic hair.

She abandoned her crotch and flailed her hand up against his face. The stubble scraped at her palm. She slid it upwards, fingers searching until they found something soft, and she dug a finger into it.

He screamed, and it was almost directly in her ear and she kept pushing. He staggered back, hands against his face. Carlotte lifted a heel and kicked him in the chest, rolling off the table as she did, and Harold fell back onto the ground.

Carlotte ran out of the workshop and down the hallway and up the stairs and through a door and then stopped, gasping for breath. She looked around, but nothing looked familiar and she couldn't tell if she was lost or just a little drunk. She could still hear Harold's faint wails behind her and she stifled a scream of her own. She wanted to drown him out.

She pushed on through one door and then another, and as she went, the rabbit in her gave way to the wolf and her thoughts focused on the Lord Orlient's face when she would burst back into the drawing room. She thought how Harold's mother would gasp when Carlotte told the world what an animal the Heir Orlient was. They would all put their hands to their mouths and the word would spread like a plague all through high society and the Orlient's name would be tainted. Their rise would be capped and they would have no one to blame for it but Harold and... her.

Carlotte stopped, hand pressed against a narrow wooden door.

They would blame Harold of course, but would they also blame her?

Of course they would. She had gone off with him hadn't she? She'd gone to his workshop and she'd bitten her lip and... God! Why couldn't she have just kept things in order? It would be her name whispered all around, and they would say that she let herself get taken advantage of, or worse, that she led Harold on. He was just a boy after all and what could boys do? God! Why had she bitten her lip? Why couldn't she have been smarter?

She sat against the wall, and one frenzied sob shuddered through her body. It came out in an unsteady breath and sounded like a cow. She clasped her hands to her mouth to keep the noises in. She didn't know what to do. She couldn't go back, not like this. The cloth at her breast was torn and the paint on her face was smeared. She thought of her sister then, and wondered what Elspeth would have done. She would have found a way out of it all. She would have known how to save herself and make Harold burn.

But Carlotte was not Elspeth. Elspeth was dead, and Carlotte would get no guidance there. She turned her eyes up to the sky lights, but God gave her no answers either. There was only one answer then. She had to escape. It was better to be a ghost than a woman wounded.

She pushed back to her feet and shoved through the narrow door into the service hallways. Elspeth used to play hide and seek with her in them at the tower, and she knew from experience that they connected almost every room with unobtrusive doors. She didn't want to go back, so she forged ahead until the hallway ended with another door. She wondered briefly if being found creeping through the walls like a rat would be an even worse outcome. She placed a hand on the door, said a little prayer that it wouldn't open directly into the drawing room, and with a deep breath, pushed it open.

It wasn't the drawing room.

It was dark, and before her eyes adjusted, she smelled shit, cleaned up but not entirely and masked with lavender and citrus. She knew the smell. When she'd been a child and her father lay dying she'd smelled it. He'd shit the bed without moving, and she remembered the maids turning him to clean the filth from his withered body. She had watched it all next to Elspeth at her mother's orders. Everything was a lesson.

There were two low-burning oil lamps on small tables in the room, and after a few moments she could see a four-poster bed opposite her with the curtains drawn up around it. The walls were all shelves, filled to bursting and half buried in a sloping bank of books that hadn't fit. The piles covered most of the floor, with only a few thin paths to navigate the room. Interspersed in that pile was all manner of exploration equipment. Metal hooks and ropes, leather repelling harnesses, and a brutal long machete sticking out of a pile like a sword in the back of a fallen soldier. The room was not small, but she felt a sudden claustrophobia, as though the room was made of books and it was all collapsing in on her.

She stood at the threshold for several moments wondering if she should go back, but peeking out from the shelves on an adjacent wall was a door, not a narrow servants door, but the kind that would lead back to a hallway where real people walked. If she went back... she couldn't. Of all the possible endings to the day, running into Harold alone would be the worst, so she went in, picking her steps carefully around the piles.

Then she heard the whispers.

She became aware of them like realizing a spider had crawled out of her hair and down her neck, and when she became aware she yelped and whirled around. The whispers had no origin at first, and she turned in a full circle searching for them, her breath caught in her throat. She stopped her turn at the bed and held completely still, struggling to hear over the sound of her heart. They were faint, just an edge above silence, and they were coming from the bed. She was sure of it.

It was just a person, some sick Orlient family member... only, Harold's mother, father and three sisters had all been in the drawing room. They had no other relatives that lived here, and Carlotte had spent many evenings at the manor. Perhaps then it was a sick servant that - no, no, a sick servant wouldn't be put up in the manor. They would deal with their ills in whatever hovel they lived in. She was letting her mind run away with her. She was an adult, a Ryker lady who did not believe in ghost stories and who did not jump to faulty conclusions. She moved forward, and before her fear could stay her hand, Carlotte threw the curtains aside.

A man lay in the center of the bed with the blankets drawn up to his shoulders and his hands clasped around a book on his belly. He was thin, the skin of his face drawn back over his cheekbones like a roasted animal. In the lamplight he looked pale as snow. His eyes were open, fixed on some point above him, and his lips moved, whispering continually into the dark.

The fear left her. It was just a sick old man. Some secret invalid of the Orlient's. Curious. Perhaps something she could use against Harold if he tried to make a fuss about today's fiasco? She stooped down to hear his words better.

They were too low to make out. Something about the dark? Complete gibberish. An old invalid's nightmares. She straightened and looked around the cluttered room for a sign of who this man was. Assuming all this was his, the equipment was that of an explorer. She picked up a book from the nearest stack and wiped the dust from its cover.

-Catalog of Amaranthine Ruins-

A historian then?

She looked around for something juicier, and her eyes fell on a small leather journal laying beside the lamp on the bedside table. There was a band around it fixed with an iron lock. That was promising. She cast about for a moment, looking for the key, and then, realizing it was hopeless in all this mess, tucked it under her arm. It was time she made her escape.

5

The driver took Saara from Inquisitor's Yard in the Old Town to the Tower DeSheras in the Nouvre Vil and unlike the other carriages she passed along the way, Saara kept her shutters open. She liked to watch the familiar streets and shops roll by, and to look out and make eye contact with the pedestrians, hoping to see someone she knew staring blandly back, unable to place Saara's face in that gilded frame. She loved it most of all when she saw first the spark of recognition and then the inevitable spasm of disgust. She kept the shutters open, even when the traffic came to a standstill at the Old Town Gate and the pedestrians stood so close that Saara could reach out a hand and touch them. The carriage was tall, but because she was sitting, her head was only slightly higher than theirs, and when the wind blew just right, it would sweep the smell of a hundred bodies into her face. She reveled in it. She was so close that she could see the sweat beading under the rim of their caps, and yet the distance from where she sat down to where they stood, was unbelievably far. The inch of wood that separated her from them was thicker than the city's walls.

She stopped enjoying the view once they left the Nor-so and began the winding trip up the West Hill to the Tower DeSheras. The wealthy flats gave way to tall houses, which gave way to estates, and every foot they climbed reminded Saara how far up she still had to go.

The Tower DeSheras sat at the highest point of the West hill and it soared another two hundred feet into the sky. Saara had been to the wide viewing deck at the top, where Carlotte's great grandsomething built their telescope, but from the road the tower looked sharp as a needle stabbing up at the heavens. There was a sprawling garden at the base of the tower, and a wrought iron fence around it which curved out as it rose up, looking simultaneously like the petals of a flower and a line of spears waiting for the enemies to charge. She wondered briefly if anyone ever had. The fence was older even than the tower, and it wasn't hard to imagine some pike addict or poor cobbler throwing themselves at it, striving to get to the riches within, only to be disemboweled by the fence like a sausage on the end of a fork, cleaned up and thrown into a garbage heap before it gave anyone else subversive ideas. There was an order to things, and that was not the way to cut in line.

Saara leaned out of her window and rapped her knuckles against the carriage's door. The driver looked over his shoulder.

"Let's go in the east," she said.

The driver stared back at her, letting the horses lead themselves. "East, Saara?"

"I got a stutter? Yes. East."

The man chewed his lip for a moment, the bristles of his mustache undulating, and then turned his gaze forward. "Right you are."

The fence had four gates, one at each cardinal direction, and the bars of each had been bent into a tableau, showcasing the scientific achievements of the DeSheras family. The east gate was the most massive, and showed the same DeSheras who had built the tower seated with his beard wrapped around his ankles, his eye glued to his telescope, and his right hand documenting his discoveries. It was a warning to all who entered that they would be measured against giants.

As the carriage approached, two men in DeSheras livery pulled the gate open. The path from the east gate was longer than the other entrances, winding like a snake through curated gardens and pruned hedges before depositing them at the tower's front door. Every turn revealed something more elegant than the last. Here a great willow tree that made a tunnel of the path, there a hedge carved into a herd of galloping horses. The trees were explosions of reds and yellows, marking the beginning of autumn, and an acceptable number of leaves had been allowed to fall and decorate the ground. At the winter solstice ball all the leaves would be gone, any hangers-on clipped away to keep them from marring the skeletal silhouettes. The carriage pulled up and Saara hopped out, pulling a crate off the bench with her.

The wide stone steps to the entrance were meant to inspire awe, inviting the climber to look up at the tower's height. Saara knew there were pipes beneath the stairs that transmitted the sounds of her steps to a room just beside the door, so she wasn't surprised when the door swung open before she could knock. A servant stood in greeting, bowed almost parallel to the floor.

"Welcome to the tower De-- oh," Aedgar said. His face dropped and he sprung upright. "What are you doing here?"

Saara didn't stop her climb and shoved past him.

"Coming inside. What does it look like?"

The tower was made up of circles of rooms stacked on top of each other, with the space in the middle empty save for stairways that criss-crossed from floor to floor. They each came from a different angle, forming a star shape that twisted as it rose. There were a lot of stairs in this tower, and Saara felt she knew each and every step. One should know their enemy.

"You're not supposed to be here!" Aedgar said, appearing beside her. "You know what Enriq said."

Saara pulled her eyes back down to earth.

"What care have I what Enriq says?"

"Because he speaks for the Lady DeSheras. No staff through the front."

Saara trudged toward the staircase, trying and failing to find a comfortable way to hold the crate. "I'm not staff, and Enriq is not my master."

Aedgar grabbed her arm. "It's not just you who will suffer. If the Lady DeSheras saw--"

"She's at the exhibition," Saara interjected "Let go of my arm."

"If she saw, she could fire you... and me!" He snapped a finger. "Like that!"

Saara leaned in close.

"If she fires you, it'll be because you're a shit. Let go of my arm."

He held on for a few moments, but then gave in. "Carlotte let trash into the tower and before long she'll sweep it out."

"Go back to your job, Aedgar. Opening doors so I can walk through them."

She felt his desire to call back, but he was too far away and he would never yell in the tower. Not Aedgar, the man who'd served the DeSheras family for longer than Saara had been alive.

Saara was getting soft. She felt it when she climbed these stairs. It felt harder every day. When she'd been rough and fresh off the street, lean as a whip, she would have vaulted up them, but now she felt the weight she'd packed on. She was still strong, but she ate well here.

In addition to the grand foyer, the bottom floor had a sitting room, a dining room, and a few guest quarters for when the family entertained Rykers who couldn't get up the stairs, and Saara wondered briefly if that would be her someday, when she took her place among the elite. She chuckled. She wouldn't mind getting well and truly fat, like the Lord Orlient. Thick thighs and a belly past her tits would be a surer sign of wealth than diamonds on her fingers.

The second and third floors were art galleries that hid servants' quarters, kitchens, laundries and various domestic work rooms. The Rykers didn't like to see such things. There was another set of stairs in the walls that she was supposed to use, but with the exhibition happening, there was little risk of being caught. The fourth floor had the bulk of guest rooms and the fifth floor had the main dining hall, ballroom and exhibition hall. The sound of the party greeted her before she arrived.

All the important Rykers in Sheras were there, waiting for the Heir DeSheras' newest discovery, and though this was neither Carlotte's first nor would it be her last, this one had a special buzz to it, as though it was expected to be Carlotte's pinnacle. It wouldn't be, Saara knew. Carlotte would never go quietly into the night.

"Girl!" A voice called from across the landing and Saara knew it was directed at her. She ducked under the velvet rope that blocked off the upper levels and resumed her climb before the Ryker could ask her for more wine or where he could take a shit. She wished Carlotte didn't make her wear the livery of the house. It made her look like a fucking servant.

The sixth through tenth floors were where Carlotte and her mother, Cainia, spent their time. Each floor had bedrooms, libraries, and laboratories so that the members of the family could do their work without going up and down the stairs. The sixth was also where they dined, usually separately. Carlotte controlled the seventh floor, but Saara didn't stop her climb there. The eighth was Cainia's and the ninth had been the Lord Carlin DeSheras' domain before he died, but ever since Saara had worked for Carlotte, she knew it to be an extension of the eighth. Cainia was like a gas, able to fill whatever space she had available. It was only the dead that kept her from consuming the tenth as well, because the tenth had been Elspeth's.

Saara hadn't known the girl, but Aedgar had told her stories, and from what the older maids said, the tenth floor hadn't been changed in all the years since Elspeth's death. These rooms had been, and always would be for mourning, and that was where Carlotte would be. They were where Carlotte always went before these sorts of things.

Saara shouldered open the door to Elspeth's bedroom. The curtains were drawn and it was dark inside.

"Ma'am?" she called, and for a moment wondered if she'd been wrong, but then Carlotte spoke.

"Did you get it?"

"Yes, Saara said.

Carlotte's voice came from the corner of the room, where Saara knew there was a chair beside a statue of the prophet. "Took you long enough."

"Yes, Ma'am," Saara said, though she wasn't late.

Carlotte was silent for several moments, and then spoke.

"Well, I suppose we should go then, shouldn't we."

It wasn't a question, but it seemed close to one. Saara frowned. Carlotte didn't usually ask her questions.

There was a rustle of cloth, and then Carlotte emerged from the darkness. She was taller than Saara, and as thin as a woman who'd never lifted anything heavier than the dress she was wearing. She had a habit of skipping meals when she was deep in her work, and it showed. Her arms were the same thickness from shoulder to wrist. Her chest was flat, but the dress she wore was tight enough in the front to give her a bit of cleavage before billowing out at the waist. She had a leather apron on top, but unlike the ones she wore in the lab, this was delicate calfskin and it followed the folds of her dress. Her hands were covered in similar gloves that went up to her elbow, and her dark brown hair was tied back with a ribbon of the same. She was some ten years younger than Saara, but the air of superiority made Saara constantly feel like a child beside her. It was an image, the perfect image of a woman bred for greatness. Brilliant, rich, incapable of manual labor, and beautiful. Ryker perfection.

Carlotte stopped just before passing her, and Saara caught the barest whiff of brandy.

"Saara... do you..." she began, but her voice trailed away.

"Yes, Ma'am?"

"Nothing..." she said, and then she took a deep breath and straightened her back. "Come along, Saara. Don't drop the box."

That was more like it. That was the woman Saara knew and tolerated.

Carlotte cut a swift pace and glided down the stairs while Saara tried not to roll down behind her. As she turned at each landing, Saara saw Carlotte's face harden and her speed increased. She was like a galley cutting through the sea, building speed and momentum with each stroke of the oars. They passed the seventh floor, and then the sixth, and then Saara sprinted down the stairs to unclip the velvet rope that blocked the fifth landing while balancing the crate atop her leg.

The exhibition hall was filled with laughter and chatter and the clinking of glass, but as Carlotte entered and cut through the crowd, the sound quelled, and when she mounted the stage against the long wall of the room, the rest of the crowd quieted too. A hush of whispers and rustling settled, and Saara took her place at the back of the stage, ready for her cue.

On the stage was a table covered in white sheets that peaked and valleyed with the objects underneath. The objects had been set for several days so that Carlotte could practice her speech. Saara had heard it so many times she knew it by heart.

Carlotte took a moment and looked out at the crowd of Rykers before her. There were near a hundred starring back up at her, all of them important, most of them brilliant, but Saara would have bet all the gold she'd stashed away under the floorboards of her room that Carlotte was looking behind the Rykers, behind the tables where bent necked servants stood with platters of wine, liquor, and sweet treats, and at the tapestries that hung on the back wall. They were a chronicle of the DeSheras family, from Haakon DeSheras, who'd built the tower, looking through his telescope, to Kaiden DeSheras, mounted atop the Nouvre Vil walls he'd built, to Elspeth DeSheras, standing in the midst of the Amaranthine Ruins she'd spent her short life unearthing. The dead of Carlotte's family keeping watch on this hall of scientific discovery and judging the weight of Carlotte's actions.

Carlotte took a deep breath, and tore the first white sheet away. Underneath was a tank of water with a large volcanic rock in its midst. It was riddled with little caves and tunnels, and in those tunnels lurked reflective eyes. They were long snakelike fish with stunted faces, and with the sudden light they moved, slithering out of their holes, like worms out of an apple, to see what threat loomed.

"These are shaker fish," Carlotte began, "taken from the waters off the coast of the Greenwall. They stick to the rocky shallows and hide where the Freelanders hunt for clam and urchin meat, and when a Freelander gets too close-"

Carlotte snapped her fingers.

"He dies."

A few murmurs rustled through the crowd but Saara saw more than a few Rykers who looked unimpressed. A showcase of strange animals was not what these people expected from a DeSheras exhibition.

"Touching a shaker fish causes paralysis and seizure. Many victims bite through their tongues as all their muscles contract at once, like a man long affected by tetanus. Sometimes their hearts stop beating, and sometimes they just fall and drown in three feet of water, unable to swim, unable to control their movements. This is well and interesting, but what is more interesting is why? Is it poison? I know of no poison that can affect the body so suddenly and completely at a touch. Is it an affliction of the mind? No, again too sudden. How is it that something outside of a human can control a human's movements instantly?

"Kalidia DeSheras, my Grandmother, proposed that there was an animal force that moved the muscles of all living things. I'm sure you've read her treatises. Some power exists which human and animal brains access to make muscles contract. You can hardly doubt it. Something makes us move."

Carlotte lifted a delicate, leather clad hand and clenched it into a fist.

"Perhaps then, that is what the shaker fish use, bypassing their victim's brains and applying the animal force directly to the body in a brute force attack that overpowers whatever animal force the victim's brain provides."

She paused, and Saara thought she saw a few raised eyebrows, though she couldn't tell if they were genuine. Rykers were always acting. It made them hard to read.

"But what is this animal force? One might say it is the soul that gives us life, that the soul is the difference between a living man and a corpse, but if the animal force came from the soul, then animals would not move. We can not deny that animals live, so either animals have souls, and these shaker fish overwhelm their victims with a superior soul, or the animal force is entirely separate."

Another pause, though she wasn't waiting for an answer.

"It is separate, of course, and unlike the soul, it is tangible. It is not even intrinsic to animals. It is in the air. It is in metals and salt and I'm sure in much more. We've only to find the means to extract it. I have found one such way."

Carlotte raked the crowd with her gaze.

"I give you, the DeSheras Pile."

Carlotte whipped the next sheet away, revealing a cluster of wood and metal towers. Each was half the height of a woman, with a core of stacked metal and cloth disks held in place by wooden dowels that ran from the towers' bases to their cone shaped tops.

"Specifically piles of copper, zinc and cloth soaked in brine, connected via copper wire here and here and here." She guided a finger along the connections and then looked back out at the crowd.

"The animal force is here. It is in these metals, and together with the brine, we can pull it out. Saara!"

Carlotte snapped her fingers again and Saara strode forward, thumping the crate down on the table. Carlotte crossed behind the table to stand beside her as Saara pried at the lid with a crowbar. It was all choreographed. Carlotte had forced Saara to practice the movements over and over to keep the flow unbroken, to keep the audience's attention. The lid hit the floor, and Carlotte extended her hand out to Saara without looking, almost carelessly. Saara reached into the crate and placed into Carlotte's hand, a human heart.

The crowd gasped. The heart had been cold, and the blood that soaked it had coagulated into a syrup that dripped from Saara's fingers and down Carlotte's glove. It was not the first heart Saara had held since entering Carlotte's service. The horror of it had long become clinical.

"This is the heart of Mister Guillerme, a criminal executed by the Mareshal's inquisition just this afternoon."

Saara pulled a large candlestick out from behind the table and placed it in front of Carlotte, where she nestled the heart like a relic on an altar. Then, Carlotte picked up the instruments of her device.

Copper wire wrapped in cloth ran from the bottom of the far left tower and from the top of the far right, each ending with a polished wooden handle and a copper spike. Carlotte held them by the handles towards the audience.

"The animal force flows like water in a pipe, and like gravity to water there is a force which guides it from one place to another, so long as there is a connection."

Saara looked out into the crowd. Their eyes were all fixed on Carlotte and the heart. In the city these people would have balked at such grotesqueness, but here there was no hint of revulsion. To the Ryker, it was not a human heart before them, it was a science experiment.

"How do I know that I have the animal force here in my DeSheras piles? Because it is the animal force that makes a heart beat."

Carlotte touched one copper spike to the left side of the heart, and then tapped it with the right, and the heart convulsed. It contracted and syrupy blood oozed out of the main artery and vein. The crowd gasped again at the phantom movement and Carlotte watched them with a hungry glee. All of their eyes were fixed on it, waiting for it to move again. With a twitch of her wrist, Carlotte touched with the right spike again and the heart beat again. She tapped eight more times, giving a second between taps and the heart beat like it was alive.

Saara was already moving before the tenth, preparing the second item from within the crate.

"I'd like to introduce you to Mister Guillerme himself," Carlotte said, and Saara revealed the criminal's head.

Saara held it by the hair like a warlord showing a decapitated foe. The man's face was slack, eyes half open and mouth and mustache sagging around a tongue pressed up against the lower lip. Brown paper was wrapped around the stump of his neck with twine, but the blood had soaked through and dripped back into the box in slow globs. Saara placed it down on the table in front of Carlotte. It squelched.

"He was a criminal in life, but in death he is a scientific achievement. When he died, the animal force left him, but when the animal force is returned, he regains the semblance of life."

Carlotte pressed the spikes to either side of Guillerme's face, and it seized. The jaw clamped shut and all the muscles contracted. His eyes flew wide open, and the skin on his forehead contorted, and then Carlotte pulled the spike away, and the face went slack again.

A collective breath released in the crowd, and everyone was silent. Carlotte let the moment last for three, four, five seconds, savoring each one.

"But what is the animal force? It is in these metals and this brine. It is in all of us, keeping our hearts beating and our lungs breathing, and--"

Saara nodded to the servants who stood at the ready by the windows. They pulled on the draw strings and the room was plunged into darkness. Saara ducked under the table where many more of the piles were gathered. Carlotte handed her down one of the spikes and Saara connected it to the piles below and handed Carlotte up a new handle and spike.

"It is in the air. Because... the animal force is lightning."

Carlotte held the spikes close together and lightning jumped from one spike to the other, lighting up Carlotte's face in a white flash. The air sizzled, and Carlotte pulled the two ends apart.

There was silence, and the smell of burning, and the darkness seemed absolute after such an intense flash. Then, the servants uncovered the windows, and the room filled with the evening light. Carlotte let out a long breath, and seemed to deflate a little with it, looking suddenly tired.

"A treatise with details of my findings has been printed. You can find them on the back tables, or with any of the servants," Carlotte said, and then the crowd erupted into conversation.

It had gone well and Saara had performed perfectly. It was the most important exhibition Saara had been a part of and one she was intimately involved in. She had helped Carlotte with the research. She had sourced the body parts and procured the metals and manufacturing to make sure it all happened, and Saara couldn't help but be pleased. This was the work of the Rykers. It was hard, and it was never straightforward, but Saara needed to get used to it, because one day soon, she wouldn't be under the table anymore.

Carlotte peeled off her gloves and then made for the stairs at the side of the stage, while Saara hurried behind, wiping the blood off her hands with a white cloth to make herself presentable. Carlotte stopped just before descending.

"Help with the pamphlets," she said.

"Pamphlets? But--"

Carlotte descended, not waiting for Saara's response, and was submerged into the crowd. Saara stood for a moment. None of the Ryker's eyes were on her. They were all turned inward, speaking with each other or clamoring for Carlotte's attention.

Saara took in a deep, shaky breath, and then walked around the edge of the crowd to where the servants were handing out pamphlets.

The crowd engulfed Carlotte like a pool of water. It pressed in, filling all the empty spaces around her and demanded her attention like a diver's body demanded breath. They wanted details about her work. She told them. They wanted to know who she'd built on. She listed the names. They wanted to know if she'd worked with anyone and owed them credit. No. If she would work with anyone. Maybe at some point. If she'd work with them specifically. No, her schedule was very busy. If she'd like to see their work. Again her schedule was full. If they'd make an exception. Sorry, no. And then again and again and again, to an ever changing parade of faces which she tried to keep straight, but couldn't. She should know them. These were the important ones and her mother would know them. It was her duty as a DeSheras to know them, but Carlotte had no memory for it. She never had. As the evening dragged into night and the servants lit the chandeliers and filled the exhibition hall with candlelight, the faces all seemed to meld together into one indistinct mass always wanting the same thing: recognition by the Heir DeSheras.

She didn't see the Orlients though. She was sure of that and she was grateful for it, though she kept telling herself that she would stand strong if she did. Each new face gave her a stab of anxiety that it would be Harold, or his sisters, or his mother, or his great barrel of a father, but they never were. That was good. She wondered if Harold would be wearing an eye patch next time she saw him.

Something touched her elbow and she swiveled around, ready for another repetition, but it was just Saara. Her face was all pinched up like she was upset about something, but then again the woman always looked like her pants were on too tight. Carlotte didn't have the patience to figure it out. She was hungry, suddenly starving, and she felt that if she tried to answer another one of these questions she would keel over and dry heave.

"Get me something to eat," Carlotte snapped, her voice low so only Saara would hear her.

"Ma'am?"

"Food. Meat. Go!" and she shooed the woman away, turning back to the circle of Rykers who wanted her attention.

It had changed. Lady Aeshire had pushed her way in, and the Lord Anselle stood beside her. He owned most of the fishing and shipping boats that used the Sheras' harbor and was a biologist of some renown. Half of his expenses went to her family for dock fees. He had an ebony cane with a silver ball top and the traditional Ryker mustaches. Another man stood at his side, his son, and save the mustache and the robes of clergy about him, he looked identical to his father, if a bit fatter. Carlotte could not recall the priest's name. He'd done nothing of scientific relevance that she knew of. If he had, he wouldn't be a priest.

The Lady Aeshire was speaking of metals. Carlotte had missed the first half, but she put together an appropriate response.

"The animal force varied depending on the metal I used, but I've no doubt there is a better configuration. After all, I don't think we are made of zinc and copper disks."

"Quite, quite," the Lord Anselle said. His mustaches were like a re-curve bow, dropping around his mouth and then shooting straight out to the sides. "It is good to see such humility in such young blood, but I wonder, what exactly is the application for all this." He thumped his chest where her pamphlet was sticking out of a pocket. "There's no mention of it here."

It took Carlotte a moment to decode what he'd said. She'd had this conversation so many times and her perception of social cues was blurring. She needed to lie down. "Current application? Little, I'm afraid, but there are many paths to follow."

The Lord Anselle grumbled, and then cleared his throat. "Have you read my treatise on the interdependency of biological systems? I imagine you were just a babe when it was exhibited."

"I believe so," Carlotte said. She had. Her tutors had made her read it and analyze it, and now she tried to pull its contents out of all the other treatises and texts locked in her memory. "One system fails and then they all do?"

"Quite. Your work made me wonder. This animal force." His speech was segmented as he put his ideas together. "If a wound, a matchlock shot say, breaks apart a heart, stopping that system, which in turn causes the others to fail and the man to die, and if, somehow, one could repair the heart, or replace it... if one could fix the other damages that occurred in the other systems as a result of the first failure, then the body would be still dead. Unmoving. Unbreathing. But if one then, to this perfectly repaired body, applied the animal force..."

There was a pause and Carlotte felt her focus come back to her, like she'd drunk a cup of strong black tea.

"Then..." Carlotte said, "Assuming it was very precise, too much causes damage to the tissue, but if it was the right amount in the right places... The systems would restart, I suppose."

The Lord Anselle nodded somewhat gravely. "Quite."

"That would be the discovery of a lifetime," The Lady Aeshire said.

"Wait, what is it you're discussing?" the priest said. The Lady Aeshire carried on as though he hadn't spoken.

"Do you think it could be tried on some criminal or something?"

"You'd have to fix the damage though..." the Lord Anselle mused.

"And that's difficult," Carlotte said. Her mind began to rush through the problems and possible solutions. "The body degrades after death in ways that are difficult to see. The hearts I used in my research became less responsive in the days after harvest."

"Harvest?" the priest said. "Are you--"

"The one I used today was just hours old."

"Perhaps someone who only died of a stopped heart then?" the Lord Anselle said.

"Do people die just from that? No other cause?" the lady Aeshire asked.

"Of course, so far as we--"

"You're talking of bringing the dead back to life!" the priest roared.

The circle quieted, and several of the people in adjacent circles of conversation quieted too and turned their attention to the priest. His gaze jumped back and forth between Anselle, Aeshire, and Carlotte, each look trying to pierce its way inside.

"You can't bring the dead back to life! It's not possible, nor--"

"Possibility is--"

The priest threw up a finger to quiet his father. "Nor is it moral to try. The dead belong to God." He looked around the circle again. "To do such things is blasphemy."

"Blasphemy?" Carlotte whispered. How could it be that the church, the supposed house of God, followed such ridiculous dogma. Her voice rose and cut across the circle. "Since when is it blasphemy to learn? That is what God put us on earth to do."

"What we speak of is theoretical," the Lady Aeshire cut in, "None I know have the knowledge or ability to heal a corpse, or reverse rot."

"Because that is not God's will! There are limits. Limits! To what should be learned. This is why our nation has turned away from God--"

"Turned away from--" Carlotte began, but the priest cut her off.

"Limits! For the sake of our Lord, Li-"

"No!" Carlotte shrieked. All of the dreariness was gone and her focus was white hot on the priest's fat face, his jowls jiggling with his indignation. "Don't appeal to me with your moral outrage! You speak from feeling, not from the mind that God gave you." She stabbed her finger at her own skull. "What about medicine? If death is the providence only of God, then surely if you were shot we should not help you. If you catch cold, we should not care for you. If you choke on your food, we shouldn't intercede, No! To do so would impinge on God's domain!"

A hand touched at her elbow but she flung it off. These priests were all the same. Thinking that their evocation made them better and more enlightened than the real Rykers who actually moved society forward. They thought they knew God because they kept a house for him, but Carlotte knew that the Church wasn't God's home. God lived in the city. He lived in the workshops and laboratories of the Rykers. Carlotte had felt him when she was on the edge of a discovery. She'd felt him when the DeSheras Pile had worked, and she'd felt him every time before when it didn't.

The circle was quiet and those around the circle had grown quiet too. The only whispers came from the edge of the room where they asked what was going on. The priest worked his jaw for a few moments before he found his words, but he never broke eye contact with Carlotte. His outrage protected him from hers.

"And what if you did, Mademoiselle DeSheras? What if you brought a corpse back to life? Instilled unnatural life in it and brought its-" he waved his hand angrily at his father, "systems back into working order? It would have no soul. You would create an abomination. A soulless, thoughtless and listless man."

"And it would be a scientific achievement worthy of the age," she sneered. The priest raised his eyebrows, and his chin shook.

"The Amaranthine had no limits, and look what happened to them."

Carlotte blinked at the man. She felt the hand on her elbow again and someone was trying to whisper in her ear, but she wasn't listening. She looked at the Lord Anselle for support, but there was none there. She looked to the Lady Aeshire and her eyes were on her hands, clasped at her stomach. Had she gone too far? She became aware of the eyes on her, all around, and nothing like they'd been when she was on the stage.

"They were Godless," Carlotte muttered.

"They were prideful," the priest said. His voice took on the timbre of a sermon. "Evil things happen to those who walk Godless paths to hell and think they are above it." He frowned and lifted his chin. "You of all people should know."

"What?" Carlotte hissed. She could hear the lesser Rykers around her whisper her sister's name. "What was that you said?"

"Evil things. Like suicide."

Carlotte's fury came surging back, like the waters from a tidal wave. Someone said her name, but she had no senses for it. They were all focused here.

"My sister died in an accident!" she yelled. "She died doing the work that you and your kind refuse. She worked while you got fucking fat on--"

"Carlotte!"

The hand at her elbow seized her and flung her backward and around.

"What?!" she screamed, and saw Saara there, pulling at her elbow with one hand and holding a plate of roasted meats in the other.

"You are needed, Ma'am. You are needed."

Carlotte saw the panic in her maidservant's eyes. The hall was quiet. Not a soul spoke. Carlotte felt the blood rushing in her temples.

She'd gone too far. Much too far.

"Needed?" she croaked.

"Yes, your... Mother."

Carlotte nodded. "Take me then."

Saara turned and pushed through the crowd. Carlotte rushed after her and tried her best not to cry.

6

Carlotte had gone too far. She knew it, but she tried not to think about it. She sat in her big chair by the fireplace in her library, perched atop the cushion with her legs against her chest. She'd engulfed herself in a thick blanket and left the window open so she wouldn't get too warm. The blanket was heavy, and the weight around her shoulders and the feeling of her legs pressed against her chest and the way that the fire flickered made it easy to pretend like she was somewhere else, an explorer in some faraway place, starring into a campfire after a day of uncovering the world's secrets. There were no social mores out there in the wilderness, no standards to which she had to conform. There was only the work. And God, of course.

A cold draft came through the window and Carlotte nestled deeper into the blanket. Her left thigh hurt. There was a long scratch there from Harold's fingers and it burned like hell now that she was alone with her thoughts. Today should have gone so well. It was supposed to have been church and then preparation and then a masterful exhibition, rife with applause and professional jealousy. Those things did go well, she supposed, the things that she'd planned for. It was everything else that went badly. There was a lesson there somewhere, but Carlotte was too tired to figure out what it was.

She didn't want to sleep yet though. Her mind was racing and she knew that if she lay down she'd be confronted by everything. By Harold's hand scratching up her thigh. By the Lady Aeshire's face as she wouldn't make eye contact. By the look of Saara's panic when she'd given Carlotte an excuse to leave.

Carlotte realized she was cringing and pulled her thoughts back to the present. She needed something else to think about.

Carlotte looked at the invalid's journal on the table beside her. She'd cut the leather clasp and skimmed through it after Saara had pulled her away from the hall. It was diverting, but it was, all of it, nonsense. It turned out the invalid was one Lord Ryliar Orlient, apparently Harold's uncle. Carlotte hadn't heard of him, but she'd never had a memory for the history of other peoples' families.

The journal was part diary and part notes on his research, not into black powder like the rest of the Orlients, but into some Amaranthine ruin. It started with a description of his expedition to a forest south of Bergshalen, where he thought this "Lok Secrak" was located. He described his journey by ship around the cape and then down the coast, stopping at Stak and Kelsiki before resupplying at Domsar where he hired laborers. He took a barge up the Cobalt to the Splitting, where they had been forced off the river by the Bergshalen Army. This was some thirty years ago during the first war with the Freelands and Ryliar wrote at length about the hardships of war, though to Carlotte's knowledge, the fighting never made it as far north as the Cobalt. Bergshalen stayed neutral throughout the first one, but Ryliar made it seem as though they were practically dodging cannon fire. He emphasized over and over how pointless and small it all was. "The struggles of little men doing little things, while God thundered above them."

It seemed the final destination of Lok Secrak was a secret to his men. He told them they were looking for a ruin called Steuersak, for which he gave no location in the journal beyond "the foothills of the hedgehog kingdom, which I found evidence of in the Royal Bergshalen Library, several years before." He spent several pages on his negotiation with the Bergshalen soldiers to get across the splitting, and then Ryliar seemed to have lost his taste for writing, because poof, they were at the Steuersak ruin.

It wasn't innocent though. Carlotte saw signs of his insanity from the beginning, and by the end, his mind had truly fallen. It could very well have been entirely fiction. She hadn't heard of half of these places, hadn't seen them on any map, and if Ryliar actually went looking for these things, then it was no wonder that the Orlient's kept him hidden away. This was dangerous stuff. The kind that ruined families. The kind that Carlotte's mother had burned after Elspeth's death.

Aside from the look on Elspeth's face, it was the smell of burning paper that Carlotte remembered most vividly from her sister's death. A fire in the laboratory had destroyed much of Elspeth's things, but Cainia finished their destruction. She incinerated all the papers and statues and artifacts and what wouldn't burn she'd crushed and what wouldn't crush she'd tied in bundles and had taken off the coast and sunk a mile out to sea. Her mother's fear had seemed to be for their safety back then, for the fear that whatever had killed Elspeth was lurking in the items she'd excavated in the frozen north, but when Carlotte got older she realized that wasn't it at all. It wasn't until she heard the whispers of the girls behind her back and became aware of the sidelong glances at social functions that she understood. DeSheras was the most powerful family in the city, and such rumors were common and baseless, but if they became more than rumors, if proof was found, then they could lose everything. The quickest way to fall in Ryker society was to go chasing magic.

Carlotte flipped to the interesting bit at the end.

"It all points to this 'center,' this Lok Secrak. Among scholars, it is commonly believed to be some kind of heathen heaven, but I believe that is wrong. It is a real place. It was not a metaphor. It was their capital. How do I know this? Because there is a map here in Steuersak, carved into a stone wall, with all the major, very real, very verifiable, Amaranthine ruins delineated. Between them are the Amaranthine roads that we walk on every day in Sheras, which connect all the ruins. That is why I believe that Lok Secrak is real, because it is on the map. There is little wonder why we've never found it before, because it is deep in the Greenwall, beyond where men of good sense do tread. I have come further than any before me since the Amaranthine Empire fell. I know the path to the center!

"The porters were expecting to go back to Sheras with the

finish of the Steuersak excavation, but I've redirected my remaining funds to extend the expedition to see if this Center can be found. Viggal believes it is a fruitless waste of capital, and a senseless risk to travel through the Freelands, but it is not his decision. The rewards are too great. The knowledge of the Amaranthine. The power! For Sheras! For the Ryker Dominion! For the Orlient name!

"I will not count my cattle though until I make it through the jungle. I am not naive. I know that disappointment is as common as dirt in the pursuit of discovery, but if Lok Secrak exists, then the myths of what resides there may exist too! Weapons that controlled fire, statues that move of their own accord, and crown of it all, Kel Shoatone. The Re-Creator."

Carlotte closed the book and put it back on the table beside her. It was madness, clearly, and yet... something about it seemed familiar. The journal abruptly cut off when the last page ended. There was obviously more. Somewhere in that mess of books and equipment in Ryliar's room, there was at least one more journal.

Carlotte shrugged off the blanket, pushed to her feet, and walked to the large map that hung opposite the fire. It was expansive, cataloging the entirety of the continent, from the cape of Sheras in the North to the southern coast of the Greenwall, from Domsar Bay in the east, past the Bergshalen mountains, to the vast deserts of the west. She traced a finger along Ryliar's supposed journey, ending at the massive Shafala forest that separated Bergshalen from the Freelands and the Freelands from the Endless Sands. That was where the journal left off. She trailed her finger then across the western Freelands to the Greenwall. There was nothing drawn there on the map, just a few trees along the edges and then a great dark shaded expanse until the sea to the south.

Carlotte frowned. Half the journal was nonsense, so Steuersak and this Lok Secrak were probably nonsense too. She'd seen the man who'd written this and his mind was completely gone. Minds didn't go suddenly. They went slowly. He was probably half gone even as he wrote it.

Something nagged at her though, a bit from the end of the journal. Kel Shoatone. The Re-Creator. She'd heard that name before, though she couldn't quite place it. It hung in the back of her mind, just on the edge of memory. Perhaps in some fairy tale, she'd read?

There was a knock at the door.

"I don't want to be disturbed," she called over her shoulder, but Saara's voice came through the door even so.

"Your mother has sent for you."

"Actually this time?" Carlotte asked. She felt a weight in her chest that made her feel very young.

"Yes, Ma'am," Saara said, "in the laboratory, eighth floor."

Carlotte had a brief fantasy of ignoring it. It was a good fantasy, but unrealistic. The Holy Texts were clear on obedience to parents. She reached into a pocket on her dress and clutched at the prayer beads there. God was interesting that way. His laws did not always lead her down the easiest paths, but he made the paths she walked easier.

Carlotte smoothed her dress, somewhat rumpled from her perch on her chair, slipped back into her boots, and left her library. Saara had already disappeared, so Carlotte walked up only with God. She tried at first to go with purpose, but as she went it felt like the air thickened and her pace slowed. By the time she reached the laboratory door, her feet seemed to weigh a hundred pounds, and her hand gripped the beads so hard she was afraid they'd crumble. She stood for several seconds before she knocked. She would be strong. She hadn't done anything wrong after all. Not really. She needed to be strong like Elspeth would have been. Carlotte remembered when Elspeth had told her mother she was leaving. She'd watched it in secret from the door way, watching her mother scream and yell and watched Elspeth let it flow around her like water around a boulder. Carlotte knocked.

There was a moment of silence, and then-

"Come in."

Carlotte opened the door. Her mother sat beside a small table with a slate in her lap and a piece of chalk in her hand. She wore a white smock over her work dress with a cuff of white cloth around her right wrist which she used to smudge away marks on the tablet as she worked. Large sheets of slate lined the walls and they were all covered in scribbles and numbers and letters. Her mother had long forgone physical science and now preferred the theoretical, working on her theory of infinitesimals for several years now.

There were several sheaves of paper on the table and more than one pen and inkwell so that no matter where she was in the room she wouldn't have to reach far to immortalize her thoughts. Carlotte understood some of what was on the boards. She had a firm grasp of the mathematics of shapes and functions, and she saw some calculations for the area of rectangles beside some new symbol she didn't recognize. It wasn't the only one. There were all kinds of symbols on the boards that her mother had probably made up, and from the few conversations she'd overheard her mother have with the other mathematicians, the whole discipline seemed fabricated. Theories of approximations of the areas of curved shapes and infinitesimally small cross sections of those shapes... It wasn't real, and yet, it described reality, like a poem that got at the true essence of a feeling.

Her mother didn't look up from her slate, and Carlotte stood, listening to the scritch scratch of the chalk on the board and the rasp of her mother's sleeve. It was a petty power play, not acknowledging her, but it was effective. A pit grew in Carlotte's stomach as she watched her mother work, like a girl waiting for her punishment. She felt the urge to start babbling, to explain herself, to try and head it all off, but no. She gritted her teeth and steeled herself. She'd be damned if she spoke before her mother.

She glanced around the room again, looking for something to distract her mind. She wondered if the symbols were partly code to protect her mother's work from some jealous Ryker who wandered in. Never mind the locked door, or the servants, or the gates, or the fence. She imagined the Lord Orlient scaling the walls and smiled. That made her think of Harold though, and that thought made the scratch on her upper thigh hurt. She felt his fingers again... scrabbling, scrabbling at her skin like a crab--

"What happened?" asked her mother, her eyes still on the slate tablet and her hand still scribbling across it.

"What do you mean?"

Her mother paused, then glanced up at her daughter. Her eyes were cold.

"I just... I mean, a lot's happened. What part did you want to know about?" What little strength Carlotte felt while she'd waited to speak was gone. She was like a little girl again, hands drawn together in front of her, fiddling with her skirt while the adults yelled at her, while the strap hit her, while she held back the wails...

"I was at the exhibition. I saw that disgrace," Cainia turned her eyes back to her tablet. "Tell me about the Orlients."

Carlotte opened her mouth, but she didn't know what she was going to say. She'd thought about it a lot that night, while she sat by the fire after the exhibition, but she couldn't put it to words. She could play it through in her mind, each movement, each touch mapped perfectly in her memory, but the words just didn't seem to work. Even with her mother sitting down, it felt like Cainia towered over her.

"Well?" Cainia asked. Skritch scratch. Skritch scratch.

"I went there... and-"

"I'm aware. I know you were there for three hours. Then you disappeared. Then Harold disappeared and neither of you came back."

Carlotte swallowed. Her thigh burned like she'd rubbed it in lemon juice.

"He invited me to see his workshop..."

"And?"

"I kissed him."

Carlotte didn't know why she was having so much trouble. Every time she started talking it felt like she was going to choke. It was ridiculous. *She* was being ridiculous. Cainia rubbed a mark away with her cuff.

"I know it didn't end there, Carlotte. You'd have come back to the party if it had."

Carlotte wondered who'd ratted her out to her mother. Who had talked to her at the exhibition? One of the petty Rykers no doubt, the ones who had something to gain by being on Cainia DeSheras' good side.

"Don't make me ask again, Carlotte."

"No," Carlotte said. "I tried to end it there but he... he tried to go further. I said no but he pushed me onto my back and I..." Carlotte's throat closed up and she wanted to scream in frustration but she couldn't even breathe. She didn't know why her body was betraying her like this, why it was being so stupid.

"Did you?" her mother asked. She looked at Carlotte now from beneath her brows. There was fire in her eyes.

"Did I what?"

"Let him in."

Carlotte stared across at her mother.

"Absolutely not," Carlotte breathed.

Her mother matched her stare for a few moments and then nodded and looked back down at her slate. "That's good. Men don't brag about *not* fucking a girl. This will all blow over in a few weeks." Her chalk scratched across the slate.

"That's it?" Carlotte asked, her voice small and cracked.

"Unless there's something else you haven't told me?"

"No, I-"

"Then what else would you have me do?" Cainia raised her voice. "You went back to his laboratory alone. You shouldn't have done that and you certainly shouldn't have kissed him. The impropriety of it all speaks volumes."

"But... All the other girls--"

"The other girls?" Her mother's voice was suddenly very hard. "Why do I care what the other girls do? I care what *my* girls do and *my* girls seem to have a habit of throwing their lives away for little and nothing!" Carina lifted her head and mumbled a prayer upwards. She tossed her slate onto the table and stared hard at her daughter. "You screwed up. You were sloppy and it reflects badly on this family. Keep your head down, spend the next few weeks working on something that won't get the inquisition hounding at our backs and the marriage will go ahead as planned."

Carlotte took a step backward. "I'm still to marry him? Mother... he tried to rape me."

Cainia watched her for a moment and then stood. Her heavy chair squealed across the stone floor behind her. "Come with me," she snapped, storming past Carlotte and pulling her through the door by the wrist.

They went down the stairs and into the grand exhibition hall where servants still worked, cleaning and resetting the room from the fervor of the party.

"Out!" her mother screamed, and the servants scattered to the nearest exits like cockroaches when a lamp is lit, leaving them alone in the room. The stripped-down tables sat at awkward angles in a line where the servants had moved them to clean the floors beneath.

Cainia heaved Carlotte towards them. Carlotte let out a little squeak as her shoulder tweaked, and she just managed to catch herself on the edge of the table before being lain out across it. Her mother stood just beside her and pointed violently at the first tapestry on the wall, at Haakon DeSheras.

"Dead," she said and then pointed to his wife, Alotta, beside him with her counting machine. "Dead." She repeated this, going down the line, pronouncing each of them dead, shouting the word into Carlotte's ear. Finally she pointed at the last, Elspeth, standing amongst the Amaranthine ruins.

"Dead," she said and then grabbed Carlotte's chin and turned it towards her. Cainia was strong, and Carlotte felt like a puppet in her hand. She winced, waiting for the stinging pain of the slap... but it didn't come.

"I am too old to continue this family, and your sister is dead," her mother whispered, her face so close Carlotte had trouble seeing it in focus. "You are the only one left."

"But mother--"

Cainia thrust a finger onto Carlotte's lips. "He is taking *your* name. Only our prestige allows that and if nothing is done, that prestige will fall. Orlient forges build all the Mareshal's guns with iron from Orlient mines. His wealth grows every day and his influence grows with it. Our rents keep us above for now, but if things continue as they are, the Orlients will eclipse us, and then Harold will not take your name, and this family will be... dead."

Cainia released Carlotte's jaw and stepped away, flinching as though she'd touched something dirty.

"If that were not enough," Cainia continued, "the Lord Orlient is in bed with the inquisitors and through them with the Mareshal. The Mareshal gives him a damn monopoly and he bargains at council to let more of the bastards in!"

Carlotte lowered her eyes. She'd never had much of a memory for politics. It distracted her from her work. Cainia pointed a finger at her.

"You don't have to worry about it. All you have to do is marry Harold and I," she pointed at her chest, "I will keep this city from falling into shit. Marry the brute, fill yourself with children, and I will do the rest. Do you understand me?"

Carlotte gave a meek nod.

"I need your words, Carlotte."

"Yes, mother," Carlotte said.

"Good. I don't want to hear another word about this," Then she strode out of the exhibition hall, stopping just before the door. She turned back to Carlotte. "Your sister didn't care for her family duties. She preferred to follow her heart. Her whim. Look where that got her." Cainia turned and slammed the double doors behind her.

Carlotte was suddenly very alone.

A great sob rose up in her and her body sagged against the table. It screeched across the floor with her weight and she slid down to the ground. The sob came up from deep inside her and it was all she could do not to wail. Her stomach heaved, her diaphragm convulsed, and she clapped a hand to her mouth to keep the sound in. She couldn't let her mother hear her. She couldn't bear that. It rolled, muffled, out of her for several minutes and it was all she could not to lie on the floor and kick her arms and legs like a child.

Was this to be her life then? Powerlessness? She, the Heir DeSheras forced to marry... Harold. Carlotte suddenly understood why Elspeth had left. It was so clear to her now because Carlotte could see the walls of the tower for what they really were. A prison. This tower, this name, this life was a prison and Elspeth had no choice but to flee. When they married, Harold would beat her and no one would listen to her pleas and she'd be forced into obscurity by him and--

Carlotte lifted a hand and slapped herself, but there was no strength behind it and she barely felt anything. She grimaced and did it again, and again until her cheek finally began to sting.

"Shut up," she whispered and slapped herself once more, this time catching her face well and the sudden pain made her nose tingle and her tears come stronger. She squeezed her eyes shut to force them back inside.

"Shut up!"

She took in a deep breath and opened her eyes. The room

swam around her for a few moments, blurred by her tears. She blinked them away until she could see clearly and pressed to her feet. The tapestries were in front of her, and all of her ancestors looked out from their tableaus like monarchs from their throne rooms. These people didn't achieve what they'd achieved by giving in to their childish notions. They waded into the maelstrom of life and demanded their place in it.

Carlotte's eye drifted left, to the last tapestry on the wall. Elspeth looked implacably out from the ruin, clutching some artifact in one hand, while the other rested on the head of a pickax, as though she'd done the actual digging.

"Why did you go?" Carlotte asked her sister, but of course, no answer came back.

Had she been trying to escape the tower? Perhaps that was part of it, but Carlotte knew her sister to be stronger than that. So was her mother right? Had Elspeth been following her whim and ignoring her familial duty? No, that didn't track either. Elspeth had been strong, stronger than Carlotte could ever hope to be, and Carlotte knew she wouldn't have backed away unless she had something more important to do. But what was so important in Amaranthine ruins? That was where the rejects went, where the Rykers who hadn't the capacity for real science studied the past instead of the future.

Carlotte barely remembered the two days she'd had with her sister before Elspeth had locked herself in her laboratory for the last time, but she remembered enough to know the gist of the conversation. Magic. She'd never told her mother about it, but she knew Cainia had a suspicion. It had ruined Ryliar Orlient, and it had—

Kel Shoatone. The re-creator.

Carlotte suddenly placed Ryliar's words, the ones that had been on the tip of her tongue before. Elspeth had said those same words, that day by the lake, the last day Carlotte saw her. She was sure of it, the memory blazoned in her mind. What did it mean that both Ryliar Orlient and Elspeth had said those exact words? A myth perhaps? Some common Amaranthine story they'd both found remnants of? That would make sense if they had found the same story and had gone after the same figment of legend.

But there had been something else that day. It felt like Carlotte was crawling through a dream, reaching through the mist at memories she'd pushed far away. Elspeth had brought something back and given it to Carlotte.

A thing, a thing that she'd put under a floorboard in her bedroom when her mother had set to destroying everything Elspeth had brought back from the mountains. Carlotte hadn't wanted it burned, so she'd hid it, and kept it a secret lest her mother find it and take it and destroy it like the rest. It was a little thing... A little thing that made light.

Surely Carlotte couldn't be remembering that correctly. It was like remembering some ridiculous factoid she'd believed as a child that she hadn't thought about with her adult brain. Carlotte remembered it as a little round ball of metal that opened up to make light. But that hadn't been real. It couldn't be. It was just some fake memory she'd concocted... right?

Carlotte left the exhibition hall, passing a few servants who were waiting for her to leave so they could get back to cleaning. She climbed the stairs up to her bedroom and considered the floor. Where had that loose board been?

She got down on her knees and started knocking at the boards, listening to their sounds. There was stone just beneath, and her knocks sounded back sharp. She kept tapping, and then, just beside the headboard, the knock came back hollow. Carlotte clawed at the board, trying to get her nails underneath it, but the floor had been resealed since she was a child, and she yelped as one of her nails tore. She growled, pushed to her feet, and rushed to the wall, yanking up and down on the bell rope that rang down in the servants' hall.

"Madame?" a servant called from the door only half a minute later. Carlotte recognized him but didn't know his name.

"Saara. Now."

"Yes, Ma'am," he said and disappeared.

"And tell her to hurry!" she called after him, resisting the urge to stick her finger into her mouth. It bled where the nail had torn.

Carlotte went back to her floorboard and knocked again, as though if she forgot where it was the whole memory would disappear.

"Ma'am?" came Saara's voice, low and scratchy.

Carlotte stood. "Come here."

The bull of a woman approached and Carlotte pointed at the floorboard. "Get rid of that."

"What, the floor?"

"That board there."

Saara looked down at the floor, thoroughly confused, and then back up at Carlotte.

"How?"

"Pry it up! Break it! I don't care, just get rid of it!"

"Right," Saara said and knelt down, pulling the knife from the sheath on her belt. "You sure? This is nice wo--"

"Now!"

"Right." She stabbed its tip at the edge of the board and then worked it back and forth until she could get it under. She pried it down, and with a crack, the board popped out.

"Huh," Saara said, "Wasn't nailed down. It was loose--"

"Good. Get out."

"What?" Saara asked, looking up at Carlotte. She had a stupid look on her face. The angle made her brow look like a shelf.

"Get. Out," Carlotte growled, and Saara heaved to her feet and trudged out the door, shrugging to the other servant on her way out.

"Close the door!" Carlotte yelled, and the door slammed shut.

Silence.

Carlotte knelt and reached for the board. It was sitting askew in its place and Carlotte pulled it reverently out, as though she were Elspeth, uncovering some ancient tomb in the frozen north.

Beneath the board was a hollow, little more than a crack between two stones where the mortar had been gouged away. Carlotte remembered suddenly the last time she'd seen it, on the day her sister had died. She'd run here after seeing Elspeth's horror-filled death mask. She'd run here and hidden away that thing Elspeth had given her.

She hadn't imagined it. The little gray ball was there, nestled amongst some dried-up taffies. Carlotte reached down, grabbed the ball's silver chain, and pulled it up. It was cold, and when she held it up to the light, its surface glinted, polished smooth. Little lines wrapped around it like a coiled-up armadillo, but when she brought her other hand up to touch it, its surface was smooth. It was just a ball, nothing more, but she remembered it opening. Had that been real? Or was it part of the story she'd told herself?

Carlotte fingered at it, trying to find a catch or an edge that she could claw at, but there was nothing to find and she only managed to smear blood across its surface. The memory was just there, like she was looking for a book, but couldn't remember the author or the title, only the shelf on which it stood. She closed her eyes.

Elspeth had leaned in while Carlotte held it and whispered something... Had she told her? Carlotte reached back, cobbling the memory together like she was stacking stones to build a wall.

Elspeth had told her... on the carriage ride back to Sheras.

Lix.

Carlotte looked at the sphere in her hands, the word held on the tip of her tongue. Did she want to say it? If she did, she'd know, and then all this would be proved a childish fantasy, the dying breath of a little girl trying to avoid her responsibilities. If she said nothing...

"Lix," Carlotte said, and the light began to shine.

She gave a yelp as the thing receded in on itself, revealing the pebble of pure white light beneath. It was impossibly bright, like a hundred candle flames compressed into the space of one with none of the heat. She stared into it, and her eyes went blind to everything else. As the world around her faded away, she saw the symbol at the light's center: a dot with two offset lines.

Carlotte closed her hand around the pebble and felt it curl closed. She leaned back against the bed, thoughts racing through her head.

"No," she said, pushing them all to the side. She was getting herself excited, like a child with a toy. This wasn't... magic. There was no such thing, no matter if Elspeth and Ryliar both wrote about this re-creator, no matter if the thing in her hand was impossible.

Carlotte opened her hand again, and the the ball was dark and gray once more. It wasn't impossible. She knew better than to think such things. If it was impossible it wouldn't have happened. This, whatever it was, was just something she didn't understand. Elspeth had found it in the Amaranthine ruins, and the Amaranthine technology was famously advanced. This was just physics like everything else in the world, and this was certainly part of the world. A curiosity. Like lightning had been before she'd delved into it and started to uncover its secrets.

Carlotte considered the pebble in her hands for a long moment, wondering if she should just stick it back into the hollow and move on with her life. She had plenty to study in the last months before she'd be forced to do her familial duty. She should just put it away. She knew it was just some yet-to-be-understood science, but others might not think so, and with the inquisitors getting more uppity, and after her performance at the exhibition that evening, it would be entirely better if she just left the thing alone.

"Yes," she whispered, "best I just put it away."

Carlotte leaned forward and put the board back into its place. She stood, smoothed out her dress, and moved to the door before realizing she was still holding the pebble in her hand. With a shrug, Carlotte pulled the chain over her head, and tucked it into her bosom, feeling its cold surface between her breasts. If it was so trivial, then there really was no harm in keeping it.

7

"Sorry, Friend. Not buying Matchlocks."

Aethan stared blankly across the counter at the man. The counter was in a little hut that jutted out from the side of a warehouse, and his deflated muffin of a hat was his badge of office. He gave a conciliatory grimace and clasped his hands in front of him.

"I'm sorry, Friend. No procurement officer in the Dominion will buy them from you."

Aethan's mouth drifted open for a few moments before he could get any words out.

"The Mareshal decide to give peace a chance?" he finally sputtered. The man behind the counter laughed.

"No, no. I think not. I doubt the Mareshal even knows the word."

"Then..." Aethan cast about for a reason but none came to mind at first. Then he frowned.

"The war is over mate. You'd refuse to trade with me because I'm--"

The clerk raised his hands.

"No, no, no! It's not that! Not at all. You folk are good with me!" he reached out a hand to Aethan. "Honestly, friend. I'm not buying Matchlocks from anyone."

Aethan warily reached out his left hand and awkwardly gripped the man's. The man didn't seem to mind and shook it warmly.

"Jaaque. Jaaque Akar," the man said.

"Aethan. Just Aethan."

"Just one name? Must make things confusing for the tax man."

"Good thing the Freelands ain't got those."

The man laughed.

"Confusing but simpler no doubt. I like that."

The man pulled his hand away and Aethan looked down at his. It was the first time he'd been touched in weeks.

"Then...?"

"Flintlocks, friend," Jaaque said. "New rifles from the Orlient forges. Don't need a match. More reliable."

"Orlient rifles are crap," Aethan said. Jaaque shrugged.

"These can fire in the rain, Friend. There's no match to give soldiers away neither. They say it's going to change war forever."

Aethan turned and regarded the cart behind him.

"Will anyone here buy them?"

"Maybe for scrap. How many rifles you say you got?"

"A hundred even."

"Could get a few Rakes if it's good steel."

"It is," Aethan said, but all of the guns' worth was in their craftsmanship, in the rifling of the barrels, in the strength of the steel and in its lightness, in the delicate crafting of the trigger and the comfort of the rifle against a soldier's shoulder. He'd paid nearly three pounds of gold for them. A couple of gold Rakes would be...

"No. I'll look elsewhere," Aethan said and turned back to Jaaque who raised one eyebrow. "I know I can't sell to the people here. I know the laws." He thought for a moment. "Is there a place that can guarantee my cart and merchandise while I deal with some business in Sheras?"

"I'll hold it for you. A silver bit a day locked in the warehouse here, and I'll sell it for scrap you leave it longer than a month."

"I'll be back for it end of the day. Need the bit now?"

Jaaque shook his head and stuck out his hand, the left one this time.

"You seem good for it."

"Plus you've got the collateral," Aethan said and gripped the man's hand properly.

"Sorry for your timing, Friend. Had you come last year, you would have gone away a richer man. Truly I feel for you."

"Thank you... Friend," Aethan said and then stalked back to the cart.

"What business takes you into the city?" Jaaque called out.

Aethan rooted around in the cart beneath the guns and pulled a few paper-wrapped packages out of the straw that cushioned the rifles. He pulled his pack from beneath the bench and shoved the packages on top of the gold within.

"I've got to see a captain about sea passage."

"Your things would probably be safer in my warehouse. City's a dangerous place."

Aethan grunted and started unhooking Toktok from his cart's rigging.

"I'm sure they would be," Aethan said and then looked up at Jaaque with a grin. "But you've got to forgive an old man his fears."

Jaaque barked a laugh and came around the counter to help with the horse.

"I'll be damned if you're half my age," Jaaque said, and then quieter, "Just be careful in there. Things are changing on the streets. Sheras has a Grand Inquisitor now. If you've been here before, I wouldn't bet on it being the same." He held out a layaway receipt.

Aethan took it, shook the man's hand again, and then hefted the pack onto his shoulders. The weight of it gave him more than a little comfort. He watched the man take his cart away and then pulled himself up onto Toktok's back and led the horse onto the road.

The city of Sheras was massive. New Freedom was the only city in the Freelands that had a chance of being larger, and then only in geographical area. Sheras was uncomfortably dense and was older than most cities on the continent. It was the end of an Amaranthine road that ran up from somewhere in the Greenwall and ended some hundred yards into the Sheras Bay. The city had been started around a few massive Amaranthine ruins that were gathered around the dock. The early Dominioneers had built a wall around it, and Old Town came into existence. Then the city had grown and filled up with people and the people spilled out beyond the walls and thus, the Nouvre Vil, the second section of Sheras, was born. The aristocracy fled Old Town and built their villas in the Nouvre Vil and eventually, they too built a wall. In time the Nouvre Vil also filled up, and the Dominioneers built homes outside the Nouvre Vil walls and thus the Outer City was born.

Aethan clucked his tongue and Toktok ambled up the road into said Outer City. Sheras had not bothered to build a third wall, and so the city kept expanding. It didn't really have a start. It just came into being. First Aethan passed a few more warehouses, and then the buildings became more common, and then, without him noticing an incremental difference, the city was all around him. The Amaranthine Road, which ran directly north-south and which the locals called the Nor-so, became so choked with pedestrians that Toktok slowed from a walk to an amble.

The situation with the guns was a setback, a big one, but he had two bad choices: Take them back to the Freelands and take a modest loss, or try for Bergshalen in the mountains to the west. If the Dominion was arming up, then Bergshalen was arming up too. The Dominion's invasion ten years earlier would be fresh in their minds. He needed to move quickly though. If this flintlock was as monumental as the clerk made it sound, then soon matchlocks everywhere would be close to worthless.

He put his right hand into his pocket and worried at his slaver bones with his thumb and pinky. Whatever happened, he still had his forty pounds of gold and the packages from the cart. He always smuggled a little pike into the Dominion when he traded here. The arbitrage was excellent, and it was good to diversify. Bluebacks didn't need much evidence to see the money-grubbing Boneman they expected. A Freelander selling guns to the Dominion? Stereotype confirmed. No need to look beneath the guns in the straw that cushioned them.

The buildings that lined the clogged street were made of wood with stone facing and had tenements above storefronts with pleasing balconies looking out over the street. The masons and carpenters had done a fine job matching the architecture to the road, but Aethan knew it was only a facade. It was only along the Nor-so that the Outer City looked so affluent. Were he to go a block east or west, he would see the true state of things: ramshackle tenements and sagging hovels, people so jammed together they could barely find a corner to sleep in.

Despite the crowd, Aethan stood out like a sore thumb. He saw a few others who could be Freelanders, or perhaps Niquari from across the desert, but from atop his horse Aethan caught more than a few angry glares. The war was years ago, but it seemed grudges held strong, especially the ones backed by old bigotry. Slavery may have been illegal in the Dominion, but thinking a man should be free was much different than thinking he should be equal. Aethan pulled his floppy hat low over his face and pressed on. Trouble was the last thing he needed. Aethan had left his pride at the Greenwall.

He reached the Nouvre Vil Gate, and the traffic came to a standstill. The wall had been built over the Nor-so and the masons had built ledges along the sides of the gatehouse passage where bluebacks stood and looked down at the people walking by. The bluebacks were not alone, Aethan noted, for another figure, clad all in black with white trim on his coat and a white feather spouting from his black hat stood amongst them.

An inquisitor.

There hadn't been inquisitors at the Gate last time Aethan had come through the city, nor the time before. Jaaque was right. Things had changed. Aethan thought of the woman the inquisitors had burned out in the country and he shivered. He pulled his hat low over his face and pulled his hands into the sleeves of his coat. He wasn't ashamed of his skin, but if they didn't happen to see it, that would be okay with him. The guards didn't stop him. They didn't seem to be stopping anybody. They just glared down from on high.

The Nouvre Vil was instantly richer. The buildings there were taller and grander, with columns supporting the second levels and large glass windows that looked out across the road. This was where the Rykers and the rich laypeople lived. Just beyond the Gate was a large tavern and inn where the rich went to slum, and the poor went to act rich.

A line of boys lounged against the stable wall watching the people flow by. They started upright when Aethan pulled his horse out of the street, but a moment later when they'd gotten a good look at him they relaxed back against the wall.

"Boneman," one of them muttered and the other sniggered. Aethan pulled an eighth out of his purse.

"You better than this?" Aethan asked. They looked to one another for a moment, and then the biggest boy pushed off the wall and took Aethan's reins.

"Almost as if everybody's money spends the same," Aethan said.

He dismounted and his backpack clinked as he hit the ground. The boy sneered, but Aethan paid him no heed and pushed through the tavern's door. He didn't blame the boy. It was the way of things. Hatred could not be helped. It was just another reason to get his fifty pounds and quit the world.

The tavern was just as dark as he remembered, and he had to take a moment to let his eyes adjust.

"Excuse me," he said, catching a barmaid by the arm as she walked past, empty mugs in hand.

"Sit down and I'll come to you," she said.

"I'm not here for a drink," he said. She turned to look at him.

"Then you came to the wrong place."

"Looking for a man. Roland."

Her eyes narrowed. Aethan reached into his pocket and pulled out two eighth bits. He placed them on the bar. She raised an eyebrow. Aethan grimaced and then reached into his purse and added a silver bit. She raised her eyebrow higher and Aethan shrugged. He could only be pushed so far. After a moment she put down the mugs and slid the coins into her apron.

"He's not here."

"When will he be here?"

"He's dead," she said.

Aethan frowned.

"Dead?"

"Inquisitors cut off his head."

He stared at her.

She raised an eyebrow. "You be wanting that drink now? I'd say it's on the house, but you already paid me."

"No," Aethan said. "No thank you."

Aethan turned and walked back outside, pushing too hard on the door so it slammed open. The boys lining the wall all looked at him.

"Fuck," he said.

He stalked out into the milling Nor-so.

"Fuck," he said again.

Pedestrians flooded around him and he felt like a rock in a river, altering the flow, but doing nothing to change its course. He didn't know this city. Roland had always been his man. Now he had to find someone else to sell an illegal--

Someone slammed into him. He staggered to the side and struggled to keep his pack from falling off his shoulder, having a terrified image of it hitting the cobbles stones and all his coins spilling out, his vials broken, and the rabble around him swarming over it like pigeons at bread.

He regained his balance and swiveled around to see that a woman stood before him. She had long brown hair that hung tangled and dirty around her face. She was awkwardly tall, only a few inches shorter than Aethan, and she wore a filthy dress that clung to a frame as straight as a little boy. She clutched a ratty violin case in one hand while the other grasped open and closed at the air, as though she'd dropped something but forgotten.

"I'm so--" she began, her voice low and breathy, but she trailed off. Her whole body leaned to one side and then she snapped back up in an instant. Her eyes darted back and forth. "I'm sorry I--" and she drifted off again.

Pike.

He reached out to steady her, but when he touched her shoulder her eyes dialed in on his face.

"No!" She lunged forward and darted around him. He spun with her, trying to grab a hold of her dress but his hand closed around nothing. She melded into the crowd like a fish dropped back into a river.

"Girl!" Aethan called. He grasped the straps of his pack as tight as he could and bowled through the crowd after her, shoulder-checking people out of his way. "Girl!"

It was lucky they were both tall, when he straightened he could see her head bobbing through. She was moving faster than he, slipping through the gaps between people like a cat through a fence while he charged through like a bull.

The crowd slowed at the Gate, and tightened around Aethan, pressing in on all sides. He could see her head still, a dozen yards ahead of him. It was too tight for both of them. They were slaves to the flow.

He wanted to shout an explanation to her, to get her to wait for him but what would he shout? Wait, I want to sell you pike? They entered the Nouvre Vil Gate and the Inquisitor's eyes roamed over the crowd again. He saw her come out the other side and dart away when the crowd thinned. He willed the crowd forward. He strained at them, and the man in front of him grumbled back at him. The man turned to say something louder, saw the color of Aethan's skin, and minded his own business.

The man surged forward as soon as he could, and Aethan darted at the opening. He knocked a few more people to the side and then turned down the same street as the girl. He saw her dart around a corner two blocks down.

"Fuck," Aethan muttered. The girl was fast. The side street had a fraction of the nor-so's traffic and he broke into a sprint. His heavy pack thumped and clinked against his back with every step. He felt all forty unwieldy pounds of it. He should have left it with the clerk.

The quaint facade of the outer city faded as he left the nor-so behind. The buildings changed from sturdy wood and stone to precarious structures of wood and cloth that all seemed ready to fall over were it not for the neighboring building falling the opposite way.

He turned again and again, only just keeping track of the girl and falling deeper and deeper into the outer city slums. The paved road gave way to mud and the tenements grew more condensed, crammed together in ever tighter quarters, a shit away from a cholera outbreak. Kids played in the mud while adults looked out glassless windows at him running past. Aethan lost track of the turns he'd taken, but he was gaining on her. She was a bit closer with every corner. They turned down a long straight street and Aethan surged forward putting everything into his sprint.

"Wait!" he shouted, and she turned thrusting out with a blade. Aethan slid to a stop, almost tumbling over in the mud.

They stared at each other, both gasping for breath. The vacant stare in her eyes was gone, replaced by a wild but focused fear. She was coming off her high, experiencing the ripples. He'd seen it all too often on the streets of New Freedom. In a few minutes, she would be gone again, lost in the depth of the next wave. Aethan unclenched his fingers from the straps of his pack and lifted his hands, palms out. The evening was lengthening, and the low sun cast long shadows from the buildings around them. Aethan could feel eyes on him. He saw them peeking out from the windows. He saw them leaning out from doors.

"What do you want!?" the girl said. "I'll drop you in the mud you keep coming at me!"

"Where do you buy it?" he asked between gasps.

"Buy it?" she asked.

"The pike."

The girl stared at him. The knife's point shook in front of her. It was a tiny blade, probably made to skin fruit.

"You chased me across the Outers to ask a question?"

"I wouldn't have chased you if you hadn't run. We could have done this," Aethan waved a hand towards the Nouvre Vil walls rising a mile or so behind them, "back there."

"Why do you want to know?"

"My man died, and I'm not from here. Didn't know who else to ask."

The girl narrowed her eyes.

"Listen," Aethan continued, and pulled a few eighths out of his purse. "You tell me, and I'll pay you."

The girl bit her lip.

"Come on. Easiest money you ever made. Just tell me who, and point me in their direction."

They watched each other for another long moment, and just as Aethan was about to pull more money from his purse, she dropped her blade to her side but kept it firmly in her fist.

"Ghost," she said. "That's where everyone gets it now. Go back down here three blocks, go west for five, then left. Big house. Won't miss it." She motioned with her chin back down the way they'd just run.

"Three back, five west, turn south," he repeated. "Ghost?"

"Yep. Ghost."

"Okay. Thank you." Aethan straightened and stepped towards her. She stepped back and stabbed out with the knife again.

"Whoa," Aethan said. "Just trying to pay you."

"Just drop it."

"In the mud?"

"Yeah."

Aethan looked down at the sucking sludge beneath him. "I could just hand it to you."

"Mud's fine."

"Right." Aethan dropped the coins and then turned and walked away. He looked over his shoulder a few steps later, and she hadn't moved, still with knife outstretched, her eyes hard and focused in between the ripples. He could probably just wait for it to take her and then take his coins back, but Aethan wasn't a thief. He was a murderous monster, and he sold things to help Dominioneers kill each other and themselves, but he wasn't a thief. A man has to draw the line somewhere. When he reached the end of the block, he looked back again, but she was gone. The evening had swallowed her whole. He found himself wondering if she could play that violin, or if it was just a bit of loot to trade for more pike.

He followed her directions, and she was right. He couldn't miss it. In the middle of the crowded slums, a house stood looking like it belonged on the nor-so with a stone foundation and a clean, well-mannered stoop. Two men stood on either side of the entry stair lit by the fading glow of twilight and oil lamps hanging from the eaves of the porch. Even amidst the thickening gloom, the house stood out like a blooming flower amidst a pile of shit, so much wealth right up against so much poor.

"Hold," came a deep voice from the first of the two men. Aethan stopped, keeping his hands tight to the straps of his pack where they could see them.

"The hell you want?" the second man said. His voice was nasally and high.

"Here to see Ghost," Aethan said. The deep voice laughed.

"You can deal with us, Freelander. An eighth for a dab. Two full bits for a vial."

Aethan raised an eyebrow. The price had gone up since last he'd been in Sheras. Maybe he could make up for the misfortune with the matchlocks.

"What's that per pound?"

"You want to buy a pound?" the second voice asked.

"No, sorry," Aethan said, "I want to sell you ten pounds."

They were both silent for a moment, and then at a nod from the second one, the first turned and walked up to the house's door. He was a hulking man. Even slouching his head was higher than the door frame. He rapped twice and a moment later it opened, spilling more warm light out onto the porch. A woman stood there, wearing canvas pants and a long knife strapped at her side. Her skin shone olive in the lamplight in the way of those who came from across the sea. She was further away from home than he was. Not that he had a home, and if she was here, working for these people, it was probable she didn't have a home either.

"Ten?" she said, and the big man nodded. She stepped past him, carrying a lantern before her, and descended the stairs, stopping just before she stepped into the mud of the street.

"Show me," she said. Aethan pulled his pack around in front of him, careful not to jiggle the coins inside, and withdrew one of the packages he'd smuggled across the Dominion beneath his guns. He pulled off the paper that swaddled it and held it aloft in the light.

It was molten silver, glittering in the lamplight as it swirled in the glass, veins of subtle variation in the color twirling in tiny eddies. They called it quicksilver in the Freelands where it was legal, but here where possession, production, and distribution were punished by a short fall and a quick stop, it was called pike.

"Pure. From the edge of the Greenwall," Aethan said and the woman nodded.

"Wait here." She withdrew back through the door. Aethan slid the jar back into his pack and the two men resumed their positions, dark statues guarding the light. There was no conversation, not between the men and not with Aethan, and in the silence, the gloom faded to night. There were still noises: a baby crying through some window, a racking cough down some street, but given the multitude of cramped tenements around them, it was strange that there were not more sounds of people. Aethan glanced over his shoulder, but the alley was still.

The racking cough sounded again, closer. He looked down the

alley but could see nothing. There was another sound of something dragging through the mud, keeping pace with the cough.

"Haakon?" the larger of the two men asked. The other nodded.

They did not seem worried, but Aethan couldn't keep the chill from creeping through him. His whole body was tense, and he braced himself against whatever was coming.

The sound drew nearer, and then a ghoul shuffled into the light. His clothes were burlap, and Aethan could just make out the word SHERAS stamped in all capitol letters across one shoulder in the way that shipping sacks were stamped on the docks. He wore no shoes but had wrapped more of the burlap around his feet, with one foot swollen to three times the size of the other. His skin was gray in the lamplight, like a corpse wandering the streets in a cheap funeral shroud.

"A dab please, and another." The man wheezed, revealing as he spoke a single brown tooth set into blood-red gums.

"You'd better have money," the taller man growled and Haakon nodded. He lifted both hands straight out, holding a dirty bronze eighth in each like they were relics of the Dominion's God.

The bigger man held a hand over the railing, and Haakon pressed the coins into it. The man snapped his hand away as soon as he held the coin, and Haakon clasped his hands together with his thumbs on his forehead.

"Thank you, thank you, sir. Thank you."

Two bronze eighths was not a lot of money, but it should have meant the world to a man as destitute as this. An eighth could rent a cheap roof, or buy a hot meal. The man needed one. He was bent over nearly in half, and the burlap across his back jutted up with each bump in his spine. The skin on his forearms hung from the bone like there was nothing else beneath it.

The bigger man nodded to the other, who turned to a little table behind him. They all stood in silence while the dealer was bent over the table, and the rasping of Haakon's breath was the only sound.

There was a sparkle in Haakon's eye as he watched the large man work, and his mouth seemed exceptionally wet, hungry for what was to come. It was the only spark of life in the man. The hunger.

The second tough turned and held out a paper-thin scrap of iron with two shining drops of moonlight quivering on top of it. He held it down from the railing and Haakon reached up to take it and for a moment Aethan could feel Haakon's withered hands against his own.

Aethan shook the feeling away. Pike may have been the man's poison, but his disease was poverty. New Freedom was full of such wraiths, wandering the streets in search of just another drop of quicksilver, but the drug was not confined to the slums. Aethan knew that the Freeland elites, the self-described captains of industry, used the drug just as often, but instead of on dirty scraps of iron, they kept whole ounces of it in crystal vials in cabinets made of glass. They mixed it with their liquor and smoked it with their tobacco, and looked down on the wraiths in the streets like they weren't the same creatures at their core.

Haakon pulled the scrap of metal close to him, cradling it like a child, and shuffled away down the alley, disappearing into the darkness just as he had emerged.

Who was Aethan to deny Haakon his choices? Who was Aethan to claim to know better what Haakon should do with his money? The Korkin masters had made choices for their slaves, and the Freelanders had slaughtered them. It was self-aggrandizing for Aethan to feel any kind of guilt for Haakon's suffering because it took away Haakon's agency. It made the man into a puppet who only danced to Aethan's actions. So what if Aethan was profiting from Haakon's poison? Who was Aethan to deny Haakon his right to choose his own death?

Or maybe all that was just an excuse for Aethan to comfort himself while the world around him fell to ashes.

The door opened and the woman looked out at him, tiny between the two bruisers.

"We can deal," she said and then motioned with her head into the house.

"I'd rather deal out here," Aethan called back.

"It's in here or not at all, friend," the woman said. "We'll give you six hundred Rakes for it, but we don't deal that kind of coin out in the open."

Aethan's stomach dropped. The price *had* gone up. Six hundred

Rakes was almost thirty pounds of gold. It was a good price. If they were selling dabs for an eighth each then they could get north of eight hundred Rakes for it on the street. A reasonable markup. A damn reasonable price. Perfect to get him in the door.

Aethan licked his teeth and watched the three of them watching him back. He couldn't go in there, not willingly. He'd have to be an idiot... but he'd have to be an idiot not to, right? Six hundred rakes. Six hundred rakes when the rest of his merchandise was practically worthless. The kind of arbitrage that came around once in a lifetime.

"It's yes or no friend. Ghost won't come to you," the woman said.

"Yes," Aethan said. "Fine."

The woman smiled and stepped across the threshold, holding the door open for him. It was a goddamned reasonable price.

The two men parted as he approached and after another moment's hesitation, Aethan stepped through the doorway. The woman closed the door behind him, and Aethan let out a breath. He'd expected the two bruisers to follow him in, but maybe he was just being paranoid. It was a reasonable price. This ghost fellow would make a pretty bit of coin off of him. There was no reason for violence. No reason for treachery. If they made a good deal, then this ghost could get another good deal out of Aethan next time he came through. Ghost had no idea that this price was enough to make this Aethan's last trip. No, it made good, sturdy business sense to make a reasonable offer and follow through with it.

The interior was well-lit with lamps along dark paneled walls. The small woman led him past a meeting area and a kitchen, both empty, and then past several closed doors before she stopped at one that ended the hall. She opened it, and warmth billowed over them. A roaring fireplace stood at the far wall and in front of it, just to the side was a large desk made of the same dark wood as the walls. A man sat behind it with long bone-white hair that rippled down the sides of his face. The man, Ghost presumably, watched him enter while he rested one hand on a small chest sitting atop the desk. A chest big enough for six hundred rakes perhaps?

Aethan stepped into the room and then noticed the second

person, sitting at a small table in the shadowy corner. Then, like noticing one ant and suddenly being aware of standing in the middle of the hive, Aethan saw the rest of them. A woman lounged against the other corner with silver daggers glinting on her belt. Three smaller but grim-looking men flanked the fireplace, their brown clothes blending into the wall behind them. Two big men stood to either side of him by the door, ready to cut him off if he tried to run back. Metal slid against leather behind him.

"Fuck..." he whispered.

"You must be new here," Ghost said. His accent was strange, seeming to be foreign but from where Aethan couldn't tell.

"Six hundred is a reasonable price," Aethan said with half a breath and Ghost smiled. Aethan heard a click and glanced over at the woman seated behind the table. There was a glint of metal beneath it. A crossbow?

"Zero is far more reasonable," Ghost said. Aethan almost cried out at the words. He was so close. So close to his fifty pounds of gold. So close to being done with all this. So close he could smell the timbers of his house. He could hear the gentle lap of the lake against his dock. The blessed solitude of it all was so close he could almost touch it.

"Do you always kill your suppliers?" Aethan asked. He felt his eyes grow wet and his left leg began to tremble.

"No. You're not a supplier. You're a competitor," Ghost said.

Aethan swallowed. Regret was pointless. He never could have turned away. No matter the risk, his standing here was inevitable. He had to go forward always. Always. The price had been too reasonable.

Aethan summoned the image of Ashatee's lake, felt his toes dangling in the water, and withdrew into himself. He saw Ghost's mouth moving, but his focus was within. He was running through the familiar corridors, a horror rising in him with every turn. In a moment he was there, standing amidst the charred bodies of his old friends. Bulwark's bubbled face stared up at him, Weed's eye accused him, and the darkness of the jungle barred down. He gripped the mausoleum door, and the stone was cold. There was no time to consider. He heaved it open, and the vines that overgrew it snapped apart, and then the blackness was there, the infinite dark.

He was vaguely aware that Ghost's monologue was ending and Ghost signaled with one hand. Aethan had no time.

It had been almost a decade, but the formulas came back to him. He set his parameters and began laying his instructions in the silvery runes that hung before the darkness.

Then the knife slid into his back.

Aethan screamed. He called it, and the darkness came, surging out the door like a dam released. It flowed through the unfinished instructions and followed them exactly. Heat. Unimaginable heat.

The world around him exploded. The floorboards, the chairs, the people, the very air combusted. Ghost's mouth dropped open. The woman with the crossbow squeaked, and then her face and throat peeled away and nothing more came out. Ghost did not scream. None of them did. There was no time. The room vaporized, and the walls blew away, and the stone around him bubbled. His own clothes burned away. He felt the knife in his back drip out of him. He watched the pikelord's house turn to hell.

The doorway inside him bulged open, stretching out, distorting. He reached out to pull it closed, but the door seemed warped. Its hinges no longer seemed to function and he felt stretched himself, like the pit of his stomach was twisting and yawning. Aethan threw all of his focus at it, willing the door to shut. The flood of darkness slowed and then reversed, and the door pulled itself back into a meaningful shape. He heaved it closed, and had just enough calm of mind to throw up a few more instructions before the darkness left, to take its heat with it. The mausoleum door thundered shut, and Aethan collapsed.

He opened his eyes, not remembering having shut them, and saw a land changed.

The house was gone. Falling ash was all that was left of the roof beams and walls. The closest tenements on either side of the house were also gone, and the ones beyond were in flame. The men and women who'd been in the room were streaks of ash on the ground, quickly disappearing in the soot that fell like black snow. Fire raged in a ring around him, but the air he breathed was frigid. The darkness never affected the one who called it, but once the door shut that protection was gone. The stone beneath his feet that had bubbled was now frozen and hard. His feet were bare on the ice, and the air sucked his heat away while people fifty strides away were burning to death. Shivers racked through him. People were screaming. Shouts of "Fire!" and cries of pain all jumbled together in a cacophony of panic. He looked down and saw, just behind his heels, a mound of gold. His gold.

Aethan cried out, feeling like he'd suddenly lost an arm. He reached his hand down to it to scoop it up, but it was hard, fused to the rock beneath, and colder than ice. He had to go. There was no time to get it back. People would come and they would see him and they would try to take him, and then what would he do?

In a mad rush, he stumbled away from his gold, from everything he was, and ran down the alley, naked as the day he was born.

There was a boom and Saara jolted awake. It wasn't terribly loud, but it was clearly audible, and for a moment she wondered if she'd dreamed it. Then she heard movement through the walls and knew that whatever it was had woken the servants. Saara rolled out of bed and opened her window. She was lucky to have one. Only those servants on the outer edge did. The new staff slept in cramped boxes of darkness that could only be lit by candles they couldn't afford.

She was Carlotte's assistant though, so she had a window and because it was in the Tower DeSheras, it gave a magnificent view. It looked out over the walls of the Nouvre Vil, over the slums in the Outer City, and into the farmland that stretched to the horizon. She'd never been to those farms. She'd never had the need. She'd been to the outer city plenty, though. She'd been born there and it was only by luck and will that she'd scrambled out.

Her uncle had given her that luck, and when she'd first taken the job under Carlotte, she'd looked out on the city and tried to pick his warehouse out of the massive sprawl. She couldn't see it, of course; her view was expansive but everything in it was small. From her window, the outer city was more an idea than a place, a pretty backdrop dotted with pinprick lights at night. She couldn't see the crime from where she stood, or the suffering, or the pain. It was a backdrop, a story from a song she'd heard in some tavern. It was as far away from her as the Freelands in the south, as the endless sands in the west.

When she opened the windows this time though, the twinkling lights were dulled by a great fire deep in the slums to the west of the Nor-so. It was several blocks at least. Saara heard gasps to her left and poked her head out to see Emmanuel and Justine, a senior cook and a scullery maid, leaning out of his window. Justine was wrapped in sheets and Emmanuel's chest was bare against the wind.

"Is it the smelters?" Justine asked him.

"Must be. Fire that big."

"The forges n' smelters are closer to the wall," Greta yelled from Saara's right. She was an old laundress. She'd been in the tower since before Carlotte was born.

"Then a cook fire?" Justine asked.

"Cook fires don't make booms like that," Saara said.

"Aye," Gretta called out. "Sounded like a cannon."

"A cannon?" Justine squeaked.

"No," Emmanuel said, "It wasn't a cannon. I'll--"

"Maybe it was. The Dominion's got a lot a enemies! I'll bet we're under attack!"

"Attack!"

"Nonsense!" Emmanuel snapped. "The Freelanders have never been this far north." Then he spoke softly to Justine. "We're not under attack."

"Not the Korkin slaves," Greta cackled, "Hill Folk from the west, come to take out their hatred on the dominion."

"Hill folk!" Justine cried.

"Shut the hell up, hag," Emmanuel yelled, then quietly to Justine, "There's no hill folk."

"Better she be scared than caught unawares," Greta yelled, "The Hill folk are coming, and they got violence on their minds! They're savages--"

"I said to shut it!"

"Savages who love to rape and murder and--

Saara pulled back into her room and closed the shutters behind her. She could still hear the servants yelling back and forth, but she had no business in it. She crawled back into the warmth of her bed. Some folk in the outer city were no doubt having the worst night of their lives, but there was nothing Saara could do about it, and it was no concern of hers to worry about. She'd clawed her way out of the Outer City, and she wasn't about to crawl back in.

Aethan's flight down the streets of Sheras seemed to him like a dream. It was not he who stumbled naked, burned, and bleeding between the tenements, lit orange by the inferno behind him. That was someone else. Some unfortunate soul living the desperate fruits of a well-deserved life.

The people around, who gathered on stoops and hung out windows, did not see him go; the unfortunate were common in Sheras. Instead, they pointed behind him and shouted to each other, all saying the same thing, each one a beacon, calling attention back behind Aethan at the hell he'd left there.

He turned down one road, and then another, and another, turning at random, and soon he found himself in an alley crowded with heaps of garbage. The walls closed in closer and closer until they jammed together, and Aethan could go no more.

He stopped at the dead end for a long moment, his heart pounding in his chest, and the dream-like quality of it all fell away. He was really there, and he was overcome by the immediacy of it all. He felt his bare feet, numb with cold and torn up by the rough streets. He felt the pain of the knife wound in his back and the dribbling of the blood down his buttocks and hamstring. He felt the night air seeping into his bones, the shivers deep, and his breath short. And worse than it all, Aethan felt his mangled hand ache as though the shot from ten years ago had just torn through it.

Aethan shuffled through the refuse and slid down the wall. It was cold, and he knew the dawn was many hours away and that the air would only grow colder. He would freeze here or bleed out, and Aethan wondered if that wouldn't be such a bad thing. It was gone. Everything was gone. His pike. His gold. Even his guns and horse. He had no money to retrieve them. All he had was his life, and that seemed less than worthless then.

And what had he lost it for? For the privilege of murdering another hundred people? Two hundred? He didn't know the number. Couldn't summon the energy to really think about it.

It wasn't his fault. The pikelord, Ghost, was to blame. It was he who'd betrayed Aethan. The price had been so reasonable and had the man made good on his word, he would be alive, and all those others around would be alive, and all those homes wouldn't be destroyed, and Aethan could have given up on his guns and retired at his cottage by the lake and known peace and quiet.

Aethan dropped his head and then knocked it back against the wall behind him. He let out a little sob, and then he knocked his head back again, harder, squeezing his eyes shut and gritting his teeth.

"Those with power are responsible for it," Ashatee had said, sitting by the fire outside her hut.

Aethan remembered her face that night, the wrinkled skin a landscape of mountains and rivers in the harsh and flickering shadows. Aethan had watched the fire in her eyes, its reflection far more enchanting than the fire itself. The bones from their dinner had lain beside them, cleaned to the white.

"This forest would burn were I not deliberate in my instruction," she'd said. "It would be reduced to ash if I lost my judgment. When gods lose their temper, the world burns."

"You don't believe that you are a god," Aethan had responded.

"No," she'd answered. "But to all of… them, we might as well be."

That was why she'd sheltered herself in the Shafala Forest, far away from them, from the people who might make her do horrible things, who might push her to destruction. It was why she did not drink or smoke. It was why she spent so much time contemplating the lake and why she lived to embody its calm.

A drop of water splashed against his eye, and he opened it just in time for another to smack into his nose. Aethan gave a little choked laugh, and the smattering of water turned into a steady rain. He looked up the alley and saw a boarded-over balcony sheltering some garbage from the water. Aethan stood and pushed the garbage aside to get out of the rain and nearly tripped over a girl.

She lay curled up amidst the trash, one hand gripping a little knife and the other holding tight to a violin case. It was the pike addict from before.

He stared at her for a long moment, watching the rise and fall of her chest, so fragile, so vulnerable, so incapable of destroying anything but herself. Did that make him better than her? Or was it the other way around? Ashatee would have scoffed at the question.

Aethan turned and slogged back up the alley. He didn't know where he was, so he kept walking until he could see the Nouvre Vil wall, and then put it to his left shoulder, knowing he'd have to cross the Nor-so eventually. He began to jog, and the knife wound in his back seared with every step. He knew where he was going, but he didn't know what he would do when he got there, not exactly, at least.

When he saw the Nor-so, Aethan turned right, running down the parallel side streets to avoid the few who walked at night in the rain, and only when the side streets became wide open patches of ground, when the city grew more and more spaced out, did Aethan merge onto the Amaranthine road. He continued down until the buildings were few and far between, and the clerk's warehouse rose up on the right.

It had been closed for the night. He shook the shutters of the little kiosk the old man had occupied, but they were locked from within. Aethan went around the building until he found a pair of bay doors, large enough to get his cart through and pushed at it. It was also barred from the inside. He wondered if he could break through but then dismissed the thought. The noise would wake someone.

He couldn't feel his feet anymore, but he limped on until he came to a door in the back with a chain and lock holding it shut. Aethan looked over his shoulder again and then reached out for the chain and delved deep within for the second time that night. He ran through the corridors of the self and came before--

He froze.

The door within had changed again. Gone was the mausoleum, and in its place was the pikelord's house. There were differences — this house was rundown and broken with gaps between the door and frame, a sagging balcony above, but undoubtedly, it was the house he had just destroyed. It sat in the Greenwall, and the devastation of what he'd done there remained. Bodies of soldiers still lay burnt, but now there were new casualties. There were poor women of Sheras, and children too, clutching each other in their deaths.

Aethan fled the corridors within and sagged against the door. He balled up his fists and took a shaky breath. He had to go back. He had no choice.

He returned, and this time, he steeled himself to the horror and guilt and trudged through the ash and bone and up the stairs to the door. Fire flickered around its edges, but when he pulled it open, there was only the infinite dark beyond.

He took his time and set his runes carefully and only let a little of the darkness through, just enough to heat the chain until it dripped in rivulets through his fingers. He shook the metal from his hand and then took the heat away and pushed through and into the dark warehouse.

It smelled dry like dust and leather, and there were no sounds save the distant scratching of a rat. His own door was still open, and part of him still stood in the dark flow. He used a series of symbols that Ashatee had taught him and that he had never quite understood, and the air above the pinkie of his maimed hand began to glow in the shape of a candle flame.

The light only shone a few yards, but he made no move to increase it. He did not want to draw attention.

The depot was laid out into long rows of wood and iron shelves, with perpendicular aisles breaking them into sections. They were tall, twice Aethan's height at least, and were filled with boxes and sacks, all carefully labeled with a precise and clear hand. He moved quickly down an aisle, passing iron ingots, sacks of grain, and long reams of cut wood. He glanced at the shelves as he passed, but he doubted the old man would have unloaded his cart and mixed his guns with the Dominion Army's goods.

He passed more shelves and then came to a line of pallets, carts, and wagons, and there, at the end, sat his. It was secured in place with wooden blocks under the wheels, parked closest to the large bay doors that had been barred from the inside. He wouldn't have to move anything to get his cart out. Aethan let out a pent-up breath. Finally. A bit of luck.

A sharp click sounded from behind him, and Aethan froze.

"Best not to keep an open flame here, friend. Fire can do a lot of damage."

Within, Aethan choked off the flow of darkness, and the glow atop his pinkie disappeared. There was the sound of metal sliding on metal, and then light spilled around him.

"Turn around, friend."

Aethan did so.

The old man had traded his clerk's hat and jacket for a woolen sleeping cap and robe. He carried a lantern with the shutter drawn up in one hand and a short gun in the other. It was pointed at Aethan's head. Aethan had seen such guns before but had always discounted them as novelties. There was no reason a foot soldier could not use two hands, and on horseback, it was difficult to keep the match lit. Hand cannons some called them, though this one looked lighter, thinner, and there was no glowing match atop the trigger mechanism.

"Flintlock?" Aethan asked.

The old man nodded.

"I've never had someone rob their own merchandise from me. Never been robbed by a naked man either."

"I've... run into troubles and can no longer afford the rent," Aethan said.

The old man raised an eyebrow.

"Some bad trouble indeed. Aethan, was it?"

Aethan nodded.

"Perhaps you should have asked nicely," the old man said.

Aethan could not remember his name. "Would you have granted it?"

The old man frowned. "I don't know. Hard to say now. I could shoot you, you know? All of this belongs to the Mareshal. Breaking in here is like breaking into the High Fortress. I could shoot you where you stand, and the inquisitors wouldn't even question me."

"It won't hurt that I'm from the Freelands," Aethan said.

The old man frowned. "It's not about that. I was ready to keep my deal with you. A silver bit a day. We agreed. We shook."

Aethan looked down the barrel of the gun and knew that his situation was hopeless. There was pity in the man's eyes but also some anger. Aethan might be able to play on it to get the man's forgiveness. He could probably even take his cart with him, but then what? He would be naked and without coin, and the Nouvre Vil Gate would be swarming with soldiers and inquisitors after the fire. He needed to lay low for a few days before attempting to get Toktok back from the stable boys, but how would he survive until then? He had no food. No shelter. No medicine for his wounds.

Aethan had known all these things on the journey here, and he had known that the old man wouldn't give them willingly. He had hoped to take them in the night, the old man unaware, but now the old man had seen him and would call the inquisition.

"Would you have let me go?" Aethan said. His voice quivered.

"Well, I suppose-" He cut off mid-sentence and squinted at Aethan's hand. "What happened to your candle?"

Aethan set new limits and specified the distance. He hung new runes before the darkness and then beckoned the darkness through.

"I'm sorry," Aethan said.

The man's clothes combusted, and he was wreathed in flame. His finger squeezed, and a bullet shot out, tearing a gash in Aethan's right tricep. Aethan grunted and slapped his maimed hand to the new wound. The old man staggered back and forth, dropping the gun and the lantern and beating at himself. He screamed. Aethan gritted his teeth and focused on the runes in the darkness, making sure they didn't let the warehouse burn. The old man collapsed to the floor. His scream guttered out, and he shriveled in on himself. His mouth worked open and closed, but nothing came out. His skin blackened and cracked. His eyes sizzled away, and his lips curled back to reveal an old man's ground down teeth. The man stopped moving, and Aethan closed the door.

He left the corridors within and sat on a crate for a long moment, holding his arm and watching the corpse. The smell of burnt flesh filled the air, and Aethan's stomach roiled. Such a familiar smell...

Aethan tore his gaze away and looked down at his arm. It was bleeding bad, worse than he'd thought. He had two choices. Find a binding, or open up the door again and cauterize it. Aethan pushed to his feet, picked up the old man's lantern, and went in search of cloth.

He found a doorway, and behind it, a set of stairs led up to a loft space with a desk, a few chests of drawers with some books on top, and a basic bed. The space looked out over the warehouse. Aethan's light must have been a beacon to the old man. Aethan opened the chest of drawers and pulled out clothes. He ripped apart a thin nightshirt and tied the cloth tight enough around his arm to stop the bleeding. He did the same for the wound in his back. Then, he went looking for something to wear.

He found a shirt, pants, and socks, and he took a long coat that hung from a hook on the wall and a pair of black boots from beside the bed. They didn't fit well, but they fit well enough, and they were warm.

On the desk sat the old man's pen and ledger. He opened the top drawer and found a small leather pouch of powder and a similar pouch half filled with shot. He pocketed these and went through the other drawers. He found a small wooden strong box banded with iron. Ashatee could have opened it. If Aethan tried he'd probably destroy the contents. The old man must have a key somewhere.

Aethan went back to the bed, and there, on the bedside table, next to a plain gold ring, was a key on a chain. He took the strong box out of the desk, placed it on top of the ledger and with the key, opened it.

Coins lay in neat rows within. They were mostly silver and bronze but there were a few gold at one end. A quick count showed less than twenty gold rakes worth in all, barely a quarter of a pound. He reached to take a few coins, just enough to get his horse out of the stables at the inn and to fund a journey west to Bergshalen, but he ended up taking them all, dumping them into one of the coat's pockets.

He went to leave but stopped at the top of the stairs and went back to the ledger. On the last page, left open by the old man, was a tally of what the man had received and what he'd paid. Aethan's name was there, on the last line, and the words "Cart. Guns. Layaway." Aethan stared at the t-chart for a long time. It was a simple thing, a line between two lists separating what was owned and had been paid for it. Aethan could add the old man's coins and clothes, and the cart and the guns, to the left column and it would be everything Aethan had in the world. But what had he paid? On the right he'd have to write his pounds of gold and his pike, Ashatee's respect, his friends, the family he'd left behind for the war and never seen again, the Greenwall, his hand, the pikelord's house, the lives of those who'd lived around it, and now, to end it all, the old man. The lists seemed... uneven. At the top of the page was a name beside the word "Clerk".

Jaaque Akar.

Aethan remembered the old man grasping his hand and greeting him the day before. He remembered the man's voice, how genuine he'd been when introducing himself. Jaaque.

"I'm sorry," Aethan whispered. He ripped the page from the ledger, crumpled it in one hand, and then pushed it into his pocket.

"I'm sorry," Aethan repeated. "Never again," he said. "I'm sorry. I'm sorry. I'm sorry."

8

Carlotte awoke with her hand closed around Elspeth's pendant. She pushed herself up and sat at the edge of the bed, thinking back on the night before. She hadn't slept well. She'd woken just after falling asleep to some sound and then she'd woken every half hour or so. She wondered if maybe the events of the day before had been a bad dream, but she toed the edge of the loosened board and felt the pendant hang heavy on her chest. Carlotte blew all the air out of her lungs and held them empty for a moment. The day before hadn't really been anything. Nothing had changed. The day's events had just been a reminder of how things were, how they had always been. Yesterday she'd been forced to wake up from her distracting dream and now she just wanted to fall back asleep. But that was not what Rykers did. That's not what Elspeth would have done.

Carlotte pushed to her feet and rang for a bath to be prepared. She soaked for half an hour, organizing her day in her mind, and then organizing the days after. Her marriage was in just under six months, and she needed to use that time effectively. She needed to do work. To keep making a name for herself.

She got out of the bath and dressed. She had no plans to leave the tower, but she had the maid put her in one of her stiffest corsets, and made the woman tighten it good and proper as a reminder of what her purpose was. Life wasn't supposed to be comfortable. She couldn't go back to sleep. There was no light she looked forward too, only a grim purpose that she was determined to follow. There was no end point. There was only her duty and her work and she was going to do them well until she died.

"Pull," She hissed and the maid heaved on the cords for all she was worth. They finished dressing in silence and Carlotte turned down the make up. The corset was enough. A butler appeared at the door to her bedroom and Carlotte motioned him over.

"I'll breakfast in my laboratory today. Two eggs in butter. Toasted bread and a sausage."

"I apologize, Madame, but your mother has asked that you breakfast with her. It's just been served in her dining room. Sixth floor."

Carlotte's stomach dropped as far as it could in a corset so tight. She nodded.

"I'll be right down."

"Madame," said the butler. He inclined his head and left the room.

"We'd best do the make up then," Carlotte said, and the maid got to work.

The table was large and there were place settings out for a dozen guests, but there was food only for two. Her eggs, bread and sausage were on a plate, steaming as though just arrived. It probably had. Good service was all about timing, after all.

Her mother sat at the head of the table with a hard-boiled egg and some kind of hash meat. Probably duck. A bowl of salt sat between the two places, along with a pitcher of water and a steaming kettle. Other than the two butlers who stood like statues against the wall, they were alone.

One of Cainia's hands held a fork, and the other leafed through some papers beside her. She had her spectacles on, sitting at the edge of her nose.

"We never breakfast together anymore," her mother said. "I thought this would be nice." She lifted her nose to peer at Carlotte over the rim of the lenses and motioned at the place beside her with the fork. "Sit."

The butler pulled out Carlotte's chair, and she sat. She couldn't ever remember a time when they had breakfasted together alone. While Elspeth had been off on her adventure, they'd sat at this table every morning, but Carlotte hadn't eaten. Her mother ate and judged while Carlotte was quizzed by her tutors. Her mother liked to watch.

"Do you have any questions about our conversation last night?" her mother asked.

Carlotte shook her head.

"You sure?"

"Yes, Madame. Very clear."

Carlotte looked down at her plate. She could feel her mother's eyes boring into the side of her face. The woman could make her feel like a little girl at a glance, reduced to three feet tall, fighting the urge to keep her thumb out of her mouth. She was being ridiculous. Her feelings were often ridiculous. It was God's will that she follow her mother's word, and this was why: she couldn't be trusted to keep her priorities straight.

"Thank you for reminding me how things are. I can get... difficult. I know."

"That's good to hear," Cainia said. "Now eat, and sit up straight. You look like a croissant."

Carlotte blushed and straightened her back, lifting from the back of her skull like she'd been taught. Posture had been a harder subject than algebra, even with the corsets. Carlotte picked up her silverware and began to eat, cutting the food into tiny pieces so her mouth was never too full to swallow and speak.

Her mother looked back down at the papers and forked a tiny piece of duck, putting it in her mouth so deftly and gracefully that Carlotte wondered if the metal had even touched her mouth.

"A letter came from the Lady Layara Orlient this morning, sending her regrets that they could not attend your exhibition. Something came up."

"Oh," Carlotte said and took a nibble of sausage. She wanted to just shove the whole thing in her mouth. It's what she would have done in her laboratory.

"She said she looks forward to tea next Sunday and hopes that I will attend with you."

"Will you?" Carlotte asked.

"Of course not. That would lend her little gatherings too much credence, but you will, and I think this will all turn out just fine. I'd expect an apology to be forthcoming. You still are the prize of the city," her mother said, and moved one of her pages to the side.

"Thank you," Carlotte said.

"It's not a compliment. You're the heir DeSheras. It's a fact."

They lapsed into silence, and Carlotte wondered what apology Harold could possibly give that would mean anything.

Sorry for the rape?

The scratch on her thigh burned. Maybe he'd send her a room full of flowers, or a cart full of chocolates that she could never eat--

Carlotte pushed the thoughts away and tried to be positive. Things were what they were, and it was her job to make the best of them. Perhaps he'd send her a handwritten letter, dictated by him personally, explaining his regret at such brutish actions, explaining that he'd never act in such a way again. It wouldn't be much. It wouldn't take the experience back, but Carlotte reckoned it wouldn't make things worse. Maybe the whole thing would turn out to be a good thing. Set the boundaries nice and early and clearly.

Come at me, and I'll scratch out your eyes.

"What will you do until the wedding?" her mother asked.

Carlotte swallowed the bit of egg she'd been chewing. "I'll continue my studies, try to get another treatise out before-"

"Of course you will, but on what? That business with the animal force seems difficult to continue down."

"I'm not sure. Maybe something new. I was thinking... something of the Amaranthine?"

Her mother's fork stopped in the air, and she turned her eyes slowly to Carlotte's. There was death behind them.

Carlotte gave a weak smile. "A joke, Mother."

Her mother said nothing.

"But not a very good one. I'm sorry."

"Hmmm."

"I'll probably work on other applications of the animal force, other ways to generate it."

Cainia finished her bite, and Carlotte touched her empty

teacup. A gloved hand appeared from over her shoulder and filled the cup from the kettle.

"Perhaps you should spend some time with me at council. It's high time you learned how this city is run. You'll have to lead it someday after all, if everything turns out." She frowned and looked back down at the papers.

"Everything alright?" Carlotte asked, and sipped at her tea. It came out more like a slurp, and Carlotte's mother glared up at the sound.

"I'm sure it will be," Cainia said. She opened her mouth and then closed it. She glanced up at the footman behind Carlotte and flicked her eyebrows. The two men bowed and exited the room.

The unease in Carlotte's stomach grew and she took another sip of her tea, trying to quell it.

Her mother spoke. "The Lord Orlient is angling hard. I'm not sure what the Mareshal has promised him, but I'd imagine it has to do with that family's meteoric rise. All those arming contracts are practically a monopoly. He's fighting to let more soldiers into Sheras, and more inquisitors. For law and order, apparently." She gave a humorless laugh.

"But..." Carlotte racked her brain for details on how the Ryker council functioned. She'd had civics classes during her tutelage, but the subject had never interested her. It was all so common and distracting. "Surely our family still controls more-"

"Of course we do, but the Orlients are not the only family that uses their iron. He gives good prices, and the Aeshire vote his way, and the Balit and the Macron..."

"Is he succeeding?" Carlotte asked.

Her mother sat back in her chair, eyeing her daughter.

"Sheras has a Grand Inquisitor now."

The unease in Carlotte's stomach grew worse.

"Why would the council agree to that?"

"It was a close vote. But some are worried about Korkin revolutionaries. And there is some trouble to the west apparently... It's all a ploy. I feel a draft coming. And more soldiers mean the Mareshal will request higher taxes. And we'll have to raise our rents, and our tenants will get angry, and we'll need more soldiers to keep them down. It's a vicious, well-orchestrated circle."

There was a knock at the dining room door, and they both looked up to see Enriq slip apologetically through. He was her mother's assistant. He looked worriedly from Carlotte to Cainia, and Cainia nodded.

"The fire, Madame. If it was an accident, it was a big one. The fire boss says black powder was involved."

Cainia placed her spectacles on the table and pushed her plate away, rubbing at her temples. "Suspects?"

"The captain on scene said a Freelander was seen running off."

"Of course there was," Cainia said.

"Fire?" Carlotte asked.

Both of them looked at her.

"You didn't hear it? There was an explosion in the night," her mother said.

Carlotte looked down at her plate. "I did hear it. I thought I'd dreamt it."

"You need to get your head out of the clouds. This is our city, our livelihood, and you need to pay attention." Cainia turned to Enriq. "Who saw this Freelander?"

"Some tenants. Very poor. Easily bought."

"Ha." Cainia barked with absolutely no humor. "He couldn't even be bothered to try."

"You think it was the Lord Orlient?" Carlotte asked quietly.

Her mother scoffed. "Black powder, Carlotte. And the Korkin rebels attacking the Sheras slums? Whatever actually happened, that story is for the benefit of the Mareshal. It gives credence to his fearmongering."

Cainia considered her daughter for a long moment and Carlotte squirmed under her mother's eyes, her hand fingering at the pendant hanging beneath her dress. Enriq coughed.

"You'll be coming to Council with me this evening. But in the meantime, I want you to go to the scene of the fire."

"To the fire? Why?" Carlotte asked.

"It's time you got involved."

9

Carlotte hadn't wanted to come—Saara had seen it in her face on the ride down—so her mother must have ordered it. Cainia DeSheras was the only force in the world that seemed to have some sway over Carlotte. Saara wasn't sure Carlotte had ever been to the Outer City before. She'd ridden through it, with the shutters closed tight against the stink of poverty, but to actually go there amongst the filth and the rabble was surprising.

Something was wrong with Carlotte. Something had made a chink in the armor of cold intellect and poise she wore so consistently. She, who hated wasting time, had spent the entire jolting ride in silence, staring at the closed shutters as though she could see through them, her fingers fussing with something underneath her blouse. The books Saara had brought for Carlotte to read sat untouched on the cushion beside her, and by the time the footman pulled the door open, Saara had grown quite uneasy.

That changed when they stepped out into the rubble.

The devastation was impressive. Almost twelve blocks had burned down before the fire crew could put them out, and here, where it started, there was nothing left but ash, broken stone, and scorched earth that radiated out from the center of the destruction. Carlotte's melancholy changed to disgust, and as they picked their way through the carnage her disgust changed to confusion and then to pensivity, her lips pressed together and her brow furrowed.

Carlotte stood at the origin, like the centerpiece on some enormous table, holding her overcoat tight around her against the ash that swirled in the wind like snow. A blueback captain stood on one side of her, and the fire boss stood on the other.

This section of the slums was actually owned by the DeSheras family. They didn't own the buildings, just the land, so they had no need to pay for reconstruction. The city was filled to bursting, and once the ash and rubble was clear, slum lords would be clamoring for the right to build on it and pay the DeSheras rent. It was a good system. Brilliant even. This was how the Rykers stayed in power, how the DeSherases stayed at the top of that power, by squeezing everyone around them for all they were worth. It was a dirty business, and a good one. Saara admired it greatly.

"It must have been a black powder," the captain said. The boss shook his head. He was some minor Ryker lord, and he wore his mustaches long in a caricature of the traditional Ryker style. They hung down on either side of his face, swaying with his head. Every time he spoke, he looked directly at Carlotte, like a puppy looking at its master. The DeSheras family did own the fire crews after all.

"I've seen blasting powder at work, and they don't look like this. There wouldn't be this much damage."

"You told my man that it was black powder," Carlotte said, and the little lordling bowed his head. His mustaches hung down from his face like a dead jellyfish.

"Yes, Madame. I did, and I'm sorry. I hadn't seen the origin yet. We were still putting out the fire, Madame."

The captain harrumphed and swiped at a fleck of ash that had settled on his chest. It made an ugly gray smear. He frowned even deeper. "Put enough powder together, and it'll destroy a mountain."

"Enough will blow apart a mountain. There'd be pieces. But this..." he turned slowly, taking in the whole area. "There's nothing left."

"Have you seen a hundred black powder barrels explode? A thousand?" the captain asked.

"No, but-"

"Then how do you know what that would look like? Black powder is the only logical explanation."

"It's the only thing that-"

"Too big," Carlotte murmured, and the men turned to her, their argument stopped dead in its tracks.

"What was that? Madame?" The Captain asked.

"The blast marks." She motioned to the long black streaks that radiated out from her in every direction. "The blast came from here. Right here," and she dragged the toe of her maroon velvet shoe in an arc in front of her. "A hundred barrels of black powder would take up more room." The men looked at each other.

"Well, maybe so, but like I said, no one's seen a-"

"How much would that cost?" Carlotte said to the fire boss.

"My lady?"

"A hundred barrels of black powder. How much would that cost?"

The fire boss blew out his cheeks. "I've no idea. A few thousand Rakes, I'd think."

"A few thousand." Carlotte turned her gaze to the Captain. "Why would someone need that much?"

"I didn't say it was a hundred, just a lot. And these were no doubt criminal types. This whole slum is full of criminals. We don't even patrol down here. Our soldiers would get mugged," the Captain finished, but Carlotte didn't break her gaze, and after a moment, the Captain cleared his throat and continued. "Who's to say why criminals do what they do. Perhaps it's for some gang's dominance or what have you."

"Dominance?" Carlotte asked. "A hundred barrels of powder seems enough to supply an army."

"We do have reports of a dark skinned man running out from here. Perhaps it's linked to the Korkins."

"The Freelanders, you mean, Captain," the fire boss corrected.

The captain waved his hand. "Whatever it is they call themselves. We've directions from the High Fortress itself to be on the lookout for spies and saboteurs and whatnot. Perhaps this-"

"You think this was a foreign attack? Here. In the slums?" Carlotte motioned at the devastated area around them and at the leaning buildings beyond. "Strange target."

"To seed discord, Madame."

"Amongst who?"

The captain opened his mouth several times and harrumphed

once before speaking. "Perhaps there was something here they wanted to destroy. Some... strategic target if you will."

"What was here?" Carlotte asked, and the captain threw up his hands.

"As I said, Madame, we don't send patrols here, and I'm not familiar with the area."

Carlotte turned to the fire boss, who nodded his head as he spoke.

"The area is zoned for residential use. But no doubt there were some illicit businesses."

Carlotte waited for a few moments, looking from one to the other.

"That's all you two have for me? Zoned for residential use? Illicit businesses?"

The two of them looked down at their shoes. Saara smiled at their discomfort but wiped it away when Carlotte glanced up at her.

"Something to add, Saara?"

The two men looked up, glad that her mistress's attentions were on someone else.

"Ghost lived here, I think."

"Ghost?"

"Ah, um. A pikelord- dealer. He had a big house that I know is- was around here somewhere."

"You don't know where it is?" Carlotte said.

Saara shook her head. "Not exactly, Madame."

"Then..."

"Well," Saara said, and scratched subconsciously behind her ear. "There's stone here about. And I don't think many of the builders here sprung for stone foundations. So, it was probably something nice that burned down, and that's the only nice thing around that I can think of."

Carlotte's eyebrows rose at that, and she frowned a little. Saara got the feeling that she was going to barf all of a sudden and cursed herself. There would be a time when people actually listened to her, actually wanted to hear what she had to say, but that wasn't now. Now, she was in the background.

"Huh," Carlotte said. "I hadn't noticed. Good eye."

The nausea was replaced by a very warm, very fuzzy feeling.

"Verify that for me," Carlotte said, and Saara nodded furiously.

"And how, pray tell, do you know anything about Pike and it's dealers?" the Captain asked.

Before Saara could answer, Carlotte threw up a hand. "Please. She's with me, Captain."

"Of course, Madame," and he took an awkward step back.

"So," Carlotte said. "I'd like another explanation. I don't like black powder for this. The fire boss here seems to think it would look different. So if not powder, then what did this?"

There were a few moments of silence as Carlotte looked back and forth between the two men.

"Go on. Take a look around. I'd like a real answer, please."

The captain took in a deep breath and straightened his back.

"May I speak honestly, Madame?"

Carlotte narrowed her eyes but nodded.

"This *was* black powder. I know it because I've seen this before."

Carlotte's eyebrows raised almost to her hairline. The fire boss cut in, unbelieving.

"Where?"

The captain grimaced and glanced up at the sky.

"In the Greenwall. Ten years ago during the last Korkin war."

"The Inferno at Greenwall," Carlotte said, her voice hushed. "You were there?"

"I was with the regiment that came after."

"You came after?" The fire boss cut in, "Then how do you know that was black powder?"

"Because," the Captain answered, leaning down towards the fire boss's face. "That's what the Inquisitors said. A whole gaggle of them investigated, and they said it was powder."

The fire boss bristled. "Just because the Inquisitors-"

"Are you saying the Inquisitors don't have the right of it? They speak with the voice of God! God and the Mareshal," the captain spat.

Saara saw Carlotte's face darken at that, but she said nothing, and the fire boss wilted. "I'm only saying there might be more to it."

"Apparently," the Captain continued, paying no heed to the fire boss. "The regiment was bringing up carts of powder through the Greenwall. Several hundred barrels." The captain motioned with his face to the surroundings. "Barrels all blew in the fight and the whole place looked like this, but worse. Half a square mile of trees cleared. Bodies..." The captain trailed off.

Carlotte looked thoughtful and more than a little disturbed. Then her eyes narrowed. "Were there no bodies here?"

"There were. Not right here," the fire boss said. "But there were many in the surrounding area. Some eighty or so people died."

"I didn't see any on the way here," she said and then glanced up at Saara, who shook her head.

"The inquisitors took them," the fire boss said.

"The inquisitors?" Carlotte breathed. "Why would they take the bodies of fire victims?"

The fire boss shrugged and held up his hands.

"Captain?"

"I wasn't informed," the captain said. "It was that inquisitor Hawthorne who came, and his rank is superior to mine. I don't question those above me."

"No," Carlotte said, "I don't imagine that you do." She looked down and kicked at the stone beneath her, sending ash swirling around her like fallen autumn leaves in the wind. The Captain took a step back, but the ash settled on his coat just the same.

"Have you ever seen a fire so hot it melted stone?" Carlotte asked, and the three of them leaned in to look at Carlotte's feet. She was right; the stone was melted, as though it had been soft candle wax, pressed down with a giant thumb. The granite was hardened over black and glassy. Carlotte kicked more of the ash away, and Saara wondered if her shoes would ever recover.

"I... No, Madame. I've never seen that before."

"Nor I..." the Captain said, and then the breath caught in his throat. They all stared wide-eyed at the streak of ground underneath the ash. "Is that-" the Captain croaked.

"Gold," Saara breathed.

The ride back to the tower started as silently as the ride from it. Carlotte sat across from Saara, fiddling at something under her shirt with one hand and the drawstring to the bag of gold with her other.

It had taken the rest of the morning to chip the metal off the ground, and though a fair amount of stone had made its way into the bag with the gold, Saara could hardly imagine the value of what they'd found. Pounds of gold. Tens of pounds of gold. Enough to buy a few townhouses in the Nouvre Vil, or a few blocks of slums and start a rental empire. It belonged to Carlotte, of course. It had been on her land and no matter the fact that Saara had chipped it out of the ground and carried it to the carriage, no matter the fact that a third of it would change Saara's life for ever and it was but a drop in the infinite coffers of the DeSheras family, it belonged to Carlotte. Everything in this world seemed to.

Carlotte opened her mouth, and Saara's attention snapped into focus. It hung open for a moment, but then she closed it, and the silence stretched on.

"Madame?" Saara ventured, knowing it was a gamble to say anything. Carlotte was just as likely to snap as ask for a cookie.

Carlotte's mouth opened again, and Saara leaned in closer.

"What do you think it was?" Carlotte said.

Saara couldn't remember the last time Carlotte had asked her opinion. Come to think of it, she wasn't sure Carlotte ever had. This was a moment.

"Ah..." Saara began, searching for something clever and insightful to say. She had no doubts why Carlotte hired her. Carlotte needed someone with a little grit, who wouldn't balk at getting a severed head from Inquisitor's Yard, and who could carry it up eight flights of stairs, someone who carried a knife at her hip and another in her boot in case things got hairy. Carlotte hired her because she was rough, but little did Carlotte know she'd also hired someone quick and smart. The perfect combination of ruthless and witty that would make the perfect Ryker. All Saara needed was the chance to show it.

Unfortunately, at this moment, nothing came to mind. "Black powder," she finally managed.

Carlotte's eyes rolled over to the closed shutters. "You're not that stupid," she said, and Saara wasn't sure if she should take that as a compliment or an insult.

Saara searched again. "A turf war, maybe? The gold... if it was Ghost's place, maybe it was a deal gone wrong."

"Seems a lot a money," Carlotte said, tugging again at the drawstrings on the canvas bag. "Is that normal for a... deal?"

Saara shook her head and looked down. "No, Madame. That does seem a lot."

"The why doesn't concern me. I want to know how. How does one melt rock?"

"What about what the Captain said? About that business in the Greenwall?"

"Pfff," Carlotte huffed, tossing her hand through the air. "I'll take advice from bluebacks when I take advice from dogs."

"And the inquisitors who t--"

"Even less reliable. Duplicity in place of stupidity."

"You think they know what it is?" Saara asked. She was getting the sense that Carlotte was after a bouncing board more than any actual contribution, which Saara was happy to oblige.

"I think they have an idea, but no, I don't think they know, not really." Carlotte reached up to her breast and clamped her hand around whatever lay beneath her blouse.

"There is more to the world than people will ever understand. Far more. And just because we can't see something doesn't mean it isn't there. It could be hiding in the darkness somewhere, and we just need to know where to shine the light... My sister told that to me. In some fashion or another." Her face fell, and she released her grip on her collar. She pulled at it to get the fabric to smooth out, but the cloth was linen, and the creases remained visible.

"Or perhaps... It's nothing," Carlotte said. "Perhaps I'm imagining patterns in the randomness."

"I'm sure you'll figure it out, Madame. You always do."

Carlotte turned her eyes to Saara and smiled. "I do. I need you to do something for me."

"Of course, Madame. I'm at your command."

Carlotte reached into one of her pockets and pulled out a journal. It was leather bound with a severed locking strap that would have kept it shut had it not been cut.

"I found this book," Carlotte said, turning it in the air and then tossing it. Saara caught it.

"It's a journal of one Ryliar Orlient."

Saara scrunched her brow. "Ryliar? I don't-"

"The Lord Orlient's brother. Harold's uncle."

Saara frowned down at the book. She was getting a bad feeling about all this. "I didn't know he had one."

"Neither did I, which says something. It's the first of a series," Carlotte said.

Saara resisted the urge to open the journal; that would be inviting scorn, so she nodded and handed it back across. "Very interesting. Do you have the others?"

"No, but I know where they are. On the second floor of the Orlient's manor, there is a dark room with an invalid lying in a bed, surrounded by books. That invalid is Ryliar, and somewhere in the stacks around him are the rest of the journals." Carlotte leaned forward. "You, Saara, are going to get them for me."

"Me?"

"Did you change your name?"

There was a painful pause that stretched out for several moments.

"You want me to ask for them?"

"No. I don't want the Orlients to know you've taken them. I don't want anyone to know."

Saara blinked. "How then?"

"I'm not the street girl, am I? Break in and steal them."

Saara's jaw dropped, and she made a forceful effort to close it again. "Madame. I don't- If I get caught, I could be..." Saara trailed off. The head in a box she'd purchased from Inquisitor's Yard stuck in her mind.

Carlotte blinked slowly. "Then don't get caught, Saara."

"For a book?"

"For several, if you can find them."

"Madame-"

"Saara. We are not the Korkins. You are not my slave. If you don't want to do this, you don't have to. I can always find someone else to help me."

"No!" Saara shouted and then blushed at her tone. One of Carlotte's immaculate eyebrows raised in a severe arch. "Of course. I'm your woman. Of course, I'll help."

Carlotte nodded and gave a brief, fleeting smile. "Should I let you out here?"

"Madame?"

"I assume you'll need to put some things in order."

"Oh. You'll want those books as soon as possible then?"

Carlotte gave the smallest of nods, as though the full movement of her head was beneath her.

Saara's gaze went vacant for a moment, staring out through the walls of the carriage and into the nether beyond, and took a big breath in through her nostrils. Then she pulled her lips back into a tight smile and nodded. "Yes. Here is fine."

Saara was disappointed to recognize the kid who lounged at the corner just off the Nor-So. His name was Jean, and he perked up when she hailed him, and he told her things she didn't want to learn about things she already knew too much about. She asked after Bracille, and he told her where to find him: on the sidelong street by the smelters, looking after some rat who did him dirty.

"Slum Tax?" Saara asked, and Jean nodded. She frowned and muttered her thanks, turning to walk away.

"You should come around sometime, Sarry!" Jean shouted after her. "Scram'll cook a pig if you do. I know he will."

Saara looked over her shoulder, not so far that she could see him, just enough to show him the profile of her face. "Yeah, Jean. Sometime," and then she hurried away.

Living in the tower so long, she'd almost started to think about the Outer City like Carlotte did, that it was just one big mass of slum, an endless expanse of poverty and crime and dehumanization. It wasn't though. There were richer parts and poorer ones, workshops and corner shops and businesses and trades of all kinds, and as Saara walked through it, taking side roads to avoid the Nor-so traffic, slipping through an alley that cut through a wide block, she felt the familiarity of it all. She knew where the best blocks for burglary were, the ones most likely to have valuables but close enough to the slums to avoid the bluebacks. She knew where the Brackle Boys ran and where the Sanjid territory ended. She knew where the sidelong street by the smelters was, and if Bracille was chasing slum tax, then she knew where to start looking for him. She felt like a wagon wheel sliding into a well-worn rut, exactly where life wanted her to be.

125

Saara rounded the back road where the smelters dumped their slag for the orphan boys and girls to pick through and caught sight of a lookout at the entrance to a narrow alley just down the way. When she came closer, he gave her a hard look and dropped a knife from his coat sleeve into his hand. Saara came on anyway and the man moved forward but then stopped a few yards away from her.

His craggy face broke up into a big grin. He mouthed "Sarry," and because he didn't speak, Saara knew Bracille was working. The big man's name was Hugo, and Saara wasn't happy that she knew it, but she let him bury her in a hug all the same.

"Where you been, Sarry?" he whispered in her ear. "Heard you was up in the Vil, like a right proper lady."

"Aye," Saara said and pulled gently out of his grip. "You know me. Fine as salt and half as sweet. Looking for Bracille."

There was a thud and then a cry from the alley and then another thud. Hugo didn't seem to notice.

"Betcha are." He winked at her and then motioned towards the alley, bowing down as he did so. "M'lady."

Saara punched him in the shoulder as she ambled past but it had no force to it. Hugo winced dramatically all the same. Saara entered the alley, picking her footfalls carefully so as not to make much noise. Bracille liked to work in silence. He said it made the point stick better.

She saw him at the end of the alley, crouching amongst the refuse, three men standing around him looking down. The alley stank like shit. The tenements on either side dumped it out their windows more than likely. It was a familiar smell. Nostalgic. Almost.

There was a man sitting against the wall. More like a boy, actually. Couldn't be twenty years yet, his face covered in dirt and acne. He'd a muscular build to him, skin sticking straight to the muscle, the kind of build one gets from working hard on not a lot of food. He looked the way Saara used to look. There was blood running down his face from a cut on his scalp, and one of his eyes was swelling up above a cheek bone that looked broken. There was hate in his eyes.

"You're a tough bastard to look at me that way after what I've given you," Bracille said. His voice was soft and smooth but the slum accent was heavy in it. One hand rested open over one knee, and the other gripped a well-worn steel knuckle. There was blood on it.

"I see the hate in your eyes, clear as a Ryker's riches. That kind of hate leads to vengeance. To retaliation."

The boy on the ground said nothing, only breathed hard keeping his eyes locked on Bracille's. Bracille looked up to one of the men standing above him.

"Give him your knife."

The man pulled a little knife from his belt, no more than two inches long, better for peeling fruit than killing, and threw it down onto the ground by the boy. The boy's eyes flicked to it.

"You want it?" Bracille said. "That blade there is vengeance. That blade there is retaliation for what I done to you. Pick it up."

The boy didn't move.

"You want to stick it in me? Go on and pick it up then. Stab me." Bracille held his left arm out wide and tapped at his chest with the right.

"You do it here, you might even kill me. I won't stop you."

"I touch it, you'll kill me," the boy said.

Saara couldn't see Bracille's face, but she knew there was a look of well-acted confusion on it.

"Kill you? For touching a blade I gave you? That's no crime to me. You already committed your crime. You tried to collect slum tax in my slum. You tried to make yourself a little kingdom in my empire. That was your crime, and I repaid you for it." He lifted the steel knuckle. "You'll wear that repayment for the rest of your life. Now the question is... what are you going to do next?" Bracille held his empty hand out to the boy and stuck his steel knuckle out to the side.

"There are two options that I see. You could give into that feeling in your chest, give into that hate, pick up that blade and stick me with it, but once you start that retaliation, me and my boys will stop it. Forever."

Bracille gently knocked the boy's shin with the steel knuckle. "That is the path of vengeance. Or, you could take the learning I just gave you and put all this retaliation behind you. What's it going to be, Marco?"

The boy's eyes flitted to the knife and then back to Bracille's outstretched hand. He flinched as the knuckle tapped against his shin. The men standing around were silent as the grave. Saara glanced up at the windows and saw faces staring down from the shadows of their homes. Ghosts witnessing Bracille's power. No one moved. No one spoke.

Then, Marco took Bracille's outstretched hand, and Bracille pulled the boy to his feet. Bracille gripped his shoulder with his empty hand and held the bloody steel knuckle to Marco's cheek, holding it like a mother holding a son. Blood dripped from the boy's chin.

"You chose good, Marco. Now get out of here," and he shoved the boy stumbling down the alley. The men moved aside to let him pass. They all watched him go.

"One of these days, someone's going to put that knife in your throat," Saara said.

Bracille turned to look at her.

"Sarry!" one of the men cried out. His name was Shamble.

"Back from the Vil ya twat!" another named Jarund yelled and the two of them buried her in a hug.

"Fuck!" Saara wheezed, "I'll pay what I owe! Don't break my ribs."

They laughed and released her. She made a show of being out of breath.

"You coming back home, Sarry?" the last one asked. He was smaller, younger even than the boy they'd just beaten.

"No, Rold. I still got business in the Vil."

"Then why are you here?" Rold asked. And Jarund slapped him on the back.

"To see Bracille ya twat. What else?"

"Maybe she wanted to see us!"

"You think she wanted to see your pimply little face? Ha!"

Rold's face reddened. "Shut up, Shamble, Your face's got more craters'n cobblestones. You should come round, Sarry. Bet Scram'll cook a pig if you do."

"So I keep hearing," Saara said.

Jarund shoved at Rold's back and started walking down the alley. "Come on ya twats. Let the two birds talk."

Rold squawked at the push, but the two others herded him out of the alley, and the brief moment of sound ended. The alley was cast back into silence.

Bracille was not smiling. His mouth, handsome but worn, was turned down at the corners. Saara couldn't tell if it was concern or pain. Maybe it was both.

"You're not coming back," Bracille said. It wasn't a question, just a statement of fact.

"No," Saara said anyway.

Bracille nodded. "Your bitch sent you then?"

"She's not my bitch."

"Right. You're the one wearing the collar."

Saara frowned. She hadn't been expecting much, but... she didn't know what she was expecting. For Bracille to bury her in love like the others? Saara grunted out one dry laugh.

"What?" Bracille asked, and Saara shook her head.

"This." She gestured around her and then pointed to the steel knuckle in Bracille's hand. "That. We do it because we have to, right? Because it's the only way out of the gutter? Yet, I get out, and you hold it against me. Like a crab pulling its buddy back into the pot."

Bracille frowned. "Why are you here, Saara?"

"I got a task needs doing."

"Ah. So your family is what, just a bunch of thugs for hire then?" Bracille came up close to her and hissed the words.

"You're not my family," Saara said.

"You want to say that to Jarund? To Jean?" Bracille said.

"That something you want me to do?" Saara spat back. "Want me to ruin your little fiction?"

"It's not a fiction."

"Yeah? Easy to preach family when you're the one in charge."

Bracille put his hand to his eyes and took in a deep breath. His jaw was sharp and covered in stubble. She could see the muscle pulsing beneath his ear. She knew what it felt like when it pulsed like that. She knew where to massage it to make it calm.

"Look," he said, his voice taking on a softer tone, "I don't want it to be like this."

"Then don't make it. I'm not here to hire you. I just need a lead."

"A lead for what?"

"The Orlient manor. I need an in. A maid or a butler who is malleable. Someone in debt, preferably. Or who hates. Hate is harder. But it'll work."

"You're breaking into the Orlient Manor?"

"Yeah. You got a lead or what?"

Bracille watched her for a long moment, and Saara's annoyance turned towards discomfort.

"Why are you doing this?"

"What does it matter to you?"

"If you get caught doing something like that, Inquisitor's Yard will take your head."

"I know the risks."

"Then why? To settle Ryker scores?"

"Because," Saara said, and she stepped even closer to him. She was just inches away, and the smell of him was in her nose and it brought memories to the back of her mind. She grabbed his hand, the one with the steel knuckle, and shook it. "Because if I'm going to do this. I want it to be for something."

"For the Rykers?"

"For myself, Bracille." Saara took a step back. "So, you got a lead or what? I don't want to stay here any longer than I have to."

"Too good for the outer city now?"

"No. And that's the problem."

Bracille rubbed at his jaw, and his skin rasped across the little hairs. It made his face look dirty, and Saara guessed she liked dirty, a little, in spite of herself.

"I'll pay you," she said and opened her purse. "If that's what it'll take." She fished out some silver and held it in front of her. Bracille eyed it, and then after a moment's hesitation, took the coins out of her hand.

"Aye. I think I know someone who can help. Debt. Not hate. A woman. Scullery maid."

Saara nodded and pulled out another piece of silver. "Give this to her then. Let her know I mean business. She doesn't have to agree to anything to keep that. It's on the house."

Bracille nodded and shoved the money into his pocket.

"Gatehouse Tavern. This afternoon," said Saara.

Bracille nodded again and gave a weak smile. "Take it you won't come back for dinner? Apparently, Scram'll cook you a pig."

Saara gave her own weak smile and shook her head. "Thank you, Bracille. I owe you one."

"No, you don't." He turned and started off down the alleyway. "That's what the money's for."

10

The woman's eyes were hungry. She watched Saara in the focused manner of a street urchin, unsure if a stranger was reaching for a coin or a blade. Saara rooted around in her purse, making sure the maid heard the clink over the tavern noise. After a few moments, Saara pulled out some coins and placed them in a neat stack in the middle of the table.

Five full gold rakes gleamed there in the half-light from the chandeliers. Five gold rakes from Saara's own stash. Carlotte would reimburse her, of course, but seeing her hard-earned money out in the open still made her nervous.

The woman's hand twitched, and her eyes darted up to Saara's. It was a lot of money, especially to someone like this maid. Subsistence living was how the Ryker's kept these people in line. Give a woman nothing and she'll kill you to eat, but give her just a little and she'll raise your children, cook your food, and clean your shit. She'll be grateful to do it. Give a woman a little more, though, and she'll have time to think about how unfair it all is.

"What'da ya get? An eighth a day?" Saara asked, laying her street accent on thick.

"Two," the woman mumbled.

"Ah. How nice of the Orlients. So that means this is..." Saara leaned back in her chair and made a big show of thinking. "Just shy of half a year of work for you."

The woman said nothing, and Saara rocked forward. "All for an hour of work for me."

"What do I have to do?" the maid asked.

Saara smiled.

"I need access to Ryliar's room."

The woman's eyes widened. "Ryliar?"

"The invalid on the second floor."

The woman looked over her shoulder and then pushed her chair back. "I don't know what this is, but it's not worth-"

Saara snapped out her hands and grabbed the woman's wrists. The woman let out a little squeak, and Saara pulled her in so that the table edge cut into her armpits. The pile of gold sat undisturbed just a foot from her face. "Six months of work is six months of your life. I know you've got debts. I know you've got a family you never see out past the wall. This gold right here is freedom. This gold right here is slack in the rope around your neck."

"I don't want-"

"I'm not going to hurt him," Saara said. "I just need a few books from his room. The Orlient's won't even know they're gone."

"Books?" the woman whispered. Her throat was crushed against the wood.

Saara released her, and she sagged back. Saara half expected her to run out the door, but she didn't.

"What do you want with books?"

"My reasons are my own. Borrow me a maid's get-up, take me to his room, give me a few minutes to find the ones I'm looking for, and we're gone. Then, your life gets a good bit easier. Saara flicked at the stack of coins, and they spilled over each other. "We got a deal?"

The woman looked at them for a moment, and then up at Saara, and then back down at the coins. She nodded, and Saara swept up all but one of the rakes.

"One now, the rest after. I want to do this today. When and where should I meet you?

The woman picked up her coin and held it, feeling the weight of it and digging her nail into its golden face. "Just before sundown, when the lords and ladies are having cocktails. There's a gate round back on the north side. Servant's entrance."

Saara nodded. "Do I need to warn you about ratting me out?" Saara asked, and the woman shook her head.

"Because," Saara continued, "don't think for a minute you can get some reward out of it. Inquisitor's Yard will take my head, but they'll take yours with it just for meeting with me."

The woman nodded again.

"Good," Saara said and stuck out her hand. The woman took it and they shook.

"Odette, was it?" she asked, and the woman nodded. "Don't be late."

Saara went to a tea shop to pass the time and asked the server to bring her something that would wake her up. It was black, and it tasted like dirt, but she forced herself to savor it all the same. That was what the Rykers did, and that was what Saara was going to do.

She leaned back in her chair and closed her eyes to feel the sun against her face. This shop was cheap and away from the Nor-so, and it had tables outside in the sun when the weather was nice. If the place sold liquor it would have been her favorite in the city, but it was all for the better. She shouldn't be drinking before what she was about to do. It was risky enough sober.

The sun was blocked from her face, and when it didn't pass, she opened one eye to see a man silhouetted against the light.

"Miss Akar?" The man said.

Saara lifted a hand to shade her eyes. "Ah. Val."

He didn't wait for her to invite him. He stepped forward and pulled out the chair across from her, dropping his sheaf of papers on the table as he sat.

Saara steadied her cup against the shaking. "Long time no see, Val. How's the family?"

He paused, hand up to the golden rim of his glasses. "They're well. Kept as well as they can be."

"That's good." Saara took a sip from her tea. It was already starting to get cold. That was the trouble with tea in Sheras. Even in the sun, the thin cups never held in the heat for long.

"I'm terribly sorry to be a bother, Miss Akar. I hope I find you well."

"Did you follow me from the tavern?"

There was a pause, and Val pulled the spectacles from his face and wiped at the rims. They shone in the sunlight, bright and polished as a mirror.

"I thought I'd speak to you there, but you had company."

"Yes. That's creepy, Val. What do you want?"

Val nodded, perched the rims back on his nose, and pushed the sheaf of papers towards her. "I've finished a treaties on the cultural differences between North and South in regards to ancient Amaranthine Culture."

"That a working title?"

Val frowned. "Well. I suppose. Do you think I should change it?"

Saara took another sip of her tea and let out a breath through her nose. "It doesn't matter. The Heir DeSheras won't read it."

Val's face fell even further for a moment, but then he bunched it up and pushed the papers even closer, jostling them up against her saucer. "Please, Miss Akar, if you could... just show them to her. I think-"

"She doesn't ask my advice for reading material, Val. I'm sorry. I'm not that kind of assistant."

"If you could just put them on her desk then-"

"Which one?"

"What?"

"Which desk? She has several," Saara said.

His lip quivered, and his mustaches quivered with them. He wore his mustaches short, in the style of Rykers two generations ago, wrapping around his mouth and meeting the scruff of hair on his chin.

"Listen, Miss Akar, I know I've asked before but this," he jabbed at the papers, "this is really something. This is good. The kind of thing that Elspeth would have died for."

Saara raised an eyebrow.

"Sorry. Turn of phrase... I mean to say, the kind of thing that the late Elspeth DeSheras would have cherished."

Val hunched further in his chair as he spoke, his long back crimped to half its height. He was clean, impressively so, with his facial hair finely trimmed and his fingernails clear, but though his clothes were pressed and spotless, they were also old. His coat showed numerous mendings, a patch at one elbow, a seam on his breast where one shouldn't have been. Only his spectacles showed any sense of wealth, but even then, the frames were of a style older than his beard. They swirled in delicate arches and spans, like a spider web designed for a queen of old, as out of place amongst the Ryker as she was.

"Carlotte isn't Elspeth," Saara said.

"I've heard she's just as smart. Perhaps even more so," Val replied.

Saara nodded. "But she isn't interested in this," and she poked at the sheaf of papers with her spoon. It left behind a droplet of tea, which Val quickly dabbed up with his sleeve. "She's interested in lightning recently, and in God. Do you have a treatise on that?"

"That is not my forte, Miss Akar. I deal with antiquity."

"She's not going to sponsor your work, Val, and I can't change her mind. She is not Elspeth. She is obsessed with the future, not the past."

"This is our future," Val replied softly. He stared down at the papers for a long moment and then looked up. "You won't help me then?"

"Not with this. I can't. The store going poorly?"

"It's not a store," he said, a touch of anger in his voice as he pulled the stack of papers back towards him. "It's a library. We charge only if people want to take the books home..." The anger left his voice, and he lifted a hand to his temples and rubbed at the graying hair there. He wasn't old, perhaps just north of forty, but the years had taken their toll on him. More than their fair share. "Not well, though," he said. "I've taken to renting out the front apartment."

Saara raised an eyebrow. "You living with your mother and sister then? In that tiny room?"

"No, no, no. That wouldn't do. I've been sleeping between the stacks. It's not all bad," Val said, lifting his eyebrows and forcing his mouth into a smile. "Makes it more convenient for my studies. Thank you for your time, Miss Akar."

Saara put a hand down on his manuscript before he could lift it off the table. "I can't help you with this, Val. The Heir DeSheras doesn't listen to me about these things. But I could put in a word with the staff. Get you a position. They're always hiring. A clerical position at the docks, or some such, or an accountant for-"

Val lifted his hand to stop her. "No. Please. Thank you, but no. It's not a Ryker's place to work. It's to study. And that's what I'm going to do. Again. Thank you, Miss Akar," and he pushed to his feet to walk away.

Saara sipped at her tea and scowled. It was cold. And it still tasted like dirt.

Odette was there when she said she would be, standing by the servant's entrance in her maid's get-up with a similar outfit draped over her arm. Her head was half bowed, but it swiveled back and forth, and when Saara stepped out from behind a hedge, Odette nearly jumped.

Odette cursed and held out the clothing.

"The Rykers are sitting down with drinks." She shoved the clothes into Saara's hands and turned her back. "Be quick about it!"

"Watch the attitude," Saara said, unbuttoning her shirt. "Rykers love drinking. We'll have plenty of time."

"It's not them I'm worried about. It's the rest of the staff."

Saara stopped with her pants pulled halfway down her thighs. "Is there a problem?"

"No," Odette hissed. "Shouldn't be. Just, please, hurry up."

Saara changed, and then pulled her purse from her pants and slipped it into one of the frock's pockets. She considered her knife. There was nothing it could do for her in the Orlient Manor, so she put it on the ground and tucked it under the pile of clothes so it wouldn't be visible if someone came upon them. Saara dressed and then let Odette pull her hair out of her bun and up into a bonnet. The outfit was typical, gray and black, with a smock of pristine white around the hip. The skirt ended just above her ankles, showing off the blocky black shoes Odette had given her. They were a drab mockery of something Carlotte would have worn. The heeled shoes Carlotte wore were slender and delicate and made Carlotte look as though she weighed nothing at all. These looked ready to support a woman made of stone.

"Not a great fit," Saara said, wiggling her foot in them. "It chafes."

"That's just how our shoes are," Odette said and pulled Saara up close to her. "Keep your head down and follow just behind me. There will be people in the gardens. Don't look at them. Don't look at anyone. Got it?"

Saara swung her arm but stopped just before her hand hit the woman's face. Odette turned her head to look at the hand floating beside her and then back at Saara. There was fear in her eyes, but not of Saara.

It made Saara nervous. She should be nervous. It was no joking matter what they were doing, what Carlotte had asked-- had told her to do... She remembered the man's head from the exhibition. She remembered the way the blood dripped like syrup down her hands, coagulated and cold. Saara relaxed her arm and let it settle on Odette's shoulder, as though she'd never thought to do anything else.

"Of course," Saara said and gave a curt nod.

"Come," Odette said and hurried through the gate.

Saara kept her head down and focused on Odette's heels clicking against the cobblestone path. The bonnet's long edges were like horse blinders on either side of her face, and she could just make out the edge of vegetable patches on either side of her. She could hear the scritch and scratch of metal digging somewhere to her left.

"Ay, Odette!" A voice called out from the left, and Odette grunted back at them without turning. She stopped at a door, and Saara waited while she fumbled with a key in the lock. She opened the door and ushered Saara over the threshold, shutting the door behind them. Saara looked up to see an unadorned hallway with narrow walls, barely enough room for two to squeeze past each other. Servant's corridors. Odette shoved past Saara and hurried down the left. They turned again and again, passing doors and other passageways, occasionally going down stairs just to go back up another flight when they reached the landing. Saara questioned Odette after the second dip.

"Underpass for a hallway," she whispered, glancing down each direction at an intersection. A bonneted woman walked away from them down the right with a bundle of cloth dragging behind her.

Odette waited for her to turn a corner before motioning Saara down the left passage.

"Underpass?" Saara asked.

"So we don't walk in their halls."

"Ah," Saara said. The servant's passages in the Tower DeSheras ran through the outer walls like arteries feeding the Ryker heart at the center.

"Is it always so empty?"

"It's shift turn," Odette grunted. "It'll be swarming in half an hour."

Saara hoped the books would be easy to find.

They went up a set of stairs and down another corridor that ended with a door. Odette stopped beside it. She nodded at Saara's unspoken question.

"Right then," Saara muttered and pushed through.

The room was dark, but then her eyes adjusted, and the little oil lamps beside the bed came into focus. The bed was surrounded by books. A sea of books, stacked and leaning and lit with the oil lamp's soft orange glow. It smelled like shit and citrus and lavender.

"Go," Odette hissed. "Grab the book, and let's go."

"Grab the... How the hell am I supposed to find a book in all this?" she whispered.

She stepped over the threshold and looked around at the shelves, at the stacks along them, at the fallen stacks that tumbled down from the walls like snow drifts.

"You don't know where it is?" Odette asked. There was panic in her voice.

"No, I... just give me... ten minutes."

"We don't have ten minutes!" Odette said.

"Well, that's what I need!" Saara said. She looked around at the larger, normal person-sized door across from them, the only space in the forest of books. "I'm not leaving until I get it, so watch the door until I do."

"I can't go out there. Maids can't be in the halls."

"So what? They see you, you'll get a whipping. They see me, and we'll both taste the inquisition's axe."

Odette snarled.

"Ten minutes. That's it. Then we're gone."

Odette strode towards the door.

"Wait," Saara hissed, and Odette looked over her shoulder. Saara motioned at the bed. "What about him?"

"The doctors haven't woken him for twenty years. I doubt you'll manage it. Just don't touch him."

"Right."

Odette went through the door and shut it behind her. Saara turned to look about her at the room. Where the hell was she supposed to begin? She had no time to think about it.

Saara started with the stack closest to the door. She lifted the first book and strained her eyes at the words on its spine.

"Meso-Ama-amaranth-ian lin-qoo-is-tics," she mouthed quietly. She had no idea what that meant, but it wasn't what Carlotte was after. She needed a journal. A leather journal with a lock.

She tossed the book to the side and started flipping through the books, looking for anything that looked vaguely like a journal. She found a couple, made a new stack with them, and went on to the next stack. After two stacks, she realized it was still taking too long and began scanning down the stacks, looking at the spines for anything sitting at a jaunty angle. If there was a lock on its face, it wouldn't lay flat.

She could hear whispers behind the drapery, and at first, she thought it was her own imagination, but as she worked towards the bed, she was sure of it. They were just perceptible, just loud enough to hear over the sound of her own heart hammering faster and faster in her chest. How the hell was she supposed to do all this in ten minutes?

She had to go faster.

She worked her way across the room towards the bed, shoving books out of the way, eyes peeled for a lock. The whispers were louder there by the bed, as though the invalid was trying to get her attention but couldn't speak up. The words felt like they were drilling into her skull, demanding to be heard. Finally, Saara stood and ripped back the curtain.

He was not an intimidating man. He was small and old. The skin of his face was stretched over his bones, and his eyes were sunken deep and stared at the ceiling. His lips moved. The rest of him was still as the grave. His hand rested on his stomach, clenched around—

A journal.

This was it. Saara knew it. It looked just like Carlotte's had, leather and closed tight with a lock.

Saara needed to go, and Carlotte would have to be content with the one journal. The most expensive damn journal Carlotte had ever bought. Saara reached down, gripped it with one hand, and pulled.

His grip did not give. So she got a firmer grip on it and reached out with her other hand to peel the man's fingers away. His hands were as cold and ungiving as iron. She braced herself and pulled harder, and the man screamed.

The scream lasted for one second, two, and then, when Saara let go of the journal, it ended in an instant, returning to his mumblings as though nothing had disturbed him. Saara was frozen in surprise, and then the door banged open, and Odette was in the room.

"What are you doing? I said don't touch him!" she cried.

"I need that book," Saara said, pointing to it. Odette grabbed at her shoulder but was unable to make her budge.

"Please, you have to go. We have to go! Someone will have heard that and-"

"Uncle?" came a call from beyond the hall. The two women hushed. There were footsteps beyond the doorway.

"Harold," Odette whispered, all color draining from her. She looked into Saara's face, as though looking for salvation in it, and then rushed to the door.

Saara had seen Harold, met him on several occasions with Carlotte. If he saw her, he might recognize her. She had to hide.

"Girl!" came Harold's voice from behind the door. "What-what are you doing here? Was that my uncle?"

Saara cast about herself. There was nowhere to hide. She dropped to her knees and pulled up the skirt on the bed. She scooped out the books that were sitting beneath and sent them sliding across the hardwood floor.

"I'm sorry, monsieur, I was just checking him and-"

"You are not in charge of his care. I know those girls."

Saara heaved herself into the cavity she'd created and dropped the black skirt back down just as the door creaked open. The skirt hung a few inches off the floor, letting in a strip of light that touched upon her arm. She did not move. Movement would give her away like scurrying rat.

"Yes, monsieur. I'm sorry, I was trying to help out."

They were in the room now. Odette's voice was clear, and Harold's boots clicked against the floorboards.

"Get out of here, girl. My uncle gets the care he needs." Harold said.

"Yes, monsieur, of course, monsieur." Then Saara heard the servant's door open and close. Saara could see Harold's shoe, shiny brown leather with a bright golden buckle across the top. Saara held her breath. Silence settled, and from it, she could hear the whispers again.

"...the dark... it lives in the dark... it eats the light... it eats-"

"Uncle," Harold said. The commanding tone he'd used with Odette was gone and replaced with something soft, something unassuming and natural, and with the slight slur of liquor. "Haven't changed, I see."

Then his hand came into view from beneath the bed skirt. The floor felt like the brick wall of a firing squad against her back, but he just picked up a book, one that she had tossed to the ground earlier, and she heard him place it on top of one of the stacks. He sat on the edge of the bed, and the slat bed frame sagged slightly over her with the extra weight. He was silent, and the whispers filled the silence.

"Still going on about that, are you?" Harold gave a little chuckle. "I hope that woman didn't bother you. Ah, I should have gotten her name. I'll ask Jean. He'll know. These... people... they have no respect. Not really. Not the way they should. They bow and scrape well enough, but leave them alone and... this is how they treat you."

His shoe kicked at another of the books Saara had pulled out from beneath the bed. It spun across the wood until it slammed up against another stack. As it settled, Saara noticed it was a leather journal with a lock on its face. She felt a little twitter in her stomach.

"No respect."

Saara had a sudden image of Odette cast out, the five gold pieces gone in a few months. Destitute. Children starving. She shoved the thought away. What's done was done. Morals only ever got in the way, and it wasn't her fault anyway. Carlotte had put her up to it. Saara was just like Odette, a cog in the great machine of Ryker society.

The bed slat creaked, and Saara's attention focused back on the present.

"My friends told me I should be forceful," Harold said, his voice even softer now. "They said that was what women really wanted." There was another long pause. "I told mother what happened, and she looked at me like I was a criminal. She told Father, and he nearly tore my head off. I risked the family's future, apparently... I must take after you, Uncle. Putting father's plans in jeopardy by following our hearts." A pause. "She was the one who kissed me."

He was talking about Carlotte, unless he had been kissing other girls. Saara thought back to the night before, at Carlotte sitting in her sister's room all in the dark. Something had been on her mind. Something hard.

"Then she bit her lip," Harold said. "How else was I supposed to take that? I was just trying to do what she wanted!" His voice took on a whining quality. "She struggled, but I thought that was just her being coy or something. Inquisitor Lucien said girls do that sometimes. He said they have to make a show of it for their image of purity."

Saara's curiosity darkened into pity. It seemed even the Heir DeSheras was vulnerable to men.

"I'm supposed to fix this, but I don't... Lucien came to tea, and he said she'll have to marry me anyway. He said her name is on the line now and that she's still just playing coy..."

This pause stretched on for a long, long moment.

"I don't want to marry her, Uncle. I don't want to marry a bitch who would do something like this to me. I don't deserve it."

The bed creaked as he stood.

"But I don't have a choice. That's what mother says. None of us do. Responsibility is the yoke of the Ryker." His shoes turned so the toes pointed at her. "You shrugged it off, though, didn't you?

And now look at you... No advice, Uncle?" He laughed weakly again. "I'll see that the girl is removed." Then he left the room, closing the door gently behind him.

Saara waited a full minute after she heard the click of the latch, processing what she'd just heard, and then slid out from under the bed and grabbed the locked journal from the floor. She turned back to the invalid, eyes staring unblinking towards the ceiling, lips whispering, and the other journal clutched like death in his hands. It was too risky to try and take it again. Saara crossed to the servant's door, opened it, and nearly screeched at the sight of Odette standing just behind. Her eyes were wide and a little wet.

"We have to go. Now," Odette said, and her voice cracked at the end.

Saara nodded, and they both hurried down the hallways. They went downstairs and turned and turned and went down and up and Saara was thoroughly lost. The careful progression that had marked their venture into the manor was gone, and now they practically ran.

"Odette!" A strong male voice called from behind them. "Is that you, Odette? I'd like a word!"

"Don't stop!" Odette hissed, and they tore around a corner, almost bowling into a bonneted girl with a bushel of vegetables in her arms.

"Odette?" The girl squeaked as they shoved past her. Saara could see the door to the garden just a few strides ahead.

"Sorry, Rochelle, just a moment," Odette stammered and ran for the door.

"Odette!" the male voice called again from back beyond the turn.

Then they were out and running through the vegetable garden, out the servant's gate and then behind the bushes where Saara's clothes lay in a dirty pile.

Odette braced herself against her knees and breathed hard. Saara threw the bonnet to the ground and pulled the maid dress over her head, eager to be back in her own clothes and out of this place. She shimmied out of it, threw it on the ground and looked up to see Odette, still out of breath, standing on top of her clothes, one blocky heel pushing the cloth into the dirt.

"Give me my money," she said, and though her voice cracked, there was fire in it.

Saara squatted down and fished her purse out of the dress's pockets and then stood back up, dressed only in her underwear. The cold Sheras air prickled her skin.

"Not going to let me dress first?" Saara asked, and Odette glowered.

"Not on your life."

Saara considered her for a moment. Odette didn't have a blade, and she didn't look strong. Saara could be at her in a second, an elbow into her face and a knee into the side of her leg and she'd be mewling in the grass like a babe without a tit to suck. But why?

"Fair enough," Saara said and opened her purse. She pulled out four gold coins. "One and four makes five full rakes." She held them out. Odette didn't move.

"Give me five more," she whispered.

"The deal was five total," Saara said.

"That was before I lost my job."

Saara raised an eyebrow.

"I didn't hear-"

"You know well enough what's going to happen when I go back in. I'll be sacked. I wasn't supposed to be in the halls. The Lord Orlient saw me. I wasn't supposed to be there," she said, her eyes going far away for a moment and rushing back to the present. "I've got kids. Two daughters. With this..." she looked down at the gold in Saara's hand ... "we'll be on the streets in a year."

Saara stared back into the woman's eyes and frowned.

"You got your book. Give me a life," she demanded, her voice fierce.

It was true. Once a girl like this was fired from one house, no other Ryker would hire them. She'd have to find some other living if there was one to be had. She felt the weight of the purse in her hand. There was more in there. Much more. She'd been planning to bill Carlotte for ten rakes anyway. But...

A breeze blew through, and Saara suppressed a shiver. She dropped the purse to her side and stepped forward until she was an arm's distance from the woman. Odette took half a step back, her heel still digging Saara's clothes into the dirt.

"You sold your job to me. For five rakes," Saara said and tossed the gold into the dirt behind her. "Now get off my fucking clothes."

Odette stood her ground for a moment, her eyes darting from Saara's face to the gold behind her. Saara took another step forward, and Odette wilted. She fell away and scrambled around Saara to gather up the coin. Saara pulled her pants on and slipped her knife and purse away before shrugging on her shirt.

"Do you enjoy what you do?" Odette asked.

Saara turned to her. A lock of hair had come loose from the bonnet and hung across her face.

"Do you enjoy helping the Ryker's use us for their little squabbles?

"Who said I work for Rykers?" Saara asked. She hadn't mentioned the DeSherases, not that she could remember.

"Who else would sneak into the Orlient manor just to steal a book no one wants?"

Saara looked down at the journal in her hand. It was shabby-looking in the light of day. The leather was worn, and the pages yellowed. The lock was dull gray with hints of rust inside the mechanism.

"Whoever you work for," Odette continued, her voice getting screechy, "We are just pieces in their games. Your master gets a book, and I lose my livelihood. Your master gets a book, and you risked your life-"

"You agreed to the price-"

"Because I need the damn gold!" Odette screamed, and Saara flinched backward, her eyes flickering to the servant's gate. "I've two daughters. How could I have turned it down? What choice did I have?"

"Someone will have heard you," Saara said and took a step back.

"I'm glad I'm done with them. Done serving them. I'm glad I'm out of the fucking grind. I'd rather lose everything than serve them one more-"

Saara heard nothing more because she turned and ran toward the Tower DeSheras that rose above the city like a beacon of authority. Saara ran until the woman's screeches muted to nothing.

Then she stumbled back into a walk, breathing hard. She didn't like running. Didn't like it at all. It was something a Ryker never did because they were never in a hurry, never in a rush. Running was what the little people did. Saara stopped and looked back to where she had come from. The Orlient manor was not very tall and she couldn't see it over the trees and buildings between, but she hawked and spat towards it.

"Bitch," Saara muttered and shook the image of Odette out of her head. She was just like Bracille and Jerund and Scram. Little people who couldn't bear to see her rise to something more. Crabs, the lot of them, pulling each other back into the pot. Saara wasn't a crab though. No. She wasn't on the menu, and soon, she'd be the fucking cook.

11

Carlotte emerged from the carriage at the Senate building, and Saara was there, holding out a hand to help her down. Carlotte raised an eyebrow, and Saara nodded and slipped a leather journal partway out of her pocket. Carlotte glanced at her mother walking ahead of her and then at the footmen around them. She shook her head, and Saara slipped the journal back out of sight.

"As effective as ever," Carlotte said. "Any issues?"

"Nothing of concern."

Carlotte stopped and turned to look into Saara's eyes. Saara straightened her back and lifted her chin.

"Nothing of concern?" Carlotte repeated.

"Nothing that will blow back. I promise."

Carlotte watched her for a moment and wondered what would have happened if the Orlient had caught Saara. Would Saara have made up a story? Or would she have given up Carlotte's name and thrown the family into scandal? Even if she didn't, Saara was a known entity. Someone would recognize her as Carlotte's assistant. It had been dumb to send Saara out like that. Exactly the kind of foolishness she should have grown out of by now. She felt a sudden surge of anger at Saara for allowing her to go through with it.

"Good," Carlotte managed. "Thank you." And then she turned and followed her mother into the building.

The Senate, like most of the buildings in Old Town, was a re-purposed Amaranthine structure, and like all those other buildings, its proportions were massive. It was one large room with a pit in the middle that descended in concentric steps until it bottomed out at a central circular floor. It had the look of a strip mine carved out of marble. The scholars had many theories on what the Amaranthine had used it for, but none of them had answers. Not even Elspeth had been sure.

The Rykers used it as Senate chambers, with the thirteen voting senators sitting at desks on the bottom level. On the level behind and above sat the advisers and contributing guests. The next few levels were for the non-voting Rykers, arranged in blocks by family and by importance. Behind and above them was the general gallery, where the non-landed people of Sheras could sit and watch the decisions of their city be made for them. Normal sized steps had been added to make the descent easier.

Carlotte's mother was already making her way down to take her place at a desk slightly elevated over the others. Enriq was beside her, speaking into her ear and carrying a case of papers.   As they approached the Ryker levels, an usher stepped into their way. He opened his hands in an apologetic manner. "Madame DeSheras-"

"She's with me," Carlotte said, not stopping her descent and forcing the man to leap out of her way.

"Madame, unless she's an adviser to-"

Carlotte swung around and glared at him. His arm was out, blocking Saara's path.

"She's with me," Carlotte repeated. She took a step back up so she was only a few inches from the man.

"Madame, I'm sorry, but the rules are-"

"What's my name?" Carlotte asked.

The man fumbled. "Madame?"

"What is my name?" Carlotte repeated.

"Madame Carlotte DeSheras."

Carlotte climbed another step. "De. Sheras," she said. "Imagine making an enemy of the DeSheras for something so silly."

"Imagine," Saara repeated. She had a wry smile on her face.

The man kept his arm out between them for several moments,

and then Saara stepped down and pushed his arm out of her way. He let it drop and then mumbled an apology and turned away from them.

"You didn't have to do that," Saara said as they descended.

"Of course I didn't," Carlotte said. She saw her mother at her desk, watching them descend while Enriq whispered into her ear. Carlotte couldn't read her expression. "But he didn't need to stop me. High on his own petty power..."

They took seats at the front of their section and looked out onto the Senate floor. Each of the desks was lit by a beam of light from above. The room was large, and though there were windows on the walls, the bottom of the pit would not naturally have enough light to see. To remedy this, a system of mirrors had been rigged at the windows and along the ceiling to cast daylight onto the floor. A catwalk had been built between them where men could adjust the mirrors as the sun moved across the sky. The old Amaranthine ceiling had several doomed recessions. Early records said they had once contained glass balls, and some of the Amaranthine scholars suggested that they had been used to light the space. No one had ever come up with a method, though, and now the craters just served as places to anchor the catwalk.

Then, there was a crack of a gavel, and the council was underway.

"The senate has convened," Carlotte's mother called out, her voice filling the chamber. "I, the Lady Cainia DeSheras, fill the first seat."

The woman to her left stood up in her own beam of light. "I, the Lady Sondra Macron, fill the second seat."

The next man stood. "I, the Lord Eman Chartay, fill the third seat on behalf of the honorable Lord Jasail Toussaint."

"Toussaint?" Carlotte repeated.

"Minor Ryker from Irondale," Saara said, leaning over to whisper in Carlotte's ear. "Bought half a block down by the Gate a few months ago."

Carlotte glanced sideways, surprised Saara knew that. "Not so minor now," Carlotte said. "You've done your research."

"Thank you, Madame."

"I assume the Orlient are funding his seat?"

Saara nodded.

"Humph," Carlotte grunted.

It wasn't unusual. There were thirteen senators, each representing a thirteenth of the land in the old city and the Nouvre Vil. The outer city didn't count. Any Ryker who owned qualifying land could pledge their percentage of the city to any other Ryker, and once a Ryker had one thirteenth, they were a senator. It was an old system, designed to keep the Senate beholden to the landed Rykers they represented, but the majority of the city was in the hands of just three families: the DeSheras, who owned about a quarter, the Aeshire who owned about an eighth, and now the Orlient who were buying up land as fast as they could pressure minor Rykers off of it, trading villas in the country for townhouses in the city. These families funded themselves and then pledged their remaining land around to buy influence. Three other Senators always voted with Carlotte's mother. If they didn't, Cainia would remove her support, and they'd lose their seats.

"How much land do the Orlients own now?" Carlotte whispered.

"At last count, a little more than the Aeshire," Saara said.

Carlotte raised her eyebrows. The Orlient had risen from country Rykers to the second most powerful family in Sheras in the span of twenty years. When she married Harold, they would represent almost half the city. Carlotte glanced across the chamber at the Orlient's box. She didn't see Harold there, and she let out a breath she didn't realize she'd been holding. She wondered at that marriage. How it would work if the thought of him left her so tense?

"The Lord Orlient," Carlotte heard her mother say, and the words snapped her attention back to the proceedings.

Harold's father stood at his desk, and the downward light above him cast long shadows beneath his brow. "Why, Esteemed Lady DeSheras, are we speaking of normal doings while our city is under attack?"

There were murmurings in the galleries all around.

"Under attack?" Cainia said. "You are referring to the fire?"

"I am referring to the explosion in the outer city," the Lord Orlient boomed.

"Are we so sure it was an attack?" another senator asked. She was the Lady Enritte, and her seat was entirely funded by the DeSheras. Carlotte wondered if she'd been primed to ask the question by her mother.

"What else could it have been?" the Lord Orlient said.

"Criminals, perhaps?" the Lady Enritte answered. "It is the outer city after all."

"Criminals? Madame, a theft is criminals. A back-alley murder is criminals, but an explosion that leveled several blocks? An explosion that killed several hundred Dominioneers? That! That is an act of war!"

"Lord Orlient!" Carlotte's mother cut in, rapping one of her rings against her desk. "If you demand that we speak of this now, then I demand that we do so with the facts on the table."

Cainia waved a hand over her shoulder.

"The Senate recognizes the Lord Gregory Clos, Captain of Public Security."

A man stood in the advisor's box behind Cainia and then tottered slowly down the steps with Enriq holding his arm. He was the captain of Public Security, and he was a second son in a Ryker family that owned a few farms in the country side. He had no land in Sheras and so he had no vote. Thus, he could not be bought, the official line went, but Cainia had chosen him because he was so deeply in debt to the DeSheras, so deep that he had to take a post and work for a living, so deep that if he ever stepped out of line, Carlotte's mother would take all his family's land, and they would no longer be Rykers.

He walked to the center of the floor, and a man on the catwalk above shifted a beam of light to illuminate him.

"There was an explosion," the Captain said. His voice was weak, but such was the shape of the building that it filled the chamber even so.

"In the outer city last night. It started a fire that destroyed several dozen tenement buildings. After speaking with several knowledgeable Rykers familiar with such things, we believe the explosion to have been from a large quantity of black powder. Smuggled in over time by the drug gangs that--"

"Excuse me," the Lord Orlient boomed. "But what need would

gangsters have for large quantities of black powder? What need would anyone have for large quantities of black powder other than war?"

"Lord Orlient," Carlotte's mother broke in. "Let the man speak."

"There is no evidence," the Capitan went on, "for any act of war-"

"Except for the large quantities of black powder!"

"Lord Orlient," Carlotte's mother tried, but he boomed over her.

"And what of the Boneman fleeing the scene?"

"There is no evidence-" the captain tried.

"Enough of this no evidence. Did you do no investigations at all?" the Lord Eman Chartay yelled, adding his voice to the ring.

"Lord-"

"Lady-"

"I say-"

"Enough!" Cainia yelled and slammed the top of her desk with her fist over and over until the Senators finally quieted.

Harold's father still stood at his desk, watching her mother like a hawk from shaded brows.

"The Captain is tasked with this city's security," Cainia said. "The soldiers under his command are the ones that keep us safe, and we will let him finish speaking."

There was a moment of silence while Cainia looked around the circle, waiting for someone to challenge her. Then, she raised a hand to the captain in the middle of the floor. He cleared his throat.

"There is no evidence of an act of war. There were some reports of a naked Boneman fleeing the fire, but there are many Bonemen settled in the outer city, some from before the first liberation war. If this sighting was more than a shadow of imagination, then it was likely a resident, roused from their bed in the night and fleeing the fire. Why else would the man be naked?"

"Did you hear anything about a Freelander?" Carlotte whispered.

Saara shook her head.

"Mother thinks it is an invention of the Orlient," Carlotte

mused.

Harold's father was still standing, and he raised a hand, casting a shadow across his desk. "In the search for evidence, I'd like to call another witness," he said.

"Who?" Cainia asked.

"The Grand Inquisitor of Sheras."

Carlotte sat up a little straighter in her seat and looked up at the dark adviser's box behind the Lord Orlient, looking for the white feather that the inquisitors were known for.

"Was the Grand Inquisitor there?" her mother asked.

"Was the Captain of Public Safety there?" The Lord Orlient said. "The Grand Inquisitor's men are well placed in the city and have already gained much vision into its dark under workings. We all appreciate the work of the Captain, but we can also acknowledge that there is more going on in this city than his bluebacks can see."

Carlotte's mother was silent for several moments, and then, "Very well. Announce him."

"The Senate recognizes the Grand Inquisitor Gerard of Sheras," The Lord Orlient said, and finally sat back down.

The captain tottered back to his seat, and another man stepped out into the circle of light. He was tall and thin, and his clothes looked more like a robe than an inquisitor's uniform. His face was old, lined with creases and sprouting with white hair. His mustache was in the traditional Ryker fashion, though so far as Carlotte knew, there were no Rykers in the inquisitors' ranks. The Mareshal would not have allowed it.

"My inquisitors," The man said, his voice clear and clipped, "have looked into this explosion. The Captain of Public Safety is right. It was centered on a house owned by a man named Ghost, who has dominated much of the illegal drug trade in our city."

"Our city?" Carlotte whispered.

Saara shook her head in agreement.

"Our streets have been flooded with the old Korkin drug called 'pike'. It is made through a complicated process of distillation from a plant that only grows south of L'Epineux. Pike is made in the Freelands by the Bonemen, and a Boneman was seen fleeing the streets where the explosion took place."

Carlotte's mother spoke. "You would have us gather then, that the Freelands smuggled hundreds of barrels of black powder into Sheras to destroy a few blocks of poor tenements? Hardly a military target."

The man lifted his palms up and turned slowly, looking at each senator in turn. "I am saying what we know. Perhaps it was an attack meant to drive us apart. In which case, it seems to be working. Or perhaps the drug house was a staging ground, and the powder was meant for some other target. Perhaps then this was a fortunate accident. Or perhaps, perhaps, it was not black powder at all. Perhaps it was some new weapon, and this was just a test of its power."

Carlotte leaned forward in her chair. She turned to look at Saara, and Saara looked back, eyebrows raised. Others were talking now. The chamber was filled with whispers and murmurs.

"It's not black powder," Carlotte whispered. "He knows it wasn't."

"A new weapon. Is there evidence of this? Or is this all just supposition?" Cainia asked.

The Grand Inquisitor shrugged again. "It was probably just black powder. But what I can tell you is that there is something going on in this city, in our Dominion. Whatever happened in the outer city does not happen in the normal course of things. It is distressing that we don't have more information."

The Grand Inquisitor bowed and moved out of the spotlight.

"Thank you, Grand Inquisitor," The Lord Orlient said. "It is distressing. I'd say it is unacceptable. Now it is only some poor tenements, but where next? The Nouvre Vil? The docks? This very Senate itself."

"Please, now you are fearmongering," Carlotte's mother said.

The Lord Orlient pounded a fist on his desk. "I am spreading the appropriate concern. We deserve answers. Our city deserves security. Security that the Captain of Public Security apparently cannot provide. It is high time that we joined the other cities in the Dominion and accept the Mareshal's help in securing our city from threats, domestic and foreign! I move that we transfer the soldiers under the Captain's command to the Grand Inquisitor and-"

The Senate burst out into an uproar along with much of the Ryker galleries. The Lord Orlient pounded on his desk and shouted above the din. "And give the responsibility of this city's security to the Grand Inquisitor."

"Here here!"

"This is a blatant power-"

"The Mareshal wants to help! Let him!"

"Shall we give our lands to the Mareshal next?"

"Let the Mareshal give us the security we need!"

Cainia lifted a hand, and a great horn sounded from above. It drowned out all the arguments and continued until the chamber stopped shouting, and Cainia dropped her hand.

"Captain," she said when the chamber was silent once more.

"Yes, Madame," the Captain of Public Security answered from the box behind her.

"If anyone in the galleries calls out again, have them escorted from the chamber. They are here to witness, not to add their opinion," Cainia growled.

"Yes, Madame," the Captain repeated, then he called out to the bluebacks that stood at several points throughout the chamber. "You have your orders, men."

"And this Senate," Cainia continued, "will be orderly. I will not remind you again."

"I need not repeat my proposal," the Lord Orlient said, sweeping his eyes across the circle of Senators. "Who supports it?"

Several hands went up. Cainia lunged forward in her chair.

"I was elected to lead this Senate, Lord Orlient! I call for the vote if there will be a vote at all!"

"Then call it, Madame," the Lord Orlient said.

"How many hands went up?" Carlotte whispered.

Saara leaned in. "Six, Madame."

"Plus the Lord Orlient himself. He has the majority. And my mother will have to call the vote."

Carlotte felt a tightness rising in her stomach. Sheras was the last major city of the Dominion to maintain some independence from the Mareshal. The lord Orlient was selling Sheras to the Mareshal one piece at a time.

"I'm surprised the Lord Balit is in favor," Saara said.

Carlotte glared at her. "Why? The Balit are war hawks. They vote with the Orlient in practically everything."

Saara opened her mouth, and then closed it again. She looked like a fish gulping water.

"Well?" Carlotte said.

"I've heard that Sanjid's gang by the foundry are in bed with the Balit family. If the Inquisitors clamp down on the outer city, then the Balit will lose a lot of money."

"The Balit run with criminals?"

Saara shrugged. "That's what I've heard."

Carlotte looked across the Senate floor at Lord Balit. He was a small man who dressed opulently. His fingers glittered with rings. He watched the ongoing exchange between her mother and Harold's father with a faint smirk on his lips. Either he didn't think the Inquisitors would actually do anything, or Saara was wrong.

She leaned back to Saara. "Are you sure?"

"I... uh--"

"I need you to be sure, Saara."

"I... yes," Saara said.

"Go. Tell Enriq."

Saara stood and made her way quickly around the gallery until she was behind the DeSheras advisor's block. Carlotte watched her lean over the partition and whisper into Enriq's ear. Enriq nodded and descended to the Senate floor. While the Lord Orlient was raging on about her mother stymieing the process, Enriq whispered into Cainia's ear. Her mother looked up and across the Senate at Carlotte. One eyebrow raised.

Are you sure? That eyebrow asked.

The pit in Carlotte's stomach grew. She wanted to shrug. She wasn't sure. But like she had told Saara, she needed to be. So Carlotte nodded.

"Lord Orlient," Cainia said, standing at her desk. "I will call a vote, but I will not hand over the security of Sheras without some assurances. If the Grand Inquisitor is to take control, then let him prove himself and his order by ridding our city of this 'pike' and eradicating the gangs that infest the outer city."

The Lord Orlient looked taken aback at the sudden acquiescence, as though the step his foot reached for was suddenly not there.

"The Grand Inquisitor will crush them," he said.

Carlotte watched the Lord Balit and saw the little smirk fall from his face. He sat a little more upright. Carlotte knew her mother saw it too.

"Let them start in the foundry district. My sources tell me it is especially rank with corruption."

The Lord Orlient nodded, and a smile spread across his face. "It will be their first order of business."

The Lord Balit looked about ready to speak, but before he did, Carlotte's mother called out.

"Then I call the vote. Vote against if you want to retain our city's autonomy from the Mareshal, and vote for if you want to give up our agency and let the Mareshal's inquisition persecute the gangs of the outer city and *all* those who profit from them."

Cainia placed both hands on her desk, as did the Lady Embry beside her. The Lord Aeshire raised his, as did the Lord Macron and the Lord Chartray. The Lord Orlient raised his and looked around the circle, counting the votes. Six up, six down. The Lord Balit sat with his hands in his lap, beneath the desk.

"Lord Balit," The Lord Orlient said. "Your vote, sir."

The Lord Balit's eyes were locked onto Cainia's. Now Cainia wore the smirk, and the Lord Balit nodded and scowled. He lifted his hands and placed them flat on the desk before him.

"Six for, seven against. Sanity prevails," Carlotte's mother said.

The Lord Orlient's mouth opened and then closed. Cainia looked up at Carlotte and gave a slight nod. Carlotte felt the blood rise in her cheeks. Saara sat back down beside her, and Carlotte could not keep the glee out of her voice.

"You would make an excellent Ryker, Saara," Carlotte said, and then Cainia called the next agenda item into discussion.

12

There were two things on the walls that forced me on to Lok Secrak. The first was the existence of the black city itself, the mythical point where the Lord God cast down his judgment upon the Amaranthine, but though that was a revelation worthy of a hundred expeditions, it was not the catalyst that thrust me forward. It was the other mural, the one on the opposite wall, a bas-relief in the grandiose style of the Amaranthine, a 20-foot figure, disfigured and decomposed and being reconstructed. Kel Shoatone. I have no doubt of this. The relief could be nothing else.

The map was truth. It marked all the places on the continent where the granite still stands and where ruins are known to be found. It is truth, and thus it is not a far stride to the bas relief being also truth. I will go seek it out. I must.

Of course, I know that even this proof could be folly. I am a Ryker. I am a scientist. I know the commonality of failure, but the rewards this would bring, the understanding of God's creation this would reveal... the applications it could have... I must go. For why else do we, the Ryker, exist but to unravel and catalog the tapestry of creation?

Carlotte looked around at her laboratory. The shaker fish swam in slow circles in their tank around the pocked rock in the center. Beside them was the DeSheras Pile, a dozen clustered towers, the culmination of all her work for the past two years. A curiosity really without an application. The animal force was groundbreaking, and yet, if all she could do with it was make a dead man grimace, then why should the world care? Why should she?

"It is a piece of the work," she said.

The fish made no reaction to her words.

She had done her part for Rykerdom and now her duty turned to politics and child rearing. This would all be her legacy, and when she died, the artists would weave a stack of copper, zinc, and cloth into her hand on her tapestry in the exhibition hall. She wondered if her great-great-grandchildren would have trouble remembering her name, if she'd just be a face in the middle of the line, the boring one with the stack of salt and metal.

Carlotte lifted Ryliar Orlient's second journal in her hand. She'd read it three times since Saara had brought it to her the night before. It was packed with information, but it was also filled with holes. It was a diary, not a treatise or a guide. The location of Steuersak was still left out. The path from the ruin to Lok Secrak was unclear. He went south through the Shafala forest and met a Korkin slave by a lake, and the slave gave him direction into the Greenwall. He followed her direction and found the entrance to the black mountain. Carlotte didn't know what an entrance to a mountain was. Perhaps it was a pass? A cave? She didn't even know there were any mountains in the Greenwall. She was missing key information. Ryliar made reference to things she did not understand. She was not an Amaranthine Scholar, and she had not done research in the Great Bergshalen library where Ryliar found his knowledge. Or maybe she didn't understand because the author was a catatonic lunatic, and she was not.

It was foolish. All of this was. It had been foolish to send Saara after the journal. What if she'd been caught? It would have been a black mark against Carlotte's name. She'd be the center of the ladies' gossip, and for what? A mad man's ramblings about mystical technologies from a people cast down by God for their arrogance? Ryliar Orlient was a nobody precisely because he'd gone after this. Because to go after this crap was to go after myths and superstition.

Carlotte realized her hand was gripping Elspeth's pendant through her shirt. She looked up at her Pile and then down again at the journal.

"What's the point," she whispered, "You're to marry in six

months anyway."

She thought of Harold and the way his eyes blurred into one with his face pressed close. The scratch on her thigh stung, and her stomach turned. She wondered what Elspeth would do in this situation. Carlotte reached up and tugged at one of the ropes that hung from the wall.

There was a knock at the door, and then it opened cautiously.

"Saara," Carlotte said, and the butler disappeared, closing the door silently behind him.

It didn't take long for Saara to knock, and when Carlotte bade her enter, the woman was out of breath, and her face was flushed.

"Yes, Madame?" Saara wheezed.

"I need..." Carlotte began and wondered what it was she needed. She wondered if she was really going to go down this path. No. She wasn't going anywhere. She was going to marry Harold and do her duty as the Heir DeSheras, but Elspeth would never have built herself into a corner. That was all Carlotte was doing. Keeping her options open.

"I need you to put an expedition together for me."

"An expedition?"

"I assume you know what that is," Carlotte snapped, and Saara's eyes widened like a cow's. The bun atop her head was so tightly bound that Carlotte wondered how the woman's eyebrows ever came back down.

"Yes, Madame. Of course. An expedition... to where?"

"To..." to where indeed. Carlotte looked down at the journal in her hands. To Steuersak? She didn't know where it was. To the black mountain? Even less of an idea. If she made this journey she'd have to go where Ryliar went. She'd have to pick up the same clues he did, put the puzzle together herself. It was dangerous... beyond sense, really, but then, all of this already was. And she wasn't even going to go anyway.

"To Bergshalen," she said, and Saara's eyes nearly popped out of her head.

13

The door creaked when Saara opened it and again as it shut behind her. The library was in twilight, the shutters closed to keep the wind from disturbing the books, and as the room receded back between the stacks, it became dark as night. Val was hunched at his desk, which was pushed up close to the shutters where the thin slats of golden light glinted off his gilt frames and gave him something to read by. He wrote with his left hand while the other traced his place in a great tome and his eyes flicked between the book and a propped up work bound in leather with the DeSheras' crest emblazoned on its cover.

"Finally brought my- Ah. Miss Akar."

"Val?" Saara said and cocked her head. There was a strange expression on the man's face.

"Sorry, for a moment I thought you were your uncle."

"Jaaque? Were you expecting him?"

"No, no, he's just overdue on a return."

"The Mareshal is stockpiling. I'm sure he's just busy with his warehouse. I'll ask after it next time I see him." Saara frowned. "It's been a while... I hope I didn't disturb you."

Val looked at her, blinked, and then looked back down at the tome.

"I've lost my place."

Saara didn't know what to say to that.

"No, it's fine," he said, pulling himself to his feet with more effort than a man his age should need. "Of course it's fine. I was working on a translation using a text by the Mademoiselle Elspeth DeSheras. The Amaranthine symbolic meaning was quite complicated. Elspeth really was something special. Genius. She would have shed light on many dark places."

Saara pulled up the other chair to the desk and plopped down in it. She leaned back and took a deep breath, and the air smelled musty and stale and much like her uncle. He had brought her here when she was too old to be enchanted and too young to appreciate it, and he would borrow books from Val and take them to his warehouse and make Saara read them out loud at the little desk in his office while he leaned over behind her. She had hated it, of course. She'd done her best to learn as little as possible.

Saara's fingers dug into the upholstery on the chair's arms and she thought that she should go see her uncle soon. Once she had time. She shook the thought away and looked up to see Val looking curiously down at her.

"Miss Akar?"

"Do you know anything about Bergshalen?" she asked.

Val blinked. "The Hedgehog Kingdom? Well, I've read some things. I doubt I know more than any tutored child."

"Well, I wasn't a tutored child," Saara said. She leaned forward to rest her elbows on her knees. "I know a little. I know Rykers aren't supposed to go there. But that's about it. This is a library, right? You're a librarian. Aren't you supposed to know things?"

Val pulled his pen out of the inkwell, wiped it off with a little black towel for just that purpose, and then plugged it with a glass stopper. He clasped his hands in front of him and leaned down on his elbows. "Why do you want to know?"

"Do me a favor, Val. Give me an overview." She slouched in the chair and let her knees fall comfortably open. Val gave a little frown and she realized she looked rather improper to him. This was not how Ryker ladies sat. But she wasn't a Ryker Lady. Not yet.

After a moment, he spoke. "Bergshalen has never liked foreigners, that's where they get their name--"

"Hedgehogs aren't friendly?" Saara asked.

"They're thorny," he said and glared at her for the interruption.

"Bergshalen's always been prickly but there were still traders and diplomats and the like. We had a consulate in their capital, I believe, but that all fell apart during the second liberation war."

"That war was with the Freelanders," Saara said.

Val nodded. "It was, but then came the battle of the split."

Val looked at her, and Saara blinked back. "That supposed to mean something to me?"

He sighed, stood, and then walked to the shelf behind him and ran his finger along the book spines.

"I'll have to chastise your uncle, if he ever brings back my book, for educating you so poorly." Val pulled a book from the shelf. He placed it on the desk and flipped through the pages.

"Amongst the people, I'm remarkably well read," Saara said.

Val scoffed. "Pah! The people..." He flipped the book around so that she could read it.

The page was a map of the continent, with the Ryker dominion at the top, the massive Freelands in the middle, the Greenwall at the bottom, the Grand Sea on the right edge, and the endless sands on the left. The Bergshalen mountains rose above the Shafala forest, which separated the continent from the desert, and in the center of the mountain, the artist had drawn a sleeping hedgehog, with long spikes protruding all around.

"The Cobalt feeds the Ryker Dominion, and the Free Freeflow feeds the Freelands." Val put two fingers on the page, one at the mouth of each river, Domsar bay in the north and the Fertile Delta in the Freeland south. He dragged his fingers along each river until they met in the foothills of the Bergshalen mountains. "The Splitting," Val said, "is where each of those rivers begin. There are, of course, countless tributaries that feed into these rivers, but the bulk of their water comes from Bergshalen, and that water is vital to both states.

"The war was bitter and hard. The Mareshal's Men were stymied at the Spine, bogged down in the Greenwall, and engaged in countless fronts along the Freeland coast. It looked much like the first liberation war twenty years before, and so the Mareshal invaded Bergshalen and took the Splitting, violating Bergshalen's neutrality.

"The Mareshal made to dam the Free Flow, to divert all the

water to Domsar. The Freelands couldn't allow this, of course. It would have started a famine. Millions would have died. So the Freelands invaded Bergshalen as well. This became the most important battle of the war. Both sides poured everything into it, and once Bergshalen had time to properly mobilize, its army came to bear as well and attempted to push both the Freelands and the Dominion out. Tens of thousands died on each side."

There was silence for a moment.

"Shit," Saara said.

Val nodded. "Indeed. It's difficult to sustain that much blood. After a month, a three-way armistice was signed. Part of that agreement was Bergshalen closing their borders entirely."

"No one can go in?"

"There are exceptions, of course," Val said, closing the book and standing to replace it on the shelf. "There is a town to the Southeast of the Splitting where they let traders in. And skilled artisans and extraordinary persons always find ways through."

"Extraordinary persons?"

"Brilliant artists, innovators, scientists. But not Rykers. Expressly not Rykers. No aristocracy or leaders from either nation. Pain of death they say. Though I've never heard of a Ryker trying."

"Huh," Saara said and leaned back in her chair. Val turned around by the bookshelf and looked at her. None of the slits of light hit him there and he seemed almost a phantom in the darkness.

"Are you going to tell me why you asked?" he said.

Saara considered giving a snide remark, something trite and coy like Carlotte would have said. She considered being mysterious and making Val draw it out of her like the Ryker ladies at DeSheras functions, but Saara wasn't that kind of lady. "I have a job for you."

Val scowled. "I understand that we see the world differently," he said. "You are a proud working woman, and a very fine one by all accounts, and so to you this," and he waved a hand at the library around him, "must seem like a willful attempt to maintain my own poverty. If you were me, you would find some occupation, some service to pull you out. That is what you would do because a working person is what you are, and you should take no shame in that, just as I take no shame in being a Ryker. It is not my place to work. It is not my place to clerk or account or... labor."

Saara sat back in her chair. "God, man. You really are something else. Do you think you're better than work?"

"It's not a matter of better. It's a matter of principles, of place and the way things should be."

Saara wondered what he would think if he knew her ambitions. She was, without a doubt, his superior. She'd grown up in the streets of the outer city, poor as a stray cat before her uncle took her in, and now she'd bet her purse that she had more in it than Val had to his name. With what Saara had hidden away in her little room, she could buy his books, his papers, his ink, his pens, his library, and the apartments above it. She could buy everything he had down to the land itself, and he was too high and mighty for labor? Of course he was. He was a Ryker, and she was not. He could own land, and she could not. He was in his place, and she was in hers, and that was something she could not argue with.

Saara rolled her eyes. "Do you really not want to hear what I have to say?"

"I don't want to hear you offer me a job out of pity. I won't... I can't bear that anymore."

His voice sagged a little at the end, and Saara noticed how sagged he was too. His back was hunched, and his arms hung limply at his sides, and Saara wondered how she looked to him. Was he thinking the same things in his head? That he was a man of principles and good sense and why should it be that this woman has everything that he does not? That thought gave Saara pause. For all the Lord Vaalier Saadermont's bluster, he really was a good man. Had he not lent Saara's uncle books without charge? Had he not talked to her and her uncle like an equal? Perhaps if Rykers were like him, if he were not the exception, then being a Ryker really would mean one was a better person... Or maybe Saara was just filling herself with shit.

Saara rubbed her eyes.

"It's more an opportunity than a job," she said, "and I'm not even sure it's going to happen. Or when. Or how."

"What do you mean?"

"So you want to hear what I have to say?"

Val was still for a moment. "Not a job? Not some occupation?"

166

"Depends how you look at it. You can always say no," she said, though if he did, she had no idea how else she'd do what Carlotte had asked. Val nodded and his spectacles caught a beam of light and glinted gold.

"Tell me," he said.

"The Lady Carlotte DeSheras is putting together an expedition."

"Wha--"

Saara put up a hand cutting him off.

"I don't know what it's about. She's not in the habit of telling me these things, but she said to hire laborers, outfit them for digging, and to find an expert on the Amaranthine."

Val's mouth fell open. "Are you... offering me..." he sputtered. His mouth didn't seem to work.

Saara couldn't help but smile. "Yes. I'm asking you to be that expert. I'm sure we can give your family a stipend while you're gone to keep all this running. Can't imagine that would cost much. But!" she said, holding up one finger. "I've no idea if it's actually going to happen. The Heir DeSheras has been... erratic. And she's supposed to be getting married in a few months. So. Take that as you will."

"Of course. Yes, of course I'll go," Val whispered and Saara couldn't keep her laugh down. She hadn't seen someone so happy since... ever, now that she thought of it.

"Where are we going?" he asked.

Saara scratched vigorously at an itch on the back of her head. "Bergshalen. Though I doubt the Heir DeSheras plans to dig there. I'm supposed to 'find a way in,'" she said.

"But she's... and I'm-"

"Rykers. I know. So, sit back down, tell me how to put together an expedition, and help me find a way to crack the Hedgehog Kingdom."

14

Carlotte threw herself into her work. She went to the council meetings with her mother, and while the senators droned endlessly on, she thought of her pile and of her lightning and the implications it might have. When she was in the tower, she studied. She poured over the chemical treatises in her library, hypothesizing new applications and methods of generation, and when she felt her brain was about to explode, she'd pick up one of Elspeth's few remaining books. Carlotte's mother had burned most of them with the rest of Elspeth's things, but there were still a few texts on the Amaranthine, and by Friday, she'd read them all. Every time she opened a new one, she told herself it was just a curiosity, and when Saara would come to her each night with details on expedition preparations, how she'd found a scholar, how she'd reserved passage on a boat, how she'd hired the violinist, Carlotte told herself it was all just an exercise in possibilities. She wouldn't actually go, she knew. She couldn't. She had duties in the city. She had duties to her family.

"A violinist?" Carlotte asked, just because she was curious.

"That prodigy, Visoletta Corlionne. She's our way in. Bergshalen lets in great artists and the like. We just pose as her entourage."

It was actually rather brilliant. Carlotte felt a fleeting spasm of guilt that she'd put Saara to all this work for nothing. But then again, that's what Saara was for.

Harold's apology never came, but Carlotte told herself it was because whatever gesture the boy planned was a big one. He would come with a gift of thirty white horses, a promise to be better etched onto every saddle. He'd spend a fortune on diamonds and prostrate himself at her feet, begging her to forgive him. It would be lacking, but it would be good all the same. Carlotte would accept his apology with draconian conditions, she would finish her work on the animal force, and then she would marry, he would give her children, and she would lead her new family in further cementing DeSheras power. This she had to do, and this she would do, but there was no harm in a bit of fun and fantasy. A few pounds of gold here, a few there. It was nothing to her.

Carlotte sat in her library, a book on Amaranthine architecture in her lap, and a knock sounded at the door.

"Enter," she told Saara, but when she looked up, it wasn't Saara at all. It was some butler. He looked familiar.

"The Madame Cainia DeSheras requests your presence in the drawing room, first floor."

Carlotte frowned. "First floor," Carlotte repeated. "She isn't alone then?"

"No, Madame."

"Right." Carlotte looked down at herself. She wore a comfortable wool dress. "Send Selene up to my room. Have her bring another maid. Tell my mother I'll be just down."

The butler nodded and closed the door behind him. Carlotte shut her book and sat forward, clasping her hands together and bowing her head to them. She felt suddenly sick, a nausea deep in her abdomen. Harold was here. He'd come for the apology. The scratch on her thigh had healed, but at the thought of seeing Harold, it burned all the same. She had run through his apology a hundred times while she'd sat in those agonizing sessions at the senate, how she would put him in his place, how she would make him wait for her forgiveness, but now that the moment had come, she wanted to hide away in her library. She wanted to lock the door and never come out, but she was a Ryker and didn't have the luxury of such frivolity.

So, instead, she prayed, apologizing to God for all her

trespasses against him, and begged him to give her strength. It worked some. When she stood and walked to her dressing room she did so with firm purpose, and as the women helped her dress and put her face and hair together, she managed to keep her lunch on the inside.

Carlotte descended quickly, muttering the Lord's prayer as she went to keep her pulse from racing, but when she turned on the final landing, she froze.

There were soldiers in the grand foyer. Four crisp, blue uniforms stood straight as arrows by the front door, and beside them were three men dressed all in black with white trim and a white feather pluming out from each of their trifold hats.

Inquisitors.

Here, in the DeSheras tower.

All of their heads turned up to her, and for a moment, Carlotte felt like a débutante on display, revealing herself to disappointed partygoers. She felt the blood rising in her cheeks, and then all but one bowed. The inquisitor who remained standing was taller than the others and had a nose that hooked down like a beak. He looked at her like a vulture looks at the dead.

"Madame DeSheras," came a voice.

Carlotte saw her mother's assistant, Enriq, down by the door to the drawing room. His voice broke the inquisitor's glare, and remembering himself, the inquisitor bowed his head with the others. She descended. There were other butlers in the foyer, standing along the walls, all of them looking on edge. Carlotte looked to Enriq and saw the same worry hiding just behind his servile smile, but before she could ask him what this was all about, he pushed open the drawing room doors and announced her.

"The Lady Carlotte DeSheras."

The drawing room was filled with evening light, igniting the room of pink and yellow pastels in a warm glow, but in the room's center stood a man clad all in black. Her mother sat opposite him, straight backed but relaxed, arms laid out on the arm rests, and with a dull glare that said this man was important, but less important than her. Carlotte recognized him from the Senate meeting some weeks before. It was the Grand Inquisitor. Carlotte could think of no reason why he would be here, let alone why she would be called to meet him. Carlotte looked around the room, expecting Harold to be standing somewhere just out of sight, but when Enriq closed the doors behind her, the three of them were alone.

"Grand Inquisitor, may I introduce the Heir DeSheras, my daughter, Carlotte." Her mother waved a hand at an empty chair beside her.

The Inquisitor turned to her. He had seemed tall at the Senate meeting, but in person he seemed taller still. He towered above her, and his black vestments hung on his frame like a scarecrow. "Mademoiselle, I am honored," he said and gave a slight nod of the head.

Carlotte would have curtsied, but her mother's demeanor told her not to, so she nodded in return. "Inquisitor," she said.

He smiled, but the gesture was only in his lips. His eyes did not change. "*Grand* Inquisitor, but please, call me Gerarde. I would never insist on titles with such a *grand* family. Please sit."

The Inquisitor sat himself, and then picked up a cup of tea that sat on the table beside his chair. He spoke again. "We were speaking of Sheras, Carlotte, and how relaxing I find it. The Capitol is filled with paranoia. The High Fortress even more so, not that it's unwarranted, but it's good to be around less important people who don't need to take so many precautions."

Carlotte looked from her mother to the Inquisitor and didn't know what she was supposed to do. "Paranoia?" she said after several moments when the silence seemed to stretch on too long.

"Of assassination, Mademoiselle. The world is a strange and difficult place. More so than ever these days. I'm not sure how much you hear up here at the edge of the world, but the Mareshal hasn't left the High Fortress in years. He leads from within and leaves it to his Inquisitors to carry out his will."

"Gerarde," her mother said, "You came here and asked to speak to my daughter for some reason, and we are busy people. For Rykers, you see, the work never stops. So please, get to the point of this visit."

Gerarde's smile fell away, and he put his cup back on the table. "Despite the proposal that you defeated in the Senate, my purpose in Sheras remains the same: to ensure that this city remains stable and peaceful. The Dominion is surrounded by enemies: The

Korkin agitants, Bergshalanese, Hill Savages disrupting our colonies, other... more singular threats. If the Dominion is to survive on this continent, then we must be as one. A united Dominion is a strong Dominion."

"And?" her mother asked.

"And I'm here to ensure it stays united. So tell me, Carlotte, why did you go to the Outer City after the explosion?"

"Pardon me?" Carlotte said. She looked to her mother, and her mother's eyes narrowed at the Inquisitor.

"The fire. You were there the next day, poking around. Why?" he said.

"Because I sent her," her mother said. "Are you following my daughter?"

"Me? No. Nor are my men. We tend to have more important things to do, but when the Heir DeSheras crosses beneath the Nouvre Vil wall, people talk. So why did you send her then?"

Her mother's lips curled up, and all pretense of nicety left her face. "Because the fire was on my land. Because the Fire Crew is in my employ. Because it is my responsibility to know what goes on in *my* city."

The old man took in a deep breath. "We are at war, Madame-"

"Really? Because last I heard the war ended ten years ago," Cainia snapped.

Carlotte felt again like a child, sitting meekly in her chair while the adults argued above her. She made a conscious effort to pull her shoulders back and keep her chin up.

"The hostilities with the Korkin slaves, perhaps, but the threat continues. The threat is insidious," the Inquisitor said. "It burrows into our society and tries to consume us from within. It tries to attack us from within-"

"Oh, don't give me that drivel about the naked Freelander," snapped Caina. "This was no act of war, no matter how you dress it up."

The Inquisitor turned to Carlotte. "I don't know what it was, but it was interesting, wasn't it, Carlotte? Not like a normal fire. The stone melted like it was. The complete destruction."

Cainia's glare moved to Carlotte, and Carlotte forced her chin to remain up. She hadn't mentioned the stone to her mother. Or the gold.

"Interesting, no?" the Inquisitor continued. "My men are flummoxed. But you, Carlotte, are a scientist, a Ryker tasked with understanding God's creation. So what do you think happened?"

Both of them were staring at her now.

"Black powder," she said and the man's face did not move. Her fingers gripped each other in her lap so hard it hurt.

"Really? Black powder. That's what you think happened?"

"What else could it be?" Carlotte managed after a moment, hating the fact that this man made her feel so small. She, a Ryker, a DeSheras!

"Hmm," Gerarde grunted.

Cainia stood, and Carlotte followed suit.

"I think it's time you leave, Gerarde. The Heir DeSheras is not some mere citizen you can bully around, and we are not here to answer your questions. You should remember that you are in Sheras at the Rykers's invitation."

Gerarde nodded and then stood.

"Of Course, Madame DeSheras. I apologize for the tenor of this conversation, but I remind you that we are on the same side. I represent the Mareshal, and the Mareshal is the Dominion's security."

Cainia clapped once, and the drawing room doors swung open, revealing Enriq with the gaggle of inquisitors and soldiers behind.

"Inquisitor," she said and lifted her hand towards the door.

"*Grand* Inquisitor," he corrected softly but with no lack of authority in his voice.

He stepped towards the door but then stopped and turned. "I almost forgot. I did come for one other reason, as a favor to the Family Orlient, who has been so kind to me." He snapped his fingers, and one of the soldiers came forth with a black, wooden box.

Cainia motioned toward a table, and Enriq took the box from the soldier and placed it where indicated. "Thank you," Cainia said, "But surely the post would have sufficed."

Gerarde shrugged. "I suppose, but important gifts should come from important hands, no?"

He turned to Carlotte. "It is a gift, Mademoiselle, from your beloved, Harold. I was so happy to hear of your engagement. The DeSheras past bonded to the Orlient future. Ah. It is a match made by God himself. I do hope your coming travels do nothing to jeopardize it. It would be a shame if Harold was forced to marry another."

His words hung in the air for a moment. Carlotte's stomach tightened.

"Travels?" Cainia said.

"Or so I assume. My men say that woman of her's is buying passage to Domsar, and arranging for a riverboat up the Cobalt! Passage for thirty, they said. A right expedition, I don't doubt. Or... am I mistaken, Mademoiselle?"

Carlotte said nothing, and for a few moments, no one else said anything either, until her mother broke the silence.

"That will be all, Gerarde."

He nodded, and stepped into the foyer and then out of the tower, his retinue falling in line behind him as he went.

Silence.

"The doors, Enriq," Cainia said, and her manservant pulled the drawing room shut and Carlotte was alone with her mother for the third time that month. It must have been a record.

Her mother said nothing and Carlotte felt herself shrinking away, younger and younger, a little girl fiddling with her dress, sucking on her thumb, sinking with the dread that she was in trouble.

"An expedition?" Cainia said. "To Domsar and then up the Cobalt. To... where?"

"It's not... I'm not actually going anywhere. I was just exploring options and-"

"Not actually going? But you've got Saara buying boats? Exploring options to run away--"

"I'm not running away, I'm-"

"What else would you call this!?" Cainia screeched, and Carlotte recoiled backwards, nearly stumbling over her chair. "You have one task! To marry Harold Orlient and make children! This family has money, it has power, it has prestige. What it doesn't have is heirs! It was Elspeth's responsibility to bear and then she died and now it's yours. You will not fail me. You will not go on an expedition to

God knows where, and you will not fail this family."

"Mother. I know my responsibility. I'm not running away," Carlotte said. "But... I've found something, mother, and it might change everything."

Cainia's gaze was that of a gorgon. "Something more important than your family?" her mother said.

"I..." Carlotte began and then thought better of it. She needed to think this out. She needed to appeal to her mother's scientific nature and--

"Well?" Cainia snapped.

Carlotte flinched away from her, and her words poured out all in a rush. "The fire. I didn't tell you about the stone. The way it melted and the blast marks came from almost a point, far too small an area for the amount of black powder it would have taken. Whatever happened there- it's something new. Something different. And the Grand Inquisitor knows it. That's why he came here and why he raised a fuss!"

"What are you saying, Carlotte?"

Carlotte felt what little confidence she had slipping away. "I... I... found a journal. In the Orlient manor. From Harold's Uncle. Ryliar. And it speaks of-"

Cainia held up a hand and cut her off. "Ryliar..." she repeated, her face drifting away in memory, and then her eyes widened. "That's right. Errik had a brother..." Her mother's face shot back to her. "Magic," she whispered.

Carlotte held her breath, waiting for the explosion.

Her mother's eyes turned upwards. "Must I lose my entire family to this?"

"No, mother, please. The things I've found in that journal. The wonders and... and mysteries to uncover. Scientific advances we can't even dream of. The Amaranthine could bring the dead back to life! Mother. Think of what that would mean for this family if we found it!"

Her mother looked at her, and her eyes were suddenly wet. She sniffed in and put her fingers to the bridge of her nose. Carlotte was stunned. She'd never seen her mother like this. "That's what Elspeth said before she left. Before *she* ran away."

She rubbed at her eyes, whisking the wetness away, and then

looked up at Carlotte. "It is the Ryker's oldest folly, Carlotte, to study..." She dropped her voice to almost a whisper for the next word. "Magic. At best, you'll come back discredited and humiliated. At worst, you'll end up like Ryliar Orlient. Or your sister."

"Elspeth found things. Wonderful things," Carlotte said, and her hand went to her chest and gripped at the pendant hanging there beneath her shirt.

"And they drove her to suicide. And to Hell."

"She didn't commit... it was an accident." Carlotte's voice nearly cracked.

"You saw her," Cainia said. "The froth on her lips. The bottle in her hand. The fire she set to burn her notes away."

"No," Carlotte said.

Cainia reached out and lifted Carlotte's chin to face her. Her grip was gentle but hard and unforgiving. "Adults do not get to ignore facts, and certainly not Ryker Ladies. Learn from your sister's mistakes and do what she would not. Whatever she saw, whatever happened to her, she would not want you to experience because she would want you to take your rightful place as my heir and make your family proud."

Carlotte stared into her mother's eyes, and for the first time in a long time, she saw something of the mother she'd known before her sister had left all those years ago. She saw tenderness... and it made Carlotte angry that such feelings still existed in her mother, and that she reserved them until now.

"How would you know what Elspeth would want," Carlotte said, not moving her eyes from her mother's. "You were the one who drove her away."

It seemed that time froze for a moment, and then, as though it went faster to catch up to itself, her mother pulled away from Carlotte, like a snake rearing to strike, and slapped her.

It was not soft, and the heel of her mother's hand hit Carlotte's cheekbone and her palm rapped across Carlotte's ear, flinging her to the ground. Carlotte shrieked and scrambled away, and her ear rung with the impact.

"You are beyond reason. You are still a child, and you will be treated as such. Enriq!" her mother screamed, and the doors flew open. Carlotte saw the man at the door. He stared back at her. She saw other servants behind him, all watching with wide eyes.

"Madame?" Enriq said.

"Put men at the door. Carlotte is not to leave the tower until her wedding night. Search her rooms for money and remove it. Get no money for her if she asks and tell the rest of the staff to do the same. And tell Saara to cancel her plans."

"Yes, Madame," Enriq said.

Cainia flowed past him and up the stairs.

Enriq looked to Carlotte for a moment, saw her on the floor, cradling the side of her face with her hand, and then he bowed. "Mademoiselle De Sheras," he said and then closed the door.

Carlotte sat and stared at the closed door. Her face ached. She wondered if it would bruise. Maybe that would be a good thing. Her mother was right. She was acting like a child, and the thought of it made her want to cry and what was that impulse but the reaction of a child? Carlotte dug one nail into her wrist, pressing hard and scraping back so the pain flared up and took her mind away from everything, but her mind found a way around it and came back, and now her soul hurt and her face hurt and her wrist hurt too. Another misstep in a life full of them.

What was she playing at? She had seen Elspeth's body. She'd seen the white froth and the bottle, but that wasn't her sister. She knew her sister. She remembered the fire in Elspeth's eyes when she'd spoken to Carlotte of what she'd found in the north, buried in the mountains beneath the ice. She knew that Elspeth never would have taken her own life, never would have damned her own soul to Hell. So how horrible must it have been? Whatever she'd found out? Whatever she'd seen?

Or maybe her sister was more like Carlotte than Carlotte cared to admit. Maybe her mother was right, and Elspeth couldn't handle her responsibility and ran away, just like Carlotte couldn't. Maybe what she found amounted to nothing, and Elspeth couldn't bear the thought of bearing children and being remembered for wasting her time. Better an eternity in Hell than an eternity remembered as a fool.

Carlotte *had* led Harold on. She had created this situation for herself. She had bitten her lip. Had she pushed him away? Or had she opened her legs? Had she fabricated this whole thing just so she could play adventurer in the garden, discovering bugs and slaying hedges, playing in the mud while the grown-ups did real work? Why did Elspeth have to die? Why couldn't she be there for Carlotte? God, Carlotte missed her.

Carlotte was spiraling. She had to pull herself out, so she reached into a pocket on her dress and pulled out her prayer beads. "God, help me," she began. "I believe in God, the almighty and the one true father, creator of the earth and the life above." She moved her fingers to the next bead. "I believe in the prophet, the soul given by God to guide the sinful through all life's troubles. Torn though he was, and battered through the Amaranthine cruelty, broken though was his body, whole was his soul, and it rose from the dead on the third morning. I believe in my subservience before him, the Lord God, and the Prophet, his messenger." She moved to the next section. "I am a sinner, I am weak, and I am nothing before thee, God. I am a sinner, I am weak, and I am nothing before thee, God. I am a sinner, I am weak, and I am nothing before thee, God," and she continued through the admittance until her fingers picked their way around the ring of beads and finished where she'd started. For all her failings, it was her weakness of faith that was her worst. Through God, she should know her place and she should know her duty and she should have the strength to do it.

Carlotte looked up from the floor at the box the Grand Inquisitor had brought. It was of ebony from the Freelands, and was carved with a fine design where the impressions had been filled with white glazed ceramic, giving it the impression of an overly decorated spider's web. A simple red ribbon was tied in a bow, holding the lid in place.

Carlotte stood and walked to it. She pulled the ribbon away. All she had to do was lift.

"God, give me guidance," she whispered. "Show me my mother is right and I've been making this all up. Show me so I can be strong and do my duty. Harold will be good, and he will be a gentleman, and I will know that I've been a child, and I will not make excuses for my actions."

She heard nothing in reply, but she knew God heard her. He always did. He was always listening.

With a deep breath, she lifted the lid, and there, settled in an interior of plush scarlet silk, lay the flintlock pistol that he'd shown her in his workshop.

"A gun," she whispered to herself. "He gave me a gun."

She reached in and lifted it. It was heavy, like she remembered, but balanced well with extra weight in the handle. She thumbed over the detail. It was an intricate scene of stags and foxes jumping through a forest, fleeing the hand that held it and rushing towards the barrel. It must have taken hours of fine work to accomplish.

It was beautiful, and Carlotte wondered if a brute could make something so delicate.

There was a card nestled in the silk, written with an elegant flowing hand. She lifted it.

"Dearest Carlotte," the letter read, "the last time we met was unfortunate, and I hope it will not build up between us like a secret in the dark. Come to my family's estate tomorrow noon, and we will put it behind us. Your betrothed, Harold."

She starred at the card and read it again and then a third time.

"He didn't even apologize," she said. "He didn't..." and she trailed off, eyes unfocused. She stood there for several minutes, thinking of the life that was before her. The paths it would take. The ways it would end and the insignificance she would leave behind.

Then she felt a rush of warmth, and she knew it was God giving her strength, holding her up so that she could do her true purpose.

"Thank you," she whispered and let the card flutter from her hand and shoved her way through the drawing room doors.

15

"Twenty-seven silver pieces?" Aethan asked.

"Yup."

"For this decrepit thing?"

"Twenty-seven," the stable woman repeated. She stood with her arms folded across her belly.

Aethan closed his mouth, which had been hanging open, and looked back over the wooden slats at the half dead donkey still chewing the same mouthful of feed he'd been chewing when Aethan had gotten there.

"That's robbery," he muttered.

"Robbery? Not if you agree to buy it. Not if it's a mutually agreed upon contract. Isn't that the way of you Freelanders?"

If he'd been in the Freelands he wouldn't have had to buy a shitty donkey in the first place.

"Look boy," the woman continued, managing to look down at him, despite being shorter. "For some reason I can't get my head around, you want the cheapest beast I got. You don't want a horse, don't even want a shitty horse. You want Greg here. Now, I'm not asking questions. I'm not running off to the bluebacks to let them know how strange it is a half baked, half gimp Korkin runaway is looking to buy a dying donkey. I'm just telling you the price is all."

Aethan moved his maimed hand behind his back.

"How much for that horse then?" He tilted his head toward the gray gelding in the next stall.

"A hundred gold rakes."

Aethan nodded. Overpriced. Hilariously overpriced. An image came to his mind of the Dominion woman on her knees, eyes wide while the flesh burned from her bones. Then he thought of Jaaque's corpse, of Jaaque's mouth wide open in a silent scream. Aethan frowned and shook the image away.

He reached into the pockets of the coat he'd stolen and fingered the slaver bones he had there. They were new. His old ones, the ones he'd had from before the Greenwall, the one's he'd taken from the gibbets over his father's land, had burned away with the rest of this things. These ones were rough, the edges not yet worn. He doubted they were actually slaver bones. They probably weren't even human. The little Freelander shop he'd bought them from also sold pork. Aethan dug beneath them and counted out the coins for the donkey.

The donkey was slow, but it could bear the weight of the cart. It swayed from side to side as it went, stumbling slightly every few steps. He just needed it to get through the Nouvre Vil Gate, then it could fall over and die as it pleased.

The outer city had erupted with bluebacks the morning after the fire at the pikelord's house and Aethan had spent the last few weeks renting a room from a distrustful old couple who wanted nothing to do with Aethan, but wanted very much to do with his money. The room had an empty window with wooden shutters that Aethan kept open so he could watch his cart parked just outside. He'd run a rope from it's hitch, through the window, and around his wrist, so that he'd wake if someone tried to take it. No one did. The blueback presence never really died down, but he was out of time. If he waited any longer the inn would sell his horse.

Greg walked slower than the crowd until the people all became one mass, squeezing through the Nouvre Vil Gate. It would have drawn too much attention to pull the cart through himself. Where is your horse? Why didn't you get your horse before you got your cart? Where did you keep the cart? What do you know about the body we found there?

The questions swirled through Aethan's head faster and faster as the flow pushed his cart forward and beneath the massive wall.

The raised sides held several inquisitors, with their white feathers swaying back and forth as they looked up and down the passage, studying the travelers. Aethan could feel their eyes on him, gathering to him like moths to a flame, but he resisted the urge to pull his hat down. They would see him. There was no avoiding it. The worst he could do was seem that he had something to hide. Instead he gripped the reins between the thumb and pinky of his maimed hand, and slid the other into his pocket, to rub at the slaver bones there.

He forced himself to breathe. He saw them speaking into each others' ears, whispering back and forth about him. His hand trembled. His breath was shallow. They would come for him. They would stop him. And he would either die, or everyone else would.

And then he was through. He emerged from the dark of the passage and the inquisitors' eyes slid back to the crowd. He pulled Greg over to the inn and then turned and looked over his shoulder at the Gate. Nothing. They couldn't care less about him.

Aethan grimaced, and wondered what he actually would have done if they'd tried to arrest him. The same as he had done before, no doubt, and the other people in the crowd would have paid the price. But he didn't have to think about it. It had not happened.

Aethan rubbed again at the little bones in his pocket, his fingers already learning their edges and indentations. They were good bones, even if they were just a pig's. Aethan was not above such things.

"Guns you say?"

"Guns," Aethan repeated. "Matchlocks that your trade depots wouldn't buy."

The clerk took in a deep breath and grimaced. He was a big man and sat behind a counter in the Customs House. The room was divided up into cubbies, where other men sat and collected fees and taxes from the long lines of merchants and passengers looking to rent space on the myriad ships in the Sheras Harbor. The man in front of Aethan spilled out over the sides of his little stool, with his shoulders hunched over like the walls were closing in around him and his legs taking up all the space underneath the table. One of his meaty hands clutched a tiny pen, glistening with fresh-dipped ink, and the other held his place in the massive ledger before him. Aethan thought of the page he'd ripped out of Jaaque's own ledger. The one still in his coat pocket.

"Guns," the clerk said again, keeping his teeth in a grimace. "Sorry, friend, but you can't ship weapons here."

"You can't ship weapons to other countries," Aethan corrected. "I want to ship them to Domsar."

The man blinked at him.

"Which is in the Dominion," Aethan clarified.

Aethan didn't typically travel by boat in the Dominion. The rules were almost impossible to keep straight, but he'd done enough research to know what he could and couldn't do. His goal was not Domsar, but from the Dominion's capital, the road to Bergshalen was considerably shorter.

The clerk sighed and pushed his ledger to one side of the table. He reached under the counter to pull out another tome and dropped it in front of him. The table bent slightly from the impact.

"Rules, Laws, and Regulations of Sheras and Dominion Shipping and Transit."

"That's what I was told last I was here," Aethan said.

The man didn't answer but methodically leafed through its pages. He found the page he was looking for, and scanned down it with his finger until he found the appropriate passage.

After another moment, he lifted his head and hissed through a grimace again. "Sorry friend. It is not permitted to transport by ship or over water any guns, blades or other weapons intended to sell or gift to any foreign country, people or persons."

"Well," Aethan said, trying hard not to be frustrated. "It's a good thing I'm going to Domsar. Which is in the Dom-in-i-on."

"Ah, but it is the intent that matters, not the location."

"Look, I'm trying to-"

"What's going on here?" A sharp voice cut Aethan off and a better dressed clerk wearing a badge of office stepped into his field of vision.

"Oh for blessed fuck," Aethan whispered.

"He'd trying to ship guns, sir."

"Can't ship gun's over sea. Not to other kingdoms."

"That's what I said, sir!"

"Then what's the problem?"

"I," Aethan said, holding his good hand against his chest, "am shipping them to Domsar."

"Ah," the manager said and turned to the clerk with a knowing air. "Domsar is in the Dominion."

"Yes, sir!" the clerk said and then pushed the "Rules, Laws, and Regulation of Sheras and Dominion Shipping and Transit" across the counter. The manager bent over the book and then snapped upright.

"Ah," he said.

"It's about intent," the clerk said.

The manager turned back to Aethan. "It's about intent," the manager repeated.

"I intend to sell it in Domsar," Aethan said through clenched teeth.

The room was hot with the weight of all the people jammed into the building, making Aethan sweat despite the chilly air of mid-fall. He felt a headache coming on.

"But you can only sell weapons through the government trade Depots, you see--" the manager began.

"I know! I'm not new to this!" Aethan snapped.

The manager raised his eyebrows, and Aethan mouthed an apology. He wasn't supposed to make a scene.

"Well then, you see, all the trade depots buy from the same lists, so if you can't sell the weapons here in Sheras, then..." He trailed off for Aethan to finish the sentence.

Aethan did not, but the clerk kindly obliged. "Then he can't sell them in Domsar either!"

"Correct." The manager looked meaningfully at Aethan. "Which, because you are not new to this whole thing, you know. Which means?"

Again, the clerk filled in for Aethan, who just gave a stony stare. "That he knows he can't sell them in Domsar and..." he paused for emphasis, "intends to sell them outside of the Dominion!"

The manager rapped his knuckle against the counter. "Precisely."

Both of them looked at Aethan, and the clerk took in another long hiss of breath. "So sorry, friend. But there is nothing we can do."

"I..." Aethan took in a deep breath of his own. "I just... really, really need a break here. Is there anything I can do?"

The two Dominion officials were quiet for a moment, and then the manager spoke, turning his head slightly away to look at both him and the clerk.

"Are you...?" the manager said.

"Are you...?" the clerk echoed.

"Offering a bribe?" the manager finished.

Aethan paused for a moment before answering, wondering if that was an invitation to offer or an invitation to get himself thrown in prison. It didn't matter. Aethan didn't have enough money to make a real bribe, not anymore.

"No, sirs," Aethan said, his voice falling. "I just wondered if there was some rule in there that would help me out."

"Ah," the manager said.

"Ah," the clerk said and sucked in another breath between his teeth. "So sorry, Friend, but there is nothing we can do."

"Right," Aethan said, "Thank you," and he turned to push his way out of the Customs House.

He stepped out into the open air and took a deep, calming breath. The air outside was cool and smelled strongly of the sea. He turned and looked out at the water lapping against the Nor-so, which continued on after the land ended, jutting out several hundred yards into the bay. Other wood and stone docks branched off from the ancient Amaranthine structure like the legs of a centipede, glaringly imperfect next to the Amaranthine granite.

With a huff, Aethan turned away from the water and trudged across the street to where he'd left his cart in easy sight of the Customs House. Why the denizens of the Dominions consented to live under such tyranny was beyond him. The largest dock in the whole damn world and none of the ships could take him the two-days journey down the coast.

TokTok and Greg stood at the side of the road next to the cart just where Aethan had left them. Aethan passed an eighth to the boy he'd hired to watch them, climbed aboard his cart, and trundled back down the Nor-so. He wasn't looking forward to another pass through the Nouvre Vil Gate, but he had no choice. It didn't feel much like he had any choices recently, not since he'd decided to step into the pikelord's house. He felt like a mine cart, trundling into the darkness on a predetermined path.

With the way by sea blocked to him, there were two routes left. One went south of the mountains and would take near three months, and the other went north of the mountains, through an old Amaranthine pass, and would take about six weeks. He knew the southern route, had traveled parts of it before, but he didn't know the northern one. He'd heard mention of it and seen it on maps, but that was it. Aethan looked over his shoulder at the cart full of expensive and obsolete weapons. He was in a race against time. He had to beat the flintlock technologies spread west, or his cart full of weapons would be a cart full of scrap. Once again, there wasn't much of a choice. He nodded at the sky, pulled Jaaque's wide-brimmed hat down low over his eyes, and rode down the Nor-so.

16

"What did I tell you?" Aedgar asked.

Saara rolled her eyes and pushed past him. He stepped in front of her, but Saara planted her feet and shoved the box she was carrying into his arms.

He caught it clumsily and stumbled back into the foyer. "You're supposed to use the servant's door!" he groaned.

Saara took the box from him. "If Carlotte tells me to do it, I'll do it. Otherwise, piss off, Aedgar."

He huffed and closed the door behind her. Saara stopped at the foot of the staircase and prepared herself for the climb. God, she hated those stairs. They were truly a reminder that life was suffering.

"Miss Akar!"

Saara turned to see Enriq gliding across the marble floor. Saara set the box down and leaned against the balustrade.

She didn't much like Enriq. He was a tall and judgmental man who had been licking Cainia's ass for so long he'd forgotten what anything other than shit tasted like, and if the staff's whisperings were to be believed, its wasn't just metaphorical. The Lady Cainia DeSheras certainly hadn't had any other male company since Saara had been there. Not that Saara didn't do her own share of ass licking, *metaphorically*, but her's was in service of a great end. Enriq had been in the tower for decades, and he would stay there until he became too old for Cainia to have a use for him.

"There was a dispute in the drawing room this morning," he said.

Saara raised an eyebrow. "A dispute?"

"The Lady Cainia has ordered Madame Carlotte to remain confined to the tower. She is to have no access to money, and you," Enriq said, "are to stop your travel preparations immediately."

Saara's eyes went wide. "What happened?"

Enriq waved a hand through the air. "Nothing to concern yourself with."

"It sounds like it concerns me."

"And yet, it doesn't. Do I make myself clear, Miss Akar?" He stepped closer and looked down his nose at her.

Saara stepped forward to match him. "You've made Cainia clear," Saara said and then wrinkled her nose. "Your breath smells like shit."

He flinched back, and Saara turned around and lifted up the box. It hadn't gotten any lighter.

Saara began her climb. She would ask one of the other servants what had happened. Probably Selene. Nothing happened in the tower that Selene didn't gossip about.

As she finished the first flight, Saara began to smile. All things considered, this was the best possible outcome. She'd wasted good favors on the violinist, and Val would be crushed, but she had no business going on an expedition. She knew the tower. She knew the city. She didn't know the rest of the world, and she didn't see the point in learning about it. Saara crested the fifth landing and paused, realizing Carlotte would be in a ripe mood. Saara considered just going back down to her room to let Carlotte cool off, but no, Carlotte was expecting her, was expecting the box of books. Carlotte wouldn't take her imprisonment lying down. She'd be busy as a bee with her work on the animal force, and Saara would be there to help her with it. Saara kept climbing. She'd probably come out ahead from all this. She'd bought a lot of things with Carlotte's money for the expedition. She could sell it off easily enough, and she doubted Carlotte would ask for the money back. She never did. The proceeds would go into Saara's little hidden compartment in her room, her Ryker fund, the funds she'd use to buy some land when this all paid out.

Saara got to the seventh floor and knocked on the door to Carlotte's laboratory. No answer. She knocked on the door to Carlotte's study. No answer. It was always the last one she tried. She knocked on the bedroom door. Nothing. Either Carlotte wasn't taking visitors, or... she was in Elspeth's room. Saara groaned and looked at the stairs behind her. When she was a Ryker, she would build an estate with only one floor. Lady Akar, the Flat Lord, they'd call her. Saara grimaced and resumed her climb. She really needed to stop eating so much.

With a harrumph, she stepped onto the ninth platform and took a moment to get her breath under control. Carlotte always looked at her funny when she was out of breath, and Saara wasn't trying to give Carlotte anything to snap at.

Saara knocked at Elspeth's bedroom door.

"Enter," came the reply, and Saara eased the door open with one hand, balancing the box on one knee.

Carlotte stood on the open balcony directly opposite the door. Elspeth's bedroom was on the western curve of the tower. Her room looked out over the Nouvre Vil and the outer city and off into the Dominion countryside twenty-four and half miles away. Saara didn't know that number off the top of her head. It was listed on a bronze plaque mounted by the balcony door. There was one at each balcony in the tower, put there by one of Carlotte's ancestors who'd decided to calculate the distance to the horizon at every point. Because science, apparently. The sun had just gone down, and there was an orange and pink glow on the clouds silhouetting Carlotte.

Saara waited by the door, but Carlotte didn't turn around, so Saara put the box down by Elspeth's bed and then joined her mistress on the balcony. The view was only slightly hampered by the wire cage that encircled all the balconies above the third floor. She assumed they were strong enough to stop one from falling, but Saara had no desire to test it.

Saara coughed to remind Carlotte that she was there, and Carlotte patted the stone railing at her waist in response. Saara moved as she was bade and wondered how many others, even among the Ryker class, had witnessed such a view.

"You heard?" Carlotte asked, still looking out.

"I bit. I heard the outcome."

"And?"

Saara looked at Carlotte, but her mistress's face gave no hint. She was so young, and yet she looked so stoic and... miserable. "I'm sorry. Whatever it was. I'm sure it must have been difficult."

"It was."

There was a long pause.

"Can I trust you, Saara?" Carlotte asked.

Saara looked up sharply, the sudden excitement of impending opportunity coursing through her. "Of course, Madame."

Carlotte nodded. "I... I still want to go. To Bergshalen."

Saara nodded understandingly. "I know, but your mother-"

"Can not get wind of it," Carlotte hissed. She stepped closer to Saara so they were only inches apart. "We need to go now. Tomorrow, if at all possible."

Saara blinked, unsure of what to say. A pit was forming in her stomach, and it wasn't because of the dizzying height.

"Madame-"

"My mother will have the doors watched, but I can get out. I'll need a carriage and horse with drivers that aren't part of the household. They should meet me just outside the west entrance to the tower grounds."

Carlotte pointed down to the gate in the fence below. Saara gripped the stone railing and looked down.

"I've a private errand to run," Carlotte went on. "Give me the carriage and a cart and drivers, and I'll meet you and the rest of the expedition by the Nouvre Vil Gates just before the sun sets, when the traffic is most chaotic. We will be gone from Sheras before the night is complete."

Saara looked up, and she must have looked panicked because Carlotte's face softened and she reached out a hand to rest lightly on Saara's shoulder, just barely touching the skin of her neck. Saara wasn't sure the last time Carlotte had touched her like that, if she ever had.

"I know what I'm asking, Saara. You've been there for me these last few years. You've helped me in all my pursuits, and I see you. Please. Help me, and I will be indebted to you." Carlotte looked into Saara's eyes for a long moment. "Will you do this for me?"

Saara looked back, her mouth agape. "I... Of course, Madame," Saara said, and then after a pause, "I am your woman."

"Good." Carlotte's light touch turned to a hard grip and pulled Saara back into Elspeth's room. There was a framed map of the continent on one wall, and Carlotte pulled Saara up to it. She pointed to Sheras in the upper right corner.

"We cannot go by sea," she said and drew her finger down the coast. "Nor can we go by road through the Dominion proper." She drew her finger south across the land. "The Inquisition will be watching, and they will turn us back."

"The Inquisition?" Saara asked, feeling several steps behind.

"We go west," Carlotte bulled on. "North to Irondale and then up the Iron river through the mountains and to the colonies. From there, across the badlands to Thorlaille and then to the splitting. It will add some time, some weeks to the journey, but it is the only way. The Inquisition will not be strong here," she said, tapping on the Dominion frontier beyond the eastern mountains.

"Everything I've prepared is for the ships..." Saara said, barely above a whisper.

Carlotte nodded. "You'll need to rearrange. Carriages. Supplies. The works. Will the violinist still be available?"

"I'm not sure. I'll need to reach out..."

"Good. And Saara, you must find someone else to make the arrangements. The Inquisition is watching you. They saw you secure the ships," Carlotte said, and a spasm of annoyance crossed her face. It was gone moments later.

She pulled a piece of paper from a pocket and held it out to Saara. "I'll need these things taken from the tower. Let no one know your purpose. Go. You have much to do," Carlotte said and then turned and went back out onto the balcony. She resumed her position against the evening sky, the silhouette almost identical to when Saara had entered.

In a daze, Saara backed out of the room and closed the door. She turned and grasped the wooden railing and looked down through the crisscrossing staircases to the floor of the tower.

Could she do this?

She'd be directly disobeying Cainia's order, and Cainia would see that Saara was fired even if Carlotte tried to protect her. But if she didn't, Carlotte would fire her. Cainia wouldn't do Saara any favors for ratting out her daughter, and Saara would be back out on the street, her dreams of being a Ryker squashed.

From her vantage point, the flights of stairs below seemed to swim back and forth. Saara gripped the balustrade harder. She wasn't at the top yet, but she was so close, and she had so far to fall. Enriq said that Carlotte had no access to money, so Saara would have to front it. The gold she had squirreled away to start her life as a Ryker would be spent on carriages and supplies and men, and when this all went to shit, she'd have nothing left. Nothing to show for her years under Carlotte's collar.

Saara looked across the chasm before her at the last flight of stairs, the ones that led to the roof, out of the tower, and into the fresh air. She was so close.

Carlotte was risking much too, Saara knew. She was running out on her marriage, on her mother, on her city. If she came back empty-handed, she would return to gossip and ridicule, and her position would be irreparably damaged.

Saara's legs steadied, and the vertigo finally left her vision. There really was no choice. She had tied herself to Carlotte, and if Carlotte fell from her tower, then Saara would fall too.

"What's it like?" Jarund asked, striking the flint and then cupping his hands to blow on the pipe until the brown leaf glowed red.

"Hmm?" Saara said, pulling out of her reverie. They sat in the kitchen at The Den, where Scram would be cooking if it had been any decent hour. It smelled warm. Saara knew that wasn't a proper smell, but there was no other way to describe it. Burning wood and simmering soup and the feeling of coming into the warmth after a childhood full of cold.

"The Vil. Living there an all," Jerund said. He breathed out a cloud of smoke and then held the pipe out to her.

She shook her head. "It's different."

"Nicer than all this, I'd imagine." Jerund motioned around him with the pipe, and the smoke from its cup twirled in the air.

Saara thought about her little room in the servant's area of the tower, how the warmth from the furnaces didn't always make its way through the hallways to compete with her shutters. She grunted out a chuckle. "Not always. You don't have to stay up with me."

"Nonsense. You barely come round for five years and then twice in a month. Gonna get my gettin' while the gettin's good."

Saara laughed and sipped at her water. She wished it was something else. Tea even. She'd been up for more than a day, and the warmth of the room and the good company, and good memories got her sleepy. Saara looked to the door in the corner that led out into the alley. That door was where the good memories stopped, back before her uncle came to Sheras, before the Den had taken her in, after her mother had died and she had to beg for coin on the Nor-so. Saara wondered how many starving children were out there right now, unable to join the ranks of the privileged poor.

"So why you do it then?" Jerund asked. "If it ain't so nice?"

"Good food."

Jerund laughed a big belly laugh and then cut himself off, remembering people were asleep elsewhere in the Den.

"And lots of it too I don't imagine," Jerund smiled. He reached out and pinched at her arm, and Saara smacked him away. "Bet you've thickened out in all kinds of places."

"You keep talking like that and I'll cut your dick off, friend," Saara said, putting on a nasty glare.

Jerund giggled and took a puff of his pipe and the smoke got in his lungs wrong and got him to coughing. Saara smiled despite herself and clapped the big man on the back. Then, there was shouting in the streets.

They both looked up sharply, and then Jean burst through the door, soaking wet. Rain pelted down outside.

"Bracille!" he screeched and Jerund was up, the pipe smoking and forgotten on the table. Jerund took the boy by the shoulders and held him firm.

"What's wrong, Jean?"

"It's Rold. We was slinging down by the smelters. Sanjid's boys was there. Rold threw knife."

"Fuck," Saara whispered, all her good memories suddenly drowned out by a flood of bad ones.

"Bracille!" the boy shouted again. "They're gonna kill him,

Bracille!"

The door into the Den opened, and Bracille came through. There were others behind him. Scram, Jenny, Shamble, and more. The kitchen was suddenly very crowded.

"Bracille!" the boy cried.

"What happened?" Bracille asked.

"Rold got into it with Sanjid by the smelters," Jarund said.

Bracille nodded and looked to Jean. "Rold still there?"

"I don't know," the boy said. There were tears in his eyes. "Rold was running. Westward. They were looking to kill him, Bracille."

Bracille nodded and then began spewing orders. "Scram, stay here with Jenny. Lock the doors tight. Keep steel ready."

"Right, Boss," the old cook said.

Jenny nodded beside him. Bracille continued.

"Emande with me to the smelter. Shamble, Jerund, and Saary, take east, north, and south of the smelter and look for Rold. You find him, you yell-"

"Woah," Saara said and stood. "I'm not part of this, Bracille."

The room was silent, save for Jean's sniffling, and all eyes were on her.

Bracille stepped close to her.

"I'm not part of the Den anymore," Saara said, holding up her hand. "I made that clear when-"

"I've got four boys out there doing your Master's bidding, Saara. Four boys that should be looking for Rold."

"Bracille-" she began.

"Rold needs you," he said, cutting her off. "You come here out of the blue and ask for help twice, and you-"

"I paid you. Both times," Saara hissed.

"This is family, Saara. If you leave him to die, then that's on you." He turned to the others. "Jean. Take me and Emande to where you last saw Rold. Everyone understand?"

"Yes, Boss," they all said in unison.

"Go," he said, and they all trundled out the door.

Jenny ran off into the den, and there were only Scram and Saara in the kitchen. Scram looked at her the way he used to when Saara would come asking for food before supper was ready. "God damn it," she said, and ran out into the rain.

It was coming down hard, and the others were already out of eyesight, but Saara knew the way. She knew the Den's territory better than she knew herself. Some buildings had changed, but the streets were the same. The rain ran down her face and down her back, and as she ran she felt the burn in her legs and felt the adrenaline run, and it felt good.

She crossed south of the smelters, and when she emerged on the other side, she saw Jerund coming out of his own alley. They both shook their heads and looped back to take other streets. There was no need to talk. They were wolves in the pack, running together with one singular purpose.

She heard yelling and followed it, coming out into a muddy street and seeing Shamble splashing through. He waved his hand in a circle and then pointed north. Saara immediately turned down the nearest alley, sprinting for all she was worth.

The breath hissed out of her, and she heard more yelling and a scream, and then she barreled out of the alley onto another street. Two men ran towards her, and she saw Shamble running after them. Saara scrambled back into the alley and waited. One, two, three, and then she charged back out, catching the leader in the side with her shoulder, sending both of them tumbling in the mud.

Saara landed hard, and the breath whooshed out of her, but she scrambled to her feet while the man she hit tried to do the same.

"Scarbe!" the other man yelled. He drew a long knife from his belt, and Saara drew hers, but then Shamble roared in. He held a carpenter's hammer in one hand and a hatchet in the other, and at the sight of him, the man with the knife turned and ran on.

Saara took the initiative and jumped at the man she'd hit. She kicked at his knee, and he screamed and tumbled back into the mud. Shamble came up and kicked him hard in the face, and his head snapped back, cutting his scream into a gurgle.

There was more yelling behind them, and Shamble turned back, staring into the downpour. "Bracille needs us," he said.

"What about him?" Saara asked.

"Bring him."

Saara nodded and pulled a blade out of the man's belt and stuck it through her own. She grabbed him by the collar and hauled him to his feet, old muscle in her straining for what felt like the first time in years. The man tried to say something, but blood and water poured down his face into his mouth, and all that came out was a garbled moan.

"Move," she growled and half-carried him after Shamble, who'd disappeared back into the darkness.

The night was ending, and the faint glow of dawn was beginning to show through the downpour.

She followed the shouting, and as she came closer, the sounds became words.

"You're in Den territory!" came Bracille's voice.

"Because this boy started shit! He killed Leon," came another.

Forms took shape. A group of men standing on two sides of a street. Bracille stood out in front, flanked by Jerund and Emande. Across the length of mud stood others. One form kneeled in the muck.

"They was slinging on our side of the-" cried the kneeling one. It was Rold. He was cut off with a thump as one of the men knocked him onto his side.

"That true, Sanjid? You breaking the lines?" called Bracille.

"Blood for blood," One man on the other side said. He'd a long beard and a bald head. Saara recognized him. It was Sanjid, famous as any in the outer city.

"The lines are their own issue," Sanjid roared. "It is murder we speak of tonight. Leon is dead, and we will have our vengeance." He drew a long blade from his belt, and the ringing of the scabbard pierced the rain.

"No!" cried Bracille.

"Whatever you take from Rold, I'll take from Scab!" Saara yelled, and the two sides turned to her.

"That your name? Scab?" Saara whispered.

"Scarbe," the man in her fist gurgled.

"Scarbe!" Saara yelled. "This piece of shit," and she dug the point of her knife into his side, not enough to do any real damage, just enough to make him scream and drive the point home.

The rain came down, and the dawn grew brighter. The rest of the two sides were slowly coming into focus, two little armies fighting over lines in the mud, fighting over the Rykers' scraps, and here Saara was right in the middle of it, just like she'd never left.

"You want to start a war, Bracille?" Sanjid said.

"Give us back our man, and we'll give you yours. The happenings here can be settled later. I'll see to any wrongs my man has done."

Sanjid barked a laugh. "You'll see to it, eh?"

"You have my word," Bracille said.

There was a moment's silence, filled only with the pattering of the rain and the ragged breathing of Scarbe. Then, Sanjid motioned with a hand, and one of his men kicked Rold towards the other side. He floundered in the mud, half running, half crawling to Bracille's feet.

"No hard feelings," Saara said into Scarbe's ear and released him. He sagged down and stumbled across the street. One of his crew caught him and snarled at her. Saara shrugged and set her hands on her belt.

"Blood for blood, Bracille," Sanjid said. "This isn't over until we get what's owed."

"Get back on your side of the line," Bracille said. "And fucking stay there."

Sanjid nodded and then turned and walked away. His crew turned and went with him, some of them walking backwards to keep Bracille's side in sight until they were gone.

"Blood for blood," Sanjid called out from the rain and pre-morning gloom.

"You okay, Rold?" Bracille asked.

"Am ahkay," he said, the words all bungled up. His face was swollen, and blood ran from several places.

Bracille walked up to him and took the boy's face in his hands. "Your nose is broken," he said.

"I-- Aack!" Rold screamed as Bracille snapped the boy's nose back into place with his thumbs.

Bracille let him go, and the boy sagged down. Jerund stepped forward and held him up.

"Let's get back," Bracille said. He waved a hand over his head, and the crew turned and trundled home through the muck. Soldiers marching to their captain's order.

The mood cheered when they returned. Bracille gave the boy a stern warning and said that there would be consequences for his actions, which Rold took in solemn form, blood dripping onto the floor, but then Bracille smiled, patted the boy on the back, and said he was happy to have him safe. There were more slaps on the back and talks of being wetted on the streets. Then Scram pulled out some bad wine, and they drank and toasted the night.

Saara sat in the corner, watching Rold's face, and wondered how it would look when it healed. One of the boy's teeth was loose, and with a cheer, he pulled it free, and there was another round of toasting.

Bracille sat opposite Saara on the other side of the room, and when the dawn came fully, and the crowd disbursed to their daily duties, he caught her eye with his.

"Go on. Get some sleep, Rold. You worked all night," Bracille said and Rold stumbled deeper into the den to fall asleep in some corner.

Then it was just her and the man she used to think she loved.

"Slinging," Saara said. "The Den selling pike now?"

Bracille nodded, his lips a firm line. "Ghost is gone. Market opened up. Sanjid's doing it too, and the rest of the crews."

"No wonder things got bloody."

Bracille knocked his knuckle against the wall. "Gotta pay the rent somehow. Your Ryker friends don't let up."

Saara gave a weak smile but said nothing. Bracille put his head in his hands and rubbed at his temples. "My boys should be back with news of your new crew soon. And your supplies. It was quite a laundry list you gave them."

"And I paid well for it. You'll pay the rent easily enough for the next few months."

She'd given him a big chunk of what she had. Her life savings half gone in a day for Carlotte's fancy.

"That you did." Bracille leaned back and finished his wine in a single gulp. "I need something from you."

"You want me to take Rold," Saara said, and Bracille looked up. "How did you-"

"Sanjid will kill him first chance he gets, and that'll start a war. Pike gets people's blood up. It's nasty business. You should stay out of it."

"It's not that simple."

"I know. That's why I left." Saara motioned to the mud on her clothes and then to Rold's blood on the floor. "To leave all this, you actually have to leave."

The door opened, and a lanky fellow stepped through. Regie. He'd come to the Den about the time Saara had. "Shit. What'd I miss?" he said, looking from them to the blood to the wine.

"A lot. How'd it go?" Saara asked, standing.

"Fine. Good. Got a crew together. Cook. Lady's maids. Laborers. Two old soldiers. The whole lot."

"Good folk?"

"I dunno. Didn't have much time to dig."

"And the carriages? The supplies?" Saara asked.

"Yeah. Got the lot," he yawned. "We'll have it waiting for you at the gate a bit before evening time."

"Thank you," Saara said. She grabbed his forearm and shook it once. "Really. Thank you."

He gave a big grin that split his face in half. "Course, Saary. Anything for you. And your coin."

"You'll take him then? You'll keep him safe?" Bracille called out from his side of the room, the same pensive frown on his face that she'd found so attractive for so long.

"I will. He deserves better than this. Everyone does."

Saara left the Den that afternoon and headed to an inn middle-way down the Nor-So in the outer city. There was a girl posted up under the stable's awnings waiting for her. She waved a roll of parchment when she saw Saara. Saara held out her hand.

"Silver," the girl said. "I ran it to the theater and waited all night for a reply. Not having you cheat me."

Saara flipped her the coin and took the paper. Saara braced herself and then opened it, moving her lips with the letters.

"What's it say?" the girl asked, leaning around her to look at it. "Spent all morning wondering. Hoped it was a love letter. Seems awful short, though."

"Oh thank God," Saara breathed.

"Good news?"

"Yes."

"Want me to take back a reply? I'll do it for another eighth. I could be your personal messenger!" the girl said.

"I'm alright. Thanks, kid," Saara said and turned to go.

"Well, what's it say?!" the girl yelled after her. "I have to know!"

"It says I'm leaving Sheras," Saara responded and stepped into the Nor-So traffic.

There were still a few hours until she needed to be at the gate, and Saara wanted nothing more than to crawl up to her room in the tower and sleep those hours away. She couldn't, though, not with her last hours in Sheras, the city where she'd spent her entire life. Saara needed to see her uncle before she left.

Jaaque Akar hadn't been there when her mother died. He'd been in the south, working for the Mareshal, but he'd sought her out when he'd been reassigned to Sheras. By then, Saara hadn't needed him. She'd been tight with the Den, but when that began to sour, he'd given her the tools to start a better life. He'd taught her to read, sort of, and when a friend of his needed some help, he'd recommended Saara. It wasn't much of a job, body guarding for a petty Ryker, but it had started her on the path that led to Carlotte. He was the only family she had, and she was the only family he had. She needed to say goodbye. It was the least she could do.

It took her half an hour to reach the edge of the outer city, but by the time the Mareshal's warehouse loomed up before her, she still had no idea what she was going to say. She was shit at goodbyes, but then again, she was shit at planning expeditions and that seemed to be going fine. Maybe this goodbye would be like that. She'd say just the right thing, give him a firm handshake, lie about seeing him soon, and then make an awkward exit.

Saara crossed to the south side and waited for her uncle to finish intaking a cart full of grain. When the farmer climbed back up and drove his cart away, Saara walked to her uncle. Only, it wasn't Jaaque.

He wore the same hat her uncle wore, and the same uniform, but it wasn't him. The man in her uncle's clothes waved her over.

"You a merchant?" he asked.

"Where's Jaaque?" she said, ignoring his question.

"I don't know a Jaaque."

"He works here. He runs this warehouse," Saara said, a bit of panic creeping into her voice.

"Oh. The one who worked here before," the man said, and he frowned. "He's dead."

Saara's eyes widened.

"What?"

"It was some nasty gang business from what I hear. Burned alive," the man in her uncle's clothes shuddered. "But no worries. I can help you just the same."

"I... he's my uncle."

"Oh... I'm sorry. If you're looking for his things, the Inquisition took them. They were crawling all over the place. I'd go up to inquisitor's yard."

Saara took a step back and then another.

"You alright, Miss?" the man in her uncle's uniform asked.

Saara didn't answer.

17

"Boy," a voice said above her.

Erika had the vaguest sense it was speaking to her.

"Boy," it repeated.

"I'm a girl," she muttered.

"What?"

"A girl, I'm a girl!" she yelled.

"Do you play, girl?"

Erika looked up from the street.

"Do I what?" The light was bright, too bright for her to bear, and she shuddered her eyes back to the cobblestones. The man's right boot nudged the black case leaning against the wall beside her.

"Of course I do," she mumbled. "Why else would I have an instrument?" She chuckled. The world swam around her. She focused on a round stone between her feet and tried to anchor her thoughts to it.

"What's that, girl?" The voice was farther away than she knew it should be.

"Yes!" she moaned and reached out to the box, pulling it close to her.

She wrapped herself around it, closed her eyes, and breathed in its musty scent. It was the smell of music, like an attic, like a chest of toys that meant adventure to a child, like a package of disappointment at a life turned out all wrong. Sorrow. Sorrow was a good base for music.

"Play something for me?" The voice was an echo. Fucking pike. The ripples were worse than the dive.

"I'll give you coin."

Her heart surged at that thought. She, sitting on the side of the street, an old crate pilfered from the docks as her chair. She would set up outside a tavern and play and play until her fingers bled, until her hands ached and her neck cramped, but the music would be worth it. It would flow out like a river and wash all her troubles out with it. She would play for coin and for food, and at the end of the day, when she played her bow down to a scant few hairs, she would have made just enough to restring it.

A fool's move, the other urchins would say. Buy food, they'd say. Buy a room with a fire. Why play if you end with nothing? She would shake her head. They did not understand what it was to be an artist, a musician. If there wasn't music, there was nothing. She could last a day without food, but she couldn't live an hour without music.

"Pikey trash."

The boots disappeared, and Erika wondered why the man had stopped. People didn't usually stop and talk to her. Maybe the old violin case had brought him. It was a ratty, moth-ridden thing, but an urchin with a violin case stood out on the street. Or maybe, more likely, the man had just been the pike. Not that it mattered. The man was gone, or he never was. When the pike swam away, she would figure it out.

She bowed her head against the case and withdrew into the ripples until a faint note hit her ear. She sat upright and strained to make out another. Nothing came at first, and then the pike gave her enough room to put together a thought. A violin was playing.

Erika staggered to her feet and braced herself against the wall. The pike swam around her, and she focused on another cobblestone a pace ahead.

Go away, little fishies. Swim away.

They listened, a little, and the world calmed a bit. Where did the note come from?

She listened again. All she heard was the street.

"Shut up!" she screamed.

"Fuck off, cunt," a man said and shoved her against the wall. She ricocheted off it and fell to the stones. Some part of her hurt, but she wasn't sure what. Then, another note came, higher, floating through the air like a leaf on the wind. To the left. The concert hall was to the left. She picked up her case and staggered down the street, scraping her shoulder against the buildings as she went.

The pike faded the farther she got. Whether it was the end or just another ripple was difficult to tell, but she had a purpose, and it did not matter. The notes were clearer now, and Erika followed them.

She didn't have to go far. The grand theater was just a block away from where she'd been sitting. That's why she'd sat there, she remembered, to be close to the music.

There wasn't much good in Sheras, the Rykers saw to that, but they hadn't ruined everything. The grand theater was a remnant from the Amaranthine Empire, nearly two thousand years old like the cathedral and the Nor-so, and the Senate, where they made all the rules. The theater rose like the DeSheras Tower towards the clouds, its top often obscured by the thick mists that came in off the docks. She'd heard it was a place of worship in the empire. It was grand enough. The doors at its front were so wide that ten people could walk through abreast, and three more could walk atop each other. As if people could walk on top of each other. That would be interesting. Another ripple was passing through her.

Erika climbed the too-big steps and went to the man who sat on a stool in front of the doors. He slapped a stick against one palm, watching her as she approached.

"Screw off, urchin," the man said as though she could be stopped when music was at stake.

"I'm here to play," Erika said, holding up the violin case in front of her.

"Like hell you are, screw off."

"I am. I'm going to be late for my duet," she said, trying to keep the pike from taking her entirely.

"Yeah? With who?" the guard asked.

"With the violinist who is currently playing."

"And who is that?" he asked. The pike pulsed around her in time with the beat the man played on his palm. Like a metronome.

She watched the stick rise and fall and said nothing.

"The great Visoletta. That's who," he said.

The ripple fell off, shorter this time. Her swim was coming to an end.

"Visoletta?" she whispered. She knew of Visoletta. The prodigy with the red cloak! Erika's mother had taken her to one of Visoletta's concerts in this very theater long ago. How alike her mother had said they looked. The same age. A face so similar to her own. Two sides of the same coin. So similar except Visoletta was a prodigy and Erika was a homeless pikey.

"Yeah," the guard said. "Visoletta. Last concert before she leaves Sheras, apparently. The run got cut short."

"The last?" Erika whispered. "Let me in, I must see her before-" She surged forward, and the guard shoved her backwards. She sat down hard, crying out at the pain that flashed through her tailbone.

"Fuck off, Urchin."

There were tears in her eyes, and she wiped them away before they could fall. She picked up her case and went around the corner, suppressing a limp as she walked, not wanting to give the doorman the satisfaction of knowing he'd hurt her. He did, though, and more than just a bruised tailbone. When he was out of sight, she sagged against the wall and let herself have a good cry for a good few minutes before gathering herself up and squeezing her eyes dry.

She needed to get herself together. This life wasn't sustainable. She had to get herself cleaned up, she had to throw away the last of her pike, and she had to find work. These childish fantasies about being a musician playing for a living on the street were just that. Childish. She'd thrown away any hope of a musical life when she'd left her mother's house.

The side of the concert hall she was walking down was a thin alley, the old city having crowded in on the ancient building over time. She looked ahead of her and saw no one. She looked behind and saw people walking along the main street, but no one in the alley with her. Perhaps, if she went a little deeper, she would come to a point where there was no one in sight, and when she got there, she would make the change and take charge of her life. She would enter this alley broken and miserable, and she would exit a bright young woman ready to take on the world.

The alley turned, and on her right was an alcove with a small, old door into the concert hall. A worker's entrance, perhaps, or a stage door. The barest hint of the music came through it. She thought of how wonderful it would be to see Visoletta sneaking out the door to avoid the uncomfortable pressure of her fans clamoring for autographs. Visoletta would come out and see Erika there, all alone, and Visoletta would take her under her arm and guide her into her new life. All she had to do was throw the pike away.

It was all she had to do.

But she didn't really have much left, just enough for a few more cuts… or one really good one. Maybe, instead of wasting it, she could see off her new life with just one more go, like a drunk toasting his future with one more swig before throwing his bottle against the ground. A toast would be good. A last hurrah.

She crouched down on the floor and flipped open the latches on her case. There was no violin. There had never been. She'd found the case in a garbage pile in the Nouvre Vil, but now it held her things: some rags, her little mirror, her tweezers. She disregarded those and opened the little compartment where a violinist would have kept their resin. She pulled out a tiny knife and an even smaller glass bottle with a cork stopper and a few drops of glistening silver. She looked at it for several moments. Its beauty, the way the liquid swam in little circles, was always magic to her.

She sat and winced at the pain in her tailbone. It didn't matter. It would all be gone soon. She pulled her grimy pants down. There was a crusty cloth stuck to her inner thigh, and with a grimace, she pulled it away, revealing a mass of old scars and new scabs. She pulled the collar of her shirt into her mouth and bit down. Then she placed the knife against the freshest scab, leaned back against the door-- and the door swung open and dumped her on her back. She squawked, and the bottle flew from her hand. She scrambled on her back and caught it just before it hit the ground.

"Thank God," she whispered, then she looked down at the blood pooling between her legs. She'd gotten herself good with the knife. She sat up against the door frame, grabbed the cloth, and pressed it into the cut. A lightless hallway ran into the building, like an entrance to some ancient cave that held all manner of dreams and treasure.

She couldn't go in, of course. That would be breaking and entering. The bluebacks would take her for sure. Beat her in the alley. Leave her a broken mess. But then again, she couldn't leave the door open for just anyone to wander in. Think of the damage they could do. Erika looked down at the bottle in her hand.

"Not now, little fishes. Soon," and she wiped the knife on the cloth, and stowed it and the bottle back in the resin compartment. Then she pulled her pants up, jostling the cloth so it would stay against her cut, and hefted the case.

She stepped into the building.

"I shouldn't be here," she whispered, but she had to find someone to lock the door. It was her duty. The faint music called to her from within. There was an old oil lantern with a flint and steel a few yards before the light ended, and she took it from the wall and fumbled at it until it lit. She went deeper, and the light from the door faded to nothing. There was only the flickering light of her lamp, casting demonic shadows behind the things that littered the hall. The music got louder as she went, and the beauty of it would have paralyzed her if not for the wonder of where she was.

She assumed she was someplace behind the stage. The walls were old, and in some places, crumbling. It wasn't the original Amaranthine granite. It was the flawed attempts of the Dominion to mimic the majesty of the Amaranthine Empire. Typical Ryker hubris to take such a grand space and break it up into smaller rooms that looked as though they hadn't been used in centuries.

It looked like an old prison. Perhaps the building hadn't always been used as a concert hall. Then she realized that the music was coming from above her.

She wasn't behind the stage. She was under it, perhaps only a few yards from the great Visoletta. She saw stairs in one corner and rushed up them as fast as she could without making a racket. Maybe she could find a way to the wings and see the concert!

At the top of the stairs was another hallway. She stopped and listened. The violin's haunted wail was coming from her left now. She was level with the it, and she tried to reach it, but all the doors were on her right. One of them was ajar, and Erika stopped and peered through. There were lanterns inside and what looked like racks of clothes. A dressing room. Visoletta's dressing room?

She reached out and touched the door with a trembling hand, and Erika wondered if it trembled because of Visoletta or because of the pike.

She stepped inside. There was a closet in the corner, and a suitcase open beside it. A mirror was on one wall with the lanterns hung in a circle around it, and beside the mirror, opposite Erika, was Visoletta's scarlet cloak.

Erika's breath caught in her throat. The cloak was Visoletta's calling card. She'd worn it when Erika had seen her play all those years ago, when they were both children, and Erika knew Visoletta was wearing it now. This must've been a spare. Erika walked into the room and touched it. It was heavy and soft, and Oh! How it would be to stand on the Grand Theater stage with that cloak flowing around her, to play her music, to enchant the audience with every note that poured out of her like blood from a slit wrist.

Erika looked over at the mirror. There was a table beneath it, covered in brushes and rouge like rich women wore. Like she used to put on her face when she snuck into her mother's bedroom. Oh, how her mother had screamed when she'd walked in. Erika reached out and touched a brush, but then recoiled when she saw her hand. It was covered in dirt and grime. She turned to the cloak and saw the mark of her fingers on the cloth. Her breath stopped in her throat. Who was she to ruin such beautiful things?

Then she saw the washbasin by the door.

Her clothes were off in an instant, and she turned the water black by the time she was done. She returned to the mirror and looked away with disgust. She couldn't bear to look at her body.

She tore through the open suitcase and pulled out clean underthings and a floor-length black travel dress. She adjusted herself and then slid them on. Oh, how gorgeous she felt!

Now, with her body covered, she turned back to the mirror. She hated her face too, with its awkwardly large nose and chin. Erika looked down at the tools she had to work with.

She'd spent enough secret time in front of her mother's mirror to know how to disguise it, how to draw attention to her cheekbones and make her eyes seem larger. She contoured and painted, and soon, her face almost made her happy. Almost. There was only so much she could do.

Her hair was disgusting, but she doubted she could comb out the mats, so she pulled it back and twirled it into a bun. Finally, she rose and draped the red cloak over her shoulders, and stepped back to look at herself.

She almost cried.

18

"Forty-two feet," Carlotte said as she peered over the railing. She hadn't been able to find a rope, and Saara had already gone before she thought to ask, so Carlotte had made do with bedsheets tied together and then knotted to the railing. She lifted and then dropped the pile of them over the edge. Now her purpose was set. If anyone walked through the gardens at that moment, her plan would be revealed, and her window to escape would close. Carlotte pulled at the knot. It seemed secure, but Carlotte had to admit, she knew nothing of knots.

"Forty-two," Carlotte said to the ground below. "It's nothing."

The first three floors had no balconies, and the windows there were secured with iron bars. It wasn't until the fourth floor that one could actually get outside, and thus, the fourth floor was her route of escape. It hadn't seemed like a big thing when she'd planned it. She would flip her legs over the edge like a hero in one of her childhood stories and then shimmy down like a spider on silk. For a summer feast, years ago, her mother had brought aerial dancers from across the sea. They had gone up and down the ropes of silk like it was nothing. Carlotte licked her teeth. It didn't seem like nothing now. Her grandfather had made a study on how human bodies were affected by falls from various heights. If she remembered correctly, at this height, there was only a fifty percent chance of death.

Carlotte teetered back from the railing and sat on her heels as the vertigo washed over her. She pressed her face into her hands and muffled a scream. She didn't have time for this! If a servant walked through the gardens, or entered the room behind her, or saw the dangling sheets from a lower window, then she might as well kiss her God-given mission goodbye.

"Sorry, God, the balcony was just too high," she whispered and then silently berated herself for using God's name in vain. Her strength was in God, as was her courage. Carlotte slipped a hand into her pocket and felt at the prayer beads there.

"It is high," she admitted, "but you're going to do it anyway, Carlotte," she whispered, and then stood.

She put one leg over the railing, realized she should have worn pants, and then put the other over. She clutched desperately at the knotted sheet. The breeze cut through her clothing. She took a breath and then rolled over onto her belly and wedged her feet between the columns. She stood, held the sheet firmly, and then lifted one leg and wrapped the sheet around it. She lowered herself a few inches, and then, when she felt her arms could hold her weight, she lifted the other foot.

For a moment, she held herself up and struggled to create enough friction with her feet, but the angle was awkward and Carlotte became very aware of how little arm strength she possessed. Her arms burned, and she tried to put her foot back on the balcony, but her arms gave way, and without her feet to stop her, she slammed into the stone and slid down the cloth. She clutched at it, and the friction burned her hands, but she could not stop herself until her hands snagged on the first knot. Her grip almost gave, but the adrenaline gave her strength.

She hung there for a moment, swinging gently five feet beneath the balcony, her feet still some thirty feet from the ground. She swung one leg around so that the cloth was wrapped around it, and then clamped her other foot against it. Her shoe dug into her leg, so she kicked it off and then held on for all she was worth. Carlotte gave another stifled scream of frustration. Why did it all have to be so difficult? Why couldn't things go her way just once?

Because, she thought, God doesn't make things easy for his children. Not for the ones he loves the most. He beats them on the anvil of life so that they can be forged into something stronger.

She clenched her teeth and set her face and gave her weight to her feet, and then she squatted, letting her arms extend over her head. Like a giant inchworm, she moved slowly down the sheet, passing the third-story windows, and then the second, and then, with about fifteen feet to go, the knot tying the sheet to the railing gave way.

Carlotte squeaked, holding back a scream while her heart fell out of her chest. Her left foot hit the ground first. She crumpled to her knees and spun sideways, tumbling several times and then crashing into a hedge. Her mouth opened, but she let out only a gasping breath. She was hurt, but she had to move. She had to go now before someone found her. She rolled over, gasped at the sharp pain in her left knee cap, and then forced herself to her feet. She stood, and her ankle screamed, but she did not fall. She bent down to feel it. It did not seem broken, but Carlotte had to admit, she knew little about practical medicine.

The sun was maybe an hour from the horizon. She needed to go, so Carlotte gritted her teeth and limped to the Western Gate. The gardens were not guarded unless there was an event, so she was not intercepted, and when she crossed the fence, she saw a carriage waiting down the hill, out of sight from the Tower grounds.

There was a cart attached to the back and a team of two horses at the front. Three men loitered by its side, looking up the hill towards her. Their gazes were hard when she approached, and when she beckoned them to come to her, they did not."

"Oi," one of them shouted when she was within a few dozen yards. "This ain't for you. Move along."

Carlotte stopped.

"You're here for me."

"You're the Lady Carlotte DeSheras?" the lead man said.

"Like hell," said the shorter one beside him.

Carlotte stared for several moments, and then looked down and understood. Her dress had been simple but elegant, but now her leg showed through a rip up the side, and the pale fabric was marred with dirt, grass stains, and a bit of blood seeping through at her left knee. Carlotte looked up at the men.

"I am the Lady Carlotte DeSheras. I've had a difficult time getting here."

The men did not move. Carlotte breathed out hard.

"My maid servant, Saara, sent you to pick me up."

"Slack sent us," the third man said. He was the largest of the lot.

"Slack?" Carlotte asked.

"Our boss," the tall one said.

"And he sent you to pick me up. Carlotte DeSheras. That's me. Let's go."

"Prove it," the shorter man said.

Carlotte was stunned. She'd never had to prove her identity before. She was known. Everyone always knew who she was.

"How else would I know who you were here for?" Carlotte asked.

"That is true," the short man said, turning to the big one behind him.

"Aye," said the big man, straightening up and putting his hands on his hips. "But it was Raphael who said we were looking for Madame DeSheras first. This woman's just repeating what Raphael said."

The short man nodded, and the three of them looked at Carlotte.

Carlotte felt her pulse in her temple. "If you don't stop this and take me where I ask, I will have Inquisitor's Yard cut the heads from your bodies and impale them on my fence," Carlotte said, pointing back at the curved fence that surrounded the tower.

The three looked at each other.

"It is the right time," the short one said.

"And she does sound like a Ryker," the big one said.

The lead man, Raphael, shrugged.

"Right you are, Madame," he said and then climbed up into the bench. The other two jumped into the cart at the back. Carlotte waited expectantly for a moment, and then shook her head and limped to the carriage.

"God give me strength," Carlotte muttered and opened her own door. Saara hadn't gotten trained footmen, but that wasn't what Carlotte had asked for. She knew there would be sacrifices.

"The DeSheras graveyard," Carlotte called out once she'd gotten settled.

"What?" Raphael asked.

Carlotte leaned out the window to see Raphael peering back at her. "What do you mean, what?"

"I mean, what is that?"

Carlotte's temper flared, and if her knee hadn't been on fire, she might have climbed out of the carriage and throttled the man. "Down this road. Second left. Grass. Tombstones. Take me to the main mausoleum..."

The man cocked an eyebrow.

"Big stone house for dead people," Carlotte said.

"Right," Raphael said, and clicked the horses into motion.

The ride wasn't long, but she had time to pull up her dress and look at her knee. Her cap was skinned and bleeding, and the knee itself had swollen to almost twice its size. Carlotte grimaced and pushed the fabric back down. It wasn't easy. It never was.

She opened her shutters and watched the tombstones roll by. The graveyard was a partial summit on the western Nouvre Vil hill, and the DeSheras Mausoleum was at the end of it, overlooking a small bluff. It was a massive thing, marble and cold. She had been there many times.

"Help me out," she called, and Raphael jumped down from his bench to do so. "You two," she said to the two in the back when she'd exited, "Open the door."

"We're going inside?" the big one asked.

"Yes. Go," she said. The two men looked at each other and then hopped out and heaved against the heavy door, revealing a stone stairway descending into the ground, like a cave yawning up at them.

"There are lamps and flint just inside. Light them," Carlotte said, leaning on Raphael's shoulder. The man smelled like he hadn't bathed in years. Carlotte tried to keep her bile back. Her knee was locking up, but with Raphael's help, she was able to hop down the few steps to the crypt. It was a long tunnel that stretched out to the edge of the hill and then turned back, snaking around itself to accommodate the ever-increasing dead of the Family DeSheras. The crypt was cleaned periodically by servants, so there was no growth of mold or fungus, and the walls and ceiling were mortared granite that kept all water at bay. It was colder down there than on the surface, but the prickling of her skin was comfortable and familiar to Carlotte. Elspeth's grave was around two bends of the crypt, at the end of the filled spaces. There were empty spots beside and across from Elspeth. Raised daises with nothing on top of them. One for Carlotte, and one for her mother. A promise of what would eventually come.

"What are we doing here?" the short one behind her asked.

"What I tell you to," Carlotte snapped. "Set me down there," she said, pointing to the dais around her sister's tomb. Raphael set her down, and then she shooed them a few yards away.

Elspeth's tomb was just like the others, body-sized marble boxes with the dead's likeness carved into the top. The likenesses were all lying on their backs, arms held pleasantly at their stomachs, skin as pure and smooth as could be rendered. Elspeth's casket had not been opened at the funeral, Carlotte remembered, and the last time she'd seen her sister, she'd looked nothing like this. Her mouth had been open in a scream, eyes sunken and wide with terror, and foam and bile dribbling from her lips. Carlotte pushed the thought away and laid her hand on the lid.

"I miss you, Elspeth," Carlotte whispered.

The stone felt cold as ice, and Carlotte's skin was goose flesh, but she did not move her arm. Her other hand clasped the Amaranthine pendant at her breast.

"I asked you how this worked, and you said we would figure it out. You and me. I'm going to do it, Elspeth. I'm going to figure it out."

Carlotte felt tears come to her eyes, so she looked up so they would not fall.

"I know you left on purpose. I know... I know it wasn't an accident, but now I wonder if it was just another expedition into the unknown. You went to find out what happens on the other side. God sent you there to see him, and now he sends me to bring you back, so you can tell the world what you've seen. You told me of Kel Shoatone, and I will take you there."

Carlotte looked up at the men, who watched several yards away. She patted the top of Elspeth's tomb. "Remove this lid."

"We aren't grave robbers," the big one said.

"It's not grave robbing. It's my sister. And she's coming with us."

19

Her mother had been right all those years ago, Erika thought as she looked at herself in Visoletta's mirror. She was almost a mirror image of the violinist with the makeup and red cloak. There were differences, of course. Her nose was larger and her shoulders broader, but if she squinted, it could have been her printed on the broadsides.

"Visoletta!" Erika said, "Violin prodigy!" and she whispered the sound of the crowd roaring.

Then she noticed that she could actually hear the crowd roaring. The music had stopped. They'd been applauding for a while, and then, she heard footsteps in the hallway.

Panic struck. There was nowhere to run. No time to run. If she were caught, they'd take her head for sure. She looked to her left. Wall. She looked to her right. Door. Washbin. Closet. Closet!

Erika scrambled across the room, shoved her way behind the clothes, pulled her own filthy rags in after her, and shut the door just as the dressing room door swung open. Erika held her breath. She could see a thin section of the room through the space where the cabinet doors met.

Visoletta stepped into view. She was beautiful. Her hair hung in flowing brown curls around a face both delicate and severe. Her jaw was wide, but her nose was small and straight, and her eyes were green, just like Erika's. The scarlet cloak was around her shoulders with the hood down at her back. She carried her violin in one hand and her bow in the other.

"Visoletta, my dear--" came a man's voice.

"I'm not your dear," she said. The man stepped into view and put an open case down. Visoletta put her violin in and began losing her bow strings.

"Of course, I just mean to say that you are dear to me, to all of us. The performance hall, the city of Sheras, the Ryker Dominion itself! I must beg you one final time to rethink your plans."

"No." Visoletta closed the clasps.

"No one appreciates music like the Dominion does, no place as cultured, and we are your homeland! You were born not a mile from--"

Visoletta turned and glared off to the right.

"I know where I was born, Michael, and I don't need you to remind me. I've been in Sheras for months, and the audiences are petering out. This city has run its course and now I've a chance for Bergshalen--"

"The Mad Queen! She'll take your head!" he interjected.

"I'm no Ryker," she continued, "It's time I spread my music across the continent. They deserve to appreciate me, sir."

"But we do appreciate you!"

"How many times must I say no?" She yelled.

"You promised us two more weeks. Two! You'll walk out on that?" the man said, changing tactics.

"I am, aren't I?" Visoletta said.

"Well, I tried. We certainly hope you decide to come back, and that the Mad Queen lets you leave."

Erika heard footsteps.

"Your concern is touching," Visoletta said and walked towards the mirror with a bag in hand.

"Michael," she said, a different timbre in her voice. "Has someone been in here?"

Erika's blood went cold, and she clamped her hands to her mouth.

"I don't see why someone would have," the man said.

"My brushes are all... different."

"Perhaps it was the Mad Queen," he said, and the door shut.

"Goddamn ungrateful son of a bitch," Visoletta muttered, and Erika heard her swiping items off the table into her bag. She returned to the suitcase, just in Erika's view, and threw the bag inside. She snapped it shut. Then she looked towards the wall, and her eyes widened.

"Michael!" she called out, and Erika realized she was looking at where her spare cloak had hung. The one that was around Erika's neck. Erika pulled her eye from the crack and sank as deep into the clothes as possible.

"Fucking thieves," Visoletta cursed, and then yelled louder. "Michael!"

There was movement in the room: shuffling footsteps, things being moved, and then the closet door opened.

The light was not good, coming entirely from the ring of lanterns around the mirror, and as Erika starred up into Visoletta's face and Visoletta starred into hers, the violinist looked more confused than surprised, as though she'd never seen such a strange costume as was crouching in the back of the closet. Then, her eyes widened, and she opened her mouth to scream and bring Erika's new life to a quick and brutal end.

Erika leapt forward, clapping her hand over Visoletta's mouth. She only meant to keep the violinist quiet until she could explain herself, but she sprang out too quickly and slammed into the woman. Visoletta tripped over her own feet and went backwards with Erika on top of her. Visoletta's head bounced off the stone floor, and then Erika's forehead bounced off Visoletta's forehead, and Visoletta's skull cracked against the floor once more.

Light exploded in front of Erika's eyes, and she rolled off, weakly clutching at her head. She couldn't see, and she could barely think, but her fingers were wet, and when she could see again, she saw they were red.

"Shit," Erika grunted, staggering up to her knees. "I didn't mean to-- I only meant--"

She closed her eyes as pain washed through her, like a bad pike ripple, and Oh God, she could use a cut.

She opened her eyes, and she was on the floor. Her cheek was wet. There was blood there. There was blood everywhere.

"Shit," Erika said. "Oh fucking shit."

Erika put a hand over Visoletta's mouth. Nothing. A bit of blood dripped onto Visoletta's lips.

"I'm sorry," Erika whispered. "I'm so, so, so sorry."

She stood shakily. She had to get out. God, why had she come in here? Why hadn't she just stayed in her alley and gotten high? The Inquisitors would torture her now. They'd take her head and display it in the yard for all to see. She had to go. She had to go now. Erika grabbed her violin case from the table and tore out of the room and down the hallways she'd come in through.

"Visoletta?" a voice called out behind her. She did not turn. She threw open the door and ran down the stairs into the understage. It was dark. She hadn't brought a lantern. She had no time to go back, so she forged on, trying to remember the layout.

She tripped once, spilling herself and her case onto the floor, but pulled herself up, gasping at the sharp pain in her shins, and continued on.

Then she ran face-first into a wall and cried out. She stood and felt her way along the stone until it opened up. This was the corridor. She could see a faint and broken border of light around the door at the end. She ran. She tripped and then stumbled back up. She burst through the door and was bathed in evening light. Erika turned right and ran down the alley until she merged into the crowd.

"Calm down. Calm down!" she hissed to herself. If she pushed her way through, she would be seen. She had to blend in, like a fish in the stream. She needed a place to hide.

Erika saw an alley open on her left, and she cut across the street and ducked in. A boy was sleeping behind a pile of garbage, but other than him, it was empty. She let out a ragged breath and then leaned against the wall and slid down onto her butt. The cloak bunched up around her shoulders. She'd have to get rid of it and dump it with the refuse, but first, she needed a cut. She needed the pike swimming through her veins so she could just get her head straight. She pulled her ratty old case in front of her and tried to undo the clasps, except it wasn't her ratty old case. This one looked almost new, with beautiful black leather and shiny silver clasps.

Dread poured into her. She flipped the latches, lifted the lid, and there was Visoletta's pristine violin. She'd taken the wrong case.

She had murdered the world's most renowned violinist and stolen her instrument. The clothes she could explain away, but a priceless violin... Erika slammed the case shut, locked the clasps, and kicked the case away from her. It skid across the cobbles and banged into the opposite wall. She'd just leave it here. Abandon it and be done with it. She could sell the cloak. It was good material and she could get a bit of pike for it, and then she could calm the fuck down.

Erika stood and hurried back up the alleyway, but when she passed the boy sleeping behind the garbage, she looked back. She was leaving a world-class violin in an alley.

That was crazy.

Beyond crazy.

She had dreamed of a violin, longed for one so she could let out her pain into music, and here came a violin from heaven, and she was abandoning it?

"Or maybe from hell," Erika whispered, remembering the crack of Visoletta's head against the stone. Erika looked down at her hands. There was still blood on them.

"Fuck."

Erika ran back for the case, lifting it like a child and cradling it to her chest. She had to get out of town. If she kept the violin, nothing would save her here. She had to leave Sheras, leave the Ryker Dominion. She could go south to the Freelands, work the land as a labourer by day and play the taverns at night. Or she could cross the sea and learn new languages and enchant them with her Western songs. Erika snapped out of her daydreaming. She had to leave. First things first.

She walked out of the alley and into the street. There were only two ways out of Old Town, the harbor and the Amaranthine Gate, and Erika didn't have a boat. She headed for the Nor-So.

As always, the main thoroughfare was filled with people. It was evening as well, and there was a mass of foot traffic commuting home.

If news of Visoletta's death had left the concert hall, it hadn't spilled into the streets yet. Her breathing was hitched, and her grip around the violin's case was iron. Her nerves were on edge, and she really needed some pike. She didn't need much. Not enough to go swimming. Just enough to take her nerves away and keep them somewhere safe. If she were leaving Sheras, she would be going through the outer city, and perhaps she could find a dealer on the way out. Maybe. Since Ghost's house burned down, it was harder to find the stuff.

The Grand Theater was just off the Nor-so, and she veered to the opposite side of the street when she neared it. The crowd slowed, and she looked over her shoulder at the theater's steps. There were men on it, and they were shouting. Their words were drowned out by the sounds of the city, but their intent was clear. They ran into the flow of traffic. Erika had to get out of Old Town.

Erika doubled her pace, weaving through the crowd like only an urchin knew how to do.

"Think small, be small, think small, be small," she whispered on repeat, hunkering down as she dodged through. People didn't notice small people, especially small homeless people, but as she reached the gate, she realized she didn't look homeless anymore. She looked pretty damn good last she'd checked, though she was a bit dirtier, and there was blood on her face, and on her hands. She scrubbed her face with Visoletta's cloak. Her own forehead was cut, and it hurt when she pressed it. She threw the hood up and pulled it low. The Amaranthine gate was just ahead of her. Forty more feet.

The commotion was getting louder behind her. Bluebacks that had been lounging by the gate house stood up and strained to look over the crowd to see what was causing all the ruckus. In a moment, they would block off the gate, and she'd be finished. Erika squeezed into the press of people passing through the passage, was carried by their current, and then was through.

She turned immediately, splitting off from the Nor-so to a side street. She lived off these streets, and she knew a hundred ways to get to the Nouvre Vil gate. Erika went several blocks to the east, away from the richest part of the Vil filled with Ryker estates, and cut through a dark alley. She passed two men, speaking softly by the wall, and they turned to leer at her as she went. She didn't look like she belonged. Erika let out a nervous giggle, thinking on the irony of being robbed on her way out of town.

The path she took was not straight. The streets of the Vil followed the curve of the two great hills on either side and forked at odd angles around buildings that were older than the streets, but Erika ran with a purpose and knew her way, and some twenty minutes later the Nouvre Vil wall rose up above the tops of the buildings and she was almost there. The buildings here were jammed up against the wall, and there was no way to follow the wall to the gate. She would have to walk down the Nor-so itself for the last fifty yards. She squeezed through the closest alley, which was barely more than a foot-wide waterway between a tavern and a highish-class brothel.

She emerged, and the Nouvre Vil gate was ahead of her, and was blocked off completely by bluebacks. Erika's blood froze. The crowd wasn't moving. The traffic was piled up, and people were shouting, asking what was going on.

"Fuck," Erika whispered.

She turned and started pushing her way up the Nor-so as quickly as she could without drawing too much attention. She had to hide. She'd stash the cloak and the violin somewhere safe and then find a hole to crawl into. She knew of good places all over the Vil. Good rooftops. Good crawl spaces. Good--

"Visoletta!"

She stopped, just for a moment, only yards from a turn in the street. Then she pretended not to hear and strode forward.

"Visoletta!" came the cry again.

They had seen her cloak! She should have ditched it already. Stupid, stupid, stupid! Erika pushed on, willing the speaker to shut up and leave her alone.

"Visoletta!" the voice said, louder, and closer. She had to run! She had to get out before--

A hand closed on her shoulder.

"Visoletta," it said from just behind her, quieter and obviously out of breath.

For a moment, Erika tried to break away, but the grip on her shoulder was powerful, and it pulled her back, turning her. She'd been caught. The new life she'd been about to start had been cut down by her own idiocy. Why had she kept the violin? Why had she kept the red cloak? She turned.

The woman who held her was shorter than Erika and stocky in the way that hides hard muscle under a small layer of fat, the kind of body people get who work hard their whole lives and then suddenly come into money.

"Could you not hear me?" the woman asked. She grabbed Erika's hand. "I'm Saara. It's good to meet you. Come on. We've been waiting for you."

Erika gave a weak pull, but the woman's grip was iron. Erika was done, and she carried her crime in her right hand.

Erika looked down at herself, trying to remember every part of her outfit, of the way it had felt to stand in front of that mirror, of her freedom. She wasn't sure if the freedom she had lived was much to be mourned, but the loss of the life she was about to have was tragic.

Where Erika had cut through the crowd like a fish, Saara just shoved through like a bull, pulling Erika towards a line of carts and wagons a dozen yards from the line of bluebacks. The mass of people was thick here, like water filling all the gaps and crevices open to it.

Saara pulled her past the first few carts and wagons in the line, the people on them looking at her strangely, then Saara stopped by the third, a covered wagon with two women sitting on the bench.

"This is Jane and Hannah," Saara shouted to be heard over the rumbling of the crowd. "Your lady's maids as agreed. The luggage you sent ahead is in the back. We need to go." Saara motioned to Jane, and the lady's maid held out her hand. Erika stared at it.

"Up up," Saara said, and grabbed Erika around the waist and pushed her upwards.

Jane grabbed her arm and together they manhandled Erika into the space between the two lady's maids.

"As we agreed," Saara shouted, and then, with a look of physical pain, pulled a bag from a pocket and tossed it up to her.

Erika caught it reflexively. It clinked and was heavy.

"The rest will come at Bergshalen!" Saara said, and strode away.

Erika was thoroughly confused. Despite her years on the streets, she'd stayed free of arrest. In the back of her mind, she'd known it would come eventually, but she'd never imagined it'd go anything like this.

"We're off," Saara shouted. "Pass it down."

Hannah leaned around the canvas and repeated the order to the wagon behind. Saara moved to the front, called to the carriage driver, and the line moved forward, glacially slow through the thickening crowd, but they came to a halt only a few yards later.

"They aren't letting us through." Hannah said, craning her head to watch Saara argue with the bluebacks that blocked their way.

Erika shrank in her seat, clutching the violin case close to her chest.

Saara walked back to the lead carriage and spoke through the window there. Then she leaned back and shouted.

"Pierre, Haric, clear a space for the Lady DeSheras!"

Two men rode up on horseback from farther down the line. They had guns on their backs, and dismounted when they reached the front. Together, they pushed the crowd away, making a bubble of space between the carriage and the line of bluebacks.

"The Lady DeSheras?" Erika whispered.

"Ay, Ma'am," said Hannah, pointing forward. "That's Carlotte DeSheras there."

A woman stepped out of the carriage, leaning heavily on Saara's hand, with a handkerchief pressed up to her nose. Her hair was long and black, cascading in curls around a heavy white fur collar. Her long coat gathered around black heeled boots in gentle ruffles that mirrored the fur at the top. She walked with a dramatic limp, but when she reached the line of soldiers, they all stood tall. The crowd hushed at the sight of her, and through that silence, she could just make out her words.

"Do you know who I am?" Carlotte asked.

The blueback nodded. "Yes, Madame."

"Where is your Captain?"

A man stepped up from the center of the line. "Here Madame," he said.

The line of soldiers parted in unison to allow him in.

"Do you know who I am?" she asked again.

"Yes, Ma'am. Apologies for the delay, Madame DeSheras. There was a murder. By order of the Inquisition, the gates are to be closed until--"

Carlotte held up a gloved finger, and the man stopped mid-sentence.

"The Inquisition does not control this city. Not yet. Are you going to block my way, Captain?" She asked.

The soldier stood stock still for several moments, the others in line watching from the corners of their eyes.

"Surely," Carlotte continued. "You do not think that I did this murder."

"No, Ma'am." The man said.

"Then?"

Several more moments passed, and then, with strict parade precision, the Captain stepped to the side and barked. "No, Ma'am."

The soldiers turned in unison and parted wide enough for the carriage to pass through.

Carlotte nodded. "Thank you, Captain," she said, and then turned and, with Saara's help, climbed back into her carriage.

The crowd erupted back into sound. Carlotte spoke to Saara, and then Saara was shouting, and the baggage train inched forward again. The two men with guns remounted and led the way through the gap in the soldiers' squad. Erika held her breath as the line approached, but they did not see her. They were shouting and arguing and pushing back at the tide of people who also wanted to go through. Then, Erika was past them and underneath the wall, and then she was through the Nouvre Vil Gates.

Erika looked at the women on either side of her. The shock and terror of the last hour still pumped adrenaline through her, and it was starting to feel out of place. A cold wind blew through the street, cutting through her cloak.

"Take this, Miss Corlionne," Jane said and pulled a woolen blanket from the wagon behind them and draped it around Erika's shoulder.

It all clicked into place. Visoletta Corlionne. Erika thought back to what she'd heard the violinist say to the man in her dressing room, that Visoletta was going to Bergshalen.

Erika looked down at the bag clutched in one hand, the one Saara had thrown to her. She put the violin case between her legs and fumbled with the string tying the bag shut. The knot gave, and the bag opened, and gold twinkled up at her in the evening light. It was more money in one place than she'd ever seen in her life.

A giggle escaped from Erika's lips, and the lady's maids looked sideways at her. They thought Erika was the person she'd just murdered. They thought she was Visoletta Corlionne. It was all she could do not to break out in hysterical laughter.

PART TWO

THE BADLANDS

20

Carlotte's caravan passed through the outer city as the evening faded to night, and then through the farmland surrounding the city into the town of Fork. It was a little town, not much more than a waypoint for people coming and going from Sheras. It was named for the split in the road. The south road led down the Dominion countryside, all the way to the Capital at Domsar, and the north went to the base of the mountain where one could take a boat up the Iron River to the wild lands in the west. The caravan took the north road. They did not linger in the town.

A chest of books sat across from Carlotte on the place where another passenger might sit, and at each corner of the carriage were ensconced lamps, all filled with oil and ready to light. Carlotte didn't light them though. Instead, she sat in the darkness and watched the little town roll past, giving way to a black countryside.

Whatever happened next, Carlotte thought, everything would be different. She had run from Harold. From her mother. From her duty. The soldiers at the Nouvre Vil Gate would start the spread, and the news would permeate through Sheras no matter what her mother did to stop it. The Orlients would hear, and the High Inquisitor would hear, and by the end of the week the entire city would be abuzz with the shame of it. *Off to study ruins* they would say at the parties and salons, and they would shake their heads at the waste, and then in ones and twos they would whisper to each other what they were all thinking. *Magic.*

What would be waiting for her when she returned? What would her status be? What would her future hold? Carlotte lifted a hand to her breast and gripped Elspeth's pendant. Her other hand gripped Ryliar's journal at her side.

"It depends on what I bring back," Carlotte whispered.

It was now forward to glory, or backwards to shame, and that was no choice at all.

The carriage stopped and Carlotte pulled out of her reverie. She opened the shutters and leaned out into the night.

Lights had been hung on poles that leaned over the fronts of the wagons like fishing poles off a bridge, and her caravan looked like a row of glow bugs in the darkness. She heard Saara shouting, telling people to pull off the road and set up camp.

"Saara!" Carlotte called out and the shouting stopped. A lantern dismounted from a horse and came closer, bobbing and jingling with quick steps. It was Saara, her features made grotesque by the direct light of her lantern.

"We cannot stop," Carlotte said. "We must be in Irondale and then the colonies as soon as possible."

Saara held the lantern high and squinted into the night.

"It's dark, Madame, a horse could step wrong and break a leg."

"The lights aren't enough?"

"They help, but every step is a risk."

Carlotte frowned and then settled back into her seat.

"Fine. But we leave before dawn, as soon as there is light to see by."

"Do you want to see them, Madame? Your crew?"

"There is no time."

Saara watched her for a moment, and Carlotte's anger prickled at the look in her servant's eyes. Saara turned and went off, shouting again, and the caravan pulled away from the road and camp was made. Saara brought her bread and cheese and salted meat and fruit. Carlotte ate while listening to the sound of the caravan until it died away, and then to the disquiet of her own mind. She put her head out the window and saw the vague outlines of the wagons and tents in the starlight. She could see no people.

"Alone in the wilderness," Carlotte whispered.

Saara had set up a tent for her beside the carriage, but Carlotte pulled the gilded shutter shut. She sat in the dark and mouthed the Lord's Prayer. She was tired but she didn't think she could sleep.

"God did not choose me," she whispered to the darkness, "Because I am special. He gives nothing for free. He does not help those who do nothing. God chose me because I am strong."

After a moment's hesitation, Carlotte reached up and pulled Elspeth's pendant from her breast. She pulled the chain over her head and whispered the word to it. The metal withdrew from itself and the white light blinded her. She reached up and wedged the chain in the space between the shutter and the window frame, so it hung by her head and lit the carriage with cold light. She reached out to the chest across from her and pulled out a book.

There was no time to dwell on what she had done. She was on God's path now, and there was no way but forward.

21

Aethan moved his little pan deeper into the fire and listened to the crackling of the pork. The smell was close but not quite right. He pulled a few hairs from his head and dropped them into the flames. There. That was how Jaaque had smelled when he burned.

Toktok and Greg grazed just beyond the firelight where he'd staked them, and he could hear them chewing at the grass. He heard the sizzling of the meat and the snapping of the wood, and he thought about Jaaque Akar. He hadn't gone to the door within since he'd added Jaaque to his long list of murders, but he already knew Jaaque's body would be waiting for him there alongside Bulwark and Weed and all the others. It was a strange thing, the door within. How it pulled up your nightmares and made them worse. How it confronted you with all your fear to try and keep you out. It was working. He thought of all the times that he'd struggled at his campfires with flint and steel when he had an inferno at his fingertips.

Aethan pulled the pan from the fire and set it on the grass to cool. He stared into the flames and thought of Ashatee's hovel by the lake. He'd spent nearly two years there and mostly he'd sat and watched a fire. He'd gathered food and fallen wood and done exercises with Ashatee, but mostly they'd just sat and stared. Were it not for hunger and sleep, Aethan believed she could have spent an entire lifetime watching the flames.

Is that what he'd do, if he ever got his gold and bought his own house by a lake all by himself? Would he sit and watch the fire, thinking of Jaaque and Bulwark and all the rest.

"Why do we have it if not to use it?" he had asked her in one of his rare moments of courage. Her eyes had flicked up from the flames at his tone. She'd blinked at him.

"Is this all it's for?" he had elaborated, waving his arms at the forest around them. "Sitting and staring into the fire while the world out there burns?"

"This forest is not aflame," she'd said.

"You know what I mean. You know what the Pales did, what they still do, what the Dominion would do if they could."

"All I know is what I've seen. I've seen no Dominion."

"You saw the Korkin. You were their slave!"

"I am free now."

"But the others-"

"Are not my problem. Nor are they yours."

He had stalked off into the darkness then and sat amongst the nettles and the bush until his anger subsided. Ashatee merely stared back into the fire.

Now, Aethan wondered what she'd seen in the flames. Her own past mistakes? Her own massacres.

If you leave, she'd said, you will find death.

Perhaps he should go back there. The Shafala forest was not far from Bergshalen. He could sell his guns and go into the forest and sit and watch the fire with Ashatee until she died and then he could sit and watch the fire until he followed her.

Jaaque's flintlock handgun lay beside him. He considered it. He had powder in one pocket, shot in another, and a whole cart full of second tries.

In Sheras, after the pikelord's house, he'd been worried about the blue coats and the inquisitors, but now all he had between him and Bergshalen was the road. It was nothing he wasn't used to. He'd been on the road for nigh on ten years, slowly building up his fortune. His future. But now all he had was a cart full of outdated guns and a few more memories to keep him company.

Aethan patted the handgun, and then ate the pork, trying his best not to think about Jaaque burning.

22

Saara woke to a delicate shoe prodding her in the ribs. She opened her eyes and saw Carlotte looking down at her. Saara scrambled to her feet.

"Madame... I... you're already awake?"

"I did not sleep," Carlotte said. She turned and surveyed the little camp inside the circle of wagons. Other than the old soldier standing watch on top of a cart, nothing stirred.

"I was just about to get up. Have us off before the dawn," Saara said, and then panicked about her state of dress before remembering that she'd slept in her clothes from the night before.

Carlotte nodded. "Wake them, feed them, and then line them up before we set off. I must meet them. Set things straight."

"Right, Madame. I thought... You were worried about time last night."

"Priorities, Saara. They've changed. This is important, but I still want to be in Irondale by sunset. There can be no other delay," Carlotte said. Then she turned and limped back across the grass to her carriage.

"Right," Saara said. She walked to the luggage cart and squatted down beside it. Rold lay beneath it, wrapped in a blanket and curled in a ball, a pack under his head and his mouth hanging open with a line of spit dribbling down his split lip into the grass. His face was a mess, but despite the damage, he still looked young. Too young to have experienced a beating like that.

"Fucking hell, Bracille," she whispered and then knocked on the wood of the cart.

"Rold," she said.

He sat up with a start, and Saara shot out her hand to stop his head from smacking against the wagon's underside.

"Wha..."

"Time to get up. Get your shit together, and get something to eat. The lady is going to inspect us, and then we're off."

"Inspect us?"

"Just stand in line over there when I tell you to," Saara said. She stood up, moving on to the tent just beside.

"Saary!" the boy called and scrambled out after her.

"We ain't in the Den anymore. My name's Saara. Or Ma'am. Yeah. Call me Ma'am." Saara bent to pull the tent flaps aside. The faces of two men stared blearily back at her.

"Kent, right?" she said, and the man on the left nodded. "Get breakfast up. Something quick. We're off before the sun comes up." She dropped the tent flap and moved on.

"Ma'am? You?" Rold said, running up beside her.

"Yes, me."

Saara opened the next tent and ordered them up.

"You ain't a Ma'am."

"I am now," Saara said, turning on the boy. "I didn't ask for you to come with me, but here you are. So do your job and stay in line."

Saara stopped in front of the violinist's tent. It was a nice one. Good waterproof canvas, erected high enough that a person could stand inside it, and Saara knew that it was filled with the pillows and bedding someone of Visoletta's station required. She reached for the flap, thought better of it, and walked over to the violinist's wagon. She knocked on the wood.

"And what exactly is my job?" Rold asked.

Saara turned and looked at him. His face looked worse than it had the night before, or was that two nights before? She'd slept for maybe five hours in the last sixty, and she felt a little sick to her stomach. She needed some of that dirt tea now. Rold looked back at her with an expression that might have been nervous. It was hard to tell with all the swelling.

"Yeah?" a woman's voice said.

Saara turned to see one of the violinist's lady's maids peering out from the wagon.

"Up," Saara said. "Food, then the Lady wants to inspect us. Can you wake up, Visoletta?"

"Sure. Now?" the woman said, looking as tired as Saara felt.

"Yep," Saara looked over her shoulder to see Kent in his bare feet, leaning into the cook wagon and pulling out packets of food. "Breakfast is on. Then we're off."

Saara turned and headed towards Val's tent.

"Saary!"

Saara turned on the boy. "What did I say?!" she snapped.

Rold took a step back. "Ma'am, I meant. God, what's your deal?"

"My deal is that I spent the night before last saving your life when I should have been asleep." She turned and called towards the tent. "Val. Up."

"Bracille saved me," Rold said. "The Den did, cause the Den looks after its own."

"Whatever," Saara muttered and turned away from him to see one of the laborers blocking her path. He was lanky, in a long dark jacket and calf-high boots. He chewed while he looked at her from beneath his tricorn hat.

"Slack, right?" Saara said.

The man spat black spit onto the grass. "Name's Slack Gin, and I'd appreciate it if you let me give my boys orders," he said in a thick old Korkin accent. "It helps clear up misunderstandings."

"Your boys?" Saara said.

"Yeah. Doss, Boris, Raphael and Kent. I brought them on. I pay them. I give them orders."

Regie had told her about the arrangement. She'd seen this kind of shit before. Hell, she'd basically run with one at the Den. Boss puts together a crew, rents them out as a unit, skims off the top. Typical street shit. She wondered if it was worth resisting.

"Well. Get breakfast on and camp packed. The lady wants us lined up for an inspection, and then we go."

"Right ya are," Slack said and winked at her. Then he turned and sauntered away, calling out orders Saara had already given.

"I didn't ask to be here either," Rold said, following behind her.

"Nope. You have Bracille to thank for that," she said, and moved to the last tent.

"What is it you got against the Den?" Rold asked, "The Den saved me. Bracille saved me. Saved you, Saary."

Saara turned around and took the kid by his shoulders.

"I know," she said, and then made an effort to soften her tone. "I know what the Den means and how it helps, but I also know how it hurts. The Den is the reason you got off the street, and it is the reason your face looks like a half-cooked slab of beef. Bracille's got you slinging pike now for fuck's sake. He's the reason you killed a--"

"And you ain't killed?" he asked.

Saara didn't answer. He pounded a fist against his chest.

"I ain't ashamed of what I did. For my crew. My family."

"I'm not..." Saara took a breath and tried to clear her head. "Look, it's too early to have this conversation. We'll talk later. Just do your job and give me space to do mine, alright."

"I don't have a job. Remember?" Rold said, crossing his arms.

She heard a rustling and turned around to face the tent. It was a blueback general issue tent, not much more than something to lie down in, and its occupant was crawling out of it. He stood, wearing only his trousers and undershirt, and glared at her, old skin wrinkling around his eyes. His name was Haric.

"I only went to sleep an hour or two ago," he said.

The other soldier, Pierre, stepped carefully down from his perch atop the cart and leaned on his matchlock like a staff.

"There can't be just two of us standing guard. We need sleep too," Haric said, and Pierre grunted in assent.

"You need another body, eh?" Saara said, turning to look at Rold. The boy frowned.

"He's no stranger to violence," Haric said.

"Mayhap the wrong end," Pierre said, and Haric burst out laughing. Rold's face may have reddened. It was hard to tell beneath the quantity of bruises.

"Looks like you got yourself a job, Rold. Hop to it."

23

Erika stood on the steps of the Grand Theater, and she'd never felt so comfortable in her life. She wore a long dress that cut high up the leg, her bountiful thigh peeking out at the crowd. The people swarmed the streets. Old Town was packed with faces, all staring up at her.

Erika lifted the bow to the violin cradled in her neck, and the crowd hushed in anticipation for the sound. She held it there, hovering above the string, and she had the faintest recollection that she hadn't played since she was a child. But that was no matter, because Erika felt the music in her, cresting like a wave through her soul. She could feel it reverberating in her breasts, straining against the fabric of her dress to be free.

Erika lowered the bow, gave a tap to the string, and a note, pure as fine silk, rang out, echoing against the Amaranthine buildings and filling the streets. The bow wanted to play. The music in her wanted to be let out. She knew it was there, and it wanted to be free.

"Visoletta."

Erika shook her head. "My name is Erika," she said. "I know who I am. Don't try to tell me my name." She lowered the bow again.

"Visoletta."

"No!" Erika shouted and threw the violin down. It smashed

onto the steps, and she felt the bottom of her stomach drop, realizing what she'd thrown away. She looked down, and there was no violin. There was only Visoletta, her red cloak billowing around her, a pool of blood seeping out from her skull.

"Visoletta, I'm-"

"NO!" Erika sat bolt upright, and for a moment, she was there on the dressing room floor. She had to get away. She had to run!

"Ma'am?" came a hesitant voice, and Erika saw the dim outline of the tent's flap and the faint blue glow of predawn creeping beneath. Erika put her hand to one side and found the violin case there, then put her hand to the other, and the bag of gold clinked. In a rush, her circumstances came back to her.

"What... What is it?" she asked, striving to keep her voice steady. A fear was settling in her.

"I'm sorry, Mistress. The boss said we're to get up. I'm sorry. I know it's early. I'm very sorry," the woman said.

The maid's voice was strange. Worried like something terrible was about to happen. Like a cadre of inquisitors stood outside the tent, waiting for Erika to come out so they could drag her away.

She considered that for a moment, and then looked around to see if she had any options. The tent was good fabric. Sturdy duck cloth that would be hard to cut through even if she had a knife, which she didn't. All she had was pillows, soft blankets, a bag full of gold, and a priceless violin. Useless. She thought of the little knife she'd kept in her old case and wondered if that dull old thing could have helped her. Her thigh ached at the thought. No. If she'd had her old case, she'd be swimming with the pike right now. God, this tent would be a great place to swim. She put her head in her hands and then recoiled, feeling a bit of roughness on her cheek. She needed tweezers and a mirror. She needed so many things, but she only had one option, which meant she had none.

"Miss?" came the maid's voice again.

Erika had forgotten her name.

"I'm coming," Erika called, "give me a moment." And she fumbled at the clothes she'd crawled out of a few hours before. It had been luxurious to actually undress for sleep and to lie on those soft things with only Visoletta's underclothes between her and the sheets. It felt even better to put them back on, marred as they were by her flight through the city. She noticed a bit of blood on Visoletta's cuff, and she spent a moment rubbing at it before giving up and pulling the shirt on. She tied the cloak around her neck and smoothed out the fabric against her body and held back a groan at the feeling. It was beautiful. It was dark and there was no mirror in the tent, but she could feel the beauty on her, like a summer sun on her face when her eyes were closed. It was how she was supposed to look, how she was supposed to feel, and she found it was so beautifully tragic that this moment, the moment she felt more like her true self than any other, might be her last.

Erika took in a deep breath and faced the tent flap. If there were a battalion of bluebacks and inquisitors out there to take her away, then she would be taken like this. Beautiful and true. She lifted her chin and stepped out into the morning air.

There were no inquisitors, no band of thugs to take her away, just the two lady's maids, hovering before her, one holding out a bit of bread and salted meat in both hands like a supplicant at an altar. Erika blinked around at the little camp, waking up and slowly coming together, shockingly calm and anticlimactic.

"I'm sorry, Miss," the one with the bread said.

Erika peered down at the bread and meat, and the maid cringed.

"It's what the cook gave us."

"I see," Erika said, though she didn't. The predawn was dim, and in the half light, Erika couldn't see what was wrong with the food. So far as she could tell, there were no maggots or mold in it. It looked practically fresh.

"I-" Erika began, but the woman pulled the food back and turned, like she was trying to hide it with her body. Her eyes were shut tight, and her face was a grimace of... fear? Erika looked up at the other maid, expecting to find the woman just as baffled as she, but the second woman seemed just as terrified as the first.

"I'm sorry," the first said. "I'll talk to the cook. Get something better for you. This is a disgrace--" She turned and scampered off toward the cook wagon, and then it all clicked into place.

"No! Come back-- what's her name?"

"Hannah, mistress," the other maid said.

"Hannah! Stop!" Erika called, and Hannah stopped, mid-stride

242

like she'd seen a bear approaching.

Erika hurried over to her. Hannah turned. She was a plain woman, perhaps ten years older than Erika was, with blond curly hair so dark it was almost brown.

"Please, Mistress. I need this post. I've got family back--"

"It's fine," Erika said, and pulled the food out of Hannah's stiff hands. She could feel the other maid beside her. Jane. Jane was her name.

"If I ask you a question, will you answer truthfully?" Erika said.

Hannah's pale face nodded. "Of course, Ma'am."

Erika considered her words carefully. "I've had... many servants, in my time. Have you ever worked for me before?"

"No, Ma'am," the first said.

"No, Ma'am," the second echoed.

Erika nodded. That was good. "And have you-- what have you heard about me?"

The two glanced at each other, their worry only compounding.

"I won't hold it against you. I promise I won't," Erika said.

"I-- I've heard from other women… that you're… particular," Jane said, after spending some time looking for the word.

"Yes, particular," Hannah echoed.

"That you expect a certain way of things," Jane continued.

Erika nodded. Ah. So Visoletta was a right bitch. She looked down at the food in her hands and caught sight of the blood on Visoletta's cuff. Visoletta's blood. She looked up at the women and then around at the little caravan. She looked at the two old soldiers, leaning on their guns while they spoke to the boy with the bruised face. She wondered what they would do with those guns if they found out who she really was. Would they shoot her on the spot and leave her in the road to die? Or would they beat her and take her back to Inquisitor's Yard?

So... she should play the part then? Right? If a bitch was what everyone expected of Visoletta, then a bitch Erika should be.

Erika swallowed and looked back at Hannah's face. She saw the weak being terrified at the power of the strong, terrified that her life was in another's hands. Hannah felt on the edge, but wasn't that just where Erika was?

"Well," Erika said. "Everything you heard is garbage, I'm not-- I don't want to be particular, and I don't want you to fear me. I left Sheras, and I'm not going to be the person I was there. I'm going to be me. Someone new, and someone who doesn't expect things in a certain way."

The women's faces turned from fear to confusion, and Erika let out a little laugh. All of this was... beyond her. If she was to be caught for being a nice person, then fuck it.

Erika stuffed the bread into her mouth and took a much too large bite.

"If goo!" she said though the crumbs, and the women's faces fell even further into confusion.

24

Just before dawn, Carlotte emerged from her carriage in the coat Elspeth had worn for her final exhibition. It was long and brown and tight beneath the breast before flaring out at the waist. It ended at her ankle, in line with the grey dress beneath, and at its collar was a thick fur that bristled out in all directions. Elspeth had never been one for extravagance at her exhibitions. Her clothes had always spoken of adventure and command, and Carlotte had been stunned when Elspeth had emerged upon the stage in this, the way her eyes seemed so full between the fur that framed her face like a halo.

Carlotte held out her hand for Saara to help her down, and Carlotte imagined herself descending with all the majesty that Elspeth had. The image was only slightly ruined by Carlotte's limp. The crew was set out in a line, and they watched her approach. One big man was still eating, his bread and jerky in either hand. Another had a face almost entirely hidden behind cuts and bruises. They weren't the crew she had imagined, but she would work with what God provided.

Carlotte stopped at an appropriate spot before them and took in a deep breath. They watched her. One coughed. Another spat black into the grass. Carlotte looked to the cart behind her carriage, where Elspeth's coffin lay, and then she began.

"My name is Carlotte. I'm sure you know my family name, but I will not utter it here because, on this expedition, it does not matter.

In Sheras, my name matters, but we go north and then west and then still farther west until we leave the colonies behind, and the meaning of my name dwindles to nothing. This is not an expedition of Rykers, this is an expedition of this company, and I am merely this company's captain."

Carlotte paused. There was no response.

"Our purpose is across the Badlands to Bergshalen and then south into the Shafala Forest to a place that I have found reference to. There we will uncover mysterious things, great things that will change the Dominion and the world. You came here for coin, but you will remember this trip for the glory of what we find and the history that we will make."

Again, there was no response. Her words had been good. Carlotte had taken some time the night before composing them, following advice she'd found in a book on proper expeditions, but the crew didn't look motivated. They looked tired.

"Do you have any questions?" Carlotte asked.

For a few moments, there was silence. Then a thin man in a long coat stepped forward. He chewed, and she could see where the hunk of blackleaf bulged out his underlip. "Name's Slack Gin."

Carlotte nodded in acknowledgment.

"Me and my boys appreciate the work," he said, and several other men in the line nodded. "But if we're going Bergshalen way, then why aren't we taking the river? There's a war in the Badlands, or don't you know?"

One of the men gave a short laugh, and Carlotte's gaze hardened.

"The savages in the hills?" Carlotte asked. "Some have become civilized, and the rest have been driven back to the mountains. All that remains of Hill Savages are the stories, Mr. Gin. By all accounts, the colonies stretch nearly to Thorlaille. There is nothing to be afraid of unless the dark still scares you."

The big man with the food laughed, but quieted down when Slack Gin glared at him.

"Of course, Madame," Slack said and gave the slightest of bows.

"There is no need for that. Saara, introductions if you will."

Saara snapped to and went down the line introducing each of

the crew. First was Jane and Hannah, handmaidens to the violinist. The two servants were thin and looked somewhat older than Carlotte expected they actually were—a hard life, no doubt—but the violinist herself was the most surprising. She was Visoletta Corlionne, one of the most famous violinists in the Dominion, though Carlotte had never gotten around to hearing her play. She was as wealthy as a Non-Ryker could be, but she clutched her violin case with one hand and a small leather sack in the other like she was afraid someone was about to take them. She wore the red cloak she was famous for, but her supposed fiery red hair seemed more like strawberry gold. She was awkward and tall, but Carlotte knew well enough that it was difficult to live up to one's hype. Carlotte was glad to have her all the same. She was their ticket into Bergshalen, and it would be good to have someone of culture to speak with on the long trip through the colonies.

Next were Pierre, Haric, and Rold, the company guards. The first two looked past their prime, old men retired from the Mareshal's ranks. They carried matchlocks and long knives at the hip and stood straight as the DeSheras tower. The third, Rold, was quite the opposite. If Saara had dug Pierre and Haric from some veteran's hall, then Rold had been dragged straight from Inquisitor's Yard, freshly beaten for theft. He was of middling height and wiry with thin muscles, and he looked very young compared to the men beside him.

Then there were the three laborers who had picked her up outside the tower: Doss, Boris, and Raphael. They stood beside a thin old cook with a sagging pot belly named Kent. Slack Gin was their taskmaster, and Carlotte figured she'd need to bring him into her circle of officers. She should take advantage of preexisting power structures.

Then there were Ari and Renee, her own handmaidens. They were young, and they clutched at each other like they were sisters, though their features looked nothing alike. Perhaps sisters by necessity?

Finally, there was Vaalier Saadermont, a middle-aged expert on Amaranthine culture and a Ryker-

"Ryker?" Carlotte said, interrupting Saara's introduction. The man had stood hunched like a clerk, but at Carlotte's words, he straightened somewhat and smiled. His spectacles were a dull gold in the predawn light.

"Yes, Madame. My father was Ruesseu Saadermont, and his father was Jeantelle Saadermont. We've owned land in the Vil for centuries."

Carlotte had never heard of them. She wondered to whom he pledged his vote.

"I was a great admirer of your sister," he added before Carlotte could speak to dismiss the company.

"My sister?"

"Yes. I've read all of Elspeth DeSheras' treaties. I started my studies of the Amaranthine when she was just a child, and she surpassed me in only a few short years."

Carlotte nodded. "She was brilliant."

"Yes. The day she died... so much knowledge was lost."

"Indeed." Carlotte's sudden sadness must have reached her face because Vaalier's eyes widened.

"I'm so sorry, Madame, I did not wish to-"

Carlotte held up a hand.

"It is nothing. We go in her footsteps. But," she said, turning her attention to the wider group, "more importantly, we go in God's footsteps."

Carlotte closed her eyes and took in a deep breath. "God is here with us. I feel him here. Would you lead us in a prayer, Vaalier?"

"A prayer, Madame?"

Carlotte opened her eyes and looked at the wide-eyed scholar. "You are faithful, are you not? Come, we must be off soon, but we have time for a resuscitation of faith and three of sin."

"I... Of course, Madame," he said, and then his gaze went far away, struggling to recall.

Carlotte did not judge him harshly for it, but Carlotte knew that she had God behind her, and she would thank him for his faith in her.

"I believe in God," Vaalier began, slow and steady. "The almighty and the one true father, creator of the earth and the life above. I believe in the prophet--"

He continued, and as he spoke, the first rays of dawn came and set his golden spectacles a twinkling. Carlotte kept a hand in her pocket, picking her fingers across the prayer beads there. She felt God on one side of her, and Elspeth on the other, and she knew that this was the beginning of greatness. This was the adventure she had been born to take.

"Amen," Vaalier said.

"Amen," the line echoed.

Carlotte answered a moment later.

"Amen."

25

"People choose to live here?" Hannah said, her voice muffled by the cloth held over her mouth.

"Where there's work, people go," Jane answered, equally muffled.

Erika's own face was buried in a scarf fetched by Hannah from some of Visoletta's luggage in the back. They were not alone. Everyone they passed had cloth around their faces, even the destitute huddled in the alleyways.

The air was thick with soot. It mixed with mist from the river, buoyed up by a cold, biting wind from the mountains, and formed a grey fog that clung to the people moving through it. It stuck to their faces and their clothes and turned everything to a dull, grimy grey. Erika clutched at Visoletta's cloak, as though she could protect it from the air.

"My brother used to live by the smelters, worked them too before they shut down," Hannah said.

Erika lifted a finger and caught a bit of black floating on the breeze. It stuck there.

"He said this stuff was killing him," Hannah finished.

"How's he now?" Jane asked.

Erika flicked her finger, but the ash stayed attached. She rubbed at it with her thumb, and it melted onto her skin like a bit of paint.

"Dead two years back," Hannah said.

Erika wiped her finger against the bench seat. Jane only grunted.

The road ran parallel to the river, where great wooden wheels tore the water into a white fury. They followed it until the avenue opened up into a town square. There was a stone fountain in the square's center, but the water did not flow, and as their wagon rolled past Erika looked down and saw a pool of black water, filled with floating scum.

The wagon train stopped in front of a three-story building that looked like it had once been grand. There was a stable to one side, and twisting columns flanked its wide entryway. Erika was struck with deja vu, but before she pushed the feeling away, she realized it was a real memory. She'd been here, at this hotel, before it had been stained with soot. The columns had been white, imitations of Amaranthine Granite, and the door had been surrounded in gilt filigree, a provincial imitation of Ryker style.

"Come," her father had said, slapping her manfully on the back, "and watch your Pa make a deal. Come and learn our business."

Erika cringed at the awkwardness of the memory. It wasn't so long ago. A decade at most, it was hard to remember, but it was a different life to her, and a most unwelcome one.

"Miss?"

Erika looked down. Hannah was below her, holding up a hand to assist her. Erika hefted the bag of gold in one hand and the violin in the other, and then, without letting go of either, let the woman help her down.

Saara strode out through the inn's front door and began distributing keys. She handed one to Jane.

"For Miss Corlionne," and then handed another. "Attendant room, just adjacent."

Hannah nodded.

"Enjoy the beds. It'll be three days on a boat after this."

"Right," Hannah said, and then turned to Erika. "Ready, Miss?"

Erika looked back up at the wagon behind them, piled high with luggage.

"Do we--"

"Jane and I will bring up some luggage, miss. The rest will keep in the wagon. Unless... do you want us to bring it all up?"

"What? Oh, no. No. Just a... change of clothes, I guess," Erika said.

Hannah led her inside, and Erika's memories flashed up stronger. She remembered walking in. Things had seemed bigger then. The Maitre d'Hotel had sat at the desk across from the door. It was still the same. Hannah led her past the man and ascended a flight of stairs and entered a hallway with numbered doors along either wall. Hannah found the correct one, inserted the key, and pulled the door open. She bowed her head and stepped aside so Erika could enter.

It was a large room, several paces from one wall to the other, with a wardrobe in one corner and a four-poster bed with heavy velvet drapes just beside it. Several glass windows ran along one wall, letting the evening light through the gray sheen of soot. Erika could just make out the river through the window. A vanity sat between two of the windows with a mirror propped up on its surface.

Hannah hissed through her teeth. "I'm so sorry, ma'am, I'm sure Miss Saara gave us the wrong key."

"What?"

"The room. It's so small--"

"No, it's... more than enough," Erika said. She laid the violin and bag of gold on the bed and walked to the vanity, brushing her fingers along the mirror's edge. Hannah came in behind her and walked to the windows, fussing at the latch.

"Oh, it's been nailed shut... For the vapors, I'll bet. How will you..." Her eyes trailed to the chamber pot beside the bed. "I'll just... just call out, Jane and I are next door and I'll wake up and take it down for you--"

Erika turned to the woman and put a hand on each shoulder. Hannah flinched at the contact.

"It's fine. I'll be okay. In fact, don't even worry about me. No need to check on me tonight. I'll be out in the morning... Believe it or not, I've been in worse."

Hannah gave a weak smile. "Oh, I'm sure. Traveling all over the Dominion like you do." Hannah's face lit up a bit. "Are you going to practice tonight, Miss? I've heard that you practice your music every day."

"Well, I... um-"

"Would you mind if I listened? I've heard fiddling but never a real violin, and I've heard they can sound like angels."

"They can," Erika said, and she saw herself standing on the stage at the Grand Theater, Visoletta's cloak billowing with the movement of her arms, the music pouring out of her. "But not tonight," Erika said, and Hannah's face fell. "I don't feel the music tonight. I played so much in Sheras that I need some time to refresh myself."

"Maybe later? On the boats tomorrow?"

"Yes, maybe then." Erika looked back at the vanity and self-consciously rubbed at her chin. "I left in such a hurry-- did a box, my box, of cosmetics make it into my luggage?"

"I believe so, Miss. Would you like me to bring it up?"

Erika nodded, and Hannah dismissed herself, bowing as she closed the door behind her. Erika sat on the bed and gasped at the feel of it. She lay back and the mattress seemed to envelope her, giving where she was and filling where she was not. The blankets of her tent had been luxurious, but this was something else entirely. A real bed. A real mattress. When was the last time she'd lain in one? When she was a child. Back when she still had a family?

"Stop it!" she hissed, pulling herself back up. She was indulging herself. It had ever been her weakness. Her father had told her often. It was easier to pretend her responsibilities away. Easier to just get high.

The thought of pike hammered at her. It was a dull ache behind her eye that would only grow the longer she went without it. Another day or two and she'd give up the whole bag of gold for just a drop. Erika had no time for soft beds. She needed pike, and she needed to get out of town. Out of the Dominion if she could manage it. Erika unfastened Visoletta's cloak from her neck and let it drop onto the bed. She wouldn't make that mistake again. The thing was beautiful, so beautiful, and the leaving of it felt like the leaving of treasure, but it was a flame in the night, and she could never hide while she wore it. Erika pushed to her feet and tried the window, but it was nailed as tightly as Hannah had said. She looked around the room. Nothing came to mind. She absently put a hand to her face and recoiled. She needed pike, a way out, and a pair of tweezers.

She found the tweezers in one of the bags that Hannah brought up a few minutes later, and set to ridding her chin of the offending hair. Then she spent a few more minutes scouring her face in the mirror for anything else that could be plucked away. The mirror was amazing. Magnitudes easier to use than the little scrap of polished metal she'd kept in her old violin case. She could see every pore in this one, and while she'd never enjoyed the look of her face, if she focused on pieces of it, the lips, the chin, the brow, the eye, then it wasn't like she was looking at herself. It was an artwork she was creating, and when she pulled away, it could be anyone. Erika wiped away the makeup from the day before and put on a simpler look, accenting her eyes to draw attention away from her chin, brightening her lips to--

Erika stopped. She was doing it again. Any second, that Saara woman would burst in and proclaim her for the fraud she was. Any second, the news of Visoletta's death would catch up to them, and Erika would be finished, but here she was painting her face just like she had at her mother's vanity, pretending to be anyone other than the stranger who stared back at her.

Erika felt the feelings rise up then, the old ones that she always hoped would die on the street. The self-pity. The weariness at the unfairness of it all. Why couldn't she just sit here and paint her face and be the violinist extraordinaire? Why couldn't that have been her life? Why couldn't this, this body, this person, be the truth? Erika reached out to the mattress and touched the cloak, and it was so soft that tears came to her eyes.

"Miss Corlionne?"

Erika spun in her seat and nearly dashed all the brushes to the ground. Saara stood behind her at the open door, one hand up on the frame and the other resting on the knife at her hip.

"Yes?" Erika said, her voice sticking in her throat.

Saara looked strangely at her. "Madame DeSheras wants you downstairs for dinner."

"Dinner," Erika repeated.

"Yeah. It's not a request," Saara said, and then turned and left.

Erika watched after her for a moment, wondering if she should make her escape now. No, that would be foolhardy. Tonight, after dinner, when the others were all asleep. She'd been Visoletta Corlionne for at least a day, she could be the woman for a few hours more. She reached for the cloak and fastened it around her neck.

Erika made room in the bag of cosmetics, stuffed the bag of gold into the bottom, and then pushed the bag under the bed. Hannah had left the room key on the vanity. Erika locked the door behind her and went down to dinner.

The common area was mostly empty, but loud. Most of the caravan members were seated at a long table in the center, talking amongst their groups while a woman slid mugs of beer between them. Hannah and Jane were seated with the Lady DeSheras' lady's maids at the end. Hannah made to stand when she saw Erika enter, but Erika waved her down. There were a few others, some locals in fancy but dirty coats at the bar and a Freelander nursing a mug in the corner. Saara stood against a door frame on the opposite wall. When she met Erika's eye, Saara ducked in, and Erika followed.

It was a much smaller but much nicer dining room, with a few glassey-topped tables surrounded by high-backed chairs. The Lady DeSheras sat at one with the other Ryker, Vaalier something, beside her. The Lady looked divine. She'd traded her travel clothes for a black dinner dress with a high collar that lengthened her neck. Her hair was simple, brought up into a bun with a needle through, and a few strands loosely tucked to frame her face. Erika had seen her before, when she'd addressed the group that morning, but now she saw the Lady DeSheras in the manner she was meant to be seen, and by God, she was beautiful. The epitome of grace and womanhood. Erika felt awkward and dirty by comparison. She looked down at the red cloak about her and took comfort in it.

The other Ryker looked up at their entrance and stood. The Lady DeSheras stayed seated.

"Thank you for joining us, Miss Corlionne," the Lady said. "It is good to savor the little decorum we have left before venturing into the wilderness."

"Yes, Madame DeSheras, I am at your service," Erika said, giving a curt bow like her father used to give to Rykers. Then she wondered if she should have curtsied, and did that as well. Saara sat down, and Erika followed suit. There was wine in front of each of them. Carlotte took a sip from hers, perfect rose lips pursing at the cup's edge, and then spoke.

"The structure of authority will be shallow on this expedition. I meant what I said this morning. This will not be an exercise in bringing Dominion hierarchy into the wilds, but there will still be some sense of place. I may be this Expedition's captain, but I will, at times, need your distinguished advice. Miss Visoletta Corlionne, you will, of course, have control of your lady's maids, and Monsieur Vaalier Saadermont, Saara is at your disposal if you should need anything at all."

"Thank you, Madame DeSheras," Vaalier said, glancing at Saara while he said it.

Saara gave a smile that didn't make it to her eyes and then gave the barest nod of her head.

"Let us dispense with the honorifics until we return to Sheras. Call me Carlotte."

"Of course, Madame. My family and friends call me Val."

Carlotte and Val looked to Erika, skipping Saara, and Erika stammered at the sudden pressure.

"Eri-- ah, Visoletta is fine," she said. The dead woman's name felt weird in her mouth. It was the first time Erika had claimed to be her. Until that moment, everyone had just assumed.

"Very Good," Carlotte said. "I want to clear the air. The crew knows that Bergshalen is our destination, and I know they wonder why we don't go there by sea and river. I don't mean to keep secrets, but it is best that the truth not be public until we are out of the Dominion proper. I've had some trouble with the Grand Inquisitor. Nothing serious. Mostly a family affair, but if we went south, the Inquisition would turn us back, and I *need* to make this journey.

"We go to study the Amaranthine. It's why you're here, Val. I have records of fantastical things, things which will catapult Dominion science forward a hundred years, even if we only find a tenth of what has been written. Of course... we could find nothing... but it is worth the exploration. One cannot fear failure and know success."

Carlotte took in a deep breath and let it out through her nose. She swallowed, and the smooth undulation of her neck caused

Erika to lift a hand to her own.

"My sister studied the Amaranthine, and I mean to finish her work."

They were silent for a few moments, Carlotte staring through the middle of the table, before Val spoke.

"I agree wholeheartedly, Mad-- ah, Carlotte. This will be a defining expedition, I have no doubt, but if I may ask a question?"

Carlotte looked his way without moving her head and then gave a slight nod.

"Why Bergshalen? I know there are ruins there, but... as happy as I am to have Miss Corlionne on this expedition... surely there are easier sites of worth. Your sister did much of her work in the mountains--"

"We are not going to Bergshalen for their ruins or their artifacts. We are going for their books. I've a lead and a trail to follow, and that trail starts in Bergshalen's Royal Library."

"A trail to where?"

Carlotte watched him for several long moments, like she was trying to see through him.

"Lok Secrak."

Val's face froze, eyes wide. Erika looked to Saara, but she gave no sign of surprise. Erika opened her mouth, but then closed it again before the question could get out.

"You know it then," Carlotte said.

"I know... of it," Val breathed. "Lok Secrak, The Center. There are references to it scattered about the continent. A place of fantastical things. Most consider it to be a Pagan heaven. Your sister--"

"It's not."

"How do you know?"

"Because people don't put heaven on maps. My source found a map in a ruin called Steursak, which then followed to Lok Secrak."

They were all silent for a few moments.

"And you don't know where Steuersak is," Val said. "Hence the libraries of Bergshalen."

Carlotte nodded.

"There will be plenty of time to get into the details on the road. Saara, see the food brought in."

"Yes, Carlotte--" Saara trailed off, her bored and stoic expression changed to insecurity and fear.

Carlotte looked back at her, one eyebrow raised.

"Madame," Saara finished and pushed to her feet. She looked at Erika, and then at Val, and then turned and strode out of the room.

"Hmmm," Carlotte said, strumming a set of perfect fingernails across the table. "Let's talk of something else. She turned to Erika.

"Visoletta. I'm glad you could make this trip. You serve a purpose, yes, but it will be nice to have some culture while we journey through the wilds. I apologize, but I've never had occasion to hear you play. I've been invited, but things always get so busy."

"Oh," Erika said, doing her best to smile like a rich person. Did rich people smile differently? "I understand. Busy life."

"I heard you play a few years ago," Val said, "You looked so young on the stage, but I don't know if that's just because I feel so old."

Erika laughed. "I hope it was good?"

"Oh," Val said. "I don't think I exaggerate to say it was divine."

Erika blushed. She was well aware that the compliment wasn't really to her, but it felt good all the same.

"I'm glad, all I want is for people to enjoy music as much as I do," Erika said, one part of her mind drifting off to the stage, to the image of her in the billowing red cloak, tremors of energy pulsing through her as she played the strings.

"An admirable focus," Carlotte said, and then turned to Val. "Tell me of the Saadermonts. My mother would kill me if she caught me not knowing a Ryker family in Sheras."

Erika lifted the glass of wine and took a long sip. It was good. Really good. She took another and then forced herself to put the glass down. Val droned on about his family, but Erika was focused inward. The ache behind her eye was growing sharper, and her forearms were feeling itchy. She needed to focus. All the compliments in the world wouldn't save her if they caught on to who she really was. An urchin. A fraud. A murderer. By God, she just needed some pike.

She lifted her head at the sound of footsteps. Two servers entered, bearing trays stacked with food. The smell almost pulled Erika out of her seat. Roasted lamb and gravy with potatoes and sautéed sprouts and bread that smelled fresh and hot. Saara came behind them and watched as the trays were placed. Erika reached out for the food, like she was going to grab it in her hands and stuff it into her mouth, and then stopped. She waited until she saw Val fork a piece of lamb onto his plate, and then she dove in, piling her plate with food. Carlotte smiled, not seeming at all tempted by the feast.

"Best eat, and drink too. We might get some hot food in Forepost and then... Whatever it was we ate last night until we cross the badlands."

Saara still stood behind the empty chair she had vacated, one hand tensed on the chair back.

"Go," Carlotte said, and she finally leaned forward to pick at the meal. "Enjoy your night. Just make sure we're on time tomorrow."

Saara frowned but nodded. "Right. Of course, Madame."

Erika watched Saara turn and walk out. She could sense the drama there, which Val and Carlotte seemed entirely oblivious to, and then promptly forgot it herself, as she stuffed fresh buttered bread into her mouth.

"I think," Carlotte said, considering the almost empty wine glass in front of her and then placing a finger on its base and pushing it away, "I'll bathe."

"Bathe?" Val repeated and snapped upright.

Carlotte raised an eyebrow.

The bottle of wine sat empty on the table, and another sat empty beside it. The conversation had alternated between stressful and confusing as it had shifted from Erika speaking vaguely about Visoletta's life to Val and Carlotte discussing Amaranthine archeology. Erika had drunk nearly a full bottle herself, and it had calmed her down and had taken the edge off the pulsing behind her eye. If she settled back in her seat and closed her eyes, she could almost will the headache away.

"Join me?"

Erika opened her eyes and caught Carlotte looking at her.

"Me?" she squeaked.

"Well, it would certainly be something if I asked Val," Carlotte said.

Val coughed.

"Come," she said, "It's the last bath we'll have for days. Perhaps even weeks if one can't be found in Forepost. Who knows how... colonial the colonies are."

"I... I don't like being naked in front of--"

"Oh my!" Val stood up, his chair screeching across the floor. "It's time I take my leave. Thank you for the evening." He turned, stumbled over his chair leg, and then left the room.

Carlotte laughed a golden, glittery sort of laugh. "So crude, Visoletta, but there will be a curtain. We are not savages." She stood and snapped her fingers. "Come, come," and limped out of the room.

Erika stood and accidentally knocked the table back with her hips. A plate of sauce fell and shattered on the ground. She followed Carlotte out to see her glaring across the hall. The expedition's members were sprinkled across the room, talking and drinking and yelling. Slack Gin lounged against a table, his long legs spread out, taking up as much room as possible while Hannah sat on one side, laughing a honking sort of laugh.

Carlotte reached out and grabbed one of her own maids' shoulders, Ari was her name. The woman turned with a sneer on her face that melted instantly to beaming servility.

"Madame! I--"

Carlotte held up a hand.

"Where's Saara?"

"Ah, I ah... She was in the corner and then... maybe she stepped out?"

"Hmmmf," Carlotte grumbled. "Get Renee and pull me a bath. Have Visoletta's maids do the same. And give me a hand to it."

The woman nodded and got up. She gathered Renee and then pulled Jane out of her conversation. Jane looked up at Erika, and Erika looked at the ground. A few moments later, Erika looked up, and the lady's maids were gone, and Carlotte was limping away with her arm over Ari's shoulder. Erika followed.

The bath room was small with paneled wood floors, walls, and ceiling, and was filling quickly with steam. A curtain hung, dividing the room into two, with a brass bathtub and a small table with a mirror, a comb, and soap on each side. A large metal tank sat above a furnace on one wall with brass pipes leading out, which the servants used to fill the tubs. Jane appeared from around the edge of the sheet.

"Miss Corlionne," she said, giving a conservative nod, and then gestured behind.

Erika went to her tub and found Hannah standing beside it, looking down at the ground. Erika heard the sounds of lacing being undone on the other side of the curtain and recoiled as Hannah approached her.

"Miss?"

"I... I can undress myself," Erika said. "Thank you."

"But--"

"Of course, Miss," Jane said, stepping up to pull Hannah aside. "We'll be just outside."

"No, please. Go back to the party. I'm sorry I pulled you away."

Hannah looked at her for a few moments, and then at Jane.

"Right you are, miss. Call if you have need," Jane said, and they disappeared around the sheet.

Carlotte dismissed her own lady's maids to wait in the hall, and then Erika heard a splash of water. Carlotte hissed in pleasure.

Erika looked at her own bath and the bits of vapor that steamed up. No one could see her. She looked around to be sure, but there was no real barrier either, just the sheet and the agreement not to look around it. One person could walk in at the wrong moment and ruin everything. But who would? They thought she was Visoletta Corlionne. It would be terribly improper.

Erika undid Visoletta's cloak, then undid the corset tie from around her waist, and then dropped her petticoats to the floor. She stepped out and then undid her shoes and rolled down her stockings. She folded them all and put them in a pile on the floor. The white stockings were torn and almost brown with muck. Erika stood in only Visoletta's shift. She glanced at the edge of the sheet again, and then in a flurry of motion, tore off the shift and crawled into the tub. The sudden heat made her squawk, and a good deal of water splashed out onto the floor. She reached for the bar of soap and lathered it up as quickly as possible until a layer of bubbles and soap scum covered the water.

Carlotte's golden laugh tinkled beyond the curtain.

"You're not at all what I expected," Carlotte called.

Erika sank lower so that just her eyes were above the water. She shouldn't have come here. She should have just gone to her room and waited for her chance to run. If she'd said no, Carlotte probably would have listened, but she was always giving in to nonsense like this. Too afraid of how things would look if she didn't act just so.

"I expected a harpy to be honest," Carlotte giggled. "Who knew Visoletta Corlionne was so humble and common?"

A moment of silence passed.

"That sounded rude. I did not mean it as an insult," Carlotte said.

"It's alright, Madame," Erika said, "I've been called worse."

The silence filled the room again, and Erika let herself relax a little and let her head lie back against the hot brass. The heat seemed to fill every inch of her, and she visualized the dirt falling away from her skin, leaving behind pink, soft, womanly flesh. She closed her eyes and took a shuddering breath. A small moan escaped her lips.

"My sister was always blunt, and so was my mother," Carlotte said. "I always wanted to be like my sister and nothing like my mother. Seems I'm caught." Carlotte laughed again.

Erika dunked her head under the water and then took the comb from the table. She stuck it in her hair and weaseled it back and forth, trying to work through the knots. The silence stretched on, and Erika felt expectation in it. Of course there was. Carlotte had invited her to keep her company.

Erika thought about what to say. Some personal fact? But Erika didn't know any personal facts about Visoletta. Did she have siblings? Were her parents still living? Would Carlotte know the truth even if Erika said it? The point was academic anyway. She had to lie, and it was better to keep lies as close to the truth as possible.

"I thought I wanted to be like my mother, but she turned out not very sweet at all," Erika said.

"Mothers are difficult. I suppose yours must have done

William Zimmerman

262

something right for you to end up like you are."

"Common?" Erika asked.

Carlotte rewarded her again with her golden laugh. "I like you, Visoletta. I'm glad you're on this expedition."

Erika stopped working at the knot in her hair. "Really?" She looked at the sheet as though she could see through it.

"Really," Carlotte answered. "I just wish my sister could have been here too. Really been here. She promised me we'd figure things out together. Long time ago. I think she would have loved this."

"I'm sorry. How did she die?"

Carlotte didn't answer for a long moment, and Erika wondered if she'd said something rude. Was it rude to ask a rich person how their sister died?

"An accident. Long time ago," Carlotte said finally.

Erika heard Carlotte stand up, and water falling into the tub, and then wet feet hitting the wooden floorboards.

"I think I've had too much to drink," Carlotte said. "Nothing good ever comes of it."

She called for Ari and Renee. Erika listened to them towel Carlotte off.

"Good Night, Visoletta."

"Good Night, Carlotte."

Then Carlotte, Ari, and Renee were gone. Erika was alone. Like she was used to.

Erika submerged herself again and pressed against the sides of the tub so she wouldn't float back to the top. The heat came at her from every direction, and she could hear nothing but the hum of the water and the course of her thoughts.

She thought about what she would do. She'd run out in the night and find a place to stock up. She'd get a new cloak, some provisions for the road, and a good bit of pike. Then she'd what? Take a boat back to Sheras, or around to Domsar? No, if she went missing, the first place Carlotte and Saara would look for her was the docks. So, then a horse? Where did one even buy a horse? How much did they cost? The bag of gold had seemed like so much wealth, but after a horse and provisions and pike, and clothes, how much would be left? She'd be on the road, alone, with a horse she didn't know how to ride. She couldn't go back to Sheras. She'd have to go south. To where? Some farm town where she could what? Be a servant girl? Live in tiny servant's quarters? How long would it take them to find out her secrets? Where would she find pike?

No, not a farm town. Domsar then. She knew cities. She knew how to find dealers. She could sell the horse, and when the money ran out... what? Back to the streets. Perhaps she could actually play the violin. She couldn't use Visoletta's. Someone might notice. So she'd have to get a new one. But how much were those?

Erika's pulse quickened, and the voice in her head was screaming at her to breathe. No matter what she did, she was fucked. There was no way out. If she left, homelessness, if she stayed--

Erika burst out of the water and gulped in a lungful of air. She collapsed against the side of the tub and felt a sob rack through her. She looked up and into her own face reflected in the mirror on the table. The hate swelled in her. Hate at her nose and her chin and the lump in her throat and the stranger's body she knew was beneath it.

She lashed out. The mirror flew from the table, hit the sheet, and shattered on the floor. She looked at the mess for a moment and then collapsed back into the tub, resigned.

Her future was fucked because her past was fucked and there didn't seem to be anything she could do about it. Go back to poverty for the rest of her life, or live like Visoletta Corlionne for a month or two until the law caught up with her and sent her to Inquisitor's Yard. A long life of the same suffering she had grown to know so well, or a short burst of the life she deserved.

The answer was obvious.

"Miss Corlionne?" came a squeak from the other side of the sheet.

"Hannah?"

"Yes, Miss Corlionne."

"I thought I told you to go back to the party?"

"I did, Ma'am, but then I came back just to make sure everything was alright. And then I heard--"

"It's alright. I'm fine," Erika said. "I just knocked over the mirror, is all."

Hannah was silent for a moment.

"Is there glass on the floor?" Hannah asked.

"There is," Erika said.

"I'll get a broom then."

Erika soaped up the water again to make sure the top was opaque and then waited until Hannah walked around the sheet and began cleaning up the glass. Hannah put the big pieces in a bucket and then swept the smaller bits into a little tray. It was difficult with the wet wooden floor, but Hannah kept at it until it was all done. Then she looked down at the pile of dirty, folded clothes.

"Would you like fresh clothes, Ma'am?"

"I'd like a fresh everything."

"Ma'am?"

"Fresh clothes would be great."

Hannah nodded and then made to leave.

"Hannah, I know you've heard bad things about me, but this is going to be a long trip, and I don't want you to be scared of me the whole time. I won't bite, I won't fire you, and if possible, I'd like to be your friend," Erika said.

Hannah looked back at her, and then, for the first time since she'd come around the sheet, gave a nervous little smile.

"Right, Miss."

"Would you do me a favor, though?" Erika asked.

"Of course."

"What do you know about buying pike?"

26

When Aethan awoke, the depression had settled in fully. He looked at his fire pit from the night before and chronicled the steps it would take to get back on the road. With great effort, he forced himself to do each step one at a time.

None of his feelings were new. He'd had them to some degree all his life, but they'd gotten worse in Sheras. The tide of feeling would near have drowned him if not for the fear and panic of his leaving. Now he was out on the road and safe, and the tide bowled him over.

When the hope was in him, Aethan felt that the world was basically a light place, and his sadness was an aberration. He felt in those times that his feelings were a result of his circumstances, and if he could fix those, if he could get his money and his house by the lake, then it would be okay. It seemed that the sadness cast a veil over his eyes that made the world appear dark and miserable, but in those times of hope, he knew the darkness to be false, even when he was deep in it. The world wasn't dark. His eyes were.

But now the hope was gone in him, and it was like waking up from a dream. He knew now that it was the light that was the lie. He had been wearing glasses of gold that made the world shiny, and now they were gone, and he could see things for what they truly were. Dark. Desolate. A mirror of the door within. Perhaps that was why the door within showed such horrible things, because it showed the truth.

Aethan considered Jaaque's handgun, and then packed up his things and set off down the road. Until he decided to use the gun, he might as well continue on.

He arrived in Irondale in the late afternoon. It had changed since last he'd been there. He'd heard tale it used to be an idyllic hamlet nested at the base of the mountain, with the Iron River bringing freshwater fish and ore from the small mining outfits scattered along the foothills. If that was the truth, then it was long over by the time he'd come three years ago to sell pigs. The town had already started going the way of industry. Gray smoke had filled the air then, and now gray soot covered its buildings.

The firebrands in the Freelands would use this as evidence of the Dominion's corruption, but if Aethan was honest, much of the Freelands were going the same way: the poor getting poorer, the revolution leaving them behind in the name of freedom. The world wasn't changing for the better or the worse, it was just changing, just stirring the suffering around.

He came to the big hotel in the center of the square and paid the stable boy to take his cart and beasts.

"You know any place to sell a donkey?" Aethan asked.

The stable boy turned to look at him. His face was covered by a gray scarf so that only his eyes and spiked gray hair showed over the top. "That donkey?"

"Yeah. Greg's his name."

The boy gave the donkey a look over. "Not that I can think of. Looks ready to die."

"Figures," Aethan said and strode into the inn. He thought about giving the stable boy a threat. The ol' I'll cut open your sack if anything happens to my things, but just the idea of putting on the airs exhausted him. So what if the boy took his beasts and stole his guns? If the boy did, Aethan would just paint one of the inn's rooms red for the trouble. Aethan fingered the handgun in his belt and wondered what it would taste like. Would it just be cold steel? Or would there be a hint of powder to it? Aethan decided it would be better to think about it while he was drinking. He hired a room and ducked into the adjoining tavern.

It was a big room just off the foyer with long common tables in the center, smaller tables along the wall, and a bar at one end. It was mostly empty, with just two gray figures at the bar and a woman who stood behind it talking to them real low. Aethan sat in the corner.

He decided to get drunk and ordered two beers to get started. He drank them and ordered two more, and by the time he'd finished the fourth, he was buzzing and his thoughts were farther away from the gun at his waist and closer to his bladder. He resisted the urge to pee. Once the seal was broken he'd be stumbling out to piss every twenty minutes.

When the woman came in, he was on his fifth. Her shoulders were wide, but her hips were wide enough to match them. She wore pants and a roomy shirt, and he could see the gleam of a knife's pommel at her belt. Aethan watched her argue with the Maitre D'hotel, and when she bent over to lean against the man's desk, Aethan felt a stirring in his loins. She came to some agreement and walked back out of the inn.

He drained the last of his glass. He felt like he'd missed something. Like he'd glimpsed a bit of the shiny world, and in a blink it was gone. He laughed like Ashatee used to, a single huff of breath through the nose. It was the drink. The drink and the time gone without. How long had it been? Certainly not since he'd left the Freelands six weeks ago. There had been that woman who owned the hostel by the Freeflow. Harcine. One of those made-up names that were popular these days. Something new and not part of the Korkin past. She'd been nice. The kind of nice that made him think on staying on a few weeks longer. Not that she'd have him if he did. But the thought-

She came in again.

This time she carried a chest against her thighs, holding it in both hands and leaning back so that its weight was on her hips. She went to the stairs, glared at them for a moment, and then hoisted the chest up higher, the muscles in her arms bulging out against her skin, and climbed away. A train of people followed: men and women both, most looking rough and poor, but a few ladies done up like maids, and one woman looking rich enough to own the rest. They went up to their rooms, and Aethan ordered a sixth.

The crowd came down to the tavern and spread out. A few

gray folk straggled in too and sat at the bar, and by the time he got his seventh, the room had turned into quite the gathering. The long center tables were filled, and most of the smaller ones too.

The woman came in again, walking across the room like she owned the place. Her hair was pulled back into a bun, tight against her head. She hadn't changed upstairs. She wore the same pants that hugged tight around her ass and were tucked into her boots. She spoke to the barmaid, passed some coin across, and disappeared into a side room.

She was like a cat, appearing and then darting away. The group was obviously from Sheras, but the woman walked as though she knew exactly where she was going. Her hips did not sway as she went, as was the style of the rich Freeland ladies, and though she wasn't tall, her strides were long and sure and loud against the floorboards.

Aethan couldn't hold his bladder any longer and stumbled out into the gray evening to piss against the side of the building. There was a lot of beer to piss away, and when he returned his table was taken. Four gray locals sat there with drinks in their grubby hands, looking over at the party from Sheras with annoyance. Aethan spied a stool at the bar and stumbled over to it, pushing between two gray folk to sit down. He rapped his little finger against the wood to get the barmaid's attention. The gray man on his right turned around, looked down at Aethan's hand, scowled, and then pushed away.

Aethan was vaguely sure he'd been slighted. If it wasn't his skin, it was his hand, but hell, if the folk of this town wanted to give him space, he wasn't going to say no. The barmaid served him. He took a long pull at his beer, and when he put it down, the woman was beside him.

"Beer," she said.

Her voice was remarkably smooth, but with an edge that bit through the clamoring of the crowd. She glared forward while she waited, an angry slant to her brow and her lips in a frown as tight as the bun on her head.

"Something you want, friend," she said, and Aethan realized he'd been staring.

"Can I buy you a drink?" he asked.

She turned back to face forward. "I've got my own money."

"Well, so do I. Doesn't mean I'd say no to a free drink."

"Right."

Aethan saw her jaw flex.

"As you will," she said.

Aethan paid for her drink, and they both stared at the wall behind the bar, draining their cups like there was a competition in it. Giving away money wasn't usually in his nature, but it wasn't really his money, he reckoned. It was Jaaque's. Jaaque was buying this woman a drink. Aethan was just going through the motions for him.

Aethan looked behind him at the room of people. Laughter. Camaraderie.

"Why aren't you with them? You came in with them."

"You talk a lot, do you?" she said.

"No," he answered, "Not usually. But I'm a bit drunk, you see."

She grunted in response and took a long drink. The stirring in his pants was becoming more urgent, but Aethan wasn't quite sure if it was just because he had to piss again.

"Do you..." he began. She turned an eye to him, and Aethan finished his thought. "...Wanna fuck?"

27

"What?" Saara asked. She turned fully to face him, having heard him very clearly but not believing what he'd said.

The Freelander went on in that queer accent Freelanders had. "You look like you are miserable and could use a distraction."

"What's it to you?"

The man tapped his left temple. "Because I am miserable and could also use a distraction."

Saara felt that her mouth was hanging a bit open, and she shut it. He was right. She was mulling a lot of things in her head: the way Carlotte had just dismissed her, the way Carlotte had relaxed the hierarchies and then snapped them back into place for her, the way she'd spent almost everything she had on this expedition, and the way that Carlotte didn't seem to care. She was thinking about how if this expedition failed, she would have no money, no job, and no family. The thoughts swirled in her head, and it was all she could do not to–

"Sure," she heard herself say.

The Freelander looked surprised, like he hadn't thought it would work.

Hell, Saara hadn't thought it would work until she'd said yes. She pushed away from the bar. "You coming?"

He nodded and shoved to his feet.

She turned, her beer forgotten, and started back to her room.

No. It wouldn't do if someone saw the man coming out or into her room. Nor would it look good, she supposed, if someone saw her going into or out of his room. She growled, as though she could threaten her anxieties away.

"Your room. Where is it?" she asked and mounted the stairs.

"First on the right, Maitre D' said." He pulled a key out of one pocket.

Saara took it from him and plowed ahead. She found the door, shoved the key into the lock, and shouldered it open.

It was a simple room. She saw the bed and stopped looking. She grabbed his shirt, pulled him roughly inside, checked the hallway, and then closed the door and clicked the lock into place. The room was dark with the door closed, and she stumbled to the bedside table and fumbled for half a minute trying to get the candle to light. When it did, she pulled her shirt over her head and then turned to see him sprawled out on the bed, watching her, fully clothed.

She suddenly felt a fool. "We doing this or not?"

"I... yes," he stammered and started at his buckle.

Saara pulled off her undershirt and caught a good whiff of herself. It wasn't great. The Freelander stopped what he was doing and stared at her chest. Saara felt the simultaneous urge to hide them and give them a shake. She couldn't remember the last time another person had seen them in this context. Had it been Bracille. No, there must have been another. Saara growled the thoughts away and sat down on the floor to unlace and wrench her boots off. There passed several moments of silence except for the sound of buckles and laces and buttons being undone, and then she wiggled out of her pants and stood, naked as the day she was born.

The Freelander undid his last button and stood as well. His pants fell to the floor, and he stepped out of them. They stared at each other. He was lean mostly, with a bit of fat around his belly, but his muscles looked hard enough beneath his skin.

Saara stepped up to him, a desperate desire pushing her forward. He reached out for her, and she put a hand up on his chest. She closed her fingers around the hair there and then let it fall down, gliding past his chest muscles and past his belly and--

"Oh," he said.

Saara pushed him back, and he lay out on the bedsheets like a prince on his chaise. She climbed on top of him and felt herself wet with a need. She lowered herself down, inch by inch, anticipating penetration, until she sat flat on his pelvis. She frowned.

"What's wrong?" she asked, and the urge to cover herself flared up again.

"Nothing, I'm just... a little drunk. Just give it a little..." he trailed off.

"A little what?"

"A little," he said, and flexed his stomach so there was some room between their hips, and reached a hand down between them. She scoffed and reached her own hand down. Her hand felt his wrist and then his hand and then-

Saara looked down, squawked, and then threw herself back onto her feet. He looked confused for a moment, and then he followed her gaze to his hand. It was a horrid, twisted thing, the three middle fingers missing entirely and the space between his thumb and little finger torn halfway to his wrist. The skin around it was lumpy and ridged and pale, a mass of scar tissue that twisted around his hand in a pink spiral through his skin.

He sat up, placed the mangled hand in his lap, and looked down at it.

"It's from the war. The second one. Not old enough for the first," he said, and then looked back up at her.

She tore her own gaze away and looked him in the eyes. They were a light brown, almost green, she noticed.

"Is it a problem?" he said.

She shook her head. "No."

"Okay." He slid his hand to the side and hid it beneath his leg. "Just give me a moment," and he began to work on himself with his other hand.

She watched him fondle himself for a moment, the awkwardness turning almost unbearable, and then she dropped to her knees and pushed his hand away. "I can do that better," and she took him into her mouth.

He grunted and leaned back onto the bed again. His hips writhed as she worked, buttocks clenching and unclenching, and his hands, both the mangled and the whole, grasped at the sheets.

He tasted like sweat and leather, and he smelled as unwashed as she did. She closed her eyes and focused on her mouth and tongue, and pushed the smell of him and the sight of his hand out of her head. He stiffened enough to poke her in the back of the throat, and she pulled away and climbed back on top of him. She took him inside her. They moaned in unison, and she bucked her hips to match his own writhing.

She knew it wouldn't last long with the way his stomach was flexing and for a moment she was afraid he would not last till she finished, but he reached down with his good hand and laid it against his stomach, crooking up a finger that gave her something to rub against and she felt the release building within her.

His breathing quickened, and hers matched pace. He reached up his other hand and grabbed at her head, and then the tie on her hair fell away, and her hair tumbled down over her shoulders. He dropped his hand behind her back, and she felt the claw push her forward and down so her body was parallel to his, and her hair cascaded around their faces, and she was unable to control the course of action other than to grind against him. Her pubic hair tugged at his and rubbed against the skin and hurt, and she ground it harder. He held her firm, sawing in and out, slamming into her, and, as a scream rose from both of them, he grabbed her face with both hands--she could feel the uneven scar tissues against her right cheek--and he kissed her violently. She screamed into him and he into her, and she felt his semen rush inside her, and she felt her muscles clench and clench and clench.

He released her face, and she collapsed beside him onto the mattress. The sheets were damp beneath her, and the room's air was cool on her skin. Her breathing slowed, and her mind came back to the wider world. She wondered if anyone had seen them go out together. The room was full. Someone must have. There would certainly be talk.

"Thank you," he said.

"You're welcome," she answered, staring up at the ceiling.

She replayed the evening in her head. The way Carlotte had asked her to set up a dinner for Val and the violinist, the way Carlotte had asked her to stay, and then... the way Carlotte had told Val that Saara was at his service, the way Carlotte had dismissed her, the way Carlotte had phrased it, like Saara was being released from an awkward situation back to where she belonged. With the crew.

It had been such a vague promise, years ago. "To be a Ryker is to be of extraordinary ability. To be one of use, you must prove your ability, your service, and your loyalty," Carlotte had said. Carlotte had been just a girl, really, back then, not yet twenty, but with the same surety of purpose and vicious intent. Carlotte had looked at her with those calculating eyes, and the insinuation was clear. It was an offer. A fee for hard work to be done. It was the promise that ran Saara's life.

Had it been clear? Had Carlotte been telling the truth?

Saara shoved the thoughts forcefully out of her head. She didn't have the luxury of these thoughts. She had put everything on the line for this expedition. She'd already made her plan, and now she could only follow it through.

Saara blinked at the piles of clothing on the floor. Hers were all about, and his was in one pile beside the bed. His shirt and pants lay atop his long brown overcoat. It was so familiar to her, just like the one her uncle had worn when he'd found time to leave his warehouse. Like the one her uncle had worn when he dragged a teenage Saara down to Val's library to learn to read. Another piece of her life apart from Carlotte gone. There wasn't much left.

She got to her feet and began dressing.

"Leaving already?" Aethan asked.

"You wanted a fuck, you got a fuck." She pulled her pants up and looked for her belt.

He watched her for a moment and then spoke again. "That was a nice distraction."

She looked at him.

"Yeah, it was." She put on her shirt. "I needed it."

"Me too," he said, and then, after a moment. "Do you want to talk about it?"

"About what?"

"Whatever it is that made you so sad before. And now."

"I'm not sad!" she snapped. "I'm just--no. I don't want to talk about it. Certainly not with you." There was venom in her voice. Probably more than she intended, but she was too tired to care.

Too over everything. Maybe her beer was still on the bar.

"I get it," he said, and turned away from her to look up at the ceiling. "Will you be here tomorrow? Because if you are then--"

"No. We are shipping out in the morning, up the Iron River. So you'll have to find another pity fuck tomorrow night."

"Up the Iron River?"

"Yeah. That a problem?"

"No," he said. "I just, that's my route too. Your party doesn't look like miners. Or colonists."

Saara narrowed her eyes at him.

"What is it to you?"

"Nothing. Just... I could use a distraction on my way west."

A long moment passed, and Saara said nothing.

He continued, "And if you were desperate enough to say yes to a stranger asking for a fuck, then I'd bet you could use a distraction out west too."

Saara crossed her arms but didn't contradict him. She thought about the road ahead. She thought about her worries and her doubts and how, for a few minutes, she hadn't thought about them at all.

"Where are you headed?" she asked.

"Bergshalen."

28

A successful expedition starts with an exceptional captain. There are many qualities required—see chapters four, five, and six for details on required knowledge, faith, and personal discipline–but more important than all is the captain's ability to hold firmly to hierarchy whilst still being a man of the laborers. In the wild recesses of the world, there are no Rykers, no societal structures or armies to enforce them. There is only the captain.

The captain must hold to a hierarchy or risk anarchy and failure. The captain must always hold dictatorial power, must project strength, and yet must appear to be friendly and 'one of the boys'. The crew should view the captain's word as law, the captain's lieutenants as an extension of this law, and yet the men must believe the captain appreciates and wants the best for them. It is the relationship of a family. The father is the captain. His children must believe he loves them and yet obey every command. He must appear to be their friend and their counselor and their punisher. The lieutenant then takes on the mother's role. An extension of the father's will. A dictatorial power over the children and yet still in service to the father. The children must see no argument between the father and mother. They must see a united front, a singular message that comes from the father. If the father must punish the mother, he must do so in private, where the children cannot--

Carlotte skipped ahead. The book was written by an ancestor of hers, one Gordon DeSheras, who'd made a name for himself taking biological expeditions down to the Greenwall and the Korkin Empire back when the Korkin Empire was still a thing. He'd penned it some hundred years before, and Carlotte was determined to glean what knowledge there was to be gleaned, regardless of the misogynistic trite that came along with it.

The crew must then be diligently picked to ensure cohesion. Each member must have four primary qualities. First and second are a respect for authority and something to lose. Do not pull from the dregs of society. Do not take immigrants from out country or pick your lieutenant from some disenfranchised Ryker family. Find those that have something to gain if the expedition goes well (recognition for the lieutenants, money for the chaff), something to lose if it goes poorly (reputation, money, lives, etc), and who recognize you as a better. Your choosing them should be an honor. Third and fourth, they must be inland Dominioneers through and through, and they must be men. Racial diversity always brings friction, and women, though their presence may seem pleasant in the manor, are strictly a hindrance in culture and morality, and--

The door opened and Saara entered carrying a breakfast tray with an egg, a peach, and a bit of bread. Carlotte closed the book and thought briefly of chucking it through a window. Alas, the windows here did not open. She wondered if she could break it with one throw. Instead, she laid the book neatly beside the breakfast tray and popped a bit of peach into her mouth. There were good ideas in the book that she would incorporate into her expedition in the next few months. She was not one to pass up knowledge just because a dead man offended her.

Ari and Renee came in then and began preparing her. Renee put together an outfit while Ari brushed and coiled Carlotte's hair, and Saara packed up Carlotte's things.

"The one with the fur, again," Carlotte ordered, and Renee obliged, unfolding Elspeth's coat and draping it across the bed. "The fur needs attention," Carlotte said, and Renee set to brushing it out. Carlotte had decided Elspeth's cloak was the look she would keep for the entire journey. It was the look that would define this expedition.

Saara looked tired, and Carlotte noticed a strand of hair hanging from Saara's usually inescapable bun. It hung to the side of her face, and as though Saara could feel Carlotte's gaze, she grabbed the hair and tucked it back where it belonged.

"The wagons are being loaded on the boat now. We're off in half an hour, Madame," Saara said and then squatted down, grabbed the chest by either handle, and heaved it up. It was quite heavy, and Carlotte was always surprised by Saara's rustic peasant strength. Saara was a good lieutenant per Gordon's rules. She had everything to lose, much to gain, and was as loyal as a dog.

"A moment," Carlotte said, and stood while Ari rushed to push a needle through Carlotte's hair to secure it in place.

While Saara held the chest, Carlotte opened it and rummaged inside until she found what she was looking for: the gun Harold had given her. Renee's eyes widened over Saara's shoulder.

"I'll be just down," Carlotte said.

Saara nodded and trundled the chest out the door. Ari and Renee helped Carlotte into a shift, stays, a dark green riding habit, and then Elspeth's coat. Renee pinned a hat to Carlotte's hair, and Ari laced up a pair of heeled boots that gave her a good three inches of height. Carlotte sent her maids away with the old clothes so that she was alone again. She lifted the gun and examined its handle. The forest creatures still ran down the barrel, and Carlotte was again amazed that Harold, of all people, had carved it. Maybe he hadn't. Likely, he had paid some artisan. The rabbit near the end of the barrel was particularly intricate, its face carved into such a delicate terror. Carlotte thought of her flight through the Orlient house and wondered if *she* was the rabbit.

She was, in part. She could not deny the fear she felt. Fear that the inquisitors would intercept them before the ship left the dock and return her to Harold's betrothal, that the expedition would be a failure, and she'd come home in disgrace. Fear that she'd end up like Elspeth. She had let that fear come across the night before with Visoletta. She shouldn't have done that.

Carlotte held up the gun and pointed it at the mirror. She made the sound of a gun firing with her mouth and mimed its recoil. She was powerful. She may be the rabbit, but she was also the thing that the rabbit ran from.

Carlotte loosened her belt and stuck the gun through it. She messed with its angle, looking at herself in the mirror, until it seemed to lie casually, easily within reach of a woman who was ready to use it. *A captain must project strength,* Gordon DeSheras had said. Carlotte set an authoritative frown, lifted her chin, and limped out of the room.

William Zimmerman

29

Once all of the expedition's carts and crew were loaded onto the ship, Saara motioned for Aethan to bring up his cart. He walked down the dock with his reins in hand, but before he could lead his horse and donkey up the gangplank, Slack Gin stepped into his way.

"Don't know where you think you're going, Boneman, but it ain't this boat."

Aethan stopped, and his gaze narrowed.

Saara stepped forward. "Slack, this man--"

"Don't bother yourself, Ma'am. I can run off this slave myself."

"I am no slave," Aethan said.

"Killing your--"

"Slack!" Saara yelled.

Slack looked over his shoulder, his lip bulging out with chew.

"This is Aethan," Saara said. "He is joining our expedition. Stop being an ass."

Slack looked from her to Aethan and back to her, and then spat a glob of black spit onto the deck. "You'd bring a murderer onto this crew?" he asked.

Saara saw a spasm of something cross Aethan's face, and he took a step back. A protective instinct sprang up in Saara.

"Aethan is a trader! And he's--"

"That man," Slack cut over her, pointing a long finger back at him. "That man and his kind slaughtered my kin! My uncle and father, and baby cousins are all dead because of him and his! My mother and I barely escaped Korka with our lives!"

Whatever feeling had washed over Aethan left, and his face set into a frown. He crossed his arms and said nothing. Saara saw Hannah from the corner of her eye, and she was suddenly aware of others gathering around them, like an audience gathering for a show that Saara was a part of. Saara lowered her voice, trying to diffuse the moment.

"The revolution was over thirty years ago. Aethan would have been a child."

"Their kind stinks with treachery," Slack cried out, "And I won't be on no crew that serves with--"

"What is happening?"

They all turned and saw Carlotte standing behind them. She was at the door to the below deck, leaning on Ari's arm. Her face was incredulous – delicate and dark eyebrows slanted, red lips in a sneer. The fur of her collar bristled up around her like a wave crashing against a mountain. Saara's stomach tightened. She grasped for something to say, some way to end this before Carlotte got herself involved. Nothing came to mind.

"Madame," Slack said, "Your girl is bringing a Boneman onto this ship. A Boneman! Them's that keep my peoples' bones in their pockets. Like goblins from stories."

"My girl?" Carlotte said. Her voice was almost silent compared to Slack's rage, but it cut through the air just as well.

"Saara," Slack said, looking suddenly unsure of himself. He gestured to Saara. "Her."

Carlotte looked from Slack to her and then back to Slack. Her sneer settled into a frown. "You mean my captain?"

"Ye, her," Slack grunted. "Whatever worth she thinks that Boneman will bring it ain't worth it. He'll cut our throats in our sleep. Just like they did my father. Mark my words."

The deck of the ship was silent then, except for the bustling sounds of a busy harbor. The air was thick with the gray smog that covered the town, though it was somewhat better over the water. The hired sailors had stopped their preparations to join the gawkers.

"Mr. Gin," Carlotte said after a long moment, "If I wanted to mark your words, I would have asked. This expedition is mine, and Saara, my Captain, speaks with *my* voice."

Carlotte glanced at Aethan and raised her voice. "Come aboard. And Mr. Gin, take a moment before the tide comes in and decide if you want to stay, or if you'd rather go back to Sheras. Alone."

Another moment of silence followed, and then Saara nodded to Aethan. Aethan clicked his tongue and guided Toktok and Greg up onto the boat. Slack watched him pass and spat another glob of black spit onto the deck.

Carlotte turned back to the door. "Saara. Show me my cabin."

"Yes, Madame," Saara said, and hurried to her.

Saara took Carlotte below deck and into the Captain's cabin. She had paid extra to oust the actual captain to the crew bunks. It was smaller than Carlotte's closet back in the tower, but it had a desk with a lamp and an actual bed. Saara had brought Carlotte's chest down fifteen minutes before, and she saw that it had been opened. A book lay on the desk, and the lamp had been lit. Carlotte had already been here.

"What are you doing?" Carlotte asked.

Saara didn't know how to answer that, so she stayed silent.

"We're not in Sheras anymore, Saara. In a week, we will barely even be in the Dominion. This expedition is only as stable as its members, and its members are only as stable as their trust is in us. You and me. Now," she paused for emphasis. "Now we've got at least one influential member who thinks we are incompetent--"

"Slack was completely out of line--"

"Then you shouldn't have hired him!" Carlotte yelled.

"Madame--" she began, but Carlotte cut her off.

"Who is this Freelander?"

"He's a... a trader."

"And why is this Freeland trader on my expedition?"

"Because..." Saara began. Because why? Because Saara had felt alone even before her uncle died, and now he was dead, and she had left the only city she'd ever known? Because she had no idea how to run an expedition and didn't know what Carlotte actually thought of her and an off the cuff fuck had been the only time she hadn't been consumed with anxiety since they'd left? Because she wanted desperately to end this conversation and do it again?

"Because he is an ex-soldier," she stammered. "He'll be good in a fight if it comes to that... And he was going to Bergshalen anyway."

"He was going to Bergshalen anyway? You just picked this person up? Saara. I don't know if this has occurred to you, but I've put everything on the line for this expedition! If this falls through, I am ruined."

Saara opened her mouth, but nothing came out. She thought of the choices *she* had made. The savings *she* had spent. The relationships *she* had sacrificed.

"You need to think your decisions through before you make them. The way the crew sees you is important, and it reflects onto me!" Carlotte snapped. "You speak with my voice, so act like it."

Carlotte turned away from Saara, and then limped to the desk and sat down. She cradled her head delicately with three fingers and looked down at the open book there.

Saara understood she was dismissed and left the room.

30

Aethan lashed his cart's wheels to eyelets set in the ship's deck and unhitched Greg and Toktok. He had agreed for them to be drafted to pull the boat, but for now they had nothing to do but eat treats from his hand.

He looked for Saara, but after going below deck, she either stayed out of sight or strode purposefully fore and aft, barking orders. Aethan was unable to tell if she was busy or actively avoiding him, and at that moment it was difficult for him to care, so he passed the time watching the sailors prepare for the tide to change. They took the boat out into the bay and let it drift slowly out to sea. The drift slowed, and then stopped, and then the tide came in, and their drift reversed, pushing them inland and up into the Iron River's mouth.

Aethan left Greg and Toktok and went to lean against the ship's railing. Teams of men swarmed around the waterwheels that dipped into the river along the shore, disengaging the mechanisms and doing something to allow the wheels to turn the opposite way. Then the boat was past the factories, and Aethan watched the outlying buildings give way to farms and pasture and then to rolling hills.

"Aethan."

He turned to see Saara standing behind him with hands on her hips.

"You've been busy," he said.

She nodded. "Tide's running out. Time for the horses."

Aethan shrugged, and then motioned to Toktok and Greg. "Do you need me to..."

"No," Saara said, "Unless they're difficult."

Aethan shook his head.

"Toktok's a dream. Greg... not sure if you want him. He might die on you."

"Is that a problem?" Saara asked.

"At this point I'll be lucky to sell him for meat."

"Right," Saara said, and then turned.

"Hey," Aethan said and grabbed her arm. He felt her stiffen beneath his fingers as she looked back to him.

"What are you doing?" Saara asked, and glared at his hand. "There's nowhere private here."

Aethan removed his hand. "Are we only allowed to talk in private?"

Saara's eyes danced around the boat, taking stock of everyone on the deck.

"Listen. I don't know how it is in the Freelands, but there are ways that things are done here."

"So, we can't talk?"

"We left dinner together last night," Saara snapped. "And now you're on the god damn boat. I think we've given everyone enough to talk about."

Aethan looked out at the ship deck. None of the crew were watching them. They were all in their little groups talking amongst themselves or helping to wrestle the horses into position. "So?"

Saara rolled her eyes and walked away.

Aethan sighed. He'd wanted to be alone, hadn't he? Wasn't that his goal? To buy some land far away from everyone and avoid people for the rest of his life? Saara was just giving him what he wanted.

He sagged against the rail and watched the boat pull up to a dock that led to nothing but a dirt road. The sailors dropped anchor, and then the horses were led down the dock and hitched into a line that would pull the boat up river.

"How do they keep the boat from hitting shore?"

Aethan turned to see the violinist on his left, leaning against the railing just like he was. She wasn't the kind of woman Aethan was normally attracted too. She was tall and gawky. Not much meat on her, but the dress she wore flowed down her arched back and then up over her backside. Her face was nothing special, hard lines and a harder jaw, but she looked vaguely familiar to him.

"What?" he asked.

"The horses are going to pull the boat upstream right?" she asked and pointed to the sailors hitching Greg into the line of horses.

Aethan nodded.

"Won't that pull the boat into the shoreline?"

Aethan ran a hand over his hair. "I don't know. Maybe the rudder pulls us back out?"

"Huh," she said. "I don't understand boats at all. I thought they were all sails and oars. I can't imagine what that is for." She pointed at the left side of the ship's front railing.

There was a thick wheel there, with the railing as its axle, and its rim was rutted as though something was to run around it.

Aethan frowned. "I've no idea," he said.

Visoletta turned her head to look at him. "I'm... Visoletta Corlionne."

"I know," Aethan said. "Everyone knows who you are."

Visoletta snorted. "Everyone thinks they know who I am." She tapped a finger to her chest. "But they don't really. Really it's just the cloak they recognize."

Visoletta gave a little twirl and the red cape billowed around her.

Aethan smiled. "I suppose no one really knows who anyone is. Not really."

"Well, who does everyone think you are?"

He lifted his good hand out to her and she took it lightly. Her hands were rough. He wondered if that was from her instrument's strings. "Aethan."

"Just Aethan?"

"The Freelands aren't fond of surnames. Father's name was Amoz, if that helps."

"Aethan, Son of Amoz," Visoletta said, rolling the words in her mouth like she was feeling each of them with her tongue. Why are you on this expedition, Aethan, Son of Amoz?"

Aethan looked back to the line of horses to see Saara arguing with the sailors setting up the team. He took in a big breath and let it out.

"I'm not sure."

Visoletta laughed again, harder this time. "I'm not sure why I'm here either. I hope it's not to pull the boat," she said.

"Miss."

Aethan and Visoletta turned to see one of the other ladies standing behind them. The maid scratched nervously at one wrist. Behind her a red tent had been pitched on the deck. Another maid stood beside that with a deep scowl on her face.

"It's ready, ma'am," the nervous one said.

"Thank you, Hannah," Visoletta said, and then took the maids arm in her own. Hannah squawked in surprise and Visoletta laughed and turned her around.

"You're coming with me," she said, and then looked back over her shoulder and winked. "Duty calls."

Visoletta pulled Hannah with her and they disappeared into the tent, followed by the third lady's maid. Aethan watched after them for several moments. Maybe this trip wouldn't be so lonely after all.

Aethan didn't get to speak to Visoletta again that day. If she emerged from her tent, then he did not see it. Instead, he watched the countryside slowly roll by, and the line of horses slowly pull them up the river. He wondered if this was any faster than just riding. He supposed there must be a reason they were on the boat, and he almost asked the sailor who leaned lazily against the helm just a dozen paces away, but Aethan's mood was settling on him. He grew suddenly very tired, and he left the railing to lie out on the deck beside his cart and watch the clouds. The day grew hot, and he thought about the flame and Jaaque's burning body. When the evening came and cold winds swept down from the mountain, he thought of his naked flight through Sheras, and the feeling of the knife in his back, how the wound still pulsed with pain. He fell asleep at some point, and when he awoke the next day, he felt as though a great weight were pressing down on every part of him. He could not muster the energy to find Saara or Visoletta, and they made no effort either. He hadn't eaten dinner the night before, and he didn't rise when Saara called out for breakfast or for lunch. He slipped in and out of a dozing sleep filled with flickering images of fire, murder, and loss, and when Saara called out for dinner, he awoke in a panic. It took him a moment to recognize where he was, and then he looked over to see the others lining up by the cook's secured cart, and he felt a pang of hunger bite through him. With a great gathering of energy, he rose and shuffled to the back of the line.

The cook stopped his ladle halfway between the pot and Aethan's bowl when he saw who held it. The man's eyes flickered up and to the side, and Aethan followed them to see Slack Gin sitting against the railing with his boys fanned out around him, watching the interaction with a lazy, disinterested glare. Aethan reached out, took the ladle from the cook's limp grip, and poured it into his bowl. He grabbed a heel of bread from beside the pot, scowled, and strode back to his cart.

"Freelander. Would you like to sit with us? Or do you prefer the company of that cart?"

Aethan stopped and turned to see the two old soldiers and the kid with the beaten face sitting in a circle just behind him. He'd walked by them without notice.

"I would not blame you if you did," the soldier continued. "People are often terrible."

The other soldier did not look up, chewing his stew intently, but after a moment of silence, he spoke. "Leave it alone, Haric. The Freelander wants nothing to do with us."

"It was just an offer," Haric said.

Aethan looked to his cart, alone in its section of the boat, and felt an overwhelming ache that was not his stomach.

"I will eat with you," Aethan said, the words grumbling out like a disused wagon wheel pressed suddenly into service. "Thank you."

Haric scooted to one side and the bruise-faced kid to the other.

Aethan sat. "Aethan," he said.

"Haric," Haric answered and then pointed to the other old soldier. "That's Pierre, and that runt with a face like ground beef is Rold."

"Ay!" Rold cried out, "I gave it more than I got it."

"Shit," Pierre said between spoonfuls of stew, "You must have right killed him."

Rold crossed his arms. "Maybe I did."

"Hear that, Aethan?" Haric said, leaning in close like they were old friends. "We got ourselves a murderer on this expedition."

"Wouldn't be the first one," Aethan mumbled, and put a spoonful of stew in his mouth. They were silent then, and when he looked up, they were all staring at him.

"I was in the war..." he said after a moment.

"Oh. That's not murder," said Pierre.

"Why not?" asked Rold.

"Cause it's not," answered Pierre.

"That's not a reason."

"Because..." Pierre looked at Haric and then at Aethan as though looking for some support.

Aethan said nothing.

"Because it's bigger than that. Murder is a personal thing, a few folk who can't figure how to be decent to one another and resort to being brutes. War is..."

"That sounds like war to me," Haric said.

Pierre scoffed. "You know what I mean," Pierre said, though it seemed none of them did.

"It's-" he waved his spoon in the air, and bits of stew splattered onto the deck. "It is the response to aggression. The... last recourse wherein a person has no choice but to fight to protect his land and his family and his people."

They were silent for a moment.

"What?" Rold asked.

Pierre flicked his spoon towards the boy. "No lip from you."

"It's not lip. It just doesn't make any sense."

"What doesn't make sense?"

"How can both sides be fighting to protect their land and their people?"

Pierre cast a desperate look at Haric.

Haric chuckled.

"Look," Pierre said finally. "There's a difference. I was in the war, and I am not a murderer. Alright?" He pointed his spoon threateningly at the Rold, who didn't look convinced, but the boy's face was so mashed it was difficult to tell what he was thinking.

"Good," Pierre said and went back to scraping up the last of his stew.

They ate the rest of their meal without speaking, listening to the murmur of conversations around them and the scrape of spoon on bowl and the creaking of the boat beneath them.

Aethan looked to Haric, and Haric gave him a smile and a nod, and Aethan gave a small one back to be polite. It felt good to give it.

"Quick," a man yelled. "Fetch the Madame DeSheras!"

Aethan looked toward the bow. The small man with the Ryker mustache and gold rimmed glasses was standing at the railing facing away from them. He turned back and waved frantically at one of the lady's maids, and Aethan saw that he held a brass spyglass in one hand. The woman went below, and the man turned back towards the front. They had been coming up on the Gladibu range for some time, and now those mountains were looming large before them.

"Who's that man?" Aethan asked.

Haric shrugged.

"Vaalier something."

"Saadermont," Pierre finished. "Low Ryker or some such."

"What's he going on about?" Rold asked.

Pierre shot a glare back at him. "You think we know?"

"Let's ask!" Rold jumped to his feet.

"Ay!" Pierre barked, "Take the dishes back first."

A crowd was forming around Vaalier, and Aethan's new group joined it. Rold shoved through to stand at the front.

Haric prodded the largest of Slack's men for an explanation.

"Does it look like I know?" the man said. "How am I to know the excitement of Rykers? Looks like a mountain to me."

"It is the lovers," came a voice behind them.

Aethan turned to see one of the hired sailors standing just behind the crowd. His hair was cut short, and his beard was worn long and braided in two strands that were flung over each shoulder like a pair of reins. It was a popular look among some sailors, affected from across the ocean.

"What are the lovers?" Aethan asked.

The sailor pointed straight down the bow at the approaching Gladibu Range. "It is the north and the south mountains. They are split by the river, and the division is so stark and so deep that the only explanation is God. Southern folk think this is called the Iron River because of the trade in iron that goes down it, but it is actually for its iron strength to cut through the mountain, like a cleaver through meat."

"Strength," Aethan glanced over the railing at the water floating lazily past them. The wide Iron River was nothing if not gentle.

The sailor continued. "The mountains were lovers whose love was so great they had no room for God in their hearts. This angered the Lord God, and he sent the river thus to divide them. Cursed to remain always close but also always separated."

"You believe this?" Aethan asked.

The sailor shrugged. "Well enough. There is little other explanation for it, and God's wrath is known to be fierce and swift."

"Huh," Aethan said, because he didn't know what else to say in such situations. There was no God in the Freelands, but God was thick in the Dominion, especially away from the large cities, and it was difficult for Aethan to tell where dogma ended and folklore began.

He didn't have to continue the conversation. Carlotte emerged from below and strode across the deck with Saara and the lady's maid at her heels. Silence spread through the crowd, and they all turned to look at her.

"Why am I here?" she asked.

"The lovers," the sailor said.

Carlotte asked for an explanation, and he repeated what he'd told Aethan.

Carlotte bristled at the answer. "Rivers cut gorges through rock all over the world."

"Aye, but you will see when we approach. This is not sloped like a normal gorge. The walls of the lovers are smooth and almost straight up and down all along the pass. There is only one explanation for it."

"You mean they are cliffs? There are plenty of rivers lined with cliffs. God is at the heart of all things, but he does not work in ways so crude as splitting a mountain because of jealousy for its love."

"You will see," the sailor said. "You will see when we arrive that I am right and you are wrong."

The sailor turned and left the crowd to attend to his normal duties. Carlotte disregarded him and motioned at the crowd. Saara pushed through them and made a path to the bow where Val stood.

"What is it?" Carlotte asked.

Val was still for a moment, but finally looked up from his eyeglass. "We are coming to the Iron Watcher," he said, holding the glass up to her. "It is one of the remaining wonders of the Amaranthine world. I have read many accounts of it, mostly by iron traders and the like."

"Nothing by Rykers?"

Val shook his head. "Some passing mention, but there are no ruins around it. Just the Watcher and the pass through the mountain. I've wondered myself why no one has made a study of it."

"Amaranthine scholars are few," Carlotte said. "Perhaps we will make a stop."

Carlotte put her eye to the glass and looked. The crowd pushed to the railing to see for themselves. Aethan found himself craning his neck to look over their shoulders.

They were still a mile off from the mountains. The foothills were around them now, rising up to each side of the river, but the Gladibu range rose up higher still just beyond. The sun touched the tops of the mountain, and they all shaded their eyes with their hands to keep from being blinded.

"I see nothing." Carlotte looked to Val beside her.

"It should come into view soon. It may be beyond the bend. I do not know."

Aethan saw no gap in the mountain, only the river vanishing into it.

Carlotte put her eye back to the glass and waited. They all waited. The foothills grew higher around them, and their grassy surfaces became broken by slabs of rock. Then the sun set further, and the mountains rose up higher. The glare was gone, and the pass appeared.

Carlotte took in a sudden breath. "What is it?" she asked.

"I do not know. No one does," Val said. His eyes flicked back and forth from the pass to the eyeglass, his fingers twitching like he wanted to take it back. Carlotte showed no sign of giving it up.

Then, Aethan could see it.

It was a pale ball floating above the entrance to the pass.

"A balloon?" Saara asked.

Val shook his head.

The crowd was silent as the boat came closer. Then details began to emerge, and he heard several gasps.

The ball was an eye of stone, white, perhaps marble, with a gray cornea and a jet black pupil. There were four spindly veins snaking out from it, tethering it to the walls of the pass in a great X. It was massive, several times Aethan's height at least, and it must have weighed many tons, but the veins were its only support and they couldn't have been thicker than Aethan's wrists. They were like leashes, and the eye seemed to surge forward to strain against them a hundred feet into the air. Carlotte let the eyeglass fall to her side as they approached. Aethan stared at the eye, and the eye stared back, unwavering, unblinking.

"No wonder no one has studied it," Saara said. "How would anyone reach it?"

"A set of pulleys, perhaps. Drop ropes from above and scale down. Or build a scaffold on a ship," Carlotte said.

"It would be a massive undertaking," Val said, and Carlotte nodded.

The boat's speed fell, and Aethan saw that the lazy river flowed faster here as it exited the pass. There was the crack of a whip, and the whinny of a protesting horse, and when Aethan turned to look, he saw a squat tower beside the road that he had not seen before, so intense was his attention on the eye. It was a dozen feet tall with a thick metal chain drooping from its top and disappearing into the water.

Their speed was a crawl at that point, and the crew threw down the anchor almost directly beneath the eye. The expedition's crew were all silent, staring up at the thing, but the sailors were busy with motion, pulling out the ramp to disembark.

"Why have we stopped?" Carlotte asked.

The captain moved through the crowd with a long wooden pole tipped with a hook, and Saara reached out to grab him. He shook off Saara's hand and thrust the pole into the water.

"There's no path for the horses," he said. Aethan looked away from the eye hanging above them and looked at the pass itself. The dirt road that had run all along the riverside ended abruptly at the wall of rock. The only way through the pass was on the water. The walls were impossibly steep. Almost straight up and down on either side, and they were smooth and unnaturally even.

"How do we get through?" Carlotte asked, peering over the railing into the water. "The current seems too fast to row."

"We pull," the ship captain said.

"Pull?" Carlotte repeated.

The captain only grunted and then began hauling the pole back in. He levered it against the railing and out of the water, and hooked to the end was the chain.

"Ah," Carlotte said.

"Wait," Saara said, stepping up to the sailor. "Who pulls?"

He blinked at her.

"Everyone, the ship is heavy with all of your things."

Saara shook her head. "The agreement was only that the horses would tow."

The captain pulled the chain up and over the wooden wheel at the left side of the prow, so that the metal settled into the rut.

"The agreement was that you would all pull your own weight."

Saara blinked at him. "I thought you meant feed ourselves."

The captain nodded. "Yes. And pull your own weight." He clapped her on the back. "Won't be long. Just a mile or so through the mountain.

The pass was narrow, barely wide enough for two boats to sail side by side, and it took them three hours to get through it. The water was fast, and the boat was heavy with all their carts and horses and bodies, and it sank deep into the river. The chain flowed up from the water, over the wheel at the front of the boat, along the deck to a similar wheel at the rear, and then back into the river. The sailors had emerged from below deck with leather-wrapped bars. They broke Saara and all the men into teams of two, then explained the process: slide the bar through a chain link, brace each side, and push. One team could not overcome the strength of the river, nor could two, but the deck was long, and the crew was large, and when teams of strong folk lined the deck from bow to stern and all struggled together, the ship moved. The teams trudged aft, and when they reached the stern, they pulled their rods free and ran back to the bow to begin the trudge again. The light of evening faded to twilight and then to a moonless darkness, and they toiled in the light of oil lamps that cast flickering shadows against the smooth wall of the pass. It was like a shadow play from an old Korkin priest, a never-ending line of dark figures struggling against a never-ending chain, sentenced to undying labor for their eternal sins. Aethan pushed and heaved until his legs left weariness behind and became numb. More than once, he thought to throw down his bar and demand a rest, but then he would look to his right and see Saara straining beside him. Her tightly bound hair sodden with sweat, the grim scowl on her face unending in its determination, the muscles in her shoulders bulging against the load. He could not quit. Not while she went on.

None of them quit, not even the small Ryker with the golden glasses, though Aethan doubted his efforts were much help, and when they finally emerged on the other side of the mountain pass, the moonlight came in, and the river opened up wide around them. The water slowed, and the resistance on the chain suddenly lessened. Aethan's legs began to give, but the captain's exhausted voice rang out.

"Not yet! To the tower!"

The expedition crew groaned, but the sailors pushed with renewed strength. Saara snarled, and Aethan shoved himself into the chain. They accelerated, and for the first time, their trudge became almost a run. He cycled through the line once, twice, three times, and then the captain called hold.

The anchor dropped, the ship lurched, and the crew collapsed where they stood. They were not individuals in that line. They had become one beast; each of them was the leg of a great centipede, and now they rested as one. The cliques that had formed were gone. Aethan lay beside Saara, and she beside him, their hands touching absently.

No one spoke. Aethan stared at the moon above him and listened to his own heavy breathing and Saara's beside him. Then, Visoletta was silhouetted above him, a dark shadow holding out a wine skin like the angel come to rescue the repentant damned at the end of the Korkin play. He pulled himself upright and took a long drink of watery wine, and then handed it to Saara. The maids were handing out skins to the others. Only Carlotte stood apart, standing at the railing and looking out at the moonlit landscape around them.

"That eye," Rold called out, breaking the silence. "The Amaranthine built it?"

"That's what you are thinking about, after all that?" One of the sailors laughed.

"It's stuck with me, too," Haric broke in. "Through all that effort, it stuck in my mind."

There were other grunts of ascent, and Carlotte turned from the railing to look back at them. The moonlight lit her from above, and the flickering oil lamps lit her from below.

"Val?" she called.

The little man with the golden glasses rose from his place amongst the men. "Yes. It was the Amaranthine. As much as we can know that anything is their doing."

"They have a flair for the dramatic," Carlotte said. "It fits with the other monuments to their hubris. Like the steps of the Grand Cathedral in Sheras. They were so taken with their own knowledge that they forgot their humanity."

"If they could build something like that--" Rold began.

"They were men," Carlotte said, cutting him off. "Men and women who believed themselves above our Lord God."

"Who were they?" Visoletta asked. She stood at the edge of the lamplight. Her red cloak seemed to be made of flame as it flickered.

"You don't know who the Amaranthine were?" Carlotte asked.

"I know a little. Some folk who fell or something. Built magnificent things," Visoletta said.

"My mother said they were damned folk," one of the lady's maids said. "She told me they were ghosts. Tried to scare me and my sister with them."

"I thought they weren't real," the big man, Boris, said. "That they were just children's tales."

"No, no, no!" Val cried, his voice sounding small in the open night. "They were real. They were people. They lived two thousand years ago. Their ruins are all over the continent. The Grand Theater and the Cathedral, and the Nor-So. Those were left here by the Amaranthine."

"What happened to them?" Visoletta asked. She did not seem ashamed of not knowing. She was serene in it. Like an inquisitive child, unafraid of judgment. "Does anyone know?"

No one answered at first. The laborers shook their heads. Pierre and Haric looked at each other and shrugged.

"Well," Val said. He winced and leaned against the railing. "Beyond the stories in scripture, the evidence we have is vague. It is not a popular avenue of study, but we know from the ruins that they were a real people and that they populated the entire continent. There are ruins high in the mountains north of Irondale, a few reported in the great desert west of Bergshalen, and if the witnesses are to be believed, there are similar ruins in the Greenwall. No books or paper writings have survived. We only have the ruins themselves, some artifacts, and a few rare carvings."

Val coughed, and Visoletta handed him a wineskin. He took a long drink and continued.

"Some ruins are in places that we would struggle to survive in, and there are carvings that show incredible things, and the things they left behind last much longer than what we can create. Many think that they were more scientifically advanced than we are. However, it is difficult to say what represents reality and what represents the Amaranthine mythology. There are depictions of moving statues, for instance, but if those actually existed, or if they are part of some heathen religious belief, is impossible to say.

"But the ruins are of similar age, and so far as we can tell, they all seem to have been abandoned at about the same time. Whatever ended the Amaranthine empire, it happened quickly."

Val blinked around at the faces all watching him.

"I could go on, but that's the gist."

"What destroyed them?" Visoletta asked.

"It's unclear," Val said. "A plague, perhaps. Or-"

"The how is unclear," Carlotte said, cutting him off. "Plague, war, or rain of fire. But the why is not. God struck them down. God gave them the gifts of knowledge and the power to live an easy life, and they became complacent. They became so enamored with his gifts that they thought themselves greater than he, and he struck them down for it. He set humanity back to ignorance so that we would discover the world's secrets for ourselves." Carlotte looked out again at the landscape, and then said quietly, "For why else do we, the Ryker, exist, but to unravel and catalog the tapestry of creation?"

A man cleared his throat, and Aethan looked to see Slack Gin rising from the deck. His hair was wet against his face, and even now his lip bulged with blackleaf. He spoke. "I was taught the Amaranthine were destroyed because they forgot their place in the hierarchy of beasts, men, and God," Slack said. He looked at Aethan and spat onto the deck.

Aethan felt his cheeks grow hot. It seemed the oneness of the crew after the labor of the pass was gone. "I was taught the Amaranthine were killed by a slave uprising," Aethan growled. "Because they were too weak and decadent to hold on to their tyranny."

Slack sneered and opened his mouth to say more, but Carlotte cut in again. "Visoletta, the crew has worked so hard for so long. Perhaps you could play something for us to end the evening. I cannot imagine a more beautiful stage."

Even in the darkness, Aethan could see Visoletta's eyes widen.

"Please!" called out Val, "It's been so long since I've heard you."

The maid, Hannah, turned to Visoletta with excitement.

"Please, Ma'am! I've heard such things!"

"I... I can not," Visoletta squeaked.

There was silence again as the entire crew of the ship looked at the violinist, who had grown as pale as the moon.

"Is it a matter of payment?" Carlotte asked.

Visoletta shook her head. "No. Not at all. It's that.. I... It's too dark and..." Her face froze. "Excuse me," she said, and then withdrew across the deck and disappeared into her tent.

"Interesting," Carlotte said, and Aethan agreed.

They slept like the dead that night, and when the sun rose and the morning grew late, the sailors gathered their energy and hooked the horses back up on the shore. The river was very wide on this side of the Gladibu mountains, and its flow was lazy and slow. The forests and green meadows were replaced by long plains of golden grass. There were farms here growing wheat and other grains, with small houses dotting the fields and clustering together at small river port villages, but as they continued on, the farms got smaller and spaced further out. The houses shrank, and Aethan was not surprised. He'd seen a few stumps, but fewer trees. Wood seemed in short supply this side of the mountains.

"How much further are the colonies?" Visoletta asked, leaning against the railing beside Aethan, Rold, and the two old soldiers.

"Already there," Haric said.

"This is it?" she asked.

"Yep," Haric said.

"You were stationed out here?" Aethan asked.

"We spent some time here after the First Lib. I remember it being more lively back then."

"It was. These farms were crawling," Pierre grunted.

"Back then, we were expanding. There were all sorts of plans for a real city further out. Maybe that's where all the action is now."

"First Lib?" Aethan asked.

"First Liberation War," Haric clarified.

"That's what you call it?"

"Aye."

"Huh," Aethan said, watching a bedraggled woman filling a bucket from the river.

"What'd you call it?" Rold asked.

"War of Ryker Aggression."

Pierre grunted, though Aethan couldn't tell if it was in ascent or descent.

"What'd you call the second?" Rold asked.

"The war of continued Ryker aggression."

They went on through the day and into the night, and they played games with Haric's deck of cards. Despite himself, Aethan found that he liked the two old soldiers and the bruise-faced kid they seemed to have adopted. They were good people, and their laughter managed to keep Aethan distracted for the most part. Visoletta would play cards with them from time to time, and when she did, Aethan thought even less about his past. She was relentlessly persistent. She didn't take no for an answer when her lady's maids tried to opt out of joining in, and then, when moods of sleepiness swept over her, she would drop her cards mid-hand and head off to her tent, mumbling a promise to return and playfully shrugging off any entreaties to stay.

Aethan was similarly immune to social pressure, but that ability had come with alienation. He didn't understand how this woman managed to be so entirely independent and also remain so radically included. He would have guessed it was because she was a woman, but she wasn't particularly attractive. Not physically, at least. When she left, Aethan found himself looking forward to her return.

Saara ignored him. He had no idea what she was doing. She spent her entire day looking busy, which was incredible on a ship that had nothing on it to do. She spoke with the helmsman, barked orders about this or that, and spent long stretches of time below deck. Aethan went below once to see what was down there, and found nothing but bunks and the captain's closed door, through which he could hear Val and Carlotte discussing the Amaranthine. He tried to put Saara out of his mind, but every time he caught sight of her, he couldn't help but think of their night together at the inn.

Carlotte emerged from below in the late afternoon when the farms began to gather more tightly. They came to a village larger than all the others, with ten-foot stone walls around a central fort that had a tower with the Mareshal's flag. The village was still small, perhaps a tenth of what Irondale had been. Many of the buildings seemed in disrepair, though Haric insisted most of them were built in the last twenty years. A few bluebacks stood atop the wall, but no one else stirred. The streets were empty, and Aethan saw no clotheslines with laundry or folks working or children playing.

"Is this our stop?" Val asked, having come up with Carlotte.

Saara shook her head. "We go further on. This is New Domsar. There is another town, Forepost, at the bend in the river. It's the farthest we can go by boat before we must take to land."

"Where are all the people?" Visoletta asked.

No one answered.

"I'd heard this place was bustling," Haric said, "before I was sent south."

Aethan saw a woman's face in one of the windows, just visible in the darkness inside the building, watching them go by.

"Perhaps they've moved west," Saara said, "to Forepost or beyond."

"Or maybe they're out working on the farms?" Rold offered.

"If they work on farms, they'd live on them," Aethan said.

"Maybe that's where they went then, to live on the farms."

"These buildings aren't temporary. People wouldn't just leave them," Aethan said.

"Perhaps," Carlotte said.

The next morning, word went around that they were coming on Forepost, and there was much energy getting ready to disembark. Aethan felt a lightness within him, an ember slowly kindled by the easy company of his new friends.

"Up straight," Haric said, prodding at Rold's hunched shoulders with a porridgey spoon. "It keeps you from falling asleep. Hand on the gun, weight on your feet. When we're off this thing, I won't have you drifting off at first watch."

"What happens if I see something?" Rold asked.

"Depends what it is."

"What am I looking for?"

"Anything out of the ordinary."

"What's out of the ordinary?"

"Anyone coming up on us that ain't from this expedition."

"Then what do I do?"

"Then yell and wake everyone up."

"I don't shoot it?"

"God, no. You're like to shoot Pierre coming back from a piss," Haric said.

Pierre grunted, and Rold protested, wanting very much to shoot something.

They pulled up to a dock, and the sailors got busy securing the boat. It was strange. The dock was well made, and a cobbled road ran from it into a town square a few dozen yards away. The square was a series of two-story buildings, equally well made, with wide roads passing through the edges at each of its four sides. In the center of the square, clearly framed by the buildings and visible from the dock, was a statue of a man in a blueback uniform. Instead of the tricorn hat that normal bluebacks wore, the statue sported a long, thin hat with a plume coming off it like a horse's mane. It was the Mareshal, Commander of the Dominion's army and de facto leader of the Dominion. Aethan had seen similar statues scattered about the country. This one pointed out to the west as though ordering a charge, or surveying land, or in casual accusation. The square was the picture of an established and wealthy frontier town, which made its surroundings all the more strange.

Around the square was a mass of ramshackle dwellings, buildings made of more canvas than wood, the kind of dwellings people made knowing they would be torn down and replaced at any moment. It looked a bit like the slums of Sheras, and a bit like the refugee camps in the Freelands during the Second War of Ryker Aggression. The only difference was that there were no people here that Aethan could see.

When Aethan's turn came, he maneuvered his cart off the boat and down the dock to park it by the others. The expedition members fussed about with this and that, hooking horses back up to carts and organizing contents. Haric was making his goodbyes to a sailor he had befriended while Pierre fussed at Rold's posture. Aethan hooked Toktok to his own cart and gathered up Greg's reins. Saara stood beside one of the carts, rummaging through its contents.

"What are you looking for?" Aethan asked, looking over her shoulder at a piece of paper she held in one hand. It was a manifest which she marked off with a stub of a pencil as she went. The letters were blocky and crude.

"This is the last bit of civilization for months and I'd rather find out I forgot the damn oats here than out there, yeah?"

"Right," Aethan said. He wrapped and unwrapped the reins around his mangled hand and watched her for a few moments, feeling like he wanted to say something but not knowing what it was.

Saara put the paper down on the edge of the cart and shoved a box aside with both hands. She froze. "Boris!" she called out.

Aethan leaned over to look into the cart. Saara had uncovered one end of a long wooden box, with the visible end cut into an angled half circle. The box was white beech, and there were words carved into the top. It was a coffin.

"What is this?" Saara asked when Boris strode up. She craned her neck to look up at him.

Boris leaned over to see what it was and then paled a little. "It's uh... You should ask the Madame."

Saara scowled.

"We picked it up," Boris continued reluctantly, "After we picked her up. At the uh..."

Saara looked back at the box, and then up at Aethan, and then shifted the cart's contents to cover it again.

"Did she say why?" Saara asked, quietly this time.

Boris shook his head. "I didn't ask. Said something about a place she was taking it."

"What place? She told you this?" Saara asked.

Boris shook his head again. "She told... her," he said and motioned with his head towards the coffin.

"You Dominioneers are strange folk," Aethan said.

Boris threw up his hands. "Don't be lumping me up with the way of Rykers."

Saara jerked her head, and Boris trotted off.

Aethan raised an eyebrow. "Do you understand the way of Rykers?" he asked.

"Do I look like I do?" Saara snapped.

Aethan's face must have seemed taken aback, because her face darkened and she snapped again. "You wanna get back on the boat? Be my guest."

Aethan stared at her and then shook his head and pulled Greg away and up the street into the square. He understood neither Rykers nor Saara. The ember that had been kindled in him felt stepped upon, and the hot sun seemed suddenly painfully bright.

Aethan stepped into the square and glanced at the buildings. Most were boarded up, but there were two that showed signs of life. One had a sign above the door that read "Food. Boarding. Goods." And the other a sign reading "Constable."

There was a man sitting in the shadows by the "Constable" door, sitting so still that Aethan did not see him at first. For a moment he wondered if the man was actually there, or if it was some statue or trick of the light, but then, after they stared at each other for a long moment, the man cocked his head to one side. He wore a blueback uniform, and there was a gun leaning beside him with a tricorn hat hanging off its muzzle. Aethan gave a cautious nod to the man, and then tied Greg to the hitching post outside the general store and stepped inside.

The bell above the door rang as he entered, but no one came to greet him. The inside of the store was much like the square outside. Many shelves ran along the walls, but few had anything on them: some farming tools, a few sacks of feed, a single box of Freeland chocolate. Little more than dust filled the rest. Aethan lifted his hand and knocked at the bell above the door again.

A few moments later, a woman emerged from a door behind a counter at the far end of the room. Her hair was tied up in a messy bun, and she'd a dour, suspicious look to her eyes.

"What are you after?" she asked.

Aethan noticed her hand rested on the hilt of a knife at her belt. "Looking to sell a beast is all."

The door opened behind him, and the soldier from outside stepped into the store. Aethan shifted to the side so he could see both, and noticed the woman squaring off to each of them too.

"I'm not buying," she said.

"She's never buying," the man said. His hat was on his head now, and he carried the long matchlock like a staff. The bayonet was missing, and the tip of the barrel was orange with rust. The flintlock hadn't made it this far west, Aethan noticed, or at least not to this backwater.

"No point in buying if you're not selling," the woman said.

"No point in selling if you're not selling what people want to buy," the man said.

The woman's face set hard. She spoke to Aethan, but kept her eyes on the man. "You a farmer? After feed? Good prices. Cheaper than you'll get anywhere else."

"Not a farmer. Just looking to offload a donkey. It's good and healthy."

"That old half-starved thing in the square?" The soldier ambled across the room and sat heavily on a stool by the counter. "Looks about to keel over any minute. What's your group after if not farming? Long way to come just to sell donkey meat."

"You with a group?" the woman said.

Aethan nodded. "Just passing through."

"To where?" they both asked simultaneously, and then looked warily at each other.

"To wherever will buy my donkey."

The man roared with laughter. "Go back down the river then! Or go up further to the mines!"

The woman eyed him with disgust. "Karl's not wrong." She said, and took her hand off the knife. "But if you won't, take the south road. There are still a few farms that direction.

"Good luck," the man laughed again.

"I'll offload the beast cheap," Aethan said, putting enough desperation into his voice to make the women think she was getting a good deal. "Five bits?"

Karl roared in laughter again. "Five! For that hunk of meat? Slaughter it and you'll get twenty pounds of good meat. Maybe."

"Look," the woman said, "I'm not looking for a deal. I won't buy it because no one is coming to buy it from me."

"Surely other farmers coming through would want a good--"

"Cheap," Karl interrupted.

"It pulled all the way up the river from Irondale with the other horses!" Aethan snapped. "The beast is strong. Hardy."

"Ain't no farmers coming through. Not any more," the woman sat wearily behind her counter, keeping an eye on both of them. Karl leered at her, entirely unfazed by Aethan's annoyance.

"Then why the store?" Aethan asked.

Karl roared once again, spittle flying from a mouth with more than a few brown teeth. "Because she has to be!" Karl's laughter died after a moment, and then he leaned back against the counter, the bulk of him sagging over the sides of the stool.

"This is Forepost. The Mareshal's manifestation of the Dominion's destiny to civilize the land out here beyond the

Gladibu. There are hillie graves beneath your feet. The town was built on the bodies that we slaughtered when we came up the river."

The man smiled as he said it, and pounded a fleshy fist weakly against the counter.

"From here west to the desert, the Dominion covering all north of Bergshalen. More land for more money for less of you folk." He waved a hand at Aethan. "Forepost was funded, stocked, and Kita here signed a thirty-year contract to run the main supply. Thought she'd be rich! But then the Second Lib went south in more ways than one, and all the troops that were out here killing the hillies left. The hillies came back, burned a couple farms, murdered a couple more farmer men, raped a hell of a lot more farmer ladies..." He rolled a hand through the air.

"So the farmers stopped coming," Aethan finished. "The war was ten years ago."

"Oh there's still some troops kickin' around, but the Mareshal's got other priorities now. Building up his forces, they say. Drilling the armies down there by Domsar for..." the man leered at Aethan, "Something."

Kita sneered. "Only ones left out there are the ones too poor to leave it all behind," she said.

"She used to have whores. Several whores. All lined up in the tavern in the next room. Now all that's left is her." He managed to both smile and return Kita's snarl at the same time. Kita fingered her blade.

"But the troops will come back," Karl mused. "One day, when they finish what they're doing down south. They'll come back and take what's owed to the Dominion. And maybe then you can get rich, Kita, and you, Boneman, can sell your donkey. Though he won't be more'in bones himself by then." And he erupted once again into laughter.

"We need to talk," Aethan said to Saara, who was still going through the cart. She did not answer him. He heard voices from behind the shuttered windows of Carlotte's carriage, so he stepped up and knocked on them.

"What are you-" Saara began, but she fell silent when Carlotte opened the window. So much about Carlotte DeSheras made her seem older: the haughty eyebrows and pursed lips, the plume of rich fur around her head, and the way she spoke as though everything she said was plainly obvious. Up close, though, the illusion fell away, and she looked as young as she actually was.

"The path forward isn't safe."

Val leaned forward from the opposite bench in the carriage. There were open books to his side and papers all around. Saara left her inventory behind and stood beside him.

"We knew that. Saara hired guns," Carlotte said.

"Forepost is abandoned," Aethan said. "The bluebacks aren't patrolling out here anymore. The hill folk are burning farms and killing farmers."

"How do you know what the bluebacks aren't doing?" Saara asked.

"I went into the square and asked."

"Who?"

"The only two people left. Everyone else has gone east, where they won't die. The farmers in the plains have mostly gone too."

"I thought the hill people had been pushed out a long time ago. I've a book here," Val said, rummaging around in a pile of them to his right. "It's all about the taming of the West. There was a large battle or something when the tribes came for blood, but they were beaten back to the mountains."

"Well, they've come back," Aethan said.

They were all silent for a moment.

"What are you suggesting we do?" Carlotte asked.

Aethan opened his mouth, but said nothing. Despite what he had heard, he realized his options hadn't changed. He had to get his cargo to Bergshalen. He was racing the clock. He could not afford to turn around. If he went back up the river, he would not make it to the Freelands alive. There, on the road, retracing his steps with all of his work in shambles. The dark would close around him, and the dark would kill him.

Aethan closed his mouth and took in a big breath, feeling the veil of depression settling on him like twenty feet of water. He shrugged. "Just thought you'd like to know."

Carlotte bit her lip, and she really did look young then. She looked inexperienced and unsure, and it struck Aethan as absurd that all these people, him included, were waiting on her word.

"Is there another way to go?"

"Not unless we go back up river and down through the Dominion," Saara said.

Carlotte shook her head. "We can't go back." Carlotte drummed her fingers against the windowsill. "You said most of the farmers had gone, but they aren't all gone. So, the hill tribes haven't invaded. They are just... raiding, and our path is well within Dominion lands."

She looked into Aethan's eyes. He could feel her wanting him to nod or smile or give her some kind of assurance, but Aethan had none to give.

"We go on," she said. "Quickly."

"Yes, Madame," Saara said, then shot Aethan a glare and hurried away, yelling at the rest of the expedition to get in order.

31

They took the road south, and Saara saw many remnants of civilization. There were irrigation ditches filled with stagnant water and clogged with weeds. There were fields in neat rows that were now overtaken by tall yellow grass. There were even a few manor houses staked out atop low hills, the ghosts of early speculators, gambling that their homes would be in the center of a thriving city ten years down the road. They were empty now. Some were boarded up, likely with the intention to return when things got better, but others had either been left open to the elements or had been opened after the fact. Some were even half finished, their frames stabbing up like bones into the sky.

An hour later, and the signs of humanity were gone. They were surrounded by hills and low ridges and shallow valleys that would become streams when rain came. Tall yellow grass covered the land like a sheet draped over the unused equipment in Elspeth DeSheras' laboratory back home. The road was just a strip of dirt kept bare by the continued tread of boot, hoof, and wheel upon it, but the grass was returning now. Little tufts of it grew from the middle of the path where wagon wheels were less likely to roll.

Eventually, the road crested a hill and a little valley opened up beneath them. There was a small river at its bottom, flowing vaguely south-west, and it looked as though there had once been a grove of trees that ran along it. Now the trees were stumps, and the flood-lands around the river were carved up into checkered plots. Many had been overtaken by the grass, but a few were still being tended.

The road ran along the top of the ridge, and as they rode along it, the farmers toiling in the fields lifted their heads and watched them pass. Aethan went down to the first few, and Saara made an excuse to follow. He tried to sell his donkey, but none of them had any money, and Aethan wasn't interested in what little they had to trade.

Saara asked them if they were worried about the hill tribes. They did not answer, and instead just said that the bluebacks would return. The Mareshal wouldn't abandon them here forever, and until then, God would protect them. Aethan and Saara stopped going down after the first three.

They made camp that evening near the water on a stretch between plots, and Saara caught Aethan's eye as he unhitched his horse.

"Scout a bit with me?" she asked.

"Scout? For what?"

"We might find something interesting... or fun," she said, and then coughed uncomfortably when Aethan didn't seem to understand.

"Oh," he said, and then after a moment nodded.

They went up the road a ways and fucked behind a hill.

She hadn't realized how much stress she was holding in her body until she lay there, feeling the glow of her orgasm slowly fade. She took a deep breath and glanced over at him, breathing hard beside her. A bead of sweat raced down his chest to pool in his belly button. She smiled and pulled her pants back on.

"I'm glad you came along," Saara said, and then laughed.

"I'm sure," Aethan said.

Saara stopped mid-buckle and looked over at him. He was on his feet, fastening his own belt.

"What?" she asked.

Aethan seemed to consider this, as though she'd asked something difficult.

"I take it you'll go back to ignoring me then?"

She straightened up, and he continued to button up his shirt, not looking her in the eye.

"Is this not convenient for you?" she said.

"It isn't. Call me a southerner but I actually prefer the women I fuck to talk to me."

Saara's temper flared. "No one forced you to come back here."

"I know!" he snapped and then took a big breath through his nose and ran his hand over his hair. "Oh, do I know."

He squatted down and tugged at the horse's tether to loosen it from the ground.

"What did you think this was?" Saara asked.

He didn't answer.

"You're mad at me for ignoring you, and now you won't speak to me?"

"No. It just. Isn't. My. Business," he grunted, heaving at the stake with each word. He stood and pulled it from the loosened ground. He handed her the reins to her horse, but she caught his wrist and held on tight.

"You're the one who came onto me at Irondale."

"And you're the one who asked me to come with you." He yanked his hand away and turned to mount his horse.

"What do you want from me?" she cried after him.

He spun around. "To talk to you. Not here. Not behind a hill. Over there. With them. Let yourself be seen with a *Boneman*," he snarled, emphasizing the last word.

"It's not about you being a Freelander," Saara said. "Its about how it looks to fuck someone I just met. It makes me look like... one of the crew."

"Aren't you?" Aethan asked.

Saara shook her head. "No. I'm not."

"Then what are you?" he asked.

Saara didn't answer, and he scoffed and mounted his horse.

"So is this over then?" she called after him.

He shrugged, but did not look back.

Saara fumed for a few moments, letting her emotions wash over her in quick succession, and then felt a chill go through her and realized her tits were still out. She buttoned up and hoisted herself into the saddle, wondering how Aethan was the one who felt used.

When dinner was served, Carlotte and Val sat in Carlotte's carriage with the oil lamps burning. Saara brought them their food, and Carlotte thanked her. Saara stood by the steps, with her own food clutched in one hand, but Carlotte did not invite her up. Before the silence could stretch out any further, before Carlotte said something that cemented her gathering feeling in reality, Saara trudged away.

The rest of the crew sat in a circle around the cook wagon's light. She saw Aethan sitting and staring absently into the fire. She took a step towards him and then stopped. The awkward violinist, Visoletta, sat beside him. She said something, and Aethan turned to her. She said something else, and Aethan laughed.

Saara sat down in the grass where it was dark and leaned against a wagon wheel. She bit into her bread and barely tasted it.

"Saary?"

She looked up and saw a dark figure standing just a few strides away from her. "Rold?"

"Yeah," he said. He stepped closer, and she could just make out his face in the light from the distant cook fire. He held one of the soldiers' rifles like a walking stick.

"Are you on watch?"

"I'm supposed to be. But what am I supposed to watch? The dark be dark?" He sighed and then sat down heavily beside her.

They sat there for a few moments, and then Saara scooted over so he could rest his back against the wheel with her. He spoke. "Thank you."

"There was plenty of room," Saara said.

"No, about taking me with you."

"Oh," Saara said. "Sure."

"I know I was in trouble. You saved my life."

That hung in the darkness for a few moments, and then Saara felt herself reach out and squeeze Rold's knee. "Don't mention it, Rold. I've got you."

32

The cook fire swam in tiny circles as the ripple settled into Erika. She looked to her right and saw Hannah watching the flames. Boris sat beside her, his mass making Hannah look tiny, like a child and a giant. He had an arm on the ground behind her, not touching, but too close to be an accident. His face was close to her ear. He was saying something about his home. Some farm he grew up on. Hannah nodded and blinked slowly. She turned and caught Erika's eye, and they looked at each other and then burst out in giggles. Boris thought she was laughing at what he'd said, and his face split into a smile. Erika brought a finger to her lips, swearing Hannah to secrecy, and Hannah giggled more.

The ripple was fading. Erika could feel it coming and closed her eyes until it did, until the pike settled. When she opened them, she saw Jane looking worriedly at them both. Erika smiled and rolled her eyes to her left, to the Freelander and the soldiers. Haric was speaking of the war, some story about a shit pit and digestion issues. Pierre and Aethan focused on their food, but Erika could see that Aethan was enjoying the story.

She watched the muscles in his neck work when he swallowed, and the way the firelight played across his wide nose and full lips. She noticed the way he smiled before he laughed when he found something genuinely funny, the way those lips would pull back and bare his teeth before the laugh came, the way he tried to stifle it as soon as it did. Haric was good at making him laugh.

"Why are you friends?" Erika wondered. They all looked at her, and she realized she'd spoken it out loud. That happened sometimes, thoughts becoming words all on their own when the pike swam through. "Sorry," she said, "I didn't... You were all in the war. On different sides."

Haric grimaced. "We believed in the first war. By the second... The young soldiers called us greybacks. They said the dye had left our coats."

"I like the term," Pierre said, looking up from the fire. "I wear it with more pride than I wore the blue."

He sat just beside Haric, closer than was absolutely necessary. There was plenty of room in this wide-open country.

Aethan nodded, his smile now a neutral frown.

"But they were the Mareshal's wars," Haric said. He looked at Aethan. "I hold no ill will, and I hope it was not I that shot your hand."

"No, I do not think so," Aethan said, and raised the mangled hand up to consider it. It looked gruesome, split down the middle with pink scar tissue all around it.

"Why did you believe in the first one?" Erika asked.

Haric grimaced again. "We were defending the Dominion," he said.

"Defending? The Dominion invaded the Freelands," Aethan said. There was no anger in his voice.

"We were told you were coming," Haric said. "When I was a child, I lived in a small village north of Domsar, and during the revolution, we heard such stories from the merchants and passers-through. Murders and rapes. Women and children burned alive. Bodies hung up all over the towns. My mother said the Korkins had it coming, 'bringing devils from across the sands.' Her words, not mine, but the sentiment was common. Then there were stories about the revolution spreading to the parts of Korka that had no slaves, small villages like Grassonne being overrun, and every Korkin executed or trussed up in gibbets to starve. The Mareshal's recruiters swept through our town then. They came to find soldiers for the Mareshal's army, to strike at the heart of the Devil before the Devil could strike at us. I joined and... well."

He fell silent, and then Pierre patted his knee. Haric grasped the other soldier's hand with his own. They held their hands together for a moment, squeezing hard, and then a quick release. Most everyone else was looking at the fire, but they were all quiet and listening.

"Was it true?" Ari asked. Carlotte's maid sat beside Slack Gin, across the fire from Erika. "The murders and rapes. The people in gibbets left to starve?"

"Some of it," Aethan said before Haric could speak. His eyes were locked onto the flames as he spoke, and they glittered in the flickering light. He rolled something gently between the fingers of his good hand. She could faintly hear whatever it was clacking.

"I have no sympathy for the Korkins," Aethan continued. "Perhaps an individual story is tragic, but the Korkins were either slavers themselves or complicit in the practice. They wanted to be our masters. After the revolution, all the plantations were divided up between the slaves who worked them. I was born on the same plot of land that my father was born on, and his father before. But when I was born, it wasn't just our responsibility to work, but our right to own. The old Korkin owners had built the gibbets that loomed over the farms, and they would use them to starve disobedient slaves to death in the sight of their kin. When the revolution happened, the old Korkin masters were put in those same gibbets and never taken down. The bones were supposed to remind us what happened to tyrants or something. The gibbet atop my father's plot had the old master's young daughter in it. I was told her name at one point, but I can't remember it now."

They were all silent. The fire crackled. Erika heard the faint breeze rustling through the sea of grass around them.

"A young girl," Slack Gin sneered, pulling them all out of Aethan's story. "Is it her bones you rattle in your hand?"

Aethan looked down and opened his hand, and Erika saw bits of white bone there.

"These?" he said, "No. My father carried her's though."

"A noble revolution indeed."

Aethan looked up, and the two of them glared at each other over the fire.

"Evil begets evil," Aethan said, enunciating each word clearly.

316

"A fine way to dismiss genocide," Slack answered.

Aethan was silent for a few moments, rolling the bones back and forth in his hand. They reminded Erika of Carlotte's prayer beads.

"Imagine," Aethan began, "that I beat your daughter. That I raped her and then when your wife put up a fuss, I sold her away to another man who looked like me. Imagine that I took your daughter every night, and if you lay still on your bed of earth, you could hear her cries faintly on the wind. Imagine that you tried to tell another man who looked like me what I had done, and they beat you for saying it. Imagine everyone who looked like me looked at people who looked like you as though you were less than dogs. Imagine this was the way you were treated, and the way your father was treated, and the way his father was treated. Imagine all that and tell me you would not do to me and my family what I had done a hundredfold to you."

"I wouldn't put a child in a gibbet," Slack spat. "An innocent."

Aethan shrugged. "Fine words from someone who hasn't felt the lash."

"Hey now," Haric interjected. "There's no need to get worked up."

"And you have?" Slack snarled at Aethan, ignoring Haric. "You weren't even born. You felt no lash either, and now you spout the propaganda of your state! You Bonemen make it worse with every telling. You conjure slights to justify your evil."

"Now you're just making things up," Aethan said.

Slack jumped to his feet, and Haric did the same, and then others jumped up all around the fire.

"There'll be no fighting in my camp!"

All of their heads except Aethan's snapped around to see Saara standing at the edge of the firelight, a hand on the hilt of the blade at her hip.

"Unless that fight is with me," she finished.

Slack scowled all the harder, and he spat black into the grass. He turned his gaze to Erika, and Erika instinctively winced back.

"Why don't you play us something, violinist?" he said.

"Oh please!" Hannah cried, the words slurring out. "Please play!"

"I..." Erika swallowed. Now they were all looking at her. "No, I cannot," she said.

"Why?" Slack said. "We've traveled for a week, and I've never heard you so much as tune the thing."

"I... I can't..." Erika said, a ripple was coming in. She could feel it gathering behind her eyes. She saw herself walking to her tent and pulling out the violin. She could feel the smooth wood on her fingers, the way the strings bit into her fingertips. She felt the music she would play, a sweet sadness that would speak of the past's hatred that these two men carried on, that spoke of the Korkin girl's tragedy, of the boy who grew up beneath her bones, of the beauty of freedom that emerged from the ashes of revolution. Erika's song would rise, nipping at the heels of a note, a note that longed to be played, but never was until the end, when she'd draw her bow across the strings and release the note, the feeling, the rebirth, like a note from God herself.

"Are you listening to me? Why?" Slack asked.

Erika was aware that she hadn't moved. Her arms were wrapped around her knobby knees, and his tone made her suddenly want to cry.

"Because she isn't a minstrel," Aethan said. "Let Visoletta alone. She'll play when she likes."

Erika turned to him, grateful for the intervention. Then she felt a drop of rain on her head. She lifted her gaze skyward, and the clouds opened up.

It came in a flood, the whole sky filling with water and the ground around them turning to mud before they could even stand. The cook fire sputtered. Everyone scattered. Jane grabbed Erika with one hand and Hannah with the other, and dragged them to the tent. Erika pulled away from Jane's grip, tilted back her head, and raised her arms out to the sides. The rain soaked her through. The drops hit her face like hail, and then Jane shoved her through the tent flap.

She collapsed onto the canvas floor and was overtaken by giggles. Hannah joined her, their laughter growing with each other's cries until they were both gasping for breath. The rain beat at the tent, threatening to find its way through the seams, but Visoletta's tent was well made and did not leak.

Jane fretted around the two of them, stripping off their cloaks and fussing at the clothes beneath. Erika had just the presence of mind to bat her away before the woman undid her dress entirely.

"I'll undress later. Just bring me a blanket," she said.

"But... everything is getting wet," Jane said.

"It will dry eventually. Nothing stays wet forever," Erika said.

Jane begrudgingly handed Erika a blanket, and Erika wrapped herself in it so only her head was sticking out the top, a mountain of cloth with an Erika top. Jane continued to fuss at Hannah, and Hannah let her strip her naked and dry her off.

Erika watched and admired: Hannah's wide hips, her full breasts, the thickness of her thighs, the lips of her vagina just visible beneath the hair at her crotch, things she'd trade everything she had for. She giggled at that. No doubt these women would trade everything they had for Erika's things... or, Visoletta's things rather. Jane wrapped Hannah in a blanket and sat her down next to Erika, and then began taking her own wet things off.

"Are you okay?" Erika asked, and Jane glanced up sharply at the question.

"What?"

"You look upset. You should take a swim," Erika said, motioning with her head to the pack where the pike was hidden. Jane followed her eyes and scowled.

"That stuff ruins people."

Jane looked at Hannah and scowled even deeper.

"That stuff almost ruined Hannah once."

"I know," Erika said. "She told me."

Jane's eyes widened. "And you still--"

"Why are you always so serious?" Erika laughed.

"Because one of us needs to."

"Why?"

"Because otherwise we'd all be out in the rain getting soaked to the bone."

"So?"

Jane didn't answer, she just busied herself with her laces.

"Visoletta," Hannah said, slurring slightly with her eyes closed.

"Yes?" Erika answered.

"Why don't you ever play? Don't you like it?"

Erika froze at the question, but it didn't seize her heart like when Slack had asked. Coming from Hannah, there was no malice in it, no expectation.

"Because," Erika said, "This won't last forever. The way my life was, the way it will be when this is over, isn't a good life. This will end eventually, and we'll be forced back to the way things were before we left Sheras. And if I play, it will be like it was before, and this feeling will end."

"How weird," Hannah mumbled. "I always imagined it would be so fun to play music."

Erika smiled.

"Me too," she said.

Erika wouldn't allow Jane to take Hannah out of the tent. She insisted they sleep there, and Jane relented. They curled up in Visoletta's extra blankets and fell asleep to the sound of rain pattering against the canvas. Jane had left the lamp burning, and Erika knew she should get up and retract the wick. She didn't though. Instead, she looked up at the seam of the tent above her and thought about the night while the last waves of pike went through her. She played the night's events over and over in her head, changing them each time. She thought about the cut of Aethan's jaw and the way he had defended her. Had he looked at her after he'd said it, or had he been watching the flames, or had he been glaring at Slack? Perhaps he'd looked at her and then guiltily looked away when she had turned to face him. He had spoken because he hated Slack. He had spoken because he loved Erika. No. Of course not. Erika flipped onto her side and faced the tent wall. The light of the lamp flickered strange shadows on it. If Aethan felt anything at all towards her, then he felt it for Visoletta, not for Erika.

She sat up and looked at the violin case lying by the entrance. What was so different between Visoletta and her? Talent? The right pieces? Why couldn't she have those things? Why did Visoletta have them, and she did not? The jealousy rose swift in her, threatening to boil its way out in sobs.

Erika crawled out of the blankets and over to the violin case. She put her fingers on the wood, on the metal latches. She undid them one by one, controlling the movement of the metal so it made no sound. She lifted the lid and beheld Visoletta's violin.

It was red in the lamp light. Delicate and smooth and shining with some glaze or oil. She reached out a finger and placed it gently on a string.

"G," she whispered, a memory flooding through her. Her mother towering over her. The violin teacher lecturing.

Erika's hands trembled. She grabbed the violin by its neck, the strings making a dull hum as she gripped them, the body making a hollow clunk as she lifted. Her other hand found the bow and pulled it out of its nook. The violin slid into the crook of her neck and she held the bow over the bridge, hovering just above the strings.

What would it sound like when she played? She heard her mother's screams. Her mother's hatred. She heard the sounds she used to make on the violin, like a cat screaming in the night, each harsh sound making her mother angrier.

But she also heard another sound, a note, and then another and another. It rose from her fingers, beautiful and pure, the ache in her soul made real as sound.

She moved her bow with each note, gliding back and forth an inch above the strings.

Then the light shifted.

She twisted and saw Jane sitting up. Her body blocked the flickering lamp.

"Ma'am?" Jane whispered.

Erika grunted, and then as quickly as she could without looking like she was caught with her dress up, put the violin back in its case and clicked the latches shut. She turned with an explanation at the tip of her tongue, but then stopped. Jane opened her mouth, but Erika cut her off.

"Good night. Jane," she said, and then crawled back to her spot on the other side of Hannah and slipped beneath the blankets.

"Turn out the light, please," she said, and turned to face the opposite wall. She could see Jane's shadow still sitting upright for several more seconds, and Erika could feel the unspoken question heavy in the air. Then Jane's shadow lay back, and the light went out.

33

When Saara called a stop, Aethan pulled his cart off the dirt road and into the grass. He unhitched Toktok and Greg and lengthened their leads so they would have room to graze, and then set about flattening a bit of grass to have a place to lie when dinner was done.

"Why are you here?"

Aethan looked up to see Rold leaning over his cart. The boy was still mottled with bruises, but they had healed enough that Aethan could read his face. There was no venom there, just bored curiosity. He'd plucked a long strand of grass and chewed absently on one end, letting the curly top hang lazily out of his mouth like a caricature of a country farmer.

"Shouldn't you be on watch?" Aethan asked. He pulled his bedroll from behind the bench seat and undid the ties.

"Nah. Pierre's doing first. I got third in the morning. Real excited to get up early to watch nothing do nothing."

"Better nothing than something when on watch," Aethan said.

Rold continued to chew his grass, disagreement plain on his face, and looked back at Aethan expectantly.

"Saara invited me," Aethan said. "I'm a trader bound for Bergshalen. Seemed convenient to travel together."

"Aye, but what are you trading?"

Something about the boy's inflection caught Aethan as strange. He looked up from his bedroll and looked harder at the kid. Rold shrugged, and he looked suddenly like he was trying a little too hard to appear uninvested. Aethan looked around the gathering camp and saw Haric look away. He looked at Visoletta, and she suddenly became embroiled in a conversation with Hannah. He looked at Rold, and the boy's cool demeanor turned to embarrassment. They looked at each other for several seconds across the top of his cart.

"There a bet going?" Aethan asked.

Rold pulled his lips back into an awkward smile. "Yeah..."

Aethan rolled his eyes, but he didn't actually feel any annoyance. He reached out and undid a few of the ties holding the oilcloth over the top of his cart.

"He's opening it!" Rold shouted, and everyone's attempt at being preoccupied vanished.

Visoletta, Hannah, the soldiers, Boris, and Kent all ran over to look into the cart.

"It's spice, I tell you!" Boris said.

"It's gotta be a mix! Diversify!" Kent yelled over him.

Aethan pulled back the cloth, and a hush came over the group.

"Ha!" Pierre shouted and pumped one fist in the air.

It was the most excitement Aethan had seen on the old soldier. The others swore. Haric said somethings about someone's mother, but then placed a congratulatory hand on Pierre's shoulder.

"How could a man who lost half his hand to a bullet sell guns?" Haric bemoaned.

"There's some powder in there, too," Aethan said.

"Dammit to hell," Boris swore.

Pierre held out his hand, and the others all reached into their pockets to drop coins into it.

Hannah started to do the same, but Visoletta stopped her and gave coins to Pierre for the both of them.

"What were your guesses?" Aethan asked.

"Chew," Hannah said.

Visoletta blushed and gave an embarrassed smile. "I was hoping it was chocolate."

"Chocolate?" Aethan said. "Wouldn't the heat--"

"I know!" she protested. "But I can dream, can't I?"

Visoletta leaned over the cart and looked down at the guns in their neat, shiny rows. She stuck out a finger and traced it along the metal. "Why are you selling guns?" she asked.

Most of the others had drifted away; only she and Hannah remained.

"I thought they'd sell well in Sheras. I've gotten good prices for matchlocks there before."

"Huh," Visoletta said. "I really wish it were chocolate. You would have had an eager customer all this way." She sighed. "Unfortunately. I've no use for these. They are pretty though."

She laughed and then took Hannah's arm and walked away. Aethan watched her go, her red clock billowing up on the tall grass beneath it, and he thought of the box of chocolate at the general store in Forepost. He found himself wishing he'd purchased it.

The day had been long, and the sun had been hot. He had spent it sweating atop his cart and thinking of evil things that he had done, but when Rold had talked to him, and even more so when Visoletta had, he had not thought of those things. He had thought instead of Rold's childish charm and Visoletta's awkward honesty. He had thought of how he looked forward to the next day when he could pull his cart up to ride alongside hers when the ground was flat enough and talk about whatever it was she found interesting.

Now he watched her walk away, and he felt so very alone. He thought again about the evil things he had done, and how, if things did not go well, he would likely do them again.

He did not go sit by the cookfire that night. He had looked forward to it throughout the afternoon, but now it felt undoable. The effort to smile and laugh, and make conversation that would make Visoletta and the others like him was unachievable. He would say something wrong. He would laugh at the wrong thing. They would know him for what he was, and they would hate him for it. Instead, he watched the fire from afar and thought about Ashatee by her lake in the woods, alone.

"Aethan."

He looked up to see Saara standing a few yards away from him. One hand was on her hip, the other hung loosely at her side. Aethan thought about the fight they'd had the night before, about how he felt used by her, about how he wanted to actually talk to the women he fucked.

"Would you like to scout a bit with me?" Saara asked.

Aethan nodded.

The days of their journey were like the land itself in Saara's mind, unending and unremarkable. The golden grass stretched from horizon to horizon, unchanging from mile to mile, and the days similarly repeated. She woke early each morning and got Kent cooking. She served Carlotte with extra bits of fruit and got the camp moving. Carlotte would complain that they were too slow, and the others would complain that she was too fast. They would set out on the dirt road that ran occasionally along the little river, and they would pass scattered farms with miserable Dominioneers toiling in the sun. Her thighs would ache. Her hamstrings would cramp. When the sun dimmed, she'd find a flat place off the side of the road and call them all to camp. They'd eat hard bread and jerky and cheese and a few shriveled bits of apple, and then she'd go to Aethan. He would look grimly at her, and then he would nod and they'd fuck hard and rough behind a hill or off in the grass far enough away that their grunts and slaps of skin against skin would not be heard by Carlotte or the others.

It was bestial, the kind of sex she used to have with Bracille, but without any of the side bits. There was no holding, no emotional weight, nothing she had to carry with her afterwards. It was just a few minutes of mindlessness, where nothing mattered but the edge of the coming oblivion. There was no Carlotte in those moments, no expectations, no dreams, no Bracille, no uncle, no family, no responsibility, just the orgasm and the release and the slumping off and the few moments of heavy breathing where they lay side by side and stared up at the stars.

There were so many stars out there in the badlands, where the lights of Sheras did not drown them out. There were more stars than she had thought existed, and the longer she gazed upward, the more stars she counted.

Aethan would stand, pull his shirt back over his chest, and Saara would trudge back to her bedroll to sleep for a few hours before she woke and began it all again.

It was the fifth day she thought, though it could have been the sixth, and she was riding at the rear of the expedition alongside

Rold. Pierre and Haric often rode their horses together at the front of the line, where dust wasn't kicked up by the others, but occasionally one of them would take a break and ride in one of the carts and let Rold borrow the horse. Saara enjoyed watching the boy's efforts. It made her feel right skilled at horsemanship.

"So what's back in Sheras for you when you get back?" Saara asked.

Rold looked over at her, and then panicked when he accidentally tugged the reins to the side. He got the horse under control, assumed a nonchalance, and then shrugged.

"I'm sure Bracille will have something for me," he said.

Saara frowned.

"You really want to spend your life breaking noses in the Outer?"

Rold shrugged again.

"Better than getting my nose broke."

They rode in silence for a few minutes. Saara liked that they didn't have to always speak when they talked.

"Did they tell you why I left the Den?" Saara asked after a long moment.

Rold nodded. "To study the stars," he said.

"What?"

"That's what Bracille said."

Saara let that sit for a few moments. She didn't know what she'd been expecting exactly. Something harsher and more condemning. Something to say she'd made a mistake, to warn the rest against following her example.

"Really?" Saara asked.

"Aye. He said you needed to do great things to be happy." Rold glanced sidelong at her. "You don't look happy."

She looked ahead of them at Aethan riding alongside Visoletta. The violinist leaned lazily against her cart's railing and gave the Freelander her full attention. Every so often, she laughed loud enough for Saara to hear, and Aethan made no effort to pull his cart away. Saara couldn't imagine the Freelander saying anything funny. He barely said anything at all, and when he did speak, it was some complaint or grunt. Saara found that she wanted to know what he had said.

Saara sneered, then she forced a smile and looked back at Rold. "Doing great things takes a while. You should try it."

"Hmpf.".

"I'm serious," Saara said. "When this is all over, you should come to the Nouvre Vil with me."

"What?"

"You can always go back to the Den if you don't like it. But give it a chance. I could use an assistant, and you could learn to do great things."

Rold was silent and looked a little stunned at the possibility. Saara had been him once, an orphan in the Den's embrace. She'd never let anyone mash her face that badly, but she'd been through her share of beatings. If her uncle hadn't found her, she'd probably still be there. She'd probably have Bracille's kid running around or stuck up her snatch, and she'd be the queen of that shitty house in that shitty place.

Saara pulled her mind out of the past and imagined herself as a freshly minted Ryker stepping into a property she had purchased, on land that she owned, with Rold at her shoulder. The kid was tough, but she'd make him tougher. She'd put him through the ropes like Carlotte had put her through. She'd even get Val to teach the boy how to read.

"It's hard work," she said, "but it's good work that will lead--"

There was a scream.

Saara's head snapped up, and she saw the Violinist's head snap forward as well. Saara kicked at her horse, and the beast surged forward, barreling straight for the back of Visoletta's cart. Saara tugged madly to the left.

"Fucking- thing-" she grunted.

The horse went off the road. She turned it forward again, almost fell off, and then drove it through the grass past the rest of the expedition. The road curved around the base of a low hill, and as she rounded it, she saw Ari and Renee at the front of the caravan driving one of the cargo carts. They had pulled their horse to a stop. Ari had a hand over her mouth. Renee held the reins in limp hands. Saara pulled up and let her horse come to a standstill.

Before them was a farm, and on the farm there was a tree, one of the few she had seen standing in the past few days. It was a little thing, an apple tree no more than ten or fifteen years old, planted next to the stream and sagging under the weight of strange fruit.

Six bodies hung from the tree. They were mutilated and burned so badly that Saara couldn't tell their gender or age, but from the size, two must have been children. The largest body bowed its branch low, and the remains of its foot dragged in the water. A farm surrounded the tree, but it was all ash. A little farmhouse that stood beside the tree was now only charred timber sticking out of rubble like the rib cage of some massive beast.

Saara turned to warn the expedition away, but Carlotte had already stepped out of her carriage, her back straight like a metal rod had been jammed through her spine. Val peered out after her. The entire caravan drew up off the road in a wide arc, all looking at the scene before them. Carlotte stood in the middle of the road. Her eyes were wide, and her jaw was clenched tight. Her nostrils flared with her breath.

"Who did this?" someone asked.

There was no answer for a long moment, and then Aethan spoke. "The hill folk."

"The hill folk are dead! The bluebacks drove them off!" Slack snarled.

"And now they're back." Aethan looked across the circle at Saara. "They did warn us in Forepost."

"They did?" Slack said.

Aethan said nothing. Saara didn't know how to answer. She looked to Carlotte, but she was still frozen in the center of the path, her eyes darting from one detail to the next. Saara willed her to say something, to give a command.

"We should never have come here," Ari said.

"What did they warn us of?" Kent asked. There was panic in his voice, and it was spreading through the group.

"Carlotte!" Saara hissed.

Carlotte turned to look at her, but did not speak. Her eyes were wide, and Saara realized Carlotte didn't know what to do. How could she? She was barely out of childhood. She knew more about books and learning than Saara could imagine, but she knew nothing of this.

It was up to Saara, but she didn't know what to do either. What could they do? Cut down the bodies and dig graves? How long would that take? Did they have shovels? Of course, they had shovels, but what cart were they in? No no no, they just had to move. They had to get out and away from this place.

"Everybody--" she began, but her voice was small and no one heard her. She took a deep breath and tried again. "Go on down the road! Do not stop. Just keep going!"

The conversation petered out. They all looked at her. Saara saw Rold on his horse at the back. His eyes were wide.

"Yeah," Slack called. "Come on boys. This ain't our business."

Slack snapped his reins, and his cart moved up the path. After a moment, the cook wagon started moving, and then Carlotte turned and stepped back into her carriage.

"What about them?" Visoletta cried out.

Carlotte froze halfway up the steps.

"We should bury them..." Visoletta began. "Are they not Dominioneers, Carlotte? Don't they deserve a burial?"

"A burial," Carlotte said. She looked at Saara.

"We don't have time. We should leave this place," Saara said.

"Right," Carlotte said, and then stepped in and closed the door behind her. Saara motioned to Boris on top of the carriage, and he snapped the horses into action. The other carts began to move as well, but Visoletta held out a hand to stop Hannah.

"We should cut them down at least," Visoletta said. She turned to Aethan, who also hadn't moved. "Shouldn't we?"

The Freelander was silent for a moment as the other carts trundled away, and the two of them looked at each other. He nodded.

Aethan climbed down from his seat and held his reins up to Visoletta.

"Hold this, would you?"

She took them, and then after a moment, handed them to Hannah.

"I'm helping," and she climbed down from her seat. Aethan held out a hand to help her down.

"I need a knife," she said, "Or shears or something."

"I've a blade," Aethan said, and they walked into the ashen field.

They walked close together, like a couple walking into a field for a picnic.

"Fuck," Saara muttered and hoisted herself out of her saddle. She handed her reins to Jane and trudged across the field, watching Aethan hold Visoletta up on his shoulder while she hacked at the knots with his knife. Her dress bunched up, revealing slender calves that Aethan held to keep her steady.

When the bodies were down, Saara helped arrange them in a line along the riverbank. Saara tried to keep her stomach calm, but when she pulled on the leg of the biggest one, the charred skin slid off in her hand, and she vomited into the water.

They washed their hands in the river when they were done, but the soot wouldn't come all the way off. Eventually, they gave up, and stood around the family... were they a family? Saara didn't know. None of them ever would.

"Does anyone know a prayer?" Visoletta asked.

"Freelanders are not known for their prayers," Aethan said.

Saara shook her head.

"Someone should say something," Visoletta said. She stood very close to Aethan, both of them apart from Saara.

"Why don't you?" Saara said. "I thought you were an artist."

They both looked up at her.

"Not that kind of artist," she said.

"Well, maybe you should play them a song. Or are these people as undeserving of that honor as we are?"

There was a moment of uncomfortable silence.

"Saara--" Aethan began.

"It's with my things. With the cart. Otherwise..."

"Otherwise, what? You'd play for them? For these poor shits in the ass end of nowhere?"

Visoletta grew red in the face and looked down at her hands. They were blackened with soot just like Saara's. She began to rub at them. Aethan reached a hand and placed it over hers. It was his mangled hand, the one missing fingers and split down the middle like a tree struck by lightning. Saara remembered when she'd first felt it that night at the inn. Visoletta didn't recoil as Saara had. Instead, she grasped it with both hands and stopped her rubbing. Saara felt the need to vomit again.

"Let's go then," Saara said, her voice a little choked. "We should get back."

Aethan and Visoletta nodded. Their hands fell apart, and the three of them turned and began their slow trudge back across the ash.

When they caught up with the Caravan, Carlotte held a white handkerchief out of her window. Saara rode up, and Aethan pulled his cart up alongside. Val's glasses glinted from the darkness within. Carlotte looked out, the panic gone from her face, but Saara could see one hand thumbing through her prayer beads in her lap.

"Hill folk?" Carlotte asked.

"Who else?" Aethan said. "They did warn us."

Carlotte frowned. "There is no other path," she said.

"Perhaps they are to the west," Val said. "We passed many farms, all of them were fine, but there were paths that branched west. Did we investigate them?"

Carlotte looked to Saara. "Did we?"

Saara shook her head.

"Why not?"

"There was no reason to..." Saara said.

"We should start scouting, at least," Aethan said. "Run some patrols. See what's coming."

Carlotte's head snapped up. "Are we not already? Isn't that why I'm paying for soldiers?"

Saara had the brief thought that Carlotte hadn't technically paid for anything yet, not until she paid Saara back.

"I... I've been scouting ahead-" Saara began.

"Ahead?" Carlotte snapped. "Because nothing can come from the sides?" The scared young woman who had been frozen at the sight of the burned bodies was completely gone, and the mistress of the tower was back. "Go," she commanded Aethan and waved a hand. "Scout, and send out the soldiers too."

Saara glared at Aethan, but the man was already turning away.

"God help us," Carlotte said. She looked at Saara. "Hurry this expedition along."

Saara gave Aethan her horse, and he gathered Pierre and Haric. They spoke together in a circle, and then all three trotted off in different directions.

It was difficult to lead from the top of Aethan's cart, but she pushed the caravan as hard as she could. She did not have the freedom of her horse, but her voice carried well enough. They went on through the day, and none of them protested when Saara did not call for lunch. When the sun began to drop in the sky, Haric returned.

He rode in hard. His beast was lathered, and he looked exhausted. His breath was heavy. He was not a young man.

"Madame!" he called, and Saara jumped off the cart and ran to meet him by Carlotte's carriage.

"There's another farm burned," he gasped.

"On the road?" Carlotte asked.

"No, a smaller path breaks off ahead, goes west a long spell."

"West!" Val cried. "They are to the west!"

Haric shook his head. "They are close – it was still smoking. More bodies. Burned bodies." Haric put a hand to his chest as though to help him breathe. "An hour's hard ride."

"Another burned farm?" Hannah asked. The rest of the caravan was bunching up around them.

"Not here, away to the west! It's fine--" Saara began.

"An hour's ride, he said!" Boris said, his voice high for such a big man.

"A hard ride!" Saara said.

"We should go back!" Slack called.

"Go back?" Carlotte said. She opened the door and stepped out of the carriage. Saara looked from her to Slack to the other worried faces, feeling the situation slipping through her hands like water through a sieve.

"Yeah. Go back," Slack said. "Back to where people aren't being hung from trees and burned."

"There is no other route," Carlotte sneered.

"There's the water," Slack argued. "I've never heard of someone going by land to Bergshalen. The water would have taken us two weeks!"

"We can't go by the water," Saara interrupted, drawing everyone's eyes to her.

"And why not?" Slack asked.

"Because..." Saara started, not knowing how she was going to finish. Because Carlotte is on the run from her own mother?

"Because," Carlotte said, her words clear and strong, "This is the way that I chose to go."

"And what if we choose to go back now?"

Carlotte glared at him with all the malice of the nobility regarding the peasantry. Slack was above her, sitting atop his wagon, but Carlotte's contempt could not be diminished.

"You are free to do so. You'll forfeit all your earnings, and you won't be taking any of my property. That cart you ride. The horses that pull it. The food you've been eating and the gun that Haric will shoot you with if you try to take any of it with you."

The crowd was silent. Haric looked nervously between Carlotte and Slack, not enjoying what he'd been volunteered for.

"Go. Go, Korkin. Get off that cart and walk back if that is what you wish. I am no slaver."

Slack licked his teeth and then spat black onto the ground.

"Or," Carlotte continued, "Get your cart in line and follow along." She paused. "Saara."

"Yes, Madame?"

"Take the rear. If anyone tries to leave with my property, put a knife in them."

"Right," Saara said.

At a word from Carlotte, Haric trotted off again, riding along the tops of the hills around them where he could see farther over the land. Saara returned to Aethan's cart and resumed her position at the back of the line. She waited for Slack to turn his cart around, and wondered what she would do when he did. Stab him? How? Run up and jump onto the cart? Not likely.

It didn't matter. He did not turn. Several hours later, when the sun hung low in the sky, Pierre appeared on top of a hill with Haric, and the two of them rode back into the line. Saara ran again to meet them.

"Another farm!" he cried.

"Burned?" Carlotte asked, leaning out of the carriage. Saara could see Val just behind.

"No!" Haric cried. "It's fine. Completely fine!"

"West," Val said, sinking back into his seat. "They are west.

We've passed them."

There were a few exhalations of relief, Saara among them.

"Were there people there?" Visoletta asked.

"Hmm? People?" Haric said. "No, it was abandoned. But all in one piece."

"Maybe that's why they didn't burn it," Visoletta said.

"These hill folk are savages," Val said. "You saw those bodies and the farm around it. They had no need to burn that field, but they did! All they know is destruction."

"So this means that they won't find us?" Visoletta asked. "We're safe?"

There was silence then for a few moments.

"They could still be out there," Slack said. "This proves nothing."

"Will you go back?" Carlotte asked. "I told you already that you could, but if we've passed them, then you might walk into their path, Mr. Gin."

Carlotte ordered the soldiers back out, and they continued on for half an hour more. Now that the immediate danger was passed, the grumblings about food began to surface. When Pierre and Haric came back down to report that they'd seen nothing, Carlotte motioned to Saara, and she called them all to camp.

"Where's Aethan?" Saara asked.

Haric pointed to the southwest. "Saw him last out that way."

"Lend me your horse – he has mine. I'll go get him."

Haric gave her the reins, and she jumped into the saddle.

"Rains coming," he said.

She looked at the gray clouds gathering above them. "Might hide our tracks?" she said.

Haric shrugged. "Hopefully they are far enough that it won't matter. This would be a shit place to die."

Saara nodded and then led Haric's horse to the top of the hill.

She could see more from up there, the endless yellow plain stretching in every direction. The sun was low, and its golden evening light lit the landscape like a painting. She shielded her eyes against it while she surveyed. Then she saw him, a few hills to the south, watching the land just like she was.

"We're stopping," she said when she pulled her horse up next to him.

"Why?" he asked. He had unbuttoned his shirt, and his chest glistened with sweat. "It's still daylight. We should get--"

"Because the Madame DeSheras said we were stopping," she snapped.

Aethan closed his mouth and considered her like her uncle used to when she'd show up unannounced after a month of silence.

"Then you should tell her to keep going."

"Listen, Freelander, this isn't the south," Saara said, letting her annoyance come out sharp. "Here, there is a hierarchy."

He set his jaw. "I am not the enemy here."

"You certainly haven't been a friend."

"What are you talking about?"

"Really?" she asked, slapping her riding crop against her leg. "You made me look like an idiot with Carlotte. The patrols. Fuck, she thinks I'm an idiot."

His eyes narrowed. "We needed a patrol."

"Then you should have told me, on the long goddamn walk back from cutting the bodies down."

"I didn't know Carlotte would-"

"How could you not know? Do you not pay attention? I have to impress her and she doesn't need any help thinking that I'm a fucking peasant!" Saara said.

"I can't be expected to read your mind, Saara."

"I don't. I expect you to pay attention instead of focusing on the fucking violinist."

He was silent for a moment, and Saara couldn't look at him, so she turned and looked into the sun instead and took comfort in the pain.

"Visoletta?" he said.

"Shut up."

"What does Visoletta have--"

"Shut up!" Saara hissed and grabbed Aethan's shoulder. She pointed into the setting sun. Aethan shaded his eyes.

"Is that a person?" Saara asked. The light made her eyes water, but she saw the vague shape of a man on a horse at the zenith of another hill.

"I don't know, it might be-" but then the figure moved,

disappearing behind the hill.

"It was," Saara stammered. "It was a person."

"Haric? Pierre?"

"They're back at the camp. Maybe they didn't see us," Saara said.

"The sun is in our eyes, not theirs," Aethan said. "They don't know where we're camped, though."

Saara looked over her shoulder and saw the dark tendrils of the cook fire smoke curling up into the gray sky.

"Aethan," she said, and pointed at it. "Do you think they could see that?"

"Fuck. Back. Back!" he cried, and his horse leapt forward down the hill. Saara snapped her crop against her horse's flank and galloped after him. The ground was uneven and each of the horse's foot falls felt like a hammer against her ass, jolting her organs and wrenching her breasts painfully up and down. She prayed that the horse didn't stumble, that the horse knew better where to put its feet than she did, that the hill tribes wouldn't come over the hill, string her up from the nearest tree, and burn her alive. A part of her noted that there weren't any trees around.

Aethan pulled up on his reins at the top of the hill that overlooked the caravan, just starting to take on the semblance of camp. They both looked back the way they'd come.

"What do you see?" Aethan asked.

"More," she answered. "You?"

"Definitely more."

She tried to count them, but they were far away and they were moving. Moving towards them.

34

Aethan tore down the hill with Saara on his heels, their horses' hooves pounding against the earth. The camp was coming together, most of the tents half raised, and the expedition turned their faces to watch them come. Kent sat over his cauldron while Raphael stuffed grass into the fire beneath it. It burned fast and hot, catching the logs to flame and belching gray smoke into the sky.

Visoletta's tent was already set up, and Jane fussed at the toggles. Visoletta and Hannah were nowhere to be seen. Aethan pulled hard at the reins, and the horse reared up and screamed.

"Pack it all up. We have to go!" Aethan shouted.

"We just set up," said Jane.

Carlotte stepped out from her carriage, and the golden evening light hit the fur around her shoulders and turned the brown hair to fire. She was a débutante, beautiful and striking, as out of place as a glass of wine on the porch of a burning house.

Saara pulled up behind him and jumped from her saddle. "They're coming." Her voice was harsh and choked.

"Who's coming?" Carlotte asked.

The camp was silent, as though they did not already know the answer.

"Horsemen. Dozens," Saara said.

"The hill folk?" Carlotte said.

"It can be no other."

The camp was still for a moment, and then the moment passed, and it erupted into motion.

"Get that God damned tent back in this cart!" Slack screamed. Black spittle flew from his lips as he jumped up into the driver's seat.

Kent slammed the cover back on the cauldron and scattered the burning grass and embers from beneath it. The other laborers ran back and forth and threw rolls and packs and pots into their carts without thought for order. Hannah and Visoletta emerged from their tent. Their faces were slack, and their eyes blinked slowly at the motion around them.

"What's going on?" Visoletta murmured. Her lips barely moved as she talked.

"We're going?" Hannah asked.

"Pack up your things. Now!" Aethan said, but Visoletta stared uncomprehending back at him.

"Help me!" Jane cried, struggling with the tie she'd just fastened.

"There's no time," Aethan said and jumped down from his horse. He grabbed the tent in a bear hug, feeling wooden poles snap, and threw the whole thing into the violinist's wagon.

Then the rain started to fall.

It came down in a patter, and then in a drizzle, and then in a torrent. It was chaos around him. Aethan helped where he could, throwing things in carts, hitching spooked horses, getting people moving. He looked ahead and saw Slack wiping at his horses, pulling at the reins to turn them off the path. Aethan ran forward and grabbed his arm.

"Out of my way, boy!" Slack screamed.

"You're going the wrong way!" Aethan yelled to be heard over the rain.

"We're going back!" Slack wrenched his arm away. "Tell that bitch to try and shoot me!"

"The horsemen are coming from the north. You'll run into them."

Slack stared down at him, water cascading out from the front fold of his tricorn hat.

"I won't stop you," Aethan said and released the man's arm. He gestured south with his chin. "Go and die."

Boris crouched in the back of the cart, gripping the wooden sides as though they were careening down a hill. His eyes flicked from Aethan to Slack's back. Aethan grimaced at him and then lifted his hands.

Slack looked up at the hills and then screamed. "We should've turned back! We should've gone back!"

Aethan turned and ran to his cart.

The others were already moving, and by the time he got Toktok hitched, he was at the back of the caravan. Aethan coaxed Toktok on, and the horse pulled harder than he had in years. Greg wasn't keeping up. The old donkey fell behind, his lead drawing out farther and farther until the cart was pulling him forward, his feet stumbling beneath him.

"Sorry, friend," Aethan whispered. He severed the lead, and Greg was swallowed by the storm. Aethan added Greg to the ledger in his mind. Another friend lost.

They continued on for many long minutes, but soon the pounding of the rain softened the earth, and the pounding of their hooves and wheels mashed it to mud. He noticed the slowdown a few minutes later. Toktok was straining harder but going slower. Ten minutes after that, they were at half the speed they started, then at walking speed, and then they weren't moving at all. The cook wagon's wheel had sunk deep into the mud and snagged a rock.

"Can we get it out?" Carlotte said from her window, yelling to be heard over the wind and the rain and the shouting of Boris and Kent and Doss as they tried to heave the cart free.

"It will take time!" Saara said.

"We don't have time," Aethan said, joining the discussion. Pierre and Haric crowded in.

"How far were they?" Haric shouted.

"A few miles," Saara answered.

"Will they find us?" Carlotte shouted. "Will the rain have erased our tracks?"

Saara looked at Aethan.

"Perhaps," he yelled. "But the road only goes two ways."

Carlotte nodded. "Options?"

"We fight. Try to scare them off," Pierre said.

Haric shot out a hand and gripped Pierre's shoulder.

"No. We run. We leave the carts behind and go. It's not worth the risk!"

"There aren't enough horses for everyone," Saara said.

"We ride two to a horse then."

"We can't leave this behind," snapped Carlotte.

"We can't fight them," Haric said. "We've only got two guns."

"Two?" Saara asked, "Aethan's cargo is all guns and powder too."

"They're matchlocks, girl," Haric responded. "As good as clubs in this rain."

"They can't fire wet," Carlotte said.

Haric nodded. "The match has to stay lit, and the powder tray must stay dry!"

"Are they dry now?" she asked, yelling over Haric.

Aethan nodded. "The cart is lined and covered with oilskin."

"We'll build a fort!" Carlotte said.

"What?"

"A dry place to fire from. Circle the carts, knock one over, and ·cover the space between with the oilskin or tent canvas. We can fire from underneath it. And this carriage too. Fire from its windows."

Haric looked at her blankly.

"Move. Move!" Carlotte shouted and pushed the carriage door open. She took Saara's hand and stepped into the muck. The rain plastered the fur around her shoulders into a wet mass.

"Leave it," she shouted to the men laboring to free the cart. "Empty that one. Flip it on its side."

They looked at her, confused and exhausted.

"Did she stutter?!" Saara screamed.

The whole expedition snapped to it, unloading the boxes of supplies onto the ground where Carlotte directed.

"Pull these other carts around!" she ordered, smacking at the cook's arm to get him moving. Visoletta's cart went on its side. Slack's cart was pulled opposite the cook's. Jane, Ari, and Renee pulled out Visoletta's tent fabric, driving nails into the wood to secure it over the sidelong cart. Doss and Boris knocked out two of the planks, creating a window to shoot through. Aethan pulled his own cart to the back and, with Haric and Pierre's help, unloaded the matchlocks under the canvas and began to load them.

The wind and the rain tugged their canvas roof back and forth, ripping at where the women had driven nails through. It wouldn't hold for long.

"This is madness," Slack yelled.

"We'll shoot. Just keep the next guns ready," Haric said.

"To hell with this," Slack yelled. He tore out of the shelter and jumped up onto one of the horses, pulling a knife from his belt and slashing at the tether as he went. The horse screamed, and he disappeared into the night. The others watched him go.

"We should run," Haric said.

Pierre handed a loaded gun to Jane and took Haric's face in both his hands.

"We can't go, Haric," he said.

"We left war behind, Pierre. We didn't leave it to die out here."

"We left. You and I. Together," Pierre said. One of his thumbs rubbed at the stubble on Haric's old cheek. "We can't abandon these people."

"Why not?" Haric asked.

"Because I want to live. I want us to live, and we couldn't live with that. Not with everything else we've done," Pierre said.

Haric's eyes scanned around them, but Aethan was the only one paying attention. The others were full of panic, making their own preparations and prayers, taking the guns Aethan handed them, not knowing what to do. Haric's eyes met Aethan's, and Haric looked quickly away.

"OK, Pierre," Haric said.

"Listen to me!" Haric yelled, pulling away from Pierre's hands. Some of those who huddled under the canvas turned to him. "We won't have time to reload. Shoot and grab another gun. Those not at the front keep the other guns dry and hand them forward. This–" he pointed to the short bit of rope smoldering above the trigger, "--is the match. It needs to be lit to fire. Pull the tray back." He did the action, revealing the indentation filled with black powder. "And pull the trigger. The match will light the powder, and the gun will fire. Drop the gun, pick up another, and repeat. There cannot be water in the barrel, the match cannot go out, and the tray cannot be wet, or it will not fire. Do you understand?"

He did not wait for an answer, because a cry came from out in the storm. It came from the north and was only just audible above the yelling and the wind, but they all knew what it meant.

Pierre grabbed an armload of rifles and then reached out and gripped Haric's hand.

"Be here, and be well when I get back," Pierre said, and then scurried out into the rain, holding his body over the guns to keep them dry.

There was another cry from the storm, and then another and another, and then the pounding of hooves could be heard over the pounding of the rain. Aethan and Haric crawled to the makeshift window in the cart. Visoletta sat at one end, holding a rifle loosely. Doss was underneath the cook cart, lying on his stomach, a rifle trembling in his hands.

"Ready!" Haric shouted, and Aethan saw the first rider materialize out of the rain. He was just a shape, no definition at all, just a smudge in his vision in the shape of a horse and a man. Then there were others. Then there were many.

Lightning flashed, and Aethan saw swords held high, faces covered in fabric, and horse hooves sending up sprays of earth and water.

A boom of thunder came from directly overhead and drowned out Aethan's cry, so he screamed it again.

"Fire!"

The guns exploded by her head, and Erika cried out and let go of whatever she had been holding. It was a gun. Why had she been holding a gun? The rain lashed against the wooden slats she leaned on, wooden slats she vaguely remembered had once been her cart. She reached out a hand and touched the gun in the mud. It was metal and cold and repellent to her. Why was she here?

The ride had been so stressful. She and Hannah had taken a swim first thing when they'd made camp, and those first ripples were always so strong. Then the ripple had passed, and they were out in the rain. Jane was panicked. She had begged them to help, and she and Hannah had done what they could, but the ripples came again, and now here she was.

Something shoved into her, and she collapsed into the mud. Guns fired again. The little fort, patched together like children playing at war in the streets, filled with smoke. War. They were being attacked. She had to help.

She pulled herself upright and gasped in a breath of air. Hannah was beside her, cowering. Erika grabbed her.

"We have to help!" Erika cried and pulled the woman up to the window with her. The pike rippled through her. This wasn't the time to be high. She needed to sober up. She picked up her gun and shoved it through the gap in the wood.

Hannah gripped the edge of the wood, and her face was filled with terror. Hannah screamed. Erika pulled the trigger. Nothing happened. She squeezed it again. Nothing.

The tray! She remembered the tray. Haric had said the tray needed to be dry. Then she noticed the little match on top of the gun was caked in mud. It had to stay lit. They needed to light it.

"We need fire," she yelled to Hannah, but Hannah wasn't paying attention. Erika grabbed Hannah and turned her face to look at her.

"Fire!" Erika yelled, and an arrow smashed into the side of Hannah's head. Blood splattered into Erika's eyes, and Hannah's body was knocked back from the force of it.

Erika scrambled back in the mud and screamed. Then the canvas above them was gone. One of the nails ripped free, and their roof became a flag whipping back and forth in the wind.

Men ran, mud and water flew, and horses charged all around the wagons. Lightning flashed, and she saw Haric fire his gun. Smoke roiled out of the barrel and was dashed away by the wind and rain. An arrow took him in the shoulder, and he went down in the mud. Erika crawled underneath a wagon, staggered to her feet, and ran.

A horse appeared in front of her. On its back, a figure all in black pulled back a bow and aimed for her heart. Then Erika was pulled sideways, and Aethan was there with a pistol in one outstretched hand. He fired, and the horse screamed and bucked, pitching the bowman over the top and then underneath the horse's body. Aethan dropped the gun and heaved Erika to her feet. He pulled her close to his face and screamed.

"Run!"

She did. She staggered against the wind and the rain and the sounds of people dying all around her, and then the pike swam back into her vision.

The drug's wave rolled over her, and she slowed to a stop and lifted her face to the sky. The sounds around her dulled, and all her attention was on the feeling of the rain on her skin, drumming a soothing staccato beat. She was a part of the storm, a stalk of wheat bending and bowing with the wind. Where was her violin? Oh, the way it would feel to play her violin in the storm, to let the storm pass through her and bring such music to the tips of her fingers.

She was lifted up into the air, and her throat was squeezed shut. She was flying, flying through the storm like a bird who could no longer breathe.

Why couldn't she breathe?

And then the horseman who had snatched her pulled her across his saddle and brought the hilt of his sword down on her forehead.

Saara didn't know what to do. She had fired the matchlock rifle out the window of the carriage at the approaching horsemen. Carlotte had fired her rifle, and then Val after. Rold handed them the other three rifles, and they fired those too. She didn't know if they'd hit anything. She could hardly distinguish the shapes that flitted through the storm. The horsemen had been ghosts, and then they were there. They were everywhere, all around them. There were more shots. Screams of men and women and horses. An arrow flitted in through the window, shattering the delicate shutters and embedding in the wood by Carlotte's head.

"God in heaven," Carlotte hissed, "I put myself beneath thy shield. Protect me, Father, unworthy as I am. My soul--"

Saara looked behind her at Val and Rold. Their eyes were wide with terror.

"Go!" Saara shouted. Val disappeared through the other door, and Rold went after him. Saara pushed Carlotte out and then followed. The world outside was even more chaotic. Pierre stood by the carriage's corner with his rifle held like a spear. The fort had lost its roof. The tent fabric ripped violently back and forth.

"Haric!" Pierre screamed, and then there was a horse. It rode by, and a wicked blade flashed, and Pierre cried out and fell to the ground, his front torn open from belly to throat.

"What do we do? Saara! Saara!" Carlotte screamed.

Saara looked at her. Carlotte was soaked through, looking like a drowned rat in the rain. Her eyes were wide, and there was blood on her face, and her lips mumbled through prayers while she waited for Saara to answer.

But Saara didn't know what to say. Saara didn't know war. She knew back-alley murders and storefront shakedowns. She took fights when she knew she could win. This was... chaos.

Carlotte reached out and grabbed Saara's shirt. "Saara!" she screamed. "What do we--"

"We run!" Saara said and then turned to look at Rold beside her and yelled it again. She didn't know where Val was. She didn't have time to know. She grabbed Rold with one hand and Carlotte with the other and shoved them toward the hill. They shouldn't have fought. They should have listened to Haric, and they should have run. They had to go into the hills. There was nowhere else to go. She ran forward and pushed at both of their backs, hurrying them through the grass.

Unbelievable pain lanced through her head, and Saara was on the ground. She rolled, fighting off a wave of nausea, and looked up to see a figure towering over her. He reached down and pulled her up by the collar of her coat. Her head lolled back, and blackness rolled through her vision.

No, she couldn't go out. Carlotte needed her. Rold needed her. She was all they had. If Saara hadn't put things in motion, they'd both be back in Sheras.

Saara opened her eyes. The face looking into hers was covered all in cloth except for a slit that revealed the eyes. His other hand lifted a club into the air.

Saara was limp. Her back was arched, and her hands dangled down by her feet, down by the alley knife sheathed in her boot.

Saara drew the knife and shoved it into her attacker's side. He screamed and dropped her. Saara fell back, pulling the knife with her, and rolled over onto hands and knees. The pain in her head was unimaginable. She wanted to lie down, to collapse into the mud and close her eyes. Just for a few moments.

She stood. Her attacker was mewling on the ground. She stepped past him. Another figure was dragging Carlotte back down the hill by her hair, and a third wrestled with Rold. She could hear Rold crying out, and she could see Carlotte kicking at the earth and scrabbling at the fingers on her scalp. Carlotte's pistol lay in the muddy grass out of reach. Saara looked to Rold, and then to Carlotte, and she charged.

She caught Carlotte's attacker in the back and looped her left arm around his neck, pulling him backwards and punching the knife low with her right arm, once, twice, three times. Her hand warmed with blood. The man screamed.

Saara released his neck and kicked him down the hill. She turned back around with Rold's name on her lips, and one foot slid out from under her. She went down hard, her chin smacked against the earth, and Saara collapsed into darkness.

Carlotte crouched over Saara and tugged at her shoulder.

"Saara!" Carlotte cried and jerked her hard. "Saara, I need you. Wake up! Wake up!"

Carlotte looked up. She could barely see anything through the downpour. Her ears were full of the pounding rain and the screaming people. She could barely hear her own voice. It didn't sound like her. It sounded like an animal. A desperate animal, scared and all alone.

There was a crack of thunder, and Carlotte cried out and scampered on hands and knees and feet and elbows through the mud toward her carriage. She couldn't run. Saara had told her to run, but Saara was dead, and where would she go? She could hide in the carriage. No, they'd look in the carriage. She could hide under it, like she'd hidden under her bed as a child. Carlotte crawled underneath and then turned to look out between the spokes of the wheel.

She saw Pierre's body just to her left, split open, and she saw depressions in the grass where she knew bodies lay, where she knew Saara lay face down in the mud.

Saara was dead, right? Had she checked her pulse? No, but Saara hadn't been breathing, but she couldn't breathe if she was face down in mud. If she wasn't dead, she would be soon.

"God help me," Carlotte whispered. Saara was probably already dead. To go out and check was just going to get Carlotte killed, and it wasn't Carlotte's place to save Saara. It was the other way around. It was Saara's job to do the saving, and it was Carlotte's job to be saved. And Saara had done it, hadn't she? Saara had pulled the man away and stabbed him like a beast possessed, and now Carlotte was safe. If Saara died doing that, then everything was going according to plan, and she didn't need to go out there. Right?

"God damn it," she whimpered. Her eyes darted left and right. She saw horses flitting through the rain, heard whoops and shouts, and the clanging of metal. She looked back to where Saara lay.

"God-" and then she broke around the wheel and sprinted to Saara's body. She tumbled, tripping on her cloak, got back to her feet, and collapsed at Saara's side. She pressed her fingers into Saara's neck. She couldn't feel anything, and then - a pulse.

Carlotte grabbed Saara by the opposite shoulder and heaved backward, straining to pull the woman over. She collapsed back down. Saara was heavy. She was too heavy for Carlotte to lift. Had the tables been turned, Saara would have carried Carlotte away, but this was too much for Carlotte. She wasn't strong enough.

Carlotte screamed and pulled again, every muscle in her body tensing, and then, with a sucking sound just barely heard over the storm, Saara came free of the mud and flipped over, knocking Carlotte onto her ass. She scrambled on top of Saara and wiped the mud off her face and out of her nostrils. The woman coughed and then vomited a little. Carlotte needed to get Saara on her side or she'd drown in the vomit. She needed to keep her off her face or she'd drown in the mud. She needed to get her out of the rain or she'd drown in that. Carlotte reached under Saara's shoulders and gripped her armpits. Then she pressed her legs into the mud and heaved the woman back a foot. She did it again and again, and then the storm was filled with orange light.

There was a great crack like the sky being ripped open, and a shock wave knocked Carlotte onto her side. She righted herself and grabbed Saara's arms to pull again, her mind racing for an answer as she strained.

It must have been thunder. Nothing else could be that loud, but the sound had come from behind her, not above. The Freelander's cart was behind her, she thought, and he had casks of black powder in his cart. Could it be that?

Explosions were terrifying, Harold had said, louder than thunder.

Carlotte turned and saw a world on fire. The ground raged with flame despite the fact that it had been soaked with rain for nearly an hour. Burning corpses littered the area around the cart, and the carts themselves were smashed to kindling. Was this the power of black powder?

Then she saw him. The Freelander, Aethan, standing in the center of the wreckage, arms outstretched to either side and head bent back, looking at the heavens.

A horse and rider raced past, and Aethan pointed a hand at them. The air between his hand and the rider ignited, and the horse and rider screamed, wreathed in flame. Then the horse fell, and shriveled, and the screaming was no more.

"Magic," Carlotte whispered.

It was real. She'd traveled for weeks to find it, and it had found her. A level of destruction without equal in the world. Power beyond all the scientific knowledge and military might in the Ryker dominion.

She was snapped out of her reverie when she noticed that the circle of fire around Aethan was expanding towards Saara. And towards her! She grabbed at Saara's arms and heaved backwards, dragging the unconscious woman through the muck, straining against the mud's force sucking her down. But the fire came on, and Carlotte knew it was foolish to think she could save Saara. She couldn't pull the woman any faster, and she was too small to pick her up and carry her. She might not even have time to save herself. Carlotte had tried. She had done the best she could do.

Carlotte dropped Saara and ran up the hill.

"No!" came Aethan's voice over the wind. "NO!" it came louder, defying the wind and the rain, as though defying God himself. Carlotte turned and saw the circle of flame pull back, the burning grass going out like like so many candles snuffed by an invisible hand. Saara's body lay just feet from the blackened circle. The ring shrank at first slowly and then with a gathering speed, racing back to the Freelander, and then it was gone. The fire was smothered and the light with it.

Carlotte turned and raced down the hill towards him, leaping over Saara and slipping in the ashen mud. She saw his form barely visible in the storm, and she saw the galloping horseman.

"No!" Carlotte screamed, but the rider did not acknowledge her. He leaped from his saddle and clubbed Aethan in the back of the head, and Aethan dropped.

"No!" Carlotte screamed, but the rider lifted him, heaved him over his horse, remounted, and sped off into the night.

Carlotte's foot caught on a body, the big one, Boris, with his mouth open and head only partially connected to the neck, and Carlotte fell. When she looked up, the rider was gone.

"No," Carlotte whispered, and then began to cry.

35

Carlotte awoke and grasped about in that amnesia that grips in the first moments after sleep. She was wet and caked with dirt, and there was blood on her hands.

This was not as it should be.

She looked down at her chest and saw the fur collar sagging off her shoulders and crusted with dirt. She must have fallen asleep sitting up... in the mud. She should be in her bed. No, she was on her expedition. She should be in her carriage or in her tent. She sat up more fully and smacked her head against something hard. Carlotte winced and looked up. A low wood ceiling. To her sides, great wooden wheels were sunk into the ground. In her lap was Saara's head. Saara had lost her little black ribbon, and her hair was loose and matted with mud and blood.

"Oh, God no. Please no," Carlotte said, remembering.

She had gone back to Saara after Aethan was taken. The other riders had left, and Carlotte had pulled Saara under the carriage and turned her on her side and cleared the vomit off her face. She had begged God not to let Saara die, not to leave Carlotte truly on her own.

Carlotte looked down at the woman's face and tried to wipe the dirt from it, but her hands were just as dirty and only smeared the muck around. She lifted Saara's head, scrambled backward, and laid it down on the ground as softly as she could manage. Then she leaned to the side to watch Saara's chest. It was still... and then it moved just so. The rise and fall were shallow, but it did happen. Saara was still alive.

Tears welled in Carlotte's eyes, and suddenly the space underneath the carriage felt unbearably claustrophobic. She crawled past Saara's body and emerged into the morning light. Her stomach heaved, but only a dribble of acid and spit came out. The back of her throat burned.

"God," she wheezed and rocked back onto her heels, kneeling before the endless golden hills beyond the reach of civilization. "God, help me."

The tears erupted from her, and sobs followed them, loud and desperate, until she began to speak through them. "God. I believe in God, the almighty and the one true father, creator of the earth and the life above. I believe in the prophet, the soul given by God to guide the sinful through all life's troubles. Torn though he was, and battered through the Amaranthine cruelty, broken though was his body, whole was his soul, and it rose from the dead on the third morning..."

Her voice steadied as she went, repeating the Admittance without thinking, letting twenty-three years of repetition and church teachings bear her along. She did not need the prayer beads to guide her through the verses or the proclamations of faith that separated them. As she went, her mind calmed and turned inwards, meditating on the suffering of the prophet in his attempts to save the Amaranthine from destruction. By the time she'd finished the cycle of prayers, her heart had slowed and her sobbing gasps had changed to deep, but stuttered, breath.

"Thank you," she managed.

Then, she looked around at what God had left for her.

She was in the middle of the Badlands. It was a week back to Forepost, and at least as much to Lake Sharathorn. She didn't see any of the horses, and the only carriages that had survived were hers and the cart it pulled.

Something glinted amidst the churned-up grass and dirt. She trudged up to it, reached down, and pulled her pistol from the muck. The creases of the bas relief on its grip were filled with mud.

If they went back, then she would go with her reputation in

tatters. She would be a joke on the lips of every Ryker, and when the Inquisitors brought her back to the tower, her mother would greet her with the same icy stare she'd had when Elspeth had come home, except Elspeth had--

Carlotte's breath froze in her chest.

Elspeth.

Carlotte spun around in a panic and then gave a strangled scream and tripped backwards. She scrambled to her feet and held the gun out with both hands. A figure stood before her with hands up, palms out. It was Jane, covered in almost as much muck as she was.

"Please," was all Jane said.

Carlotte held the pose for a moment. Her hands shook, and the tip of the pistol danced about. Then she let the gun drop and ran past Jane to the cart hitched to her carriage. She tripped on something soft and only just managed to keep herself from falling. She looked back at Pierre's body, a long gash all up through his torso, and stifled a scream. She turned away and rooted through the cart. She shoved the heavy boxes to the side as best she could, and then let out a pent-up breath.

Her hands rested against the white finish of Elspeth's coffin, and Carlotte felt suddenly very guilty for smudging her grime across it.

What had she been thinking, taking Elspeth's body from her family's crypt? What must her mother have thought when her theft had been discovered? What would her mother say when she returned? Carlotte the Mad. Carlotte the Grave Robber. She'd be lucky if Harold still agreed to take her name. Her actions had probably ended the DeSheras line. What childish fantasy had she been trying to fulfill? That she would take her sister on one final adventure? That she would take her sister into some magical fairy tale where ancient peoples could turn back time?

Then, Carlotte remembered the fairy tale she had seen with her own eyes, and her spiraling came to a stop. She looked up from the coffin, past Jane staring back at her, and to the ring of blackened earth.

"What happened?" she whispered, and then she repeated it louder and looked at Jane.

"I... I was with Hannah," Jane said. "We fired the guns and then... an arrow... and I ran into the grass and hid."

"No," Carlotte said. "What happened with the Freelander? With Aethan?"

"I did not see-"

"The fire!" Carlotte yelled. "Did you see the fire?"

Jane stood with her mouth slightly open, as though unable to process Carlotte's sudden rage. Carlotte tried to rein herself in. She took a deep breath and stroked the coffin's lid with a shaky hand.

"The fire, Jane," she said, keeping her voice as low and steady as she could. "Did you see the fire?"

"I saw the light, but--"

The carriage door opened. Jane squealed and Carlotte pulled up the pistol again, but then let it drop when she saw Val poking his head out.

"Carlotte?" he said, "And another? Who is there? Saara?"

There was blood on his face, and his spectacles were still perched on his nose, but the wires were badly bent and the glass was shattered. He squinted at her from behind them.

"Jane is here," Carlotte said. "But Saara is alive. She is under the carriage." Carlotte stepped closer to him. "Did you see the Freelander?" she asked. "Did you see the fire?"

"I didn't-- I was with you and then we fled and then--"

"Did you see the fire, Vaalier?"

"The explosion?"

"Yes," Carlotte hissed. She took another step towards him.

"I heard it, a crack like the earth splitting apart. I looked out the window, but my spectacles..." Val reached up a shaking hand to touch the wires, and then winced at the feel of them. "All that powder. I just hope it took some of those savages-"

"No, no, no. It wasn't powder," Carlotte said.

Val squinted at her. "I don't think it was thunder-"

"I know it wasn't thunder. It was the Freelander."

A breeze blew through the grass. Val reached out a hand and gripped the windowsill. "The Freelander?"

Carlotte's nostrils flared with her breath. Her jaw trembled. She held her teeth just apart and pressed her tongue into the space between. "It. Was. Magic."

"Magic?" Jane repeated.

Carlotte looked from one to the other, and they both stared back at her, the fear on their faces inching towards pity.

"Carlotte," Val said. "We've been through a lot. When we return to-"

"We're not going back," Carlotte said.

"What?"

"We can't. I can't go back." Carlotte hissed.

"Carlotte..."

"This is why we are here!" she shouted. "They took him. The riders took Aethan, and we have to get him back."

Val gave a nervous laugh. "How?"

"I..." Carlotte chewed the inside of her mouth. "I don't..." She looked around at the carnage, then at the grass-covered hills all around them. "We need to know where they went," she said. "We need a guide."

"A guide?" Val echoed.

"Yes, a guide!" Carlotte snapped. "We need a guide and we need a way to talk to them." She looked up at Jane and thrust a finger at her. "You. Check the bodies. All of them. See if anyone's still alive."

Jane just stared back at her.

"Now!" Carlotte screamed.

Jane glanced at Val, and then back at her. Carlotte could tell she didn't agree with her, but the habit of obedience seemed to be strong in her, because she gave a curt nod and went off to follow the order.

Carlotte went to the carriage and pushed Val out of her way. She reached inside and heaved the chest of books off the bench. An arrow stuck out of its side.

"Aethan is gone, Carlotte."

"I am aware."

Carlotte tore through the chest, throwing books out as she went.

"Carlotte, you-- we have been through a very traumatic experience. And I know that you think you saw--"

"I know what I saw," Carlotte hissed.

"And I'm sure it seemed very real, but this hysteria is--"

"Why do you think we are here, Val?" Carlotte snapped and reeled around to face him with a book on Animal Force gripped in one hand. "Why do you think I asked you here? I could work with anyone, any Ryker in Sheras were I looking for anything else, but I am looking for magic!" Carlotte spat the word and flung the book at him. It struck him on the cheek, and he cried out and flailed backwards. "I do not care for the past. Elspeth did not care for the past, except that we both knew it contained knowledge that was lost. Magic. That is what we are looking for, and that is what I saw last night!"

"Madame!" Jane called.

Carlotte turned to see the woman standing over one of the hill people. Carlotte turned back to Val. "There's a book in here on languages. Find it. And then... take care of Saara."

She didn't wait to watch him scramble up. The world felt like it was balanced on an edge. Her mind was only holding it together because she had a problem to solve, and if she stopped focusing on it, she felt that the world would come crashing down around her.

Jane stood by a horse's carcass. A black-clad rider still sat in the saddle with one leg trapped beneath it. Jane withdrew as Carlotte approached. Carlotte got down onto her knees and watched the person's chest.

It moved.

She waved a hand in front of their face. Nothing. She held her pistol in one hand and dug the other under the rider's armpit. She pulled. "Help me," she said.

Jane came down beside her and pulled at the other armpit. Nothing. "They're stuck fast," Jane said.

Carlotte's mind raced, feeling the world teeter around her. "We need a horse. Where are the horses?"

"I don't know," Jane said.

"Then go look for them. There! Up the hill. Look out and find one."

Jane hurried off.

Carlotte watched her go, and felt very helpless that she had nothing to do, so she went back to Val, who was cradling Saara's head underneath the carriage and wiping mud from her face. Carlotte watched them for a few moments.

"How did you know each other? Before all this?"

"I know her uncle. She learned to read in my library," Val said. "The book is on the step."

Carlotte thought of Saara as a little girl, and had trouble imagining her being young. The woman's pinched face, her bulky body, the way she'd stabbed the hill person, punching that dagger in and in and in. Carlotte bit down on her cheek and picked up the book.

The Continental Languages: Ancient and Current.

She opened it to the list of authors. Elspeth DeSheras was at the top and in the biggest print. She'd only written one chapter, but the authors were listed by importance, not by contribution. Rykers did not typically compile their work. They were miserly with their fame, but once Elspeth DeSheras had given a chapter, the others had flooded in to be associated with her name.

Carlotte flipped to the table of contents and then turned her eyes skyward and muttered a prayer of thanks.

"Part 3, section 2: 'The Hill Dialects'"

"We need to go back," Val said. "Saara has a concussion. She needs medicine."

"It's a week back to Forepost," Carlotte said.

"It's more than two to Thorlaille."

"If she can live a week, then she can live two."

"It's on your shoulders if she dies," Val said.

Carlotte thought about that for a moment. She thought about how she had dragged Saara through the mud, how she'd kept her from drowning in her own vomit, how she had left Saara behind when she thought the fire was going to overtake them. Carlotte squatted down and looked at Val underneath the carriage. There were tears behind his broken spectacles. He stroked Saara's cheek with one thumb.

"Everything is on my shoulders," Carlotte said with more conviction than she felt. "That is what it is to be a Ryker. But I need her. She will not die."

"And you get to decide that, do you?" Val asked.

"God decides, and God has decided. How many died last night? And she did not. God spared her, and God has reasons for what he does."

Carlotte stood and walked away from Val and his questions. God had decided when he sent her on this expedition. God did not take what she could not do without.

She flipped through the book. It wasn't a complete explanation of all the languages, more a discussion of their pronunciations and structure, but there was a short table of words in this section. She read and sounded out the words as she went.

Carlotte heard a sound and looked up to see Jane coming down the road with a horse in tow. It was the Freelander's horse, the one he'd always been talking to. Could witches talk to animals? She had so much to ask Aethan when she found him.

"He was grazing. His hobble was still on. I couldn't see any others."

"We work with what God gives us," Carlotte said and sent Jane off to find some rope. She returned, and Carlotte directed her where to tie the ropes and what knots to use so that the dead horse was firmly attached to the live one. When Jane finished, Carlotte held the book open in one hand and the pistol in the other, aimed at the rider's head.

She gave the order, and Jane led the horse forward. The ropes tightened, groaned, and then, as Carlotte began to worry the horse wasn't strong enough, the dead horse began to slide. The rider woke up and screamed.

It was a woman's scream.

The rider was pulled along with the horse, and her hands and free leg scrambled at the horse's body, though whether she was trying to hang on or push it off was unclear. Carlotte wasn't sure the woman even knew. Before Carlotte could call out for Jane to stop, there was a loud crack, and the rider's screams peaked and then died. The woman had fallen unconscious again. Jane looked back at Carlotte.

Carlotte chewed the inside of her cheek, and then. "Go again."

"Maybe her foot is caught in a stirrup or something?" Jane said.

Carlotte nodded. "Go again. I need her free."

Jane didn't move. Carlotte looked into her eyes.

"They killed Hannah," Carlotte said, and Jane's face hardened.

Carlotte placed the book and gun down on a dry bit of dirt and grabbed the rider by the armpits. She braced her heels into the earth.

"Go," Carlotte said, and Jane led the horse forward. Carlotte's heels dug furrows into the ground. She straightened her back against the force and then there was another snap, and the horse's body slid off the woman and Carlotte fell onto her ass.

The boot was missing, apparently taken by the horse's corpse, and it left behind a purple and bloody foot turned at the wrong angle. The ankle was ripped on one side, and a jagged bone stuck through the skin where blood bubbled out. Carlotte fought a wave of nausea.

"Twine. Find me some twine," she breathed.

Jane vomited, but only bile came up. Then she found and brought back some more rope, and Carlotte tied a tourniquet to stop the bleeding. Carlotte took a moment to gather herself and then stood. She held the book open in one hand and the pistol in the other, aimed down at the rider's head, like an inquisitor proclaiming her accusation.

"Wake up!"

Nothing happened. Not that she really thought that would work. She reached out a toe and nudged the rider's face. Nothing. She looked at Jane. No help. Carlotte placed the book back on the ground and began unwrapping the long cloth from around the rider's face.

It revealed a small, youngish face, not much older than Carlotte was.

Carlotte sat back on the ground and considered the girl and her foot, and then thought of the pain in her own ankle, still a bit sore from her fall from the tower and aggravated by her recent activity. Carlotte grimaced and steeled herself. This "girl" had tried to kill her, or kidnap her, or whatever. This girl was lucky to be alive. She was not to be pitied.

"Don't just stand there," Carlotte growled at Jane.

"What should I do?"

"Go... see what we have left. We will need packs of food and gear. I can handle this."

Jane left, and Carlotte looked back down at the hill woman. There was nothing for it. There were certain herbs and minerals that, when crushed, could wake the unconscious. She remembered them from lessons long ago, but she'd never had much use for herbology. It was a housewife's science.

"Maybe you should start learning," she whispered to herself. She was to be a wife when this was all over, after all. Carlotte scooted to a drier bit of road and then opened the book back up. She focused on the words and tried not to think about anything else.

It took half an hour for the hill woman to wake. She moaned, and Carlotte jumped to her feet. She aimed the pistol at the woman's head and held the pose until the woman opened her eyes.

"Ke sar ka'volm," Carlotte said, and put all the hate she could into her face. The book made the hill language seem rather simple, with verbs only conjugated by tense and plurality of the subject. Unfortunately, there was not a word in her book for tribe or people, so instead of "Where is your tribe?" she said what she hoped was "Where are your boys?"

The woman squinted up at her, confused, and then, when her eyes registered the gun in Carlotte's hand, fierce. She pushed herself up onto her hands, tucked her omnidirectional foot underneath her, and collapsed back with an ear-piercing scream.

"Ke sar ka'volm?" Carlotte yelled again once the screams turned to whimpers. The girl pushed herself into a sit and looked down at her foot.

"Ash'Areek," she whispered and brought a hand to her face.

Carlotte glanced through the page of terms. Though the conjugations were simple, possession was more complicated, combining with words rather than being distinct. She didn't understand, but she had studied the chapter long enough to know where to look.

"My god," the girl had said.

Then, the girl began to cry. The tears leaked from her eyes as she reached down and touched tenderly at the torn flesh of her ankle. Her breathing hitched, but she did not cry out loud. It made the pity in Carlotte well up, but Carlotte had no time for pity. She'd wasted enough already.

"Ke," she said slowly and deliberately to make up for whatever thick accent she knew she must have. "Sar ka'volm?"

"Ash'volm?" the woman asked, finally looking up. The gun didn't seem to scare her. She did not look at the barrel but into Carlotte's eyes. Her's were a dark green. She must have been much loved in her tribe.

"Ke," Carlotte repeated.

"Ash'volm... Ash'seka?"

Carlotte growled in frustration. She didn't know what that meant, and if she said yes without knowing the meaning it could confuse things more. Carlotte backed away to the nearest rider corpse and kicked it.

"Ka'volm." Then she gestured out into the hills around her with the gun. "Ke? Ke sar ka'volm."

The woman's breath came in half sobs, but Carlotte could see the wheels in her head working to understand. Then the girl spoke. "Do you speak Dominion?"

Carlotte's jaw dropped, and she stood still for several moments. "Yes. Where is your tribe?"

"Ah," The girl said. Her accent was thick, and she hit the k's hard in the back of her throat. "Ike sar ka'handay." The words modulated in pitch as she spoke -- the book hadn't mentioned the language being tonal -- and the words the girl had said sounded different. More than just an accent. Carlotte resisted the urge to hurl the book across the road. The girl lifted a hand and pointed to the northwest. "Da."

"You speak Dominion, but do you know what this is?" Carlotte asked, motioning to the gun. The woman's eyes narrowed.

"We are not savages."

"Good, then you know what it can do. What I'll do with it if you don't do as I command."

The woman bared her teeth, but Carlotte went on.

"Your tribe took something from me, and I mean to get it back. You will take me to them and--"

The woman laughed, or at least it sounded a little like a laugh that turned into a choking cough. "As you wish," she said.

"And if," Carlotte said, putting all the malice she could muster in her voice, "if you lead me astray, or try to kill me, or betray me in any way, I will take your other foot and--"

"Yes. Threat. Dominion threats are not new to me. Put me on

your horse. I will take you."

The woman closed her eyes and lay back in the dirt. Carlotte could see tears coming between her eyelids.

"Well... Good," Carlotte said. She gave the woman a quick look, but didn't see any weapons on her person. They must have been scattered during the fight. "Don't try anything," she said. The woman didn't answer.

Carlotte turned and walked back to her carriage. Val was still under it with Saara's head in his lap. Jane was crouched beside him.

"What's left?" Carlotte asked.

"Some food," Jane said. "Some tools, your clothes. Everything in this cart and carriage. The rest is burned."

Carlotte looked to the horse and then to the carriage with its cart in tow, and the hills beyond them. She doubted there were roads where they were going. Then she looked at Val and Jane and Saara, all that was left of her merry expedition.

"Can you wake her up?"

"She's unconscious. She needs a doctor," Val said.

"I need her," Carlotte said.

Val glared up with real malice in his eyes, and Carlotte took a subconscious step back.

"I suppose God has decided you don't," he spat.

Carlotte swallowed. She thought for a moment about what she was about to do, what she was about to do *without* Saara. "This is bigger than us," Carlotte tried.

But Val sneered. "I'd say you've lost your mind, but I wonder if it was already gone when all this madness began. Who but a mad woman would bring a coffin out here and keep it a secret?"

A panic rose in her. She thought of her plan, of the foolish scope of it, of her decision to leave behind her position and privilege and take her sister's body into the unknown, and the panic welled up like a great wave that threatened to bowl her over and smash her into the earth.

"And now," Val went on, "You treat your servant's life with contempt so you can run off into the wild to chase some imagining of magic."

Carlotte's thoughts focused on his words, and then on the wonder of what she had seen the night before, of the man surrounded with summoned flames that died at his calling.

"I'm not crazy," Carlotte whispered. "I know what I saw."

Her gaze hardened, and she turned away from Val and snapped her fingers at Jane.

"Saddle the horse. And fill its saddle bags with food and anything else I might need."

"We need that horse to--" Val began, but Carlotte cut him off.

"What are you going to do about it?" she asked, and then shifted the pistol in her hand.

"My God. You really have lost it," he said.

"Lions do not concern themselves with the opinions of mice," Carlotte said. "Wait here until I get back. Then we go on to Thorlaille."

"How long do we wait?" Jane asked, her eyes far away.

"Until I'm back."

"And what if they come again. The riders?"

Carlotte glanced around at the bodies and the char and the ruined caravan.

"Hide."

They sat in one saddle, smashed up against each other like a pair of lovers, except the hill woman's hands were tied to the pommel and Carlotte cradled her pistol between her belly and the woman's back. She'd had it held with the barrel jammed into the woman's side, but the angle was awkward, and the barrel was long, and she'd had to hold her arm out to the side to manage it. The ache got to her shoulder, and she'd relented. The woman was trussed up regardless. There was nothing she could do.

Carlotte craned her neck over the woman's shoulder every so often to make sure she wasn't working at the knots, but she never was. At first, Carlotte assumed the woman was waiting for her moment, like a heroine in a girl's adventure book, waiting for the captor to drop their guard and make their escape, but the sun went high in the sky and started its descent back down, and the woman just sat, hunched and silent.

Carlotte glanced down at the woman's right leg, and supposed that the heroines in those stories had never been crippled. The foot dangled, seemingly unattached to the leg above it save for the sack of broken skin that held it. It jiggled with the horse's steps and beat a steady rhythm against the horse's side.

It wasn't supposed to be like this. She'd known her departure from Sheras was rash and ill-prepared. She'd known bad things would happen, but this...

She should have been celebrated. She should have spent the last two years planning the expedition, marking maps, writing theories and predictions, consulting with other Ryker lords and ladies, and taking the utmost interest and personal care in who was going with her. She remembered the flurry and frenzy that had surrounded Elspeth's departure to the Amaranthine ruins to the north. It had been so hard to focus on her lessons with all the people coming and going from the tower. She'd wanted to go so badly, and her only consolation was the thought that one day she would have the same moment of glory. God would not forget her.

The hill woman stiffened and hissed a word that Carlotte didn't understand. Carlotte pulled back the gun and pressed it into the woman's side, and then looked over her shoulder. They'd crested a hill, and a body lay at the bottom, smashing down the grass, its gray clothing obvious amid the golden stalks.

Carlotte turned her head in a slow circle, surveying the land around them. She saw nothing. Just more hills to the horizon. Carlotte flicked the reins and descended to the body, stopping the horse a dozen paces away.

Its face was covered in grey, and one arm was thrown over its eyes like a swooning maid. Carlotte watched the body for a moment, and then moved the horse to go on.

"No. Let me see the face," the woman hissed. It was the first thing she'd said since they'd hoisted her into the saddle. Carlotte stopped the horse.

"Why?"

"Please," the woman said.

Carlotte considered it. Her instinct was to ride off anyway, but there was no reason to, other than spite. She considered that it was a ploy, but the woman's hands looked well tied. Carlotte gave the bonds a yank for good measure and then slid awkwardly off the horse.

She nudged the body with her foot. It didn't respond. She

could see now what had killed it. There was a strip of cloth, crusty with blood, tied around its midsection. A gunshot, probably. Carlotte pushed the arm off the face with her foot, and then knelt and pulled the covering away.

The hill woman moaned. It was half a scream and half a sob, a wordless enunciation of pain that Carlotte had heard before. Carlotte whipped around to face her. The woman's hands were gripped tight around the pommel of the saddle, knuckles white and shaking with strain, as though her whole body weight was balanced atop them. She moaned again, and Carlotte knew the sound. Her mother had made that sound when she'd seen Elspeth's body lying against the wall with the vial in her hand and the foam around her lips.

Carlotte looked back down and saw that the face belonged to a young man, about Carlotte's age, with close-cropped black hair and full lips pulled into a grimace. He'd been shot in the belly. He would have been in unimaginable pain until he'd collapsed from his horse.

Carlotte stood, feeling she should pray for the body or something, but of course, the hill tribes did not worship God. They prayed to spirits and animals or... something.

"I'm sorry," she said, and then felt silly that she'd said anything. This woman was her enemy. This woman and this young man had attacked the caravan and murdered her people. They had tried to murder her, and yet, here was a young woman broken in body and soul, looking at the dead body of... someone she loved. She wondered what Elspeth would have done, what God would have her do, but Carlotte did not know, and so she climbed back atop the horse while the woman sobbed, and coaxed the horse into a trot. The woman dropped down over the saddle's pommel as they went and collapsed against the horse's neck.

They went on, and the sun continued its slow descent. After half an hour, the woman's sobs were just whimpers, and another half hour after that, they were gone entirely. The sun fell further, and Carlotte pulled bread and cheese from a saddle bag and ate. She reached around to offer it to the woman, not expecting her to take it, but the woman did. She clutched it in her hands and brought her face down to eat from them. They ate in silence, and when they'd both finished, they continued the silence. Occasionally, Carlotte would ask if they were going the right way. The woman would nod or motion with her head, and they would go on.

"Stop."

Carlotte did not stop the horse.

"Are we going the right way?" Carlotte asked.

"Yes."

"Then why would we stop?" Carlotte said. She whipped the horse into a canter.

"Please!" the woman shouted, and Carlotte could hear the real pain in her voice. The jolting of the horse's gait must be hell to her broken ankle. "I don't want to die!"

Carlotte continued the pace for several moments while the words sank in, and then she slowed to a stop. The woman hissed breath through her teeth.

"If you wanted to live, you shouldn't have attacked us," Carlotte said.

The woman twisted around and glared up at Carlotte like a wounded dog, teeth bared.

"We did not strike first."

Carlotte narrowed her brow. "Strike first? We were riding down the road. We weren't hurting--"

"You think I want this!" the woman roared, and she gripped the saddle's pommel and shook at it wildly and ineffectively, making the horse give a soft nay in protest. "I will never run, I will never walk, I will never stand again, and if we don't stop, I will never breathe again." She quieted, squeezed her eyes shut, and then forced her face to relax and take a breath. "Your bit of string will not keep the rot away."

She meant the tourniquet, Carlotte realized, which had kept her from bleeding out hours ago, but Carlotte knew it wasn't tight enough. She had noticed the slow drip while they'd ridden, but had figured it would last long enough to get them to wherever the hill folk were camped. She'd made an effort not to think much further along than that. She didn't even know what she would do when they arrived, let alone what she'd do with the woman. Trade her for Aethan, maybe? Were the hill tribes the kind of people who would value a crippled woman?

"What do you want me to do about it?" Carlotte asked.

The woman took a deep breath before speaking. "Remove it."

It took Carlotte several long moments to understand what the woman meant, and not because she was stupid, she was not stupid, but because such things were not said so casually. Such things were only said on battlefields by screaming medics or by old Ryker men who'd spent their lives studying physiology, who put their hat in their lap and took a deep breath before giving the news that the limb must go.

"Remove it?" Carlotte repeated.

"Yes. Hack it off and burn the wound shut."

Carlotte's head swam at the thought, and she felt her body start to fall from the saddle before she caught herself.

"I am no doctor," Carlotte said.

"And I have no choice. The rot will set, and I will die." She gave a surprisingly girlish laugh, and the absurdity of it almost made Carlotte laugh as well. "I will probably die anyway. It is probably too late."

"No, you can't die. I need you to get me to your people!" Carlotte said.

The woman gave a slight shudder at the last word. "Then I'll make you a promise," she hissed. "I've led you true so far, but there are miles to go, and unless you do this for me, I'll lead you astray."

Carlotte shook her head and realized the woman could not see her. It was so strange to be having such a conversation with the back of the woman's head. "No."

"Then here we both die."

"I'll make you."

"And how will you do that?" the woman cried. "Will you break my other foot. Will you take my eyes and my tongue and peel the nails from my fingers? Either I die or I live. There is nothing you can take from me that I have not lost already."

Carlotte wondered if she could go on without the woman, and then quickly dismissed the idea. She could continue in the same direction they'd been going, but unless she was going in exactly the right direction, soon she would be far from her mark, and in these hills, unless the riders camped on top of a hill, she would never find them. She could probably find her way back... probably. She could head west until she hit the road and take that south until she hit her caravan. Unless, of course, she hit the road already south of the caravan, and then she would be going the wrong way, and these hills were so similar, she doubted she'd know the difference between the road she'd traveled and the road she hadn't.

Then she shook her head. She wasn't going back. She was going forward, and she needed this woman's help.

"Okay."

The woman turned her head as far as she could to the side and looked at Carlotte through the corner of her eye. "Truly?"

Carlotte nodded.

"Then start a fire."

There was no wood, so Carlotte pulled up all the grass in a five-foot radius and then dug a shallow pit in the middle to keep the flames from engulfing the hillside. The hill woman had her twist the strands of grass tightly together so they formed thick ropes that would burn a little slower. Then she guided Carlotte through the process of starting a fire. Carlotte had never learned. She knew in theory how it was done, but her servants had always lit the candles and lamps and furnaces when she'd needed them. The hill woman told her what to do, step by step, and when the fire was burning fast and hot, the woman told her to place the two spoons from the saddlebags into the flame.

It didn't feel real. It felt like she was back in her classes with a tutor guiding her through an experiment. When she helped the woman awkwardly off the horse, she was back in her medicines class, practicing with the tutor's body, placing her on the hillside by the fire with her feet uphill so that gravity would help with the bleeding. When the woman told her not to stop once she got going, to cut steadily until the foot was off, she was in the tower's gardens, doing an outdoor lesson on the concepts of field triage.

"Cut, burn, and bind," the teacher said.

"Cut, burn, and bind," Carlotte repeated.

None of it was important, of course. She'd learned the concepts, but medicine and healing were middling fields for middling Rykers, and she'd only studied them because she'd studied everything. She would never do the things she learned. Doing was for other people. For servants and soldiers, and women who couldn't handle the rigors of discovery.

So, when she'd laid out the cleanest fabric she could find, and she'd put her belt between the woman's teeth, and she'd sat upon the woman's leg, and she'd held the large field knife in her hand, it all just seemed like practice, conceptual motions that one might do one day, but when the woman dug her fingers into the earth, and bit down hard on the leather, and gave one curt nod, it was real.

The ankle hung open like a demon's maw. It had broken at one side, and severed white ligaments hung down like teeth waiting to bite onto the blade. Carlotte held the knife just before it. She had dissected corpses many times before. That's all this was. A corpse.

A corpse that bled, a corpse that would scream and thrash until it passed out.

No. She pushed the thought away. It was just a corpse, just another poor peasant who'd ended up under her knife on her laboratory table. It was all just... an experiment. She gripped just above the woman's ankle with her free hand, pushed it down hard into the earth, and began to cut.

The woman's pain began as a moan, and her foot trembled underneath her, the muscles in her leg all flexing at once. Carlotte sank all of her weight down on top of the knee and sawed the knife back and forth. The moan became a yell, and then, not a quarter of the way through, it became a scream, high-pitched and ear-piercing. The leg shot back and forth, and Carlotte struggled to keep her knife steady, but she failed to do so. The screaming rose, and Carlotte realized she was screaming too. She cut at the leg as quickly as she could, trying to inflict even more pain to make the woman pass out, but she didn't, not while Carlotte was cutting, not when she hit the bone and had to saw through it millimeter by millimeter, not when Carlotte stabbed at the last bit of skin and gristle that held it onto the woman's body. Her screams had become soul-rending sobs, and all Carlotte wanted was for the woman to shut up, for her to stop moving and stop making everything harder.

It wasn't until Carlotte pressed the red hot silverware against the stump of the woman's leg, and the smoke from burning flesh filled Carlotte's lungs, that the hill woman finally collapsed and was still and was silent.

The heat of the day did not last long after the sun sank below the horizon. The landscape was too bare, and the air was too dry, and the sky was too clear to hold any of the heat in, so Carlotte did her best to keep the woman warm. She was afraid to move her, afraid she'd hit something, or move something she shouldn't, afraid the woman would die. Carlotte draped her cloak over the woman's body and tried to keep the fire burning.

Even with twisting the grass into strands, the fire burned hot and fast, and she had to get up every quarter hour to gather more grass in an ever-widening circle of desolation around her. If the fire went out, she was afraid she wouldn't be able to light it again.

She was exhausted. The only sleep she'd managed in the last two days was what she'd gotten underneath the carriage while cradling Saara's head. That thought gave her pause, and she looked over at the woman with her cloth-wrapped stump jutting out from underneath the blanket, and wondered if Saara was still alive. Surely she was. Why else would God have let her survive the attack? She knew how that sounded, how Vaalier had taken it, how self-centered it seemed, but if there was one thing Carlotte knew, it was that God had meant for her to take this expedition. She was meant to do something great before she fell into wifedom and motherhood. She had to believe that this was for a greater purpose, and if it was, then everything that happened to her was for a reason.

Carlotte looked up at the sky. Even with the firelight, there were many more stars than she could see in Sheras. The splendors of God's creation always dimmed around human endeavor.

She reached into the pocket on the inside breast of her coat, but her fingers found nothing. The prayer beads had been lost in the fight, just like everything else. God had taken that from her as well. Perhaps it was all a test, and if it was, she would pass it the way she passed all the other struggles in her life, by putting herself to work until it was done. She pushed herself to her feet to pull more grass.

"Alakeed."

Carlotte spun around and lunged for her pistol. She stopped on all fours when she heard the hill woman's laugh. The woman had propped herself up on her elbows and was watching Carlotte scramble. Carlotte rose to her feet carefully, anger flaring up at the woman's expression. She could think of no logical reason why this savage's opinion should matter to her, but the anger remained.

"Alakeed is my name," the woman said.

Carlotte waited, watching the woman for a long moment, not sure what to do with the information.

"Are you going to tell me yours?" Alakeed asked. There was a patronizing tone to her voice.

Carlotte's embarrassed anger flashed hotter. "What difference does it make?" she snapped.

The woman shrugged and scooted herself backwards to prop her back up against the saddle bags. Her face screwed up in pain and then she spat into the dirt. Not much came out, Carlotte noticed. She should give her a drink.

"No difference. But it would be nice to know."

Carlotte pursed her lips and tried to think of a reason not to tell her, but she couldn't find one that didn't sound like a little girl throwing a temper tantrum.

"Carlotte DeSheras."

"Carlotte," the woman repeated, and let her head fall backwards to look up at the sky. She took in a deep, shaky breath. "Thank you, Carlotte."

Carlotte's mouth fell open. "You're... welcome, of course," she whispered.

"Those were your guns? Your men who fired them?"

When Carlotte didn't answer, Alakeed turned her head towards her.

"You are a woman of money. I can tell by your shoulders. You do not slump like a farmer, and the caravans that come through here have seeds, not guns, nor soldiers to fire them."

Alakeed took in another shaky breath and considered the sky. "We did not expect guns. I don't--" she cut off with a grimace, and then with a strained voice, "I don't think we would have found it worth it."

Alakeed closed her eyes and fingered a stalk of grass beside her. "I am tired of this land, Carlotte. I will show you where your friends were taken, and I will lead you out of the Badlands. And in exchange, you will fill my pockets with gold."

Carlotte frowned. It was always gold. This woman was no different from a Dominioneer. No grand ideas, no vaunted ideals, just gold. It was so depressingly predictable. Almost as predictable as the inevitable demand for more.

Carlotte walked forward until she stood almost directly above Alakeed's head. The pistol felt like a boulder at the end of her arm.

"And why would I give you anything?" Carlotte asked.

The woman's eyes glistened like water in the firelight. "Because I have nothing left to lose."

They were silent for a few moments, staring into each other's eyes.

"You already promised to help me," Carlotte said. "If you're willing to put conditions on that promise, what makes you think I will keep this one?"

"You do not know what is out there," Alakeed said, gesturing weakly to the west. "You don't know the people here, and you don't know how to get your friend back. I am the only person who can help you, Carlotte, and you are the only person who has any use for me."

Carlotte lifted the pistol and pointed its barrel at the woman's forehead.

Alakeed did not blink. "I do not want to die, but if I am left with empty pockets and this," she lifted her footless leg, "then I might as well already be."

Carlotte considered Alakeed. The skin on her forehead was beaded with sweat, and her breath was ragged and weak. Carlotte did not think she could have survived were the roles reversed. She knew nothing of this woman. She didn't know if the word of a hill savage meant anything.

In the end, this was probably better. Greed was better than promises. Greed was more predictable, but greed also made people do risky things.

Carlotte squatted onto her heels and pressed the barrel into Alakeed's hair. The woman winced a little.

"I will pay you," Carlotte said, "But I don't have it here. Not enough to fill your pockets. You will accompany me out of these lands, and I will give it to you. I agree to this, but know that it is the last deal I make with you. I will not be betrayed." She paused for effect and then leaned in even closer, so that she could whisper her words. "If I have only one action left in this world, it will be to put a ball of lead in your skull."

"Agreed," Alakeed said, and there was a fierceness behind her eyes. They were so close that Carlotte could see the woman's pores, clogged and inflamed and dirty. Carlotte could only imagine what her own looked like now.

She stuck the pistol through her belt and then sat back onto the earth, feeling suddenly like a girl in her mother's gardens, playing at an adventure instead of living one.

"So, now that we're on the same page, tell me," Carlotte said, shaking off the feeling with a slight shudder.

"Tell you what?"

"Where we are going. We're on the same side now, so we should make a plan."

"Ah," Alakeed propped herself onto her elbows again, looking a little faint. "Your friend is being taken to the border."

"To Bergshalen?"

"The desert."

"Ah," Carlotte did not try to keep the ice out of her voice. There was only one reason to go to the desert: to trade with those who lived beyond it, a strange people called the Niquari, a strange people who dealt in slaves. It was they who sold the first foreign slaves to the Korkin empire, centuries ago, and it was supposedly they who bought Korkin prisoners from the Freelands after the revolution. They did not care what kind of people they sold, only that there were people to sell.

"There is a meeting ground two days west of here where my band will meet up with other raiding parties before they make contact with the slavers. We should get to your friends before they get to the meeting place."

Carlotte nodded. "How would you propose we get them?" Carlotte asked.

"How much gold did you bring?" Alakeed asked.

Carlotte narrowed her eyes. "Some."

"I would try to buy them back. The price will be lower than you think. Despite appearances, the folk out here are not wealthy,"

Alakeed said, and smiled at her own joke.

"I'm not going to pay your people for kidnapping," Carlotte snarled.

Alakeed's smile fell, and she raised an eyebrow. "What else are you going to do? Kill them all with your little gun?"

Carlotte didn't answer.

Alakeed let herself slowly back down to the ground. "Money is easier, Carlotte. Money is always easier."

Carlotte watched her for a long moment, waiting for her to say something else, but she didn't, and Carlotte supposed she didn't need to, because she was right. Despite how it felt, money was always easier, and what was money to Carlotte DeSheras?

36

"What is it?" Aethan asked. Ashatee sat across the fire pit from him, and the light from the low flames flickered across the edge of her face in a way that made Aethan think that perhaps she did not exist and was only a phantom that haunted these woods. Ashatee spent most nights staring into the flames until sleep came to take her. In the summers, when the days were longer and her hut became stifling, they would set up the fire outside. They did not need the heat, and despite what Ashatee implied, he did not need the practice. He was beyond sparks and candle flames now.

He had pulled great balls of fire from the void and cast them into the lake, sending up bouts of steam and bringing dead fish floating to the top while Ashatee watched and quenched any sparks that might set the forest around them alight. Each time she'd asked him for more. A bigger ball, a hotter flame, a greater torrent of heat. He obliged, and as the darkness flowed, the door stretched. He watched it from within, the frame of the mausoleum distorting and bowing outward, and he felt it in his chest, like his ribs were being drawn apart into a cavernous maw.

"More!" Ashatee had shouted, and Aethan pulled up a great cyclone of heat, spiraling up into the sky and dashing the clouds to ribbons.

"Stop," Ashatee had said, and she was behind him, her hand on his shoulder. He shut the door, and the darkness fled back into the void. She looked into his eyes and squinted, looking for something. Aethan drew back.

"Did you feel nothing?" she'd asked.

"I felt stretching. There is a soreness here," he'd said, tapping his solar plexus.

"A soreness... No coldness? Nothing around your heart?"

"No. Should there have been? The door was difficult to close. Is that normal?" Aethan had asked.

Ashatee had not answered.

Aethan pulled out of his memory and stared across the fire at her.

"What is it?" He repeated. Louder this time.

Ashatee looked up at him, and Aethan looked away. Her eyes were always so judging, like she was tallying up his worth every second.

"I don't know."

Aethan looked back up at her. Her eyes were focused again on the fire.

"You don't...?" Aethan began, afraid for some reason of finishing the sentence. Like it would offend her to have her omnipotence questioned.

"The Niquari say it is God," Ashatee said. Her voice was low, and she lifted a hand to pull at her earlobe. Aethan's eyes widened.

"You've talked with the desert people?"

"I've talked with many people."

Aethan knew very little about the Ashatee. She'd lived through the revolution in the Freelands. He'd put that much together from what little she said and from her age, but he couldn't help but think she'd always been here, by the side of the lake amidst the endless trees, staring into the flames.

"They say that the Amaranthine Archmages walked through their own doors so that they could see God. And for their arrogance, God cast them down," Ashatee said.

"Ridiculous," Aethan snorted.

Ashatee looked up at him for a long moment. Her face told him to explain, but he tried to hold out, tried to make her actually ask and prove that she didn't have complete control over him. He broke, of course.

"Because there is no God," he said.

"You know this?"

Aethan was surprised for the second time that night. Even if she left the Freelands during the revolution... surely she wasn't one of those old slaves who had held on to the lies the Korkins had taught them.

"God was a Korkin device to keep us in bondage," Aethan said, quoting what he'd heard a thousand times on the streets of New Freedom. Aethan continued when Ashatee didn't speak, "And how could both slavery and a just God exist? A just God would allow no such thing." He'd also heard this on the streets, from the criers on the corners who handed out pamphlets he couldn't read at the time. This was something every Freelander knew.

"A just God," the old woman murmured, watching the flames. She twisted her earlobe back and forth. "Who says God has to be just?"

"The Korkin. The ones who invented him."

Ashatee chuckled, though it wouldn't look it to someone who hadn't spent the last year with her. Two barely audible spurts of air through her nostrils. "He," she repeated, and gave another spurt of air.

"What?" he asked. "You don't think the darkness is a God... do you?"

She looked up then, and in her eyes he saw a brief condemnation that held him fast. But then she broke the look and pressed up to her feet.

"I don't know what it is. No one does. The darkness does not wish you ill, nor does it wish you well. It just is. The door, on the other hand..." She looked down at him. "Your door is wider than it should be. Don't go too far, Aethan. Whatever actually happened, the Amaranthine went too far, and it tore them apart."

It was the smell that woke him. Lavender. Sage. An acrid burning in his sinuses. It reminded him of the Greenwall, of his mother, and of something more recent that he could not place. A strong smell, and someone screaming. That town in the Dominion countryside where they had burned the woman at the stake. He had smelled it there.

Aethan coughed, and when he opened his eyes, he saw a yellow-orange haze. He was looking through tears. He blinked them away and squinted. The light and smoke came from a brazier with a bundle of smoldering herbs in the corner of the room. No, it wasn't a room. It was a tent. The entrance flap was hung up on something and let in a shaft of daylight that pierced through the darkness in a solid beam.

Aethan coughed again and brought up his hands to wipe at his eyes, but his hands were bound behind him. He tried to crawl forward, but the bindings held him back. He turned to look at what held him, but the leash was short, and the brazier's light did not reach far. His fingers scrabbled at the dirt, and he felt metal there, an eyelet on a stake driven into the ground.

He thought of Breaker's Boulevard in New Freedom, where the cages hung from iron eyelets at uniform intervals all the way down the street. They were old slave gibbets filled with old slavers. Bones stuck out from the gaps and were worn smooth by thousands of passing hands reaching up to rub them for good luck. Aethan remembered how those bones felt beneath his fingers. He was tall and could reach bones that most couldn't, bones that were still jagged and rough, bones that he broke off and kept as his own slaver bones.

Aethan blinked and refocused on the eyelet behind him. He turned to the other side to get a better look and saw a body. A woman. Her hair cascaded down from the hood of her mud-covered cloak. He squinted at it. It looked familiar. Then he saw a patch where the mud wasn't thick and saw that underneath was bright scarlet.

"Visoletta..." he croaked. The smoke raked at his lungs.

She turned her head and looked up at him. Her eyes were hazy and wet. "Where are we?" she asked.

"I don't know," Aethan said. "The riders..."

He trailed off. Visoletta was covered in filth. She looked more like a street urchin than a virtuoso, but he saw her as she was before, the way she'd looked on the road, laughing and talking and reaching out to touch the people around her. Her hand on a shoulder. Her hand on a chest. Her hand on a knee. His knee. He saw her smile. The way she showed all her teeth and squinted her eyes and blushed and --

"Aethan?" Visoletta said, and Aethan's eyes refocused. His mind kept wandering off. He shook his head to try and clear out the cobwebs.

"What's going to happen?" she asked.

"We're going to leave. They don't know what they've taken," he whispered. Aethan closed his eyes and took in a breath through his nose. He pictured Ashatee's lake; he saw the ripples of a single pebble, and then withdrew into the corridors of the self. When he reached the door, he would let loose the darkness and burn his bindings away. He'd burn the tent around them. He'd rain fire on all those who tried to stop them. He had killed hundreds of soldiers at the Greenwall, hundreds of the guilty and innocent alike in Sheras. He had murdered an old man. These would-be slavers knew nothing of the wrath--

"How?" Visoletta said.

Aethan realized he'd wandered off again. He coughed and looked at the herbs on the brazier. "The smoke..." he started, but then he heard horse hooves.

"Oh God," Visoletta moaned.

Aethan put his face against the dirt to see through the gap in the tent flap and saw horse legs stamping and circling. He heard shouting in a language he did not know. Other shouts came in answer, and several sets of human legs ran from the periphery to take the reins.

"Oh god..." Visoletta repeated. "They've found me..."

Aethan didn't know what Visoletta meant. He squeezed his eyes shut and delved deep within himself to find the door. If only he could open it, he could burn away all of this. He'd make them pay for--

"Focus!" he hissed.

Three sets of boots hit the ground, and Aethan's eyes popped open. Legs walked towards the tent. Two sets fell behind. There was more talking, quick questions and answers, orders and acknowledgments. As they came, the angle shortened, and Aethan could only see their shins, and then only their feet. They stopped at the tent flap, one boot of black leather with a point at the toe blocked Aethan's view. Then, the tent's flap was torn open.

Light flooded the tent, and Aethan reeled back, only able to see silhouettes against the sudden brightness. The men let the flap fall behind them, and Aethan widened his eyes to see them in the brazier's glow.

There were two of them. One who stood by the entrance, a tall man with the upright air of a leader. He held a cloth to his nose and mouth. The other stood directly in front of Aethan and stared down at him. A scarf was wrapped around the lower part of his face, but above it, his skin was crossed with so many tattoos that it was difficult to tell what was ink and what was skin. He clattered as he walked. There were bits of bone strung together and wrapped around his neck and draped over his shoulders in a perversion of the cuirass of a Freeland general. Underneath it, the man wore the same faded black of the others, but the sleeves had been removed, showing lanky, muscled arms that were littered with the same tattoos.

The inked man barked out more words. The man behind grunted acknowledgment and leaned away from the inked man like he wanted to leave. The inked man pointed at Visoletta, and the bones around him clinked and rattled. He spoke, and the other man responded.

The inked man squatted down, and a foul stench washed over Aethan. Aethan gagged and coughed, and the inked man watched him squirm.

"Does she touch the void?" he asked. His voice was deep and hard, each word rumbling up from his chest and clearly enunciated. His accent was strange, lilting without harmony, like a poet marking through a poem.

"What?"

"The girl. She touch the void like you?" he asked again.

"I..." Aethan's gaze flicked away to the herbs on the brazier. Whatever they were, they were stopping him from--

The inked man reached out a hand with filthy fingernails and gripped Aethan's jaw, pulling it back to face him. "I will not ask a fourth time. Can the girl call the void?"

Aethan shook his head. His mind was swimming.

"I thought not. She does not smell of it." He looked over his shoulder at the man holding the cloth to his mouth and barked a few words. The man nodded, opened the tent flap, and barked out some more. Two large men came in, and at a command, grabbed Visoletta and pulled her out of the tent.

At first, she seemed confused, but then she began to scream and thrash. Her arms were tied behind her back, and the men held her by the armpits, but she bucked her body and kicked out with her legs until the man with the cloth over his nose punched her in the face. Her screams stopped with a crunch and a gurgle, and Aethan realized he was screaming too.

He strained forward, pulling his shoulders painfully back. He yelled in Dominion and then in Freelander for them to let her go. The inked man held tight to his jaw, pushed him back with surprising strength, and then blew into his face.

Aethan wretched. The man's breath was like decayed meat. Aethan's stomach seized, and he vomited. Nothing came up but acid that burned the back of his throat. The inked man lifted Aethan's face from the dirt and leaned in close. Aethan's instinct was to lunge forward and bite, but the thought of putting any piece of this man in his mouth made Aethan's stomach seize again.

"Shh," the inked man cooed. "She doesn't have the door, and she does not matter. By the time she gets to Niquari, she will be whole enough. It is best to let the men have their way. It keeps them from grumbling."

Aethan pulled his face away and looked back through the gap in the flap. The men pulled Visoletta through the grass away from him. Another held open a tent, and the men threw her inside.

"I'll kill you," Aethan growled. "I'll kill you."

"I do not know the Freeland tongue."

Had he been speaking Freelander? Aethan couldn't recall. He shook his head so violently that the inked man rocked warily back onto his heels. Aethan snarled and tried to put as much malice behind his eyes as possible, but his mind kept drifting back to Visoletta. To what they would do to her. What they were already doing to her. The inked man chuckled at the attempt.

"You don't know how powerful I am," Aethan said. "I've killed more than you'll ever know."

The inked man reached out a finger and gently bopped Aethan on the nose. "It is not you who is dangerous. But what lies behind."

He licked his teeth and smiled, revealing teeth oddly white for a man so ill-groomed. "Imagine my surprise, Boneman, when they told me they'd found a witchdoctor. The man said he watched you summon a cyclone of fire, and I did not believe him. A trick of the light, of the storm, and an explosion of black powder, perhaps, but not witchcraft. Not truly. But then, I asked others, and the story was all the same."

The inked man stood and went to the brazier. He picked up a bundle of herbs from the floor and held it to the coals. It lit, and fresh smoke billowed upward.

"I did not think it likely. The Dominion is not known for its abundance of witches. The Mareshal has done such a good job of killing them off. But I bought the Palamur all the same and distributed it amongst my lieutenants, and look how it has paid off."

The inked man squatted back down. "The price the Niquari will pay for you! The Dominion sold me for a handful of silver when they could have sold me for a kingdom. With your bounty, the Altishi will take back what is theirs, and maybe a little more. Maybe we will go past the watcher's eye and take a piece of the Dominion for our own. Give them a taste of conquest."

The man shook his chest, and the bones about him rattled.

"The Niquari told me stories of your people, Boneman, the way your generals wear slavers' bones around their necks. Those stories kept me alive in the markets and the brothels and under the master's whip. They gave me something to live for, and when they taught me to open the door, those stories gave me a goal to achieve.

"This," he said, and tapped at a long thin bone hanging down from his collar, "is the ulna of a blueback lieutenant. And this," he tapped another that was strung to it, "was a captain's collar. But these…" He drew out a string that was threaded with little bones that rattled against each other as he moved. "These are my favorites. The finger bones of dead bluebacks. Dead slavers! One hundred and seventeen. My men, they bring them to me all boiled and clean. Each from a different blueback!" He smiled wide, showing off his teeth, and then his eyes crinkled together in thought. "I suppose, I don't know that. They could be lying to me, and ten could be from the same man, or not even a blueback at all... Ah, well," he sighed. "It's the thought that counts. Where are your bones, Boneman?"

"I... lost them... in a fire," Aethan rasped. His throat burned.

"Ah. A pity. To meet a Boneman who has no bones. I will have to be Boneman for us both then. I am sorry for what I am going to do to you, for the sin I will commit upon you, but may it give you comfort to know that your enemies are mine, and you sacrificed for their destruction. Al'Aksahlad, they call me. I hope-"

There was a yell from outside, and Al'Aksahlad turned. He drew back the tent flap and looked out.

For a moment, there was nothing to see, just the sound of men yelling, the sound of flesh hitting flesh, and then Visoletta's body flew out of the tent she'd been dragged into. She hit the dirt and skidded. She didn't scream. Aethan heard nothing from her other than the sound of her sliding across the earth and the emergence of four men behind her. They were furious, but the man at their lead was the most so, wearing rage on his face like a theater mask. He strode up to Visoletta, who'd just risen up onto all fours, and kicked her in the stomach hard enough to lift her off the ground and send her rolling.

Al'Aksahlad bolted out of the tent, yelling in their language, and Aethan lowered himself to the floor to see through the gap.

At Al'Aksahlad's approach, the four men shrank back, but the one who'd kicked Visoletta stopped and began to argue. His words made no impact on Al'Aksahlad. This made the man angry, and he began to yell and gesticulate wildly. Perhaps she'd bitten him? He jabbed a finger in her direction and yelled the same thing three times.

"Ik'sargoth! Sargoth! Ik! Sargoth!"

There was silence for a moment, and then Al'Aksahlad stepped up close. The angry man flinched, and Aethan could see him wrinkle his nose. Aethan couldn't hear what was said, and even if he did, he wouldn't have understood it, but the thug paled and then picked Visoletta off the ground while Al'Aksahlad turned and addressed the entire group. His words were not loud, but they carried well, and all those standing around nodded soberly. Aethan could not understand their words, but a captain asserting his authority was universal. Get in line, or get dead.

They took Visoletta out of Aethan's narrow field of vision, and he screamed out her name to let her know that he was there. He was there, and she wasn't alone. For all the good it would do her.

37

Erika knelt with her forehead pressed into the sand, and her wrists cinched so tightly behind her back that she could not feel her hands. She waited for the consequences to come. The consequences had always been coming. She had been on borrowed time since Visoletta's head had cracked against the stone, and now that time was due back with interest.

She hadn't meant to kill Visoletta, but the responsibility was hers. She had trespassed. She had dressed in Visoletta's clothes, and when mistaken for a dead woman, she'd made no effort to set the record straight. Erika may have fallen into all this, but to Visoletta, Erika was a ghoul who had emerged from the night and crawled into her skin. Erika did not belong. She had never belonged.

Erika coughed and tried to quell the three that followed. Each was a knife in her side where the man's boot had broken at least one of her ribs. She tasted blood in her mouth. Metallic. She moved her tongue and prodded the loose molar on the right side. One of the punches had done that, before they'd thrown her out of the tent, after that long, horrible moment when they'd pulled up her dress and ripped her underthings away. Her eyes filled with tears again at the thought of it. Of the disgust that was almost worse than the punches and kicks that had followed. She supposed she should feel grateful that they hadn't raped her, but if her identity was the price to pay for that, then she might have chosen differently.

The theft of identity, she knew, was her true sin. The murder was a horrible thing, but it was the theft that damned her, just as the hill men had stolen hers when they'd looked at her with slack jaws and confused eyes. She couldn't understand their language, but she knew what the words they'd yelled meant. She'd heard that inflection when she was younger, before she'd learned the tricks of movement and dress that helped her appear as though her body was not incorrect.

The universe knew her sin. It had given her its gifts, and she had been naive enough to believe that she could keep them. The money, the clothes, the servants, and the respect were all illusions like the moments just after waking from a beautiful dream, where you believe that if you just keep your eyes closed, it could all be true. But waking always comes and tramples you with its bitter reality. When a kind woman gives you a silver coin, the other urchins will beat you for it. When you find a warm place out of the wind and away from prying eyes, thieves will follow you to it. When you finally have freedom, you will become a slave.

The tent opened, and a light came with it, warm and flickering, a lantern's light that lit black boots worn through to the foot in several places. These people were not well off, and for a moment, the sight of those threadbare boots, so like the shoes she'd worn in her time on the street, made her feel pity for the man.

"I... love," the man said, in a thick, halting accent.

Erika lifted her gaze higher, past the knives in his boots and on his belt, past gnarled fingers that clenched and picked at one another, and into a face with an astounded look in its eye.

"I love?" Erika asked. The pain in her ribs flared, and she crumpled back down.

The man crouched down on his heels, placing the lantern beside him, and grabbed her face gently with rough hands.

"I," he repeated in a whisper, "love."

"Love," she echoed again, and she burst into tears.

"No," he said, and wiped the tears from her cheeks. "No. I give..." he searched for the word. "Want." He pointed to himself. "Give." And then to her, while he gave a tentative, oddly nervous smile, "want."

Erika didn't understand entirely, but she lifted her numb hands behind her.

"Please," she said.

He nodded and reached behind her, letting her face down to the floor. She gasped when the knot came free and the blood rushed back into her hands. Her shoulder blades relaxed forward, and pain shot through them. The man grabbed her face again with both hands and lifted her up.

"Thank you," Erika gasped, "You have no-"

He jerked her face forward and mashed his lips against her mouth. For a moment, she did nothing, too surprised to react. Her fingers were numb, but they tingled with returning feeling. He released her and pulled away, and she recognized the look in his face. She'd seen it in the back of that dark tent that the men had pulled her into. He had sat on his haunches, and he had leered at her from the shadows, eager to partake.

He released her, and she fell. She got her hands beneath her just in time to keep from smacking her face into the dirt. It was gritty and cold between her fingers. She heard him unbuckle his belt. She was no stranger to such affairs. She could not pretend that she hadn't been forced into such situations from time to time by the underbelly of Sheras.

"No," she said, but not violently.

She turned her face up, keeping her chin down and looking up at him from beneath her eyelashes. Innocence. It always sold the best. Some of the other girls, the ones who had been blessed with more appropriate bodies, could pull off the siren's call, but it was innocence that had worked for her.

"Let me," she said, a naive girl who just wanted to please.

The man seemed to understand her, and he let his hands fall to his sides. Erika rose up to her knees, letting one hand glide gently up his leg, and lifting the other straight to his belt. The man had already pulled the extra from the loop of leather that held it down. It hung like a dead snake.

She had been offered another way. The way disgusted her, but she had done it before. There was no guarantee it would work, that she wouldn't still end up on the back of a slave caravan across the desert, or beaten to death here in the grass, but her soul was already dirty. What was a little more filth?

She let go of the belt and lunged at the knife on his waist. He saw it coming, and his hand was closer than hers. He crushed her fingers against the metal handle. She cried out, and he peeled her hand away. The passion in his eyes was gone. There was only angry lust and a cold smile.

"Sargoth," he growled, and bent her hand backwards. Pain shot through it, and it felt near to breaking. He pulled back his other hand to smash her across the face, and that was fine because the knife on his belt had been a distraction.

Her left hand pulled out the knife from his boot and jammed it up into the soft tissue between his legs. He released her hand and gasped. She knew a scream was coming, and if a scream came, then the other men would come too.

She pulled out the blade as quickly as she'd put it in, surged to her feet, and plunged it into his neck, killing the scream in his throat. She pulled it out and stabbed it in again and again, blood spurting in time with the shlick shlick shlick of his flesh being opened.

He fell with a thump, and Erika stood over him, a murderer again. Another bit of dirt on her soul. There was blood on her cloak.

She took the other knife from his belt and, holding them in each hand, faced the tent flap. She would not be seduced by life's circumstances again. Life did not care, and it could not be trusted, so when they opened the tent to murder her, she would charge out with defiance on her lips.

But they did not come. She waited another minute. Two. Perhaps they were gathering outside for the charge? All was silent. Had no one heard it? She had stopped the scream, but the exchange had made noise. The falling of the body, his gasps, and gurgles. Was there no guard?

She stepped over the man and reached to flick open the tent with the knife, but she stopped herself inches away. She was being reckless. Why did she need to see out the front? If the hill people were out there, seeing them wouldn't save her. The knife quivered. She looked down and saw that it was her hand that was shaking. Both of them were.

She turned and stuck the blade under the back hem of the tent, sawing upwards until she could crawl out. Night had fallen completely, and above was only a half moon, casting the faintest light on the camp. She could see nothing in the darkness, and she considered going back for the man's lantern, but that was foolish. Darkness was her friend.

There was another tent in front of her. She turned to either side and saw imprecise lines of tents. Two men lounged around a fire in the center of the camp, casting dice into the dirt. The fire was low, but it cast long shadows, and she could see well enough that the tents were in two circles around the fire.

Erika considered her options. Her heart was pounding. All the angry calm she'd had before was gone, and now she had to fight the rising panic. She needed a horse, but she didn't know how to ride a horse. She needed Aethan. He was a soldier. He'd know what to do.

Erika retraced the day's brutal events in her head, trying to build a map of the camp in her mind, and then set off. She picked her way through the rows of tents, doing her best to stay out of the firelight and stepping carefully over the tent pegs. She stopped when an awkward step sent pain through her ribs, or when she heard noises behind a tent's fabric. It took her a quarter hour to go a hundred feet, but she reached the back of Aethan's tent without raising an alarm. She placed her knife under the tent's hem, and an orange glow shone on the bloody blade. She began sawing upwards. It sounded like an avalanche to her, and as the knife rose, more and more light lit her. She squeezed her eyes shut and cut faster.

Two feet up, she opened her eyes and crawled into the opening. Aethan was positioned just as she had been. Kneeling with forehead on the ground and arms manacled behind his back.

Manacled.

Erika moved behind him, blinking her eyes against the smoke, and looked for a cord she could cut, but it was all metal. Dull gray bracelets fastened with iron pins and a hefty chain connecting them to a spike driven into the ground.

"Visoletta?" he croaked.

She looked up and saw him looking at her sideways. There was nothing she could do. She had to abandon him. She had to just try and run for it.

"Visoletta," he repeated, louder this time.

Erika kneeled down beside him, pushing a finger against her lips. "Shh, they will hear you," she said into his ear.

He pulled at the chains, and they clinked like alarm bells. The men would come in and pull her back out. It would be just like before. They'd beat her and cut her and pull out her teeth and--

"The smoke," he croaked.

"Be quiet!" she hissed, and then clapped her own hands over her mouth and stared with terror at the tent's opening. She couldn't focus. Why couldn't she focus? Was it leftovers from the pike? No, she knew what ripples felt like. This was...

"The smoke. Put it out," Aethan said.

Erika looked from him to the brazier in the corner. A bundle of weeds smoldered on top of a bed of embers. She remembered this from before, but that part of her memory wasn't working well. Nothing in her head seemed to be working well. Some part of her mind screamed at her to just leave. There was nothing she could do for Aethan. She couldn't cut iron. But the other part of her reached out to the embers and pulled out the bundle. It was hot, but she held it from the top where it was not burning, and turned it over. The bottom crawled with little embers, like a hive of glowing worms under an old rock. They crawled back and forth, writhing and merging and splitting.

"The smoke," Aethan croaked again, and Erika remembered what she was doing. She looked around for some method of putting it out. What even was it? Some kind of plant. Was the smoke a drug?

Focus!

There was no way to put it out, but she could move it. So she went to the little hole in the tent and crawled through. She looked for a place to put it, and then remembered that she was out in the open and anyone could see her. She froze, listening.

Nothing.

But then there was a sharp burning in her hand, and she let out a little squeal, dropping the weed into the trampled grass beneath her.

Fire!

The bundle smoked, and the dry grasses it was lying on started smoking, and in a panic, Erika kicked it. With the sudden intake of air, the bundle burst into a flaming ball and thumped against the wall of another tent. Erika's eyes went wide, and she crawled back through the hole. She had to run, but she had to tell Aethan she was going. She couldn't just leave without an explanation. But when she came back through, she saw that he was on his feet in a crouch, manacled hands awkwardly grabbing at the chain attached to the stake.

"Help," he said.

She rushed forward and grabbed the chain. Aethan strained upwards, the manacles digging deep into his wrists. Aethan was strong, but his angle was awkward, and he wasn't able to pull directly out of the ground.

There was shouting outside. They had noticed the fire. She heard several more voices and the stamping of feet. It wouldn't be long until they realized where the fire had come from. They had to go now.

Aethan sagged back down, but before he could collapse completely, Erika whispered into his ear.

"On three. One, two, three!"

They both stood, with Erika pulling backwards as much as upwards to counteract Aethan's angle. Nothing moved, and then Erika felt a shift in the earth, the slightest give, and then all in a moment the dirt and grass roots gave way. They stood with the momentum, and Aethan's weight carried him forward, pulling Erika behind him. Her forehead smacked against his back as she fell.

More shouting. The fire must have been growing. All that dry grass. She remembered the blackened valley around the pillaged farm.

"Up. We have to go," she said.

He'd fallen hard on his face with his hands still stuck behind his back. He cursed and rolled to his side. Erika grabbed one of the knives from the floor and did her best to pull him up. He was such a heavy man. He lurched towards the entrance, and Erika pulled at his shoulder.

"Through the back! The back!" she hissed.

He swung around wide, and his shoulder hit hers and sent her spinning. She steadied herself just in time to see a man step through the tent flap. With a squeak, she thrust the knife forward, and the man swung his fist. The knife went in surprisingly easily, piercing through his jacket and into his belly up to the hilt. At the same time, his fist smashed into her face. She felt the strange sensation of her jaw breaking, so similar to the subtle give in the earth before the stake had come free, except this was so unimaginably painful. The ground hit her in the chest, and her chin bounced against the dirt and exploded in pain again, like a knife had been thrust into the base of her cheek. The world seemed to fade. She saw the darkness closing like a heavy blanket being wrapped around her.

"No!" she moaned. She couldn't let it take her. She couldn't stay here. She was terrified. The man behind her was screaming, and others would be coming for her. She didn't want to be a slave. She didn't want to die.

She reached out and dug her fingers into the turf and pulled herself forward, forcing her knees under her. Her dress ripped. It had been so beautiful. She crawled towards the back opening, her face in agony, her ribs screaming with each desperate gasp.

She reached a hand through the hole and felt fingers wrap around hers. She squealed and pulled frantically back against them, but the hands were stronger, and a moment later she came out into the night. A red glow lit Aethan's face. He was crouching in the grass, his manacled hand still behind him, gripping her wrist. He looked at her over his shoulder.

"Quick!" he said. "Run!"

He pulled her to her feet and then took off around the tent. The metal stake jingled and bounced off his calves with each step. It was barbed, she could see now. Little backward hooks jutted out from it and ripped bloody holes in the back of his pants.

She heard the sounds of horses, and Aethan ran towards them. They rounded a tent, and there the horses were in two neat rows with reins tied to stakes in the ground. The fire in the camp was growing, and the horses were bathed in orange light, stomping and rearing. A man stood with his legs wide, trying to calm the beasts. He turned at their coming, but it was too slow. Aethan was already barreling at him, head down like a bull. His shoulder smashed into the man's ribs, and they both spiraled to the ground. Aethan tried to roll with his fall, but the man's body got in the way, and he just flopped off, rolling sideways like he was trying to put out a fire.

"Free the horses!" he yelled, struggling to his feet. The man he had hit was hurt bad, rolling onto his side and clutching at his ribs.

Erika turned and reached for the nearest stake. Despair gripped her. The stakes were the same ones that had held Aethan to the ground, and she'd never be able to get them out on her own. Then she remembered the knife in her hand. The one she hadn't left in the man's stomach.

The commotion had the horses panicked now, and Erika only had to saw halfway through the cords before they snapped under the pressure. The camp was fully awake. The fire had grown, and men everywhere were shouting. She freed a fourth horse and then turned.

Three men charged at her with weapons drawn.

"Aethan!" she screamed.

Two of the men had swords, and a third pulled a bowstring back to his cheek. Erika dropped the knife. She stepped back and tripped over a stake and fell onto her butt as the arrow flew past where her chest had been. One of the swordsmen was just steps away, his sword held high and swinging down. She threw her arms over her head, and then everything was fire.

The swordsmen, the bowman, the grass, and the tents were incinerated in a brilliant flash of light that burned into the back of her skull. She scrambled backwards, kicking at the ground to get away from the heat that she knew she must feel. Except, she didn't feel any heat.

Then a strong hand pulled her to her feet. Aethan. No longer manacled, towering like a god above her.

"We need to go," he said, and hurried her up onto one of the horses. "Can you ride?"

She shook her head, and then he jumped up in front of her and drew her arms around his stomach.

"Hold on tight," he said, and she did. He was firm, his stomach was tight, and his back muscles bunched as he twisted the reins.

Then, like an oven door being opened, she felt the heat all at once. She looked over her shoulder, and the wall of flame had become a wildfire spreading through the grass.

They rode hard, galloping up the nearest hill with the fires lighting the landscape. She squeezed her eyes shut and pressed her face into his back. He smelled like sweat and smoke and lavender.

They pulled up sharp, and the horse reared and turned. She would have fallen off were she not holding on so tightly. She opened her eyes and could see nothing.

Nothing.

"Where is the fire?" Erika asked.

"Al'Aksahlad," Aethan answered, as though that was an answer that made any sense.

In her first year on the street, a fire had raged through Sheras. It burned through half the outer city, and the bluebacks hadn't been able to stop it. It would have burned straight up to the Nouvre Vil wall if the rain hadn't come and drowned it.

Even with the rain coming in a downpour, it had taken hours for the Sheras fire to fully die, but this fire had disappeared in a moment. She could hear the crying of horses and men yelling to each other. The camp was still there. She just couldn't see it.

Aethan stood in the stirrups and dismounted.

"Where are you going?" she asked.

He held up his hand to help her down, and she took it. He handed her the reins.

"Hold the horse," he said and then stepped to the edge of the hilltop, looking out towards the sounds of the camp.

"What is going on, Aethan?" she whispered. She hadn't meant to whisper, but the breath seemed to have left her.

"Don't let it bolt," he said, and then he bowed his head and spoke so softly that Erika wasn't quite sure she'd heard it.

"Just leave us alone," Aethan said.

He lifted one hand, and the air in front of it ignited. There was a flash of light, and a ball of fire blossomed before him. He flicked his wrist, and the ball of flame streaked down the hill, setting the grass beneath it alight. It traveled a few hundred yards, dwindling as it went, and then exploded outwards in great arcs of light. Erika could see the camp again. The new fire lit up the night. She could see men running here and there, calming horses and pulling down tents. Aethan cocked his head.

A figure walked towards them, black against the orange glow, and as he approached, the wild fire receded from him, snuffing out in a wide arch in time with his steps.

"Fuck," Aethan said, and then exploded into motion. He reached a hand into the air and pulled another ball of flame, and as he threw it forward, his other hand went up and pulled another. He twisted and spun, windmilling his arms and sending the missiles careening towards the walking man as though he were picking and throwing apples from a tree.

They exploded, one after another, in a series of flashes a few dozen feet from the approaching man, but he kept coming. Erika almost tripped forward as a wind picked up behind her, blowing in towards Aethan. The horse neighed in fear, and Erika struggled to hold him. Aethan spun faster, throwing more and more, until she could no longer make out the movement of his arms through the brightness, and there seemed to be just a long line of fire streaming down the hill into the approaching man's path. The man stopped advancing and then fell to one knee.

Then, the heat came. It prickled her face and stung her arms despite the stiff wind at her back. It leaked out from Aethan like he was an open furnace before her. Smoke rose from his shoulders, and the grass around him caught fire. Erika cried out and stumbled backwards, pulling the horse with her. The flash fire spread, and new pockets of grass combusted around her. She backed away further and cried out as Aethan was wreathed in flame, a human torch.

"Aethan!" she screamed, but he didn't react. She couldn't see him anymore. He'd become a cyclone of fire now, and the whole hilltop was aflame. The horse screamed and reared. She tried to pull it back down, but it kicked and she let go, afraid one of the hooves would bash in her skull. It turned to run, but the fire was everywhere. There was nowhere it could go. Nowhere Erika could go.

"Aethan!" she screamed again, and her broken jaw stabbed with pain.

The horse ran. It galloped toward the flame and tried to leap through it. It emerged with its mane alight. It was a torch hurtling down the hillside, feeding its own flames with the wind from its speed. It ran, and screamed, and collapsed at the bottom of the hill.

Erika fell to her knees and whimpered, pulling her dirt-caked cloak around her to ward off the building heat. Her skin was burning, and it was getting hotter. There was no escape.

38

Ashatee was the only other person Aethan had known who could call the Darkness, and like Ashatee, Al'Aksahlad was much more skilled than he. Aethan wasn't sure how Al'Aksahlad was doing it. He was leeching the heat around him, but he was also deflecting the superheated air Aethan was throwing down towards him. Perhaps he was throwing cooled air back up at Aethan? He wasn't moving his arms, so he wasn't anchoring the darkness to anything so simple as his hands.

Aethan knew Ashatee would have had an elegant solution. She had always tried to teach him to use the darkness in creative ways, but Aethan had only learned the basic structure of the silvery symbols that told the darkness what to do. He had memorized several sequences and could link them together to do specific things, but he had never been good at doing it on the fly. Ashatee would have changed her approach with the changing circumstances, but Aethan wasn't Ashatee. So, he did what he had always done and swung his sword harder.

He stood before the door of the pikelord's house, Jaaque's corpse at his feet, his friends from the Greenwall all around, and the darkness flowed past him. It flowed through the corridors of the self, and through the silver symbols he'd hung before it. He poured heat into the air and flung it down the hillside at the speed of an arrow. He poured more and more heat, and threw them faster and faster, and as Al'Aksahlad slowed, Aethan called to the darkness for more.

His chest felt like it was opening, like his ribs were being pulled slowly apart, and the door within him warped at the edges. The doorframe bent like a bow and stretched outward, distorting into an absurd caricature of what a door could look like, and Aethan directed all of the darkness that came through down the hill.

Aethan could barely make out Al'Aksahlad, but he saw the form of a man fall to his knees. He imagined the look on Al'Aksahlad's face, the look of a boy who realized he had picked a fight with someone much too strong. Aethan called for more darkness, and more darkness came.

There was no evil like Al'Aksahlad, like slavery, like reducing men and women to chattel to be bought and sold and beaten and raped. This man was all that the Freelanders had fought against, all that Aethan had fought against all those years ago. He would destroy Al'Aksahlad for daring to sell him, for daring to hurt Visoletta, for daring to--

Visoletta.

With a cry, Aethan turned his attention to his surroundings. The hillside was burning. The horse they'd stolen was gone, and Visoletta was collapsed into a lump on the ground, her muddy red clock pulled over her like a child hiding from monsters. The fire was all around her, burning in, coming to consume her.

"No!" he screamed.

He reached for the door within, but the frame had bowed out into an almost perfect circle and had lost all semblance of being a door. The pikelord's house around it was warped too, stretching into a thin silver line on the edge of the darkness. The bodies were stretched, and flashed in and out of existence like a landscape lit by lightning. The door itself was a maw inside him, and in the maw's throat was only the dark.

"Enough!" he screamed, and heaved at the door. It took no notice. There was only the maw, stretching further open with every moment. He forced his way up close, right up to the edge, closer than he'd ever come before.

Never pass through the door, Ashatee had said. *The Amaranthine stepped through, and they lost their minds.*

The darkness was not just the absence of light, it was the absence of everything, a great and terrible infinity of nothing, and as Aethan reached out for its edges, he felt as though it was drawing him in, pulling him towards the infinite dark.

Outside, Aethan roared, and within, he focused on the edges of the maw and pulled inward with all the strength he had.

It began to close.

The darkness flowed faster, and then, as the maw continued to shrink, the flow stopped and reversed, pulling back faster and faster as the maw grew smaller. Slowly, the house around it came back into being, and the bodies fixed into place. He pulled, and the maw became a door once more.

Aethan ripped the heat around him away and sent it through the door, and then slammed it shut and fled to the world outside. He was holding his hands toward the sky like a prophet proclaiming the end of the world, and the sky rumbled and boiled in response with the massive updrafts of heat.

Aethan looked down the hill and saw Al'Aksahlad on his knees. The man stood on shaky legs, turned, and stumbled back towards the camp, where the hill men stood watching, unmoving.

Aethan turned. Much of the countryside was aflame. He had taken much of the heat from the air directly around him, and the fires beyond that still burned were only warming it slowly. Visoletta looked up at him in the middle of it all, sitting with her cloak still draped over her, and began to shiver. Aethan went to her.

"What are you?" she asked.

He was naked. His clothes had burned away, and he felt her eyes upon him.

"Just a man," he answered and held out his hand.

She looked at it, and he realized it was his left, with its missing fingers and gruesome split down the middle. A spasm of self-hatred burned through him, but before he could pull it back, she took his hand in her own.

"We have to go," he said, and pulled her up to her feet.

They turned and ran down the hill.

39

"Show me again!" Carlotte demanded. Her voice was young and squeaky in the little cave of leaves.

"Are you sure you want to see it?" Elspeth asked.

Carlotte nodded. She tried to be as cute as she could. She knew that being cute would get older people to do things for her. If it seemed earnest, they'd usually give in, and it wasn't hard to be earnest this time. She really did want to see it again.

"How does it work, Ellie?" she asked.

Elspeth opened her hands to reveal the little ball of light.

Carlotte gasped. It wasn't white like she remembered. It was red and orange, and as soon as Elspeth opened her hands, she began to close them again.

"I don't know. Not yet," Elspeth said, and opened her hands again, bathing them in orange light.

"Is it... magic?"

Elspeth smiled. "Magic is just a word for what we don't understand, Carly. Everything has a cause."

"Are you going to find out how it works?"

"I'm going to try." Elspeth closed and opened her hands again, and then repeated the motion again and again, flashing the light in Carlotte's face.

"Can I help?" Carlotte asked. The shine flickered faster and faster, seeming to get brighter, to light up their cave like they had their own personal sun.

Her mother's voice pierced through the leaves. "Carlotte!"

"I have to go, Carly," Elspeth said. She brought the light closer to Carlotte's face. It was so bright. It felt as though it burned her eyes.

"Carlotte!"

Carlotte opened her eyes. It was cold, her sister wasn't there, and the sky was on fire. She sat up. It was night, but the sky was red and orange from a pulsing glow to the west.

"Carlotte! Get me off the ground!" Alakeed was sitting up. Her eyes were wide. Her fingers were digging into the earth.

Carlotte stood and turned away from the hill woman. Alakeed screamed her name again, but Carlotte was already running up the hill, her skirts clutched in her hands. Her mind played through the possible reasons for a pulsing red sky. Forest fire? No, that didn't explain the pulse. A battle? There was no weapon she knew of that could do such a thing. A volcano then? It had to be a volcano. She'd never seen one, but she'd read of them in books. Mountains erupting with the boiling blood of the earth to destroy everything around them. No. She wasn't quite sure how she knew; she had no proof, but as she mounted the crest of the hill and peered into the distance, she knew that this was something that was not understood.

The badlands were uneven, but over the hilly horizon, she saw the pulsing orange light. Above it, the clouds were lit like a woman's face with a candle held beneath, and the clouds swirled and churned in their own private storm. It was Aethan. It had to be, but what power did he have that he could affect the very sky? Carlotte fixed her eyes on the brightest part of the light, and tried to sear its location into her memory. Then she turned and ran back down the hill.

"We need to move!" Carlotte yelled.

"You think I'm blind?" Alakeed cried. "Get me up!"

Aethan's horse pawed at the ground. Carlotte untied the hobbles and then pulled the horse to Alakeed's side. Then she stopped.

She had no idea how to get the woman on the horse by herself.

Alakeed saw her doubt and reached out her arms. "Just pull me forward!"

"I can't lift you," Carlotte said, grabbing onto the woman's wrists. Alakeed pulled hard, and Carlotte stumbled forward.

"I can lift myself, just don't let me fall," Alakeed hissed, and then scooched up so her heel was on the ground and against her butt, with her stump out in front.

"Pull!"

Carlotte did, and the woman stood, amazingly shooting up on one leg with so much force that Carlotte almost fell back onto her ass. Alakeed screamed as she rose, face paling and screwed up with pain.

"Don't let me fall," she hissed, barely above a whisper this time, and Carlotte felt the woman's weight increase.

Carlotte stuck her arms under Alakeed's armpits and held her in an awkward hug.

Carlotte heard Alakeed's ragged breath in her ear, and then, "The horse," Alakeed said.

"I... You'll fall."

"I'll be fine. Get the horse."

Carlotte let the woman's weight settle on her leg and then let her go to grab the horse's reins.

"Give me the saddle."

Carlotte pulled the horse closer, and Alakeed grabbed onto the pommel. She swayed for a moment, shook her head, and looked back at Carlotte.

Before Carlotte could think to grab her and help her up, Alakeed squatted halfway down on her one leg until her arms were stretched out as far as they'd go, and then exploded upwards. She left the ground and swung her shortened leg up and over, and for a moment, Carlotte saw her landing in the saddle like a heroine in a children's story, but she didn't. Instead, her stump slammed against the horse's rump, and she let loose a scream as her other leg flailed for the stirrup, slowly sliding away off the horse's back. Carlotte rushed forward and pushed her up.

Alakeed whimpered and pulled hard. Carlotte pushed, and then her hips went over the rim of the saddle, and she was hugging the horse's neck.

"Are you okay?" Carlotte asked, one hand still on Alakeed's butt holding her steady.

Alakeed's face was almost white. "No. I've lost a foot," she said, and then breathed out hard. "We should... go."

Carlotte ran back to their little campsite and snatched up the blankets and her pistol, stuffing them haphazardly into the saddle bags, realizing as she did so that she had no idea how to properly pack a saddle bag, or any bag for that matter. Then Carlotte kicked out the fire and used the stirrup to haul herself onto the horse behind Alakeed. She reached around her to grab the reins.

"Heeya!" she cried and snapped the leather against the horse's neck. It reared, lifting Alakeed off its neck, but Carlotte wrapped her free arm around the woman, holding her steady, and then the horse bolted forward, towards the glow.

"Where are you going?" Alakeed moaned into the wind. "You're going the wrong way."

Carlotte ignored her and galloped towards the light, the land bathed in dim orange light around them.

"Turn around," Alakeed hissed. "Al'Aksahlad. We are too late. We have to run."

Carlotte urged the horse faster towards the light. She didn't understand Alakeed, but she did understand the light. It was a beacon from God guiding her to her great purpose. God had seen her sacrifice, and God had answered.

40

Saara awoke with her head in Bracille's lap. She could feel his legs crossed beneath her, and it awoke a longing in her. She moaned and lifted a hand to touch his face, but then she saw another form crouching and watching her sleep. She sat up and promptly passed out.

The next time she awoke, she was alone, and her head rested on something soft. She reached up and touched it: a bundle of cloth. She opened her eyes and saw dirt-crusted wood panels above her. She sat up, and her mind exploded in pain. She dropped back down, and the pain flared harder. She stifled a scream and ground her teeth and was suddenly nauseous. She rolled on one side to vomit, but after a minute of heavy breathing, the nausea drifted away. There were two wheels before her: the wheels of Carlotte's carriage. She remembered the battle.

She lay for several seconds with her eyes wide but unfocused, reliving the battle in fast motion. She heard the rain and the charging horses. She saw the riders emerge from the darkness and felt the gun kick in her hands. She replayed the arrows and the screaming. She remembered the bodies, Carlotte and Rold running up the hill in the grass, the pain, the stabbing, the warm blood on her hand. Carlotte being dragged away. Rold wrestling in the mud.

Saara reached her hand up again and felt where she'd been hit. It was swollen like an egg under her skin, and her hand came back with flakes of blood.

She had saved Carlotte. She had put her knife in Carlotte's attacker three times and Rold... Rold? Had she saved the boy? She couldn't remember.

"Rold," she mumbled, and rolled onto all fours. "Rold," she said louder. She waited for the pain to settle and then crawled out into the sun. "Rold!" she shouted, feeling more like a cow than a person. The word reverberated in her head. Rold, Rold, Rold.

"Saara!"

There was a person kneeling beside her. They wrapped their hands around her, and she collapsed into them. They guided her back down to the earth, onto her back, and Saara looked up to see Visoletta's maid, Jane, looking down. Saara could barely see past the woman's face. The air around her was all white light, and her face was barely more than a silhouette, like an angel of pain coming down from above.

"The battle," Saara gasped.

"It's over," Jane said, cradling Saara's head in her hands. "Two days it's been over."

Saara opened her eyes and saw another face, Val. The frames of his spectacles had been bent out of shape, and the lenses had spider webs of cracks across them.

"Oh thank God," Val said. "Oh thank God."

"Rold," Saara whimpered, "Where's Rold?"

Neither of them answered. They just looked down from on high, and Saara felt like they were looking in at her in a grave.

"Did I save him?" Saara asked.

She remembered Rold then, not as he had been on the expedition, with his bruised face and missing tooth. She remembered him as he had been when he'd first shown up at the Den's door, a little kid dressed in rags with his hand in another boy's. His legs had trembled, and the other boy had told him not to worry, the Den would give him something to eat. The Den would keep him safe.

You'll take him then? Bracille had asked. You'll keep him safe?

"Where is he?" Saara asked.

"He's dead," Jane said. "I'm sorry."

Something clenched in Saara's stomach, and she cried out. She saw the battle again. She saw Rold to one side and Carlotte to the other. She saw them struggling for their lives.

Saara had saved Carlotte. Saara had chosen Carlotte and Rold had died.

Saara shoved Val and Jane away and rolled over and back onto all fours.

"Saara--" Val began, but Saara cut him off.

"Where's Carlotte? I want to speak to Carlotte!"

"She's gone," Jane said, her voice oddly cold.

"Gone," Saara repeated. Her hands grasped at the dirt and grass, clenching and unclenching. She took in a breath, and her whole body shook with it. "Gone," she said again, and her voice broke. Her breath rushed out in a sob. She had chosen Carlotte and Carlotte had died anyway. She stumbled up to her feet, and when she felt Val's hand at her elbow, she batted it away, nearly falling over with the motion.

"Fuck," she said. "Fuck fuck fuck fuck!"

"It's okay," Val said.

Saara turned on him. "It's not okay!" she screamed. "Everything I had was in Carlotte!"

"At least you're alive," Jane snapped.

"And what is that worth?" Saara said, "Without Carlotte... I spent the last five years... everything... without her, I have... and now... and now..." Saara broke off, and the sobs broke through her. They rolled up from her stomach and forced their way out in great, ugly gasps. Her legs collapsed under her, and she sat down hard. She cried, and Val and Jane watched her.

"This is ridiculous," Jane said.

"It's not ridiculous," Val said. "You cried plenty yesterday. Let her have her feelings. Saara was close to the boy and to Carlotte."

"Close?" Jane spat. "I was close to Hannah. Hannah's children were close to her. Hannah's head has an arrow through it, and we're crying over over this Ryker bitch?"

"Carlotte being a Ryker has nothing-"

"It has everything to do with it!" Jane hissed. "Why else are we here except that she is a Ryker? You think I could summon folk into the badlands to die for nothing?"

"I saved her," Saara said. The other two turned. "I saved her from the riders on the hill. Where is she?"

"What?" Jane said.

"Carlotte. Where is she?"

"Gone. I told you-"

"Where is her fucking body?"

Jane's eyes screwed up in annoyance.

"She's gone. She didn't die. She left."

"Left?" Saara repeated.

"One of the riders survived. Carlotte took the only horse and the survivor, and left." Jane waved a hand westward. "Out there to get herself killed."

"The riders took Aethan. She went to get him back," Val said.

"She left?" Saara repeated.

Jane threw up her hands and turned to walk away. "God in heaven. They really did hit you hard."

Val stepped up to Saara and put a hand on her shoulder. "I'm sorry," he said.

Saara didn't push his hand away this time. "I did save her..." Saara said, "And then, she left? Willingly?"

"She seemed to think Aethan was... something. I think she was in shock."

Saara blinked and stared straight ahead at the carriage. The fine craftsmanship still showed, delicate molding along the door with inlaid metal that shown in the afternoon sun, but now the battle shown on it too. An arrowhead protruded through one wall. The thin, adjustable shutter on one window was shattered. There was a brown stain on the extendable steps. It still looked functional, but any illusion of its elevated status was gone. How thick Saara used to think those carriage walls were, thicker than the walls of the Nouvre Vil, but all it took was an arrow to smash through and let the world in.

41

Alakeed slept draped across the horse's mane, and Carlotte didn't wake her. Carlotte knew the general direction of her quarry. It was burned into her mind.

The glow in the west had died out not long after they had set off, and Carlotte had traveled through the hills and valleys by the half moon. The hills were larger here and less regular than they had been by the road. Deep valleys cut between them in the landscape like the claw marks of some celestial cat. They had the telltale signs of floodpaths, with scraggly bushes amidst the grass at their bottoms and steep but short dirt cliffs along one side or the other. The sun lit her path before she could see it, hiding behind the ridges until midmorning, and when it did come out of hiding, its heat baked her. She saw movement occasionally, something scurrying amongst the dry foliage, and a few birds circled high overhead.

Carlotte stopped and reached for the water skin in the saddle bags. It was nearly empty. She had another, but she didn't want to take the time to find it. She needed to find Aethan quickly. She needed guidance, but when she reached out to shake Alakeed awake, Carlotte froze. Alakeed's stump was bleeding. The bandage was soaked through, and it dripped slowly to the grass below.

Carlotte swallowed and wondered what she would do if the woman didn't wake up. Were cauterized wounds supposed to bleed? Was that normal? She had been taught medicine and anatomy. Why couldn't she remember any of it?

Carlotte shook Alakeed violently, and she awoke, shouting out in her native tongue and grasping at the horse's neck with her hands. The horse snorted in protest, and Carlotte grabbed the woman's waist to keep her from falling off.

"Qi shan ba'Areek?" Alakeed said, grasping at Carlotte's hands around her waist to steady herself.

"I... your leg," Carlotte said, pointing down at the stump. "Is that normal?"

Alakeed looked down.

"Normal? You mean, is it supposed to bleed?" Alakeed asked.

Carlotte nodded.

"No," Alakeed said, "feet are not supposed to bleed. They are supposed to stand and run."

Carlotte tightened her face.

"You should re-bandage it. Tight this time," Alakeed said.

"It was tight the first time."

"Not tight enough." Alakeed pulled up her jacket and ripped a section of her shirt away, revealing the skin above her hip where it dimpled around the bone. Carlotte dismounted and pulled off the old bandage, trying her best not to look at it while Alakeed white-knuckled the pommel of the saddle and cursed through clenched teeth. Carlotte cinched the bandage as tightly as she could, and Alakeed hissed. Alakeed took a moment, clenching her eyes shut and breathing deep through her nose. Carlotte took the time to find the other water skin.

"How did it smell?" Alakeed said, eyes still closed.

"What?"

"My ankle. Did it smell like rot?" Alakeed asked.

"I didn't sniff it."

"Then smell it now."

"And what if I do and what if it does?" Carlotte snapped. "What then? Will you have me take it off at the knee? At the hip? Do you think you would survive that?"

Carlotte pulled the water skin out of the saddle bag and set to reorganizing it so she could reach it from the saddle.

Alakeed scowled and looked up, taking in the land around

them. "We have gone west."

"Is that a problem?"

"How could a burning sky not be a problem?" the hill woman asked.

Carlotte stopped what she was doing and watched Alakeed's face. "What is Al'Aksahlad?" Carlotte asked.

Alakeed raised an eyebrow, but did not answer.

Carlotte latched the saddlebag shut. "You said it last night, before you passed out."

She put her foot in the stirrup and heaved up into the saddle behind the other woman, her groin smashing against the woman's butt. They were not big women, but the saddle was only made for one, and Carlotte was grateful in that moment that she was not a man. She reached for the reins, but Alakeed took them in her own hands and snapped them against the horse's neck, putting it into a gentle trot.

"I know the way better than you, I think."

Carlotte placed a hand gently on the stock of the pistol stuck through her belt, but said nothing.

"I'm sure your friend matters to you, but we should turn around and leave the badlands."

"Why?"

"Why? Need I remind you of a sky on fire? Have you ever seen a thing like that?"

"No."

"Then?"

"I am not afraid of the unknown," Carlotte said.

Alakeed's back stiffened before she spoke. "There is only one explanation for what we saw."

"Al'Aksahlad?" Carlotte asked.

Alakeed rode in silence for several moments and then gave a curt nod.

"What is it?" Carlotte asked.

"It means, 'The dead man'."

"Of all things to be afraid of, dead men aren't one of them."

"The dead man. One. Singular. Perhaps the bones of a dead man would be a better translation. It is under his orders that we raided your caravan."

"So he's your people's leader?"

"My people's leader died when I was a child. Al'Aksahlad merely... gave us a direction after her death."

"Gathering slaves, you mean?" Carlotte said. She imagined Visoletta, the greatest musician in the Dominion, a slave to some foreign prince across the sands.

"Slaves. Gold. Whatever your Dominioneers bring into these lands," Alakeed said.

"I see," Carlotte said, trying to keep the budding anger out of her voice. "And this... Al'Aksahlad can put fire into the sky?"

Alakeed was silent for a moment before she responded. "He is a witch doctor of old, and he can do many terrible things. I've seen him... stop arrows in the air. I've seen him lift great mounds of earth. I've seen him pull the limbs from a man's body, one by one, without touching him."

Carlotte felt something in her flutter, that feeling she got when her future appeared before her, like God kindling a flame in her chest. She had left civilization looking for remnants of Amaranthine magic, and here two real witches entered her life. If ever there was a sign from God that she was on the right path, it was this, and if ever God made it clear that her grand fate would not be easy, it was this also.

"Magic," Carlotte whispered.

"Yes," and Alakeed spat off the side of the horse.

"I would like to meet this Al'Aksahlad."

The hill woman laughed. "If you met him, he would take you as a slave. That was my plan, you know, when you pointed that gun at me after you woke me up, and asked me in terrible Altishi to take you where your friends had gone. I thought, a gift, it is not every day a Ryker bitch offers herself up to a dying Altishi."

Carlotte shifted uncomfortably. The sun was already beating down hard, and she felt the sweat soaking her underthings.

"Why did you change your plan?" Carlotte asked.

"I decided I did not want to die."

"When you saw that dead man in the grass?"

"Yes," Alakeed said, but her voice hitched with the word. She was keeping something from Carlotte. A lie? Betrayal? If it was betrayal, it was a convoluted one.

"Who was he?" Carlotte asked. She repositioned her hand on her gun.

"Just an Altishi," Alakeed said quietly. "The thought of death is different than seeing it before you. But that is that. Al'Aksahlad was supposed to be at that meeting place I spoke of. The plan was to help you buy your friends back from the fighters who took them before Al'Aksahlad got involved, but that show in the sky means that he came to meet them."

Alakeed pulled the horse to a stop.

"He has never come to us. We have always gone to him," Alakeed said. She stared straight ahead.

Carlotte nervously fingered the butt of her pistol.

"Who is your friend?" Alakeed asked.

"A man. And perhaps another. A woman."

"What are they?"

"A violinist and... a trader. Why?"

"No," Alakeed shook her head. "Al'Aksahlad would not come for such as those." She turned in the saddle as best she could, and Carlotte could see half her face and one olive eye. Carlotte leaned warily back.

"Your friends. They are witch doctors. Al'Aksahlad would come for other witch doctors. He has made his desires to find one very clear. The fire in the sky... Was that your friends?"

Carlotte stared back at the hill woman. "Would it change anything?"

Alakeed did not answer.

"You could probably kill me here," Carlotte said, keeping her voice as steady as she could manage. "And be a poor cripple. Or you can keep the deal and maybe be a rich cripple. So. Does who my friends are change anything?"

Alakeed watched her from one eye and then turned back to look ahead. "No," Alakeed said. "I guess it does not."

She snapped the reins and proceeded west.

They rode through the morning and into the late afternoon, keeping to the valleys and avoiding high ground whenever possible. They ate the hardtack and harder cheese from the saddle bags as they rode, and stopped only to relieve themselves. Doing so was awkward for both of them. Alakeed's stump was far too fresh to bear any weight, and so, despite her surprising strength, the only way for Alakeed to squat down was with Carlotte's help.

Carlotte had never considered that she'd have to do such a thing, but her shame at seeing another woman's bodily functions was dwarfed by Alakeed's shame at being seen. She said nothing, but Carlotte saw Alakeed stare straight forward and blush as Carlotte held her, as they both pretended not to hear the trickle, or smell the stench of the solid movement.

When they remounted, smooshed into the saddle as they had been before, Alakeed thanked Carlotte, who nodded in return, and they continued on their way.

It was not until the too-hot sun was just above the horizon, when they were in the center of a large valley, that Alakeed pulled the horse up short and hissed.

Carlotte saw nothing. "What is-"

Alakeed held up a hand, and Carlotte shut her mouth. Alakeed was looking up at a ridge that rose up on the other end of the valley.

Carlotte saw nothing but rock, more scraggly bushes along the dry riverbed, the never-ending grass, and-- a glint of light in the split between two rises in the ridge. It flashed once, twice, and then four times quickly.

"Alakeed," Carlotte began, but the hill woman spun their horse around, scanning the rim of the valley around them.

"What is going on?" Carlotte hissed. "That was a code. What did it say?"

"That a stranger rides through this valley," Alakeed answered. "But I did not see who answered it."

"Would they have answered?"

"Always. Else you don't know it's been received," Alakeed said, and whipped the horse into a canter.

"What are you doing?" Carlotte asked. Her stomach tightened, and her breath grew shallow. She felt the anxiety rising up in her like it had during the storm two nights prior.

"Someone will come," Alakeed said. "We need to get out of sight."

She angled the horse parallel to their original path, climbing the large hill that bordered the valley, heading for a copse of rock that jutted out of the ground.

"What are we going to do?" Carlotte asked.

Alakeed looked west, towards the setting sun. She muttered in Altishi and whipped the horse faster.

"Answer me, Alakeed!" Carlotte cried out, wincing at the jostling of the horse against her sore thighs.

"Shut up, Sikka," Alakeed commanded. She pulled up the horse by one of the large rocks, such that the area of the far ridge, where the glint had come from, was obscured from view.

"Get off the horse."

"What?" Carlotte said. "Absolutely not."

"Do you want to die?"

Carlotte's temper flared, overpowering the fear in her stomach, and she pulled the pistol from her belt. "My name is Carlotte DeSheras and you will--"

"They are coming, Carlotte DeSheras," Alakeed hissed, swiveling in her seat to look at her, and they cannot see two of us in the saddle."

"Then you get out."

"I can't!" Alakeed said, pointing at her stump. "And do you speak Altishi?"

"A little-" Carlotte began, but Alakeed cut her off.

"Like a child from the mountains. Trust me, Carlotte. I will not betray you."

Carlotte looked at her for a moment, trying to weigh the information while the anxiety gripped her chest in a vice. Alakeed looked up at the setting sun, and then behind them. There, coming down the path, was another horse with a speck of rider atop it. It was coming quickly; it could already see them, but probably couldn't separate the two of them. The setting sun would be in their eyes, but soon, it wouldn't make a difference.

Carlotte seized Alakeed's arm. "How do I know?" she whispered.

"You don't," Alakeed hissed back. "Now get off the fucking horse."

Carlotte paused another second, and then, with a look at the approaching rider, jumped from the horse and scrambled into the grass. She turned to face Alakeed and parted the stalks just enough to see through. A calm breeze flowed through the valley and disguised any movement she made with the gentle undulating of the grass.

She was making a mistake. She could feel it deep in her heart. She could hear the horse's galloping hoof beats coming closer. Alakeed would give her up. She'd point Carlotte out, and the coming rider would kill her. Carlotte should have shot the backstabbing bitch when she'd told her to get off, then and there, but... then what? What would she have done? She had no idea what she was doing out here. She had come after Aethan and Visoletta not even half-cocked, with no plan and nothing but this pistol with one shot in it, and she was going to die and--

"Yatid ash'fantil!" Alakeed called out.

The hoof beats stopped. Carlotte could not see them through her gap in the grass, and she dared not widen it. By the sound of the horse's heavy breathing, they were only a few dozen feet away.

"Yatid ash'kisa," another voice answered. It was male, and its tone was wary.

Carlotte gripped her pistol as tightly as she could, struggling to hear over the pounding of her own heart against her chest.

Alakeed called out again in Altishi. She sounded weak and tired with none of the fire she'd had before. Carlotte saw her slumped in her saddle, her stump side facing the man. On the other side, concealed behind the Freelander's horse, Alakeed held the knife Carlotte had used to cut off the foot. Carlotte hadn't realized Alakeed had taken the knife. She wondered how long she'd had it.

The man spoke. Carlotte racked her brain to remember what she'd learned from the book, but the words were gibberish, coming too quickly to be distinguished from one another.

The man's horse drew closer, and Carlotte could see him through the gap in the grass. He was tall, head and shoulders above Alakeed, and he was all in washed-out gray. She wondered if he had been there two nights before, if he had been the one to cut Pierre open. Carlotte should not have come here. She should have listened to Valieer and gone home, crawled back to her mother, married Harold, and done her duty as the Heir DeSheras.

Alakeed's voice broke into a sob, and she slumped further. The man drew his horse up to hers. Alakeed sagged against the reins, turning her horse out, and the man reached down, grabbing hold of the leather in one hand.

Alakeed straightened in an instant and swung the knife up and into the man's neck. It bit deep into the meat behind his clavicle. He cried out, and his horse crushed against hers, trapping her stump between the two beasts. Alakeed strangled a scream and sank over her horse's neck, struggling to stay in the saddle while the man grasped at the knife she left behind.

"Grab the reins," she gasped, and Carlotte rushed forward, stumbling over the hem of her riding dress. The man flailed, gurgling, and the horse spooked, reared up, and dumped the man from his saddle. Carlotte grabbed the reins before it could bolt, but the man's foot had caught in the stirrup, and he kept thrashing, pushing at his horse's side and spooking it more. The horse reared again and tried to pull away, almost wrenching Carlotte's arms from her sockets.

"Hold the beast!" Alakeed said. "They can't see it running off!"

"I'm trying!" Carlotte cried and pulled hard, turning the horse's head towards hers.

"Shh, shh, good girl, good girl," she said, doing her best to portray a calm she did not feel. The man gurgled again, spasmed, and sagged limp.

"Good girl," she whispered, having no idea of the horse's gender, and it calmed some, snorting uneasily and stamping its feet.

"Get the mirror," Alakeed whispered, pointing to the man's body. She was pale again, her face like a ghost's.

"What?"

"The mirror. It'll be... here," she said and patted her breast.

Carlotte passed the reins to Alakeed and went to the man. She pulled his leg out of the stirrup, and it fell to the ground like a stone.

"Quickly. The sun. We have... to catch it," Alakeed urged.

"I'm looking!" Carlotte opened the man's jacket and felt vomit rise in her as warm blood covered her hands. She clamped her jaw shut and forced her hand into the pocket. There was something flat and smooth. She pulled out a metal disk, polished to a shine but smeared with red.

"Is this--"

"Yes, yes!" Alakeed said. "Give it to me!"

Carlotte exchanged the mirror for the new horse's reins, and Alakeed pushed herself back up, swaying slightly to the left. She righted herself, wiped the mirror clean on her pant leg, and led the horse out into the last rays of sunshine. She aimed the mirror at the break in the western ridge and began to flash it in a series of long and short signals.

She finished and then waited. Carlotte pulled her horse with her and peeked around the copse of rock. Nothing for long moments, and then, in that same gap in the rocks, flashes. Short-short-long.

Carlotte collapsed to her knees. Her breath came heavy, and her heart beat a thousand times a minute.

"Get on the horse!" Alakeed hissed. Carlotte looked up at her.

"Give me a minute-"

"We don't have a minute. They need to see two horses riding out of here!"

Carlotte took in a deep and shaky breath and got to her feet. She hauled herself into the recently vacated saddle and led the horse after Alakeed. She looked down at the man, the knife still lodged in the base of his neck, and quickly looked away.

"Slow. Not in a hurry. The light isn't gone yet."

Carlotte nodded and let her horse walk beside the hill woman. She reached into her coat and felt for her prayer beads. They weren't there. That's right, she had lost them. Her panic rose again, but her fingers fell on the pendant around her neck. Elspeth's light. It was cool and smooth, and Carlotte rolled the metallic ball in her fingers until dusk settled onto the valley and her breathing returned to something approaching normal.

"What did your signal mean?" Carlotte asked, trying to give her mind something else to fix on.

Alakeed was slouched over, and she turned her head to look up at Carlotte beside her. "That you were Altishi."

Carlotte nodded and waited for the hill woman to add more, but nothing was forthcoming. She took in a deep breath and held it, ordering herself to calm down and think. She had to think. Thinking was what separated her from... these people. Thinking was why she was a Ryker, for God's sake. She forced herself to think through the encounter as a scientist, looking at every movement and action as a dispassionate observer.

"That was all that you said? That I was Altishi? That was awfully long for a message so short."

Alakeed glared at her. "There was also a call sign."

"To signify who was speaking?" Carlotte asked.

"Yes. Why else would there be a call sign?"

"And you gave yours?"

"No! His!" Alakeed yelled loud enough for Carlotte to glance uneasily to where she had seen the flashing lights.

After only a moment's hesitation, Carlotte whipped her horse out in front of Alakeed and blocked her way. Alakeed opened her mouth, but Carlotte cut her off before she could get a word out.

"I am still in charge, hill woman."

They watched each other for a long moment, Carlotte attempting to embody stiff-backed authority, and Alakeed looking like a cat who'd tumbled down a cliff, but her eyes did not break contact.

"Where are we going now?" Carlotte asked. "Back up this path and around the ridge?"

"No." Alakeed pointed to the side, at the southern ridge parallel to their path.

"Your friends are that way." Her eyelids were heavy, and the muscles in her face sagged with weariness. This was all taking a toll on her.

Carlotte felt suddenly like an impetuous child. "That way? Why-"

"In the next valley, I imagine," Alakeed said.

"How can you know that?"

"Because I am Altishi and I know this land. There is no reason for scouts to be here unless they have a quarry, and if they had someone there," she pointed to where they'd come from, and there," she pointed to where the light had flashed, "then they are watching something over that ridge," Alakeed said, pointing again to the south.

"And you think that something is my people?"

"There is no one else in this land."

Carlotte nodded and looked up at the notch in the crest. "Can they still see which direction we go?"

"I don't think so. I imagine they are not even watching."

"Good. Lead us up to the crest," Carlotte said and pointed southward.

Alakeed gave a weak half-bow. "So glad we had this conversation."

She pulled the horse to the side and walked it up the valley through the long grass. Carlotte rode beside her as best she could.

"What happens if we run into more of them?" she asked.

Alakeed did not turn to look at her. "We kill them."

"Like the last man?" Carlotte asked.

"Like the last man," Alakeed confirmed.

Carlotte looked down at her hands and saw blood there that had begun to dry and turn brown. She scrubbed her hands against her dress, trying to get the blood out of the creases in her palms and off the crooks in her wrists. The blood had soaked into her sleeves. It would never come out. That stain was a part of her dress now.

Carlotte reached up to rub Elspeth's pendant with her free hand. "How do you do it?" she asked sharply.

"Do what?"

"Kill so easily?" Carlotte said.

"You didn't seem to have any trouble shooting us during the storm," Alakeed said.

"You were trying to kill me, and you aren't my own."

"Ah. Well, they are not my own either."

Carlotte fell silent and watched the shadow of Alakeed's face. The darkness grew by the minute, and with it, Carlotte could feel the temperature dropping. "I don't understand."

"They are Altishi, but they are not of my people. They are from all over the Middle Lands. Of my people, of the Haldith, there were only two of us left. All that binds me to *these* people is Al'Aksahlad, and I owe him nothing."

Carlotte digested those words, trying to make sense of them. "He isn't Altishi?" She asked.

"He was born to the Kandi in the mountains, so I suppose he is, but he was sold to the Niquari during the early skirmishes. When he came back, he was... not Altishi and not of the desert peoples.

He was only Al'Aksahlad."

"The skirmishes? Between your tribes?" Carlotte asked, trying to understand. She hadn't known there were different peoples out here, though it seemed obvious in hindsight. That language book had made no distinction beyond "hill tribes."

"No. The tribes fought occasionally, but not in a large way. I do not know what your people call them, but the early skirmishes are how we call your people's first invasions from across the eastern mountains."

"Mine?"

"Are the Dominioneers your people?" Alakeed asked.

"Yes," Carlotte answered.

"Then yes. Your people. Some forty years ago, when the Dominion first came up the river and started murdering the Gistak who lived near the Watcher's Cut in the mountains."

Carlotte remembered the Amaranthine sculpture of the great eye they had sailed beneath.

"There wasn't anyone to the west," Carlotte said, racking her brain to think of her history lessons. "The second Mareshal had succeeded the first, and after he'd consolidated his power over the north, Dominioneers had gone westward to tame the wild and empty lands that lay beyond the mountains.

"There most certainly was," Alakeed growled. "It was Dominioneers who sold Al'Aksahlad to the Niquari as a boy. It was Dominioneers who killed the leader of my tribe. It was Dominioneers who killed my family."

Alakeed was silent for a few moments while Carlotte tried to formulate a response.

"Did you really not know?" Alakeed continued. "Why do you think we are out here? You think anyone would choose to live in these garbage hills?"

"I didn't... We don't keep slaves," Carlotte protested.

"But you do sell them. By the thousands. Kill the warriors, sell the rest to the desert. That is the Dominion way," Alakeed said. "I don't blame you for this. I don't think you are personally responsible, but neither do I feel bad for the farmers and settlers we have sold to the desert. Your people made the rules, and we only play by them.

"That is not what I was taught," Carlotte murmured.

"Well. You were taught for shit, Sikka," Alakeed scoffed. "Come. The land will get more difficult near the top, and we should get there while we still have light."

42

Erika ran for what felt like hours. The rush of what she'd seen kept her going at first, but the sprint quickly turned to a jog, and Erika would have slowed further if Aethan had let her. He ran just in front of her, and no matter how she pushed herself to come even with him, she remained just behind, staring at his flexing buttocks and the rolling muscles in his back. He was lit orange by the fires at first, but as they continued, he became lit by the half moon. He was a stag, a sculpted creature exemplifying the workings of human movement. The endless sight of his body filled her with a deep yearning that was overshadowed only by her growing exhaustion.

He stopped some hours before dawn and told her to sleep.

"What about you?" she asked.

"I'll keep watch."

"All night? You need to sleep too."

"I'll wake you in a few hours, and you can replace me," he said.

The night had cooled, and now that they'd stopped moving, she could see him shivering. She sat up, and after a moment's hesitation, undid the clasp that held Visoletta's cloak around her shoulders. She held it out to him, and though he was the naked one, Erika felt she was the one exposed. She looked at the cloth in her hands. It had been a beautiful garment on Visoletta's back, and now, after two weeks on her back, it was a filthy rag.

"I'll be fine," Aethan said. "You'll get cold without it."

The chivalry of his words touched her, but the stupidity of them pissed her off. She dropped the garment on the ground and lay back down, curling into a ball amidst the grass.

"Visoletta--" Aethan said, but Erika did not answer.

Sleep came a few minutes later, but while she waited for it to take her, she was cold. She wished she still had the cloak, but at that moment she couldn't bear the thought of wearing it again. She didn't know if it was because he had challenged her, because of her guilt, or because she no longer looked pretty in it. They all seemed like good options.

She awoke perhaps an hour later, shivering. She pushed to a sitting position. Her body was sore all over, but her jaw hurt most of all, pulsing with a pain that made her want to vomit. She didn't understand how she could be both nauseous and hungry at the same time, but it felt like her stomach was turning in on itself and trying to come up her throat.

"God," she whispered, and her teeth clattered, pain flaring with each click. She willed the shiver to stop. She actually missed the streets of Sheras. At least there she knew where to beg a bite of bread, where to find a fire, where to get a cut. She thought about the ounce Hannah had purchased for her in Irondale. Erika had never seen so much pike in one place. The thought of it made her ache, the silvery look of it, the sweet pain in her thigh, the sting as it went in-- then she remembered the arrow hitting Hannah's face, and she shuddered.

She pressed her palms into her eyes, and felt sobs trying to come up her throat. She pushed to her feet instead. Once they came, she was afraid they would never stop.

Aethan sat a few yards away with his back to her, wrapped up in Visoletta's ruined cloak, and through the dim starlight she could see him shivering.

"Can't you make a fire?" she asked through her teeth, trying not to move her jaw as she spoke.

"There is nothing to burn," he answered, "unless you want to start a flash fire." He turned to look at her.

"I can't sleep. You should get some rest."

"I can't either," Aethan said, and then he stood. "No point in waiting then."

Aethan led the way and they moved off into the night. They didn't run this time. They just walked.

The stars out here were clearer than she'd ever seen them before. In Sheras, the sky was washed out by the ever-burning lamps and covered by the ever-present clouds. Erika supposed that the sky had been just as clear all along their trip from Forepost, but she hadn't really looked up before. Some of the brighter stars looked familiar, but the way they clustered and the way some showed dim and some showed bright made the sky seem less like pinpricks and more a landscape rendered in dots. There were rivers and roads, mountains and cities. It was beautiful. Beyond beautiful, but beautiful does not fill bellies, and her belly was empty.

The hunger got worse when the sun rose and continued to escalate through the morning. It became all she thought about. It overwhelmed the ache in her joints and the stabbing in her jaw and in her side. She was like an animal, singularly focused on one thing, until she looked up and saw Aethan's ass flexing as he walked, and thought about another hunger for a few moments.

They stopped every hour or so to squat in the grass and will the various pains away. Each time they did, Erika thought to speak to him, but each time she found it too difficult to begin.

They had developed a rapport on the ride south, but those gentle and lazy conversations on carriage benches were so far away that it seemed a different person had had them. That was Visoletta, not her. She had been the violinist when she'd been surrounded by her servants and her money and her pike beneath her seat, and he, on his own bench, with his tricorn hat, and his cart, and his horse, had been a handsome trader from the south. Since the battle, she had changed slowly back into Erika, the dirty and destitute street urchin, and when Aethan had erupted in fire and burned all his clothes away, he had become... a witch, she supposed. The violinist and the handsome trader knew each other. The dirty urchin and the naked witch were complete strangers.

"They are watching us," Aethan said.

They squatted in the grass at midday. She looked at him, and he pointed at a hill in the distance.

"They're waiting for us to die. Or pass out maybe."

She followed his hand and squinted in the bright sunlight. Atop one of the hills, far away, was the speck of a horse with a rider on top. They weren't moving, just watching, watching two specks sitting in the grass. She started to ask why they weren't coming for them, and then answered her own question.

"They're afraid of you," she said.

Aethan nodded. There was a long moment of silence then, as they both watched the rider on top of his hill. The grass here was dry, and it scraped against her ankles. Her stockings hadn't survived the journey.

"Are you a witch?" she asked.

Aethan took in a deep breath and let it out before he answered. "I am a man."

"A man," she repeated, "a man who becomes fire."

He turned around to look at her, and she looked back.

"Can you..." she ventured, not sure how to ask, "pull things other than fire from the air?"

"No. Well, some things. But not what we need. Not food. Not water. Not a fucking pair of pants," he growled.

"Oh."

"Are you afraid of me?" he asked.

"I don't know."

He scowled and pushed to his feet. She knew his bare feet had been lacerated by the long walk, and she felt her heart go out to him. She'd lied about not knowing; she wasn't afraid of him at all. Perhaps she should be, but instead, all she wanted was to reach out and hold him. She wanted to wrap his feet and give him sweet touches to take the pain from his bones and feed him delicious things to make him content and turn him back into the handsome trader she had known on the road.

She wanted so many things that she could not have. She couldn't hold Aethan any more than she could hold a fire, and if she tried, she knew she would be burned. It was her curse to be forever wanting. Even if they made it out of this godforsaken country, she would never have what she wanted, what she needed. It was not in her stars.

43

They continued to wind their way through the badlands heading eastward. Aethan didn't know exactly where they were, but Visoletta followed him as though he did. They were somewhere southwest of Forepost. If they continued on, they'd hit the road eventually, and then take it north to the river and do... whatever it was they were going to do next.

Aethan had had one goal for the past ten years, one thing he had been building towards, and now that it was gone... He couldn't think about the future. He could only think about his next step and the steps that had brought him here. As he walked, as the dry grass bit and cut at his feet, Aethan remembered the Greenwall.

Aethan stumbled down the overgrown Amaranthine road in the Greenwall for what felt like days. He was delirious with pain and fever, and the tree cover was thick. Day and night meant almost nothing under those leaves. It was always hot, and the air was always thick with rot. It smelled sweet and sickly, and he was all too aware of what happened to open wounds in that place. He knew something evil had settled into his mangled hand, but he was afraid of peeling the cloth away to see it. He just stumbled on, his mind going in and out of waking dreams of fire and destruction until finally there was a light. It was dim at first, but it grew brighter as he approached. In his addled mind, he thought it was the end, death coming to take him away and out of the Greenwall's hell. All his rage at the Dominion was gone in that moment, and all his impatience with Ashatee. All that was left was a great relief that his journey was over, that he wouldn't have to think about Bulwark and Weed and all the others. He reached the light, and he felt embraced by it, and then he fell into another hell.

There was no rest. There was only a twisting nightmare, dreams of Ashatee's rage, of Weed's pleading, of his father's shame. He dreamed that he killed his family, that he killed his country. He dreamed that everything he touched burned, and that the world hated him and hunted him. He dreamed that whenever he found a quiet place, a good place, he would touch it, and it would all go up in flame.

The fever broke, and he awoke on a sweat-drenched cot in a military tent filled with moaning men. His hand had been cleanly bandaged, and his uniform had been removed. Soon his lucidity was noticed, and a captain sat by his side and asked him questions.

He asked Aethan who he was and why he had been in the Greenwall, and Aethan was filled with a great fear that if he said he was a soldier, they would make him go back. He lied and said he was a trader. It was not an unbelievable lie. The army depended on traders for supply. The army could only appropriate so much livestock in the name of the revolution before the land was barren. Thinking back, Aethan believed it was his hand and not his lie that kept the captain from pressing him back into service, but the captain let him go either way and gave him a list of needed items and how much his unit would pay for them.

Aethan had no intention of filling the order, but he took the list to keep up the lie and headed north and east, away from the Greenwall and into the heart of the Freelands.

His dreams continued, but they were not quite so bad as the fever dreams. They were of burning trees and the charred bodies of his friends. He always awoke tired, stressed, and covered in sweat.

There were two places he could think to go, but he could not bring himself to head back to Ashatee in the Shafala, so he headed home.

He had not seen his father or his sister since he'd left some five years earlier — that was before he'd been wounded near the Split, before Ashatee had found him and taught him to open the door. He didn't know what his father's reaction would be, but there was no other place where he could gather himself and plan the next step of his life.

The thought of his family distracted him on the long road north, and instead of dwelling on death and fire, he thought of what his father would say and how his sister would treat him. He thought through every possible variation on how it would go, and he felt that no matter what happened, when he showed up on the doorstep of their little refurbished slave hovel, he would be ready.

There had been a great elm tree by the old master house on the divided estate his family lived on. It was taller than anything for miles around, and when he had been a child and had ridden away with his father to the market or to a gathering of the revolution, he had always known he was home when he saw the top of that tree over the horizon. He didn't see the tree, and so he didn't realize he was home until he stood in the midst of its ruin. He hadn't prepared himself for this possibility.

He had not left the fire behind in the Greenwall. It had overtaken him and arrived weeks before to wait for him with open arms. The tree was gone, burned, along with the master house and the fields, and all the old slave hovels around them. It was all ash and foundation stones and bits of charred lumber. Even the hanging gibbets with the old slavers' skeletons had been burned away, leaving only jagged black teeth that stabbed at the sky and blackened metal ribs littering their base.

He fell to his knees. There was no puff of ash. All the light ash had blown away and left only the heavy black soot that had been beaten into the earth by rain and marching boots. Whose boots he could not tell. It could have been the Dominion, but this was a strange target for a raid, and he would have heard if Dominioneers had broken through the northern line and pushed this far into the interior. The two nations had been pushing back and forth all across the border mountains for the better part of five years. The very reason he'd been sent into the Greenwall was to keep the bastards from circumventing the line.

No, it had probably been Freeland soldiers. He knew how they thought. He'd been one. They were risking their lives to protect the revolution, and so what if a farmer got robbed? So what if a daughter got raped? They were defending freedom. This evil was a small thing. Boys will be boys, and soldiers will be soldiers.

He wondered where his sister was. They hadn't been close. When he'd stolen away, she'd only been... nine, maybe? Which would make her fourteen or so when he'd knelt amongst those ruins. He wondered if she was even alive at all.

He understood Ashatee then, in her hut by the lake. He understood why she lived alone and why she did not fight for the revolution.

Aethan dug his fingers into the black earth – he remembered that clearly, the feel of the bits of charcoal mixed into the soil - and then he lifted his hands and let the earth fall through his fingers. This was what war brought. This was what the darkness brought. This was what he brought. This was what he was owed.

So he decided to be like Ashatee, but unless he wanted to live on deer and squirrel like she did, he needed money. So he stole himself a cart and a horse, and bargained against the order the captain had given him to fill the cart with goods. He fulfilled the order and used the profits to buy more. He did the calculations and settled on fifty pounds of gold. If he could get that, then he could be done. He could buy some property in the Freeland west, where there were few people and fewer conflicts, and live out his days alone. Fifty pounds. That was what he needed.

Aethan's attention drifted back to the present, and his gaze fell to his bare and bloody feet, plodding through the dry grass that felt like little stalks of razors. He remembered the weight of his pack when it had been full of his gold, how it had made every step almost fifty pounds heavier. Now, wearing nothing but Visoletta's ragged cloak around his neck, it felt even heavier: a hundred pounds, a thousand. It was suddenly unbearable.

He looked up and saw a tree. It was about as far from the tree of his childhood as one could get. It was small, dry, and devoid of leaves, and it stood in a copse of similar dried-up trees in a valley that must have once been a river.

Visoletta stopped beside him, and they looked at the trees while the sun beat down on them like a Korkin whip. He staggered towards them and let his weight fall into a space between their exposed roots. The bare branches gave little shade, but it was better than nothing.

"Are we taking a break?" Visoletta asked.

Aethan grunted.

She sat down across from him and leaned her head back against the bark. She looked nothing like a famous violinist anymore. Without the brilliant scarlet cloak, and covered in mud and blood as she was, she looked more like a street urchin. Her face was so dirty it almost looked like the shadow of a boy's beard was gracing her face.

"How long?" she asked, but he didn't answer. He was so tired. He was so done with it all.

Aethan awoke several hours later. The sun had fallen behind the horizon, and already a chill was creeping in. He didn't understand how a place could be so cold and so hot. It all seemed unfair.

Aethan looked across the copse of trees and saw that Visoletta had gathered some broken branches and stacked them carefully around a mound of pulled-up grass. She'd cleared away a fire break around the little campfire, and she sat beside it, opposite him, with her arms wrapped around her knees. Her eyes were on his.

"I didn't have a light. I was hoping you could help," she said.

He opened his mouth and then closed it again. "I... I can't," he said. Damn his throat was dry.

"Why?"

"Because..."

Because why? Because he was afraid of what would be waiting for him? Because he had drawn up to the edge of the infinite dark and was afraid that he would fall through?

He looked at her struggling to hold back her shivers while he thought on what to do, and suddenly he hated himself for keeping her cold. What was he afraid of anyway? That'd he'd die? The dehydration would do that to him soon enough. So he closed his eyes and withdrew inward.

The scene was much the same as it had been before, the jungle all around and the burnt bodies littering the ground in front of the pikelord's house. The fire licked out around the door's edge, and the bodies around him burned. He could smell the burning of the bodies and the wood. It filled his nose and scratched at his sinuses.

This time, there was a new body, but instead of lying on the ground, it knelt in the path. It was charred black, but there were hints of color to it, fabric that showed bright red in parts. Its arms were tied behind it, and its back was bent. Its head hung over its knees. Aethan moved closer, and the head moved. It tilted back, and he saw Visoletta's face.

One half was burned away, but the other side was certainly her, all the features, awkward and beautiful, sliced in half by fire. Her lips parted, and the burned side cracked. Puss leaked through and dribbled down her chin like wax down the side of a candle.

"Please," Visoletta whispered, and Aethan's chest seized up. "Please, Aethan, Please don't hurt me anymore."

Aethan fled back to the world. He gasped and opened his eyes to see Visoletta flinching backwards.

"No!" he cried and scrambled forward on his knees, but then stopped himself, realizing how he must look. "Please. Please don't be afraid."

After a moment, she rocked forward again, but her eyes remained wary, and she stayed opposite the pile of sticks.

Aethan went to the pile of branches. Everything hurt, but he squatted beside it and grabbed two sticks that were straight enough. He dug the end of one into the other to make a shallow divot in the wood. The old revolutionaries had taught him this trick during his first stint in the army before he'd been wounded, and Ashatee had found him, back at the beginning of the war when there were still old Freeland soldiers to go around. Most of the units were mixed in those days, with veterans from the first war of Ryker aggression and even a few old men from the revolution itself sprinkled in with the green boys.

Aethan used his feet to hold the stick with the divot against the ground. Then he pressed the other stick into the depression perpendicular to the first, and held it between his palms. He rubbed his hands together, rolling the stick back and forth, and pressed down, sliding his hands down the rough wood. He repeated the motion again when his hands neared the bottom, and then again and again, not giving the wood any time to cool between passes. His palms hurt, but the rest of his body already hurt, and he wasn't about to stop. A few minutes later, when the burn of the motion was settling into his shoulders, a wisp of smoke leaked up from the deepening divot. He pushed harder and twisted faster.

He focused on the smoke, but from the corner of his eye, he could see Visoletta watching him. He wouldn't look at her, couldn't, because he felt that if he did, he would see her as she was within him, a burned and boiled thing, blistered and bleeding.

He hadn't done this in years. After Ashatee, he had taken great pride in overcoming his fear of the door and lighting his cook fires with the darkness when no one was watching. And after he'd left the Greenwall, he'd kept a good flint in his cart.

The trickle of smoke became a little stream, and Aethan pulled a handful of dry grass out of the fire pile, crushed it in his fist, and sprinkled it into the smoking hole. He bent back to it, pushing harder and rubbing faster, letting the smoke grow and bending down to blow, and finally, in the midst of the smoking char, there was an ember. He dropped the second stick and put more bits of grass onto the ember, letting it grow a little larger, and then carefully placed the stick into the dry pile Visoletta had created.

She'd constructed it well enough with fast-burning tinder in the middle and larger fuel stacked on top. There could have been more airflow, but it worked fine. He blew, and the tinder caught light. The fire flared up hot as the grass burned, and then died down, the larger sticks igniting. Those old revolutionaries would have been proud.

Aethan became suddenly aware of his nakedness and sheepishly sat on the ground, taking Visoletta's cloak from around his neck and wrapping it around his waist to hide his genitals. They settled across from each other, watching the fire burn, while Aethan occasionally fed more sticks in. They had no axe to cut larger logs from the trees, so he kept the fire burning low. It was warm, and that would have to be good enough.

"Are we going to die?"

Aethan looked up and saw a desperate kind of look in

Visoletta's eyes, not panic, not sadness, just a needful look. His stomach growled loud enough for both of them to hear.

"They're watching us. Waiting for us to be too weak to resist," Aethan said. He poked another stick into the center of the flames.

"For you to be too weak, you mean," she said.

Aethan grunted. There was another long moment, and when Aethan looked up again, he saw tears in her eyes. They glistened in the firelight.

"Visoletta-" he began.

She cut him off. "Why are they even after us? After what you did?"

"Viso-"

"You burned them with... I don't know. Magic, I guess? Is that what it is? Are you a wizard like one of those stories? Or a witch like the priests preach about?"

The mania was entering her voice, and the faster she spoke, the deeper her voice went. It had always been an alto, but now it dropped even lower. He wanted to reach out and grab her and try to calm her, but he was afraid that if he touched her, it would only make everything worse.

"That's why they're after me," he cut in, and Visoletta's eyes fixed on his. "Because of what I can do. Al'Aksahlad told me after they... took you. He wants to sell me across the desert."

"We are going to die," she whispered, and this time it wasn't a question. One of the tears gathered enough to fall, and it glittered as it fell down her cheek, dragging a line through the grime of the past few days. He searched for words, but he had none to give.

They were doomed. They had no water. No food. He had no clothes. A legion of horsemen was after them, and if they came, Aethan was as like to kill Visoletta as kill them.

He heard a sob. Just one, but it was enough. He stood and went to her. She didn't cringe at him this time. He sat beside her and put what he hoped was a calming hand on her shoulder. She took in a deep breath and held it until the tremors in her chest stopped.

"So," she said, after a moment, "You can pull fire from the air. Are you sure you can't pull bread?"

The laugh escaped his lips before he knew it was there. Short and crisp and loud, and then he laughed again, quieter.

"It seems relevant," she said.

"No," he answered.

"Bread would be more useful than fire. Especially when anyone can make a fire by rubbing sticks together like a caveman."

Aethan laughed again, and Visoletta put a hand over his on her shoulder. He scooted in closer, and she rested her head against his chest. She smelled like smoke and unwashed body. He didn't mind it. The smell of sweat stirred within him, and he forgot the crippling pangs of hunger for a moment.

"Should I be afraid of you?" she whispered.

"I would never hurt you," he whispered back. Through the grime, he could see that the skin of her hand was a pale red, like she'd been out in the sun. Had that been him? He had hurt her. Another few moments and his fire would have killed her.

"What's wrong?" she asked.

She pulled away and looked at him. She was so close. Her eyes were bright, and her jaw was wide. Her nose was large, and her throat moved up and down. She looked so young, so perfect in all her imperfections.

"I will never hurt you. Not again," he said, and she kissed him.

Her lips were dry and his were drier, but her tongue was wet when it pushed against his, and the saliva was so sweet. He wrapped an arm around her and pulled her in close, letting his other hand fall to her chest. Her breasts were small, so small he couldn't feel them through her thick dress, but it did not matter.

"Stop," she said, and he did. He pulled away and looked at her.

"I'm sorry. I shouldn't have done that," she said.

"Why not?"

"Because..."

"Do you want to stop?"

"No," she whispered. "No, no, I don't, but I... Underneath this..." she tugged at the folds of her dress. "It's not what you want."

"I want you," Aethan said, and her breath came out in a quiver. "Is what's underneath this you?"

He gripped the dress beside her hand. She nodded.

"Then it's what I want," he said.

"Do you mean it?"

In response, Aethan kissed her again and pulled her hand gently away from her dress. She did not resist. Her body rolled as he kissed her, pressing up against him. One of her hands slipped underneath the torn cloak and found him. He gasped at her touch and bit her lip, and she moaned and stroked faster. He felt his climax already approaching, and he pulled her hand away. This was not like his desperate trysts with Saara, where they fucked in the grass to distract themselves from the pains of the world. This was desperate, but it was also different. They were at the end of their world, and there was nothing so important as making the moment last. He thrust his hand under her skirt and felt her body stiffen. He was surprised to find a bunch of cloth between her legs, but he'd heard of such things when women were menstruating, and the thought of her blood only made him harder.

"Aethan-" she began, gripping his shoulders tightly, but his hand pushed the tight bound cloth aside, dug for her slit and found-

Aethan froze, holding in his hand something he'd never touched on another person, had no desire to touch, something that should not be there. He looked into Visoletta's eyes and saw fear there, but the horror he felt was worse.

Aethan cried out and shoved at her, slamming her back against the earth. He rolled and scrambled to his feet away from her. He had to get distance between him and... her... him? It? The wide jaw, the bulge in her throat, the shadow on her chin, and her voice! He'd taken it for sultry but... He looked down at her lying on the ground, gasping for the breath he had knocked out of her.

Aethan blinked, and he saw Visoletta. He blinked again, and he saw someone else. He shook his head violently.

"What are you?" he demanded.

The cloak had fallen away from his lap, and he covered his genitals with his hands. Visoletta coughed and pushed herself up to sitting. Her eyes were wet.

"What are you!?" Aethan repeated.

"A woman."

"Liar! I felt--"

"I am a woman!" Visoletta screamed. Tears flowed, but her face hardened behind them. She pushed to her feet and stood opposite him, hands clenched at her side. She pounded one of them against her chest. "I know what I am!"

Aethan's jaw worked, but no sound came out. He didn't know what to say, what to do.

"I felt," he repeated, voice shaky. He stabbed downward with his finger as he spoke. "I felt what was between your legs. I felt your... cock!" The word came out like a snapping tree branch, and he felt dirty just saying it, admitting out loud that he'd touched it, that he'd held it. The word hung in the air between them for a long moment, and Visoletta looked back at him. Her chin trembled.

"What of it?" she asked, barely above a whisper.

"Women don't have cocks," he said.

"This one does."

"That... that's not how it works. You have a cock, and--"

"So then you're what, a homosexual?"

Aethan's stomach flipped at the suggestion. He'd seen homosexuals in the Freelands, lounging outside their brothels in women's clothing, calling at him to come join them. He remembered the way his comrades had sneered, the words they shouted back. He'd seen homosexuals hanged during the war. The Korkin kings were all homosexuals, he'd heard. They'd been too interested in their depravity to stop the revolution.

"I am not--" he began.

But Visoletta cut him off. "Because you wanted to fuck me! I felt it. I had my hand on your cock!" She spat the word out just as harshly as he had, "and it was hard as rock to fuck me! And if I'm a man, then you wanted to fuck a man, and that makes you a homosexual."

"I didn't know you had a cock!" he protested, taking a step back as though she would infect him somehow.

"So I was a woman before you knew, and after, I was a man?"

Aethan stared slack-jawed at her. She wasn't making any sense, and he could feel his blood pulsing in at the base of his skull, slamming pain into his head. He shook it, trying to rid himself of the confusion.

"Women," he said slowly, taking a moment between each word. "Don't. Have. Cocks."

"Then what the fuck are you?" she demanded.

Her face was contorted in rage, like a mountain barbarian bearing down with an ax to strike his head from his shoulders.

"What?"

"What the fuck are you?"

"I'm a man, I have a--"

"Men have two hands!"

Aethan tilted his head. "What?"

"Two hands. Men have two hands, and you don't have two hands. You have one hand and one fucked up claw, so I guess you aren't a man then."

"That's not how it works--"

"Why? Why isn't that how it works?"

"This happened to me. I was shot," Aethan said. He was confused as to how he was on the back foot here when he was the victim.

"So, if you'd been born with a fucked up hand you wouldn't be a man then?"

Aethan's jaw worked again. What the fuck was she talking about?

"Hands aren't what make a man a man-"

"What about becoming fire then?" she asked. "What about being a witch?"

Her voice dropped in volume, and the fervor in it went away. She took a step closer to him.

"What about pulling a wall of fire out of the air to burn men alive. That's not something a 'man' can do."

She took another step towards him, but he stepped back. She looked down at his feet, and he saw the tears well in her eyes again. The bulge in her throat bobbed as she swallowed.

"That's different," he hissed.

"Why?" Visoletta asked.

Aethan didn't answer. It was different. It was completely different and Visoletta was just... just confusing him with a bunch of words and--

"Some women are born with paper white skin and eyes red as the morning sun. Some are born with shriveled feet or bad breathing or short legs or red hair and some... some are born with cocks."

The fire crackled, and its flickering played across the side of her face. She pressed a hand to her chest.

"I feel like a woman." She tapped her temple with a finger. "I think like a woman." She placed both hands over her crotch. "And I hunger like a woman. I know what the Dominion thinks of women like me. I'm all too fucking aware of it, but they don't get to decide what I'm worth. Neither do those brutes that beat me yesterday. I thought you'd be different than them."

She gestured back to the west, from whence they'd come, and the past day's events clicked in his mind. That was why the hill men had kicked her out when they'd taken her back to do what hard men of violence always do with helpless women. When they'd found what he'd found, they'd tried to kill her. 'Ik sargoth! Ik sargoth!' they had cried, pointing at her in the trampled grass. 'Ik sargoth.'

"I'm not like them," Aethan whispered. He saw them kick her again, the savagery on their faces. He remembered how he'd felt. The hopelessness. How he'd wished more than anything that he could protect her.

"Really?" Visoletta said, "because you seem pretty fucking similar to me."

44

"Is that them?" Carlotte asked.

She sat on her horse at the top of the ridge and huddled deep into her dress, thinking of the heavy winter cloaks that lined whole closets in her family's tower.

"Who else would it be?" Alakeed grumbled.

The sun had set, but there was a fire burning in the valley below in the midst of a copse of trees. Carlotte could just make out two figures sitting around the flames, and one of them was a witch. Carlotte's stomach tingled at the thought of being so close to something so powerful. More powerful than a battalion of soldiers. More powerful than all the black powder in the Mareshal's army. She thought of the mural painted by her great-grandfather on the ceiling of the cathedral in Sheras, the image of God raining down fire on the Amaranthine, and the sorcerers atop their mountain summoning a treacherous serpent of flame. Here was one of those sorcerers. Here was something that could change the course of the world, that had changed the world. This, whatever it was, had destroyed an empire. Aethan existed. She had seen his power with her own eyes, and if Aethan existed, then what of the other things Ryliar Orlient had written of? The wonders of Lok Secrak: the machines, the golems, the recreator? The possibilities tugged at Carlotte's heart..

"There," Alakeed said, pointing to the west at a ridge that

Carlotte could only just make out in the starlight. "And there," she pointed into the blackness to the east. "Altishi."

The tingle in Carlotte's stomach was beginning to feel like acid. Aethan was so close, and yet...

"More riders?" Carlotte asked.

"At least two. Probably six around the valley." She swiped her hand across the black landscape.

"You can see them?" Carlotte asked.

"I saw him move," Alakeed nodded at the western hill. "The others are guesses. Correct guesses. If there are more riders, they are there." She pointed again to the west. "And if this man is a witch doctor, there are certainly more riders."

Carlotte looked hard at the western hill, squinting her eyes, but she could see nothing. She looked back at the fire.

"We have to go down to them."

"The scouts will see us and will call in others. They'll cut off any escape and shoot us down."

Carlotte bit her lip and watched the fire twinkle like a spinning ruby down below.

"Why aren't they attacking then?"

"I don't know, Sikka," Alakeed said. "Would you like to ask?"

"There must be a reason they're waiting.

"Perhaps Al'Aksahlad is on his way."

"Then we should go before he gets here," Carlotte said.

"They can kill us plenty well without him. They do have weapons."

"Then what would you recommend?" Carlotte snapped. She couldn't see Alakeed's face in the darkness, but she would have bet a thousand gold rakes that the bitch was smiling.

"Why would you care what I would do. I thought you were in charge?" Alakeed said.

"I'm delegating," Carlotte responded. "Delegating to you to give me fucking advice."

Alakeed laughed, and Carlotte scowled. The curse word felt dirty on her tongue. She imagined her mother's glare.

"I would go east," Alakeed said after several moments.

"East? What's east?"

"The scouts. If we go straight, they will put arrows in us before we leave the valley, but if we find and kill the scouts on the east side of the valley, then we have an opening to escape through.

"Won't they hear us coming before we find them?"

Alakeed nodded. "Probably."

"Which means?"

"We would die."

"The whole point is not to die!" Carlotte snapped.

"I didn't say it was a good idea, Sikka. Just that it's a better idea. What we really should do is ride back to your little caravan and get out of these badlands. Go back to your Dominion and enjoy your money. Looking for magic will only bring misery," Alakeed said.

"Not an option."

"Then go east. Perhaps we will get lucky, and I can convince them that I am their friend."

"Like the last one?" Carlotte asked.

"Like the last one," Alakeed echoed. "But it is up to you. You are in charge, after all."

Carlotte bit her lip again and stared down at the fire. So close she could almost reach out and take it with her hand. What would Elspeth have done?

The answer was simple when she thought about it. Rykers became Rykers because they trusted logic. They did not make rash decisions based on their feelings. They chose the option that made sense, that had the best gain-to-risk ratio. Rykers did not trust their guts. They trusted their heads. Elspeth would have done whatever was most likely to succeed.

"We go east."

Alakeed gave a dry chuckle. "Wise." She then pointed to the butt of Carlotte's horse. "I'll be needing that."

Carlotte looked over her shoulder, and after a moment of confusion, saw the short bow strapped behind her saddle and a bundle of arrows strapped beside it. She looked back at Alakeed warily.

"Can I trust you?" she asked. She could not see if Alakeed smiled.

"My mother used to say, Asa'pakar sar pasha vat telan. Self-interest is better than trust."

Carlotte regarded her dark figure for a moment and then

nodded.

"I see where you got the attitude from," Carlotte said, and she twisted around to struggle with the straps. She handed the bow to Alakeed, who braced it against the pommel of her saddle and strung it with practiced ease. Carlotte thought of the arrows smashing through her carriage's window. Carlotte handed the arrows over, and Alakeed strapped them to her own saddle and then turned her horse eastward. Carlotte made to follow, but Alakeed froze, head cocked to one side.

"Wha--"

"Shhh!" Alakeed hissed.

Carlotte shut her mouth and listened as hard as she could. Nothing. There was the wind in the grass and... the distant lark of some nightingale... Come to think of it, she'd heard no nightingales the night previously. In this land, there were only crows and vultures.

"They are moving," Alakeed murmured.

The acid in Carlotte's stomach turned to cold dread. For a moment, she could not breathe. They were coming, and they would take everything away.

"Hiya!" Carlotte snapped at the reins and brought her horse wheeling to the side. She galloped down the ridge, straight for the glowing copse of trees. She heard Alakeed behind her, whipping at the Freelander's horse and hissing Carlotte's name as loudly as she dared, but Carlotte put it out of her head. She had no time for listening. Her heart thumped in her chest. She needed a plan, any plan!

She hurtled down the hill, praying that the horse wouldn't stumble and send her crashing to her death, praying that it was actually the witch and the violinist who were down there, and praying more than anything that she'd think some way around this.

Other hooves beat in the distance. Other horses were coming. They knew she was here. She was loud enough that her mother in Sheras must have heard her. This was no place for stealth.

"Freelander!" she shouted.

The copse of trees grew as she rushed towards them. They were black skeletons dancing with the campfire. Two dark forms stepped in front of the light. The taller raised an arm into the sky, and the copse of trees erupted into fire. The light seared bright, and she let go of the reins with one hand to shield her eyes.

"Carlotte!" Alakeed yelled.

Carlotte twisted to look over her shoulder and saw the hill woman riding hard behind her, and to her right, some fifty yards away, another horse and rider galloped, closing the distance to her.

He rode high, back arched against the wind, hands free of the reins and holding a bow drawn to his shoulder. Carlotte yelped and ducked down, melting as close to the horse's neck as she could manage just in time for an arrow to whip through the air where her head had been.

Alakeed yelled in Altishi, but Carlotte couldn't bring herself to look back again, feeling like a child afraid to look over the blanket, as though not seeing the horror would make it unreal. She squinted into the blazing trees.

"Visoletta!" Carlotte cried out, and then there was a jerk in her right arm that almost ripped her free from the saddle. She turned her head and saw a bloody arrowhead hovering a few inches from her eyes. The rest of the arrow poked through her arm just above the elbow. Blood seeped through the arm of her dress. She blinked, and the arrow was still there, and then the pain washed over her. She screamed.

A man screamed behind her.

"Carlotte!" Alakeed called again.

Carlotte ignored her. She bit down on her lip, screamed through her teeth, and beat at the horse's side with her foot. Faster, faster, faster. The blood dribbled from her arm and fell against the horse's hide.

"Protect me, Father," Carlotte cried out.

Another arrow zipped by her head, this time from the opposite direction. She glanced to her left and saw another scout closing in.

"Protect me, Father!" she cried again, and then Alakeed put an arrow in the horse's skull. It buckled, sending the rider crashing against the turf and rolling over and over. She forced her eyes forward. She was almost there. It was Aethan and Visoletta! She could make out their features in the fire's light.

"My work is for thee, Father. Protect me and see me through evil. Faith, protect and-"

And then there was a wall of heat and light before her. Roaring flame shot into the space between her and the trees, and her horse skidded to a halt in the grass. Alakeed's horse did the same, pulling up beside her. Alakeed sat upright in her saddle, arrows gripped between each finger of her pulling hand, with one knocked and ready to fire.

"Freelander!"

Carlotte lifted her arm to block the heat from her face, and the arrow shifted in her arm. She yelled through the pain. "I've come to help! It's Carlotte DeSheras. Let me through!"

The heat intensified, and her horse edged backward.

"We have to go, now!" Alakeed hissed. "They are coming!"

Carlotte looked to the west and saw a horde approaching. Hundreds of riders rode across the valley in a wide, scattered formation, lit from the front in flickering orange.

"Visoletta!" she pleaded, yelling as loud as she could to be heard over the roaring of the flames. The horde was getting closer. It had already come halfway down the valley and would be on them in moments. Blood dripped down her right arm and made her hand slick. God, she couldn't think about that now.

"I came to save you!" she screamed. The heat intensified again, and for a moment, Carlotte thought they'd have no choice but to turn and run, but then, the wall fell. Gone as instantly as it had appeared.

"Madame?" came a husky woman's voice. Visoletta.

Carlotte lowered her hand. Aethan stood naked in the middle of the trees, glistening in the light of the branches, and watching them warily. Visoletta stood away to the side of him, looking as ragged as a Sheras street urchin.

"Carlotte?" Visoletta said. Her voice was disbelieving.

"We have to go!" Alakeed yelled, and Aethan raised a hand towards her.

"No!" Carlotte cried. "She's with me. Get on our horses. We have to-"

"There is no time," Aethan said, and he turned to his left.

Carlotte turned with him and saw the horde bearing down on them. The horde was too close. By the time Aethan and Visoletta got on the saddles, they would be within bowshot.

Aethan reached his hand forward and paused for a few moments, his gaze vacant, and then a line of grass between them and the coming riders combusted, creating a shorter wall of fire than the one that had cut Carlotte off moments before. The riders in front pulled sharply up on their mounts and came to a stop before the line, and those behind fell into the empty spaces between. There was the sound of moving horses and cursing and calls in Altishi, but then they settled into place, and silence fell.

"Hass!" a man near the front called out, and all along the line, arrows were knocked and drawn.

Alakeed growled and backed away, and Visoletta made a sort of whimper.

"Your arrows will burn in the air," the Freelander yelled, "and you will burn after!"

The riders made no answer, but held their bows drawn and aimed. There was a flicker in the flames that separated Aethan from the horde, as though a sudden gust of wind had blown, and the flames sputtered and went out. The ground where the flames had been glowed red, but no smoke rose. On either side of the line, a strip of frost crusted the grass. A pulse rippled through the army, and the horses all took a step closer to the line. Aethan did not cower.

"You think I need air to melt the flesh from your slaver bones?" Aethan yelled.

The army was still again.

"We've already done this dance, Aksahlad," Aethan roared.

"We should run, Carlotte," Alakeed breathed. Her eyes were everywhere, attempting to take note of every detail.

"No-"

"There is no winning this!" Alakeed hissed.

Another ripple moved through the army. This time dividing itself in half and clearing a corridor down the middle to give room to a single rider. The horse was large, several hands taller than those beside it, and on top of it rode a man wrapped in bones that clinked and rattled as he moved. His back was slumped, but even so, Carlotte could see that he was tall and lithe. His face was shaved and covered in tattoos, and the hair on his head was long and matted, rolling down his back and over his shoulders in clumps that were woven into the strands of bones.

"He's here," Alakeed whispered. "Al'Aksahlad," and there was fear in her voice.

He stopped at the head of his army, just a foot away from the glowing line, and pulled a long, curving sword from a sheath at his horse's side. He reached its point slowly forward, and its tip blossomed white with frost. He pushed it forward a few inches more, the frost spreading down as he went, and then the tip flared bright white. Al'Aksahlad pulled the sword back, and the tip dimmed instantly to black and crusted again with frost. He held it before him and looked at it. The tip was deformed and drooped downward. He reached up and hovered his other hand an inch from it, and then touched the blackened metal. He did not scream. There was no sizzle of flesh. Al'Aksahlad looked up at Aethan.

"You take away too much heat at the edges. Inefficient," Al'Aksahlad said in a strange accent. It was different from Alakeed's. It was more particular. Each consonant was sharply pronounced, like a mother making herself clear to a child.

"This heat alone will not stop an arrow," he said.

"Then try it," Aethan growled.

"You are unskilled."

"And you are weak," Aethan said. His voice was hoarse but loud. "Do not make me slaughter your people."

Al'Aksahlad looked up and down the line of glowing earth.

"I was wrong to take you. I will admit that."

"I don't need your apologies."

"I was not giving one," Al'Aksahlad said, sitting back in his saddle and crossing his arms. "I would sell a hundred thousand of you to give the west back to my Altishi. You should understand that. A Boneman, of all people, should know what a people will do to take back their freedom."

Aethan didn't answer.

After a moment, Al'Aksahlad went on. "A Dominion army is nothing to me. To their neat ranks of order and discipline, I could do with as you did with so many of mine. But though the Mareshal is an evil man, he is not a stupid man, and he knows this. The Mareshal does not send an army. He hides his armies in the fields and the villages, and if I come upon one, he burns it down. If I go too far forward, he goes behind and burns what we have built and murders the camp folk we leave behind. My ability can win any battle, but it cannot win a war... But perhaps... with two? You with all your might and hot hot fury at the fore, pushing the Mareshal back beyond the watcher's eye and into their heart! And me behind to clean up after and wash away what little surprises the Mareshal sends around. One unbeatable army is little... but two? Two could--"

"I will not join you. Be gone," Aethan interrupted.

Aethan's eyes were only loosely focused on Al'Aksahlad, and his attention seemed to split somewhere else, like a man trying to listen to two conversations at once. He stood strong, with his muscles taut and on display, but there was also a shake to them. Carlotte saw it first in one of his calves, and then saw it travel up to a thigh. She wondered at its cause. Was it some price he was paying for his magic? Or was he just exhausted? She saw no packs of food around. How long had it been since he'd eaten or slept?

"Nonsense," Al'Aksahlad said. "The Dominion will strike your Freelands. They've done it twice. They will do it a third. They make room for me in the north by gathering their forces to the south, and they will keep striking until your countrymen have been washed into the sea!"

Carlotte nudged her horse forward and opened her mouth to speak, but Aethan shot out a hand.

"Do not cross in front of me," he snapped, with his eyes still loosely focused ahead.

Carlotte pulled up sharply on the reins, and her horse snorted and stepped backwards. She glanced between the two men, trying to understand. Was Aethan afraid she'd block his view?

Al'Aksahlad scowled. "You think I need contact to kill this Dominioneer?"

"I think you should turn around and leave this valley alive," Aethan said.

Al'Aksahlad's eyes flickered over each of them. Carlotte glanced at Alakeed and saw her atop her horse, slowly sweeping her drawn bow across the line of riders, as though she could cover the whole line on her own. Her arm was shaking.

Carlotte looked back at the line of horsemen. Their own bows were all still drawn, waiting. Waiting for what?

"I want no part of your war," the Freelander said.

"You don't have the luxury of refusing action. As powerful as you are, you have a responsibility," Al'Aksahlad said. He lifted the sword as he talked, and put its tip in and out of the invisible wall, letting it flare off and on with light.

Carlotte didn't know what was going on. She didn't know how any of this worked, and what was everyone waiting for? Was there some sort of magic battle of wills going on? Or maybe they were just talking, but if so, then why were the bows still drawn? Why didn't Al'Aksahlad tell his men to put them down?

Carlotte's arm throbbed, and the adrenaline coursing through her was making her head swim. She could feel her heart pumping. She could feel her blood trickling down her wrist.

"I will not play this game anymore, Aksahlad," Aethan said. "Take your men and leave, or I will kill you all. I've murdered enough in my life. Don't add more to my ledger."

No one moved. They stayed tense, waiting on a hair trigger. For the Freelander to pass out? Was his magic taxing him or something? That sounded like something out of a fairytale, a wizard putting his life force into his magic to make it powerful. Was that how it worked?

"We are witches, Freelander. We have a responsibility to stick together," Al'Aksahlad said. He raised a finger on the hand not holding the sword, on the one that wasn't the center of attention, but that all of his men could see.

The scouts!

Carlotte twisted in her saddle, pulling her pistol out of her belt with her right hand as she did. The arrow shaft scraped against her bone, and nauseating pain shot up her arm. A man crouched behind one of the trees and had an arrow drawn, pointed at Aethan's back. She pointed the pistol and squeezed the trigger.

The muscles in her arm contracted around the arrow, and she screamed in time with the pistol's blast like thunder. The man behind the tree flinched, and his bow released.

Then, the world exploded. A great force slammed into her and threw her from her saddle into the air. Her body struck a tree from the side and wrapped around it. She felt something in her snap, and she tumbled down to bounce off the exposed roots.

Her vision darkened around the edges, and through the pin pricks of light that remained, she could see that the burning branches had become a cyclone of flame reaching up into the heavens. She sucked frantically for air, but it would not come. Her lungs wouldn't cooperate, and her chest felt like it was in a vice. All she could hear was whooshing fire and screams of men and horses. She tried to join them, but her lungs would not cooperate.

A series of shock waves pressed her back into the tree and hammered at her ears. She smelled burning flesh and hair. She felt wet and warm and crushed and broken.

Get up. Get up, get up, GET UP! She yelled inside her head.

Carlotte rolled over and pushed up onto her hands and knees. The arrow in her arm had broken, and the feathered end was gone. The wound was ripped open, and blood spurted out to the beat of her heart like a garden fountain.

Breathe. BREATHE!

Carlotte sucked, and her body seized. She sucked again and then air filled her, rushing in like water through a burst damn, filling her up to bursting. She felt the broken ends of her ribs scrape each other, and her vision dimmed. She turned her head towards the Freelander and saw hell. Fire streamed from him towards Al'Aksahlad, where it split and cooked the remains of men and horses to either side. The rest of the horde were routed, galloping back out of the valley as quickly as their mounts would carry them. Half a hundred men and horses dead at the will of one man.

In an instant, the fire was gone. Al'Aksahlad was on his knees with his arms bent before him as though they were a shield. The only sound was that of the trees, still ablaze like giant torches and lighting the whole valley. Compared to the cacophony before, it felt like silence.

The Freelander still stood sparkling with sweat. There was no arrow in him. The scout lay crumpled a dozen feet from where he had crouched, dead by her bullet, or dead by something else, Carlotte could not tell. Alakeed was laid out some twenty feet away, propped up onto her elbows and grimacing. Their horses were nowhere to be seen, run off beyond the light of the trees.

"How can you take their side?" Al'Aksahlad asked. His voice was tired, and there was a touch of sadness to it. "The Dominion has no love for you."

"It wasn't the Dominion who tried to enslave me. Nor was it they who made me watch as they tried to rape--"

"But it was the Dominion who caused it to happen!" Al'Aksahlad screamed, cutting the Freelander off. "It was they who pushed us out of our lands, who killed my people, who sold me! They are the root of all of this."

Aethan stared back at him.

"You doubt my claims?" Al'Aksahlad asked.

Aethan shook his head.

"Then why be on their side?"

"I'm not, but neither am I on yours," Aethan said.

"So you leave my people to oppression?"

"That," Aethan said, "is not my problem to solve."

Al'Aksahlad cried out and struck the ground with his fists. All of the composure he'd possessed atop his horse was gone. The bones that clinked around his neck and body no longer seemed so imposing. Instead of death, they reminded Carlotte of an old beggar man on the streets of Sheras, dangling with tin cups and metal pans, clanging and clamoring as he ambled down the street.

Carlotte heard a grunt and turned her head to see Alakeed. She'd shifted forward, getting her good leg under her, and with another grunt, pressed up to a one-legged standing position. Her stump dripped blood, broken open yet again. Al'Aksahlad turned his eyes to her.

"Samaeelee," he said, "Kasso samaee ka'handass! Ka'ravat sar--"

"My brother is dead!" Alakeed shouted. Blood leaked out of both nostrils over her lips and sprayed out as she spat her words.

His eyes narrowed.

"Rav salomleo ustab ra'handass."

"No!" Alakeed said. Her voice was raw but loud. "He died for your anger. You are not my people. My Haldith. You see an evil and think it is a solution to make us evil too!"

"You would hold us to a higher standard than they? That is no way to win a war," Al'Aksahlad said.

"The Haldith are dead. They died with my brother! All the

Altishi are gone. Now there is only Al'Aksahlad."

Carlotte remembered the man they had found on the first day of their travel after the attack, lying in the grass with a bullet hole in his stomach. She remembered the cry that had come from Alakeed and the inexplicable change of face the woman had had after the encounter.

"The Altishi only die if we let them," Al'Aksahlad said softly.

"I have bled enough for you," Alakeed said, "for this land. For this damned life. I gave you my blood, my family, my fucking foot, and you've given me nothing. I am leaving, and I will never come back, here, to this Areek efataleo sashan. You wish to make us *like* them. No. I would rather become *them* than some Aksahlad reflection."

There was silence then, save for the crackling of the branches.

"Do not follow us," Aethan said, and Al'Aksahlad dropped his head.

He put his hands down on the earth and pushed himself up to standing, now seeming very old and frail, and then turned and walked away from them, picking his way through the bodies of his comrades. He stopped and turned his head back, so that Carlotte could see half of his inked face.

"You would not be my instrument, but there is no neutrality in this world. If you will not be mine, you will be the Ryker's, and you will find in them no kind master."

Carlotte's eyes darted to Aethan, fearing that the man who became fire would turn his wrath on her, but Aethan made no move, only watched Al'Aksahlad turn back and continue on out of the valley. Then, Aethan sat down and let out a great breath.

Carlotte ignored the pain and pushed to her feet.

"You have to kill him," she said.

Aethan looked warily up at her and shook his head. "It is over."

"It's not over!" Carlotte cried out. "You heard him. He will attack the Dominion! He's a monster!"

The Freelander's face did not change. He just closed his eyes and turned away from her.

"That is not my problem to solve either."

"You kill all these men, but you don't kill him? He'll kill more. Many more! How can you let him go?"

"Because having the power to do something doesn't mean that I know the something that should be done. Not even if everyone else acts like it is obvious."

PART THREE

THORLAILLE

45

Aethan stood beyond the light from the smoldering stumps and whistled as loud as he could. He waited, listening to the wilderness and trying to pick out the sound of hooves from the commotion behind him. The women were back by the fire, and they were dealing with their various pains. Aethan thought of Ashatee's lake and withdrew into himself, not all the way through the corridors of his self, just a little under the surface so he could think clearly and listen. He whistled again, and then there it was. Hooves from the east. He waited, and a few minutes later, Toktok came out of the darkness, his bridal jingling and the packs on his saddle slapping against his haunches. Aethan reached out a hand, and Toktok stuck his nose into it, looking for a treat that Aethan did not have.

"Thank you, friend," Aethan said, and felt a great relief. Toktok looked up at him the same way he always had, and Aethan appreciated it. His life had changed a lot in the last month. It was good that Toktok was still here, and that he was the same. Aethan led the horse back to the group.

"Who is she?" Visoletta asked.

She was not speaking to Aethan. She hadn't spoken directly to him since the battle and... what had happened before. Aethan looked at her, crouched down on her haunches, staring across the little fire. She sounded the same as before. Of course, her voice was lower than most women's, but that was Visoletta's voice. It had always been Visoletta's voice, and it had never seemed wrong to him... but what was a sound when he'd felt beneath her skirts and learned the truth. Aethan turned away and began to rummage through Toktok's saddlebags.

"The one who helped me find you," Carlotte grunted.

"Alakeed," the hill woman said.

Aethan pulled some bread, cheese, and a skin of water out of the bag. He put it to his mouth and took a long draw, but stopped himself from gorging. They didn't have enough water to waste on vomiting.

Alakeed hissed and pulled herself into a sit. She was a thin woman, but not thin like Carlotte with her arms the same thickness from shoulder to wrist. Alakeed's skin clung to tight muscles, like bark clung to roots above the ground. There was dirty cloth wrapped around the stump at the end of her leg, and it was wet and brown.

Aethan's stomach growled, and he put a hunk of cheese into his mouth. It was one of the best things he'd ever tasted.

"Do you know medicine, Boneman?" Alakeed asked.

"Some. What the war taught me."

"Then come here and look," Alakeed said, and began to unwrap her stump.

Aethan went to her, but then caught a glimpse of Visoletta sitting opposite the fire in the place that they had kissed. Aethan didn't want to think about it, about... her, but she looked so miserable there by the fire. He knew how hungry she was, and how her thirst burned. He went to her and held out the water and cheese. She took them, but she didn't look at him. She didn't say anything, and Aethan didn't know how to respond to that, so he turned away and squatted down to look at the end of Alakeed's leg.

The foot had been removed at the end of the shin just above the ankle. The cut was rough, and the translucent skin that covered the stump showed red and orange and white with black veins beneath it. Blood dribbled out in several places where the thin skin had ruptured.

"Most of the flesh here is dead. Whatever you used was probably too hot." Aethan prodded at the edge of the leg, and Alakeed hissed.

She looked to Carlotte and scowled.

"I worked with what I had," Alakeed said.

"I don't think it's infected," Aethan said, though he didn't really know. It looked the same as the wounds his comrades had gotten in the Greenwall, and those wounds all rotted, and many of his comrades had died. This wasn't the Greenwall, though, and if it was infected, there was nothing he or Alakeed could do about it.

Alakeed nodded.

"I think there is some cloth in the saddle bags," Alakeed said, nodding to Toktok. "A shirt or some such. Can you fetch it?"

Aethan did, and took some dried meat out of the saddlebags too. He ate while Alakeed tore strips out of the blouse and wrapped her stump. He glanced back at Visoletta. She wasn't looking at him. She was chewing slowly and looking into the fire. He looked away.

"That cloth is taffeta from across the sea," Carlotte said. She lay on her back, eyes closed, with one elbow cradled in the other hand. She hadn't made eye contact with him either since the business with Al'Aksahlad ended, though he got the feeling she was watching him when his back was turned.

"Is it?" Alakeed asked, "It looks like a bandage to me."

Carlotte grunted in what could have been either a laugh or a sob.

Aethan looked at her. The sleeve of the arm was wet. The hand that held it was dark red in the firelight. Aethan squatted beside her. "Give me your arm."

Carlotte started at the request. Her eyes hesitated, and then slowly climbed up to his face. "You're naked," she said.

Aethan remembered that he was. Perhaps that was why she hadn't looked him in the eye. Perhaps she wasn't treating him strangely at all. He grimaced at his sudden embarrassment, and Carlotte flinched, the muscles in her neck taut, her lips pursed. No. She was afraid of him. Of course she was. That thought made him feel angry, and then the anger made him feel guilty.

"Give me your arm," he repeated with an edge to his voice. He forced his tone to calm. "That's a lot of blood. You don't have much to spare."

After a moment's hesitation, Carlotte lifted her arm, and

Aethan pulled her wrist towards him. Carlotte whimpered.

"I need a knife," Aethan said.

Alakeed tossed one into the dirt beside him. He picked it up and cut the thick fabric of her coat.

"That's Korkin cotton," Carlotte said.

"Freeland cotton," Aethan corrected her.

He pulled the sleeve of the coat away. There was more blood there. The sleeve of the blouse beneath it was stained dark red. He cut that away too, and looked at the wound. The arrow had gone through just above her elbow, scraping against the bone and piercing through her bicep. The feathered end of the arrow had broken off, and in its breaking had ripped the hole in her arm wider. The iron tip was still intact, and its base was hooked inward.

"It will bleed worse when we pull it out," Aethan said. "You're lucky it went all the way through. This arrowhead wouldn't come out the way it went in."

Carlotte's lip trembled. "How do we stop the bleeding?"

"We cauterize it, of course," Alakeed said, dragging herself to sit beside Carlotte. "And I will do it."

"Cauterize?" Carlotte said.

Alakeed laughed. "At least your arm is still attached. There are spoons in the saddlebag. Heat them, Boneman," Alakeed said and snapped her fingers at him.

Carlotte's breath caught in her throat, and her body froze.

Alakeed noticed the tension and looked from Carlotte's face to Aethan. She sneered. "Are you going to burn me, Boneman? For my insolence? Are you going to cast your spell and make my bones ash?"

She looked him in the eye, and there was a rage behind her gaze. "That is what Al'Aksahlad would do. Are all you witch doctors the same?"

Aethan leaned back.

"Alakeed," Carlotte said, a warning tone in her voice that filled Aethan with a sudden rage.

"I'm not going to-!" Aethan snapped.

Carlotte gasped as Aethan's fingers dug into her wrist.

Aethan cut himself off and let her arm go. His hand was shaking. He stood and backed away from the two women. He glanced across the fire at Visoletta, and she finally looked back at him. It wasn't a soft look though, it was a tired reproach that he could not bear.

He turned back to Carlotte. "I do not think you need to burn it," he said quietly. "Just bind it tightly."

The hill woman growled. "In these hills, we burn wounds like this."

"In the war, we would bind it," Aethan said. "But do as you will."

Aethan sat heavily on the ground and stared into the coals of the dying fire. He could still see the women from the corner of his eye.

"Bind it then," Carlotte said.

"Bah! Sikka!" Alakeed said and ripped more strips from the tattered shirt. "Weak as a kitten."

Alakeed pulled off the splinters at the broken end of the arrow and then gripped Carlotte's arm with one hand and the tip of the arrow with the other. Carlotte whimpered again.

"Are you ready, Sikka?" Alakeed asked.

Carlotte shook her head. "Why do you keep calling me that? What does it mean?" Carlotte asked.

Alakeed grinned. "It is a term of love. Small child. Mouse. Baby. Sikka."

"I am not a--"

Alakeed yanked at the arrow, and Carlotte screamed.

Aethan was growing used to the sound.

Aethan watched the embers of the dying fire. Exhaustion pulled at his bones, but he was afraid to go to sleep, afraid of revisiting the horrible things that guarded the door within. Dreams had never been Aethan's friend.

Alakeed and Visoletta had both gone to sleep, but Carlotte still sat up, staring into the embers opposite Aethan. Her right arm hung in a sling made from the last of the taffeta from across the sea, and her left hand fingered absently at something beneath her shirt. Occasionally, she would look up at him, thinking he didn't notice, and then quickly look back down. She was afraid, but there was something she wanted very badly to say. Aethan could feel it in the air between them as much as he could feel the fire's warmth.

If you will not be mine, Al'Aksahlad had said. *You will be the Rykers', and you will find in them no kind master.*

Aethan looked up and caught Carlotte's eyes. She looked down.

"Why did you come for us?" Aethan said. His voice was more of a growl than he had intended.

Carlotte opened her mouth, and then closed it again, obviously choosing her words with care. Was she careful because she was about to say difficult things, or was it because she thought him a brute on the knife's edge of violence?

"Did Saara tell you why we are on this expedition?" Carlotte asked. Her voice was soft, calming in a way that made him want to throw something at her.

"Bergshalen, for research or some such," Aethan answered.

"I-- We are looking for magic, and two nights ago, when the hill people attacked, I saw you summon a cyclone of fire."

"And why are you seeking magic?" Aethan asked.

"To understand it," Carlotte said, her voice barely above a whisper. Despite her fear, she leaned forward a little, and the embers lit her from below with orange light.

"Well," Aethan said. "I am the wrong man for you. I don't understand it at all."

"But you can call it!" Carlotte insisted. "You must know how it--"

"I breathe, too, and I digest. That doesn't mean I understand how to turn food and air into life!" Aethan snapped. The edge in his voice made Carlotte flinch, and Aethan scowled deeper.

"Stop treating me like I'm going to hurt you," Aethan growled. "I'm not a monster. Not like... I'm not a monster." Aethan finished more quietly.

"Then tell me. Tell me what you know," Carlotte said.

"No good comes of it," Aethan said.

"Knowledge is always good."

Aethan watched her for a moment, and then his gaze shifted back to the coals glowing before him. He wondered how to give Carlotte what she wanted.

"My teacher called it the darkness," he said after a moment.

"Why?"

"It's the way it looks... or, not the way it looks, but... the way it seems when you let it in."

Carlotte let the pause linger, but finally broke the silence when he didn't continue.

"Let it in from where?" she asked.

Aethan thought of the infinite dark, the infinite nothing on the other side of the door. He thought of how close he had been on the hilltop in his first battle with Al'Aksahlad. How he'd pressed up close to it and felt it pulling him in. The second battle had been easier. Al'Aksahlad hadn't believed he could win. Aethan was grateful for that.

"I don't know," Aethan said. He started to shiver. The embers were giving less and less warmth. "I don't think anyone does."

He saw himself then, as Ashatee, sitting and staring into the fire, speaking vaguely and giving only half answers. It had driven him crazy when it was he asking the questions, but now here he was being just as cryptic as she. How could he explain it, though? How could he explain the door to someone who had not stood before their own? How could he explain the manner in which the door opened, or the scenes that surrounded it? He'd often wondered what blocked Ashatee's door. At the time, he'd assumed it was horrors from the revolution, or horrors from her slavery before it, but now he wondered if perhaps it was more like his, surrounded with the horrors of her own making. And how could he explain that to someone else? How could he give a clear and concise account of all the death and evil he had caused?

"You said teacher? So it can be taught?" Carlotte asked.

"To some people. You can be taught to open the door, but not everyone has the door within them to open. Or so my teacher said."

"The door?" Carlotte asked.

Aethan waved his hand. "It's complicated," he said.

"Okay," Carlotte said, frustration leaking into her words. "What about before. During the battle. You told me not to get in front of you. Why?"

"There's... There's a limit to how far the darkness works directly. Within that limit, there are much more precise things the darkness can do. If you'd gone within it, he could have... I don't know. Set you aflame. Boiled your brain. Ripped out your eyes."

"He could do that?"

Aethan shrugged. "That's not that difficult. Well. Ripping out just the eyes is."

At that, Carlotte was silent a moment.

"And beyond that limit?" she asked.

"Beyond the limit, the act must be done and then propelled out. My teacher could do some precise things beyond the limit. But it's much harder. The world gets in the way."

"So there are rules to this darkness?" Carlotte said.

"All the darkness is, is rules," Aethan said.

Carlotte sat on that for another long moment, and then she pushed to her feet. Aethan looked up warily as Carlotte stepped over the sleeping bodies of Alakeed and Visoletta and kneeled beside him. Aethan leaned away.

"Teach them to me," she said, and her eyes glittered in the dim light.

"I'm telling you what I know--"

"No--" Carlotte insisted. "Really teach me. Teach me all the limits and the rules and the methods. Teach me to use it."

"Not everyone has the door--"

"I have it!" Carlotte hissed, and she leaned in closer. "I know I do, and I need to understand it."

"I--" Aethan began, but Carlotte cut him off in her building frenzy.

"Continue on with us. We are following a path through the Shafala and to Lok Secrak. We are going to the root of the Amaranthine empire and--"

"The Shafala forest? My teacher was in the Shafala--"

"See! You were sent by God to help me on this quest. We are going to understand magic. Truly understand it! Come with me and help me in my work and answer my questions and teach me how to open this door!" Carlotte was leaning in very close then.

Aethan pushed away from her and to his feet. "I was not Al'Aksahlad's puppet, and I will not be yours."

Carlotte looked up at him, mouth hanging open for a few moments. "This endeavor is greater than us," she said finally.

"I've heard that before," Aethan said, thinking back to the

speeches his captains had made in the war. "I want no part of your great purpose. You are wrong. Knowledge is not always a good thing. The darkness will only bring you death."

She said nothing for several moments, and then nodded her head and stood. She looked into his face, and there was no longer any fear on hers, nor any passion, just a determined bitterness.

"I'll pay you," she said.

Aethan frowned. "You'll pay me?"

"Don't you want money? " Carlotte asked. "Name your price and I'll pay it."

"I've lost more money in the last month than--"

"Then name it," Carlotte said.

Aethan thought of his guns, surely ruined in the battle two nights before. He thought of his gold, melted to slag at the Pikelord's house. He thought of his decade of crossing the continent, trading, and building up his purse, and he thought of how, at that moment, he didn't even own clothes.

"Fifty pounds of gold," Aethan said.

Without a beat, Carlotte nodded and extended her left hand, the one not in a sling.

Aethan looked down at it. "You can pay that much?" he asked.

"I am Carlotte DeSheras. I'm the richest Ryker north of Domsar. What is fifty pounds of gold to me?"

Aethan stared at her, looking for some sign of deception.

"For what exactly?" he asked.

"Answer my questions. Teach me what you know. Guide me through the Shafala and help me find Lok Secrak."

"I don't know of this place. What if it does not exist? I'll not be bound to you forever."

"Just two years. Unless we find it sooner, and I will give you your fifty pounds of gold."

Aethan stared down at Carlotte's outstretched hand. It was so small, the fingers so thin and uncalloused. Aethan thought about the gold, about the weight of it on his back. And he thought about Al'Aksahlad's final words. You will be the Rykers', and you will find in them no kind master.

Aethan reached out and gripped Carlotte's left hand in his, his hand engulfing hers. She did not flinch.

"That's a lot of money you owe," Alakeed said.

They both looked across the embers to see the hill woman's eyes glittering up at them.

"You better be good for it," Alakeed said.

Carlotte pulled her shoulders back.

"I am," she said.

Alakeed grunted. "If you cheat me, I'll put another arrow in you, but if you cheat him, I think he'll burn your heart out."

46

Saara sank the shovel into the dirt and sat down hard. The earth had been hell to turn, but now that it was in a pile beside the hole, it was loose, and it gave a little when she sat. It was midday, and the sun was beating the sweat off her brow and into her eyes. Her head hurt, both at her temples and at the place in the back where it was swollen.

Saara looked across the hole at Pierre. He was on his back, face to the sun like a boy ignoring his chores. His eyes were open, though. A boy wouldn't do that unless he wanted to lose his vision. There was a gash down his front that showed a fair bit of his insides. Every time she looked at him, she saw the strike come again, the horse and rider frozen in time in the lightning flash, the sword halfway through him. His rifle suspended in the air as though on marionette strings.

Saara thought of Rold back in Sheras, on his knees in the mud, blood all down his face. Saara glanced to her left at the first grave she'd dug. It was a little shorter than the others. She felt her face contort, and she forced it into a trembling grimace. Bracille had thought he'd saved the boy's life, giving him to Saara, but Bracille always thought he was the hero. Never mind the fact that Rold wouldn't have needed saving if not for Bracille.

"Fucking Bracille," Saara spat.

She couldn't go back. Not that she'd wanted to, but now she

really couldn't. She couldn't face him. She couldn't look Bracille in the eye and tell him what had happened. She couldn't endure his hand on her knee, gently squeezing as he sat next to her in quiet support, as though God had struck Rold down, as though it wasn't her fault, as though these sorts of things couldn't be helped. She couldn't endure the candles he would light and pass out to the Den. She couldn't endure the memorial he would give, painting Rold as an innocent, as a carefree child, and as a good soldier. She couldn't endure the little tears on the young ones' faces and the drinking after and the toasts and the knowledge that it would happen again and again and again. She couldn't. She just couldn't.

Saara stood. She pulled the shovel from the dirt and braced it under Pierre's body. He smelled terrible. Four days of rot will do that to a man. She should have done this earlier, but she'd been busy preparing for Carlotte's return. They needed to be ready. She lifted him up and over into the hole. He flopped in and landed on his side, but his head lolled skyward, milky eyes looking up through her.

"You should put Haric in there too," said Jane from behind her. Saara shook her head and threw a shovel of dirt in.

"They deserve some dignity."

"They'd probably prefer it, being honest," said Jane.

Saara stopped and turned, shading her eyes against the sun to see Jane standing there with her hands held in front of her like maids do. She didn't look a maid, though. Her dress was covered in dirt and blood. There were bruises on the parts of her arms that showed, and her lips had cracked and split. Her hair was tied back in a loose bun, and the look in her eye was one of exhaustion.

"That's disgusting," Saara said.

Jane shrugged.

"They're dead. Believe what you want, but it would save time."

"We in some kind of rush?"

"We're ready."

Saara looked over at Carlotte's carriage and cart, the only vehicles still in any shape to travel. Val stood beside the carriage, shading his eyes to watch them. When he noticed her looking back, he averted his gaze and studied the hill line. He had a bag strapped to his back and two more at his feet.

"We've *been* ready," Saara said. "When Carlotte returns with the horse, we go."

Jane looked like she had something sour in her mouth.

"She's not coming back."

Saara turned away and flung another shovel of dirt into the grave.

"I'm not giving up yet."

"When will you?"

"Can't tell the future."

Saara thrust the shovel into the ground, and Jane stepped onto its ridge, holding it in the earth. Saara looked at the shoe blocking her way. It was a working woman's shoe, brown, with a modest wooden heel. A poor person's shoe.

"Step back, Jane," Saara said.

"They'll come back and they'll kill us," Jane said.

"Step. The fuck. Back," Saara growled.

"Or what?" Jane said.

Saara dropped the shovel and turned.

"Or you'll kill me? The riders come back, I'm dead anyway," Jane said.

"We're not leaving without Carlotte," Saara hissed.

"Carlotte's gone."

"She's coming back!" Saara screamed.

Jane flinched but didn't back up.

"What's she got on you?" Jane asked. "Or are you just addicted to the taste of her fancy shoes?"

"You don't understand," Saara said.

"You're right. I don't. Because Carlotte got my friend killed. Hannah has kids. A mother she supports. But now she's a few feet underground with an arrow in her eye, and her kids and her mother got nothing."

"It's not Carlotte's fault that-"

"Of course it's her fault! *She* killed Hannah, and *she* killed Rold. I know you don't care about me or Hannah or Boris or the rest, but you cared about him. I know you did."

"Is everything alright?" Val asked, walking up to them.

They ignored him.

"The hill folk killed Rold," Saara said.

"And who told us they were no threat? Who pushed us on after that farm? Who decided to go through the badlands in the first place? Carlotte."

"You were paid. You agreed to come. No one forced you," Saara said.

"Yes. I was paid, and I took that pay because it was go off on a Ryker's ego trip or let my children starve. Carlotte could have fed my children. We live in her family's tenements. Carlotte could have waived our rent. She could have come down from her tower and kept my family from hunger, but no. She demanded I come out here to earn the right to feed my family. Taking this job wasn't a choice any more than my next breath is a choice."

Saara didn't answer. She just snarled and pushed past Jane. She had to separate herself before she broke the woman's nose.

"What is there for you here?" Jane called after her.

Saara spun around. "Everything!" Saara roared. "The only thing I have rode off into the wild and left me here. I don't have anyone to go back to. The closest thing to a family I have is buried there," Saara stabbed a finger at Rold's grave. "I've given up everything for this. If I go back without Carlotte, I'm nothing."

"You have family," Val said, stepping up to her. "Your uncle cares for you and--"

"My uncle's dead," Saara said. "That's why he never returned your book, Val. I went to see him before we left, and he was gone. Dead three days earlier, they said, and already he'd been replaced. Already, there was a new clerk at the warehouse, as though he'd never been there. As though he'd never mattered because he doesn't. He didn't. He was little, and little people are like ants in this world."

"Saara, I'm so sorry-" Val began.

Jane cut him off. "You are a little person, too, Saara. No matter how much Carlotte was paying you, you are just like me. Just like your uncle. Replaceable and little. You won't own land, you won't matter, because you aren't a Ryker!"

Saara stared back at the two of them, breathing hard through her nose.

"Not yet," she said, just above a whisper.

Jane's mouth dropped open a little, and then she let out a huff that was half laugh, half exasperation.

"What are you talking about, Saara?"

Saara looked from Jane to Val.

They looked back at her like the concussion had taken all her brains with it, but the cogs *did* work in her head. She tried to think through what she would say so that it wouldn't sound crazy, and then the looks on their faces pulled the words out of her before they were ready. "Carlotte is going to make me a Ryker."

Jane and Val were both silent for a moment. Jane's eyebrows knitted together. Val's mouth hung slightly open.

"She said that?" Jane said finally.

Saara licked her teeth, looking back and forth between them.

"In not as many words," Saara said.

"What does that mean?" Jane asked.

"It means I know what I'm owed. I've worked with Carlotte long enough to know what she means by what she says. She doesn't need to say it out right. I've given everything to her and she's going to make me a Ryker and then all of this shit will have been worth it."

There was another long silence, and Val's open mouth changed to a disapproving frown.

"What?" Saara yelled. "You got something else to say?"

She glared hard at him and then jerked suddenly forward. He squeaked and stumbled backwards. Saara turned her aggression to Jane, but the woman no longer seemed angry. Now her eyes were sympathetic. Pitying.

"Oh, Saara. She's not going to make you a Ryker," Jane said.

"If I need some stockings mended, I'll ask your opinion," Saara spat.

Jane shook her head. "Have you ever heard of someone becoming a Ryker who wasn't born to it?"

"Shut up, maid," Saara said.

"This is what Rykers do. They dangle what they have in front of you like a carrot on a stick."

"I'm not a fucking donkey!" Saara cried.

"That's not how it works," Val cut in. "Even if a Ryker marries a commoner, they don't just become a Ryker. It's not something you can achieve. It's something you're born with-"

Saara swung her fist at him, and he cried out and cringed backwards, tripping over his own feet and falling over onto his back. Her punch missed, but Saara surged forward, crouching over him and pulling him up by his collar. He threw his hands in front of his face. Saara pulled back for another punch, but Jane was on her, dragging at her elbow with all her weight. Saara screamed and heaved her arm around, flinging Jane forward to tumble down beside Val. They both looked up at her, cowering back into the dirt and grass. They were so weak, so mewling and helpless.

Saara yelled. No words, just a release of rage, and she felt all her muscles flex like she was about to burst. Then she turned away and took a few steps. Her head ached. She didn't know she had muscles in her scalp, but they were all tight and seizing up. The swollen egg above her spine burned. She put a hand to her temples. She sobbed once and then sat down. She breathed hard. In. Out. In. Out. Sounding to herself like a blast furnace.

"I'm sorry, Saara," Jane said behind her, and she felt a hand on her shoulder.

"You shouldn't try to become a Ryker any more than you should try to be a horse," Val added. "There is an order to things, and you need to find happiness in your--"

"Shut up, Val!" Jane hissed.

Val obliged.

Jane crossed in front of Saara and sat down. She took up the hand that wasn't clutched over Saara's eyes and held it in her own.

"I'm sorry, Saara," Jane repeated. "That's what Rykers do. They lie. They mislead."

Val coughed behind them, but Jane paid him no attention and continued on.

"If you gave up your life to serve Carlotte DeSheras, then you have no one to blame but Carlotte DeSheras. She is gone. She left you. She doesn't care about you, Saara, and she never did. You need to decide what you are going to do with your life. You are young. You are strong. And you don't need her. Let's go home, Saara, before those riders come back. Carlotte took five years of your life. Don't let her take the rest."

Saara didn't open her eyes for a long moment. She just breathed. She felt weak. She felt like a little girl. She wished Bracille were there to hold her, and that thought made her feel even weaker.

"Let's go home," Jane said.

After a moment, Saara nodded. "Okay."

"Okay," Jane repeated.

"Oh, thank God," Val said.

Saara resisted the urge to punch him.

"Why would she bring a coffin?" Val asked, peering at the long box in the cart. It was half buried under boxes of supply, but one end was visible.

"Because Rykers are weird fucks," Jane said.

Val bristled. "I'd appreciate it if you held in your disdain for me," he said.

Jane waved a hand. "You're not really a Ryker. You're almost as poor as I am."

"Being a Ryker isn't about money, it's about--"

"It's her sister, I think," Saara said. She hefted her pack up and thrust her arms through the straps.

"Elspeth?" Val asked.

Saara shrugged. "Carlotte was close with her. Maybe she wanted her along or something. She didn't tell me."

Jane lifted her own pack. "It's a mystery for the ages. Let's go."

Saara tightened the straps. It was more a sack than a pack, rigged together by Jane with tent canvas, and it didn't sit well. A box of dried fruit sat at the bottom, and its edge dug into the space just above her right buttock. She pulled the strap away from her and twisted it around to try and get the thing to fit better.

"Ready?" Jane said.

Saara grunted.

"Right then," said Val. He stepped forward with Pierre's matchlock grasped in one hand like a staff.

Jane followed.

Saara turned to look back at the carriage and cart, the same carriage she'd ridden in to pick up the convict's head for Carlotte's exhibition all those weeks ago. Behind it, she could see the six mounds she'd dug. One for each body, with the last holding Haric and Pierre both. The dead riders and horses lay where they'd fallen.

Saara scrunched up her face and then turned back to the path and followed after Jane. Her strides were long for her height, and a few steps later, she'd caught up to the others and slowed down to match their pace.

"This pack is heavy," Val said.

"It's a long walk," Jane answered. "And it's the only way out."

"I just, let me reconfigure..." Val said and then stopped. He shrugged his pack off his back and turned to open it up.

"We just started!" Jane protested.

"It's a long walk and I don't need this pack crippling me because--"

"For God's sake," Jane grumbled. Her pack was lighter than Val's, but Saara's was heavier than both of theirs. Saara thought about reconfiguring her own bag to get the box corner out of her back, but she couldn't find the will to care. She closed her eyes and breathed deep. The pain in her head was worse than the pain in her back, and--

"Riders!" Jane gasped.

Saara's eyes flew open, and she snapped up her head to follow Jane's gaze. A pair of horses with riders stood at the crest of the hill.

"Give me the gun," Saara demanded.

"What's going--"

"Give me the gun, Val!" Saara yelled. She grabbed it out of his hand, keeping her eyes on the riders. "Where's the powder?"

"The what?"

"The powder, Pierre's powder bag--"

"They're coming," Jane said.

Saara threw the useless gun down and shrugged the bag off her back. She reached into her boot and pulled out her knife. Making a stand was pointless, she knew. They had no cover here, and a knife wouldn't stop an arrow, but Saara didn't find she cared much. Good. There was nothing for her in Sheras, and there was nothing for her here. All an arrow to the chest would do was save her a long walk. Saara growled and marched forward.

The riders descended the hill, but they didn't charge like they had during the battle. They came slowly, at a walk. They were in no danger. They did not need to rush. They could saunter down and fill Saara full of arrows at their leisure.

But... they didn't know they were in no danger. They didn't know Saara had no gun...

Saara's march slowed, and then she stopped. Her resolve fading into confusion. She squinted and shaded her eyes with her hand.

The riders were a little closer now, and it looked like there were two of them on each horse. One to hold the reins while the other shot? They'd been able to shoot and ride during the battle. Why would they need another rider now?

"What's going on?" Val called out. "I can't see. Where are they?"

"Where's the powder, Val!" Jane squeaked, desperately sifting through the bags.

"It's not the riders," Saara said.

"What?" Jane asked.

"What's going on?" Val screeched.

"It's them. They're back."

"What?" Jane said.

"Carlotte came back," Saara said, and she broke into a run.

The horses were descending the hill towards the carriage, and Saara sprinted back down the road to meet them. All the weight she'd felt before was gone. She was lighter than air, like a wealthy child jumping out of bed in the morning, excited for what the coming day would bring, excited for the future.

"Saara!" Jane called after her, "Wait!"

But she did not. She ran back to the wagon, and when she came around it, she saw them clearly. Aethan rode one horse, naked as the day he was born, and Visoletta, looking half dead, was behind him. Carlotte rode the other, sitting behind a woman Saara didn't recognize.

Saara ran up to her and held out her arms. Carlotte took them, letting Saara half lift her from the saddle. She looked weak. Her face was paler than Saara had ever seen. There were scratches on her cheek, and one of her arms was in a filthy sling.

Val and Jane arrived, and the others dismounted, except for the strange woman dressed in gray. Saara had no eyes for them. She eased Carlotte down, and when Carlotte's feet touched the ground, Saara held her up so that there wouldn't be much pressure on them.

"You're alive, Carlotte. You're alive," Saara whispered.

"Yes, Saara. So are you, I see."

Saara could have hugged Carlotte. She could have scooped her up and kissed her.

"Carlotte, you're--"

"Let me go!" Carlotte snapped. "I can walk."

Carlotte pushed out of Saara's arms and limped toward the carriage.

"Bring me something to eat," Carlotte said. "We ran out of food on the way back."

Saara did not move. She watched Carlotte walk on. The woman on the horse did not dismount, but she clicked her tongue and led the horse to follow Carlotte to the carriage steps.

"Carlotte," the strange woman said in a strange accent, "I need help to get down."

Carlotte looked up at her, and then to Saara.

"Saara. Help her," Carlotte said.

"Yes... of course," Saara said with half a voice.

Then Jane was beside her, one hand on Saara's shoulder. "And you think she'll make you a Ryker?"

Saara did not respond.

"You are a tool to her, Saara," Jane said. "A hammer. And one does not make a hammer a queen."

47

Erika stood behind the cart and fingered at the tweezers Jane had found for her. She watched Jane sift through the trunk of Carlotte's clothing. Her's were the only ones to survive Aethan's firestorm, and Carlotte had ordered Jane to find something clean for Erika and Aethan to wear. Erika was lucky, she supposed. She was closer to Carlotte's size.

"You really don't need to," Erika said, "I can search for myself."

"Nonsense," Jane said, pulling out a handful of rose colored fabric. "You've been through hell."

Jane pulled the rest of the fabric out and held it up. It was a conservative dress, with a high collar, sleeves to the wrist, and a pleated ankle-length skirt. Jane looked to Erika.

Erika nodded. "Thank you," she said.

Jane approached, and Erika put a hand on the woman's shoulder. "But you've been through a lot too. What happened to Hannah..." Erika gave her shoulder a light squeeze.

Jane frowned at the name and looked down. Erika continued. "She was dear to me, but I only knew her for two weeks. I know that you two were close before all this and I... I'm sorry."

"Yes," Jane whispered. She was silent for a moment and then continued. "At first, I wondered if she might have survived if you hadn't pumped her full of pike."

Erika cringed back, but before she could mumble a response, Jane continued.

"But everyone died. Haric and Pierre. Boris and Kent and Ari and Renee and... In the end, I'm glad she was swimming. Maybe she wasn't terrified before she went." Jane took in a big sniff and then swallowed.

"I'm still sorry."

Jane nodded. "And before you ask, no. None of it survived. Pike went up in flames when the gunpowder blew. You're in for a rough few weeks."

Erika nodded and felt a little guilty that she had, in fact, been about to ask. She gave a weak little laugh. "It's alright. I've been through it before."

Jane held up the dress again and looked at it like she was looking for a fault. "You know, Carlotte didn't even ask about Ari or Renee after the battle. Neither did that dick, Val, with the glasses. Rykers can't be bothered to care about the help."

"Well," Erika said. "I'm not a Ryker."

Jane gathered up the dress into a bundle and looked Erika in the eye.

Erika shrank back a bit at the intensity of the stare, like an inquisitor looking for a confession, and Erika wondered if maybe Visoletta had been some minor Ryker. "Jane--"

"No," Jane said, cutting her off. "You're not rich either, are you?"

Erika froze, her chest half full of air.

"I... well..." Erika began.

"You're not Visoletta Corlionne. You can't even play the violin," Jane said. Her gaze pierced through Erika, searching for the truth in her face, and when she saw it, she nodded.

"Please," Erika stammered. "I... I didn't mean to lie. It just... It just happened, and Saara thought I was her and she--"

"You were dressed as her. You were in her red cloak."

"Yes, but I -- I should have-- I was going to get rid of it, but Saara had already seen me--"

"All those bluebacks at the Nouvre Vil gate. They were looking for you, weren't they?"

Erika gave a tiny nod. Her chest felt like she had a belt wrapped around it.

"Who are you?" Jane asked.

"I'm... Erika," she breathed. Tears welled up in her eyes, and her voice hitched. "I didn't mean to kill her. I was just trying on her things, and then she saw me, and she fell and... I got scared and ran. I was trying to get out of the city, and then Saara saw me."

Jane raised an eyebrow. "You killed Visoletta Corlionne?"

She felt pinned in place by Jane's gaze, like a butterfly in a collector's shadow box.

"It was an accident..."

"Well," Jane said, and then held out the dress. "I heard Visoletta was a right bitch. You're not my enemy, Erika, and I don't want to be yours. Would you like help dressing, or would you like a little privacy?"

Erika gulped and took the dress in numb fingers.

"Privacy, please," she said, her voice barely a whisper.

Jane nodded. "I thought so. There's more to you than meets the eye. A lot more."

Jane closed the lid to the trunk and then hefted it up against her thighs and hauled it away.

Erika took a few moments to breathe. Somehow, it hadn't gone bad. Somehow.

She peeled off her soiled things as quickly as possible and put on Carlotte's dress, putting the tweezers in a pocket for later. The rags around her nether region were disgusting, and there was no obvious replacement, so Erika decided to leave it to the wind. She couldn't fasten the back of the dress, though, so she held a hand over her breast and went to find Jane.

Jane was standing with Aethan, who was still naked. He held blue fabric in each hand.

"I can't wear this," Aethan grumbled.

Jane shrugged. "Then keep your dick out for all I care. Either way, you're sure to cause a stir when we get back to civilization," Jane said.

Erika coughed, and Jane turned.

"I need help with the back, if you don't mind," Erika said.

Jane obliged, lacing up the back of Erika's new dress with practiced hands. When she finished, Jane looked at Aethan, who

476

had wrapped the long blue skirt around his waist. It would have gone down to Carlotte's ankles, but it stopped just a bit below the knee on Aethan. His frown was deep.

"I can't wear this," he repeated. "Isn't there something else--"

"It's all there is. None of her blouses will fit, and the dresses are much too tight. It's this and the cloak or it's nothing at all," Jane said, and then hefted up the trunk again and waddled away.

Erika looked at Aethan.

Aethan looked back at her and then at the ground. "Listen," Aethan said, "I--"

Erika held up a hand. "I don't judge, Aethan. Not on something like this. I'm not that kind of person."

She turned and walked away before Aethan could say anything else. She didn't have anywhere in particular to go, so she rummaged through the cart until she found a polished tin plate and went off to make use of what sunlight was left. She sat down in the tall grass, far enough away that none of the others could see her, and angled the plate to catch the light and look at her face. She felt roughness there, and she went at it with the tweezers, finding the bits of stubble on her chin and pulling them out at the root. It was a familiar ritual, and oddly calming.

Erika changed position to account for the changing angle of the light, and something flashed in the grass. She put down the tweezers and pushed the stalks aside. There, half buried in the mud, was a gold coin.

She stared at it for a long moment before she reached out to pick it up. It seemed unreal as she rubbed at it, but when the dirt fell away, it was the Mareshal's scowling face that stared back at her. She glanced around her and then hunched over it. A few days ago, when she'd had Visoletta's bag of gold beneath her seat, a single coin would have meant nothing to her, but now...

She didn't have anything anymore. It was all gone, and Visoletta was gone too. Jane knew the truth, and how long was it before the others did too? They would be out of this land and back into civilization soon, and word of Visoletta's death would catch up with them, and then what would be left for Erika? She clutched the coin to her stomach. A gold rake could buy a lot when they returned. It could buy her passage on a ship. It could buy her new clothes. Or...

Erika felt the familiar itch on her thighs where she knew there were crisscrossing scars. It had been almost four days since she'd had a cut, and it would be at least a week until she was somewhere she could buy another. Probably more.

That was enough time to kick the urge. Right? Then she could use the coin to start a new life.

Erika tucked the coin away into her pocket and went back to her face. Every few hairs she plucked, she would drop her hand down to feel that the coin was still there. She would go to Domsar with that coin. She would start over. That's what she would do.

48

Carlotte held her lip between her teeth and prepared herself for the pain that was about to come. When it did, she wasn't ready for it, and she bit down and gasped something between a hiss and a whine. Alakeed clicked her tongue but continued to unwrap Carlotte's bandage.

It wasn't the unwrapping that hurt; it was the rough way Alakeed held her arm, and Carlotte could swear the hill woman was purposefully wrenching it back and forth just so.

Alakeed pulled away the last of the dirty fabric and then peered at the arm for a long moment. Carlotte looked down and then quickly looked away. Alakeed moved her forearm up and down, and it felt like she was being shot all over again. Carlotte hissed again, and she could have sworn she saw the ghost of a smile on Alakeed's lips.

"That hurts," Carlotte said.

"It would be strange if it didn't," Alakeed responded.

"You could be gentler."

"I could. Probably," Alakeed said. Then she leaned in and sniffed the wound. "I don't think it is rotting."

"Thank God in Heaven," Carlotte said.

"Thank the soldier that shot you for not dipping his arrows in shit," Alakeed said. She ripped off a piece of fabric from one of Carlotte's blouses and began to wrap the arm again.

"Your people do that?" Carlotte asked.

Alakeed shook her head.

"My people are all dead. Some Altishi in the west mountains do, but the Altishi in the west mountains are as different from my people as snakes are from rabbits."

"Are your people the snakes or the rabbits?"

Alakeed looked up into Carlotte's eyes and smiled.

"Depends who's asking, Dominioneer."

Carlotte looked away and let the hill woman finish. She was tired of Alakeed's mysterious little digs, aggressive little comments that seemed designed to make her appear both trustworthy and duplicitous. She didn't want to talk anymore. She didn't want to sit there in the wilderness and let Alakeed wrench at her arm. She wanted to be on the road. She wanted to be in the south, in the Shafala, in the libraries of Bergshalen. She wanted to be talking to Aethan about the deep mysteries of this "darkness." She wanted to be doing the work.

She was on the edge of something great. She could feel it pulsing just beyond her reach. She had felt it from the moment she'd set out on the journey, but now it was different, more real. Before, she had been at the start of a mountain path with a map in her hand, but now she was at the cave's mouth with nothing but a torch and her intellect to find the way through. All she had to do was venture in, and that greatness would be hers.

She glanced over at Aethan across the campfire from her, staring into the flames like some sage from a three-penny adventure story and dressed like a village fool from the same. He wore one of her wraps that barely made it around his waist and a good wool cloak of her's around his neck like a cape. At least he wasn't naked anymore. She'd seen more male genitals in the last twenty-four hours than she'd seen in her entire life. Even the cadavers from her studies had had the decency to cover that bit up. She didn't understand the attraction. Sausages had never made her tremble. She thought of Harold with his own sausage hiding behind his pants, and it made her clench and gag.

Visoletta was sitting near Aethan, and she kept glancing over at him while trying to look like she wasn't. Something had happened between them, but Carlotte didn't care to find out.

Saara appeared beside Carlotte and put a plate of porridge and dried fruit down in front of her.

"Is this all we have?" Carlotte asked.

"I... we--" Saara began, pausing halfway to rising.

"Meat, Saara! Before I pass out," Carlotte snapped.

"Right," Saara said. She picked up the plate of porridge and moved off.

Alakeed fastened the bandage, and Carlotte yanked her arm away before the hill woman could do anything else to it. She clenched her teeth at the sudden pain of the movement and caught Alakeed's smile in the firelight. She held herself back from punching the woman in the face. She'd probably just break her hand on the woman's thick skull, and then she'd have two useless arms.

"How much food do we have?" Carlotte snapped, trying to direct her feelings elsewhere before she made a tenuous situation even worse. She could feel the expedition's distrust and animosity towards Alakeed, and she didn't need to push things in the wrong direction. Alakeed had proved herself useful. They would see it in time.

"I assume you took inventory while we were gone?" Carlotte continued.

There was no response for several moments, but just as Carlotte was about to turn and repeat herself, Saara spoke. "We did. Most of the food was in Kent's cart, and that burned. We've got three weeks of food for four people. Mostly fruit and oats."

"Of course," Carlotte mused. She glanced around the fire. "So two weeks for six--"

"Seven, you mean. Or are we going to leave Hannah's murderer behind?"

Carlotte looked after the voice and saw Jane, Visoletta's maid, standing on the edge of the light. Carlotte had forgotten about her.

Alakeed growled.

"Seven," Carlotte repeated, raising a calming hand to the hill woman. "So less than two weeks, then. How long to Thorlaille?"

"We won't all fit in the carriage," Jane said. "Some will need to walk. Two weeks at least."

"Of course," Carlotte said. "We'll tighten our belts then."

"We've got plenty of food to get back to Forepost," Jane said. "That's only a week away."

"Unfortunately, we aren't going to Forepost," Carlotte said. Her irritation was making its way into her voice. She knew it didn't help, but her arm hurt and her ribs hurt and her head hurt, and Jane's voice was making all of it worse. She needed this day to be over. She'd deal with her hunger in the morning. Carlotte put a hand to her head and pushed to her feet.

"I'm going to bed. We leave as soon as the horses can see their hooves."

"I think we should go to Forepost," Jane said.

Carlotte opened one eye to see Jane step into the firelight.

Jane looked around at the others. "The expedition is ruined," she said. "Our friends died out here for nothing. I think we should go to Forepost. I think we should go home."

She didn't look like a maid standing there in the firelight. Her eyes weren't downcast. Her chin was up, and she was staring Carlotte in the eye as though she hadn't been just a bargaining chip to get Visoletta to come along.

"Well. You are free to go back to Forepost," Carlotte said. "Then we'll have enough food for two weeks. Visoletta has been through enough. I'm sure she can get on without a maid."

"You don't get to decide, Carlotte!" Jane yelled.

Everyone started at the outburst. Even Aethan looked up from the fire to watch her.

"You said it yourself. Out here, your name means nothing. You are one woman, and I am another, and I say we go back!"

"It is my expedition," Carlotte spat back. "We go on to Thorlaille with or without you."

Jane looked around at the group. "Do you, Val? Or you Aethan? Do you want to meet the same fate as our friends? There could be more hill folk out there."

"They will not follow. Not anymore," Alakeed said.

"Says the woman who put an arrow in my friend's head!" Jane snapped.

Alakeed shrugged. "Al'Aksahlad will not follow if Aethan is with us."

Jane glared at them all, looking from one to the next, but their attention seemed to fade away. Aethan looked back into the fire. Val put his head into his hands. Visoletta caught Jane's gaze, and then looked at Carlotte, and then looked at the ground.

"None of you?" Jane said. "You all just follow her like lambs?"

They did not answer.

"Visoletta?" Jane said, her voice turning a bit shrill. "You agree with this? You side with her?"

Carlotte wanted to be smug at this maid's little rebellion, but she was tired, and there was no victory in it anyway. Jane had not lost these people with her cause any more than Carlotte had won them over with her own. There were no higher aspirations in these people.

"They don't follow me because they agree with me," Carlotte said. "They follow me because I pay them."

Jane's eyes grew wide, and Carlotte closed her own as her headache intensified.

"You mean I pay them," Saara said from behind her.

Carlotte looked over her shoulder and saw Saara standing in the shadows with Carlotte's plate of porridge in one hand. It was tipped down, and the mush slopped off onto the ground. Saara's shoulders were hunched over in that cow-like way of hers, and her brow looked thick in the harsh shadow of the firelight.

"What?" Carlotte said.

"You meant to say that I pay them," Saara said.

Carlotte waved a hand and winced at the nauseous wave of pain from her arm. She should have put it back in a sling.

"Whatever. It's my money that--"

"You don't have any money," Saara said. She dropped the plate into the grass and took a step towards Carlotte.

"Your mother cut you off," Saara said. "I spent my life's savings to put this expedition together. I paid these people. Not you."

"You have no money?" Alakeed asked and frowned up at Carlotte.

Aethan's head turned from the flames to look at her. His eyes flicked with the fire's reflection.

"I have money," Carlotte insisted. She lifted her arms, careful not to move her elbow, and gasped in pain as her rib shifted.

"I am Carlotte DeSheras. I have more money than--"

"Your mother has money," Saara said. "You have nothing."

"What are you doing? This is nonsense, my name is worth--"

"Your name is all you have," Saara said. Her voice was low and quiet and forceful. "And it's worth everything."

"You see," Jane cried, voice full of victory, "You don't have any power, Car--"

"Shut up, Jane," Saara said.

"You've got no money?" Alakeed repeated, more forcefully this time. Carlotte turned to her and tried to give a calming gesture.

"What are you playing at, Carlotte?" Aethan said.

They were all around her, baying like wolves closing in to kill.

"Stop!" she cried, and held out her good arm as though to fend them off. "I will pay you. I will pay all of you. I swear I will do it. My word is worth more than gold, but I'll give you gold. That's what you want. That's what you people always want!"

"Spoken like one who's never gone without it," Jane said.

"Your mother's word is the one worth--" Saara began.

But Carlotte yelled over her. "You don't understand what we've found. You don't understand what it is that we're on to! Magic. Magic! When I come back to Sheras with that knowledge, my mother will be nothing to me. I'll be the most celebrated Ryker in history. I'll have my family's name, and it's gold, and I will pay you. I will pay you all," Carlotte said. She rotated as she talked, speaking to all of them, holding them back with her words.

"The darkness only brings death," Aethan said.

"It does more than that!" Carlotte said. "It can do more than fire and death. It is not just darkness. It is light too. It can heal. It can change the world if we understand it."

"Carlotte," Val cut in, "you don't know that what's in Rylair's journals is true. The man was mad."

Carlotte dug at her breast and fished out Elspeth's pendant from beneath her blouse. She fished it out and tried to undo the clasp, but she couldn't manage with one hand, so she bowed her head and yanked it up to bring the pendant to her lips.

"Lix," she said, and the ball opened.

White light poured out and blinded her to everything else but it. She heard a gasp.

"This is magic," Carlotte said, holding the pendant as far

forward as she could. "My sister brought it back from the Amaranthine ruins. This exists, Aethan exists, and if an eighth of what Ryliar wrote exists, then I will be the most famous Ryker in history."

She still couldn't see them, but she turned to where she remembered each of them to be. "I'll pay you everything I promised. Everything."

"To trust your word is to trust a snake," Jane said.

Before Carlotte could lash out, she felt Saara's hand on her shoulder. She turned, and the woman's face filled her view. She was very close, and though Carlotte knew that she was taller, she felt small. She felt like a little girl looking up to her mother. Saara had pulled out the band that normally kept her hair tight against her head, and now her hair hung loose around her shoulders. Her lips were curled up in a sneer. Her eyes were bright in the pendant's light. Saara's other hand clasped around Carlotte's, and the pendant's light was blotted out. Carlotte felt the thing recover itself against her palm.

Saara's other hand released her shoulder and lifted up a purse. "Everything I have, I spent on this expedition for you. This is all that's left. It's enough to restock in Thorlaille. Perhaps enough to get us to the Shafala. But it's mine. It's not yours."

Saara's grip was tight on Carlotte's hand. She saw a bulging strain in Saara's Shoulders. She'd always thought Saara a cow, but in this moment, she felt that she was staring down a bull.

"What will you give me for it?" Saara said.

"I'll pay you too, I'll--"

"You'll repay me. Of course you will. But what will you give me for this loan?"

"Interest. A fee. Whatever you--"

"I don't want more money," Saara said, and her grip grew tighter.

"What do you want?" Carlotte whispered. The woman before her was totally foreign. Gone was Saara, her maid servant. Gone was her assistant. Here was a thug shaking down a poor girl in the alley.

"I want to be a Ryker."

Carlotte's eyes widened, and Saara's narrowed.

Val spoke. "Saara. I don't mean to belabor the point, but that's not how it works."

"I've helped you for five years," Saara said. "I've given you my life for five years. Will you make me a Ryker in exchange for a little more?"

Carlotte could feel her mouth gape open. Saara's grip was mashing her fingers painfully against the pendant.

"I..." Carlotte stuttered. "I... I can't. I'll give you whatever you want, but I can't--"

Saara released Carlotte's hand, and Carlotte sagged back.

"Fine," Saara said. "At dawn, me, my money, and everything my money has paid for will go back to Forepost."

"No!" Carlotte cried. "Please. Just get me to Thorlaille, I just need-- Please--"

But Saara turned away, her hunched shoulders almost blocking the view of the back of her head. Carlotte felt herself falling, not into the mouth of the cave but away from it, falling down the mountain and away from her moment of greatness, away from God's purpose in her.

"I'll do it!" Carlotte cried, and Saara stopped. "I'll do it."

Saara turned back around. She lifted one eyebrow. "You give your word?"

"I swear it. On Elspeth's grave, I swear it. To God, I swear this."

"No!" Jane yelled.

"It doesn't work that way!" Val protested.

"I'll adopt you," Carlotte said. "You'll take my name."

"It doesn't matter!" Val insisted, pushing to his feet. "You can't be brought into Rykerdom without being born to--"

"She's always been a DeSheras. My father's bastard."

"Carlotte--"

Carlotte spun to Val.

"I'll say it's so and it will be so! I am a DeSheras, and who will countermand me? You, Saadermont of nothing and no one? You will countermand the word of Carlotte DeSheras? It's why I've been working with her. Because she's my... my sister."

The words felt wrong in her mouth, like she was selling a kingdom for a cow, but she clung to them. She stabbed them at Val like he was the one she needed to convince. He held her gaze a moment and then dropped it to the ground.

Saara stepped around and offered her hand. Carlotte took it. Saara's grip crushed her knuckles, and Carlotte made her third pact in as many nights.

49

They set out at first light each morning. Two of them walked, and the rest rode in or on the carriage. Saara penciled out their order on a bit of paper, and they all took turns except for Alakeed, who drove the carriage up top. The long hours in the sun did not bother her as much as they did the Dominioneers. Nobody argued with it, but Aethan started trading his slots in the carriage for shifts outside. It was stuffy inside with three people's feet all mashed together, and he could feel Visoletta's eyes on him, even when he looked out the window at the passing grass. Her gaze burned. He could feel it even when he stole a glance and saw her looking out her own window and paying him no attention at all. Perhaps it burned even greater then. He preferred to walk in the sun beside Toktok, talking softly to the beast while he labored. The horse had been his only friend for years, and he told Toktok how he would reward him for his hard work when this was all over. When he had Carlotte's gold in his pocket, Toktok would never have to pull a cart again. He would be free to roam, and eat apples from Aethan's hand, and do generally as he pleased.

He'd been hungry a lot the past few days, and he didn't imagine it was like to get much better. He glanced down at his belly, bare in his ridiculous outfit. Was it leaner already? Or was he just imagining it? Aethan complained to Saara that first day when she'd brought the afternoon ration, but Saara brushed him off, and Aethan didn't have the energy to fight. It wasn't like he didn't understand. They had to do it. Of course they did.

On the second night, they sat around a little fire, built with wood they'd carted along from the wreckage of the old caravan. Saara leaned over his shoulder and spoke into his ear.

"I'll give you something else to eat if you want."

Aethan looked up, and the others were all watching him, except for Carlotte, who was pointedly not. He didn't look to see how Visoletta watched. He didn't need to. He felt her burn clear enough.

Aethan nodded and followed Saara into the grass.

He went down on her but came up moments later. They hadn't bathed in weeks, and the smell reminded him of Al'Aksahlad. Saara didn't seem to mind, but she left him with a painful scratch down his back that felt a little like revenge.

"You done with her then?" Saara asked, when they lay panting next to each other. Aethan turned his head to look at her, but there was only a sliver of moon in the sky and he could only just make out the curves of her body.

"Done with who?"

"The violinist."

"What?"

She turned on her side to look at him, and he did the same. His back went cold as his sweat mingled with the night air.

"Don't. I saw the way things were going before. Did you get it out of your system out there?"

Aethan thought of Visoletta's body: the firmness of her backside in one hand, the soft squish of her cock in his other.

"There was never anything!" he snapped. He sat up. "We did nothing."

"Oh?" Saara said. "Interesting response."

"What of it?" Aethan snarled.

Saara lifted a finger and bopped him on the nose.

"Nothing at all. Just remember that I'm a Ryker now. A DeSheras, would you believe? And Ryker's don't share, Aethan."

"I'm not your plaything," Aethan said. "But I'm not fucking the violinist. And I never would. Not ever."

"Tell me how to use it," Carlotte said.

She walked between Aethan and the carriage, and when Aethan turned to look at her, he could see Visoletta sitting at the carriage window, elbow on the sill and chin in her hand. He tried to slow down and let Carlotte overtake him so he could switch her places, but Carlotte slowed with him, her attention rapt, and her breaths in little spurts from her nose.

The sun was hot overhead, and the only sounds were the wind in the grass, the creaking of the carriage wheels, the huffs of the horses, and Alakeed's endless talking. She sat atop the carriage beside Jane, having a lively and one-sided conversation. Aethan could tell Visoletta was listening because every so often her lips would twitch into a smile.

Carlotte waved a hand in his face. "We had a deal, Aethan. Tell me how to use it."

Aethan flinched away from the hand and thought about how Ashatee had taught him. He'd been bed-bound when she started, still healing from the bullet in his side. He'd had nothing to do but stare at the hut's ceiling and think on his pain. Ashatee had said it was good for him. The pain gave him something singular to focus on, until the busyness of thought was gone from his head and there was nothing but the pain.

"It is hard to begin while walking," Aethan said after a long moment.

"Can you not summon fire while you walk?" Carlotte asked.

"I can, but I did not learn it walking. Half of it is concentration."

"Half?" Carlotte asked.

Aethan nodded.

"And the other half?"

"Symbols," Aethan said.

Carlotte glanced over at him.

"Magic words? Abracadabra? That sort of thing?"

Aethan frowned, but Carlotte didn't seem to be mocking him. She watched him like a tailor examining a new fabric.

"No. There are no words. You don't need to speak or move at all. You only need to instruct the darkness on what to do."

"And you do that with symbols that you do not speak. Do you

write them down beforehand?"

"No. You just... You put them... you... It is really quite difficult to explain while we walk," Aethan said. "And besides, that is the second half. It is academic if you cannot find the door in the first place. It really would--"

"What is the door?" Carlotte interrupted.

"It is irrelevant if you can't concentrate enough to find it."

"So," Carlotte said, turning her gaze back to the path before them. "You can not teach me the symbols while we walk, and you cannot teach me to concentrate while we walk. Who knew walking took so much of a person's mind."

Now she *was* mocking him. There was an edge of nastiness to her voice.

"If you cannot teach me the practicalities while we walk, then let it be academic. I am a scholar, Aethan. You will not scare me away with academia. What is the door?"

Aethan sighed. "I don't know what it is. I don't think anyone does."

"Even your teacher? The one in the Shafala?"

"Not even her. I asked her the same question, and she could not answer."

Carlotte said nothing, but Aethan could feel the expectation.

"There is a door in some people. I don't know if it's real. Ashatee, my teacher, talked of it like it was a trick of the mind, a way to visualize the act of letting the darkness through."

"So the door is a metaphor?" Carlotte asked.

Aethan thought of the things he'd seen in front of the door. He thought of mangled Visoletta, and the warehouse keeper, and the pikelord, and the bodies of his friends arranged before it. He thought of the way that the door felt when he hefted it, the way the mausoleum had been cold and smooth like marble before the incident with the Pikelord, and the rough warmth of the wood after. He thought of the infinite black beyond the door, and how close he came to touching it.

"No," Aethan said. "It's real. But it's not... physical. It's not here. It's inside... But not everyone has it."

Carlotte's face pinched up. "And how do you know that?"

"Ashatee told me--"

"And how does Ashatee know?"

Aethan frowned. "I don't know. She knew many things--"

"Except what the door is, or what the darkness is. The answer to all my questions seems to be that no one knows. The only thing your teacher does seem to know is that not everyone has the talent--"

"It's not a talent, it's--"

"You said you can't tell, your teacher could, but you cannot, yes?"

Aethan nodded.

"Then assume I can. If God gave you the gift, then he most certainly gave it to me."

Aethan didn't know what to say to that. He absently reached for his slaver bones and then remembered that he'd lost them along with his pants.

"You will show me tonight, before you go off into the grass with Saara, since both walking and learning are too much for our delicate minds." Carlotte glared at him and then at the carriage.

"My feet ache," she said, and stomped to the carriage, opened the door, and squeezed herself past Visoletta. There was a bit of a commotion, and then Visoletta stumbled out. Aethan swallowed. Her hair was down around her face, cascading down her chest. She looked up at him, and he quickly turned away and stopped walking. He heard her sigh.

"Done walking, Boneman?" Alakeed called from her place atop the carriage.

"Need a piss, hill girl," Aethan called, and Alakeed laughed and resumed talking at Jane beside her.

Aethan did pee and then hurried to catch up. Visoletta was lagging behind a bit, and Aethan made to overtake her but then caught sight of the way the fabric of her dress fell across her backside. He felt a stirring in his pants and looked into the sky.

He didn't know what to make of Visoletta. He knew the truth. He knew what she was underneath all that fabric... and yet. Why did he react so?

"Are you going to apologize to me?"

Aethan looked down. Visoletta had stopped moving and was looking back at him. He cringed, and she scowled back. He saw himself suddenly as she must see him, a fool in a skirt and a cape, and it bothered him that he cared.

"Or you just gonna stare at my ass?"

"I was not--"

"Yes, you were, don't lie. I heard you come up and then slow down to stay behind. You don't walk quietly."

Aethan opened his mouth and then closed it again. He didn't know what to say. He was a fool, a fool who'd been stricken dumb.

"You haven't told anyone yet. So either you're such a bigot that admitting the truth would make you tainted, or... You feel bad about what you did."

Visoletta crossed her arms and glared. "You also haven't killed me, which we both know you're good at, so I'm leaning, hoping, towards the latter."

Aethan just stood and stared. Visoletta stared back. The carriage continued to trundle on without them.

"Or would you rather just get left behind in this god damn--"

"I'm sorry," Aethan said.

Visoletta raised an eyebrow.

"But you shouldn't have--"

"Don't put a but after an apology. It ruins it," Visoletta said.

She turned and walked on after the carriage. Aethan found himself hurrying to catch up.

"I don't care what you are. I'm not the kind to judge--"

Visoletta gave a bark of a laugh.

"I'm serious. I don't care," Aethan said. "I don't care what you do or how you do it. I'm not like those hill folk. I shouldn't have responded the way I did, but you lied to me and--"

"I didn't lie to you, Aethan. Not about that."

"Just because you didn't outright say it, doesn't mean you didn't lie. You acted like... You led me to believe that you were a girl." He hissed the word 'girl' as though there was anyone within earshot to hear him.

"I just acted like myself. You filled in the rest. But I'm not a girl, I'm a woman."

Aethan glanced sideways at her. She certainly looked like a woman, but there were those features: the little lump in her throat, her hands, her nose. None of it fit quite right in his view of things.

Little things, perhaps, but real and obvious when he remembered to look for them.

"You're not what people think when they say woman," Aethan clarified, and Erika waved a hand impatiently in the air and sniffed.

"Don't I know it."

"What I'm trying to say is, I'm sorry for how I reacted, but I'm not sorry for stopping it. I don't want to sleep with you," Aethan said.

Visoletta nodded. "Good," she said. "Because I don't want to sleep with you either."

"What?"

She shrugged.

"But the other night--" he began.

Visoletta cut him off. "The other night, I wanted you to fuck me because you wanted to fuck me--"

"I didn't wa--"

"Yes, you did," Visoletta snapped. "You wanted it right up until you didn't. And once you didn't, I didn't want you to, and I still don't want you to. You men don't get it. You want to fuck a thing. You look at someone who doesn't want you, and you think, I'd like to fuck that thing. I'd like to do sex to it. I'd like to use that thing. Her feelings don't matter to your desire because you are the doer and she is the done to, but that's not how women see it. We don't want to fuck, or at least I don't. We want to be desired, and we want you to want us. Yes, there's attraction and personality and all the other stuff, but that's all moot if you men don't want it. So no. I don't want you to fuck me. I don't want your pity and I especially don't want a pity fuck, so keep your dick on... your side of Carlotte's skirt."

"Okay," Aethan said after a long moment. "Fine." He didn't know what else to say.

They continued on in silence for a few moments, slowly gaining on the carriage, but as they continued on, the awkward feeling in his gut began to lessen.

"So," Aethan said, "What did you lie to me about?"

"What?"

"Before, you implied that you lied to me, but not about being a woman."

Visoletta stopped again, and Aethan stopped with her. She looked up at him, and there was a sudden seriousness in her eyes. It wasn't the anger from before. The moment dragged on longer, and Aethan felt the knot begin to retie itself in his stomach. Her eyes glistened wet.

"Visoletta--"

"No," she said, a little tremble in her voice. "That's not my name."

Aethan narrowed his eyes.

"What?"

"I'm not Visoletta. I'm not even a violinist. I'm not supposed to be here."

"I..." Aethan said, his voice trailing off as he tried to make sense of what she was saying. Her eyes darted back and forth, searching his face.

"Saara mistook me, and I never corrected her. I needed to leave Sheras, and this expedition got me out, and I just went with it. I'm me. I'm still me, I've never pretended to be any different than who I am, but my name and my past are..."

Aethan stared down at her, and a few more things made sense: why she never played her violin, why she seemed so different from Carlotte, so unlike the haughty Rykers he had dealt with before. He stared down at her and wondered what it meant that her name was not Visoletta, that she was fleeing something she had done in Sheras. He had fled Sheras himself. Aethan thought about the pikelord, and he thought about old Jaaque. Whatever her true past, it couldn't have been worse than his own.

Her eyes grew wetter the longer the moment stretched on. He had a sudden urge to wipe the tears away, but that was a bridge too far. Instead, he nodded.

"Then what is your name?" he asked.

"Erika," she said.

"Erika," he repeated, and the panic in her face lessened when he said it. He nodded toward the carriage, quickly diminishing down the rough road. "We should continue on, Erika."

She smiled. "Yes, Aethan. We really should."

50

Saara heaved herself up onto the carriage's step and handed a hunk of hard bread and cheese to Val.

He grimaced. "My turn already?"

Saara nodded.

Val's grimace deepened, but he took the food. "Can't I just stay here. There's room for four--"

"Out, Val. It's your turn," Saara said.

Val stood, and Saara swung to the side to let him leave. He jumped down and stumbled a bit as the ground caught him. Saara pulled herself inside.

Saara felt for him. She knew that the life he'd led before, nestled in his rat's nest of books, was no preparation for this. He'd been a poor Ryker, but he'd still been a Ryker, and Saara doubted he had ever gone truly hungry. Saara was hungry too, but it didn't bother her as much as it did him. She had near starved as a child, but it wasn't her memories of destitution that dulled her own pain. It was something else, something that dulled everything.

Saara should have felt different. She had a promise, an explicit, witnessed promise that she would be a Ryker when they returned, and not just any Ryker, not some poor petty landlord like Val. She was going to be a DeSheras. When she returned it would be her shit that Enriq would have to bare on his nose. That thought should have given her joy, some quantum of solace, but any pleasant reaction was overwhelmed by a cold rage at the cost, at the thought of graves, and one shorter than the others.

Carlotte sat on one side of the carriage with a book cradled in her good arm, and Visoletta sat beside Saara with her head resting against the door. Neither of them looked troubled. Neither of them looked sufficiently distressed by the previous days. Neither of them seemed sorry.

Saara placed the rest of the food on the space beside Carlotte, and began to separate it into thirds.

"I hope you know what you're doing."

Saara looked up to see Carlotte watching. Her chin was high. Saara slid Carlotte's portion across the seat, and Carlotte put down her book to take it.

"With?" Saara asked.

"Aethan," Carlotte answered.

Saara glanced at Visoletta and saw that her mouth was slightly open. Asleep. Saara frowned across at Carlotte. Even after the deal and all that they had been through, Carlotte still exuded superiority. She was so much younger than Saara, but the sharpness of her chin and the angle of her eyes communicated both authority and a belief that people like Saara should naturally obey. It gave Saara an urge to give that sharp chin a sharp smack.

"We made a deal. Who I sleep with has nothing to do with it," Saara said.

Carlotte frowned. "Our deal is not in question," Carlotte said, emphasizing the word 'deal' like it was something odious. "But have you thought about what he is?"

"What do you mean?"

"He killed a dozen men in a second," Carlotte said.

Saara had heard the story. Alakeed had told it more than once. Aethan had called fire from the sky and turned the plains to ash, killed a score of horsemen with a thought. Saara thought of Aethan. The way he always looked wounded after they fucked. How easily he turned inwards at the slightest provocation or criticism. The way he stared into the campfire like he was the only one to ever have made mistakes.

"He won't do anything. You're his meal ticket," Saara said.

"Just don't..." Carlotte said, and there was a little hesitancy in her voice. "Don't push him."

"Alright. I won't."

Carlotte nodded and then began picking at her food. Saara separated what was left into two and held out one to Visoletta. She didn't take it, so Saara jostled her roughly with an elbow. No response.

"Visoletta," Saara said, and jostled her again.

Saara turned fully and leaned over to look at the woman's face. Her forehead was beaded in sweat, and her eyes darted back and forth beneath her eyelids. Visoletta's breath whimpered slightly. Saara glanced up at Carlotte. Carlotte lifted an eyebrow.

Then Visoletta jerked up and vomited.

Thin bubbly mucus shot out and spattered against the bench beside Carlotte and down Visoletta's front. Saara reeled back. Carlotte squealed and pushed herself into the corner of the Carriage. Visoletta shuddered and then slumped back into her corner.

"What's wrong with her?" Carlotte hissed.

"She's got... some kind of sickness!"

"I can see that!" Carlotte snapped.

"I... Your dress..." Saara said and lifted a finger to point at the line of bile beneath one breast. Carlotte's hand shot to her mouth, and she shuddered.

"Stop! Stop the horses!" Carlotte yelled and thumped her hand against the door frame.

The carriage stopped, and Saara smacked into the wall. Carlotte opened the door and dashed out, barely making it a step before she retched into the grass.

"What's going on?" Alakeed called.

Aethan appeared in the window.

"Visoletta..." he breathed.

"Saara!" Carlotte cried. "Get me a clean dress, or a rag or--"

Aethan reached a hand through the window.

"Stop!" Saara said, putting out her own hand like he was about to walk off a cliff. He narrowed his eyebrows at her.

"I don't know what's wrong with her. She could be contagious," Saara said.

Aethan's hand hovered in the air.

"Where would she have caught an illness? What are her symptoms?" Val called from outside.

"The hell is going on?" Alakeed called again and began thumping on the roof when no one answered her.

"Um... She's sweating. And the vomit. And--"

"Oh, for God's sake," Jane said, appearing beside Aethan in the window. She shoved him out of the way and opened the door.

Visoletta gurgled.

"You just going to let her drown?" Jane asked and then put her arm behind Visoletta. She pulled the violinist up into a sitting position so that her chin was against her chest and the bile dribbled out onto her lap.

"Get a cloth or something," Jane said, and then looked up at Saara.

"She could be contag--"

"She's not sick. She's just..." Jane looked down, frowning hard. "Just going through withdrawal."

They were all silent.

"Withdrawal?" Val said.

"Of what?" Carlotte asked.

Saara had had one knee on the bench and she let it slump off. Carlotte stood at the other door, the horror gone and her little face pinched back up into disdain.

"Of pike. What else?" Jane said, and she waved a hand at Saara. "Get off the bench, we need to lie her down on her side so she doesn't choke if she pukes again."

Saara let herself be moved to the other bench, and Jane laid the woman down on her side.

"I need a pillow--"

"Here," Aethan said, and handed the blue cloak of Carlotte's he'd been wearing bundled up through the door. Jane slid it under Visoletta's head. Saara frowned at the display. Aethan stood beyond the window, his body gleaming in the morning light like some fucking hero in a story book giving up his cloak for the damsel.

"The most renowned musician of our age," Carlotte said, "Is a pike addict?"

"You surprised?" Jane snapped. "It's all over Sheras. Half the folk I know use it."

"But she's not..."

"Poor?" Jane asked.

Carlotte's lip curled. "A fool," Carlotte said. "Or so I thought. But I've been wrong before."

Jane and Carlotte glared at each other, Jane holding up the violinist, and Carlotte with her hand in a delicate fist at her side and a bit of vomit on her breast.

"Sooooo," Alakeed called from her place on top of the carriage, "What's going on now?"

51

"I'm sorry," Erika said again.

"You don't need to be sorry," Jane repeated for the tenth time.

They were both pressed into one corner of the carriage, and Carlotte, Saara, and Aethan were pressed into the others, their feet all mixed up together in a knot. Val was out in the pounding rain in the only scrap of tent that remained, and when the press of bodies and the scent of Erika's bile had become too much, Alakeed had hopped out to join him. Aethan didn't blame her.

"I'm sorry," Erika repeated, her eyes pressed together. She lifted a filthy rag to her lips and gave a choking cough. The smell of sick intensified. Aethan felt his own bile rising. He clenched his teeth and tried to will it away.

"My God," Carlotte hissed, and she fumbled awkwardly at the latch on the shudders.

"She'll take cold," Aethan said.

"And we'll asphyxiate," Carlotte spat. The angle was awkward, but her fingers found purchase, and she pulled.

Aethan shot out a hand to stop the shutters from opening. "She'll take. Cold," he repeated.

"Then heat the cabin," she spat.

"I'm not a trained dog," Aethan spat back.

"Please don't fight. I'm sorry," Erika wheezed. "Open the shutters, Aethan, I'll be fine."

Aethan looked from Carlotte, staring daggers, to Erika, breathing quick and shallow. Saara watched him with a dark expression. He felt her eyes cutting into him. The rain beat against the carriage. The smell grew stronger.

Aethan released Carlotte's hand and shoved the door open. Rain pelted in at an angle.

"What are you doing?" Saara demanded, but Aethan did not respond.

He shouldered out the door, getting his feet tangled up in everyone else's as he did so, and then reached back to grab Carlotte's wrist. He tugged. She tugged back.

"Let go!" Carlotte cried.

"Aethan, let go of her!" Saara yelled, surging forward, but getting caught up in all the legs.

"You want to call the darkness? Come on."

"Aethan!" Saara yelled.

"Now? In this?" Carlotte demanded.

"Close the door!" Jane screamed.

"Now," Aethan said.

Carlotte hissed her disgust and then let Aethan pull her up and out into the rain.

"Madame!" Saara said.

Aethan swung the door shut and turned to Carlotte, who stood behind him. The storm wiped at her hair, tearing strands free from the band that held it to the back of her skull. The rain beat against them, and in seconds they were soaked through. Her dress looked deflated and plastered against her body underneath, the weight of the water holding it down against the wind. Her loose hair stuck to her face. She looked so small and so wet, like a rich lady's dog left out in the rain. All she needed was a tail shivering between her legs.

"Well?" Carlotte shouted.

Aethan turned and strode off the path into the whipping grass. He sat down a few strides from the road and motioned before him. She stood watching for a moment, eyebrows narrowed, lip curled, rivulets of water running down her face. Then she sat across from him.

"The first step," Aethan yelled to be heard above the wind and rain, "Is concentration. There is a place inside. A corridor you must walk to find the door. Opening the door is the second step. First, you must find it."

"How?" Carlotte yelled back.

"Stop thinking! Withdraw into yourself."

"What does that mean? How can a person withdraw--"

"Close your eyes."

"What?"

"Close your eyes!" Aethan yelled.

Carlotte rolled them and then closed them.

Aethan crawled forward so his face wasn't far from Carlotte's. "Feel the rain--"

"How can I not feel the f--"

"Shut! Up!" Aethan yelled.

Carlotte bared her teeth like a dog, but she did not speak.

"Feel the rain. Really feel it hit your face. Feel it in your hair, on your back, on your hands. Feel each individual rain drop, and every time your mind wanders to your books, or your family, or your plans, refocus on the rain. Your entire mind. On the rain."

Carlotte's face was scrunched up tight. "And then what?" Carlotte called out.

Aethan leaned in to put his head beside her ear, and he felt a tingling as he came so close to her wet neck.

"Focus. On. The rain."

He sat back. The sky beat at him. She didn't look like she was focusing. She looked like every muscle in her body was tensed, but then again, focusing didn't look like much of anything. It had been summer when Ashatee had taught him. He'd had the buzzing of flies and gnats and the pain of the hole in his side to focus on.

What is pain? Ashatee had asked him. *Think on the pain. Examine it. What does pain feel like? Why does it hurt? What is hurt? You are lucky, little soldier boy, to have so good a lesson.*

He didn't feel lucky then. He didn't feel lucky now, sitting half naked in the rain, his anger and annoyance burning out now that Carlotte wasn't talking. She didn't look like she felt lucky either. He didn't understand why a woman like her was not running home after all that had happened, but a lot had happened recently that he didn't understand. He thought of Erika, laid out in the carriage. He thought of her lips on his. Of the way she smiled at him and talked the hours of the day away. Of the squish of her cock in his hand.

That last thought was troubling. His disgust was less visceral than it had been. The violent urge to push her away was dulled. What did that say about him?

Aethan stood and walked back to the carriage. He pulled the door open, heaved himself inside, and closed it behind him.

"Where is Carlotte?" Saara asked.

Jane didn't seem to care. Erika was asleep with her head resting on Jane's breast.

"She's learning," he said, and nestled back into the wall. "A little rain won't kill her."

52

"And there," Saara said, placing the heel of bread into Alakeed's hand, "is the last of it."

Alakeed ripped the bread in two and popped one half into her mouth. Her cheeks bulged out with it as she chewed, and not four chews later, Alakeed was swallowing. Saara took a different approach to the hunger. She slipped the last of her own bread into her mouth and chewed slowly and well. The taste of the stale bread was delicious to her, but when she finally swallowed, she had to admit she felt no fuller for the waiting.

They sat atop the caravan, the horse's reins clenched between Alakeed's knees, and they looked out at Lake Sharathorn, stretching a dozen or so miles towards the horizon and dotted with fishing vessels. At its end was a clump of buildings that was the town of Thorlaille. The end was in sight. Before night came, she would be spending what little was left of her life savings to feed and outfit the remainder of the expedition, and she would have no more power over Carlotte. Once that money was spent, all Saara would have was Carlotte's word. Saara's scowl deepened.

Aethan and Visoletta were walking out in front of the carriage, chatting on and on and on as though they were out for a stroll in the Nouvre Vil, and not at the tail end of a starvation march. Visoletta was doing much better. Her withdrawals had calmed after about a week, and yesterday she had managed to resume the walking schedule. Just in time for it to be over.

"Pah," Alakeed said.

Saara glanced over at the hill woman. She had a similar scowl on her face. Saara didn't blame her. She'd been stuck on the bench for two weeks straight. Saara didn't doubt her ass had been rubbed raw and bloody.

"Are you enjoying this hunger, Sikka?" Alakeed said, and then a grin took over her face. "Not for much longer, eh? When the Ryker makes you a sister, then hunger will be as foreign to you as I am."

"Aye," Saara grumbled, "and you'll be rich."

"Aye," Alakeed echoed, "so long as we can keep the Ryker from getting herself killed."

Saara's disdain for the hill woman had lessened. She was another of Carlotte's minions whose usefulness had already dried up, another who was dependent on Carlotte's word. She knew that Alakeed felt the helplessness. Behind all her smiles and jokes, there was a familiar rage, and at times, Saara caught her staring down at her stump leg with a deepening frown.

The road got better the closer they came to Thorlaille. It was still dirt, but was somewhat maintained. As they came down into the valley, it skirted along the edge of the lake, and if Saara had not been so hungry and if Visoletta and Aethan had not appeared to be having such a pleasant time, Saara would have thought it quite beautiful. She could hear the two talking, not well enough to make out the words, but the constant tittering of Visoletta's laugh grated on Saara's mind. She made a mental note to make sure Aethan had a private room tonight so that she could pay a visit and remind him that pleasant conversation was only good for so much. She imagined knocking on the door and there being no answer. She imagined putting her ear to the wood and hearing Visoletta's laugh from within. Her fingers clenched onto the wooden bench.

"What will you do?" Saara asked to get her mind on something else. "Once you have the money. Back to the badlands?"

Alakeed gave a dry laugh.

"They are called the badlands for a reason, Sikka."

"Then to Sheras? Carlotte might give you--"

"No, too much God in the Dominion. I will go to the Freelands, I think. It is said the only God there is gold, and I'll have enough of it to be a prophet."

"I've never been. I hear it's all degenerates and profiteers."

"Like our witch doctor friend?"

Saara looked over to see if the woman was having a go at her. But if Alakeed was, she was doing it subtly.

"He was a Freelander trying to sell guns to the Dominion. Not sure what else to call it."

"And you, Sikka? What will you do when Carlotte makes you a Ryker?"

Saara opened her mouth and then closed it again. She wasn't actually sure. What does one do after one makes it? Continue to make it, she supposed.

"Buy land," Saara said. "Out in the country around Sheras for farming. The city is always growing, and the more people, the more food they need to farm."

Now it was Alakeed's turn to raise an eyebrow.

"You? A farmer?"

Saara scoffed.

"Not me. Tenants will farm. I'll just collect the rent."

"Rent?" Alakeed asked.

"For the right to use my land."

Alakeed was silent for a moment. "Why don't they just work some other land?"

"They don't have any. Only Rykers can own land."

"Hmmm," Alakeed said. "That's a stupid system."

Saara only shrugged. There was nothing to argue against.

They fell to silence then, watching the lake roll by. It was large enough to have small waves that sloshed against the rocky shore. The plains of tall grass they'd ridden through were gone, and in their place were pebbly shores and scraggly-looking evergreen trees.

Thorlaille was larger than she'd thought. She could make out more buildings as they approached. It was still nothing to Sheras, but compared to Forepost, it was something to behold.

A few hours later, her stomach was eating itself, and the edge of the town approached. The road was well-maintained now. It was flattened, and the edges were marked out with fallen logs and piles of rocks. They passed several docks that increased in size, with small shacks built up beside them. Saara saw no one. Presumably, they were all out on their ships. She could see the boats, sailing about, with their nets dragging behind them.

They continued on, and the wall came into view. It was only a few strides high, and it was made of wood. A squat tower stood at one end beside the water, and a closed gate was beside it. Aethan and Visoletta stood before the gate. Alakeed stopped the carriage just behind them. Saara looked about but saw no one.

"Maybe we knock?" she said.

Alakeed grunted.

Saara gathered what strength she had left and swung down from the bench. Carlotte stepped out of the carriage. Her arm was out of the sling, but she was in the habit of letting it hang to one side.

"How do we pass?" Carlotte asked.

Saara shrugged and craned her neck upwards. She shaded her eyes against the late afternoon sun and saw movement.

"Hey!" she called out. "Let us--"

She was interrupted by the gate swinging open and the hinges screaming in protest. Saara looked for someone to take credit, but there was no one.

"Thanks," Saara muttered, and then followed Aethan and Visoletta in.

"Where is everyone?" Visoletta asked.

Wooden buildings rose up on either side of the path. They were well made, with wooden pillars supporting wooden eaves over porches. There was a sign in one window reading "Bits and Pieces," and beside it a wooden sign reading "Closed." Saara swiveled around and looked up at the tower, but whoever she'd seen before was gone.

"Perhaps it's abandoned," Val said, stepping out of the carriage. "Like Forepost."

Jane stepped out beside him. They were all on foot now, except for Alakeed, who still sat atop her bench.

"The lake is full of boats," Carlotte said.

"There's someone," Jane said, pointing down the street. Saara followed her finger and saw an old man leaning on a porch railing some ways down. Aethan started forward, and the rest followed.

"Excuse me, sir?" Saara called out.

He didn't respond. They got closer, and the old man took a pipe out of his coat and stuck it in his mouth.

"Sir?" Saara called.

The man struck a match and puffed at the pipe until a plume of smoke gushed from his lips. He looked up and pulled a walking stick out from behind the railing. He raised his hand in greeting and then stepped off the porch toward them. His stick scraped against the dirt.

Aethan walked up to meet him and spoke. "Where is every--"

The man lunged forward and blew a lungful of smoke into Aethan's face. It billowed around his head, and the air was filled with the scent of lavender and sage. Aethan sputtered and stumbled back, and then the doors all around them burst open.

Bluebacks ran out of the buildings. Alakeed screamed something in Altishi. Saara pulled the knife from her belt and was slammed into from behind. She fell and her chin scraped against the cobblestone. She scrambled forward and spun around. A blueback was getting to his feet, and another charged at her with a thick wooden stick clutched in one hand. He reared up to slam the club down, but Saara kicked out at his knee, and it crunched. He howled and fell backward. Saara got to her feet. The one who'd hit her from behind was still on his hands and knees, and Saara kicked at his head. Her foot caught his chin, and his neck snapped upward. She reached for the knife at her belt. It was gone. She'd dropped it, but there was no time to find it. Everyone was yelling. She saw Aethan on his side. Several bluebacks kicked at him, and the old man crouched beside him and spewed smoke over him like a dragon. More bluebacks advanced on her, all with sticks in their hands. A man all in black with white fringe and a white feather sticking out from his tricorn hat stepped out onto the road. His nose was sharply hooked. Two bluebacks pulled Alakeed down from the bench while she screamed bloody murder.

Saara reached back and pulled the knife from her boot. She tossed the thin blade from one hand to the other and spread her feet out. The three men advancing on her slowed and exchanged unsure glances with each other.

"Come on, you--"

And then there were hands on her back. She tried to spin, but more hands joined, and she was wrestled to the ground. One of the bluebacks ran forward and cracked her wrist with his billy club. Saara grunted and dropped the knife before the next blow came. Someone was on her back now, she could feel a knee crushing her neck into the road.

"Get off me," she wheezed, but there was no answer. Her arms were pulled behind her, and she felt rough cord being cinched around her wrists.

Her face was mashed into the road, but she could see that the others had stopped struggling. Aethan wasn't moving at all. The men above him were breathing hard. Alakeed didn't look to be in much better shape, on her belly in the dirt, being trussed up just like Saara was. Val was cowering on the ground with his arms around his face. Carlotte was on her ass, and blood trickled down from her hairline. Jane and Visoletta stood in the middle of it all. Visoletta's hands were in the air. Jane's were out to the side, as though to steady a world swirling around her. For a moment, all was still, and then the inquisitor made his way through.

The white feather in his hat quivered, and the spurs on his boot jangled with each step. He stopped before Carlotte.

"Do you have any idea who I am?" Carlotte asked. The familiar tone of authority was in her voice, but it was shaky and sounded weak from where she was on the ground. Saara could see her hand trembling.

The inquisitor pointed one long, gloved finger at her. "The Madame Carlotte DeSheras."

He turned and pointed again and again as he spoke. "Monsieur Valieer Saadermont. The servant Saara Akar. The Boneman witch. Ah..." His finger pointed at Alakeed, and she snarled. "A hill woman." His eyes narrowed, and he flicked a finger at one of the bluebacks on top of her. He reared up and cracked his stick across her skull. She slumped.

"You already had her!" Jane cried out.

The inquisitor's finger flipped to her. "Can't be too careful. All it takes is an instant and then... the town is ashes. Intellectual contagions, of course. You... one of the lady's maids?" He looked around at all of them again. "Mr. Gin said there were more of you."

"They're buried," Jane said.

"Ah," he said. His eyes flicked from Visoletta to Jane. "And the one that claimed to be Visoletta Corlionne?"

"Dead!" Visoletta spurted. Visoletta pointed to herself and Jane. "We were her maids."

"Hmmm," the inquisitor said. Saara saw Carlotte glance wearily at Val, but neither of them said anything. The inquisitor waved a hand. "Go. I've no mandate for the help."

Visoletta and Jane looked at each other, and then they backed away and hurried off down the road. The inquisitor turned again to Carlotte and extended a hand.

"Come, Madame. Let's get you somewhere more fitting of your station."

53

As Erika and Jane hurried down the side streets of Thorlaille, the sounds of the expedition's arrest grew fainter behind them. The city near the gate was dense, but the streets were empty. At first, it seemed a ghost town, but then Erika looked into the windows and saw the people peering around drapery to watch them go by, as though they'd been ordered off the streets. Because of Aethan? Then the inquisitor knew what Aethan was, and there was only one thing that could happen.

Erika had never seen a witch burning, but she had heard of them. They didn't happen in the city, but out in the countryside where the inquisition rooted through small towns for charlatans and traitors, witches were found and witches were burned. Small towns like Thorlaille...

Erika stumbled into a wall and cursed. She saw the sticks of the bluebacks rising and falling, beating Aethan senseless. The sickening thuds. The first few gasps of pain before Aethan had gone silent. Erika's own ribs cried out in sympathy.

She clutched at the stones, and the nausea in her stomach raged. She had put on a strong face the previous morning. She had been tired of sitting and taking Saara's dirty looks, and she had lied and told Aethan she felt fine, that the withdrawals were over. She'd lied because she'd needed out of that carriage almost as much as she needed a cut. Almost as much.

She thrust her hand into her pocket and felt for the gold coin's reassuring presence. She could do a lot with that gold coin. Maybe she could bribe a guard or hire some men to break Aethan out of wherever they were keeping him. Or maybe she could get a drop or two so that she could think straight. Erika pushed away from the wall and stumbled after Jane.

They emerged from the alley, and the city was suddenly alive. The buildings here were not made of stone, and the windows had no glass. Two children played in the dirt road, and a thin man watched them from the steps of a building where he was mending a net across his lap.

Erika looked left, and then right, and then back down the alley they had emerged from. Her heart was beating faster and faster. They needed to do something. Erika fingered the coin in her pocket.

"Where should we go?" she asked.

Jane stared at the two children playing in the street. She snarled and then turned on her heel and headed back down the alley. Erika ran to keep up with her.

"Yes, we should go back. Go back and do something. Get them free..." Erika said, trailing off. "How are we going to get them free?"

"We're not," Jane said.

"Oh, right. Then... what are we going to do?"

"I'm going to go back and demand my wages, and then I'm going to go home," Jane said.

Erika stopped, stunned, but Jane did not, and Erika ran to catch up to her.

"You're not going to leave them."

"Yes, I am."

Erika cut in front and blocked her way. Jane snarled again and put her hands on her hips.

"We need to get them out," Erika said, slightly out of breath from her little sprint. Her stomach roiled, and she felt the bile rising in her throat.

"Get them out," Jane repeated. She took in a deep breath through her nose. "I have kids. Just like those two back there, and they are waiting for me to come back. Hannah's kids are waiting for their mother to come back too."

Jane's voice broke a little, and she scrunched up her face. "So I'm going to demand my wages, and Hannah's too, and I'm going to go home to them. Get out of my way."

Jane shoved past, and Erika stumbled into the wall.

"They're going to burn him," Erika said. "They're going to kill Aethan."

Jane stopped. She stood there, frozen, for several moments, and then she turned to face Erika. "And what are you going to do about it?"

"I..." Erika glanced around, as though the answers might be plastered on the walls of the alley. "I don't know. I need you to help me."

Jane walked back to Erika so they were only a few steps apart. "You mean, you need me to do it for you," Jane said.

Erika shrank back a little at the intensity of Jane's glare, and her hand found its way into her pocket to finger the coin.

"You're a nice girl, Visoletta-- Erika, whatever your name is, and it was refreshing to see what I thought was a rich person who was kind, but you're not a rich person. You're not a violinist. You're a pike addict who accidentally came into more money than my family has ever seen, and what did you do with it?" Jane raised her hands and then let them drop at her side. "Nothing. You bought pike. You got my friend back into something she quit a long time ago. And then, then you came back from the badlands, I thought you were on my side. But you weren't. You couldn't even do that."

"I said I was sorry!" Erika cried. "I didn't side with Carlotte either."

Jane shrugged. "I know. You were on your own side. You always are. I don't owe that Boneman anything, and I certainly don't owe Carlotte De fucking Sheras anything. Maybe you do, but doing something about it would be hard, and you..." She poked her finger in Erika's chest. "You only do what is easy."

Erika felt at the coin in her pocket, and had a sudden urge to hand it to Jane. It would make a real difference in Jane's life, and if Erika gave it to her, it would prove that Jane was wrong, that Erika wasn't selfish, that she did the right thing, the hard thing. Erika felt her arm tense to do it, but her hand stayed in her pocket.

"I thought you were my friend," Erika said.

Jane pulled her lips back into a grimace. "I thought you were mine. We should have gone back to Forepost."

Then Jane turned and walked away.

Erika wanted to chase after her, but what would she say if she did? Instead, she turned the other way and walked out into the street. The children had stopped their game and were watching her now, and Erika realized that she was crying. She gripped the coin hard in one hand and wiped her nose with the other.

"Come on in now," the net mender said, and Erika didn't wait to see if the children obeyed.

She turned left and hurried down the street. She didn't know where she was going, but she knew what she was after. Thorlaille wasn't very big, and soon she emerged from a rundown lane to see another wall of the city, and against it, ramshackle huts housing an altogether different sort of Dominioneer. The afternoon was warm, and the door to one of the huts gaped open. A man lay inside. Erika could just make out the rising and falling of his chest, and in the door frame, a woman sprawled, her head back against the wood, her hands lying on either side of her, opening and closing. Erika walked and then ran to them. The woman's eyes flicked over to her as she came.

"Eh?" the woman said.

"I need a cut. Where can I get one?" Erika asked.

The woman watched her blankly, and Erika wondered if she'd heard, but then the woman raised a hand and pointed down the lane. Erika's eyes followed it to a gatehouse in the city wall. There was a wooden chair in the shade beside it, and a blueback sat there, slouched and unmoving. Beside him were more huts, and more people laid out in them.

"Which house?" Erika asked, and the woman shook her wrist, still pointing in the same direction. Erika squatted down so she was even with her.

"If you tell me, I'll bring some back for you."

The woman blinked, deep in a ripple, and then leaned slowly toward her, drifting down agonizingly slow.

"Eric," she mumbled. "Soljur."

"Soljur?" Erika repeated and looked back down the lane at the open gate. The blueback was leaning back on two legs of his chair. His gun was propped against the wall.

"Soldier?" Erika said, but the woman didn't respond.

Erika stood and walked toward the gate. She could see the road continuing out past it, south or north or wherever. Erika didn't know where she was or what she was facing, but she saw the scraggly trees and the rocky ground and the afternoon sky above. The blueback turned his head towards her and eased his chair back down onto all four legs. He reached out and grabbed his rifle and stood as she approached. She stopped a dozen strides from him. He gestured towards the open gate.

"Ways clear if you're going out," he said. His blue coat had faded to gray, and the cuffs of his sleeves were frayed at the edges. He squinted. "You new in town? Come with the Ryker?"

The Ryker. Erika thought of Carlotte and Saara and mostly of Aethan, and wondered where they were now. She wondered if Jane had gotten to them and if she'd gotten her money. She knew it must have been half an hour since she'd seen them, but it seemed to her like an instant, like she was waking up from a dream. She thought of the trek through the badlands, watching Aethan's muscles flexing as he walked naked through the grass. She thought of the way he'd kissed her and the way he'd held her before it all went wrong, and she thought of the way he would scream when they burned him at the stake.

"Miss?" the blueback said. Erika wiped her nose with the back of her hand.

"Pike," she said, and the man raised his eyebrows.

"Really now?" He glanced around the street and then laid the rifle back against the wall.

"You got coin then?"

Erika nodded. Her stomach was in her throat, and her mouth was dry.

"Ten pennies for a dab," he said.

"I need a knife too," she said. He crossed his arms.

"All I got is the pike. You wanna swim or not?"

"What about that?" Erika said and pointed at the knife at his hip. The man looked down and then pulled the blade out of its sheath. It was short, maybe half a foot long, but the sharp edge gleamed in the sunlight.

"This," he said. "Is out of your price range. You got the pennies or not?"

Erika paused. The thought of the pike made her knees weak and her mouth wet, but she thought also of Aethan, wherever he was, and what was about to happen to him. She wanted to help him. She really did. Erika looked down at the gold coin in her hand, all that was left of Visoletta's fortune. It could buy her a lot of things. Could it pay off a guard? Could it buy Aethan's freedom? Erika didn't think so, so she held it out instead. The man's eyebrows rose.

"I can't make change for that," he said.

"Give me the knife. And the pike," she said. "All of it."

54

The room seemed as though it had been made by someone who'd heard of style but never actually seen it. The wooden window frames were painted gold with filigree in thin red lines. The rug was red to match, but it wasn't large enough to cover the wooden floor, and the sun had bleached parts of it to a pale pink. Several chairs sat around the room, each with cushions of a slightly different shade of crimson, and one long overstuffed couch entirely of white. Carlotte's own dress was dark red, flowing down from a belt around her stomach to her ankles. She imagined this is what a brothel must look like, or a body being opened up.

Carlotte paced back and forth, her borrowed heels digging into the carpet with each turn, and occasionally glanced out the window at the town square. It was done in the style of many other Dominion townships, equally prepared for a parade or a desperate last defense. A large statue of the Mareshal stood in its center. Two long posts had been erected between the statue and Carlotte's window, and workers busied themselves piling wood at their bases.

Carlotte caught herself humming several times, like an endless groan that wouldn't quite come out, bubbling in her throat, threatening to burst forth into a scream. She felt dizzy and finally had to sit down to keep from falling over.

The door opened, and Enriq, her mother's assistant, stepped through. Carlotte drew back in surprise.

His lips were pressed, and his chin was lifted. He met her gaze and then inclined his head in deference, a trick Saara had never quite gotten the hang of. "Madame Carlotte DeSheras--"

"Enriq. Why are you here? Did my mother send you?"

Enriq looked up at her. "The Madame Cainia DeSheras did not wish this to happen, but she had no choice."

"Why are you--"

Enriq stepped to the side, and Carlotte's words dried up on her tongue.

"The Lord Harold Orlient," Enriq announced, and Carlotte's fiancée stepped into the room.

He stood tall as ever, back straight and with hair flattened against his scalp. He wore a black coat with white ruffles at his wrists and gleaming silver embroidery along his collar, and in his left eye, beneath the iris, was a dark red smudge. Harold lifted two fingers and motioned Enriq away. Enriq opened his mouth as though to speak, but then thought better of it. He inclined his head once more and scurried out the door. It closed with a soft click.

Harold looked down at her, and she looked up at him, and neither of them said anything. The time stretched out, and Carlotte's heart beat faster with each second. Finally, Harold stepped forward and sat in one of the chairs. He crossed one leg over the other and rested his hands in his lap.

"Why are you here?" Carlotte whispered. She hadn't meant to whisper, and she swallowed and tried again. "Why are you here?"

"To get my fiancée back. A better question is why are you here?" He cast a glare around the room and scowled, as though everything in it offended him. She couldn't quite blame him. The decor offended her too.

"The entire city is talking of your disappearance. Not just the Rykers. Your name is in the mouths of all the little Dominioneers. Soldiers. Shopkeepers. Addicts. Where oh where did the Heir DeSheras go? The stories I've heard about my fiancée. The gossip. That you ran from me to be with a Boneman. That I had you killed. Half the city thinks you killed that violinist, Visoletta Corlionne." Harold glared angrily at the crown molding along the ceiling's edge, then his gaze snapped back to her. "You didn't, did you?"

"What? Visoletta's not dead."

Harold let out a breath.

"She is. She was found dead in her dressing room, Carlotte, on the same night you left for this ridiculous expedition!"

Harold winced at his tone and forced his face into something approaching normal.

"Was this all because of that night?" he demanded.

"What?" Carlotte asked. Her heart was still pounding and she was gripping the arm rest of her chair so hard her hands were trembling. None of what Harold was saying made any sense.

Harold stood. He took a step towards her, and without thinking, Carlotte cringed back into her chair. Harold stopped and glared down at her. His hands were uneasy at his sides, opening and closing. "I'm not a monster," he spat. "You are the one who nearly took out my eye, and you don't see me acting like I was assaulted."

Carlotte's eyes widened. "You tried to rape me," she said.

"Fantasy!" Harold cried, and he waved his hand as though to swat her accusation away. "That's a gross misrepresentation, and you know it. You are as responsible, if not more responsible, for how things turned out. The way you were acting."

"The way I acted? You held me down and--"

"It was a moment of passion that you incited!"

"I told you no!" Carlotte yelled.

"And so you ran halfway across the damn world?" Harold screamed. His face was mottled with rage. "You are such a smart woman and yet--" He rapped a finger against his temple. "Think of what could have gone wrong. Your man, Mr. Gin, told us about the savages. How you could have turned around at multiple points, and yet you kept on all because of... a misunderstanding."

Carlotte was silent for a moment, and then stood. "You think I left because of you?" Carlotte said. "You think you're that important to me?"

Harold put his hands on his hips. He tapped one shoe against the carpet. "I think you're just like your mother. Unwilling to accept your own decline."

Carlotte's jaw dropped. "How dare--"

"You can't stop the way Sheras is changing. This match was a reach for my family, but now, after the gossip you've dragged your name through, it will come across as charity."

Carlotte let out a breath that was half exasperation and half laugh. "No amount of iron will make the Orlient more than an uppity country family," Carlotte spat. "I went through Irondale. I saw where you come from. Soot, misery, dreams of grandeur."

Harold looked at her, breathing through his nose in shallow huffs. "You're smarter than that," Harold said, "Irondale is industry. And growing power."

"My family is power," Carlotte hissed.

Harold took a step closer. "Not. Anymore."

His face didn't turn nasty. It didn't look like she imagined her own must have looked in that moment. It looked tired, and sad, and impatient for her to understand.

Carlotte's sneer fell. "What are you talking about?"

"This adventure of yours. You've no idea the embarrassment it's caused your mother. And with Visoletta's murder? The whole city was in an uproar. The outer city practically rioted, and my family provided a solution."

"No," Carlotte said. "My mother wouldn't let you."

"She tried. But the Balit turned, the council sided with my father, and the city invited the Grand Inquisitor to take control of the streets. He obliged. Your mother isn't in control of the council anymore, and your mother no longer controls the city. Perhaps you'll have to change your name."

Carlotte took a step back and steadied herself against the chair. He was obviously lying. He had to be lying. Her family had always controlled the council. Always.

Carlotte shook her head. "Harold. I'm not out here because I'm running from you. I'm out here because I'm on to something extraordinary. The man I was with. The Freelander your men beat, he's--"

"God in heaven," Harold swore. "So you've bought into these fairy tales."

"It's not a fairy tale, Harold. It's real. That Freelander is a—"

"Witch?" Harold said.

"Ah… yes, how did—"

"Inquisitor Hawthorne won't shut up about him. Please don't tell me you believe in this… fantasy."

Carlotte took in a deep breath. "It's… real, Harold. I've seen it."

Harold strode past her to the window and flung the curtain wide. Carlotte could see workmen gathering wood around the posts in the square. Harold jabbed a finger at the glass.

"That is what will become of your Boneman, Carlotte. He'll be burned to ash like the charlatan he is."

He turned his finger to her. "In the morning, he and that hill savage will be burned, and then you are coming back with me to Sheras. I've no wish to be crude, and I don't want you to view me as a brute, but you have no choice in the matter. You gave up that right when you ran off into the wilderness like a wild girl. We are betrothed, Carlotte. And that means something. It means we are bound to one another, and I will not let you destroy the last shreds of your credibility and your dignity by allowing you to entertain this nonsense for one moment longer."

"I'm not allowed?" Carlotte said, her hands bunching at her sides.

"No. You're not! You have one choice left, Carlotte. Will you return willingly, so you can take your rightful place in society as the Heir DeSheras? Or will you make me haul you back kicking and screaming, and dragging the last of your family's dignity through the muck?"

He took a step towards her. "I'm not your enemy, Dear. Not unless you make me." Harold turned and strode to the door. "We leave before noon tomorrow."

Carlotte straightened her back and tried to keep her lip from trembling. Harold's posture was ramrod straight. The picture of a well-bred man doing his odious duty. This would be her life when she returned. He would be her life.

"I don't want to marry you," Carlotte said.

Harold stopped. He was frozen for several moments, and then he turned, his jaw tight and his eyes deeply sad. "As though what we want ever mattered."

He turned and left the room.

55

Saara would have paced, but there was no room to do so in her little cell. A single stride took her from one wall to the other. There was not even enough room to lie down flat. If she wanted to sleep, she would have to curl up into a ball or sit against the wall like the others.

She could see Alakeed and Aethan in their own cells across from her. They sat on the floor with their backs against the stone and their hands manacled above their heads. Their ankles were similarly manacled to eyelets set into the floor, though Alakeed's stump was left free. Saara had watched with numb amusement when the bluebacks had tried and then given up manacling a leg with no foot.

They were underground, and there were no windows. The only light came from the two glowing braziers between the cells. There were herbs smoldering on top of each of them, filling the small dungeon with smoke that smelled of lavender and sage and burned the back of Saara's throat. Her head felt strange, jumping from idea to idea, never able to stay still.

Instead of pacing, Saara sat against the bars, counted her heartbeats, and thudded her forehead into the bars on every eighth beat, filling the space with a dull metallic ring.

"Qi shan ba'Areek?"

Saara looked up and saw nothing different. The orange light

was so dim she could barely make out Alakeed's shape, but then she moved, and Saara heard the clink of chains.

"You're awake," Saara said.

Alakeed did not answer for a moment. Saara heard metal rasping against stone.

"Qi shan ba'Areek!" Alakeed shouted, her voice hoarse from the smoke. There was a flurry of clinking metal, a cry of pain, and then silence.

"Alakeed?" Saara said.

"A pol kat salomleo ustal ash'ravat," Alakeed whispered, and then she coughed and was silent.

Finally, she spoke in Dominion.

"Do they think us witches, Sikka?"

Saara did not answer.

"They must to burn such Palamur," Alakeed continued. "The Boneman is here?"

"Yes, Saara rasped. "One cell over."

"Boneman!" Alakeed yelled. "Burn this place down. Kill these Assa efataleeda!"

"He's not awake. They beat him badly," Saara said.

She wasn't sure Aethan would wake up at all. She had seen many beatings in her life, and this had been one of the worst. May as well stab a man as beat him like they did.

"Ah," Alakeed said, and then quieter, "What does your country do to witches?"

"My country doesn't believe in witches," Saara said. "But in the countryside, the inquisitors burn the ones who claim to be."

Alakeed was silent for a moment.

"And we are in the countryside, no?" Alakeed laughed and then coughed. "Carlotte is getting out of a lot of debt today, eh, Sikka?"

There was a screeching of hinges, and white light poured in from the left. Saara stood and pressed her face into the bars.

"What is happening?" Alakeed asked.

A man coughed, and then she heard the sound of striking stone, and firelight flickered in the smoke. The sound of boots came down the steps.

"God in heaven, they'll suffocate in all of this!" a man said. She knew the voice, but its place eluded her.

Saara readied herself for something. She didn't know what, perhaps to throw herself against the bars and demand her freedom, perhaps to grab at whoever walked by, but when the first face came into her view, she was stunned.

"Enriq..." Saara said.

The man servant of Cainia DeSheras walked down the aisle between the cells with a torch in one hand and a handkerchief held over his face with the other. An inquisitor walked past him and tossed new herbs onto each of the braziers.

"Is that really necessary?" Enriq asked, his voice muffled by the cloth.

"It is. The risk is great, and the inconvenience is mild."

The inquisitor took in a deep breath of the smoke and blew it out like a dragon into the air. He knocked his knuckle against one of the bars, letting loose a dull ringing. "Would that we could burn them now. The stakes are ready, but Hawthorne wants an audience. Come noon tomorrow, they will be ash, and the Dominion will be that much safer."

"I am no witch," Alakeed said, and the inquisitor glanced down at her. He shrugged.

"Of course. Witches do not exist. There is only God."

"Then why all this?" Enriq asked, gesturing at the braziers. "For pretenders?"

The inquisitor swiveled on his heel to look at Enriq. The look behind his eyes was dead, like a school teacher inured to the babble of children. "Would you like to ask Inquisitor Hawthorne that question?" he asked.

Enriq shook his head, and the inquisitor nodded. He turned towards the steps.

"Be quick about your visit then, and do not touch the coals, or I will be the least of your worries."

He disappeared up the steps, and Saara heard the door slam shut. She was left with Enriq staring at her from over his kerchief, one side of his face lit yellow and orange from the flickering torch and the other in shadow. He dropped the kerchief to his side and scowled at her.

"You're not here to get me out," Saara said. It was not a question.

Enriq nodded all the same and then spoke. "The damage you have caused to our family. You've no idea what we've been through in Sheras because of this little stunt."

"What you've been through?" Saara said. "I've been attacked, Enriq. I've seen my people die. I've dug graves with my own hands."

Enriq's scowl only deepened. "And who is at fault for that?"

"Carlotte!" Saara cried and slammed her fists into the bars.

Enriq flinched, but he did not retreat.

"Tell me you would not have done the same if Cainia had ordered it," Saara said.

Enriq came a step closer. "Carlotte is not the mistress of the House DeSheras. Cainia is. She ordered you to stop, but you went on anyway. It is our duty to advise and keep the Rykers from being destroyed by their own bad ideas. Carlotte is a child, and it was your job to persuade her away from this disaster. You didn't. You failed. But, I suppose it is Carlotte's fault in the end, bringing street trash into the tower."

Saara exploded forward, slamming her face into the bars and reaching through to throttle him. He was out of her reach, but he cried out and staggered away anyway, dropping his torch to the ground.

"You little shit," Saara spat. "Asking me if I knew what damage I'd done to our family, as though you were a part of it. You are a servant, a trained dog, Enriq, and when your usefulness is up, Cainia will put you down to make room for another!"

"Then what does that make you, Saara? A dog that failed? A dog that bit the queen? The Lady DeSheras doesn't take to being bitten. She told me to bring Carlotte back... without you."

He gestured behind him at Alakeed and Aethan. "These two will burn tomorrow, but you will stay in here. The inquisition has been vigorous as of late, especially in these little border towns. Perhaps you will be lucky, and they will take you outside to be shot for a traitor, or perhaps you will just... stay."

"I am no traitor," Saara hissed.

"You betrayed the Lady DeSheras."

"I followed Carlotte."

"And that," Enriq said, "was your mistake. Goodbye, Saara.

Sheras is cleaner without you."

"Burn in hell!" Saara screamed.

Enriq did not answer. He bent down to pick up his torch and then turned and walked up the steps.

Saara heard the door open, and then heard it thud closed. Saara screamed and smashed her fists against the iron bars. They did not break, but eventually her anger did, and Saara slumped down to the floor and tried not to cry.

56

Erika reached out for her violin, scrabbling at the dirt with her fingers, but she couldn't find it. She wanted to play. She could feel the music inside her, on the edge of bursting out of its own accord. The pike swam with it. Its current rippled through her, lifting her breast to the heavens with song. All she needed was to pick up her violin and put bow to string, and her soul would speak with crystalline music.

Her fingers kept scrabbling, scraping at dirt and stone, and finally she leaned her head over and opened her eyes. The light was bright, painfully bright, but she forced her eyes open all the same.

There was nothing beside her, just the street and the muck and the detritus of the city. She turned to the other and saw Nicolette and... the other one, the man who'd been asleep when she came in and was asleep now, curled around Nicolette's frail form like a child wrapped around a knitted doll. They both lay in the dark of the hut. Erika was propped up in the doorway, half in the dark and half in the light. There was no violin in that darkness, so Erika looked down at her lap and saw the soldier's knife and the vial of liquid silver.

She didn't have a violin. It had been lost, of course, out there in the badlands. She'd taken a swim and lived a dream as Visoletta, and when the ripples had faded, when she awoke, that dream had ended. Friends were dead, Erika was nothing and no one, and the violin was lost.

Erika lifted the knife and saw a bit of blood on its edge. Her blood, she knew. She could feel the sting it had left on her thigh. She had a wild fantasy then, of pressing the blade into her neck and pressing until she could press no more. She should have played the violin. She'd only held it once, that night in the tent. She should have played it, let the music speak through her, and free her from the cage that was her place in life. Music knew no society, no rules, no shame. Music was the language of the soul, and it told no lies. But the violin was gone. Lost to the badlands, burned up in Aethan's fire.

Aethan.

Erika sat bolt upright. How long had it been? She squinted and thought very hard, trying to push the pike out of the way so she could bring her mind together. Had it been night? It had been. She had awoken when it was dark, and when she went to use the knife, it had slipped and cut her hand. Or was that a dream? Erika looked down and saw the fresh gash there, between her finger and her thumb. It was real, and now it was light, so the morning had come. Was Aethan still alive? She thought of him then, pulling her hands away from her dress that night in the badlands. She thought of how their bodies had tensed and relaxed together before it all fell apart. She imagined him burning, his skin falling away, his mouth wide open in a final scream.

Erika pushed to her feet. She had to save him. She had to do something. Was he already dead? Erika staggered out into the street, the pike clutched in one hand and the knife in the other. She looked to the gate, but it was closed, and she saw no guard. She braced herself against a wall and waited for the ripple to pass through her. It came, it crested, and then she heard a note on the wind. It pierced through the ripple and snapped her head around. Had she imagined it? No, it was real. It was long and high and brassy, a horn calling all to gather. To gather for what?

For a burning.

Acid rose in her, climbing out of her stomach and burning at her throat. She held her hand against her chest and gasped at the pain.

Aethan.

Aethan was going to die unless she saved him.

Erika stepped toward the sound and then stopped. She needed help. She spun, and her eyes settled on Nicolette and her partner in the hovel. Erika ran to them and slapped softly against Nicolette's cheek until the woman's eyes opened and slowly came into focus.

"Wha--"

"I need your help. Both of you. Come on!" Erika said, and then began slapping at the man's face. She'd not learned his name. He wasn't responding. Asleep like the dead.

"Wake him up," Erika pleaded to Nicolette. "Quick, you owe me for the pike."

"G'fuck y'self," Nicolette mumbled. She threw the crook of her elbow over her eyes.

"No, no, up!" Erika cried and started back on her, flicking at her face. Nicolette lifted her other arm to try and ward off Erika's attacks, but Erika could actually see what she was doing and darted around her defenses. Nicolette looked out from under her arm and shot out a hand, clamping hard onto Erika's wrist.

"Fuck what I owe ya. Fuck off," Nicolette snarled and she sat up and pushed Erika back so she fell on her ass.

Erika breathed hard. She couldn't do this alone. She didn't even know what she was doing, but she couldn't do it alone.

Erika looked down at the vial of pike she'd laid beside her, still mostly full. It was more pike than she had ever held in Sheras. Enough pike to swim for two weeks straight. Enough pike to never wake up again. This was all too difficult. It was all above her head. She had never asked for this, never asked to go on an expedition. She was well within her rights to just curl up in the corner and let the pike take her away.

Before she could think too hard on it, Erika held up the vial so that the silver glinted in the light of the morning. Nicolette's snarl melted away, and her cracked lips parted.

"I'll give you this. All of it. If you come with me," Erika said.

Nicolette's eyes glinted, suddenly wet. Her gaze was fixed on the swirling silver. Erika's was too. Just the sight of it made her mouth dry, made her thigh itch.

"Whadda I godda do?" Nicolette whispered.

Erika thought about it, thought about all the things she'd done in Sheras for a single dab, all the things she would have done for something like this.

"Does it matter?" Erika asked, but she didn't need an answer. She knew it didn't.

The square was large and quickly filling with people. It was dominated on one side by a three-story building with an entrance on the second floor. Mirrored staircases led up to it, splitting around a pool on the ground level. In front of the building, on either side of the great statue of the Mareshal, two wooden posts had been erected and were piled high with kindling. The crowd did not approach the posts. There were no guards to keep them away, but a bubble of empty space surrounded the posts nonetheless.

"What is that?" Erika asked. She lurked at the corner of a building, peering around into the square. Much of the town had gathered there to watch, and the surrounding streets were empty.

"What is what?" Nicolette breathed. She made no effort to conceal herself. She leaned over with one hand braced against the wall, eyes closed, and breathing heavy. Erika grabbed her by the shoulders and turned her to face the crowd.

"That."

"S'a town square. What else would it-"

"No, that." Erika pointed past Nicolette's head at the three-story building. All its windows were glass, and through them Erika could see figures standing and watching from the top level. Onlookers to the execution, above the rabble, but not above the spectacle.

"S'mayor's house."

"That's where Carlotte will be," Erika said. "Is that where the jail is?"

"No. Over there." Nicolette threw out an arm to the right of the staircases.

The mayor's house was part of a facade of buildings that continued unbroken down the entire side of the square. There were multiple doors in the wall with placards beside each.

Erika grabbed Nicolette's wrist and pulled her back up the street, and then around, taking a circuitous route to where Nicolette had pointed. Thorlaille wasn't at all like Sheras with its winding roads and narrow alleyways. This town had been planned, a part of the Mareshal's agenda of expansion, and the streets were laid out in a neat grid. Erika turned the next corner and then stopped. A blueback stood at the edge of the intersection, lounging beside a wooden door in the stone wall. Erika flinched back and pressed Nicolette and herself into a doorway. Erika motioned around the corner with her head.

"What's that?"

Nicolette looked at her, one eye shut against the glare of the late morning, and then peeked her head around the door frame.

"Closet."

"Closet?"

"Closet," Nicolette repeated.

"Why is a closet being guarded?"

"Fuck if I know," Nicolette slurred. She was pretty deep in a ripple. Erika knew that her mind was barely with her. The thought made Erika's thighs itch. Everything seemed to make her thighs itch.

"It's not the jail?" Erika asked.

"Nope," Nicolette shook her head emphatically back and forth, as far as her range of motion would allow. "Jail's down more. Is'ha couple doors. That door's a closet. Jus' a storeroom. Henri takes me there sometime for a suck." Nicolette smiled, showing remarkably straight and white teeth, "Henri gives two dabs for a suck."

The itching in Erika's thigh ratcheted up a notch. Her own ripples had passed almost entirely, and now she was left with the little nauseating tremors that followed. Only way to get rid of those was to wait or go for another swim. She shook off the thought. She still had no plan. She didn't even know where Aethan was, but she knew where he'd be soon.

"There's something in there," Erika said, "They don't guard just a closet, right?"

"Sure," Nicolette shrugged.

Erika bit her lip. She peeked at the blueback and then around the corner at the gathering crowd. An inquisitor had taken a place at the foot of the two stakes and was speaking. They would bring Aethan out soon.

"Can you get him away from the door?" Erika asked. Nicolette opened one eye and then peeked back around the corner. She laughed.

"Ya. That's Jacob," she said. She held out her hand. "For what you promised."

Erika was holding the vial. She'd been clutching it ever since she'd promised it, as though holding it tight would make her not have to give it up. She looked down at her fist then, enclosing the glass like the bars of a flesh colored prison. With an effort, she uncurled her fingers. It lay there, the silver inside swirling.

God, she needed a cut.

She could tell Nicolette to jump off a cliff. She could find herself a nice alcove and just forget it all. What had Aethan even done to deserve her help? If anything, she should let the bastard burn after the way he'd treated her, after the way he'd let her down. She lifted her hand, and the silver glittered in the sunlight.

Nicolette's fingers darted out and plucked it from her palm. Nicolette grinned wide, perfect teeth shining like the pike. Erika's legs felt weak.

"Right then," Nicolette said, and lifted up her skirts to shove the vial into a pocket. She shook her head violently, and then, suddenly full of energy, sauntered out into the street. Erika peeked out after her.

The blueback brightened at the sight of her. He puffed out his chest, and Nicolette placed a hand on her breast and tittered out a greeting. They spoke for a few moments. The blueback made to open the door, and Nicolette shook her head, motioning down the street, away from the crowd, away from the door. The blueback glanced around and then shrugged. A moment later, they were off, he chasing her down the street, giggling like a little boy. The door stood alone.

For a moment, Erika stood stunned, amazed at the ease with which Nicolette had done it. Just a titter, a gesture, and a few words, and he was salivating at her back, as though Carlotte DeSheras herself was parting her legs.

Erika scowled and went to the door. She pushed on it, and it was locked. Of course it was. Why wouldn't it be? She jiggled the handle. Still locked. She shook the door, heaving back and forth at the latch with all her weight, and the deadbolt rattled in its notch.

Another note pierced the air, this time much closer, from the square just beyond. She went and peered around the corner. The crowd had grown larger. Half the town must have been gathered there.

A door opened in the wall between the crowd and her, and with it came a billow of smoke. She smelled sage and lavender, just like she had smelled in the tent with Aethan. A man came out of the smoke, tall and thin with a black tricorn hat and a white feather pluming out from the top. An inquisitor. Erika's fingers gripped at the building's corner. Another man emerged, broad and hunched, wearing nothing but a wrap around his waist and bearing the skin of a Freelander.

"Aethan," Erika whispered.

His hands were manacled in front of him, and his back was bowed. He shuffled along with a limp. A blueback was on either side of him, holding him by the shoulders. One of them held a brazier on a swinging chain beneath Aethan's face, and smoke billowed up from it. Another blueback followed, and then Alakeed, hopping along on one foot with two bluebacks hoisting her by her armpits. Two more bluebacks followed, carrying long rifles with bayonets affixed to the tips. The trumpet sounded again, and this time Erika could see the trumpeter standing at the top of the steps to the mayor's house, making a last call to the spectacle.

She was running out of time.

Erika left the corner and went a dozen strides up the street. She turned, braced herself, and then charged at the door.

The frame splintered, her shoulder popped, and with a shattering of wood, the door broke open and spilled Erika inside. She stumbled through, bounced off a pile of barrels, and knocked her head against the stone wall. Light flashed in her eyes, and a scream of pain rose in her throat, but she stuffed a hand into her mouth and stifled it. Her vision spun, and then the pain came on in full. Her breath hissed out from clenched teeth, and it was all she could do to stay silent.

The intensity of the pain fell, and she reached up to feel her shoulder. It wasn't right. She tried to raise it, and pain lanced through her. She stopped, whimpered, and then forced herself up onto her knees. She didn't have time for any of this.

It was a store closet, just like Nicolette had said. There were sacks of grain, piles of canvas, and boxes emblazoned with the Mareshal's stamp. All very normal things to be in a closet, but there was a reason the blueback had been guarding the door. Along one wall were instruments of war. A line of rifles, boxes of shot, bayonets, powder slings, and piled in the center were a dozen barrels, each slightly larger than her head.

Erika considered her options for several moments. Perhaps the guns? Aethan had told her how to use them that night of the battle, but did she remember? She had been deep in a ripple, and she wasn't sure she could lift one with her shoulder in the state that it was. Perhaps there was a pistol here, like Carlotte had used? But what would she do with one shot?

Her shoulder was pulsing something fierce now. She grimaced and looked at the floor. Erika had knocked one of the barrels from the pile when she'd run into them, and its stopper had been dislodged, spilling a broken stream of powder across the stone. Powder. The barrels were full of black powder.

An idea struck her. She wasn't going to fight her way to Aethan, but perhaps she could distract her way to him. It wasn't quite a plan, but it was all she had. She pulled to her feet and began rifling through the boxes and sacks with her good arm, looking for anything that would--

There. She pulled a candle and a piece of flint from a box of camp supplies, and then she went to the fallen barrel and lifted it up so that the hole was pointed down and spilling powder onto the floor. The weight on her shoulder was agony, but she brought the barrel back to its friends and laid it on its side such that the trail of powder led into the hole. Then she pulled out the candle and used her knife to cut off its bottom so that it was only a little stub. She moved away from the powder and struck at the flint with her knife. Sparks showered the candle, but it didn't light. She tried again and again, whimpering louder and louder with the effort, and finally the candle flickered to life. She gave herself a moment to breathe, and then, with as much care as she could manage, wedged the candle's butt into the pile of loose powder, rocking it slowly back and forth so that it was well supported and would not fall over. She pulled her hand back just a hair, ready to catch it, but it stood. Erika crawled slowly away from it, her eyes glued to the flame. She swallowed, and a bead of sweat fell from her brow to the stone. She pushed to her feet. Her shoulder throbbed, and her ribs and jaw too, but she let out only a hiss of breath. She needed to go. She needed to go now, before this whole thing blew up and took her with it.

Erika left and closed the door as best she could with the frame shattered as it was. Any passerby would see that it was broken, but she had to hope that Nicolette would keep the blueback busy until the candle burned down, and that no one else saw the door and decided to intervene. Erika glanced around to make sure no one had seen her activities, and then hunched her shoulders and went to join the crowd.

Aethan had been tied to one of the stakes, and now the bluebacks were struggling to tie Alakeed to hers. She wasn't making it easy. She writhed and dropped her weight, and when one of the bluebacks hit her across the face, she spat blood at him and yelled all the louder. Smoke rose from smoldering herbs at their feet. Little embers on top of a pile of kindling. All it needed was a stiff breeze for the whole thing to go up.

The crowd kept back from the stakes, making an empty place between them where the inquisitor stood. He held a torch in one hand and his other hand sliced through the air with each of his pronouncements.

"What's he saying?" someone asked.

"I hear no better than you," another answered. "Who are these folk?"

Erika knifed through the crowd with a lifetime of practice, an urchin cutting through the endless throng of Sheras, until there was only one row in front of her. She stopped and waited. She could hear the inquisitor now, but she couldn't pay attention. She felt the knife tucked up into her sleeve, its edge prickling her forearm. She heard the pounding of her heart under her dress, and she watched Aethan leaning limp against the stake behind him. She braced herself and waited.

57

There was a clock hanging on the back wall of the room. Its pendulum swung audibly beneath it, ticking the seconds away, but Harold pulled his pocket watch out all the same and frowned down at it.

"I say, they are taking their time," the mayor said.

He stood to Carlotte's right beside Val. Harold was on Carlotte's left next to the Inquisitor Hawthorne, and they all looked out the large window at the crowd gathering in the square. There were bluebacks in the room too, lining the back wall by the clock, standing at attention, and making Carlotte feel like she was in a prison.

The mayor was a short man with a bald patch that covered most of his head. His mustaches were waxed out almost sideways, and when he turned to peer around Carlotte, his little beard gave him the appearance of a devil.

"A fine piece of clockmanship that," he said. "A Pierre du Pont?"

Harold glanced up. "A what?"

"Pierre Du Pont," Carlotte said. "Minor Rykers in Sheras. Watchmakers."

Harold's frown deepened. He looked down at his watch and then to Inquisitor Hawthorn beside him.

"Quite right!" the mayor said. "The best in the Dominion. I

have a Du Pont in the master bedroom. I myself am a clockmaker. More a tinkerer. The mechanics and all that. My wife, the Lady Constantineau, even did some work on pendulums before we married. Wrote some excellent papers describing the mathematics of their motion. Energy loss to air resistance and all that.

"Hmmm," Harold said.

Carlotte looked at the Lady Constantineau, sitting just behind them. Her back was straight, and her gaze was down and to the left and very far away. At mention of her name, she looked up and caught Carlotte's eyes.

"Come, Darling. You'll miss the show," the mayor said.

"It hasn't started yet," she said.

The mayor tsked and rapped on the windowsill.

"All the same," he said.

His wife rose from her seat like a ghost from a grave and came to stand beside him. She set a small handbag on the sill. Val shuffled to the side to give her room.

"What do you study now?" Carlotte asked.

"Nothing. The household keeps me busy."

Carlotte felt her gorge rise and quickly looked away and out the window. A blueback had climbed atop one of the piles of kindling and was shading his eyes, looking to the west, apparently as impatient as Harold. Carlotte felt like she was in a dream that she had to wake up from, but as long as she kept her eyes on the scene before her, she would not. Like a beaker that would not boil if she watched, she could keep dreaming and pretend that Aethan was not about to be killed, and all her hopes along with him.

"I read your treatise," the mayor said. "Animal force and all that." He leaned over to his wife. "You see, according to the Lady DeSheras' theories, lightning is inside all animals and is the thing that makes them move. Marvelous."

"Lightning?" his wife repeated. She had opened her small bag and pulled out a small crystal flask. She opened it, dabbed a bit of silver liquid onto her finger, and delicately rubbed it into her gums.

"When men are hanged," she said, "they kick. Is that why? It always seemed a desperate and pointless act."

"All human movements are," Carlotte said.

Dying men may have had the animal force, but there seemed to be none of it in the mayor's wife. There was no lightning behind her eyes. No spark. Carlotte's heart was beating faster, and her breath was short, and she reached her left hand up to grip at her elbow where the arrow wound still ached. She squeezed and felt the dull pain rise.

The mayor's wife lifted the flask towards her, an offer. Carlotte shook her head and the mayor tutted.

"Not in front of guests, dear."

"What is taking them so long?" Harold asked.

The inquisitor shrugged. "They will come soon enough. More people are arriving. The more that see this, the more striking the message will be."

Harold huffed and looked back at his watch. "I need a drink."

The mayor peered around Carlotte again.

"Wine? I've a nice cellar. Or perhaps something stronger?"

Harold made to speak and then looked to the inquisitor.

The inquisitor nodded. "It will be some time before the actual burning."

"You need an inquisitor's permission to have a drink?" Carlotte said.

Harold glared down at her. "Don't go anywhere," he said pointlessly, and turned from the window. "Something stronger."

The Mayor beamed and swept his wife and Val towards the door. Harold followed.

The mayor chattered as he went. "I've a Korkin whiskey from before the revolution. A few crates of it laid down by my father and better with every year. What say we open one and I could take a look at that Du Pont--"

His words became indistinct as the door closed behind them. Carlotte didn't take her eyes off the oval of space between the posts. She wondered what Inquisitor Hawthorn would do if she tried to leave, what the bluebacks lining the walls would do if she tried to run.

"This is a mistake," Carlotte said softly enough that only Hawthorne could hear.

He did not answer.

She could feel him beside her, a burning presence like standing beside a forge with her eyes closed.

"You've no idea what he can do," she said.

Carlotte felt him turn, and his gaze burned into the side of her face.

"Don't I? He killed two hundred and thirty-seven in the outer city."

Carlotte looked into his face. "That was him? The tenement fire?"

"You didn't know?"

Carlotte hadn't, but she felt a tiny gush of pleasure that her conviction that it hadn't been black powder had been right.

"And you care about two hundred lives from the outer city?" Carlotte said.

He frowned. "If he can do that, imagine what he could do to the DeSheras Tower."

"He could break it in two," Carlotte whispered.

"And kill everyone within. In an instant."

"But if he can do that, then think what else he could do: heat forges, turn gears, propel ships--"

"Burn a city. Destroy an army."

"But we don't even understand it!" Carlotte cried.

The inquisitor raised an eyebrow and glanced back at the bluebacks. They all stared dutifully forward, reacting to nothing.

"Is mass murder something you would seek to understand?"

Carlotte stepped towards him, and the bluebacks all tensed. The inquisitor raised a finger to them.

"How else can it be controlled?" she asked.

Hawthorne looked again out the window. "He looks controlled to me."

Carlotte turned and saw a procession cutting through the crowd. An inquisitor led the way, and behind him was Aethan. He was flanked by two bluebacks, and he still wore the wrap skirt that Carlotte had lent him. The cloak had been lost, and his face was shrouded in smoke from a brazier one of the bluebacks held. His hands were bound at his back. More bluebacks followed, and with them Alakeed, hopping along on one foot.

Carlotte felt weak. Were it not for the rigid bones of the corset, she may have crumpled to the floor. She put out a hand to steady herself against the windowsill and watched Aethan go to his death, and with him the last hopes of God's mission for her.

"Put him in a cell. Just let me study him. The gains would--"

"You think he'd let you?"

"I can work with him. He's not--"

Hawthorne scoffed. "The Mareshal tried such things, and good folk died. Free him from the smoke, and he goes from a broken man to an earthquake."

"I can speak to him. I can make him--"

"Then he may decide to soldier against us. The Freelands would bark at the chance, and when the Dominion is ash and Sheras along with it, you would wish we'd just let the dog die. The Mareshal is clear on the matter. A witch cannot be suffered to live. The danger--"

Carlotte felt she was in quicksand, her fingers sliding through mud and burying her deeper and deeper. Her corset felt oppressively tight. Her breath was coming in gasps. She changed tactics.

"They are people. Have you no--"

"People?" Hawthorn scoffed.

He stepped up and hissed in Carlotte's face, and she nearly stumbled in her heels. "Two hundred and thirty-seven *people* are dead. *They* are monsters, Carlotte, monsters who can kill thousands, who are only held in check by..." he fluttered his fingers through the air, "morality. Fragile as a house of straw, unable to stand to a gust of wind. Ask any soldier how long morality holds."

"I just want to learn!" Carlotte pleaded. "God tells us to decipher the world. Why would God make this power if we were not to know it?"

"Ask the Amaranthine," Hawthorn said.

He looked out the window and then motioned with his hand. A blueback sprang forward and came to attention at Hawthorne's shoulder.

"Fetch the Lord Orlient. The witches' deaths are at hand."

Carlotte swiveled to the square and saw Aethan and Alakeed bound to their posts. Alakeed writhed and screamed with all the panic Carlotte felt, and Aethan slumped and leaned back with all the powerlessness Carlotte had. Smoke already billowed around them.

"Please," she whispered, not loud enough to be heard. "Please," she repeated. Her hands grasped around her dress, but there were no pockets, and even if there were, her prayer beads wouldn't have been in them. They were lost out in the badlands somewhere.

"God," she whispered, "Please just give me a chance. Don't let this be the end of me. Please, God. Please."

The door behind her banged open, and Carlotte flinched.

"Finally, the Inquisition starts its show," Harold called.

His voice grated against her, and when she felt his arm snake around her waist, her stomach cringed in on itself. His fingers hooked under the hem of her corset, pressing against her still sore ribs. He smelled of whiskey.

"Miss me, darling?"

She did not answer. She couldn't. The mayor and his wife saddled up to the window next to her. He was blathering on, something about clocks. His wife stood subdued beside him, and Val stood subdued beside her.

"Please," Carlotte whispered, barely a breath.

"What's that now?" Harold said, leaning in.

"Hush," the Inquisitor Hawthorne commanded. "It begins."

And then the glass shattered.

The floor shuttered, and the thump of air that burst through the window knocked Carlotte backwards and onto her ass. She landed hard and rolled back and smacked her head against the carpet.

The world tilted around her, and her ears were filled with a high-pitched whine. She blinked and shook her head, and then rolled onto her hands and knees. The room was in shambles, the chairs knocked over, the clock smashed on the floor, and the people were in similar states of confusion. One soldier had his hand to his neck, blood seeping between his fingers. She could hear a faint screaming through the whine, as though it were miles away. She saw Hawthorne rolling over onto his hands and knees, and Carlotte felt a surge of adrenaline pulse through her.

God had given her a chance, and God would not give her another.

Val was on his back, blinking slowly at the ceiling, one lens of his newly repaired spectacles cracked.

Carlotte heaved herself halfway up and crawled over until her face was directly above his. "Get up, Val. I need you. Get up," Carlotte said.

She grabbed him and pulled at him. "Val!" She hissed.

"Yes... Yes, of course," he said, and they used each other to stand.

Harold moved, slowly rolling over. She looked at him, and he locked gazes with her. The little smudge of blood in his eye was mirrored by a cut across his cheek.

"No," Harold ordered in a harsh rasp. He reached out for her, but Carlotte turned away and pulled Val out the door.

58

The great boom caused the ground to shutter and threw Saara off her heels and into the back wall of her little cell. She lay on the floor, curled in a ball, with her hands over her head as dust and bits of rock rained down upon her.

First, she was taken by a primal fear of being buried alive, but the despair she had dwelt upon all the night before quickly took over. She felt relief that she would not have to live in this darkness forever, each undefined day wondering if this was the arbitrary length of time in which she would be taken into the light and shot. When they had taken Aethan and Alakeed, they had put out the smoking braziers and dashed Saara's world to absolute darkness. They had taken all sound with them too. The walls of this underground dungeon were thick, and she could hear nothing of the chaos that must be happening above ground. She could only hear her breathing and her heart beating weakly against her chest.

Her heart really should have been beating faster, but what was there to beat for? This was what her life had built up to. She had grown up an orphan on the streets of Sheras. She had climbed out of the gutters and into Bracille's love by cutting purses and shattering knees. She had climbed out of the slums and into the tallest tower of the Nouvre Vil by learning to read and selling her dignity, and she had seized the name DeSheras by giving up everything she had: Her money, her city, her family. She had done all this, and now she was grateful to die alone in the dark.

It was pitiful, it was disgusting, and the realization of her pitiful end made her furious.

Saara broke out of her ball and slammed her hands against the bars. The metal shifted. More dust fell upon her. The tremor in the ground had caused the walls to shift and the mortar to weaken. She braced herself against the back wall and kicked, aiming for where she thought the lock would be, but she missed. Her ankle glanced off a bar and sent a numbing pain up her leg, but she had no patience for pain.

She adjusted and kicked again. This time her boot hit the latch, and there was a screech of metal. More dirt fell from above. She kicked again and again, and dirt fell and metal screamed, and then the latch broke free of its anchor.

Saara stumbled out and caught her toe on a stone that had not been there before. Another something fell and cracked against the floor. Saara lunged forward and slammed into another cell door. Alakeed's cage. She felt her way along the wall to the stairwell. A stone block caught her foot, and she went down on hands and knees. She did not bother to stand. She just scrambled forward until she felt the first step and then climbed until her fingers felt wood. There was a lip of stone on the floor, preventing the door from opening in towards her, but between the lip and the door came a line of light. She pushed out, and the door did not rattle like a locked door would. It was completely immobile, like one that was just stuck.

Saara growled her frustration and backed carefully down the stairs, counting the steps as she did. She gathered herself and then hurtled back up and slammed her shoulder into the wood.

The door burst open, and Saara careened through and caught herself on a stone wall across the landing. There was light from her left, and when she looked towards it, her vision went white with the sudden brightness.

She could hear yelling now, and she could smell smoke. Not the lavender and sage of the dungeon. Normal wood smoke. She squinted her eyes and climbed the steps. At the top of the stairwell was a little office for the blueback on duty. It had been manned when she was brought in, but now it was empty. The desk had moved, and the things that had been on shelves behind it were on the floor. The door to the street was ajar, and it didn't look like it fit the frame. Now that she noticed it, the wall had a strange tilt to it too. She kicked the door open.

The street was in a panic. People were shouting, crying, screaming. Smoke filled the air. She shaded her eyes and squinted to her left. The end of the building from which she had emerged was in flames. A great plume of smoke billowed up, and an afternoon breeze pushed it into the street. A blueback was shouting for something. Another was trying to organize the rabble into a bucket line. All around her were pieces of building, bits of wood and stone, and sprinkled between them were mounds of fabric. A little boy pulled at one with two stocking-clad legs sticking out the back. The boy was crying, and the mound he pulled at didn't move.

A hand was on her shoulder. She spun, and a blueback with long mustaches yelled into her face. "Buckets? Where are the buckets? Does this town have a fire marshal?"

Saara narrowed her eyes at him. "I've no idea."

"For God's sake!" the man yelled. He turned and grabbed a man stumbling through the debris.

"Buckets! Where are the damned buckets?"

Saara backed up a step, tripped over some masonry, and steadied herself against the wall. She was out. She was free, and no one seemed to know that she was gone. But what to do with her newfound freedom? Run? To where? To what? The fury burning in her stomach twisted at her. No. She would not slink off with nothing but the clothes on her back. She would take back what she was owed. She needed Carlotte. She needed Aethan.

She spied a man pulling himself into a sitting position against the wall. One of his pant legs was ripped and wet. She squatted down beside him.

"Help me," he stammered, "My leg. It's-- my leg--"

"Where are the witches? Where is the Freelander?" Saara said.

The man didn't seem to be listening. He reached down with his hands to touch gingerly at his leg. "Ah!" he cried.

Saara grabbed his face and forced him to look at her. He was clean-shaven, and his face was pocked with craters. His eyes were wide, and his pupils were dilated out like tea saucers.

"Where are the witches? Where are they being burned?"

He lifted a shaky hand and pointed behind her into the smoke-filled square.

"The--there," he said.

Saara dropped his face and ran with a lilting stride. She'd twisted something in her leg when she'd kicked her way out of her prison. The smoke was funneling through the streets and dispersing out into the open square, where it hung in the air like a fog. People moved in every direction, fading in and out of the gloom like ghosts. Saara's eyes and throat burned with the smoke, and then, like an island appearing out of the mist, a stake rose up above her. It was wide at the base where kindling was stacked, and above that, a figure writhed against it, screaming like a banshee. Two bluebacks stood beside the pile, one holding a torch and the other a rifle.

"Light it!" the second shouted.

The one with the torch shook his head. "We're supposed to wait for the inquisitor--"

The second dropped his rifle and wrestled the torch out of the other's hand.

"But the inquisitor said--"

The first man's words were cut off as Saara kicked the back of his knee. He pitched forward and latched onto his partner, throwing him off balance and knocking his torch and gun to the cobbles. Saara stepped up and punched the second in the face, once, twice, and then dropped an elbow into the back of the first one's neck. They both went down, and Saara picked up the rifle. She flipped it around and bashed at the second man's face with the stock. He rolled to the side, sliding the first man off of him. The rifle smacked into the stone and jarred Saara's joints, but she did not let up. Her growl was a roar now, and she advanced on him. He tried to get up, and she kicked him in the side. He sprawled back down, and she stepped up to kick him again. He moved, and instead of hitting with the top of her boot, her toes crunched into the man's nose. His head snapped back, and Saara cursed. Pain shot up through her foot, but she snarled it away and kicked the limp man's head again.

"Lock me up, will you? Bury me alive, will you?" she screamed. She lifted her foot and stomped on the side of his head, and then turned back to the first. He wasn't moving.

"Help me!"

Saara looked up at the figure on the stake. It wasn't Aethan. It was Alakeed, straining at her bonds, blood running down from her nose and soaking the front of her shirt.

"Where's Aethan?" Saara shouted.

"Don't you leave me, Assa efatalee!"

Saara scowled, half a mind to turn and leave the savage to die, but Alakeed was useful. She was owed by Carlotte too. She was and would be an ally. That, and the bluebacks wanted her dead, and the bluebacks could go fuck themselves. Saara bent down and fished at the second blueback's belt until she found a knife and pulled it free. She dropped the rifle and clambered up onto the kindling. Her leg hurt. Her toes hurt. She grabbed Alakeed's stump leg to pull herself up, and Alakeed cried out.

"Stop moving," Saara said, and stood behind her.

She slid the knife in between Alakeed's hands and sawed at the rope. Alakeed squawked, and blood spattered onto Saara's boots. She grunted and yanked the knife back, and the rope gave way. Alakeed swung her arms forward and almost tumbled down the front of the pile, but Saara grabbed her by the collar and tugged her back.

Saara took a look at the woman balancing on one leg, and then down a few feet to the cobbles stones. She pushed the knife into Alakeed's bloody hands and then reached down and swooped her legs out from under her, holding her like a bride.

Alakeed spat foreign words, and Saara slid down the pile, landing hard on the stones. She put Alakeed down and steadied her with both hands.

Alakeed snarled, and her teeth were red. "Looks like Carlotte's not getting out of her debts so easily, eh, Sikka?"

"Where is Aethan?" Saara shouted.

"Turn around," Alakeed spat, and the blood in her teeth splattered against Saara's face.

Saara turned.

The smoke had opened up, and behind her, not a dozen paces away, rose another wooden stake and kindling. Aethan was tied to it, his chest still bare, and Carlotte's skirt still wrapped around his waist. Saara felt a surge in her chest as she saw him, a release of tension she hadn't been aware she was holding, and then she saw that the pile was on fire.

59

The building went up with a crack, like a clap of thunder directly overhead. The crowd gasped and then all toppled over in unison as the shockwave rolled through them. Only Aethan and Alakeed remained standing, bound as they were, like statues of heretical gods before a horde of prostrate worshipers. Then a bit of building fell from the sky and slammed into the cobblestones. A wail went up, for pain or fear, Erika could not tell, and then everyone was screaming. More bits of timber and stone fell, and the people began to scatter. There was no direction to the panic. They ran towards the explosion and away. They ran to the mayor's house, and they ran for the square's exits. They ran into the surrounding buildings and out of them.

The building she'd bombed was missing its top half. Smoke lit with yellow flame billowed out where its roof should have been, and a breeze that funneled through the open street brought the smoke out into the square.

Erika was one of the few whose surprise stunned them into stillness, and then she saw Aethan standing against his stake with the fabric of Carlotte's skirt fluttering around his thighs, and she remembered her purpose.

She stepped towards him and ricocheted off a man sprinting the other way. She went down hard. The knife up her sleeve bit into her forearm, and Erika yelped and dropped it. She curled into a ball, and someone tripped over her, their foot making hard contact with her back as they bowled over. She couldn't stay on the ground. She'd be trampled. Erika scrambled up, scraping her knees against the cobblestones as she did, and darted forward. She dodged a woman, stumbled over a man's body, and then caught herself against the wood of Aethan's pyre. She looked up, and he looked down, and their eyes met.

His mouth hung slightly open. The dead look in his eyes was gone. Erika smiled, and then his face turned to alarm. Erika turned just as the inquisitor tried to lay a hand on her.

It was the one who'd been preaching to the crowd. In one hand was a torch. The other one reached out towards her.

"Get away!" the inquisitor yelled.

Erika scrambled back around the pile, splinters of wood digging into her hands.

"He's dangerous!" the inquisitor said. He glared up at Aethan. "This was his doing!"

"No!" Erika cried.

But the torch had already left his hand. It arched through the air and landed atop the kindling, just a stride from Aethan's feet.

Erika grabbed wood from the pile and flung it away behind her. She tried to reach up to where the torch burned, but she was too far away. She jammed her feet into a gap and stepped up, and the inquisitor pulled her back.

His arms were around her belly, and he heaved her backwards. Erika reached out for the wood, for Aethan, but she was pulled away. She kicked and screamed and wrenched her neck to the side. His face was directly in hers, hazel eyes inches from her own, thin nose practically touching her cheek. She could not outmatch him – he was stronger than her, but she'd learned a thing or two on the streets of Sheras.

She swung her fist down, grasped at the space between his legs until she found the soft flesh, and squeezed for all she was worth. His eyes went wide, and he shoved her away, screaming. She pitched forward and caught herself against the cobblestones by the heels of her hands.

Smoke hung thick in the air everywhere now. She could still see Aethan, but he was now shrouded in it. It burned in her lungs. It made her eyes water. Erika pushed to her feet, and when she looked up again, there was a woman before her wearing a red dress, bunched up around her waist and flowing freely around her legs. Her hair was dark, and her skin was pale, like a vampire from the stories her mother had told her as a child.

The woman tore at the wood, and there was a man beside her taking the burning pieces of timber with both hands and pitching them over his shoulder. The spectacles on his face glinted in the firelight. It was Carlotte. It was Val.

Erika ran forward. Her ribs screamed. Her knees and her hands and her shoulder screamed with them, but she ran on. There was no time to stop the fire. It would burn, and all that stood atop it would burn with it. Erika hit the wood and began to climb, fist over fist, and the fire burned at her. She'd lost her shoes at some point in the struggle, and the soles of her feet burned with the palms of her hands, but she did not stop. She climbed, and when she reached the top, she stood beside Aethan and breathed in the scent of him – musty and sweaty and sour and the way he had smelled in that copse of trees when he'd kissed her before it had all fallen apart. He was speaking to her, but she couldn't hear it over the sound of blood pounding in her ears. She went behind him and tore at the rope with her fingernails. It would not give. Where was the knife? Had she dropped it? Why had she dropped it?

"Visoletta!"

Erika looked up, and two figures appeared out of the smoke. Alakeed and Saara, and in Saara's hand was a knife. It spun around in her hands, and then Saara tossed it, hilt first, and Erika snatched it out of the air. Her fingers closed half around the hilt, and half around the blade. The edge bit into her fingers, but she was beyond caring. She slashed at the rope that bound Aethan's hands, and then sawed at it. The rope gave, and Aethan's hands came free, and with them went Erika's strength, and she collapsed into Aethan's arms, which were suddenly beneath her.

60

Aethan held Erika for just a moment, the small of her back arched over his forearm, her chest lifted, and her throat bared. She had come through the smoke like an apparition, and now she felt like one, weightless in his arms. He stumbled down from the pyre. The sticks stabbed splinters into his bare feet, and the growing fire burned them. He barely felt it. He stepped to the cobbles and laid her down. He knelt beside her and cradled her head in one hand. Her skin was filthy, and it shone with wet. He drew his thumb across her cheek.

"Wake up," he said. His voice was hoarse with the smoke, and something was caught in his throat. "Wake up."

His thoughts were swimming, remembering her on her cart as she laughed, and then her face when they kicked her in the grass, and then the feel of her pressed against him, and then the pain in her eyes as he cast her away. The thoughts cycled over and over as he looked at her. The tip of her nose, the cracked skin of her lip, the bulge of her throat. He felt the tautness of her, the dry smoothness of her skin, the limpness of her muscles.

"I'm sorry," Aethan said. "I'm sorry."

He looked up and saw the chaos around him. People ran. A man lay still in the street. Carlotte was in a red dress, wrestling with an inquisitor who was missing his hat. The man shoved her away and pointed a pistol at him. Carlotte sprang in between them, her arms wide like a sail that wanted to stop the wind.

"He can't live!" the inquisitor cried.

His hat was gone, but Aethan recognized the hook of his nose. He had been in that town before Sheras, weeks before. He had burned that woman at the stake after denying her power. He stepped to the side, and Carlotte stepped with him.

"Aethan."

He looked down and saw that Erika's eyes were open. "Erika," he croaked.

She lifted a hand and grabbed onto his, but her grip was weak and slackened immediately. Her face screwed up with pain. He pulled her hand open and saw that the skin was blistered and burned.

His thoughts were gaining focus now. He took a deep breath and breathed out smoke. The square was filled with it now. He thought of her in the copse of trees, how angry she'd been at his failure, and he wondered how that angry girl had been the one to climb into the fire to save him.

"They burned you, Erika," he said.

She lifted her hand from his and touched his jaw.

"We were supposed to die out there in the grass," she said, and then smiled. "This is all just extra."

There was a crack and Carlotte cried out. Aethan looked up and saw her sprawled on the street. Blood ran down from her temple. The inquisitor pointed his gun at Aethan. Aethan judged the distance to the farthest part of Carlotte. Five yards. He glanced to the side and saw Saara and Alakeed stumbling towards them. Six yards to the right. Make it seven. Val stepped to Carlotte's side and tried to help her up. Aethan closed his eyes and thought of Erika laughing atop her cart.

"He cannot live. He brings nothing but death," the inquisitor yelled.

"No!" Carlotte shouted. "This is God's will that--"

Aethan opened his eyes, and the world was turned to fire.

61

The flash was brilliant, knocking Carlotte back as effectively as the butt of the inquisitor's pistol against her skull, and when she could see again, the world was a great inferno that ended a few feet in front of her in an abrupt line. Hawthorne was gone, his skin peeled away and his bones dissolved into ash, the gun in his hand vaporized and blown away in the gale.

And then, the wall of fire was gone. It went like a bit of gunpowder laid out on a table. A flash of brilliance, a few moments of unbelievable light, and then nothing but soot to signify its passing.

The smoke had all been burned away, and Carlotte could see clear across the square. The cobblestones she sat on were unchanged, but beyond, where the fire had been, the ground had changed to black glass. It billowed out away from her, like an ocean wave frozen in time. Where the glass extended, there was nothing. No posts, no remains, no bodies, but beyond, a few dozen yards away, beyond where the statue of the Mareshal had been reduced to a heap of black and melted stone, the eerie emptiness changed to a still burning hell. Bodies were littered around, many still burning. The mayor's manor was all aflame, and what windows had survived the initial explosion were shattered. The other buildings around the square were the same, and toiling among them, Carlotte saw the movement of people. A yell rose up, and then a chorus of faraway cries filled the air. The buildings that burned belched smoke into the sky, and the same lake breeze that had filled the square with smoke brought the billows of smoke in again like an approaching wall. It blew over them and cast them back into the shadow realm of smoke and falling ash, separate from any who were more than a dozen yards away.

"It *was* you," Carlotte said. "In the outer city. You were the Freelander running through the streets. You killed those people."

"God in heaven," Val breathed. "You really are a witch..."

Carlotte turned her head and saw Val, lying back and propped up on his elbows with his eyes like saucers. She looked behind her to see Alakeed standing on her one good leg with an arm around Saara's shoulders. They were both stunned, but Saara more so. She had never seen any of Aethan's magic after all. Aethan still knelt on the cobbles, the head of the woman who had claimed to be Visoletta in his hands.

He raised his eyes and looked at her. She did not know what she expected, perhaps a face of unfeeling stone, but it was certainly not the look of pain she received. His jaw trembled. His eyes were wet.

"I've killed a lot of people," he said.

Carlotte started to do the sums in her head. A person for every square yard? One in four, perhaps. How many yards? At least a hundred, no, two hundred across. A circumference of six hundred and twenty-eight. Thirty-one thousand or so square yards. Make it thirty. One in four, seven and a half thousand dead? No. Too many. Upper bound. Half that, maybe. Four thousand? Three? How was she to know for sure? Plus the three hundred in Sheras. And then the ones out in the badlands... she didn't know. How could she know? An unthinkable number of people. The mayor, his wife, the inquisitor, all the soldiers and villagers, Enriq-- Enriq! Her mother's right hand for decades. Gone. What would her mother do now? And Harold...

"You wanted magic," Aethan said. "I told you it brought death."

"I... This isn't what..." Carlotte began, but then she trailed off. Her thoughts were all muddled in her head.

"Pah," Alakeed spat. "I did not see you in such a state when people who looked like me were burned away."

"Magic can do this?" Saara asked. "You can do this?"

Aethan didn't answer. Ash settled on his bare shoulders and in his hair.

"Why aren't you a general?" Saara said. "Why aren't you a king?"

"I don't want to be a king," Aethan said, his voice soft, barely audible over the mounting pandemonium in the city around them.

"I just want..." He trailed off and then looked up at Carlotte.

"I just want my gold."

"Gold," Carlotte whispered, her voice having lost her. "They all died for gold?"

"No. They died for my life," Aethan said, and then he looked around at each of them. "And yours, and yours, and yours, and..." he looked down at the woman who had claimed to be Visoletta. "Yours..."

The muscles in his jaw worked, and he looked up again at each of them, a wilder look in his eye. Val took a step away, right to the edge of the circle, but did not step onto the black glass.

"I did not ask for this," Aethan snarled. "I did not make this happen. They did. And I will not apologize for it!"

No one said a word, and Aethan's eyes danced from one to the other, looking for something that none of them gave him.

"So I should let myself die?" he continued. "Would you? Or are the rules different for me because they are weak and I am strong?"

"But the people in the square. They were just--" Carlotte began.

Alakeed jumped in. "They were content to watch us burn! Aethan was right to kill them. They deserved a worse hell. I hold no ill will towards you, raka Areek. I am only thankful you are on our side."

"Deserve..." Aethan said, lingering on the word, melancholy thick in his voice. "No one deserves anything. We just are."

He fell silent, and none of them argued. Perhaps they were afraid. Carlotte was. Before, Aethan had seemed dangerous, but now he seemed capricious too, or maybe just... unconstrained. Carlotte didn't know which was worse, that he had decided to kill all the onlookers, or that he had done it accidentally. Was he a vengeful demon killing at whim, or a powder keg in a crowded theater? What was she to do with either of those? How was she to behave? How were any of them to behave?

Or perhaps they were silent because they were all murderers too. Carlotte had seen Alakeed kill in the badlands, and Saara also. She and Val had both fired guns and felt the kick of those killing shots against their shoulders that night in the rain. And Carlotte had freed Aethan, hadn't she? Or at least helped. Either she had willfully released that vengeful demon, or she had lit the powder keg while the audience was packed in tight. What had she thought would happen when she tried to pull Aethan down from that stake? What had been her end game when she put herself in front of Hawthorn's pistol? What else had she been delaying for, except for Aethan to do exactly what she had seen him do to Al'Aksahlad?

Aethan had traded those thousand lives for his own. What had Carlotte traded them for? So she could unravel the secrets of Aethan's power? Or just so she didn't have to get married? She thought about Harold then and wondered how he had gone. Had it been instant? Or was he burning to death in the Mayor's manor as she stood there thinking?

"We should go," Carlotte breathed, breaking the silence.

"Go?" Val repeated.

Carlotte nodded, her eyes fixed on a spatter of blood on the cobbles.

"Hawthorn is gone, but there are more inquisitors in this city. They will gather their strength eventually, and we should be gone before they do."

"You mean to go on?" Val stammered.

"What else would we do?" Carlotte hissed. She looked around at each of them. "You still want your gold and your titles." She looked at Val. "You still want to be a part of something that matters." She looked again at the blood stain. "Well, I still want my answers. So we go on."

Aethan nodded and rose to his feet. He stooped down and lifted the Visoletta woman. She hung limp and unconscious in his arms.

"She's coming with us," Aethan said.

"She's not Visoletta," Carlotte said. "She killed Visoletta Corlionne in Sheras and took her name. She's lied to us this whole time."

Aethan shrugged. "Her name is Erika, and she's not the only murderer on this expedition. Nor the only liar. We aren't leaving her behind."

62

They walked through the smoke and then past the burning buildings and into the city. There were some who watched them go, but most were lost in the chaos that had enveloped the town. People ran here and there, putting out fires, pulling things from buildings, weeping in the street. Aethan hadn't meant for the fire to go so far. He had been so concerned with where it should start and in what direction it should go. Of course, people other than the inquisitor had died. He shouldn't have pushed so much. He hadn't thought it through, but he couldn't admit that to them now. They were already looking at him like he *was* the monster the inquisitor had labeled him as.

They went around the town until they found the stables where Carlotte's carriage had been stowed. She rummaged through the towed cart and then, finding the coffin, nodded. Aethan laid Erika onto the seat, and then found Toktok in one of the stalls and hitched him up. Alakeed and Saara freed more horses. They hitched one beside Toktok, and Alakeed mounted a second and held the reins to a third. Saara said the bluebacks had taken her purse, but she took Val back into the city all the same, and returned with boxes of provisions. Val looked shaken. No one asked how Saara had paid.

Saara had brought clothes too, and for the first time in two weeks, Aethan put on a shirt that fit him and pants that were only a little short in the leg. Then Aethan saw to Toktok and climbed into the carriage. Erika's eyes were closed, and her hands were clutched loosely on her belly. Aethan could see the blistered skin. When he sat, she opened her eyes and looked at him.

"The others look away now," Aethan said.

"Do you blame them?" Erika asked.

Aethan looked out the window. The gilded frame was shattered. The thin wooden shutters were closed, but only one slat remained. He tried to remember what the carriage had looked like when he'd met them in Irondale, weeks ago. It had been a ghastly, ornamented thing, as out of place in the badlands as he was in the world.

"No," he said. "I don't blame them. Ashatee told me they would hate me. She warned me, but I did not listen."

Aethan felt a touch on his hand and looked back. Erika's hand was outstretched and lightly rested on his own.

"Thank you, Aethan. For saving me again."

"It was you who saved me," Aethan said, "Again."

Erika smiled. "You did not mean for it to turn out this way."

"No," Aethan agreed. He never did.

Carlotte climbed into the carriage a few minutes later and sat beside Aethan. He heard Val flick the reins and click his tongue, and the wagon moved. Aethan looked out the window and saw Alakeed sitting tall on a gray horse. Saara slouched atop another horse just beyond. She pulled ahead and led the way.

They trundled out of town and down the southern road. The day turned to noon, but they did not stop to eat. They did not speak. Carlotte sat with her thumb on her cheek and her forefingers on her brow, considering Erika before her. In her other hand, she clutched at a loop of beads Saara had brought her, and picked through them one by one, round and round. The day grew long, and Thorlaille fell far behind them. The sun fell to the horizon and then dipped below.

Carlotte reached into her blouse and pulled her necklace over her head. She brought it to her lips, and it shone with light. She hung it from a bit of splintered siding, and it filled the carriage with a bright and cool white light. She met Aethan's gaze.

"Magic is death," she said, "But it's not just death. It is not just darkness. It is light too."

"If you say so," Aethan said.

He closed his eyes and withdrew into himself. He moved through the corridors and came to the door within. When he'd destroyed Thorlaille, he had stepped over the burned bodies. He had kicked aside Erika's corpse and torn open the Pikelord's flaming door. He had called forth the darkness and let it flow through him like a torrent. It had stretched the door wide, but he had watched it and pulled it shut just seconds after.

He stood before the door now, but the scene was changed. There was no longer the Pikelord's house. The door was now just a wooden door in a wooden frame, standing free from any structure. It had a metal door knob and it sat in a field of grass that stretched away to the horizon in every direction. The field was empty except for a repeating pattern of small mounds with small wooden placards sticking out from them.

"Erika" read one, "taken before her time."

"Carlotte DeSheras" read another. "Bulwark" read a third, and "Weed" read a fourth, and Saara, and Alakeed, and Jaaque, and Jane, and Hannah, and Ari, and Renee, and Rold, and Slack, and Pierre, and Haric, and Boris, and Raphael, and Kent, and Doss, and his sister, and his father, and even Ashatee. Everyone he had ever known.

He stepped forward and placed a hand on the doorknob. He felt the cool brass underneath his palm and knew that on the other side of the door was only death. Carlotte was wrong about that. Death was the only future for him, and there was only one way out.

His hand tightened, and he turned. He pulled the door open, and there was the darkness beyond. The abyss of nothing. He felt the darkness draw at him, calling him to step through and be swallowed up by it, to give up his form and become nothing himself.

He was aware of Saara calling the expedition to a halt, and Aethan shut the door. He withdrew from the corridors of the self, and looked up to see Carlotte staring intently at him.

"You were there, at the door?" she asked.

Aethan nodded.

"I have tried every night to find it in me," she said.

Aethan nodded again. "You may not have it."

She was silent, and then she opened the carriage door and stepped out into the gathering dusk. "You will teach me all the same," she said over her shoulder.

Aethan watched her go. He knew she expected him to follow, but Aethan sat still and thought of the new scene within, of the graves all around stretching to the horizon. He wondered what end Carlotte's quest would bring, and how the darkness would claim her like it had everyone else.

Would Carlotte DeSheras be better off if Aethan stayed in the carriage and stepped through the door within, banishing himself to whatever darkness awaited on the other side? Would they all be?

Erika shifted beside him, and he looked down at her. He still held her hand, and it squeezed his, as though she knew what he was thinking.

Carlotte thrust her head through the shattered window.

"Come, Aethan. It is time you earned your gold."

About the Author

William Zimmerman grew up in southern New Mexico and spent much of his youth writing stories and pretending to be other people on stage. Now he lives in Seattle, WA, with his wife and his cat, and continues to write and pretend to be other people.

Follow him on instagram at @nogardehh
See his website at: willzimmerman.com

Acknowledgments

Thank you to Claire for your notes, your encouragement, and your endless support. Thank you to Kernie for helping me edit. Thank you to Andrew and Robby for being early readers and giving me feedback. Thank you to Tasha for pressuring me to finish. Thank you to everyone who gave me support during the process.

Thank you for reading.

www.ingramcontent.com/pod-product-compliance
Lightning Source LLC
Chambersburg PA
CBHW021938110726
47901CB00003B/883